Music and Manipulation

MUSIC AND MANIPULATION

On the Social Uses and Social Control of Music

Edited by

Steven Brown

and

Ulrik Volgsten

Berghahn Books
NEW YORK • OXFORD

Published in 2006 by
Berghahn Books

www.berghahnbooks.com

© 2006 Steven Brown and Ulrik Volgsten

Library of Congress Cataloging-in-Publication Data

A catalogue record for this book is available from
the Library of Congress.

British Library Cataloguing in Publication Data

A catalogue record for this book is available from
the British Library.

Printed in the United States on acid-free paper

To the memory of Nils L. Wallin

CONTENTS

Part III Audiovisual Media

MANIPULATION OF MUSIC

Part IV Governmental/Industrial Control

Part V Control by Reuse

ILLUSTRATIONS

FIGURES

FOREWORD

Manipulating Music—a Perspective of Practicing Composers

Music is an essential form of human communication and has probably been so since before the dawn of speech. Research suggests that there are interesting parallels between ritual music in humans and structured communication sounds used by several species of birds and mammals, providing compelling evidence for the antiquity of musical sound patterns. One of the most important features shared between these various forms of communication is their efficacy in influencing the behavior of individuals and even whole groups.

The term "manipulation" has a very broad meaning when applied to music. In the present context, we will consider it to mean a manifestation aimed at influencing a person to act or react in a desired manner. In one type of circumstance, the purpose of this music is simply to fortify the emotional experience of, say, watching a play or film. In another type of circumstance, though, the aim can be to make an individual generate a desire for a given product, service, or ideology. Music has a special way of getting past the "bouncers" of the human unconscious. This seems very paradoxical in many ways. In contrast to visual or linguistic messages, instrumental music lacks any obvious "content." While you can always argue about the contents of a text—and thus offer a contrary position—in the case of music, there are no words to oppose; it is mainly feelings, and you cannot argue against them on rational grounds.

Music can, in and of itself, provide deep emotional experiences, which in part explains its positive applications in such areas as music therapy, wherein words often fail to reach a person but music can find a way of getting through. In the world of storytelling, music can enhance the viewer's emotional experience of a visually presented narrative. But music can become a manipulative device when placed in conjunction with an intellectual message, adding new and powerful emotional dimensions to it. In daily life, a widespread application of this use is in the form of audiovisual marketing through commercials, generating an interest in consumer products. In addition, music is an important component of all kinds of propaganda, including political and religious messages of all sorts. Music is able to capture a sense of meaning through its use of several specific devices. Rhythm—the basic component of all music—can, all on its own, induce a wide range of emotional expressions associated with speed, from calmness and relaxation to stress and high tension. Harmonies allow for countless mood settings and emotional nuances. The interaction between different chords can describe a variety of things: the progress of events, the characters of a narrative, emotions such as joy and sadness, threats—you name it. In combination with well-selected instrumentation, they can also describe characteristics of an object or person: proportions, age, personality, and so on.

Last but not least is melody. Every composer of film music knows the importance of leitmotifs. A melodic theme associated with a certain character can, once established, be used repeatedly throughout the film to suggest the character's presence even when he or she is not visible. A good example of this is John Williams's music for the film *Jaws,* directed by Steven Spielberg. Early on in the film, the shark's threatening melody line, consisting of only two alternating notes a semitone apart, is established, together with a moving camera-angle from the beast's own point of view. In the first half of the film, the shark makes its presence known exclusively through these two elements: the musical motif and the subjective camera. The above-mentioned musical components provide a rich, nonverbal language capable of conveying a wide range of feelings, emotions, and attitudes to a listener. One would wish for a greater public awareness about the components at work in these potent audiovisual messages, particularly when the messages have commercial and political import. As professional composers of music aimed at manipulating people in various audiovisual contexts, we have found that our perspective on our own craft has been expanded immeasurably through our participation in the Music and Manipulation project. We would like to thank our colleagues for making our world a bigger place!

Örjan Strandberg
Bengt-Arne Wallin

Preface

Why is there music? Sociologists and psychologists of music have devised theories to explain how people perceive, respond to, and interpret music, but they have never really made a major point of asking the basic question of where this music comes from to begin with. Why is music all around us? Many theorists would prefer to think of music as just something "out there," a kind of background noise that begs our attention and challenges our interpretive powers. But that misses the whole point of music's intended purposes. What motivates music's presence in particular environments and particular situations? What do its creators and users hope to accomplish with it? These are particularly difficult questions to avoid, given music's ubiquitous presence nowadays. Music has become part of the acoustic landscape of modern society, and there is hardly a place where we can avoid it. But this is only the case because music is a functional object, usually *intended* to serve some sort of *purpose*. In other words, it is there because somebody has placed it there. But who put it there, and why is it there in greater abundance than ever before? Despite the centrality of these questions to an understanding of music's role in society, they have scarcely been addressed, least of all by contemporary theorists, who tend to treat functionality and intentionality as entirely unrelated issues.

This anthology is designed to investigate the "why's," "how's," and "what's" of music's socially influential effects. But an understanding of this requires different approaches. The fact that sociologists, humanists, and psychologists of music have no common academic journal or other forum in which to discuss their respective theories and methods signifies a state of mutual distrust. We have attempted to bridge this gap by having representatives from all three fields in this volume, thereby reinforcing an important sense of balance.

The present volume is the outcome of a conference dealing with the sociology of music that took place at the National Palace (Nalen) in Stockholm, Sweden. The organizational phase of the conference involved a very long incubation period during which funding was sought. This gave the organizers plenty of time to work through the details of the program, which were actively debated at monthly meetings over the course of more than two years. From its humble beginnings as a conference dealing with the use of music in television advertising, to one about music in all the audiovisual media, to one about music in the sound environment and the audiovisual media, to finally one about its use in live music events, the sound environment, and the audiovisual media, Music and Manipulation took shape. With the realization that musical control is a counterpoint to musical use—including such important issues as censorship, propaganda, copyright, and the music industry—a general conference devoted to nothing less than the use and control of music became the project of the organizers of the Music and Manipulation conference.

Much of the writing in this book is based on a "use/control" perspective of music, relating in various ways to a sender-message-receiver-feedback model. In this volume, it is treated variously as a theoretical model and as a map of a diverse theoretical field, with one contributor even questioning its applicability. The introduction by Brown presents a general social-communication model for music that considers the full gamut of processes from the social/economic functions motivating musical use through to the ultimate influence of this use on individual and collective behavior. Music is viewed essentially as a tool for persuasion, one whose ultimate effect is to increase cooperative behavior within social groups. This essay is based on classical models of a sender-message-receiver-feedback arrangement. Brown argues that a critical problem with receiver-based models of music is their general disregard for musical senders and thus for the whole concept of musical "use." He urges a reintroduction of the sender's perspective to models of musical communication, especially one grounded on the notion of "pragmatics," wherein musical messages are tailored to their intended purposes.

The book is then divided into two main sections, one looking at how music is used ("Manipulation *by* Music") and the other at how music is controlled ("Manipulation *of* Music"), with the word "manipulation" being used as a catchall term to reflect music's general role as a medium for both persuasion and manipulation. Regarding the first section, the book considers three general and nonexclusive forms of musical use. In the first part, "Music Events," the focus is on situations in which music is used by listeners in a more or less voluntary manner and in which music is basically the central point of a social activity. It includes ritual performance in smaller-scale cultures, as well as concerts, music festivals, folk music performances, music-club performances, and recreational choral/instrumental gatherings that occur in larger-scale cultures.

The chapter by Dissanayake extends this view of small versus large cultures to include societies of nonhuman animals. Her point of departure is the parallelism that exists between human ceremonial rituals and various forms of ritualization seen in animals, including such things as courtship rituals and displays of aggression. Both ceremonial rituals in humans and ritualized behaviors in animals incorporate behaviors taken from other contexts that are then recombined into distinctive displays or signals. Dissanayake also traces the emotional core of music back to early mother-infant interaction, whereby its deep social significance is attested.

The chapter by Martin argues that concerts in modern societies may be seen as rituals just as much as the ceremonies of smaller-scale cultures. They share the features of being done on a habitual basis and being important means for social interaction, distinction, and even display. By claiming that musical use is "bound up in complex ways with people's participation in wider configurations of [social] activity," Martin takes issue with the classical communication model. The result is an emphasis on the social patterns in which the music is heard, rather than on the senders of music. Thus, a classical concert and a pop concert are both ritualized means of reinforcing identity.

The chapter by Volgsten brings together issues from the previous chapters while suggesting explanations for phenomena discussed in the remainder of the book. The social basis of the affective core of music is seen in relation to the verbal discourses that surround any musical culture or subculture. The ethical, ideological, and identificational consequences of this coupling of affect and discourse through music are discussed, as are the outlines for a theory of musical experiences. An argument is presented claiming that discursive content is a necessary condition for music as *a human cultural artifact*. This discursive content of music is part of our conscious *and* our unconscious experiences of music. As both musical sounds and verbal discourses about music are increasingly mass-mediated, possibilities for musical manipulation increase.

The second part of this section is entitled "Background Music." Unlike music events, background music tends to be transmitted indirectly and is more often recorded than live. Brown and Theorell make a distinction in their chapter between two forms of background music. The first is what they refer to as "personal enhancement background music," which is used to support individual improvement, such as in therapeutic and educational contexts. The second is what they call "milieu music," which is the kind of music that supports the production and consumption of commercial goods.

The chapter by North and Hargreaves presents a discussion of music in business settings, including in-store music, in-office music, and telephone-waiting music. The kinds of studies that North and Hargreaves discuss, in which background music can potently yet unconsciously influence eating rates, product preferences, tolerance for waiting, etc., might be among the most compelling examples of conscious manipulation that can be found in this book. How should we react to the observation that the mere playing of background music at a supermarket wine display can bias consumer preference for the wine properly matched to the music (compared to the one poorly matched) by a factor of threefold? In response to this, North and Hargreaves point out that music is but one of a host of elements used to influence product choice in stores, that there is still too little research available to know to what extent people are oblivious to background music, and that whatever influence music might have on consumers, its effect is in no way all-encompassing.

"Audiovisual Media," the third part of this first section, considers music that occurs in a host of media, including film, television, commercials, and music videos, as well as at music events and as background music. Film and television, as larger-scale media forms, afford music an extensive role as a narrative and ideological device. As Tagg argues in his chapter, music is capable of influencing our attitudes through seamlessly coupling concepts that would be strongly incongruent if presented in verbal or visual discourse. While most listeners are fully competent at decoding music's cultural messages, very little is known about the mechanisms behind these interpretative skills. Since the potential of these media for manipulation is vast, Tagg prescribes full-scale education as an anti-manipulation strategy.

Television commercials and music videos, as smaller-scale products, are involved more in the commercial uses of music, with videos being essentially promotional devices for popular music recordings. Music occurs in 85 to 90 percent of American television commercials (Murray and Murray, 1996), and the chapter by Bullerjahn on music in commercial advertising makes clear that television is one of our greatest sources of exposure to music in Western society (see Tagg as well on this point). In addition, Bullerjahn's essay (like that of North and Hargreaves) highlights the fact that theories of persuasion play a critical role in understanding music's effects. In comparison to classical "step" models, contemporary models of persuasion incorporate the parallel roles of verbal and nonverbal routes of persuasion, especially as modulated by the personal-involvement level of the viewer of the ad. Music, like other "peripheral" elements of the persuasive message, can be effective even when (and sometimes especially when) involvement in the ad is minimal.

The chapter by Strachan moves from a view of music as an adjunct to advertising to one in which music is itself the advertised product. His essay presents a more cultural perspective but still one that highlights the economic role of videos as an advertising device for recorded music. Something on the order of 97 percent of songs on the Billboard music chart have accompanying video clips (Banks, 1998), thereby making videos a requirement for the financial success of a song and album. Strachan points out that to sell a product, videos have to be "placed" within existing cultural contexts, genres, and discourses, which are thus indirectly manipulated by the industry.

With this view of the uses of music in mind, the second section of the volume, "Manipulation *of* Music," examines two aspects regarding the control of music: governmental/industrial control and control by reuse. In the fourth part of the book, "Governmental/Industrial Control," the chapter by Korpe, Reitov, and Cloonan analyzes the governmental control of music through censorship from a cross-cultural and historical perspective, including a discussion of modern-day examples of music censorship, which are rife. It focuses especially on religion and government as the two main agents of censorship, examining a series of case studies that include Algeria, South Africa, Nazi Germany, the former Soviet bloc, and modern-day America. All forms of censorship are justified on essentially the same grounds—to protect a culture from dangerous influences. As the authors argue, music censorship turns out to be a double-edged sword in that it can, in addition to serving as a force of repression, serve as a source of protection in cases where music is an expression of hate that threatens the livelihood of various minority groups in a society.

Moreno's chapter about the uses of music in the Nazi concentration camp system looks at a situation in twentieth-century European history in which music was not only the object of rigorous censorship and propagandizing but also a tool for humiliation, deception, and torture, as part of an institutionalized program of genocide.

The following chapter by Wallis examines not only governmental but also industrial control of music. Wallis's discussion of copyright and the recording industry examines new threats to the stability of corporate oligopoly in the music business, not least by the "brave new world" of e-commerce and MP3 file-sharing technology. Peterson and Berger's (1975) classic analysis of "cycles of symbolic production" was the first demonstration of the inverse relationship between corporate concentration and creative diversity in the music industry. Based on this analysis, the expected weakening of corporate control over access to MP3 music files in the late 1990s would have predicted the potential for a strong increase in musical diversity and a decrease in homogenizing trends. However, in the end, the music industry was able to obtain large restrictions over this liberal file-sharing technology through litigation, thereby retightening its noose of control over electronic music.

In the book's final part, "Control by Reuse," the last two chapters look at reuse as a form of musical use as well as the corresponding control issues. The chapter by Stockfelt examines the historical evolution of the musical "object" and the criteria used to determine the authenticity of a given musical work. Stockfelt argues that the need for creating "works" of music as definitive objects occurs for three principal reasons: to make music a salable commodity in the marketplace; to protect composers' works and livelihood in the context of such a market-oriented profession; and to provide everyday listeners with a source of history and cultural capital.

This inevitably leads to a discussion of copyright, and the chapter by Volgsten and Åkerberg follows up on the ideas put forth in Stockfelt's chapter by presenting a more in-depth analysis of the history of intellectual property rights as applied to musical works and their composers. In doing so, it reviews the arguments both for and against musical copyright, pointing to (as does Wallis) the tradeoff between the creative and financial protection for composers that occurs in its presence versus the creative freedom that occurs in its absence. A closer look at the Lockean notion of "property," leads to the final question: Are rights right?

As stated above, the current volume presents not only the first systematic discussion of the use and control of music in society but also one of the very first to unite sociological, psychological, and humanist analyses of music. In addition—as summarized in the epilogue—the book touches on a wide range of moral issues regarding the use and control of music that have rarely been presented in one place. The social study of music is in great need of integrative, cross-disciplinary thinking. We hope that the spirit of the current volume will open both minds and doors.

Steven Brown
Ulrik Volgsten

References

Banks, J. (1998). "Video in the machine: The incorporation of music video into the recording industry." *Popular Music* 16: 293–309.

Murray, N. M. and Murray, S. B. (1996). "Music and lyrics in commercials: A cross-cultural comparison between commercials run in the Dominican Republic and in the United States." *Journal of Advertising* 25: 51–63.

Peterson, R. A. and Berger, D. G. (1975). "Cycles in symbolic production: The case of popular music." *American Sociological Review* 40: 158–173.

Acknowledgments

We would like acknowledge the work of the organizers of the conference on which this book is based, who include (in addition to ourselves) Yngve Åkerberg (chairman of the planning committee), Arne Brodd (its courageous secretary and treasurer), Professor Töres Theorell (the institutional organizer), Örjan Strandberg, and Bengt-Arne Wallin. Raija Lindblad provided spirited and efficient administrative support during the organization of the conference. The initial conference about music and television advertising was the brainchild of Nils L. Wallin, who unfortunately did not live to see the publication of this volume. We would like to express our deepest thanks to all the scholars who contributed chapters to this volume.

We are also grateful to the many funding organizations that generously contributed financial resources to the Music and Manipulation conference: the Bank of Sweden Tercentenary Foundation (Riksbankens Jubileumsfond), "The Year of the Brain" in Sweden (Hjärnåret), the Foundation for Biomusicology and Acoustic Ethology (Mid-Sweden University, Östersund, Sweden), the Swedish National Council for Cultural Affairs (Kulturrådet), the Swedish Council for Research in Humanities and the Social Sciences, the Helge Ax:son Johnson Foundation, the Swedish Artists' and Musicians' Interest Organization (SAMI), the Swedish Society of Popular Music Composers (SKAP), and the European Culture Program (EU Kaleidoscope Program).

The Division of Psychosocial Factors and Health, Department of Public Health Sciences, of the Karolinska Institutet, under the direction of Töres Theorell, served as the organizing institution for the conference, and we are grateful for its support and administrative assistance. We thank the Institute of Popular Music at the University of Liverpool and Die Hochschule für Musik und Theater in Hanover for agreeing to be co-organizing institutions for the European Culture Program grant. Olle Edström, Holger Larsen, and Hans-Åke Olsson from the Departments of Musicology at the Göteborg and Stockholm Universities also contributed in generous ways. We are especially grateful to the Bank of Sweden Tercentenary Foundation, the Swedish Society of Popular Music Composers, and the Swedish Music Publishers Association (SMFF) for their specific contributions to our work on this book. We could never have put it together without their support. Steven Brown would like to give his heartfelt thanks to Eva Götell for her generosity in providing salary support during periods in his work on the book when he had none.

Finally, we would both like to give additional thanks to Arne Brodd and Yngve Åkerberg for all the hard work they did during the follow-up to the conference and the period of our work on this book. Arne had the thankless job of not only straightening out the finances for the conference but of searching for additional funds for our work on the book, a job he did with untiring devotion. We dedicate our work on this book to Arne and Yngve with our deepest gratitude.

Contributors

Yngve Åkerberg
Stockholm, Sweden

Steven Brown
Department of Psychology
Simon Fraser University
Burnaby, British Columbia
Canada

Claudia Bullerjahn
Universität Hildesheim
Fachbereich II—Kulturwissen-
    schaften und Aesthetische
    Kommunikation
Institut für Musik und
    Musikwissenschaft
Hildesheim, Germany

Martin Cloonan
DACE
University of Glasgow
Glasgow, UK

Ellen Dissanayake
Seattle, Washington
USA

David J. Hargreaves

Centre for the Advanced Studies in
    Music Education
University of Surrey Roehampton
Southlands College
London, UK

Marie Korpe
Freemuse
Danish Centre for Human Rights
Copenhagen, Denmark

Peter J. Martin
Department of Sociology
University of Manchester
Manchester, UK

Joseph J. Moreno
Moreno Institute for the Creative
    Arts Therapies
St. Louis, MO
USA

Adrian C. North
Department of Psychology
University of Leicester
Leicester, UK

Ole Reitov
Danish Center for Development
  and Culture
Copenhagen, Denmark

Ola Stockfelt
Department of Musicology
Göteborg University
Gothenburg, Sweden

Rob Strachan
Institute of Popular Music
University of Liverpool
Liverpool, UK

Philip Tagg
Institute of Popular Music
University of Liverpool
Liverpool, UK

Töres Theorell
Department of Public Health
  Sciences
Karolinska Institutet, Stockholm

Ulrik Volgsten
Department of Musicology
Göteborg University
Gothenburg, Sweden

Roger Wallis
Swedish Society of Popular Music
  Composers
Stockholm, Sweden

INTRODUCTION

"How Does Music Work?" Toward a Pragmatics of Musical Communication

Steven Brown

Introduction

This opening essay highlights basic themes associated with the topic of music and manipulation by addressing the essential question "How does music work?" Can one describe music's most fundamental social functions and mechanisms? In order to address this question, the essay outlines a communication model for music, arguing that music is, in its most basic sense, an *associative enhancer of communication* at the group level. This view has several important ramifications: (1) music is, psychobiologically speaking, an emotive reward and reinforcer, one that acts to modulate arousal, affect, and mood; (2) music's principal mode of operation at the cultural level is associative, and this often manifests itself in specific linkages between musical structure and social meaning; (3) the objects of this association range widely, and include such divergent entities as verbal texts, group identities, social ideologies, and commercial products; and (4) music is ideally utilizable as a tool for persuasion and manipulation. This essay promotes a pragmatic approach to music, one that considers not only the "texts" and meanings of musical communication but the motivations that underlie this communication to begin with.

* * *

Music's use in contemporary society is plagued by a host of moral problems, including censorship, propaganda, quotas, commercialization, and globalization.

Notes for this section are located on page 25.

What underlies most of these issues is the notion that music has a powerful influence over human behavior and that this influence can be exerted for a host of political and economic ends. Music is a major tool for propagating group ideologies and identities, and as such serves as an important device for reinforcing collective actions and for delineating the lines of inclusion for social groups. In addition, music is one of the most important marketing tools in modern society and one of its most important economic commodities. The music industry is a $40 billion enterprise, itself a part of a much larger transnational entertainment industry. The current volume deals with the social uses and controlling mechanisms of music. As an introduction to the major themes of this volume, this essay poses the basic question "How does music work?" In other words, what are music's most fundamental functions and mechanisms? In addressing this question, I hope to highlight some of the major features of the use and control of music discussed by the contributors to this volume. My approach will be to develop a general social-communication model for music that is both interdisciplinary and cross-cultural, a model that shows striking contrasts to the dominant cultural-studies approach to the sociology of music. In elaborating this model, I hope to set the stage for the remaining chapters of the book. At the same time, I want to emphasize that in presenting this model in the introduction of the book, I am in no way implying that all the contributors to this volume agree with the perspective outlined here. Far from it. Each contributor presents his or her own perspective on music's role in society and how music both influences and is influenced by the society that uses it.

Music and Behavioral Control

The communication model to be developed in this essay will be predicated on a dynamic model of society. Music can be best understood in terms of how it influences the livelihood and survival of individuals and—most especially—cultures. My overriding hypothesis is that music is a functional object whose universal persistence over time and place has resulted from its contribution to the operations of societies. This conforms with the "functionalist" ethos in sociological theory (e.g., Kincaid, 1990), which has been much criticized (Elster, 1983). Functionalism, in this context, is the application of functional explanation to social phenomena. It is, almost by definition, holist in its outlook, viewing society as something greater than the sum of the components that make it up, namely, individual people. This is in opposition to the philosophy known as "methodological individualism" (Watkins, 1957), which is anti-holist in its orientation and which explains all social phenomena in terms of individual behavior. With this commitment to functionalism in mind, it will be necessary to develop a dynamic macrosociological perspective. The analysis of social dynamics has been the domain of both anthropology and sociology, although they have adopted very different orientations. By focusing, respectively, on small and large societies, anthropology and sociology have developed strikingly different theoretical emphases: anthropological theories have tended to focus on *consensus,* whereas sociological theories have tended to focus on *conflict.* The same applies in their approach to music: ethnomusicologists analyze small-scale cultures and the role that music plays in creating cohesion and cooperation, whereas sociomusicologists (especially those who study popular music) analyze large, industrialized societies and the role that music plays in defining social divisions among classes, subcultures, and interest groups.

Consensus and conflict are flip sides of a coin comprised of cooperation and competition. In order to understand how music operates in societies of all kinds, it is necessary to invoke large-scale sociological theories, and especially selectionist models (Boyd and Richerson, 1985; Henrich, 2004). Cooperation and competition can be unified by looking at group processes as a two-component system involving "within-group" dynamics, on the one hand, and "between-group" dynamics, on the other (Sober and Wilson, 1998). A group's chances of survival depend both on the internal integrity of the group (within-group processes) and on the ability of that group to function in relation to competing groups in a meta-population (between-group processes). The most important concept to be highlighted here is that internal cooperation is a necessity for groups to flourish at both levels. A conflict-filled social club will probably disband due to internal instability. Likewise, a conflict-laden army in which soldiers fight among themselves has little chance of success against an opposing army. Collective ventures like building bridges and waging battles require large-scale cooperation and coordination among members of a work force; one has to cooperate to compete. In sum, the long-term survival of groups depends on the balance of cooperation and competition both within and between groups.

In ethnomusicological analyses, the groups whose survival is analyzed are often self-contained though small-scale units such as tribal groups, whereas in sociomusicological analyses, they are usually groups within larger societies, such as political groups (based on ethnicity, nationality, and the like) and interest groups (based on gender, age, race, sexual orientation, and the like). I argue that music's role in both kinds of societies is fundamentally similar: Music serves principally as a cooperative device within social groups to foster both internal harmony for its own sake and group solidarity in the face of intergroup conflict (Brown, 2000a, 2003). What this implies is that music is ultimately used for behavioral control at some level, and that the consequences of this use vary strikingly depending on the side of the ingroup/outgroup divide one happens to be on. The principal difference between small-scale and large-scale cultures in this regard is that the latter societies are hierarchical and multilayered, and therefore that the relevant lines of separation between groups are to a large extent internal to the society as a whole; conflict occurs internally between competing subcultures as well externally between large-scale units like nations. This creates a much more complicated dynamic of within-group and between-group processes. Be that as it may, I argue that music serves as a cooperative device at these many levels of structure, and identify six important aspects of music's role in this area that implicate behavioral control as a major mechanism of its action (discussed in Brown, 2000a).

1. Music has an important role in bringing about behavioral *conformity* and in stimulating *compliance* with social norms. In other words, music has the effect of *homogenizing* social behavior within groups, especially in ritual contexts. Boyd and Richerson (1985, 1990, 1992, 2002) have done extensive theoretical work demonstrating that "conformist transmission" is a major force influencing intergroup processes leading to cultural evolution. It does so by reducing behavioral variation within groups, thereby intensifying intergroup differences. How music promotes conformity and compliance is best seen in the context of group-wide performance-events, where it works on at least two major levels. First, music-events themselves comprise a significant component of the activities of the groups in question, and participating in such events serves as an important criterion for membership in the group. Attendance at the event is normative, and the ritual behaviors occurring at the event require conformity to group norms. Music reinforces codes of behavior. This applies equally well to tribal rituals, classical concerts, and raves. Second, music serves as an adjunct to language to emotively reinforce group values, virtues, and normative behaviors. Musical devices such as rhythm, repetition, and polyphony act to increase the meaning and memorability of linguistic messages (Richman, 2000). So at the level of contexts and contents, music acts as a force of compliance and conformity.

2. Along similar lines, music is a communication device that serves as an important component of systems of *persuasion and manipulation*. This fits in with music's role as a "knowledge-bearing function" (Eyerman and Jamison, 1998), one that reinforces group ideologies. This point is elaborated in detail in my communication model in the following sections of the essay.

3. As a force of social conformity, music has a major role in defining and reinforcing *social identity*, serving as a socializing force that fosters *enculturation* of individuals (for further discussion, see Dissanayake's and Volgsten's contributions to this volume). People learn about the normative behaviors of their society or subculture in the context of musical rituals. In addition, music, as a cultural entity, serves as an important symbol, in and of itself, of group identity, helping to create borders between ingroup and outgroup. This has emerged as one of the dominant themes in both ethnomusicology and sociomusicology. Much work in social identity theory has shown that identity formation is basically an exclusionary process. Music plays on our most tribal instincts and helps distinguish "us" from "them." As Frith and Street (1992: 80) wrote,

"When people feel most passionately about music together it is because of its power to mark boundaries."

4. Along these lines, music serves as an important basis for *sorting* people into groups in large-scale societies, creating musical-preference groups (Mark, 1998). This can be both the cause and effect of group formation: people not only sort into groups based on their musical tastes but use musical taste as an important criterion for membership in certain groups. Music is a means of creating and reinforcing group boundaries both within and between (sub)cultures. In recent years, this notion of sorting has found a role in studies of audience "fragmentation" in mass-media studies (McQuail, 2000) whereby musical-taste groups become increasingly divergent and autonomous collectivities, creating further boundaries and further independent genre groupings (see Martin's and Volgsten's contributions to this volume).

5. Music is an important device for creating group-level *coordination* and *cooperation*. Its ability to increase arousal and synchronize movement can lead to coordinated and cooperative action. Again, such coordination can be just as useful for threatening impending enemies as for reinforcing local sentiments of goodwill. When such coordination occurs in the context of group musical performance, it tends to create a symbolic feeling of equality and unity, one that produces a leveling of status differences among the participants, thereby dampening within-group competition. One area of intense analysis in sociomusicological studies has been in the music of social protest, where it is through music that social/political movements exert much of their influence on the society at large (see the essays in Garofalo, 1992a; Wicke, 1992; Eyerman and Jamison, 1998).

6. Music is an important device for *emotional expression, conflict resolution,* and *social play.* Music and dance are, in fact, among the very few devices for channeling emotional expression at the group level (e.g., Merriam, 1964). They are therefore among the most important means for creating cohesion and resolving internal conflicts. Such channeling of group emotion can be used to promote both social harmony and ethnocentric hate.

Each of these six factors helps to promote group formation, reduce internal competition, homogenize group behavior, and intensify intergroup differences. They highlight music's functional roles at the level of behavioral control. This should be seen in contrast to cultural theories that ignore the behavioral effects of music altogether and that focus on musical signification (e.g., symbolic interpretation) as an end in and of itself. Behavioral effects are at the core of my model, which provides a general approach to analyzing music in all types of societies by considering the ongoing balance between within-group and between-group processes.

The Social Enhancement Model of Music

Having sketched the end-point of the model—the ultimate effects of music—I will now begin at the beginning, where the *functions* of music are seen as the driving force for the uses and controlling mechanisms of music. I will describe the operations of music in the form of a social communication model whose final outcomes are the behavior-controlling effects just discussed.

While music is usually conceptualized as a cultural product, it is rarely seen as a form of communication, at least not by the rigorous standards of communication theorists. Virtually all of the mainstream musicological approaches place music itself—not *the social production of music*—at their starting point. For example, musical semiotics, as a theory of musical "signs," rarely considers the social processes of musical creation (although Tagg is certainly an exception here, e.g., 1987, 1989, this volume). Likewise, aesthetic and psychoacoustic perspectives focus exclusively on perceptual processes. Finally, cultural-studies approaches place their emphasis much more on musical "consumption" and "emission" than musical production, as their overriding focus is on recorded music. As Garofalo (1992b: 19) has written: "[Cultural theorists] can be criticized for privileging the act of consumption in such a way as to ignore not only the political intentions of artists and cultural workers, but also the political economy of production and, in particular, the influential role of the culture industry itself." For these reasons, I find it essential to return to the traditional analytical framework of linear transmission models in communication research, wherein "senders" are essential components of the communication process (McQuail, 2000). Such models, while far from being unambiguous when applied to music, offer the benefit of considering the full gamut of processes from production to reception, permitting consideration of both intended outcomes and actual effects. Alternatives (e.g., reception models) that ignore senders, function, intended effects, production, context, messages, transmission modes, and the like are doomed to provide an incomplete view of how music works. In most cases, such alternative approaches can themselves be subsumed by a more general communication framework.

My goal, therefore, is to develop a sociomusicological analysis rooted in the dynamics of communication: who sends what messages to whom? what are the sender's intentions? to what extent do the receivers' responses conform with the sender's intentions? what are the conditions influencing the receiver's interpretation? and what kinds of costs and benefits are involved in this type of communication? However, there are substantial problems in creating a communication model for music. Can we unambiguously identify senders and receivers? Can we identify a message? *What* is being communicated? How are musical messages encoded and decoded?

Figure I.1 provides a schematic overview of the model, which I call the Social Enhancement Model of music, a framework for understanding group-level musical communication. In this flow diagram, three classes of processes—labeled as

Figure I.1 The Social Enhancement Model of Music

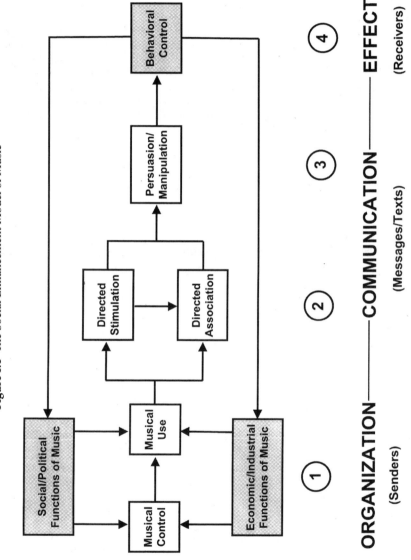

Note for figure I.1: The Social Enhancement Model of Music. The figure presents a flow diagram that outlines the dynamics of the sociomusicological processes described in this chapter. Four general processes are described as shown by the numbers toward the bottom of the figure. The first (1) is the organizational phase of musical communication, whose end result is the selection of musical senders. Musical use and control are driven by the functions of music, shown here as either social/political (all cultures) or economic/industrial (large-scale cultures only) in nature. Musical control is essentially control of use. The next two phases, (2) and (3), refer to the means by which musical messages are formed in a pragmatic manner by senders (and decoded by receivers) during musical use. Phase (2) refers to a set of two linked processes by which musical meaning is generated through either direct affective stimulation or through semiosis. Phase (3) refers to higher-level effects that impact on beliefs, attitudes and ideologies, thereby leading to persuasion and manipulation. All of this feeds onto the last process (4), which is that of behavioral control, conceptualized as the final outcome of musical communication in many contexts. This process of behavioral control then feeds back onto the initial social and economic functions underlying music use. In sum, music is viewed as an associative enhancer of social communication.

1, 2, and 3 in the lower part of the diagram—are seen as leading up to the final outcome of behavioral control. Briefly speaking, 1 refers to the organizational side of musical communication, focusing on music's social and economic functions and how these get translated into actual uses and controlling mechanisms. Stages 2 and 3 comprise the communication process itself, especially the message level. Message generation depends both on a process of affective modulation ("stimulation") and on a process of coupling these affective musical sounds to social objects ("association"). When the objects of this coupling encompass higher-order entities like beliefs, attitudes, and ideologies, music becomes a potent device for enhancing persuasion and manipulation. These latter processes are then used to promote behavioral control at some level, as described in the previous section of the essay. Finally, behavioral control itself feeds back onto the social and economic functions of music, thereby completing the loop. This creates the potential for both musical change and social change. The three parts of the model will be described in sequence below.

One of the goals of this model is to provide a view of music that applies to all types of cultures, both small and large. While there are many differences between the uses of music in different types of cultures and contexts, I believe that an extremely important difference lies in the mode of transmission—the "medium," if you will. I make a fundamental distinction here between *direct transmission* and *indirect transmission* of music (Burnett, 1996; McQuail, 2000). Direct transmission can be thought of as live performance of music, while indirect transmission consists mainly of the emission of pre-recorded music through speaker systems, either public or personal. The latter is usually associated with notions of mass communication. Direct and indirect transmission differ in many important respects in addition to the live versus recorded transmission route. In the case of direct transmission, musical senders are visible, identifiable, and often personally familiar people, whereas in the case of indirect transmission they usually are not. Direct transmission is usually associated with definable music events in which people gather together for some specific and common purpose (whether for music listening or otherwise), while indirect transmission is usually not. For this reason, the receivers of directly transmitted music are clustered both spatially and temporally, whereas those of indirectly transmitted music are widely dispersed in both senses. In general, the latter audience is much larger than the former and is significantly more non-interactive, anonymous, and amorphous. Indirect transmission is usually associated with the concept of "mass culture," which itself is generally characterized as non-traditional, non-elite, mass-produced, popular, commercial, and homogenized (McQuail, 2000). But I will not focus on those aspects here. The important distinction for my purposes relates to the communication arrangement itself. In the case of direct transmission, senders and receivers are relatively easy to identify, whereas in the case of indirect transmission they are much more elusive. To understand the latter situation, one has to rely on theories of mass communication. However, my approach will be to apply such theories to *all* musics transmitted by the indirect channel regardless of their genre or social function (i.e., not only popular music).

As cultures expand in size, complexity, and technological sophistication, and as the major route of musical communication changes from direct to indirect transmission, there is a dramatic shift in the basic unit of cultural transmission of music: a change from *performances* to *phonograms*. This has many important ramifications. Phonograms are cheap to replicate and easy to disperse geographically, whereas performances are neither of these. Transmission of phonograms, therefore, has an explosive potential to influence cultural exchange and mediate cultural domination. This greatly complicates a process of musical communication that is already quite complex even when restricted to a single culture. Moreover, as phonograms are virtually always economic commodities, the shift from direct to indirect transmission is accompanied by a tremendous expansion in the commercial importance of music, including the industrialization of music production. This highlights the point that in many cases of direct transmission, especially in small-scale cultures, the senders and receivers of music tend to be the same overall individuals, whereas in most cases of indirect transmission there is not only a social separation between musicians and nonmusicians but an economic distinction between "producers" (phonogram producers, that is) and "consumers."[1] So while music that is directly transmitted is often under cooperative and interactive control, music that is indirectly transmitted is often under the strict control of market forces, leading to the creation of "culture industries" (Horkheimer and Adorno, 1944/1972).

Despite these differences, what unites direct and indirect transmission of music is the underlying process of communication, which begins with senders' intentions and ends with receivers' responses. Situations of direct transmission allow us to define a relatively straightforward network of senders and receivers in the communication process, especially in the case of music events. Indirect transmission, in contrast, poses many challenges to understanding such a process. However, a lapse into non-communication-based frameworks that ignore musical senders and messages only makes matters worse as such models end up missing critical information needed to understand how music works.

Function, Use, and Control

I now go on to present the three phases of the Social Enhancement Model. The first phase comprises organizational processes related to the use and control of music at the social level whose end result is *the selection and arrangement of musical senders*. It is important to keep in mind that musical production and organization vary strikingly with the mode of musical transmission. Where it is direct, production deals with the contexts and mechanisms of musical *composition* and *performance*. Where it is indirect, production deals mainly with the contexts and forms of the *emission* of pre-recorded sounds. (I retain the use of the word "production" for the latter process even though no musical performance may occur in real time.) In both cases, senders comprise not only composers and musicians but the organizers of musical performance-events and emission-events.

One of my strongest tenets is that the use and control of music are motivated, specified, and controlled by social and economic functions (figure I.1), especially those related to behavioral control. Music is produced with social goals, costs, and benefits in mind, and this is usually related to group or subgroup function. Many contemporary approaches ignore the production of music altogether and therefore reduce music to a kind of environmental noise that impinges on unsuspecting listeners. By contrast, my model focuses on the *uses* of music (rather than its meanings or effects alone) and seeks to understand them in terms of social and economic functions. But what is the difference between use and function? Despite an abundant literature devoted to the study of music from the cultural-studies perspective, little mention has been made of the social functions of music, least of all from a cross-cultural vantage point. For this, one has to turn to the anthropological literature. But then the focus invariably shifts toward small-scale cultures and direct transmission of music, leaving a gap in the understanding of indirect transmission to mass audiences.

One of the few people to analyze the functions of music as well as clarify the dichotomy between function and use was Alan Merriam in his classic text *The Anthropology of Music* (1964). Merriam's analysis provides a useful starting point for my discussion: "When I speak of the uses of music, I am referring to the ways in which music is employed in human society, to the habitual practice or customary exercise of music either as a thing in itself or in conjunction with other activities.... 'Use', then, refers to the *situation* in which music is employed in human action; 'function' concerns the *reasons* for its employment and particularly the broader *purpose* that it serves" (p. 210, emphases added). From this analysis we can see that uses tend to be contexts or situations, whereas functions tend to be purposes or reasons. Functions are broad in scope and few in number, while uses are particular and many. As a general tenet, I would state that *use emanates from function* (see figure I.1). While it is true that a given use may have several functions and that a given function can be subserved by a host of uses, it will be instructive to think of musical uses as emanating from and being motivated by particular functions of music. One of the most important pieces of evidence that musical use is dictated and driven by social function is that in small-scale societies—where direct transmission and ritual music are the rule—the performance of musical works tends to show strong context-specificity, or what ethnomusicologists refer to as "functionality." Each musical form is inextricably associated with a particular social function or activity; likewise a given social function or activity requires performance of the appropriate musical form in order for it to be complete and proper (e.g., Arom and Khalfa, 1998).

Would it be possible to identify a set of broad functions that effectively encompass all the uses of music? Merriam (1964), working from a functionalist anthropological perspective, identified ten basic functions of music cross-culturally: emotional expression; aesthetic enjoyment; entertainment; communication; symbolic representation; physical response; enforcing conformity to social norms; validation of social institutions and religious rituals; contribution to the continuity and stability of culture; and contribution to the integration of society. In a similar vein, Dissanayake, in discussing the social purposes of ritual music in her chapter in this volume, identifies six general functions: display of resources; control and channeling of individual aggression; facilitation of courtship; establishment and maintenance of social identity; relief from anxiety and psychological pain; and promotion of group cooperation and prosperity. By focusing on ritual music in small-scale cultures, both Merriam and Dissanayake see music as functioning to increase cooperation and affiliation within social groups while at the same time downplaying internal competition and hostility.

But what about the functions of music in large-scale cultures? Are they the same as those seen in the cultures that Merriam and Dissanayake describe, or are they radically different? There seems to be much overall similarity but at least three major levels of difference. (1) I described earlier the hierarchical nature of large-scale societies and the conflict between cooperation and competition among the multiple, overlapping layers that make them up. Music's functions in large societies must be seen in light of the more complex balance of within-group and between-group forces. All of the functions that Merriam mentions are things that support within-group solidarity. By contrast, Dissanayake presents important functions, such as courtship and resource display, that have the clear potential to foster within-group competition. Furthermore, most contemporary discussions of popular music in Western culture focus on the potential of music to create social *divisions* within large societies along the lines of age, race, ethnicity, gender, sexual orientation, political orientation, and so on. So if music is functioning to promote the solidarity of groups, it is very often doing so in order to fuel opposition to other groups, to create difference. (2) For this reason, and for reasons related to the predominance of indirect musical transmission to temporally and spatially dispersed audiences in modern societies, a function related to *identity formation*, rather than social action per se, becomes highly accentuated (see the chapter by Martin, this volume, for a more detailed discussion). This has given lots of fuel to semiotic and cultural-studies approaches to music and their focus on signification for its own sake. (3) A new class of functions that are essentially absent in small-scale societies—*economic* functions—emerge in large-scale societies (see figure I.1). This applies mainly to cultures where music-making and music-producing are economic activities and, most especially, where a commercial music industry operates. The contention that economic functions may be among the most competitive functions of music has driven much Marxist thinking about the music industry (e.g., Horkheimer and Adorno, 1944/1972). Merriam doesn't include them in his anthropological discussion because music-making is generally collective and consensual in small-scale cultures, and the functions of music are mainly religious/political. But in societies where music-making is a professional specialization, where musical consumption (by either direct or indirect transmission) becomes an economic activity, and where music is used to promote other economic processes, a separate set of economic functions emerges as active determinants of the use and control of music. In sum, while music in large-scale cultures has political functions related to conformity, compliance, cooperation, and coordination, just as in small-scale cultures, much of the political emphasis is shunted toward group identity (rather than group action), and economic functions emerge as novel functions of great importance, two phenomena related to one another by the dominance of indirect transmission of recorded music.

Having discussed use and function—where use emanates from function—I would like to contrast this with "control." Control of music can involve suppression or imposition but its basic concern is to regulate facets of use. As shown in figure I.1, I conceptualize musical control as being *the control of use* and argue that use is the most salient target of control. It is a way of biasing use in certain directions by selectively favoring or disfavoring particular components of a music-culture. What aspects of musical use are controlled? To answer this question, it is instructive to look at the targets of musical censorship and propaganda seen throughout history (see Korpe, Reitov, and Cloonan, this volume): performance contexts, locales, composers, performers, song texts, musical works, genres, instruments, modes, intervals, rhythms, timbres, and so on. The important point to emphasize for my purposes is that *control is driven by exactly the same social and economic functions as use, and works to achieve behavioral control in a similar manner.* As is described elsewhere in this volume, musical control can assume at least three major forms: control by tradition (Dissanayake, this volume), governmental control (Korpe, Reitov, and Cloonan, this volume), and industrial control (Wallis, this volume).

The product of this interplay between function, control, and use is the organization of musical-performance events (direct transmission) and musical-emission events (indirect transmission), as dictated by social concerns related to behavioral control. This, in effect, creates a selection and arrangement of *musical senders*, whether it involves live performance or the activation of sound systems. In the case of direct transmission, it involves specification of the contexts and contents of music to be performed, including the selection of musicians, musical works, performance arrangements, and performance styles, often as an accompaniment to other social functions: hunting, political rallies, worship, dance, and so on. Functionality might or might not be an important consideration here.

In the case of indirect transmission, a much more complicated arrangement is obtained because sending is spatially and temporally displaced from performance. This creates two types of sending processes: *recording* and *emission*. The first is typically the domain of the music industry as part of the process of phonogram production. Although some phonograms are recordings of concert performances, most are studio recordings organized by agents and industry executives, and economic functions are the dominant driving force for this. It is through the emission process that the senders and receivers of indirect transmission are defined, and this process takes many forms, depending completely on the particular uses of the music. The predominant one in contemporary society is far and away the most amorphous one: private listening to phonograms by individuals (see Brown and Theorell, this volume). The sending process in this case is difficult to specify beyond the musicians themselves and their industry handlers. The receivers will be comprised of a large, undifferentiated, and unorganized aggregate of people. But there are less amorphous arrangements. For example, owners of businesses can play recordings in stores in order to attract customers and enhance sales. The senders in this case will be not only the people who recorded the music but those who control the emission of the music, where the receivers are the customers in the store. Likewise, one can think about films, where underscored music is composed to enhance the narrative properties of the film, as received by audiences of film viewers. In a similar fashion, the directors of television commercials often select well-known songs to be played in their commercials to influence customer affinity for advertised items. The sender is both the recorder and the emitter, and the audience consists of a dispersed aggregate. The bottom line is that senders and receivers must be analyzed on a *case-by-case basis* in terms of the transmission events that characterize musical communication. For indirect transmission, emitters are just as important as performers, and often times have interests, intentions, and agendas that differs greatly from those of the performers, thereby raising important concerns about the moral rights of composers and musicians (for further discussion, see Volgsten and Åkerberg, this volume).

Directed Stimulation and Directed Association

With this notion of musical "senders" in mind, I go on to discuss the second phase of the model, which deals with the communication process itself and most especially with the generation of socially meaningful *musical messages*. From the production side, it deals with how senders formulate messages in order to convey their meanings. From the reception side, it deals with how receivers decode these messages and interpret their meanings. It is important to emphasize that these two general processes involve essentially inverse mechanisms, as described by simple information-transfer models of communication. Therefore, I do not make any point of distinguishing production and reception mechanisms at this stage, emphasizing that they are, for the most part, inverse forms of processing.

An analysis of musical messages is intimately related to the complex problem of musical meaning or musical semantics. What does music mean, and how do people use music to express their meanings? The dominant framework in this area of musicology comes not from communication studies but from linguistic theory, as represented by the field of musical semiotics. The overriding emphasis of theories in musical semiotics is on the search to define the nature of musical semantics vis-à-vis linguistic theory. As a result, language serves as the standard against which theories of musical meaning are measured (see Monelle, 1995). This has generated a long-standing discussion about the nature of musical "signs," as modeled after the semiotic formulations of Ferdinand de Saussure and Charles Peirce (see Turino, 1999). However, I argue that such a view of musical meaning is limited and places too much emphasis on language in explaining music. In addition, musical semiotics is a theory of message *interpretation* and thus gives little consideration to musical senders or the social functions of communication. In my opinion, a view of musical meaning based on messages and communication rather than signs and language holds greater promise in explaining how music works.

Many theories in musicology make a binary distinction between two levels of musical meaning (reviewed in Feld and Fox, 1994). The first level deals with intrinsic emotive meanings, and is described by what I shall call "effect theories" of music, which I define as theories that explain music's emotive effects as a causal function of musical structure. The second level deals with linguistic, connotative meanings, and is typically described by musical semiotic theories. This distinction between meanings based on musical structure and musical association is very common in the literature. Designations for this distinction include: intrinsic/extrinsic; musical/extramusical; absolute/referential (Meyer, 1956; Feld and Fox, 1994); and acoustic/vehicle (Brown, 2000b).

My approach to this problem will be to argue that the semantic level of music should be represented as a linked pair of nested hierarchies, as shown in figure I.2 (see also Volgsten, this volume, for a discussion of the hierarchical levels of music). The top part of the figure shows a *musical hierarchy* representing various

Figure I.2 A Hierarchical View of Musical Semantics

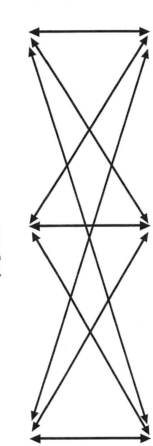

MUSICAL HIERARCHY

scale   rhythm   volume ⟶   motif   work   genre   repertoire
interval   tempo   melody
chord   progression

SEMANTIC HIERARCHY

EMOTIONS ⟶   SYMBOLS ⟶   ATTITUDES

emotion   word/text   ideology/text
mood   object   historical period
               person   geographical region
               place   social activity/function
               event   social identity

STIMULATION   ASSOCIATION   PERSUASION

Note for figure I.2: A Hierarchical View of Musical Semantics. The figure presents a conceptualization of musical semantics as a linked pair of nested hierarchies. The top part of the figure shows a *musical hierarchy* representing various levels of musical structure, from the most fundamental level (left) to the highest level (moving rightward). The lower part of the figure shows a *semantic hierarchy*, describing the musical meanings that are typically ascribed to components in the musical hierarchy. The hierarchy, again, proceeds rightward to higher levels of meaning. A progression is seen from (1) a level of emotional meanings to (2) a level of simple associative meanings to (3) a level of beliefs and attitudes. Musical semantics is basically concerned with defining the relationship between elements of these two hierarchies for particular musical messages. The interaction between the two hierarchies is highly multivalent, as shown by the crisscrossing arrows in the center of the figure. The vertical arrows occurring on line with the three categorical headings of "stimulation", "association" and "persuasion" show the most common means of linking the hierarchies, but many other connections are possible.

levels of musical structure. The lowest level of the hierarchy includes the structural features of music that effect theories typically describe: scales, intervals, melodic contours, chords, rhythms, tempos, volumes, timbres, etc. Higher up, and more inclusive, are motifs, melodies, and short progressions. Still higher are sections and musical works, with the highest level consisting of musical genres and entire cultural repertoires. This hierarchy is nested in the sense that anything at a higher level necessarily incorporates elements of all lower levels. Next, the bottom part of the figure shows a *semantic hierarchy*, demonstrating the musical meanings that can be typically ascribed to levels in the musical hierarchy. Such a semantic hierarchy shows parallels with that between icon, index, and symbol in Peircian semiology (Turino, 1999) although I do not make use of such concepts here. The lowest level typically involves affective ascriptions related to emotion, mood, and arousal, as described by effect theories of music. Higher levels in the semantic hierarchy deal with symbolisms, usually of the linguistic variety, as described by semiotic theories. Whereas a single chord is usually limited to a certain emotive meaning, a motif or phrase can have broader connotations, to include a word, object, person, event, place, and so on. A musical work can have even richer connotations, such as a verbal text, philosophy, historical period, social activity, social function, and the like. A musical genre can signify whole cultures, subcultures, geographical regions, social identities, and other similar things.

There are two important points to emphasize in this scheme. The first is the *nested* nature of the semantic hierarchy: higher-level meanings necessarily incorporate lower-level meanings. Symbolization of a geographical location by a musical motif, for example, necessarily incorporates the affective meaning of the chord as well. To my mind, the weakness of semiotic formulations is their inability to deal adequately with this kind of hierarchical arrangement, especially in relation to the affective properties of music. If I am correct in assuming that music's semantic system is hierarchical, then semiotic theories, as a class, should be seen to contain effect theories, even if this is not generally mentioned by semiotic theorists. The second major point to highlight is the *multivalent* nature of the interaction, as shown by the criss-crossing arrows in the center of figure I.2. Structural elements of music can acquire a host of meanings, and particular meanings can be instantiated at many levels of the musical hierarchy, using a large variety of musical devices. The vertical arrows on line with the three categorical headings of "stimulation," "association," and "persuasion" show the most common means of linking the hierarchies, but many other connections are possible.

Given these two hierarchies, the pragmatic task for the sender is to create musical messages that effectively unite musical structure and semantic meaning. Theories that describe the outcome of this process fall into the two categories of effect theories and semiotic theories depending on the level of the semantic hierarchy invoked in the message. I will maintain this dichotomy between effect theories and semiotic theories in the current discussion for historical reasons, as the theories have been so radically different in kind. To make these theories compatible with my model, I will convert them into communication processes: what I will call *directed stimulation* and *directed association*. My use of the word "directed" in both cases implies not only a sense of communicative intent but the pragmatic concern of senders to select sound devices that are appropriate to the messages being communicated. Stimulation and association are shown as parallel processes in my flow diagram (figure I.1) as they are parallel perceptions of musical sound patterns. The principal way in which stimulation and association differ here is simply at the level of the semantic hierarchy at which connections are made to musical structure. Aside from that, the two processes of message formation will be formally equivalent.

Directed Stimulation. Directed stimulation refers to the process by which the sender uses musical devices to produce rather immediate effects on attention, arousal, emotion, and mood in the receiver while making minimal use of external referents. Such effects are generally perceived as resulting from properties intrinsic to the sound patterns with little mediation by linguistic or extramusical meanings. I use the generic term "stimulation" here to imply that the effects on arousal and emotional state cover a large spectrum of responses. Message generation by directed stimulation is based on two related elements: *formulaic devices* (a musical lexicon) and *content matching* (pragmatic rules for creating meaningful messages). Both processes suggest that music has clear design features for communication. Devices refer to a series of formulas that can be used by musical senders to communicate intended messages. They include scale types, melody types (contour), rhythm types, tempos, volumes, registers, and the like. They can be used in a highly combinatorial (syntactic) fashion. Such devices can be either universal or culture-specific. The existence of formulas implies that there is a musical lexicon that is shared between the senders and receivers of musical communication within a culture and that defines the borders of that communication. Given this lexicon of devices, content matching, then, refers to the pragmatic process by which musical senders fashion their sounds so as to fit particular intended meanings. It is like choosing one's words and intonation properly when communicating something linguistically.[2] The sounds should fit the message. This is not just about expectancy or convention but about rationality and interpretability. Messages that are mismatched to content are misinterpreted or ignored by receivers. When Plato says that "the mode and rhythm [of a song] should suit the words" (*Republic* 398d), he means not only that language should take priority over music in creating songs but that the composed music should fit appropriately to the linguistic content of a song. Adorno (e.g., 1941, 1945) was wrong in his claim that commercial popular music was the principal genre employing conventionalized formulas. In fact, they are a prominent feature of every musical genre and tradition— improvisational as well as notated—if only because they facilitate communication. Cinema (Gorbman, 1987) and Western opera (Swain, 1997) provide a wealth of examples of such conventionalized formulas. Several empirical studies have demonstrated that people's verbal/emotive interpretations of musical passages are remarkably uniform (Tagg, 1987, 1989, this volume; Sloboda, 1991; Krumhansl, 1997, 2002; Sollberger, Reber, and Eckstein, 2003). Moreover, North and Hargreaves (1996) have demonstrated that people show highly convergent interpretations of which type of music they feel is appropriate for a given social activity or social context. There is thus an empirical basis for saying that the musical lexicon of a given culture is more or less shared by the members of that culture.

Formulaic devices are widely discussed in the musicology literature, and are well described by what I am calling here "effect" theories of music, which are the principal theoretical frameworks of the fields of music psychology, psychoacoustics, musical aesthetics, music physiology, and all areas of applied musicology (e.g., music therapy, commercial advertising). The power of music has been described from time immemorial in terms of its effects on people (Orpheus), animals (the dolphins of Orion), plants (growth stimulation), and inanimate objects (the walls of Jericho). The general idea behind effect theories at the semantic level is that features of musical structure intrinsically convey or communicate aspects of emotional expression without any mediation of cultural interpretation or convention (see caveats in Brown and Theorell, this volume). They thus place a strong focus on musical structure and have a definite nativist/universalist flavor to them.

Effect theories, whatever their form, suffer from a major weakness. They are exclusively *perceptual* theories: they completely lack the sender's communicative perspective. They tend to be individual-level theories that place receivers in a social vacuum. Music is viewed as appearing "out there," ready to impact on a passive listener. The sounds are environmental and purposeless. Because such theories rarely make mention of musical context, social function, communicative intent, musical taste, and the like, they are highly asocial and deterministic. Scott (1990) has rightly described such theories as reducing music to the level of a "mood-altering drug." The best way of overcoming these weaknesses is to *re-introduce the sender's role*. The manner in which this can occur in the context of directed stimulation is through the pragmatic process of content matching: musical sounds should correspond, in some significant way, with the ideas being communicated by the sender. Once that condition is imposed, content matching is relatively straightforward to predict using the lexicon and formulas of effect theories as guides. Content matching places the communication process on an equal playing field for senders and receivers. The same is true of speech, where words and prosodic devices are selected in a pragmatically appropriate manner to convey intended meanings during discourse events.

Directed Association. I now go on to discuss the second component in my dichotomous scheme. Directed association can be thought of as the process by which the sender uses musical devices to produce symbolic associations between musical structure and cultural objects. This process is similar to directed stimulation except that it occurs at a higher level of meaning-generation along the semantic hierarchy, namely, linguistically mediated associations. Theories of directed association are described by semiotic theories, which look to musical structure as a means of verbally associating, connoting, signifying, representing, etc., a broad array of cultural objects. Whereas effect theories are intrinsic and nativist, semiotic theories are extrinsic and cultural. I emphasize again that semiotic theories implicitly incorporate effect theories of music to the extent that musical semantics is an intrinsically hierarchical process, which is what I am arguing. In linking cultural objects to musical structure, semiotic theories are implicitly connecting the underlying affective associations of musical structure through a kind of piggy-back process. Thus, it is not sufficient for associative theories to be purely interpretive, as they often are in text-based cultural-studies models; they must be affective as well.

What semiotic theories share with effect theories is a focus on formulaic devices and content matching. This is another piece of evidence that semiotic theories contain effect theories. However, the formulas generally occur at higher levels of both musical structure and semantic meaning than those described by effect theories. Consider the following example. The Muslim call to prayer (*adhan* in Arabic) functions as a signal to bring worshippers to the mosque for a ceremony involving prayer as well as the cantillation of the Quran. The meaning of the call's sounds can achieve signification on many different levels. To any listener, the structural elements of the call (e.g., its scale, melodic contour, intonation pattern, free rhythm, vocal style) evoke certain emotive responses, as predicted by effect theories. To a worshipper in Cairo within listening distance of the minaret, the call's presence serves as a signal indicating the time for prayer, and its words remind the person of Allah's expectations that one go the mosque and pray. A visitor from Tunisia hearing these same sounds would be struck by the difference in their style and presentation compared to the call in his home in Gadès. His local call would represent something personal and Tunisian. It would be a symbol of his identity, and the Egyptian call a symbol of difference. The same call used in a travel documentary about Egypt would function as a musical tag for a particular geographical location and its culture. It would serve as a generic example of Middle Eastern music.

The major point is that there is a complex network relating features of the musical hierarchy to those of the semantic hierarchy, making musical semiotics a complicated affair. Musical signification can occur simultaneously at many levels which themselves may be hierarchical and multivalent. There is a one-to-many relationship between music's components and what they can signify. That said, the major weakness of semiotic theories is similar to that of effect theories: the *intent* behind this whole web of signification is simply missing, and music's presence is seen as some kind of background noise whose meanings impose themselves upon unsuspecting listeners. Most semiotic theories of music are individual-level theories that focus solely on the interpretation of musical symbols. My proposed solution to this problem is to focus less on signification per se and more on *how signification is used* in the service of communication. My prescription is the same as before: re-introduce the sender into the context of musical communication, especially in relation to content-matching processes and the design features of musical messages. Content matching assumes that a type of rational correspondence is sought between what is being communicated and the properties of the message, again with the caveat being that both universal and culture-specific elements are employed.

Persuasion and Manipulation

We now move to the last stage in the communication model as well as the last level in the semantic hierarchy: persuasion. Synthesizing theories of stimulation together with theories of semiosis leads me to the general theme of this introduction—that music works principally as a type of *associative enhancer of communication*, and that this very often occurs in the service of persuasion. This is the principal means by which music operates at the social level, and the basic concept underlying the Social Enhancement Model. Music functions to enhance and reinforce those things with which it is associated, to amplify and give salience to the messages being communicated. This concept can effectively tie together many disparate ideas about the nature, functions, and mechanisms of music in many different contexts and cultures. Again, I emphasize the importance of the hierarchical nature of message formation: musical persuasion usually requires a form of association, which itself usually depends on affective stimulation. What makes persuasion different from simple associationism is its higher-order semantic nature, usually involving beliefs, attitudes, values, and ideologies rather than simple object-significations. And as with the other levels in this dual hierarchy, formulas and fit are important factors in determining the effectiveness of communication.

Although most research on persuasion occurs in non-naturalistic settings (Petty and Cacioppo, 1986; Petty, Wegener, and Fabrigar, 1997; Wood, 2000; Albarrancin, 2002), the phenomenon of persuasion permeates all aspects of human life, from the simplest dyadic interactions to group decision-making to the alluring messages emanating from mass-media sources. Persuasion is a central component of the operations of religion, politics, commerce, and family (Jowett and O'Donnell, 1999). It is not only about how attitudes are changed but how they are *maintained* and *reinforced* despite an onslaught of factors designed to weaken them. As shown in my flow diagram (figure I.1), persuasion is used principally for the purposes of behavioral control. It is used to create compliance, conformity, and cooperation for the purposes of reinforcing group affiliations, justifying collective actions, swaying purchasing behavior, and the like. Persuasion figures prominently in most contexts in which music is used (see below), mainly group-ritual events (such as religious rituals), public places (e.g., stores, restaurants), and the audiovisual media (film, television, commercials, video). By capitalizing on the processes of stimulation and semiosis, music effectively plays into systems of beliefs and attitudes, thereby influencing motivation and behavior.

The central feature of persuasion as a form of communication is that the sender is trying to influence—not merely inform—the receiver, with the intent of modifying the latter's attitudes and/or behavior. Persuasion is usually thought of as an honest, consensual, and interactive process in which the sender's intentions to influence are clear and open (Jowett and O'Donnell, 1999). Its desired outcome is voluntary change, not coercion. Such a transaction is usually socially positive for both the sender and receiver, often resulting in mutual need satisfaction. In other words, it is a cooperative arrangement in which the social rewards of the communication process—be they at the levels of emotion, motivation, or action—are shared more or less equally between the sender and receiver. Persuasion is typically contrasted with *manipulation*,[3] where the main difference lies at the level of the sender's intentions: manipulation implies that the sender's intentions are both selfish and concealed (though the message need not necessarily be false or socially negative). In this regard, manipulation is a type of deceptive communication in which the receiver falsely expects to benefit by acting in the interests of the sender. In general, sender and receiver reap asymmetrical social rewards from such a transaction, with a strong bias in favor of the sender.

How can this distinction be applied to musical communication? The contrast between honest and deceptive signaling permeates evolutionary theories of communication, where *all* acts of communication are viewed in individualist terms as forms of manipulation (Krebs and Dawkins, 1984). Likewise there is a broad sense in which all music can be said to be manipulative to the extent that it influences a person's emotional state and tendency to act. This is the everyday view of music as a powerful modifier of people's emotional responses and manner of behaving, as described by "effect" theories of music.

In this broad view, music is non-manipulative only to the extent that it fails to have an impact on a person's emotions or motivations, in other words, to the extent that it produces *no effects*. Be that as it may, all music is produced with the intention of being manipulative (i.e., affective and motivating). When this concept is extended into the realm of behavior, it essentially reduces to the evolutionist's claim that all communication is manipulation. But this catch-all description permits little functional distinction between different types of use of music.

Contained within this global and monolithic view is another that says that the term "manipulation" should be reserved for *deceptive* forms of communication in which the sender's intentions are both selfish and concealed. By this criterion, a distinction can be made between manipulative and non-manipulative uses of music, where manipulative uses are defined as deceptive, and non-manipulative uses as honest and cooperative forms of communication. In the latter case, music is used to signal something socially positive for both the sender and receiver, and it is done so in an open way. The social rewards are shared more or less equally among the participants. This, then, reduces to the definition of true persuasion as described by communication theorists.

The view of manipulation that I will adopt in this essay will sit somewhere in between the broad and the narrow viewpoints just described. On the one hand, I will argue that most uses of music are driven by social and economic functions that lead to behavioral control at some level. However, I will acknowledge that such uses cover a broad gamut of communicative possibilities, from cooperative to competitive, altruistic to selfish, open to concealed, voluntary to coercive, and honest to deceptive. The limiting factor in this analysis will be an ability to distinguish persuasion (honest and cooperative) from manipulation (deceptive and selfish) in most circumstances. Elements of both types of communication will be present in almost all cases. The bottom line for me is that *music is usually used to influence behavior (manipulation in the broad sense)* and that *this often makes use of deceptive devices in order to achieve its effects (manipulation in the narrow sense)*. So while I am not saying that all musical communication is self-serving and deceptive, I am arguing that music's uses must be analyzed on a case-by-case basis in terms of senders' intentions, receivers' actions, and the social functions underlying communication. I believe that most cases of musical use will be shown to involve a combination of honest and deceptive elements.

How does musical persuasion work? The scientific study of persuasion offers a diverse array of theories. However, theories that focus exclusively on networks of interacting beliefs (i.e., propositional statements) are ill-equipped to deal with the influence of non-verbal factors like music on attitude or behavior. So one must look to theories that incorporate non-linguistic elements into the influencing process. The most important in this regard is the "elaboration likelihood model" of persuasion (Petty and Cacioppo, 1986; see also the chapters by North and Hargreaves and by Bullerjahn, this volume), which is both influential and controversial. According to this model, there are two parallel routes for processing messages. One is directly related to the message's (linguistic) content, and the other is peripheral to it. These are modulated independently. They are referred to, respectively, as the "central" and "peripheral" routes of processing. Importantly, the central route always involves linguistic statements and their interaction through networks of persuasive argumentation. They comprise the message in the crude sense of the term. Peripheral factors tend to be non-linguistic, affective cues, including such things as music, images, source characteristics (e.g., reputation, attractiveness, credibility), and so on, so the peripheral route is very often paralinguistic to the central route's verbal channel. These two routes serve as mutually reinforcing elements in the influencing process. Much research has suggested that peripheral cues are more significant during low-involvement processing and central cues during high-involvement processing (Petty and Cacioppo, 1986; for a classic example involving music, see Park and Young, 1986), but this dogma has been challenged (MacInnis and Park, 1991).

To a reasonable approximation, music would seem to work through a peripheral route of persuasion, operating more as a *reinforcer* than a direct message. As a peripheral cue, music is used to do many things, including (Huron, 1989; Dunbar, 1990): engage attention; enhance mood or emotion; act as an object's identity-marker, thereby enhancing message memorability; non-verbally comment on or describe narrative features; enhance message credibility; and provide unity and continuity. Such effects must be analyzed on a case-by-case, basis as the uses of music are so incredibly diverse. In addition, it is very important to distinguish between attitude *change* and attitude *reinforcement*, as the literature on persuasion has had an overwhelming focus on the former. An important generalization that has emerged from persuasion research is that deeply felt attitudes are quite resistant to change and that only unfamiliar, lightly felt, peripheral issues that do not matter much or are not tied to personal predispositions are subject to change. In the case of deeply held religious and political beliefs, music's major persuasion function might be related to the maintenance and reinforcement of beliefs already held about group identity and collective purpose. In contrast, in the case of lightly felt beliefs about everyday consumer goods where people's attitudes are swayable, music may serve more as an instrument of attitude change. In the one case, music directly reinforces beliefs of central importance (verbal texts about gods, historical epics, norms, collective activities, etc.); it is acting as a direct complement to the elaboration of issue-relevant arguments by the central route of processing. In the other case, it is complementing what is already a peripheral route of persuasion; for example, it is used to enhance the appeal of visual images in television commercials. It is difficult to make hard generalizations here as music's uses are so diverse. However, a persuasion perspective offers a valuable analytic approach to understanding music's mechanism of operation in many, if not most, contexts of use.

Understanding How Music Works:
Toward a Pragmatics of Music

The perspective of this essay and book calls for the introduction of a pragmatic approach to the sociology of music. This approach considers not only music's effects and meanings but the uses to which music is put in order to convey these effects and meanings, all within the context of the motivations that underlie them. Pragmatics is a branch of linguistics that considers the practical details of how people frame their messages in the context of discourse. It deals with people's intended meanings, assumptions, purposes, and goals, and the kinds of actions they are performing when they communicate (Yule, 1996). Pragmatics looks beyond formal considerations of semantics and syntax to more practical concerns for how people construct meaningful messages to suit their audience and the context of their presentation, all in accordance with their motivations and desired outcomes. In reality, all communication—be it linguistic, musical, gestural—is guided by pragmatic concerns. Because music has not traditionally been conceptualized as a communication system but rather as an art form, pragmatics has rarely been considered an essential part of musicological analysis, a situation which is dubious on both psychological and sociological grounds. It is currently sociomusicological dogma that artists are products of their society who create their works with particular audiences in mind, even if those are specialist audiences made up of peers and insiders. However, even much contemporary thinking in the sociology of popular music downplays the motivational side—and therefore the pragmatic side—of musical communication and instead places the analytic focus on listeners and their interpretation of musical symbols and texts, as if these symbols and texts simply appeared out of nowhere, like the "invisible music" of shopping malls. While it might at first seem vulgar or cynical to think about music as a persuader and/or manipulator, it is only too easy to identify such a role for music in social life.

To sum up, the Social Enhancement Model of music is a communication model that considers the full gamut of processes, from the social/economic functions motivating musical use to the ultimate influence of this use on individual and collective behavior. Music basically operates as an enhancer of persuasion processes, which themselves depend on more fundamental processes of stimulation and semiosis. As a communication system, music uses a lexicon of well-understood acoustic devices that are employed in a pragmatic manner to fit the content of the intended message. The notion of pragmatics places music firmly in the sphere of communication, with the focus on the senders and receivers of musical messages.

Overall, this volume makes a plea to implement a communication model in musicology, especially one that considers musical use and control from a pragmatic perspective. This perspective, while commonplace in linguistics, is all but absent in musicology, and it is hoped that this book will help stimulate work in this area. Understanding the relationship between music and society will never come about by seeing music's social effects exclusively from the listener's perspective. This relationship must be seen equally well from the *user's* perspective in terms of the power relations that allow music's affective and semiotic devices to perform their special magic.

At the experiential level, the magnitude of our exposure to music is ever-increasing. Every acoustic niche is becoming filled with music. The roller coaster rides at Disneyland now come complete with Wagnerian orchestral scores supplying crescendos at just the right moments. People walk away from these rides feeling exhilarated. What was in the olden days merely a visual-kinetic experience has, in our time, become an *audio*-visual-kinetic experience in which a musical composer has carefully designed a correspondence map between the contours of the melodic line and those of visual space. The German comparative musicologist Erich von Hornbostel called this type of association between music and space "melodic dance" in 1904. Nowadays we seem to go through life experiencing a type of melodic dance wherever we go. The real question from the standpoint of the current volume is whether we dance freely or whether, like wooden puppets, we come with strings attached.

Notes

1. The cultural-studies term "consumer" has come to be used for describing *all* listeners of music, regardless of the transmission mode for music.
2. At the interface of music and speech, we see a wonderful example of the use of musical formulas and content matching in the case of mother-infant communication (Fernald, 1992; Papousek, 1996; Dissanayake, 2000a, 2000b).
3. Many texts contrast persuasion with *propaganda*, but I will use the more general term "manipulation" in the remainder of this introduction.

References

Adorno, T. W. (1941). "On popular music." *Studies in Philosophy and Social Sciences* 9: 17–48.
_____ (1945). "A social critique of radio music." *Kenyon Review* 7: 208–217.
Albarrancin, D. (2002). "Cognition in persuasion: An analysis of information processing in response to persuasive communications." *Advances in Experimental Social Psychology* 34: 61–130.
Arom, S. and Khalfa, J. (1998). "Une raison en acte: Pensée formelle et systématique musicale dans les sociétés de tradition orale." *Revue de Musicologie* 84: 5–17.
Boyd, R. and Richerson, P. J. (1985). *Culture and the Evolutionary Process.* Chicago: University of Chicago Press.
_____ (1990). "Culture and cooperation." In J. J. Mansbridge (ed.) *Beyond Self-Interest* (pp. 111–132). Chicago: University of Chicago Press.
_____ (1992). "Punishment allows the evolution of cooperation (or anything else) in sizable groups." *Ethology and Sociobiology* 13: 171–195.

_____ (2002). "Group beneficial norms can spread rapidly in a structured population." *Journal of Theoretical Biology* 215: 287–296.

Brown, S. (2000a). "Evolutionary models of music: From sexual selection to group selection." In F. Tonneau and N. S. Thompson (eds.) *Perspectives in Ethology.* Vol. 13: *Evolution, Culture, and Behavior* (pp. 231–281). New York: Kluwer Academic/Plenum Publishers.

_____ (2000b). "The 'musilanguage' model of music evolution." In N. L. Wallin, B. Merker, and S. Brown (eds.) *The Origins of Music* (pp. 271–300). Cambridge, MA: MIT Press.

_____ (2003). "Biomusicology, and three biological paradoxes about music." *Bulletin of Psychology and the Arts* 4: 15–17.

Burnett, R. (1996). *The Global Jukebox: The International Music Industry.* London: Routledge.

Dissanayake, E. (2000a). "Antecedents of the temporal arts in early mother-infant interaction." In N. L. Wallin, B. Merker, and S. Brown (eds.) *The Origins of Music* (pp. 389–410). Cambridge, MA: MIT Press.

_____ (2000b). *Art and Intimacy: How the Arts Began.* Seattle: University of Washington Press.

Dunbar, D. S. (1990). "Music, and advertising." *International Journal of Advertising* 9: 197–203.

Elster, J. (1983). *Explaining Technical Change: A Case Study in the Philosophy of Science.* Cambridge: Cambridge University Press.

Eyerman, R. and Jamison, A. (1998). *Music and Social Movements: Mobilizing Traditions in the Twentieth Century.* Cambridge: Cambridge University Press.

Feld, S. and Fox, A. A. (1994). "Music and language." *Annual Review of Anthropology* 23: 25–53.

Fernald, A. (1992). "Human maternal vocalizations to infants as biologically relevant signals: An evolutionary perspective." In J. H. Barkow, L. Cosmides, and J. Tooby (eds.) *The Adapted Mind: Evolutionary Psychology and the Generation of Culture* (pp. 391–428). Oxford: Oxford University Press.

Frith, S. and Street, J. (1992). "Rock Against Racism and Red Wing: From music to politics, from politics to music." In R. Garofalo (ed.) *Rockin' the Boat: Mass Music and Mass Movements* (pp. 67–80). Boston: South End Press.

Garofalo, R. (ed.) (1992a). *Rockin' the Boat: Mass Music and Mass Movements.* Boston: South End Press.

Garofalo, R. (1992b). "Understanding mega-events: If I are the world then how do I change it?" In R. Garofalo (ed.) *Rockin' the Boat: Mass Music and Mass Movements* (pp. 15–35). Boston: South End Press.

Gorbman, C. (1987). *Unheard Melodies: Narrative Film Music.* Bloomington: Indiana University Press.

Henrich, J. (2004). "Cultural group selection, coevolutionary processes and large-scale cooperation." *Journal of Economic Behavior & Organization* 53: 3–35.

Horkheimer, M. and Adorno, T. W. (1944/1972). *The Dialectic of Enlightenment.* Translated by John Cumming. New York: Herder and Herder.

Huron, D. (1989). "Music in advertising: An analytic paradigm." *Musical Quarterly* 73: 557–574.

Jowett, G. S. and O'Donnell, V. (1999). *Propaganda and Persuasion.* 3rd ed. Thousand Oaks: Sage Publications.

Kincaid, H. (1990). "Assessing functional explanation in the social sciences." In A. Fine, M. Forbes, and L. Wessels (eds.) *PSA 1990: Proceedings of the 1990 Biennial Meeting of the Philosophy of Science Association* (pp. 341–354). East Lansing: Michigan State University Press.

Krebs, J. R. and Dawkins, R. (1984). "Animal signals: Mind reading and manipulation." In J. R. Krebs and N. B. Davies (eds.) *Behavioral Ecology: An Evolutionary Perspective.* 2nd ed. (pp. 380–402). Oxford: Blackwell Scientific Publications.

Krumhansl, C. L. (1997). "An exploratory study of musical emotions and psychophysiology." *Canadian Journal of Experimental Psychology* 51: 336–352.

_____ (2002). "Music: A link between cognition and emotion." *Current Directions in Psychological Science* 11: 45–50.

MacInnis, D. J. and Park, C. W. (1991). "The differential role of characteristics of music on high- and low-involvement consumers' processing of ads." *Journal of Consumer Research* 18: 161–173.

Mark, N. (1998). "Birds of a feather sing together." *Social Forces* 77: 453–485.

McQuail, D. (2000). *McQuail's Mass Communication Theory.* 4th ed. London: Sage Publications.

Merriam, A. P. (1964). *The Anthropology of Music.* Evanston: Northwestern University Press.

Meyer, L. B. (1956). *Emotion and Meaning in Music.* Chicago: University of Chicago Press.

Monelle, R. (1995). "Music and semantics." In E. Tarasti (ed.) *Musical Signification: Essays in the Semiotic Theory and Analysis of Music* (pp. 91–107). Berlin: Mouton de Gruyter.

North, A. C. and Hargreaves, D. J. (1996). "Situational influences on reported musical preference." *Psychomusicology* 15: 30–45.

Papousek, M. (1996). "Intuitive parenting: A hidden source of musical stimulation in infancy." In I. Deliège and J. Sloboda (eds.) *Musical beginnings* (pp. 145–170). Oxford: Oxford University Press.

Park, C. W. and Young, S. M. (1986). "Consumer response to television commercials: The impact of involvement and background music on brand attitude formation." *Journal of Marketing Research* 23: 11–24.

Petty, R. E. and Cacioppo, J. T. (1986). "The elaboration likelihood model of persuasion." *Advanced Experimental Psychology* 19: 123–205.

Petty, R. E., Wegener, D. T., and Fabrigar, L. R. (1997). "Attitudes and attitude change." *Annual Review of Psychology* 48: 609–647.

Plato (1987). *The Republic.* Translated by Desmond Lee. 2nd ed. London: Penguin.

Richman, B. (2000). "How music fixed 'nonsense' into significant formulas: On rhythm, repetition and meaning." In N. L. Wallin, B. Merker and S. Brown (eds.) *The Origins of Music* (pp. 301–314). Cambridge, MA: MIT Press.

Scott, L. M. (1990). "Understanding jingles and needledrop: A rhetorical approach to music in advertising." *Journal of Consumer Research* 17: 223–236.

Sloboda, J. A. (1991). "Music structure and emotional response: Some empirical findings." *Psychology of Music* 19: 110–120.

Sober, E. and Wilson, D. S. (1998). *Unto Others: The Evolution and Psychology of Unselfish Behavior.* Cambridge, MA: Harvard University Press.

Sollberger, B., Reber, R. and Eckstein, D. (2003). "Musical chords as affective priming context in a word-evaluation task." *Music Perception* 20: 263–282.

Swain, J. P. (1997). *Musical Languages.* New York: Norton.

Tagg, P. (1987). "Musicology and the semiotics of popular music." *Semiotica* 66: 279–298.

_____ (1989). "An anthropology of television music?" *Svensk Tidskrift för Musikforskning* 71: 19–42.

Turino, T. (1999). "Signs of imagination, identity, and experience: A Peircian semiotic theory for music." *Ethnomusicology* 43: 221–255.

von Hornbostel, E. M. (1904/1975). "Melodischer Tanz: Eine musikpsychologische studie." Reprinted with English translation as "Melodic dance: A musico-psychological study." In K. P. Wachsmann, D. Christensen, and H-P. Reinecke (eds.) *Hornbostel Opera Omnia* (pp. 204–215). The Hague: Martinus Nijhoff.

Watkins, J. W. N. (1957). "Historical explanation in the social sciences." *British Journal for the Philosophy of Science* 8: 104–117.

Wicke, P. (1992). "'The times they are a-changin': Rock music and political change in East Germany." In R. Garofalo (ed.) *Rockin' the Boat: Mass Music and Mass Movements* (pp. 81–92). Boston: South End Press.

Wood, W. (2000). "Attitude change: Persuasion and social influence." *Annual Review of Psychology* 51: 539–570.

Yule, G. (1996). *Pragmatics.* Oxford: Oxford University Press.

Manipulation by Music

PART I MUSIC EVENTS

Chapter 1

RITUAL AND RITUALIZATION
Musical Means of Conveying and Shaping Emotion in Humans and Other Animals

Ellen Dissanayake

Introduction

Emotional experiences of music are notably difficult to describe and have resisted philosophical and psychological as well as vernacular explanation. This essay uses a new departure by taking an ethological approach to questions of musical experience—that is, treating music as a behavior that evolved in ancestral humans because it contributed to their survival and reproductive success. In particular, I describe interesting and suggestive similarities between the evolutionary (biological) process of ritualization in animal communication and the ritual (cultural) uses of musical behavior in human rites or ceremonies. In both ritual and ritualization, stylized (i.e., formalized, rhythmically repeated, exaggerated, and elaborated) sounds and movements are important means of shaping the responses of participants, as they are in music. The ethological view of emotion as a motivator of behavior similarly brings a fresh approach to the understanding of possible sources of musical emotion, permitting a preliminary "ethological taxonomy" of four types of emotional response to music. Finally, surveying the uses of music in some thirty traditional societies I describe six general social functions of ritual music that have counterparts in animal ritualizations and parallels in the uses of music in modern societies.

* * *

In the preface to his magisterial *History of Music Aesthetics*, Enrico Fubini (1990) well described the difficulty of explaining musical experience:

Since ancient times, philosophers, intellectuals and musicians have written about music and have clearly believed it to have a particular status among the arts, being endowed with special powers.... Both the fascination it has always exerted and its extreme elusiveness are due primarily to the nature of its expressiveness: it expresses something, and yet, despite the complexity of its 'language,' it says nothing definite about anything; while everybody, even the strictest of formalist thinkers, seems to concur in ascribing to music a certain power of expression, nobody has yet succeeded in defining clearly what it is that music expresses or how it does so. (pp. xi–xii)

One who wishes to add to this long and abstruse discourse about musical experience should have good reasons for doing so. My excuse here is that I intend to look at the subject in a heretofore untried way—that is, as an ethologist or biological anthropologist, who approaches music as a behavior that evolved in ancestral humans because it contributed to their survival and reproductive success. I will be specifically concerned with musical emotion—how music produces emotion, and what musical emotion *is* or *does*. In an ethological view, the biological purpose of emotions is to motivate behavior—to make us respond appropriately to the sorts of occurrences in the environment that could affect us, for good or ill. In this sense, then, musical experience was originally functional.

This approach is unfamiliar, and carries with it assumptions and questions that deserve treatment much more extensive than I shall be able to provide in a single essay. As a preliminary step, however, I will describe interesting and suggestive similarities between the evolutionary (biological) process of "ritualization" in animal communication and the ritual (cultural) use of musical behavior in human rites or ceremonies. This comparison will, I hope, provide a useful framework for understanding (a) some of the ways that music creates and shapes ("manipulates") emotions, and (b) the social ends that these emotional dispositions serve. My examples will come from selected small-scale traditional societies, whose members lead subsistence lives more in character with those of ancestral humans than our lives today in complex, postindustrial, modernized societies. Quite clearly, however, it is from these complex societies that our present ideas about music have come. Thus to begin with, it will be useful to look—somewhat summarily—at a few general differences in the ways in which music is regarded and used in non-Western societies as compared to the modern West.

Traditional Musics Compared with Western Ideas about Music

Although the term "music" does not mean the same thing in all cultures—indeed, most societies have no concept or word for "music" in a Western sense—the activities of singing and otherwise making and participating in music appear to be universal in humans. That is, "human sound communication outside the scope of spoken language" (Nettl, 1983: 24) exists in all known and described human societies, and has observable effects on its makers and listeners.

Musics in traditional societies of Africa, Oceania, Australia, North and South America, and Asia sound very different from one another. Nonetheless, they share certain characteristics of conceptualization and behavior that, in some respects at least, differentiate them from present-day ideas about Western music, which have been affected, among other things, by the historical process of modernity. (See also the last section of this chapter.)

In the modern West, music—although difficult to define—typically refers to formalized melodic and rhythmic sounds produced by the human voice or other instruments. In small-scale societies, however, a phenomenon that we would call music (say, melodic vocalizing or drumming) may well be categorized somewhat differently and overlap with phenomena that a Western observer would probably consider irrelevant. For example, what might be identified as the "music" of the Kaluli of the Southern Highlands of Papua New Guinea, because it sounds like "song" or "humanly organized sound," is regarded by its makers as being but one of a variety of sounds shared to greater or lesser degrees by natural and animal agents—for example, rain, waterfalls, crickets, and birds, as well as humans (Feld, 1984: 389). Alternatively, a traditional society's ideas about its music might exclude elements that a Western observer would consider essential or make distinctions we ignore. The Venda of Southern Africa deny, as we might not, that there is a continuum between speech and song, but within the realm of what they consider to be music they distinguish, as we do not, between melodies that are free or lyrical and melodies that are dominated by the tone patterns of words (Blacking, 1982: 19). Nonmusical sounds (including distress calls of a chicken dragged on the ground from house to house, gunshots, blacksmith bellows, and cacophony from striking household utensils) may be recontextualized by the Anlo-Ewe in Ghana to become "musical" sounds in healing and exorcism practices (Avorgbedor, 2000).

To Western minds, music is generally considered to be a rare talent possessed by only a few. As a consequence, most contemporary thinkers who have pondered the evolutionary contribution of music to human life regard it as an inexplicable "mystery" because it is so unevenly distributed among individuals (e.g., Barrow, 1995). If one looks at traditional societies, however, it is evident that "music" is as broadly endowed as any other human capacity, and virtually everyone participates in music making. Although some societies have musical specialists, in most others, like the Kaluli, skill in "musical" activities such as song, stylized weeping, whooping, cheering, humming, drumming, and identifying bird, animal, and other environmental sounds is acquired naturally, rather like learning to talk and understand speech. Differences in performing and composing ability are attributed to differences in individual interest and desire, not to special endowment (Feld, 1984: 390).

In traditional societies also, unlike in the modern West, music is typically—like speech—a multimedia activity (Blacking, 1982: 16). That is, singing or playing an instrument are inseparable from gestural movement (in both performer and audience), whether as dance or beating time with the body, hands, or feet. For example, the Kalapalo of central Brazil "cannot easily" sing a tune without the movement of the body, especially the legs; a listener might swing in his or her hammock or merely tap a hand on a nearby housepost (Basso, 1985: 250).

Traditional music is rarely an end in itself, but a means to social ends (e.g., Sugarman, 1988: 2), and to varying degrees is integrated with other activities of life. Whereas in modern societies we tend to think of music as something set apart as a performance by specialists for somewhat detached appreciation by individuals in an audience, traditional music is generally integral to ritual ceremonies that are performed with a particular important pragmatic end in view (Kapferer, 1983: 188; Seeger, 1987: 7). These ceremonies usually require community participation and, along with the music that is essential to them, are considered to be vitally necessary to the maintenance of the society. As Anthony Seeger has claimed for the Suya people of the Northern Mato Grasso in Brazil, it is not the economic system that created the ritual but the ritual that mobilizes men, women, and children to be willing participants in the economic system (Seeger, 1987: 132).

More than in modern societies, traditional music is associated with the supernatural (Nettl, 1983: 40)—with a non-mundane time or realm or state that is frequently created, sustained, or reaffirmed by its performance (e.g., Shapiro and Talamantez, 1986; Seeger, 1987: 85, 131). Frequently, for example, music is used to communicate with powerful beings (e.g., among the Kalapalo of central Brazil, where they are "sung into being" [Basso, 1985: 253], or the Nigerian Yoruba, where they are "danced into existence" [Drewal and Drewal, 1983: 105]), or to assist participants into a trance state (e.g., Katz, 1982; Roseman, 1991; Becker, 2000) in which the ritual's transformative purpose can take place,[1] since music is frequently thought to have transcendent and transformative powers (e.g., Basso, 1985; Sugarman, 1988; Norton, 2000) and to structure the participants' reality (e.g., Kapferer, 1983).

This brief and necessarily incomplete introduction to the practice of music in traditional societies should make clear that in order to understand music as an evolved human endowment, it is essential to think of it more broadly than is customary in the modern West. It is possible that the earliest human music included sounds or activities that are not today considered to be music (e.g., movement or dance); ancestral music would have been almost certainly primarily communal and participatory rather than solitary, remote, and impractical. Indeed, judging by music in traditional societies of today, it would have been essential to—even coextensive with—ceremonial occasions in which important social purposes were addressed.

I will describe these social purposes in a later section, and return again to the aforementioned contrasts between traditional and modern ideas about the nature and practice of music at the end of the essay. First, however, let us examine suggestive parallels between human ceremonial ritual—in which music appears to be a universal and necessary component—and the defining features of what students of animal behavior call "ritualized" behaviors.

Ritual and Ritualization

The term "ritual," as the British anthropologist Jack Goody (1961) claimed some forty years ago, has been applied by anthropologists and others to a wide assortment of acts and beliefs. Here I will follow Julian Huxley and others (Huxley, 1966; Watanabe and Smuts, 1999) by approaching human ritual through an understanding of the term "ritualization," which has a precise meaning in the study of animal communication.[2]

Before beginning this discussion, however, let us digress and briefly review what is meant by the term "evolution by natural selection." Natural selection is the process by which species change (evolve) over time. Breeders of plants and animals exercise *artificial* selection, choosing to cross individuals with certain desirable traits (e.g., coat color, shape, size, hardiness, speed, milk productivity) for particular purposes. In natural selection, the environment does the "choosing," so that over generations the individuals who are best adapted to existing environmental circumstances tend to predominate.

Charles Darwin's theory of evolution by natural selection arises from applying logic to three natural history observations: (a) *superabundance*: biological organisms have the ability or tendency to reproduce themselves far more than is necessary to maintain their numbers (e.g., over a lifetime, one frog lays thousands of eggs); (b) *variation*: each individual differs from others of its kind, and these differences are inherited from parents and passed on in varying combinations to offspring; (c) *limited resources*: if every frog egg resulted in a mature frog, there would not be enough ponds and insects to sustain them. It follows that if resources are limited and there is a superabundance of individuals, there will be some kind of competition or struggle for these resources. It also follows that individuals whose differences enable them better to acquire resources and escape harm will be better able to survive and pass on their more adaptive traits to offspring, who in turn will do the same.

Not only anatomy and physiology are affected by selective forces. Psychology and behavior too have evolved to "fit" or "adapt" individuals to a way of life in a particular environment. For example, within a genus (say, Felidae), some species (lions) have a way of life (on the open savanna) that promotes sociality and group hunting, while other species' way of life (tigers in dense jungles) fosters asociality and solitary hunting. Not only behavioral systems of social interaction but of mating, parenting, acquiring food, and defense—individually called "behaviors" or "behavioral mechanisms"—evolved to suit the members of a species to their particular environmental niche and its required way of life.[3]

In 1914, while studying the courtship behavior of birds (specifically, the great crested grebe), Julian Huxley proposed that highly stereotyped communicative signals in animals have evolved by natural selection in the same way as have more instrumental behaviors. He coined the term "ritualization" to refer to the process by which selection gradually alters certain behaviors into increasingly effective signals (Watanabe and Smuts, 1999). In the 1950s, ethologists—biologists who specialize in the study of animal behavior—expanded Huxley's insight and described how the process occurs (e.g., Tinbergen, 1952, 1959).[4]

In ritualization, components of a behavior that occurs as part of normal, everyday, instrumental activity—such as preening, nestbuilding, preparing to fly, or caring for young—are, as it were, "selected" or taken out of context, "ritualized," and used to signal an entirely different motivation—usually an attitude or intention that may then influence (affect or manipulate) the behavior of another animal. For example, the head movements used by gulls to pluck grass for building a nest may be co-opted and ritualized to signal aggression (thus driving another gull away), or behaviors derived from feeding young (e.g., touching bills, offering a token with the bill, coughing as if regurgitating) may become ritualized and used for courtship (attracting a mate).

In the course of ritualization, particular changes occur in the original behavior pattern so that the resulting signal becomes prominent, distinctive, and unambiguous, and consequently is not confused with its precursor (Smith, 1977; Eibl-Eibesfeldt, 1989). Compared to the original instrumental or "ordinary" precursor behavior, ritualized movements become "extraordinary" and thus attract attention. They typically become (a) simplified or formalized (stereotyped), and (b) repeated rhythmically, often (c) with a "typical" intensity (Morris, 1957)—that is, with a set regularity of pace. The signals are frequently (d) exaggerated in time and space, and (e) further emphasized by the development of special colors or anatomical features.

A good example of a ritualized behavior occurs in pheasant courtship where males try to entice females by scratching and pecking at the ground as if finding food, just as hens peck to attract their chicks. The food-acquiring movement originally used instrumentally in parental behavior is co-opted for the quite different signaling function of attracting a mate, and may become further altered (ritualized—formalized and elaborated) as in the impeyan cock pheasant who, while pecking, adds a deep bow. When a female comes to investigate he spreads his wings and tail feathers, keeps his head down, and remains still while his fanned-out tail moves slowly and rhythmically up and down.

Another member of the pheasant family, the peacock, also initially scratches and bows to attract a hen, but adds even more extravagant variation to his spread tail, which has evolved to become particularly conspicuous with beautiful colors and patterning, and quivering movement. Although his beak still points downward as in other kinds of pheasant, the peacock's lavish courtship display otherwise contains little of the original food-enticement movements from which it was phylogenetically derived (Eibl-Eibesfeldt, 1971).

Human ritual ceremony, with its associated and necessary arts, has obvious parallels with the biological display of ritualized signals (Dissanayake,

1979, 1988, 1992). Watanabe and Smuts (1999) have listed characteristics of biologically evolved cooperative (as contrasted with agonistic) ritualizations in non-human animals that suggest an evolutionary substrate for human culturally created rituals. That is, ceremonial rituals, like ritualized behaviors, draw on gestures or behaviors from other social contexts and recombine them into distinctive displays or signals. These recombined displays now relate not to instrumental activities (e.g., ordinary motor behavior, everyday discourse, making and using everyday functional objects), but to specialized social communication. The ceremonial displays become "ritualized" to the extent that they circumscribe a repertoire of possible behaviors and establish a formalized framework of interaction that participants recognize as such and choose to conform to. Finally, the displays literally embody in communal participation the mutual coordination they presuppose (Watanabe and Smuts, 1999).

In a traditional North American wedding ceremony, for example, the church or hall is specially decorated with flowers; bridesmaids wear special clothing and walk solemnly in a measured tread to a musical background before the more splendidly attired bride, who is accompanied by her father. Using formal, archaic language, the officiating cleric follows a prescribed sequence of actions and words. Guests, also specially garbed, occupy prescribed places depending on their relationship to the bride or groom, and sit or stand at prescribed times. These various components of the ceremony have been extracted from their ordinary contexts (e.g., occupying shelter, covering the body, moving from place to place, interacting with friends and parents, falling in love, deciding to marry, speaking), made special and distinctive (with flowers, music, fine fabrics, arresting language, artificial movement, and prescribed spatial and temporal arrangement), and recombined into a formalized or stereotyped event that participants recognize and experience together as "a wedding." Such rituals or ceremonies have characterized human groups for thousands if not tens of thousands of years.[5]

It should be noted that a large proportion of the distinctive recombined components of human ritual ceremonies resemble (or in fact *are*) what we call the arts—dance and mime, poetic language, visual display, and "music" (song). Indeed, one can view ceremonial and other arts as ordinary behavior (i.e., ordinary bodily and facial movements, ordinary speech, utilization of ordinary objects and surroundings, and ordinary prosodic vocalizations) made *extra*ordinary through essentially the same operations or procedures as in animal ritualizations: formalization (stereotypy), repetition, exaggeration, and elaborations of various kinds.

Of course, human arts and rituals are culturally created, in contrast to the ritualized behaviors of animals, which are instinctive. The peacock is not free to experiment with his display, nor can a robin decide to behave like a peacock. Their partners would not understand such "creativity" and would not agree to mate and produce offspring endowed with similar ingenuity. Although human societies develop widely diverse ceremonies/arts, which may alter gradually over time, it is important to note that ceremonies/arts appear to be intrinsic and essential in all societies. One can confidently propose that the inclination to make ordinary behavior extraordinary, in circumstances about which people care greatly, is part of our biological nature (Dissanayake, 1992, 2000b).

In the case of human ceremonies/arts, one might ask *which* gestures (or behaviors) from *which* ritualized social contexts might be the substrate for cultural recombination and elaboration. If we think of *Ur*-music as combined vocal and kinesic movement (which, we saw, is how it is manifested most often in traditional societies today, as well as by young children) rather than in its restricted and individualized current Western sense, we can hazard an informed speculation. In other publications (Dissanayake, 1999, 2000a, 2000b; Miall and Dissanayake, 2003), I have suggested that culturally created human music is drawn, at least in part, from biologically evolved competencies and sensitivities that were originally developed in interactions between mothers and young infants.

Interestingly, one can consider mother-infant interaction itself as a biologically ritualized behavior, where visual, vocal, and kinesic expressions drawn from adult affiliative contexts—e.g., smiles, nods, soft undulant sounds, touches, caresses—are simplified, stereotyped, repeated, and exaggerated in order to temporally coordinate and emotionally unite the mother-infant pair. Infants are born ready to respond to and coordinate their own behavior with these very signals, and especially to their dynamic variation.

In creating ceremonial rituals, ancestral human groups could draw upon the evolved competency to formalize, repeat, and exaggerate that had been developed in kinesic-vocal-facial modalities with adults to infants, and elaborate these even more in the dances, songs, and imitations that comprise "music" in traditional if not in modern Western contexts. Formalization, repetition, and exaggeration of body movements, vocal sounds, and facial expressions are emotionally evocative to infants, and when manipulated further, dynamically and temporally, in deliberate creations by individuals or cultures, are attention-getting and affecting to adults. Music in ceremonial rituals then can be considered as deliberate cultural formalization, repetition, exaggeration, and elaboration of evolved sensitivities to vocal-gestural features that in their evolutionary origins conveyed emotional messages between mothers and infants.

Sources of Musical Emotion

The subject of "emotion" is specialized and complex, and use of the terms "emotion" and "feeling" is variable and imprecise among psychologists as well as lay persons (Griffiths, 1997). Unfortunately, this essay is not the place for an analysis of the conceptual and scientific problems, although such an analysis would be desirable. One could perhaps speak of affect with less ambiguity, using the work of Paul Ekman and colleagues who describe six cross-culturally produced and recognized affect programs composed of identifiable coordinated physical and physiological responses (e.g., Ekman, Levenson, and Friesen, 1983). However, for a study of emotion in music, these basic affects (happiness, sadness, fear, anger, disgust, and surprise) seem limited. Not all music can be so simply or distinctly characterized, even as happy, sad, or surprising (and less so as fearful, angry, or disgusted), nor will it unfailingly be recognized as such across cultures, as the facial expressions of affect programs have been shown to be.

Yet it is commonly agreed that music has "emotional" effects of some sort on participants, although the nature or source of "musical emotion" resists easy explanation. I suggest that an understanding of how emotions are manipulated in ritualized behaviors—and, by extension, in human ritual ceremonies—can contribute useful insights into the more complex problem of the nature of musical emotion in general.

Preceding sections have described how, in the biologically evolved process of ritualization in animals, elements from ordinary instrumental behavior become formalized or stereotyped, repeated with a typical regularity or intensity, exaggerated, and elaborated. Such operations upon ordinary behavior seem intrinsically to attract attention, indicate the motivation of the actor, and—significantly—influence the emotions and hence behavior of the recipient. Interestingly, these same operations of formalization, repetition, exaggeration, and elaboration are also characteristic in culturally created ritual ceremonies—composed of "arts"—in human societies, where they also attract attention and influence emotions and behavior.

Anthropological studies of human ritual typically emphasize its importance for passing on information and group tradition, functions that have been essential in the nonliterate societies that characterized humans for 99.9 percent of their history. It should not be overlooked, however, that rituals accomplish these practical purposes by shaping and even creating *appropriate feelings* in their participants. Radcliffe-Brown reminds us that ceremonies change or structure feelings: they "maintain and transmit from one generation to another the emotional dispositions on which the society depends for its existence" (Radcliffe-Brown, 1922/1948: 234). Rituals compel participants to feel (or "go through the motions of feeling") emotions appropriate to the purposes of the ritual—e.g., confidence, pride, joyfulness, well-being, resolve, release, and unification. But how do they do this?

Salience—prominence or emphasis of any sort—is potentially *emotional*. In the generalized, unremarkable state of ordinary consciousness in which most of daily life is spent, we do not experience "emotion" so much as what might be described as mood fluctuations, like corks bobbing gently this way and that on a "stream of affect" (Watson and Clark, 1994: 90) whose eddies are more or less good (positive), bad (negative), or indifferent. Emotion enters (or potentially enters) the scene when there is some discrepancy or change, provoking an interest. We appraise a salient or novel cue, anticipating what it means for our vital interests. Salience, novelty, and change in themselves are neither positive nor negative—they may lead to anxiety, intense fear, relief, curiosity, or delight. But an unexpected or markedly salient event seems to trigger a readiness for emotion, if not a full-blown emotion (Ellsworth, 1994).

Formalization, repetition, exaggeration, and elaboration are all ways of giving salience, hence emotional or potentially emotional significance, to stimuli. In ritualized behaviors in animals, the marked signals are organized in time, thereby not only capturing but manipulating the attention of the recipient. The temporal progression has the power both to convey and shape (also to "tune," integrate, or synchronize) emotion: in response to various ritualized signals, an animal may fight, flee, or coordinate its movements and sounds with the signaler to mate or, as shown above with human infants, to form and maintain an emotional bond.

I suggest that the component operations used in ritualized behaviors—formalization or regularization, stereotypy, repetition, exaggeration, and elaboration—are also prototypes for the creation of expressiveness, and hence "emotion," in music (and the other arts). As described, infants are born ready to recognize, attend to, and respond to these operations on vocalizations, gestures, and facial expressions as presented to them by adults in coordinated interactions, and adults attend to and respond to these features as presented to them aurally, kinaesthetically, and visually in the arts (Dissanayake 2000a, 2000b). Both mother-infant engagement and music are temporal (or sequential) structures in which changes unfolding in the present create, *and are*, the experience (Stern, 1995; Volgsten, this volume). They are capsule or prototypical examples of shaped emotional experience, exercised for their own sake—although, unknown to the participants, parent-infant mutuality contributes to each partner's biological fitness, and musical sensitivities originally predisposed us to engage in and respond to fitness-enhancing ceremonial rituals. They are like play, "not for real," although they have real benefits.

In music, emotion is conveyed, aroused, and shaped by changing, ongoing fluctuations in feeling state that occur in response to the music's temporal unfolding. Otherwise ordinary sounds (as tones or beats) are given salience: they are formalized (patterned or regularized), repeated, exaggerated, and elaborated in not-quite expected ways, creating interest and perhaps uncertainty. Like the infant with its mother, the listener may detect some discrepancy or novelty in an ongoingness, and become alerted to what comes next, which either bears out or subverts one's expectation. As Robert Jourdain (1997: 312; see also Meyer, 1956) has said:

> Music sets up anticipations and then satisfies them. It can withhold its resolutions, and heighten anticipation by doing so, then to satisfy the anticipation in a great gush of resolution. When music goes out of its way to violate the very expectations that it sets up, we call it "expressive." Musicians breathe "feeling" into a piece by introducing minute deviations in timing and loudness. And composers build expression into their compositions by purposely violating anticipations they have established.

To be sure, not all music (or art) is "expressive" in the sense that I have outlined above or that Jourdain and Meyer identify. Pygmy women's music, which may constitute the "world's oldest stock of sound" (Lomax, in Thompson 1995: 206) superimposes rich polyphony upon a polyrhythmic continuum in an "infinite sound" of "chaotic unity" (Meurant, 1995: 180). In such musics, musical emotion may result less from manipulation and resolution of uncertainty than from the contagion and conjoinment of sensory immersion and vocal and kinesic synchronization with others.

At this point, taking the foregoing discussion into account, I propose a speculative, preliminary "ethological taxonomy" of four types of emotional response to music. In specific instances, these may overlap, and a particular work may include more than one type of response. With the appropriate changes, these could be applied to other arts.

Appeal to Inherent Sensory and Cognitive Dispositions

In the arts, as in life, our attention is pleasantly drawn to sensory elements that have inherent visual, aural, cognitive, and emotional allure: bright colors, smooth and skilled movements, euphonious sounds, or fascinating and intriguing subject matter. Among these appealing elements are repeated, or predictably regular, sounds or bodily movements, which (as with repetition of visual shapes, or patterns) seem to be intrinsically satisfying or pleasurable. Although positive responses to specific entities may be culturally conditioned, evolutionary psychologists (e.g., Thornhill, 1999) suggest that many aesthetic percepts are innately predisposed because they signal youth, vitality, and other features that would have indicated evolutionary advantage in ancestral times. For the Igbo people of Nigeria, as for many human societies, the most valued aesthetic qualities are brightness, clarity, precision, balance, and harmony, and these—rather than dullness, clumsiness, and debility—are understandably identified with personal and social worth (Willis, 1989). At least some musical sounds and patterns have intrinsic appeal because of sensory and cognitive features related to exercise of vitality and competence; these pleasurable stimuli are building blocks to be further formalized, repeated, exaggerated, and elaborated to varying degrees.

Association and Connotation

People everywhere are drawn to experience intrinsically pleasant occasions where there is beauty, laughter, and enjoyment. Elements of such occasions may then become associated with them, as when the mere sound of music in itself is associated with festivity, power, and control of disorder (e.g., among the Yoruba [Waterman, 1990; Lawal, 1996] and Tiv [Keil, 1979] of Nigeria). In lowland regions of South America, "wherever music is heard, something important is happening" (Seeger, 1987: 7). For the Sambia of Papua New Guinea, the

sounds of flutes may evoke the combined fear and excitement of ritual participation (Herdt, 1982). In the Kalapalo of central Brazil, sound—as expletives,
speech, and song, which in rituals are transformed into one another—serves as
a code for interpreting states of mind, that is, for conveying ideas about feeling,
personal identity, and the emotions that accompany transformative changes in
one's personal relations (Basso, 1985: 91).

In modern Western societies too, various musics conventionally set the
scene, in life or in mediated entertainment, for—say—suspense, solemnity, gai-
ety, or romance. Music may be comfortably constant and familiar, or regularly
and predictably unfolding, and foster joyful participatory emotion. Humans
seem to find inherent pleasure and well-being in keeping together in time
with others (McNeill, 1995), which connotes, because it demonstrates, accord.
Simply engaging in music, where participants and audience are spatially and
temporally coordinated (whether by unison, overlapping, or antiphony), is
itself not only a metaphor for but a means of actively constructing or displaying social order and harmony.

Intensification

Music may also be associated with trance states (e.g., Javanese [Kartomi, 1973]).
In the ceremonies of many groups, musical (and hence psychological) tension
builds steadily over time (e.g., in the Eskimo/Inuit [Freuchen, 1935], Cubeo
people of the Northwest Amazon [Goldman, 1964], Sinhalese [Kapferer, 1983],
Kalahari !Kung [Katz, 1982], and Suya [Seeger, 1987: 5]), eventually resulting in
trance, catharsis, or a similar sense of transfiguration or transcendence. Inten-
sification of volume and tempo in music parallel and thus assist physiological
and psychological excitement, leading to emotional discharge.

Expectation, Disruption and Repair—Heightened Affective Moments

The emotion produced by music may not be unalloyed pleasure or climactic
catharsis, but a state of anticipation and uncertainty that can be manipulated
along what might be called an *emotional trajectory*.

Infant expectancies in dyadic interactions with adults are organized according
to three principles of salience (Beebe and Lachmann, 1994) that have suggestive
similarities with musical experience. The first, expectable ongoing regulation,
refers to the characteristic and predictable way in which an interaction unfolds,
comparable to the comfortable constancy of musical experience described
above. Other interactions are organized by violations of expectancy (disrup-
tions), which may be mild or severe, and ensuing efforts to resolve or repair
these breaches. In such interactions, infant experience is organized by a second
principle, that of contrast, disjunction, and difference, in which the gap between
what is expected and what is happening may be either repaired, leading to experiences of coping, "effectance" (Gianino and Tronick, 1988: 63), and righting,

or inadequately resolved (in mismatchings), leading to frustration and distress. In the third principle, heightened affective moments, infants may experience a powerful state transformation: one dramatic moment stands out in time.

These latter two principles seem to have counterparts in musical experience in those cultures where music has acquired an emotional depth and complexity apart from its "functional" uses in ceremonial rituals. In literate societies, where musical scores can be written down and even mechanically printed, composers can expend considerable time and thought in planning and elaborating the emotional effectiveness of their creations, and performers can practice and perfect their reconstruction of the composer's intentions. However, improvised musics can attain similar if not equal complexity, and emotional force (e.g., in the art of Taqasim in the Arab Near East [Racy, 2000], and in modern jazz). It is usually these more elaborated, subtle, and sophisticated instances that are the subject of academic or critical studies of musical emotion and musical meaning by psychologists and philosophers of music. Although *what* musical experience expresses remains ever elusive and fascinating, as the excerpt from Fubini stated at the beginning of this essay, an ethological description of the means by which musical emotion is engendered suggests that sophisticated musical emotion arises from the manipulation of expectations using the same fundamental structural features (formalization, repetition, exaggeration, elaboration) as in ritualized behaviors in non-human animals and in mother-infant interaction. That is, it is built upon universal psychobiological sensitivities and capacities that are—in some societies, using their specific tonal and rhythmic systems—additionally manipulated for maximum emotional effect.

Social Functions Served by Ritual Music

It is important to note that ritualized behaviors in animals, which have evolved because they contribute to individual survival and inclusive fitness, occur in biologically important contexts: they threaten, show dominance, and display resources, or indicate submission, appeasement, and willingness for interaction. Interestingly, human ritual ceremonies occur in similar if not always identical circumstances, and engaging in them may also affect survival and reproduction.

From an examination of ethnomusicological studies of rituals in more than thirty traditional societies, I have artificially extracted six general social "functions" that appear to be achieved through these rituals, and—I will argue—facilitated through the formalizations, repetitions, exaggerations, and elaborations of their music, since music is integral and even primary to shaping the behavior and feelings of participants. (One can hardly imagine a ceremony without its music.) Many rituals (e.g., *kaiko* in the Maring of Papua New Guinea [Rappaport, 1967]) of course address within one ceremony a number of functions that are listed separately here.

The first three social functions listed below—display of resources, control and channeling of aggression, and facilitation of courtship—have clear counterparts in ritualized behaviors of other animals. One could perhaps make the case, with certain accommodations, that rudiments of the last three functions—establishment and maintenance of social identity through rites of passage, relief from anxiety, and promotion of cooperation—exist in animal rituals as well. It should be noted that, as presented here, the latter three functions are rather broad: individual components might well be extracted for separate attention (e.g., relief from anxiety here subsumes both "mourning" and "healing," and the promotion of cooperation can be accomplished in diverse ways, as will be discussed below).

Display of Resources

Display may be by individuals, families, or an entire social group. Examples include display of male strength and vigor as in the Suya of Brazil (Seeger, 1987: 97) and male or female beauty and skill, as in the East Asian Hmong (Catlin, 1982, 1985, 1992), where the best singers push the chest voice so high that controlled falsetto breaks are possible, creating a sobbing effect that heartrendingly depicts the tension of singing, and at the same time the skill and strength of the girl. (See also other East and Southeast Asian peoples, such as the Maranao [Cadar, 1973, 1975], and the Kmhmu [Proschan, 1992].) Family prestige and power, as in the Pacific Northwest Coast Makah (Goodman, 1992), may be displayed within the group, or one society's resources shown to a neighboring group. There are parallels to these displays in the animal world, and Rappaport has expressly likened the *kaiko* dancing of Maring males (which indicates their interest in females, their availability, and their differential strength, endurance, wealth, and beauty) to animal ritualized epigamic or amatory display, and the density or population size of males revealed in *kaiko* dancing to ritualized epideictic display in animals, which shows the strength of one group to another (Rappaport, 1967). Evolutionists commonly attribute the selective value of successful individual ritualized display in both animals and humans to gaining or solidifying prestige and power, and to acquiring mates.

Control and Channeling of Individual Aggression

Human display may be indicative not only of strength, skill, and other resources. It may be additionally perceived as more or less "aggressive," as in Rappaport's analysis of Maring ritual, in which he compares the Maring stake-planting ritual to animal ritualized threat display and their "small" or "nothing" fight to animal ritualized territorial display (Rappaport, 1967: 193–195). Eskimo/Inuit song duels (*nith* songs) and taunts, similarly serve as ritually acceptable ways of resolving a grudge or dispute (Hoebel, 1968; Balikci, 1970; see also Basso [1985: 246] and Sugarman [1988: 36n18] for examples in other societies). The evolutionary value of redirecting or defusing aggression in ritualized behaviors has been well studied in non-human animals.

Facilitation of Courtship

Ritualization of courtship behavior in birds has been well studied (e.g., Huxley, 1914; Tinbergen, 1952). Humans too have developed cultural rituals that allow a courting pair to coordinate body rhythms and otherwise assess one another's compatibility (e.g., Cadar, 1973, 1975). For example, young Hmong males and females together sing improvised courtship dialogue songs while simultaneously tossing a ball back and forth under the scrutiny of family, friends, and outsiders. Initially the young man invites the girl to play ball, and then begins to sing or entreats her to sing. She must first profess shyness or lack of ability, whereupon he continues to urge her participation, which demands of her considerable strength and ability (see above). Tossing the ball while singing allows the opportunity to demonstrate interest by variations in eye contact and facial expression, as well as displaying the girl's ability to remain calm in a stressful social situation, and also to be entertaining and playful (Catlin, 1982, 1985).[6]

Sometimes a courting couple may interact by playing instruments or moving to music as a substitute for the interaction of actual lovemaking. In antiphonal love dialogues, common in some East and Southeast Asian peoples, the courting couple use repetition and variation, as well as enjambment and pauses, to create suspense, anticipation, and surprise and thereby increase the partner's involvement and pleasure (Proschan, 1992: 16). In the Medlpa of highland New Guinea, beautifully adorned young couples sit side by side and sway their bodies toward and away from each other, while moving their heads in parallel, to a background of adults' singing. Then placing their foreheads together, they turn or roll their heads (which must always be touching) from back to front, and when their cheeks are together, make a bow. During bouts of several repetitions of this activity, each couple creates its own common synchronous rhythm, not necessarily that of the vocal background. They adjust to one another—the young man initiating and controlling the form of the movement and the young woman the fine variation in speed (Pitcairn and Schleidt, 1976).

Music additionally allows lovers to "say things" that might otherwise be awkward and embarrassing. For example, Hmong and Kmhmu males play love songs on a strummed, mouth-played bamboo instrument that conveys all vowels and most consonants, and the young woman may reply on a flute-like instrument of her own (Catlin, 1982, 1985; Proschan, 1992). The lovers may together create a secret language of love, with metaphoric uses of these musical "words," to confuse any elder who might be listening.

To find the function of music to be in facilitating courtship, and hence mating, has made sense to evolutionists from Darwin (1871) to the present (e.g., Miller 2000a, 2000b). Although it is questionable whether music originated in or was driven solely by competitive sexual display (see Brown, 2000; Dissanayake 2000a, 2000b), it is clear that it may serve to display the charms of either sex to the other and may be used to facilitate a romantic mood.

Establishment and Maintenance of Social Identity through Rites of Passage

Prominent among this functional category are rites of passage (e.g., Kubik, 1977; Shapiro and Talamantez, 1986; Seeger, 1987; Naroditshaya, 2000) that occur at points of life transitions (e.g., birth, puberty, marriage, death). Although non-human animals do not mark rites of passage, the establishment and reiteration of social identity *as status* is important in many species, and these ends are frequently achieved and periodically reaffirmed by ritualized display, as described for humans in the first social function, above. However, human rites of passage go beyond status displays, conferring or recognizing a wide array of cultural as well as biological individual identities such as that of child, adolescent, adult, marriageable or married person, parent, warrior, widow, member of this or that subgroup, and so forth. This important function of ceremonial music deserves separate treatment.

In the eight-day puberty ceremony of Mescalero Apache girls in North America, where each is transformed into the female deity and literally "sung" into womanhood, ritual music not only creates emotional responses during individual segments of a ceremony, but organizes its overall time-frame as well. Pulse, repetitions, change, and silence—elements that in music help to mark the passage of time—are carefully structured and give the ceremony a grace, flexibility, and logic felt by participants and audience alike (Shapiro and Talamantez, 1986). Diverse, imprecisely timed activities of the first day gradually resolve to close coordination between song structure and action, which focuses attention on specific ritual actions and enhances them, and finally to an achievement of timeless transcendent presence. Repetition occurs in the pulses of rattles and jingling cones on dresses; the return of strongly contoured refrains, chant-like verses, and other ritual markers; and the grouping of four formulaic songs marked by glissandi and emissions of ritual smoke by the medicine men. The clear contour of melodies with octave leaps, triadic outlines, and sectional structure provides an analogic design that matches other parts of the ceremony, from the shapes of tipis against the sky to painted geometric designs. On the last morning, with a hand raised to the sun, the singer breaks the overall symmetry of the ceremony, and with the dismantling of the ritual tipi, and giving away of food and sweets, the ordinary sense of time and space returns. The music ends, as does the sacred time that was in large part created by the music (Shapiro and Talamantez, 1986).

Relief from Anxiety and Psychological Pain

Although human groups do not generally perform rituals with the overtly expressed intention of relieving anxiety or of providing a sense of control over threatening outer circumstances, these functions frequently accompany rituals performed for other ostensible purposes, e.g., those meant to heal illness or resolve dissent (Katz, 1982; Kapferer, 1983; Seeger, 1987); to expel or avert evil (e.g., Speck and Broom, 1951/1983; Avorgbedor, 2000); to provide an analogue of escape from oppression (as in the metaphor of "flight" encoded in Big Drum songs and dances on the small Caribbean island of Carriacou [McDaniel, 1998]); or to mourn the dead (e.g., Goldman, 1964; Feld, 1982; Basso, 1985; Tolbert, 1990; Seremetakis, 1991; Knopoff, 1993). Ritual expression of individual emotion that is usually repressed (e.g., in the Bedouin [Abu-Lughod, 1986]) and Thule Eskimo/Inuit [Freuchen, 1935]) may additionally provide a sort of emotional relief, release, and even refuge during psychologically troubled times (e.g., Greek women [Seremetakis, 1991] and Karelian women [Tolbert, 1990] in ritualized lament—see below). Such functions resemble what in the modern Western psychotherapeutic tradition is called displacement, sublimation, or fantasy. In many ceremonies, participants enter altered psychological states and make contact with a supernatural realm, and one can suggest that this too is in the ultimate service of dealing with uncertainty.[7]

It is in mourning and healing rituals, especially, that musical form seems to be widely used to manage and shape human feeling. These rituals are important because even as they heal individuals or assure the safe passage of the deceased person's spirit to its ancestral home, the ceremonies provide an institutionalized outlet for individual pain, fear, grief, and anger. At the same time, they reassert group loyalties as members fulfill their ritual obligations (Knopoff, 1993: 149; Averill and Nunley, 1993).

Although many analyses of the lament tradition, in Greece and elsewhere, have emphasized the importance of *verbalizing* one's grief, it is obvious that the verbal narrative is but one component of the total mourning performance. Antiphonal singing of laments is recorded in the Homeric epics, and indeed ritual lamenting occurs not only in Mediterranean cultures but, until recently, in northern Eurasia, highland New Guinea, Africa, China, tribal India, Indonesia, and the Americas (Holst-Warhaft, 1992). Elizabeth Tolbert (1990) has described in detail the Finnish-Karelian lament (*itkuvirsi*), which uses a highly metaphoric language and powerful improvisational manner of performance, reminiscent of a shamanistic trance (Tolbert, 1990). Karelian laments, sung at both weddings and funerals, are performed only by older women in an ecstatic style that is a mixture of weeping, speech, and song. They are not simply or primarily a personal expression of grief but the sacred language of these two important rites of passage—where through marriage a girl leaves her home as well as her girlhood, and through death a person leaves his or her life and loved ones.

On the most general level, the Karelian lament is iconic for a sigh, using a terraced, descending melodic contour (with fluid pitches and irregular rhythm), repeated and endlessly elaborated with microtonal and microrhythmic variations that express, with intensifying emotional involvement, that a successful contact with the other world has been made and that spiritual power is present. This ambiguity and instability of pitch, mode, range, and phrase structure is as necessary to the effectiveness of the lament as predictable pattern and control is to other types of ritual music.

Interestingly, in highland Papua New Guinea, Kaluli women also perform improvisational "melodic-sung-weeping" at funerals, using a descending melodic contour (Feld, 1982: 16). In addition, Kaluli men have also incorporated stylized weeping and sobbing into a ceremony, *gisalo*, that is expressive of feelings of loss and abandonment but occurs on occasions of marriage, pork distributions, and other formal exchanges where the virtue of reciprocity is implicit and, in the ceremony, emphasized (Feld, 1982, 1984).

A cross-cultural study of the lament would serve as a prototypical illustration of the use of formalization, repetition, exaggeration, and elaboration in order to create a cultural object (here, a stylized vocal performance) from a natural emotional state (weeping in grief). The psychological value of the lament, like other examples of using music to relieve anxiety (e.g., special performances that use songs to heal in the Temiar of peninsular Malaysia [Roseman, 1984, 1991]), probably inheres in assisting the ability to cope (see next paragraph).

Promotion of Group Cooperation and Prosperity

The first three described social functions of ritual music—display of resources, control and channeling of aggression, and facilitation of courtship—have counterparts in ritualized behaviors of other animals and are congruent with evolutionary models of individual fitness maximization. The fifth function of ritual music—relief from anxiety and psychological pain—seems to have less application to ritualized behavior in animals. Apart from redirecting aggression, the ritualized behaviors of non-human animals cannot be said to relieve anxiety, enable repression, or provide the illusion of coping with troubling events—certainly not to the degree that occurs in human rituals.[8] However, insofar as rituals and their music successfully perform these functions in humans, they promote fitness. Studies show that the debilitating physiological effects of stress are reduced when individuals have a sense of control over uncertain circumstances (Whybrow, 1984; Sapolsky, 1992; Huether et al., 1996), even if this sense of control is illusory.

With the fourth and sixth social functions of ritual music—establishing and maintaining social identity through rites of passage, and group cooperation and prosperity—there are few, if any, convincing parallels with other animals and a more controversial claim for evolutionary benefits.

The current specialized controversy among evolutionary scientists over the level at which selection occurs—gene, individual, or group—need not concern us in this essay, except to say that the widely observed and enduring use of music for group coordination strongly reinforces claims for group selection in humans. Indeed, music may be the first cognitive adaptation that is not completely explainable by individual selection mechanisms (Brown, 2000), and thus is an important arrow in the quiver of advocates of group selection arguments.

Virtually every serious non-biological writer on the function of music names its contribution to the integration, stability, and continuity of the society, culture, or social group that engages in it (e.g., Merriam, 1964; Lomax, 1968; Nettl, 1983), and many of the other functions that such writers mention can be subsumed in this larger category (e.g., enforcing conformity, entertaining, and symbolic representation [Merriam, 1964]). Additionally, music is part of rituals that enculturate the young (e.g., Kubik, 1977; Comaroff, 1985; Seeger, 1987); transfer cultural information (e.g., Vinnicombe, 1976; Guss, 1989; Kaeppeler, 1990; Seremetakis, 1991; Knopoff, 1993); and embody community identity (Solomon, 2000), and these too contribute to social integration and prosperity.

In this same category might also be included ceremonies for assuring abundance of food and fertility of women, longevity or survival, and well-being (e.g., Lawal, 1996); for neutralizing (or providing an antidote to) evil (e.g., Keil, 1979); for creating social harmony and dissolving social tension (e.g., Basso, 1985, Sugarman, 1988); as well as maintaining egalitarianism (Roseman, 1984) and communal intimacy in the face of potential or actual anarchy and chaos (Sarno, 1993). One could also mention here ceremonies that entertain and celebrate, and that engender and express feelings of pleasure and well-being, cheerfulness, and fellowship (e.g., Drewal and Drewal, 1983; Seeger, 1987; Waterman, 1990; Lawal, 1996).

In point of fact, one might say that in general, *all* rituals serve to maintain the well-being of the society and its individuals, because they join individuals in common cause. Even ceremonies that incite a group to hate or attack another group promote cohesion and cooperation among the ritual's participants. By "making society work," cooperative rituals are integral, not dispensable (e.g., Seeger, 1987: 131f.). A society of uncooperating individuals is not likely to thrive and maintain itself over generations, and music appears to have been one of the indispensable means for instilling and maintaining group cohesion and hence perpetuation.

Music Today

What is usually uncritically considered to be "music," at least in the academy—Western classical music and perhaps jazz—has developed over the past two centuries within an aesthetic or "high art" tradition where music, like art in general, is considered nonfunctional ("for its own sake") and generally listened to with full attention in special settings, or on recordings in the home (see also Martin's and Stockfelt's contributions to this volume). However, although music today is loosed from its original integral structural roles in society, and appears in other respects, described at the beginning of this chapter, to be obviously different from music in traditional societies, one can nevertheless detect multiple robust ties to its initial roots.

Music today, for example, is not as conceptually isolate as purists might claim. Words are integral to the "musical" melodic or rhythmic components in genres as diverse as *Sprechstimme* and rap. Nor is our appreciation of music invariably disinterested or detached. At the personal level, even classical music may frequently be moved to—involuntarily or inconspicuously at concerts (with the toes inside one's shoe, one's tongue inside the mouth, or one's fingers) or privately at home with more unselfconscious head and body movements. At concerts featuring popular music, such as rock or country and western, toe-tapping, clapping, or head-nodding is expected, and even participative dancing is common. More generally, music today is integrated with life—although frequently serving as background—with Muzak in shops and elevators, and radio or recorded music in our homes or cars.

Music still remains associated with the supernatural in religious activity, and many lovers of music attest to feeling "transformed" by certain musical experience as well as bonded to the emotional associations that these evoke and represent.

Music today steadfastly remains socially important for holidays and other ceremonial observance, both sacred and secular, and it is certainly essential to the maintenance of *sub*cultures within the larger society—that is, a member of the subculture necessarily "knows the score" of the popular rhythms and styles that define it. In this capacity, music articulates the values that are both tacitly and explicitly expressed by the subculture, and its simultaneous, often commercial, representation as a fad or fashion.

However, music's most important social uses today are, arguably, at the level of the macro-economic: to sway emotions for entertainment and distraction and to condition and persuade people to buy things, since nearly all modern social activities, including music, are designed around the goals of the marketplace (see Bullerjahn and North and Hargreaves, this volume).

Although it would be difficult today to claim that music is integral to the working of our society in any larger sense, or that it contributes to individual or group prosperity outside the marketplace, many of its earlier functions persist, particularly in popular music. It still allows individuals to show off, and is frequently important in courtship—to set a "mood," to express one's sentiments, and to accompany dancing. The sound of music itself can uncannily re-create in memory a time, place, and emotional state, with surprising emotional strength. It still entertains, though we are audience more often than participant.

Music remains integral to rites of passage—as in weddings and funerals—and to nearly any ceremonial occasion. It can still heal, as employed in music therapy or in fundamentalist and charismatic religions. It still "says things that cannot be said in any other way," and otherwise allows for fantasy, displacement, and sublimation. It still eases labor and tedium, as when we listen to recorded music or sing to ourselves while working or driving.

Music is still able to create social harmony and solidarity, whether in small groups singing songs around a campfire, military recruits marching and chanting in time, or the well-being felt after sharing a musical occasion with others. It still enculturates and transfers cultural information, as is evident in nationalist music, global youth culture, or any subculture, as well as in advertising and marketing.

In modern societies, as described, all these functions of music have been influenced by modernity, particularly its individualism, pluralism, secularism, consumerism, media proliferation, and reliance on technology. Yet it is still possible in music to set aside, to some degree, everyday knowledge and experience so that, like those who live in the traditional non-Western societies described above, we can enter an "extra-ordinary" state, sometimes even feeling transformed. Music everywhere shapes or gives form to feeling, and has multimodal associations with bodily life and with the natural landscape that are beyond the resources of talk. Also, as in the non-Western music traditions mentioned here, we are susceptible to deviations from the expected as well as to confirmation of the expected, to alternation and overlap, as well as to synchronized participation, all of which are iconic for the creation and expression of intercoordination and community where boundaries are collapsed and individuals feel at one—with others or with their deeper selves.

Notes

1. Trance states have different purposes in different rituals—for healing (e.g., the Kalahari Kung [Katz, 1982]), managing grief (e.g., the Amazonian Cubeo [Goldman, 1964]), relieving anxiety (e.g., folk trance in Java [Kartomi, 1973]), achieving contact with supernatural beings or a supernatural world (e.g., the Malaysian Temiar [Roseman, 1991]), and for other occasions where "transformation" from one state to another is considered desirable.

2. According to Julian Huxley (1966), "ritualization may be defined ethologically as the adaptive formalization or canalization of emotionally-motivated behaviour, under the pressure of natural selection so as (a) to promote better and more unambiguous signal function, both intra- and inter-specifically; (b) to serve as more efficient stimulators or releasers of more efficient patterns of action in other individuals; (c) to reduce intra-specific danger; and (d) to serve as sexual or social bonding mechanisms." He defines human ritual as "the adaptive formalization and canalization of motivated human activities so as to secure more effective communicatory ('signalling') function, reduction of intra-group damage, or better intra-group bonding."

3. Behaviors generally require a facilitating environment in order to develop smoothly, but they are inherited, with greater and lesser degrees of lability in expression, as predispositions. They are not (or are rarely) mechanically "determined." "Ritualization" is a behavioral mechanism. A ritualized behavior has evolved gradually over time through natural selection because individuals who performed it enjoyed comparatively higher survival and reproductive success.

4. Tinbergen (1959) succinctly defined ritualization as "adaptive evolutionary change in the direction of increased efficiency as a signal."

5. I generally use the terms "ritual," "ceremony," and "ritual ceremony" interchangeably, referring to human behavior. "Ritualized" and "ritualization" generally refer to behavior of

non-human animals (although I point out later in the chapter that human mother-infant interaction appears to be in part a biologically evolved ritualized behavior).

6. After marriage, women's songs of a sensual nature are avoided and replaced by more "functional" songs (lullabies; mowing, sowing, harvesting, and weaving songs; and wedding or mourning songs). Traditional Hmong women were reluctant to sing even in the presence of their infant sons and particularly in front of males, including male relatives, in order that their songs not be interpreted as an "invitation." Post menopausal women, however, could sing in the presence of men (Catlin, 1982: 78–80).

7. In this "therapeutic" category, one might also even include rituals that relieve labor and tedium, such as those that assist with or physically coordinate work (e.g., rice planting and harvesting in the Kpelle people of Liberia [Schmidt, 1990], or rice pounding in central Java [Kartomi, 1973: 202]).

8. The chimpanzee male "rain dance" described by Jane Goodall (van Lawick-Goodall, 1975) might be considered a rudimentary instance of the emotional release of individual and perhaps group anxiety in a non-human primate during a time of uncertainty.

References

Abu-Lughod, L. (1986). *Veiled Sentiments: Honor and Poetry in a Bedouin Society*. Berkeley: University of California Press.

Averill, J. R. and Nunley, E. P. (1993). "Grief as an emotion and as a disease: A social-constructionist perspective." In M. S. Stroebe, W. Stroebe, and R. O. Hansson (eds.) *Handbook of Bereavement: Theory, Research, and Intervention* (pp. 77–90). New York: Cambridge University Press.

Avorgbedor, D. (2000). "*Dee Hoo!* Sonic articulations in healing practices of the Anlo-Ewe." *The World of Music* 42: 9–24.

Balikci, A. (1970). *The Netsilik Eskimo*. Garden City, NY: Natural History Press.

Barrow, J. (1995). *The Artful Universe*. Oxford: Clarendon Press.

Basso, E. B. (1985). *A Musical View of the Universe: Kalapalo Myth and Ritual Performance*. Philadelphia: University of Pennsylvania Press.

Becker, J. (2000). "Listening selves and spirit possession." *The World of Music* 42: 25–50.

Beebe, B. and Lachmann, F. (1994). "Representation and internalization in infancy: Three principles of salience." *Psychoanalytic Psychology* 11: 127–165.

Blacking, J. (1982). "The structure of musical discourse: The problem of the song text." *Yearbook for Traditional Music* 14: 15–24.

Brown, S. (2000). "Evolutionary models of music: From sexual selection to group selection." In F. Tonneau and N. S. Thompson (eds.) *Perspectives in Ethology* 13 (pp. 231–281). New York: Plenum.

Cadar, U. H. (1973). "The role of Kulintang music in Maranao society." *Ethnomusicology* 17: 234–249.

_____ (1975). "The role of Kulintang in Maranao society." *Selected Reports in Ethnomusicology* 2: 49–62.

Catlin, A. R. (1982). "Speech surrogate systems of the Hmong: From singing voices to talking reeds." In B. T. Downing and D. P. Olney (eds.) *The Hmong in the West: Observations and Reports* (pp. 170–197). Minneapolis: Southeast Asian Refugee Studies Project, Center for Urban and Regional Affairs, University of Minnesota.

_____ (1985). "Harmonizing the generations in Hmong musical performance." *Selected Reports in Ethnomusicology* 6: 83–97.

_____ (1992). "*Homo Cantens*: Why Hmong sing during interactive courtship rituals." *Selected Reports in Ethnomusicology* 9: 43–60.

Comaroff, J. (1985). *Body of Power Spirit of Resistance: The Culture and History of a South African People*. Chicago: University of Chicago Press.

Darwin, C. (1871). *The Descent of Man and Selection in Relation to Sex*. London: John Murray.

Dissanayake, E. (1979). "An ethological view of ritual and art in human evolutionary history." *Leonardo* 7: 211–218.

_____ (1988). *What Is Art For?* Seattle: University of Washington Press.

_____ (1992). *Homo Aestheticus: Where Art Comes From and Why*. New York: Free Press (reprinted 1995, Seattle: University of Washington Press).

_____ (1999). "Antecedents of musical meaning in the mother-infant dyad." In B. Cooke and F. Turner (eds.) *Biopoetics: Evolutionary Explorations in the Arts* (pp. 367–397). New York: Paragon House.

_____ (2000a). "Antecedents of the temporal arts in early mother-infant interaction." In N. L. Wallin, B. Merker, and S. Brown (eds.) *The Origins of Music* (pp. 389–410). Cambridge, MA: MIT Press.

_____ (2000b). *Art and Intimacy: How the Arts Began*. Seattle: University of Washington Press.

_____ (In preparation). "Ritualized features in mother-infant early interactions as a source for adult affinitive cultural behaviors."

Drewal, H. J. and Drewal, M. T. (1983). *Gèlèdé: Art and Female Power Among the Yoruba*. Bloomington: Indiana University Press.

Eibl-Eibesfeldt, I. (1971). *Love and Hate*. New York: Holt Rinehart and Winston.

_____ (1989). *Human Ethology*. New York: Aldine de Gruyter.

Ekman, P., Levenson, R. W., and Friesen, W. V. (1983). "Autonomic nervous system activity distinguishes between emotions." *Science* 221: 1208–1210.

Ellsworth, P. (1994). "Some reasons to expect universal antecedents of emotion." In P. Ekman and R. J. Davidson (eds.) *The Nature of Emotion: Fundamental Questions* (pp. 150–154). New York: Oxford University Press.

Feld, S. (1982). *Sound and Sentiment: Birds, Weeping, Poetics and Song in Kaluli Expression*. Philadelphia: University of Pennsylvania Press.

_____ (1984). "Sound structure as social structure." *Ethnomusicology* 28: 383–409.

Freuchen, P. (1935). *Arctic Adventure*. New York: Farrar and Rinehart.

Fubini, E. (1990). *The History of Music Aesthetics*. London: Macmillan.

Gianino, A. and Tronick, E. Z. (1988). "The mutual regulation model: The infant's self- and interactive regulation and coping and defensive capacities." In T. Feld, P. McCabe, and N. Schneiderman (eds.) *Stress and Coping* (pp. 47–68). Hillsdale, NJ: Erlbaum.

Goldman, I. (1964). "The structure of ritual in the northwest Amazon." In R. A. Manners (ed.) *Process and Pattern in Culture* (pp. 111–122). Chicago: Aldine.

Goodman, L. J. (1992). "Aspects of spiritual and political power in chiefs' songs of the Makah Indians." *The World of Music* 34: 23–42.

Goody, J. (1961). "Religion and ritual: The definitional problem." *British Journal of Sociology* 12: 142–164.

Griffiths, P. E. (1997). *What Emotions Really Are: The Problem of Psychological Categories*. Chicago: University of Chicago Press.

Guss, D. M. (1989). *To Weave and Sing: Art, Symbol and Narrative in the South American Rain Forest*. Berkeley: University of California Press.

Herdt, G. H. (1982). "Fetish and fantasy in Sambia initiation." In G. H. Herdt (ed.) *Rituals of Manhood: Male Initiation in Papua New Guinea* (pp. 44–98). Berkeley and Los Angeles: University of California Press.

Hoebel, E. A. (1968). *The Law of Primitive Man*. New York: Atheneum.

Holst-Warhaft, G. (1992). *Dangerous Voices: Women's Laments and Greek Literature*. London: Routledge.

Huether, G., Doering, S., Rueger, U., and Ruether, E. (1996). "Psychic stress and neuronal plasticity. An expanded model of the stress reaction processes as basis for the understanding of adaptive processes in the central nervous system." *Zeitschrift für Psychosomatische Medezin und Psychoanalyse* 42: 107–127.

Huxley, J. (1914). "The courtship habits of the Great Crested Grebe (*Podiceps cristatus*) together with a discussion of the evolution of courtship in birds." *Journal of the Linnean Society of London: Zoology* 53: 253–292.

_____ (1966). Introduction. In "A Discussion on Ritualization of Behaviour in Animals and Man. Organized by Sir Julian Huxley." *Philosophical Transactions of the Royal Society of London, Series B. Biological Sciences* 772: 249–271.

Jourdain, R. (1997). *Music, the Brain, and Ecstasy: How Music Captures Our Imagination*. New York: Morrow.

Kaeppler, A. (1990). "The production and reproduction of social and cultural values in the compositions of Queen Sálote of Tonga." In M. Herndon and S. Ziegler (eds.) *Music, Gender, and Culture* (pp. 191–219). Wilhelmshaven: Florian Noetzel.

Kapferer, B. (1983). *A Celebration of Demons: Exorcism and the Aesthetics of Healing in Sri Lanka*. Bloomington: Indiana University Press.

Kartomi, M. (1973). "Music and trance in central Java." *Ethnomusicology* 17: 163–208.

Katz, R. (1982). *Boiling Energy: Community Healing Among the Kalahari Kung*. Cambridge MA: Harvard University Press.

Keil, C. (1979). *Tiv Song*. Chicago: University of Chicago Press.

Knopoff, S. (1993). "*Yuta Manikay*: Juxtaposition of ancestral and contemporary elements in the performance of Yolngu clan songs." *Yearbook for Traditional Music* 24: 138–153.

Kubik, G. (1977). "Patterns of body movement in the music of boys' initiation in south-east Angola." In J. Blacking (ed.) *The Anthropology of the Body* (pp. 253–274). New York: Academic Press.

Lawal, B. (1996). *The Gèlèdé Spectacle: Art, Gender, and Social Harmony in an African Culture*. Seattle: University of Washington Press.

Lomax, A. (1968). *Folk Song Style and Culture*. Washington, DC: American Association for the Advancement of Science.

McDaniel, L. (1998). *The Big Drum Ritual of Carriacou: Praisesongs in Rememory of Flight*. Gainesville: University Press of Florida.

McNeill, W. H. (1995). *Keeping Together in Time: Dance and Drill in Human History*. Cambridge MA: Harvard University Press.

Merriam, A. (1964). *The Anthropology of Music*. Evanston, IL: Northwestern University Press.

Meurant, G. (1995). "Aesthetic." In G. Meurant and R. F. Thompson (eds.) *Mbuti Design: Paintings by Pygmy Women of the Ituri Forest* (pp. 127–183). London: Thames and Hudson.

Meyer, L. B. (1956). *Emotion and Meaning in Music*. Chicago: Phoenix.

Miall, D. and Dissanayake, E. (2003). "The poetics of babytalk." *Human Nature* 14: 337–364.

Miller, G. (2000a). "Evolution of human music through sexual selection." In N. L. Wallin, B. Merker, and S. Brown (eds.) *The Origins of Music* (pp. 329–360). Cambridge, MA: MIT Press.

_____ (2000b). *The Mating Mind: How Sexual Choice Shaped the Evolution of Human Nature*. New York: Doubleday.

Morris, D. (1957). "'Typical intensity' and its relation to the problem of ritualization." *Behaviour* 11: 1–2.

Naroditskaya, I. (2000). "Azerbaijanian female musicians: Women's voices defying and defining the culture." *Ethnomusicology* 44: 234–256.

Nettl, B. (1983). *The Study of Ethnomusicology: Twenty-Nine Issues and Concepts*. Urbana: The University of Illinois Press.

Norton, B. (2000). "Vietnamese mediumship rituals: The musical construction of the spirits." *The World of Music* 42: 75–97.

Pitcairn, T. K. and Schleidt, M. (1976). "Dance and decision: An analysis of a courtship dance of the Medlpa, New Guinea." *Behaviour* 58: 298–316.

Proschan, F. (1992). "Poetic parallelism in Kmhmu verbal arts: From texts to performances." *Selected Reports in Ethnomusicology* 9: 1–31.

Racy, A.J. (2000). "The many faces of improvisation: The Arab Taqasim as a musical symbol." *Ethnomusicology* 44: 65–96.

Radcliffe-Brown, A. R. (1922/1948). *The Andaman Islanders*. Glencoe, IL: The Free Press.

Rappaport, R. A. (1967). *Pigs for the Ancestors: Ritual in the Ecology of a New Guinea People*. New Haven: Yale University Press.

Roseman, M. (1984). "The social structuring of sound: The Temiar of peninsular Malaysia." *Ethnomusicology* 28: 411–445.

_____ (1991). *Healing Sounds from the Malaysian Rainforest: Temiar Music and Medicine*. Berkeley and Los Angeles: University of California Press.

Sarno, L. (1993). *Song From the Forest: My Life Among the Ba-Benjellé Pygmies*. New York: Houghton Mifflin.

Sapolsky, R. M. (1992). "Neuroendocrinology of the stress response." In J. B. Becker, S. M. Breedlove, and D. Crews (eds.) *Behavioral Endocrinology* (pp. 287–324). Cambridge, MA: MIT Press.

Schmidt, C. (1990). "Group expression and performance among Kpelle women's associations of Liberia." In M. Herndon and S. Ziegler (eds.) *Music, Gender, and Culture* (pp. 131–142). Wilhelmshaven: Florian Noetzel.

Seeger, A. (1987). *Why Suya Sing: A Musical Anthropology of an Amazonian People*. Cambridge: Cambridge University Press.

Seremetakis, C. N. (1991). *The Last Word: Women, Death, and Divination in Inner Mani*. Chicago: University of Chicago Press.

Shapiro, A. D. and Talamantez, I. (1986). "The Mescalero Apache girls' puberty ceremony: The role of music in structuring ritual time." *Yearbook for Traditional Music* 18: 77–90.

Smith, W. J. (1977). *The Behavior of Communicating: An Evolutionary Approach*. Cambridge, MA: Harvard University Press.

Solomon, T. (2000). "Dueling landscapes: Singing places and identities in highland Bolivia." *Ethnomusicology* 44: 257–280.

Speck, F. G. and L. Broom. (1951/1983). *Cherokee Dance and Drama*. Norman: University of Oklahoma Press.

Stern, D. (1995). *The Motherhood Constellation: A Unified View of Parent-Infant Psychotherapy*. New York: Basic Books.

Sugarman, J. C. (1988). "Making *muabet*: The social basis of singing among Prespa Albanian men." *Selected Reports in Ethnomusicology* 7: 1–42.

Thompson, R. F. (1995). "Impulse and repose: The art of Ituri women." In G. Meurant and R. F. Thompson (eds.) *Mbuti Design: Paintings by Pgymy Women of the Ituri Forest* (pp. 185–214). London: Thames and Hudson.

Thornhill, R. (1999). "Darwinian aesthetics." In C. Crawford and D. L. Krebs (eds.) *Handbook of Evolutionary Psychology: Ideas, Issues, and Applications* (pp. 543–572). Mahwah, NJ: Erlbaum.

Tinbergen, N. (1952). "Derived activities: Their causation, biological significance, origin, and emancipation during evolution." *Quarterly Review of Biology* 27: 1–32.

_____ (1959). "Comparative studies of the behaviour of gulls (Laridae): A progress report." *Behaviour* 15: 1–70.

Tolbert, E. (1990). "Women cry with words: Symbolization of affect in the Karelian lament." *Yearbook for Traditional Music* 22: 80–105.

van Lawick-Goodall, J. (1975). "The chimpanzee." In V. Goodall (ed.) *The Quest for Man* (pp. 131–169). London: Phaidon.

Vinnicombe, P. (1976). *People of the Eland*. Pietermaritzburg: University of Natal Press.

Watanabe, J. M. and Smuts, B. B. (1999). "Explaining religion without explaining it away: Trust, truth, and the evolution of cooperation in Roy A. Rappaport's 'The Obvious Aspects of Ritual.'" *American Anthropologist* 101: 98–112.

Waterman, C. A. (1990). *Jùjú: A Social History and Ethnography of an African Popular Music.* Chicago: University of Chicago Press.

Watson, D. and L. A. Clark. (1994). "The vicissitudes of mood: A schematic model." In P. Ekman and R. J. Davidson (eds.) *The Nature of Emotion: Fundamental Questions* (pp. 400–405). New York: Oxford University Press.

Whybrow, P. (1984). "Contributions for neuroendocrinology." In K. Scherer and P. Ekman (eds.) *Approaches to Emotion* (pp. 59–72). Hillsdale, NJ: Erlbaum.

Willis, L. (1989). "*Uli* painting and the Igbo world view." *African Arts* 23: 62–67.

Chapter 2

Music, Identity, and Social Control

Peter J. Martin

Introduction

The focus of this chapter is a consideration, from a specifically sociological point of view, of the "effects" of music on people in everyday social settings. It is argued that, to the extent that they depend on a "sender-receiver" model of musical communication, studies of mass media effects—including those of Adorno and the critical theorists—fail to take account of the significant ways in which musical meanings are constituted through, and embedded in, wider configurations of social relationships. Rather than conceptualizing music's effects in terms of the sending of a "message," or attempting to decipher the decontextualized "meaning" of musical texts, sociological studies are increasingly concerned with the actual use of music in everyday settings in which social processes confer meaning on music, and vice versa. These points are illustrated with reference to empirical studies of the actual use of music as an important and effective element in the process of establishing a secure sense of personal identity. The implication is that music's power to "manipulate" cannot be assumed, and that rather than inducing passive conformity, popular music in particular may be effective in facilitating the active assertion of self in the increasingly unstable social circumstances of late (or post-) modernity.

* * *

In this chapter I will be mainly concerned with exploring some implications of the idea of the manipulation of people by music in "everyday" social settings—that is, those that are neither formal rituals, nor events predominantly organized around audiovisual media experiences. The topic thus brings into

---

References for this chapter begin on page 72.

focus the question of the place of music, and the uses that are made of it in people's everyday lives, and—more generally—the issue of the extent to which their thoughts, emotions, and actions are influenced by music.

In considering these matters from a specifically sociological perspective—which is what I propose to do—it soon becomes clear that neat distinctions mentioned above appear increasingly problematic. Attendance at, for example, classical or rock concerts, or at a jazz or folk club, may appear to the sociologist as a pattern of activity that in many respects exhibits the characteristics of a more formalized ritual, or as one that has been seen as fundamental to the social organization of earlier societies. Thus, for example, Small (1987: 6) has argued that the symphony concert is indeed a ritual, "a celebration, undertaken not fully awares [*sic*], of the shared mythology and values of a certain group within our deeply fragmented society." And in another fragment of that society, Thornton (1995) in her study of "club cultures" found that young people's attendance—carefully dressed—at "alternative" club venues was an important means by which they asserted their independence from mainstream culture, thus acquiring "subcultural" capital.

Clearly, such activities may be described in just the same ways as more formal rituals. They are regularly undertaken and organized according to quite strict conventions, and their effects are similar: the generation of a sense of group solidarity and personal identity, and an affirmation of the divisions between insiders and outsiders, "us" and "them." Moreover, the audiovisual media now play a very considerable part in our everyday experiences of music—as, for example, when we watch television, go to the movies, or experience "background" music in public places—so that the separation of the audiovisual media from everyday social experience is, increasingly, problematic.

The initial distinctions, therefore, between ritual, audiovisual, and everyday contexts of music use are not easy to sustain. My aim, however, is not to dwell on issues of classification, but rather to suggest that from a sociological point of view, as the two examples above suggest, music in everyday contexts must be understood as *embedded* in patterns of everyday social activities, and thus may be only a part—an important, even crucial, part—but a part nevertheless of a larger complex of activities. In comparison with the number of analyses of individual pieces of music, abstracted from any actual performance context, or of musical perception under "experimental" conditions, there are in fact relatively few studies of "real life" music use, but what they do suggest is the operation of a kind of circle of interpretation—some would call it hermeneutic—through which the social activities receive their meaning from the music, and vice versa.

One important implication of this is that the widespread assumption of music as a form of communication in which a "message" is passed from a "sender" to a "receiver" may not provide a satisfactory model for the understanding of musical effects, whatever they may be (see Brown, this volume, for a different point of view). The "message" model, if I may call it that, is sociologically unsatisfactory in several ways, as has often been pointed out (e.g., Denzin, 1992: 115ff.). Blumer, for example, in a significant departure from the earlier position of the "Chicago school" sociologists (Denzin, 1992: 116), pointed out that mass media messages and their effects cannot reasonably be isolated from the dynamic social contexts of their production and appropriation. The "message" model seems to imply, for example, that both the active "sender" and passive "receiver" are individuals, isolated from any actual social context of music use, and to assume that the "message" is both unambiguous and effective in producing an appropriate reaction in the "receiver." Above all, "Account must be taken of a collective process of definition which in different ways shapes the manner in which individuals composing the 'audience' interpret and respond to the presentations given through the mass media" (Blumer, 1959/1969: 188). In the present context, Blumer's insistence on the fundamental importance of this collaborative process of interpretation is highly significant. What I will suggest is that studies of music use in "real life" contexts serve to emphasize the serious sociological limitations of the "message" model, and that such studies, if pursued more vigorously, would lead to a greater understanding of the ways in which music and its effects are inevitably implicated in wider patterns of social activity.

In order to avoid any misunderstandings, I should immediately make it clear that I have no wish to deny the value of, say, musicological analyses of particular musical "texts," or of systematic psychological studies of responses to music. Such studies derive from certain specific—and quite different—academic discourses, and we have much to learn from them (see the chapters by Bullerjahn and North and Hargreaves in this volume). In considering the actual use of music in everyday situations, however, we are led into the sociological domain, where music making and hearing are seen as sets of social practices in which people are collaboratively involved.

In what follows, therefore, I will draw on an inevitably selective and limited number of studies of music use—most of them relating to popular music—to consider some of the sociological issues that have emerged, with a particular emphasis on the relationship between music and personal identity. As I have already suggested, participation in sets of activities organized around music can create or reinforce a sense of being a particular kind of person, of belonging to a particular group, and by extension may lead to the designation, definition, and possible denigration of "others." But if music can thus be seen to affect the development of individuals' sense of self and others, is it not therefore a prime example of manipulation, in Foucault's use of the term? Could music not constitute a "dividing practice," through which "the subject is objectified by a process of division either within himself or from others" (quoted in Rabinow, 1991: 8). Inevitably, as I shall suggest, things are not so straightforward. In conclusion, I will consider some implications of the discussion for our understanding of the concepts of manipulation and social control.

Popular Music in Use

For Adorno and the critical theorists, the nature and effects of the "culture industry" were of fundamental importance in their search for an answer to the question of why the exploited mass proletariat generated by modern capitalism had failed to develop the kind of oppositional class consciousness envisaged by Marxist theorists. Thus, in their *Dialectic of Enlightenment*, Adorno and Horkheimer famously described the "culture industry"—that is, the business processes through which culture in the form of standardized, mass commodities was produced and distributed—as above all generating "mass deception" (1944/1979: 120ff.). Adorno's view was uncompromising; indeed, the tone of his remarks makes the term "manipulation" seem quite mild: "In contrast to the Kantian, the categorical imperative of the culture industry no longer has anything in common with freedom. It proclaims: you shall conform, without instruction as to what; conform to what exists anyway, and to that which anyone thinks anyway as a reflex of its power and omnipresence. The power of the culture industry's ideology is such that conformity has replaced consciousness" (Adorno, 1963/1991: 90).

From this point of view, and particularly for Adorno, popular music can be nothing more than a commodity produced by the "culture industry," inescapably trivial and aesthetically degraded, producing and reproducing the "regression of listening" that characterized mass audiences (Adorno, 1938/1991: 40f.). "There is actually a neurotic mechanism of stupidity in listening, too," says Adorno, "the arrogantly ignorant rejection of everything unfamiliar is its sure sign" (pp. 44f.). The synthetic products of the music business have now swept away all traces of the authentic voice of the working people. Once, in an earlier era, the "power of the street ballad, the catchy tune and all the swarming forms of the banal" were used to attack "the cultural privilege of the ruling class." Now, however, the masses are deluded into a preference for the very music that degrades them: "The illusion of a social preference for light music as against serious is based on that passivity of the masses which makes the consumption of light music contradict the objective interests of those who consume it" (Adorno, 1938/1991: 30).

Even in its details, popular music represents and reinforces the annihilation of the autonomous individual that the critical theorists took to be fundamental in the totalitarian society of capitalist industrialism. "The concepts of order which [the culture industry] hammers into human beings," writes Adorno, "are always those of the status quo"—as when, for example, syncopated effects, and other "rhythmic problems," are "instantly resolved by the triumph of the basic beat" (Adorno, 1963/1991: 90). It is hardly surprising, therefore, to find that in the view of one commentator, "Adorno identified popular music as part of the effort of late capitalism to transform man into an insect" (Brunkhorst, 1999: 143). For the critical theorists, therefore, the principal function of popular music was to "affirm" the values and normative patterns of mass society and thus to reconcile the "humming millions" to their existence as workers and, increasingly, consumers; in filling people's heads with simple tunes and escapist fantasies, it inculcated an ideological acceptance of, and an unquestioning obedience to, the status quo, while concealing the exploitation and mystification on which it was based.

There could hardly be a stronger statement than this of the idea of music as manipulation, and on a massive scale. Interestingly, much American writing of the 1950s on the "mass society" thesis adopted a similar position with regard to popular music, assuming that its endless succession of ephemeral love songs and "Moon in June" lyrics effectively reflected and reinforced conventional morality (Hirsch, 1971: 373). In contrast to Adorno's despair, however, American commentators of the 1950s took some consolation from this. They agreed that the music itself might well be "standardized trivia," but at least it had the merit of encouraging social stability and celebrating the American way of life; in the language of 1950s sociology, it could be seen as contributing significantly to the "functional imperatives" of both socialization and social control. All this was to change, of course, with the volcanic eruption of rock 'n' roll in the mid 1950s and the emergence of "oppositional" youth cultures in which music was a major component, culminating in the overt challenges to conventional morality and established institutions in the "countercultural" music of the late 1960s.

Almost as soon as it appeared, rock 'n' roll was condemned as a force that would corrupt youth, undermine the family, and destabilize American society (see the chapter on music censorship by Korpe, Reitov, and Cloonan, this volume). Much of this moral panic, as Ward (1998) has shown, was orchestrated by white supremacist Southern politicians, whose main agenda was driven by their resistance to integrationist policies which presented a challenge to their particular way of life. In the present context, what is significant about this movement is the set of assumptions that it made—which critics of styles such as "rap" still tend to make—about the music and its effects. Much of the evidence which was used to characterize pop music styles as *either* affirming conventional morality *or* presenting a threat to it was based on "content analysis" studies of song lyrics. Methodologically, the limitations of this procedure are clear enough and similar to the issues raised by the "message" model of musical communication: the words of a song are treated as a "text" independently of the music (which is then ignored), and both are decontextualized. It is further assumed that this "text" has an unambiguous "meaning," and that this meaning is effectively and unproblematically communicated to those who listen to the song.

It was against this background that Hirsch took the simple—but at the time quite novel—step of examining the actual use of pop music by real high-school teenagers. The results, which have been echoed in various subsequent studies, were instructive, and quite damaging to the conventional wisdom—whether of critical theorists or conservatives—about popular music and its effects. Not only did it emerge that there was a variety of interpretations of song lyrics, but even in the case of big-selling "protest" songs, "the vast majority of teenage listeners are unaware of what the lyrics … are about" (Robinson and Hirsch, 1972: 231). Moreover, any analysis that neglects the actual *sound* of a record is unlikely to capture the essence of what it does for people: the rhythm, the "feel," or what jazz musicians call the "groove" of a recording may give it its attraction, irrespective of the "content" of its lyrics. In general, as Denzin (1969: 1036) put it: "There may be little correspondence between the intended and the imputed meanings" of such cultural objects, so that "an art object, because it may not invoke the intended response in the audience, cannot be taken as an a priori valid indicator of a group's perspective." This is an important point, since it concisely but directly challenges all those interpretations that in some way consider musical styles as to be "reflections" or "representations" or "articulations" of the central values of social groups, whether these be whole societies, dominant classes, or oppositional subcultures (Martin, 1995: 160ff.; DeNora, 2000: 3).

It is also significant that empirical demonstrations of the inadequacy of the critical theorists' model of "mass society" have been complemented by theoretical analyses that cast doubt on the validity of their assumptions about the culture industry and its manipulative effects. Honneth, for example, has argued that there is a specifically "sociological deficit" (1993: 187) in Horkheimer's programmatic formulation of critical theory: a preoccupation with large-scale economic forces, on the one hand, and psychoanalytic theories, on the other, led not only to an impoverished concept of culture—which simply serves to "reflect the behavioral constraints of the economic system back upon the individual psyche" (p. 208)—but, crucially, to an almost total neglect of the actions and interactions of real individuals and groups. In Honneth's view, Horkheimer's perspective "screens the whole spectrum of everyday social action out of the object domain of interdisciplinary social science" (p. 210). In other words, the critical theorists' fixation with political economy and psychoanalysis led them to ignore precisely those phenomena that are the object of sociology as an "autonomous science" (p. 211). Horkheimer sees modern society only as a mass of atomized and passive individuals, with a consequent disregard both for the particular cultural and institutional configurations that constitute the social environment of real people, and for the specifically sociological process through which such configurations are enacted.

The implication of such studies is that, from a sociological point of view, the meaning and effects of music must be understood though an examination of the contexts of its use. Yet, Honneth contends, under the increasing influence of Adorno, the project of critical theory was gradually reoriented: so far as the analysis of culture was concerned, there was less and less emphasis on Horkheimer's original interest in an interdisciplinary theory of social action or of institutions, and in its place a growing preoccupation with the "ideological-critical deciphering of the social content of the work of art" (p. 211). Thus, Adorno's aesthetic commitments pre-empted the development of a sociological approach to music (and literature) focused on "social mediation" (p. 212) and concerned with examining the ways in which cultural objects are used and interpreted by real people in real situations. This is a significant omission, since what studies of the actual use of popular music emphasize is the extent to which it is bound up in complex ways with people's participation in wider configurations of activity. It should not be simply assumed that they actively "listen" to it with the close attention of the symphony concert-goer (although they may do so); what may be far more important is that the experience of the music helps to define them to themselves and others as certain sorts of people. Indeed, another important implication of studies of popular-music use is the extent to which musical meanings are derived from non-musical sources—"significant others" such as friends or fellow students, or authoritative opinion leaders like DJs or critics. Indeed, just as in the worlds of classical music, or jazz, or folk music, an array of journals and magazines does much to constitute the discourse that provides possible ways of hearing specific sounds, songs, styles, bands, singers, and so on.

In short, what I am suggesting is that, sociologically speaking, the use of music in everyday situations is not effectively conceptualized as the communication of messages from senders to individual receivers, but is to be understood as a collaborative process involving a network of relationships in which the music derives its meaning from the pattern of social activities in which it is embedded, and vice versa. In other words, musical meaning is not to be found "in" the text, nor does it have autonomous effects; rather, it may be more useful to think in terms of a reciprocity of effects linking music and the configuration of social activities in which it is inescapably embedded. Such a conclusion not only reveals the distinctive perspective of the "sociological gaze" as it is applied to music (Martin, 2000), but indicates some of the ways in which it differs from other, equally legitimate, approaches—such as those of the musicological analyst or the cultural critic. Indeed, DeNora (2000) has characterized recent sociological work in this sphere as marking "a shift in focus from aesthetic objects and their content ... to the cultural practices in and through which aesthetic materials were appropriated and used ... to produce social life" (p. 6).

Music and Identity

A similar perspective has been developed in some of Simon Frith's more recent work: "[T]he issue is not how a particular piece of music reflects the people, but how it produces them, how it creates and constructs an experience—a musical experience, an aesthetic experience—that we can only make sense of by *taking on* both a subjective and a collective identity" (Frith, 1996a: 109, emphasis in original). As this quotation indicates, Frith's position emerged in criticism of "reflection" theories that seek to demonstrate a correspondence, or some sort of "structural homology" (Shepherd, 1991: 89), between social

groups and the styles of music they produce, whether affirmative or oppositional (see also Middleton, 1990: 147ff.). But what does it mean to say, as Frith
does, that music can "produce" people? What this definitely does *not* mean is
that there is some sort of Foucauldian "discourse" that manipulates people in
the sense that "it" constitutes their subjectivities. What I think it does lead us
to appreciate is the often neglected social dimension of musical experience, the
ways in which having a musical experience inevitably involves us in relationships with others, whether they are present or not. In listening to or performing music, we must, as Schutz (1964) argued, "tune in" our subjectivity to that
of others as we follow the succession of sounds in "real time"—thus constituting the intersubjective "we" that is the foundation of all social experience.
For present purposes, one important implication is that rather than viewing
collectivities—societies, groups, subcultures, and so on—as existing prior to
the music or other cultural phenomena, which then express "their" values, it
is more productive to examine the ways in which a sense of participating in a
distinct collectivity is *produced* through such collaborative activities and experiences (Frith, 1996a: 111).

Thus, the sociological importance of music, and popular music in particular,
lies in its power to construct "our sense of identity through the direct experiences it offers of the body, time, and sociability" (p. 124). All such experiences
are "obdurately social" (Frith, 1996b: 277) in the sense that they involve the
establishment of a relationship between "inner" subjectivity and the "outer"
world of collaborative cultural practices. In a "mass" industrial society music
can thus provide a strong source of meaning and belonging: it affords, in short,
"a way of being in the world" (Frith, 1996a: 114) and is a highly salient aspect
of the process through which aspects of identity—gender, age, ethnicity, class,
religion, and so on—are established, maintained and changed.

It seems too that music, as a specific form of cultural practice, is particularly effective in contributing to the process of identity formation. As Shepherd (1991) has argued, music, as a sonic medium, has an immediacy that
purely visual media may lack, affording the sensation that significant sounds
are—in a quite literal sense—resonating within us. Indeed, in considering
the implications of the recent revival of sociological interest in the aesthetic
(as opposed to the cognitive) dimensions of cultural practice, DeNora (2000)
has emphasized the particular power of music to act as a constitutive, rather
than simply reflective, medium: "Its temporal dimension, the fact that it is a
non-verbal, non-depictive medium, and that fact that it is a physical presence
whose vibrations can be felt, all enhance its ability to work at non-cognitive or
subconscious levels" (DeNora, 2000: 159). In this short essay it is impossible to
elaborate on this point; to anyone interested in the "effects" of music, however,
it is unlikely to be contentious (for further discussion, see the chapters by Dissanayake and Volgsten, this volume).

In any case, what is empirically undeniable is the persistence and strength
of the attachment that people in modern industrial societies have to music,

both as "consumers" and performers. It is this attachment that sustains the recording industry and also ensures that, for example, in every town and city in the developed world—and many outside it—there are dozens, sometimes hundreds or thousands, of aspiring musicians in a wide variety of styles (see Finnegan, 1989). For the sociologist this phenomenon has a particular fascination. Why should music matter so much in contemporary culture? In the remarks above, I have suggested that this may well have something to do with the effectiveness of music, not in stupefying the masses (as Adorno thought), nor in either representing or challenging conventional morality (though it can contribute to these things), but quite simply in its ability to give people a sense of secure identity—whatever they wish that to be—and a sense of belonging at a time when the accelerating pace of economic and technological change is making it increasingly difficult to achieve continuity and stability in social life (Sennett, 1998). Some remarks by Bernard Sumner, a musician who achieved success in the late 1980s with the Manchester bands Joy Division and, later, New Order, may serve to illustrate the point. Sumner was describing the effects of the dispersion and physical destruction of the community in which he spent his childhood: "By the age of twenty-two, I'd had quite a lot of loss in my life. The place where I used to live, where I had my happiest memories, all that had gone. All that was left was a chemical factory. I realised then that I could never go back to that happiness. So there's this void. For me Joy Division was about the death of my community and my childhood" (quoted in Haslam, 1999: xxiv).

From this perspective music appears not as the manipulator of passive victims, but as a means through which individuals can actively construct a sense of self and proclaim a distinct identity. Indeed, one of the most promising areas of recent research in this field concerned linking the evident fragmentation of musical styles to the active process of identity construction that, it has been argued, is increasingly typical of late-modern, mass consumption societies—particularly in view of the declining salience of such "traditional" factors as class, occupation, locality, and gender (Bennett, 1999: 606). It may be added that such a view of the fragmentary and constructed nature of the self is neither new nor distinctively postmodern. In his classic essay, "Metropolis and Mental Life," first published in 1903, Georg Simmel suggested that while the modern city exposes the individual to intense psychological pressures, it also affords liberation from traditional community roles and thus an unprecedented degree of personal freedom (Simmel, 1903/1997: 180). Simmel goes on to anticipate a strong theme in postmodern thought by remarking on the ways in which, through their choice of conduct and consumption patterns, people may seek both to assert their identities and secure social distinction. In the context of the present discussion, the significant point is the extent to which, a century after Simmel was writing, music—and especially popular music—has become an important means by which people seek to achieve these ends. Why else does Elvis Presley remain "The King" to those whose teenage rebellion took place more than fifty years ago? Why else do the fans of heavy metal stay attached to their guitar heroes three decades after they first appeared?

Moreover, despite the continuing trend toward global concentration in the music business, with four international corporations selling around 80 percent of all recorded popular music, an unprecedented range and diversity of music styles is now available on the market (see Lopes, 1992). Technological developments, too, have had the effect of empowering individuals in ways that give them the potential to resist the "culture industry": since the 1970s the increasing availability of low-cost recording equipment has meant that aspiring musicians are no longer dependent on orthodox companies in order to record their own music, and by the end of the twentieth century the Internet was becoming recognized as a potential threat to the companies' control of distribution networks (see also Wallis's and Volgsten and Åkerberg's contributions to this volume). These are excellent examples of the way in which, as Marx put it, constant development of the "forces of production" inevitably undermines the existing "social relations of production," and as such may be considered one of the inevitable contradictions of capitalism. Here, however, the essential point is that the availability of a wide diversity of music styles and access to recording and distribution are important in that they give people increasing opportunities to select, construct, and express through music a vast range of possible cultural identities. Indeed, one of the notable developments facilitated by new technologies for recording, producing, and reproducing music has been the increasing involvement of young people as producers of their own sounds and aural environments, and the consequent erosion of the distinction between the production and consumption of popular music (Willis, 1990: 82). I will return to this point below.

Music in Social Context

The discussion so far has suggested that the "message" model of communication that underlies much thinking about music, manipulation, and mass culture is sociologically unsatisfactory, and that a concern with the examination of actual music use by real people requires consideration of the wider context of social activities in which music is always embedded. There can be little doubt that in recent years there has been a significant reorientation in sociologists' perspectives on music, with a movement away from the traditional concern with deciphering the meaning of musical "texts," and a corresponding increase in analyses of the ways in which music is *used* by people in real situations (see, for example, Becker, 1989; Martin, 1995/2000; DeNora, 2000). Among these, several authors have highlighted the significance of music as a medium through which individuals and groups seek to sustain and assert a sense of identity, often in the context of institutional changes and cultural instability that threaten the continuity of their experience. To amplify the above remarks, even if briefly, it seems appropriate to provide some examples of recent studies in which music may be seen to play a role in the establishment of social relationships and the formation of personal identities.

Music and Social Distinction

The Gentlemen's Concerts in Manchester was a society of subscribers founded in the late eighteenth century that attracted the leading citizens of the city at the very height of its ascendancy as the world's "first industrial city." Subscribers to the Gentlemen's Concerts thus included some of the world's leading capitalist entrepreneurs, and since there was no established court or group of aristocrats in their city, their activities give us an interesting insight into the formation of the new industrial bourgeoisie (Allis, 1995). It has often been asserted, by Adorno among others, that the "classical" music that emerged between the 1770s and 1830s is an expression of the rise of bourgeois ideology, epitomized by Beethoven's "middle period" works (Witkin, 1998). So, did the Manchester Gentlemen's Concerts promote the "classical" music that has been seen as expressing the essence of their world-view? In general they did not. Throughout the nineteenth century, the programs were of a light and heterogeneous nature. Top soloists were engaged from all over Europe, and paid handsomely, but their performances were often treated disdainfully by the audience—in fact, time after time the concert managers had to post notices asking the subscribers to refrain from disrupting performances by talking, smoking, entering and leaving, and walking about the hall. Yet for more than fifty years the Gentlemen's Concerts was the most socially exclusive society in the city. In short, the history of the Gentlemen's Concerts casts considerable doubt on the widespread assumption of the affinity between "classical" music and the new bourgeoisie (Martin, 2006) and, of particular interest in the present context, is an excellent example of an organization whose formal aims were musical, yet whose primary purpose was to afford its members the opportunity to claim and display social distinction, to publicly affirm their sense of belonging to the dominant social grouping.

Nor is this merely a retrospective interpretation: on 27 December 1883, the *Manchester Guardian* declared that the Concert Hall was "as much a social as a musical institution" where people went to see and be seen (Allis, 1995: 110). Just as the primary purpose of early Italian opera houses was "to show off the ruling groups of a petty Italian state" (Rosselli, 1991: 57), the Manchester Gentlemen's Concerts provided a means by which the subscribers affirmed their social status and sense of identity to themselves and to each other, and in doing so distinguished themselves from the vast majority of the city's population. Of course some, probably many, of the subscribers were motivated by their love of music in itself; equally, however, it seems undeniable that the whole configuration of activities revolving around the Gentlemen's Concerts can only be understood in terms of what Bourdieu (1986) calls the pursuit of social distinction, itself founded on a "network of oppositions" that "has its ultimate source in the opposition between the 'elite' of the dominant and the 'mass' of the dominated" (p. 468).

Music in Everyday Life

The example of the Gentlemen's Concerts may serve to suggest some of the ways in which music may be, as I have suggested, embedded in a wider pattern of social activities. But it may be objected that this example does not link the music *itself* with the process of identity formation. This issue is examined in some detail in DeNora's work on *Music in Everyday Life* (2000), which focuses on the part played by music in the everyday lives of women. On the basis of her ethnographic studies, DeNora reports that music is indeed often used by women "as a key resource for the production of autobiography and the narrative thread of self" (2000: 158), and she examines the more specific processes through which the use of music can be seen, for example, to extend bodily capacities, to facilitate concentration, to manage emotional states, to produce particular memories, and so on (p. 160). In doing all these things, DeNora emphasizes the properties of music itself as a physical, sonic medium: "Its temporal dimension, the fact that it is a non-verbal, non-depictive medium and that it is a physical presence whose vibrations can be felt, all enhance its ability to work at non-cognitive or subconscious levels" (p. 159).

Yet, and this is an important point in the present context, DeNora also emphasizes that the ways in which music produces effects cannot be adequately understood simply as a stimulus which acts upon people: "Rather, music's 'effects' come from the ways in which individuals orient to it, how they interpret it and how they place it within their personal musical maps, within the semiotic web of music and extra-musical associations" (p. 61). This, then, is an *active* process of meaning-creation in which music is an important element in the "definition of the situation" achieved by people in particular social contexts. To repeat, sociological interest is focused on this process, and its role in the constitution of social order, as opposed to a concern with the musical "work" as a "meaningful unit" per se (ibid.).

Music and the Constitution of Identity

Similar themes are pursued in Andy Bennett's account (2000) of his investigation of the ways in which popular music styles are used by young people in the process of establishing and sustaining their own sense of identity. For Bennett, as for DeNora, the links between popular music and personal identity are of considerable sociological importance; moreover, the use of music by young people is essentially *active*, and rooted in the particular circumstances of their local social environment. Thus, Bennett is critical of theorists of globalization (and, by implication, "mass culture") who diagnose not only the homogenization of cultural experience but the reduction of individuals to passive consumers—indeed, his argument is entirely consistent with Honneth's view of the "sociological deficit" inherent in the mass culture thesis. Bennett accepts that young people do make use of "musical and stylistic resources appropriated from the global culture industries"; what this involves in practice, however, is "the use of such resources in the articulation of collective sensibilities which are both constructed and acted out in response to given sets of circumstances encountered in the everyday lives of particular groups and individuals. As the physical territory of everyday life, it is the 'local' that serves both as a basis for social action and for the collective identities forged as a result of particular forms of social action" (Bennett, 2000: 197).

This emphasis on the active constitution of a sense of identity in the context of local cultural environments has been an important element in the influential work of Paul Willis (1990); he too, like the authors considered above, has placed considerable emphasis on the significance of music in this process. Given the erosion of traditional institutions and the continuing dehumanization of work, it is increasingly only in their so-called leisure time that young people have the chance to establish their sense of identity and exercise their "creative symbolic activities" (Willis, 1990: 15). While it is true that the clothes, the videos, the computer games, the magazines, the radio and TV shows—and the music—that form such a large part of "common culture" are mass-produced commodities of the culture industry, Willis is concerned with the "grounded aesthetics" through which the meanings of such items are "selected, reselected, highlighted, and recomposed" (p. 21) so as to create the symbolic worlds of the young, rather than simply "received" by passive consumers. Indeed, for Willis "Consumerism now has to be understood as an active, not a passive process. Its play includes work" (p. 18). As far as popular music is concerned:

> The cultural meaning of Bros or Morrissey, house or hip hop, Tiffany or Tracey Chapman, isn't simply the result of record company sales campaigns, it depends too on consumer abilities to make value judgements, to talk knowledgeably and passionately about their genre tastes, to place music in their lives, to use commodities and symbols for their own imaginative purposes and to generate their own particular grounded aesthetics. These processes involve the exercise of critical, discriminating choices and uses which disrupt taste categories and "ideal" modes of consumption promoted by the leisure industry and break up its superimposed definitions of musical meaning. (p. 60)

Given the strong claims that Willis makes, it is worth noting that his conclusions are based on many years of ethnographic work among young people, in marked contrast to the theoretical presuppositions and speculations of those who criticize "mass culture" in general and the music business in particular. Indeed (just as Hirsch's studies demonstrated back in the 1960s), detailed empirical investigations of real people in real situations tend to reveal a rather different picture from that painted by the "grand theorists" of mass culture. So as a final example I will refer to *The Hidden Musicians* (1989), Ruth Finnegan's exhaustive anthropological study of music-making in an English town, and in particular to her conclusion that, in this context, participation in music-making (in all styles) gave the many individuals involved a sense of "achievement in a valued activity and a well-founded sense of identity" (1989: 328). Moreover, Finnegan wants to emphasize that this process of collaboration with others in musical projects is "structured in recognized pathways" that, while not imposed by any external or bureaucratic authority, nevertheless have "a real existence outside and, in a sense, independent of individuals, giving them, as it were, one road to live by with all the detailed expectations about behaviour, content, ritual, values, and social relationships that this implies. Such musical pathways—not so unlike those of religion—also constitute symbolic constructs within which people can create and control the world.... To be involved in musical practice is not merely an individual matter or, indeed, asocial withdrawal ... but *is* to be involved in social action and social relations—in society" (p. 329).

Conclusion

I have suggested that general theoretical accounts that regard music in general and popular music in particular as a means by which people may be manipulated or controlled have tended to oversimplify a set of relationships that is far more complex—and far more interesting from a sociological point of view—than the theorists have allowed. Often such accounts rest on various *assumptions* about how music "works," or how it has the effects it is supposed to have, which are not well supported by the (relatively few) empirical studies of actual music in use. Such studies, however, do lead us to an understanding of music as inevitably implicated in wider configurations of social action in which there may be a reciprocal determination of meanings between the music and the activities. Such a perspective suggests the inadequacies of simple models of musical "effects" that presuppose the communication of a message from sender to receiver.

In contrast to the notion that music somehow acts on a more or less passive listener, I have emphasized some of the ways in which people may actively use music in the process of establishing and maintaining a distinct sense of self, an identity that, though constantly evolving, provides both psychological security and a sense of belonging to a wider community. Just as Foucault realized the limitations of his early work on manipulation and the various "techniques of domination" and turned to the investigation of "techniques of the self" (McNay, 1994: 134), so we are now, I suggest, in a position to move beyond the straightforward idea of social control as either external or internal coercion (or some mixture of the two), and to examine the ways in which the "effects" of music are generated in and through the activities of real people in specific social situations. Moreover, as I have suggested, some recent studies have begun to explore the *active* process of identity formation associated with modern patterns of popular music use, in relation to lifestyle choices and selective commodity consumption.

In saying this, however, I should emphasize that I am not claiming that individuals have the ability to define meanings or construct selves entirely as they please: on the contrary, it is precisely in the engagement between individual subjectivities and the "objective facticities" (Berger and Luckmann, 1991: 78) of the social world that the process of self-formation is carried out. Furthermore, while I wish to emphasize the active aspect of this process, and the relative autonomy of individuals as they seek to "identify" themselves, it must be recognized that all these activities are pursued, and "ways of being" are achieved, in an *engagement* with the cultural and institutional parameters that constitute the "objective facticities" of global capitalism.

Willis is surely right to emphasize the active and creative ways in which young people use music (among other cultural resources) as an important means through which they "make sense of the social world and their place within it" (1990: 82): claiming and proclaiming particular identities, asserting differences, and experiencing a sense of belonging in a world of increasing insecurities. However, as Willis also notes, the activities that sustain such "grounded aesthetics" may be primarily defensive, in that they above all "enable survival: contesting or expressing feelings of boredom, fear, powerlessness and frustration. They can be used as affective strategies to cope with, manage, and make bearable the experiences of everyday life" (p. 64). Described in this way, they appear as coping strategies, rather than resistant or even radical ones. I suspect, therefore, that for the critical theorists the "symbolic creativity" that Willis identifies might simply be regarded as a more sophisticated form of "mass deception" in which, for example, the achievement of a sense of particular identity is little more than an instance of what Adorno called "pseudo-individuality": "The peculiarity of the self is a monopoly commodity determined by society; it is falsely represented as natural" (Adorno and Horkheimer, 1944/1979: 154). Does it matter whether we buy CDs of rap or heavy metal, girl bands or grunge, acid jazz or disco, as long as we keep buying *something*? Trumpets may have brought down the walls of Jericho, but they have not so far made much impression on what Marx called the "financial system" of the modern world.

References

Adorno, T. W. (1938/1991). "On the fetish character of music and the regression in listening." In J. M. Bernstein (ed.) *The Culture Industry: Selected Essays on Mass Culture* (pp. 26–52). London: Routledge.

_____ (1963/1991). "Culture industry reconsidered." In J. M. Bernstein (ed.) *The Culture Industry: Selected Essays on Mass Culture* (pp. 85–92). London: Routledge.

Adorno, T. W. and Horkheimer, M. (1944/1979). *Dialectic of Enlightenment*. London: Verso.

Allis, W. (1995). *The Manchester Gentlemen's Concerts*. Unpublished M.Phil. dissertation, University of Manchester.

Becker, H. S. (1989). "Ethnomusicology and sociology: A letter to Charles Seeger." *Ethnomusicology* 33: 275–285.

Bennett, A. (1999). "Subcultures or neo-tribes? Rethinking the relationship between youth, style, and musical taste." *Sociology* 33: 599–617.

_____ (2000). *Popular Music and Youth Culture: Music, Identity and Place*. London: Macmillan.

Berger, P. and Luckmann, T. (1966/1991). *The Social Construction of Reality*. London: Penguin.

Blumer, H. (1959/1969). "Suggestions for the study of mass media effects." In H. Blumer, *Symbolic Interactionism: Perspective and Method* (pp. 183–194). Berkeley: University of California Press.

Bourdieu, P. (1986). *Distinction: A Social Critique of the Judgement of Taste*. London: Routledge.

Brunkhorst, H. (1999). *Adorno and Critical Theory*. Cardiff: University of Wales Press.

DeNora, T. (2000) *Music in Everyday Life*. Cambridge: Cambridge University Press.

Denzin, N. (1969). "Problems in analysing elements of mass culture: Notes on the popular song and other artistic productions." *American Journal of Sociology* 75: 1035–1041.

_____ (1992). *Symbolic Interactionism and Cultural Studies: The Politics of Interpretation*. Cambridge, MA: Blackwell.

Finnegan, R. (1989). *The Hidden Musicians*. Cambridge: Cambridge University Press.

Frith, S. (1996a). "Music and identity." In S. Hall and P. DuGay (eds.) *Questions of Cultural Identity* (pp. 108–127). London: Sage.

_____ (1996b). *Performing Rites: On the Value of Popular Music*. Oxford: Oxford University Press.

Haslam, D. (1999). *Manchester England: The Story of the Pop Cult City*. London: Fourth Estate.

Hirsch, P. M. (1971). "Sociological approaches to the pop music phenomenon." *American Behavioral Scientist* 14: 371–388.

Honneth, A. (1993). "Max Horkheimer and the sociological deficit of critical theory." In S. Benhabib, W. Bonss, and J. McCole (eds.) *On Max Horkheimer: New Perspectives* (pp. 187–214). Cambridge, MA: MIT Press

Lopes, P. (1992). "Innovation and diversity in the popular music industry, 1969–1990." *American Sociological Review* 57: 56–71.

McNay, L. (1994). *Foucault: A Critical Introduction*. Cambridge: Polity.

Martin, P. J. (1995). *Sounds and Society: Themes in the Sociology of Music*. Manchester: Manchester University Press.

_____ (2000). "Music and the sociological gaze." *Svensk Tidskrift för Musikforskning* [Swedish Journal of Musicology] 82: 41–56.

_____ (2006). *Music and the Sociological Gaze*. Manchester: Manchester University Press.

Middleton, R. (1990). *Studying Popular Music*. Milton Keynes: Open University Press.

Rabinow, P. (ed.) (1984/1991). *The Foucault Reader: An Introduction to Foucault's Thought*. London: Penguin.

Robinson, J. and Hirsch, P. M. (1972). "Teenage response to rock 'n' roll protest songs." In R. S. Denisoff and R. A. Peterson (eds.) *The Sounds of Social Change* (pp. 222–231). Chicago: Rand McNally.

Rosselli, J. (1991). *Music and Musicians in Nineteenth Century Italy*. London: Batsford.

Schutz, A. (1964). "Making music together." In A. Schutz, *Collected Papers*, vol. 2 (pp. 159–178). The Hague: Martinus Nijhoff.

Sennett, R. (1998). *The Corrosion of Character: The Personal Consequences of Work in the New Capitalism*. New York: Norton.

Shepherd, J. (1991). *Music as Social Text*. Cambridge: Polity.

Simmel, G. (1903/1997). "The metropolis and mental life." In D. Frisby and M. Featherstone (eds.) *Simmel on Culture* (pp. 174–185). London: Sage.

Small, C. (1987). "Performance as ritual: Sketch for an enquiry into the true nature of a symphony concert." In A. L. White (ed.) *Lost in Music: Culture, Style and the Musical Event* (pp. 6–32). London: Routledge.

Thornton, S. (1995). *Club Cultures: Music, Media, and Subcultural Capital*. Cambridge: Polity.

Ward, B. (1998). *Just My Soul Responding: Rhythm and Blues, Black Consciousness, and Race Relations*. London: UCL Press.

Willis, P. (1990). *Common Culture*. Milton Keynes: Open University Press.

Witkin, R. (1998). *Adorno on Music*. London: Routledge.

Chapter 3

BETWEEN IDEOLOGY AND IDENTITY
Media, Discourse, and Affect in the Musical Experience

❦

Ulrik Volgsten

Introduction

Music as a human cultural artifact presupposes two things. The first is an affective substrate that has its source in early non-verbal communication. Music builds on the same affective qualities as does communication between mother and infant. The second presupposition is verbal discourse. Music as a human cultural artifact requires verbal discourse about itself. In other words, for our sound-making to become music, we need to talk about it. Why this is so will be argued here in a rather novel manner. Although I shall not present any definition of the term music, I suggest as one condition that to have a full sense of music the listener must be able to ascribe a social functionality to it. To have a full sense of music—whichever it may be—one must first of all have the cognitive capacity to separate sound from function. This is what enables musical and cultural pluralism and the ethical dimension that pluralism involves (and should not be mistaken for a functionalist sociology with its moral commitment to a preconceived social order). Once sound-making becomes related to verbal discourse and turns into music, it is also transformed from a merely social activity into an ideological expression. Musical sound thereby becomes a very subtle ideological manipulator in that—by utilizing the earliest means for human socialization—it *affectively articulates* the discursive contents to which it is bound. Although mass-mediation obstructs discursive (i.e., ideological) control, the inevitable ideological impact of music has consequences both for our identities and our actions, as reference to various kinds of discourse will make clear.

Notes for this chapter are located on page 97.

* * *

According to Ellen Dissanayake (this volume), music is one particular way of making ordinary behavior extraordinary. In a process that resembles ritualized behavior among non-human species, music is a means of promoting various social functions, such as the channeling of aggression, the facilitation of courtship, and the establishment and maintenance of identity. Music is able to fulfill these functions because of its close relationship to early mother-infant communication. What is particularly interesting about this is that the non-verbal communication that music draws upon for its impact on the listener is of an *affective* nature. Early communication between parent and infant is not primarily conceptual; it seems, rather, that conceptual learning and communication in the infant requires the capacity to experience the world affectively. The linking of music to feelings in various ways has a long history that can be traced back via Schopenhauer and Rousseau to Plato and the myths of antiquity. What Dissanayake brings into focus is a contemporary field of research that may explain music's social functionality with psychological credibility.

Sociologists of music have also argued for music's role in the socialization of human beings. Like Dissanayake, they have focused on the shaping of both individual and cultural identities. Rather than music being simply a way of expressing social values and identities, Simon Frith has argued that music actively partakes in the production of these identities. "Identity," he says, "is not a thing but a process—an experiential process which is most vividly grasped *as music*" (Frith, 1996: 110; emphasis in original). Accordingly, it is not the case "that a social group has beliefs which it then articulates in music, but that music, an aesthetic practice, articulates *in itself* an understanding of both group relations and individuality, on the basis of which ethical codes and social ideologies are understood" (p. 110f.; emphasis in original).

An important part of what happens in such cases, I will argue, is that music (or more correctly, musical sound) activates and articulates particular verbal discourses that the listener has already internalized, or comes to internalize, as part of his or her world view. These verbal discourses transform musical sound making from a merely social phenomenon into an *ideological* one in that they sanction certain kinds of actions at the expense of others. Rather than conforming to a Marxian or Nietzschean notion of ideology, this comes close to Ward Goodenough's (1981) anthropologic definition of culture as the "standards for deciding what is, standards for deciding what can be, standards for deciding how one feels about it, standards for deciding what to do about it, and standards for deciding how to go about doing it" (p. 62). As I hope will become clear, this "culturalist" notion of ideology and those of personal and cultural identity have important denominators in common.

That language is ideological has been shown by others, so I shall not argue for it here. With reference to both Foucault and Adorno, Peter Martin makes an important claim in his contribution to this volume, namely, that the ideological content of music is not passively internalized by the individual subject; there is a dialectic between the various cultural and individual uses that music is put to, leading to a diversity of ideological content. Moreover, listeners may not only assign to music content unforeseen by senders and producers; they may also be capable of critically evaluating (either consciously or unconsciously) any discursive content the musical sounds may convey (cf. Eco, 1967/1985; Hall, 1980). This becomes increasingly the case when music (both its sonic and discursive components) is disseminated through the mass media.

For example, one can mention Charles Hamm's 1992 analysis of Lionel Richie's hit *All Night Long*. Richie's song took on an unforeseen ideological content that enabled it to function subversively against the apartheid regime in South Africa, while it strengthened the identity of opposing groups. (On apartheid censorship, see Korpe, Reitov, and Cloonan, this volume.) While perhaps marginal from a global perspective, such an example complicates the idea of manipulation since the notion of a "sender" is blurred once mass-mediated musical sound (whether taped from radio or purchased on CD) is used in contexts unforeseen and uncontrolled by its commercial producers. The example also indicates that the fact that the content (of the "message") is more or less concealed does not necessarily make it deceptive to the "receivers." On the whole, though, verbal content shapes our musical experiences as much as our musical experiences affect verbal discourse. Assuming Martin's thesis, what I will do in the following pages is argue that what makes these internalized discourses function so effectively is the fact that they are *affectively articulated* by musical sound and that they become, to paraphrase Adorno (1970/1984), an integrated part of the musical experience.

With a slight change of emphasis, I will add to Frith's discussion of identity production by saying that when we hear music, bonds between us and the music, its style and style adherents, are cohered to and strengthened. Attending to music creates, for better or worse, a meaningful backdrop for one's personal self and one's mental states. Music, when it functions socially, acts as a mediator of social relations. The listener becomes a "friend" (or "enemy") with the music and, by extension, with others. The ideological dimension appears when we consider the specific contents of the discourses that are affectively articulated through musical sound. The contents of these discourses are either accepted or rejected by the listeners' belief systems, and so they logically sanction certain kinds of action at the expense of others.

In addition to experiencing musical sound within a discursive context, the listener knows—or at least has good reason to intuit—that others also have invested in an affective relationship with it. Whether the verbal content is something the listener already knows or something that he or she comes to know along with the musical style, the important point is that musical sound affectively articulates this content against and with the listener's personal moods, emotions, and other mental states.

This brings us back to the issue of affect, or more precisely, how affect relates to ideology and identity production. The notion of affect suggested here resembles that of Susanne Langer's (1948) when she spoke of music as "the logical expression" of the "morphology of feelings" (pp. 176, 193). However, music is more than just some sensory stimulus for us to cognitively respond to. The role of affect in music differs in important ways from a view such as Leonard Meyer's (1956), according to which music is "an art which is essentially without external referents ... a more or less closed system" (p. 89). I do not intend to make an aesthetic point here. Every culture or subculture has its own norms for a correct understanding of music, and for distinguishing aesthetically relevant content from individual associations and outgroup standards. But with its roots in early mother-infant communication and the shaping of personal identity, music is an inherently social phenomenon, and, as we shall see, because of verbal discourse musical sound inevitably becomes ideological.

More specifically, music's strength as an ideological expression—its manipulative force *par excellence*—comes from the capacity of musical sounds to affectively articulate the verbal discourses to which they become indissolubly tied. Affect is what makes music's ideological dimension both subtle and powerful. Accordingly, I will begin by clarifying the notion of affect, its functional origin in early parent-infant interaction, and its subsequent role for our musical experiences. Then I give examples of different kinds of mass-mediated discursive content in music. Finally, I will argue for the necessity and omnipresence of discursive content in music, and the ethical consequences that this entails.

Affect, Music, and the Development of the Self

Let us start from the beginning. As pointed out by René Spitz (1965: 44), the newborn's perception of the world is limited to the experience of "pure *differences.*" A newborn cannot perceive any *thing* in the world, it has not yet formed any concepts for particular objects. Instead it experiences abstract quality-changes such as rhythm, tempo, duration (Spitz, 1965), intensity, and shape (Lewkovicz and Turkewitz, 1980; Meltzoff, 1981). This experience of various abstract quality changes is an *amodal* perception (Stern, 1985): instead of distinguishing between different sensory modalities it functions as a "common sense," enabling the comparison between different modalities of sensory stimulation (cf. the notion of *imagination,* as discussed by Johnson, 1987).

Physiologically, we may assume that an experience of abstract quality-changes consists of "a temporal pattern of changes in density of neural firing. No matter if the object [is] encountered with the eye or the touch, and perhaps even with the ear, it ... produce[s] the same overall pattern of activation contour" (Stern, 1995: 84). As a result of these patterns of firing being hedonically appraised (cf. Berlyne, 1971), the phenomenological experience is *affective.*[1] As Daniel Stern puts it: "[W]henever a motive is enacted (whether initiated internally or externally, as in drinking when thirsty or receiving and adjusting to bad news), there is necessarily a shift in pleasure, arousal, level of motivation or goal achievement, and so on, that accompanies the enactment. These shifts unfold in time and each describe a temporal contour. The temporal contours, although neurophysiologically separate, act in concert and seem to be subjectively experienced as one complex feeling" (p. 84). In other words, to hear a melodic contour is fundamentally to feel it. This is how, for instance, two-month-old babies can react differently to different kinds of prosodic speech patterns. The effects are similar for both American English and Mandarin Chinese: falling speech melodies soothe, rising melodies attract attention, bell-shaped and falling melodies maintain attention, while bell-shaped and unilevel voice melodies discourage ongoing behavior (Papousek, Papousek, and Symmes, 1991).

The notions of "affect" and the related "affect attunement" (which will be described below) are elaborated by Stern in a theory about the human being's development of a sense of a *self*, as articulated against an *other*. In the following, I will regard Stern's developmental trajectory for the human being's sense of a self as a parallel to the human being's sense of that other which is excluded by the self—in this case music. In other words, I suggest that Stern's model can be regarded as a parallel to a model of how we come to experience music. This will show how affective experiences are necessary for both our capacity to experience music and the development of the human self. The relation between the two indicates the submersion of music in matters of socialization and identity.

The Development of a Musical Self

In the development of a *sense of self*, the amodal qualities of sensation to which the newborn child attends (e.g., prosodic contour) constitute the earliest temporally organized islands of coherence and coordination in an otherwise non-differentiated chaos. These experiences serve as the earliest points of reference between which significant relationships can subsequently be inferred. Most notably, the child will increasingly experience the difference between events that it may enact itself and those that are beyond the limits of its own immediate volition. While the experience of being the agent of certain coherent events but not of others gives the child a first sense of *self versus other*, the regulation of the infant's affective state by another's ministrations leads the child to a second level, a sense of *self with other* (Stern, 1985).

This feeling of togetherness—which is radically different from the earliest non-differentiation and symbiosis with the mother (cf. rather the notion of "trust" in Giddens, 1991)—is further enhanced through *affect attunement*. In affect attunement, more or less unconscious communicative behavior depends on the amodal similarities between the infant's behavior and the parent's. Without necessarily being aware of the fact, the parent attunes to the child's activities, not by imitation, but by performing an analogous action that retains the amodal properties of the original action. The attuning activity performed by the parent shares with the child's activity the underlying affective contour. Both are similar to the respective agents with regard to the amodal qualities of shape, rhythm, and intensity (as experiments show, whenever the mother misattunes, for instance by exaggerating intensity or showing no sense of rhythmical timing, the child reacts by becoming confused or upset).

A consequence of this "analogous translation from perception of another person's behavior [into] feelings [through] the transmutation from the perception of timing, intensity and shape via cross-modal fluency into felt vitality-affects in ourselves" (p. 159), as the sense of a self in relation to others develops, is an intuitive understanding of other people's affective states: "[W]e may gather from someone's arm gesture the perceptual qualities of rapid acceleration, speed, and fullness of display. But we will not experience the gesture in terms of the perceptual qualities of timing, intensity and shape; we will experience it directly as 'forceful'—that is, in terms of a vitality affect" (p. 158).

We should pay attention here to Stern's cautious use of quotation marks when writing of "forceful"; it is still too early to speak about conventional labels or culturally encoded emotions. Nevertheless, this experiencing of affective contours—"perceived in another's overt behavior becom[ing] a virtual vitality affect when experienced in the self" (p. 158)—points further from the level of self versus other to the level of a *subjective self*. At the level of a subjective self, actions acquire social significance. It is at this level that affective contours become related to the context of purposeful interaction, whereas earlier amodal perception was merely affective. It is at this level that a sense of intentionality occurs—the self having already been articulated against and with an *other*: now this relationship takes on a rudimentary dimension of subjective purposefulness.

This development of the self is furthered by affective contours coming to function in succession as *protonarrative envelopes*, articulating the child's earliest sense of desire and motivation, which adds a narrative-like structure to the perceived world: "The elements of plot get temporally distributed on a line of dramatic tension. And the dramatic line of tension is invariably synchronous with the temporal feeling shape. This is natural, since the motive-goal-tension is played out in terms of temporal shifts in arousal, pleasure, motivational strength, and goal attainment. In a sense, the perceived plot is superimposed or rather dispersed along the temporal feeling shape, which then acts as the line of tension to carry the narrative" (Stern, 1995: 91).

When affective contours are experienced as linked together, they function as protonarrative envelopes, as a supportive scaffold for the narrative distribution of perceived and successively denominated objects and events. Subsequently, language and narrative itself provide unifying themes that further extend the affective contour. Along with the acquisition of language, the sense of a subjective self will help to shape the child's beliefs about its personal history and character, eventually enabling a sense of a *verbal self* (Stern, 1985). As Stern says, the role of language for the verbal self "is not primarily another means for individuation, nor is it primarily another means for creating togetherness" (p. 173). The uniqueness of language is that it "ultimately brings about the ability to narrate one's own life story with all the potential that holds for changing how one views oneself. The making of a narrative is not the same as any other kind of thinking or talking. It appears to involve a different mode of thought from problem solving or pure description. It involves thinking in terms of persons who act as agents with intentions and goals that unfold in some causal sequence with a beginning, middle and an end" (p. 173f.).

Levels of Self and Levels of Music

We have already seen how two-month-old babies react similarly to prosodic contours in different languages. Even before this happens, within the first three days of life, a newborn baby is capable of distinguishing its mother's voice from other female voices. It not only recognizes its mother's voice but shows a clear preference for it (DeCasper and Fifer, 1980).

As experiments show, neither frequency nor amplitude in isolation is recognized, leaving as the only available parameter of significance the characteristic prosody of the mother's voice, the amodal properties of its melodic contour (Mehler et al., 1978; Fernald and Kuhl 1987). Moreover, it has been shown that at four-and-a-half to six months of age, babies prefer certain phrasing in music. In one study (Krumhansl and Jusczyk, 1990), Mozart minuets were divided into temporally separated segments that either did or did not correspond to the phrase indications of the score. The infants under study faced a loudspeaker playing the versions with temporal separation between phrases significantly longer than they faced a differently placed loudspeaker playing versions that had pauses inserted within phrases. Although we may not be innately "hardwired" to prefer correct Mozartean phrasing over stylistically deviant versions, there is reason to believe (as we shall see in a later section) that what makes infants attentive to deviations in motherese are its similarities with classical music in matters of phrasing.

If we add these findings to Stern's developmental model and translate the sum into a model for music perception, we can hypothesize that it is at the early stages of self development—the development of our senses of *self versus other*, and *self with other*—that perception of musical phrasing begins. That we experience short musical phrases as cohesive gestalts depends, in other words, on the same principles of categorization as does the child's preference for its mother's voice. To carry the parallel further to Stern's sense of a subjective self, it is the affective substrate of these vocal phrases, amodally perceived, that enables the intuition of an affective core underlying the other's behavior, an intuition of the other's affective states. Stern likens this to art in general, which "translates" into feeling. It would thus be the affective contour caused by its melodic counterpart that makes us experience music "directly as force-ful." And once affect attunement (together with the linguistic competence of a verbal self) is employed, we are subsequently able to denote the musical phrase in terms of being "masculine" or "feminine," of being "happy" or "sad," or of being expressive of any other kind of emotion.

Attunement to the affective properties of melodic contours may also explain the personal character of perceived contours. The individual prosody of the mother's voice is detected by the newborn, though it can not be said to have any social significance; it is not yet associated with meaningful action. Nevertheless, the significance of affective contours, inferred through affect attunement, leads Stern to talk about personal *styles* of behavior. In many children's games, the repetition of affective contours functions as themes with variations, enabling the child to identify the caregiver on the basis of the latter's individual style of varia-tion. As behavior is successively categorized, conventional behavior and action can be ascribed to particular agents on the basis of the personal style-code of its performance. Hence, affect also "concern[s] the manner in which conventional-ized affect displays such as smiling and other highly fixed motor programs such as walking are performed. This is where the exact performance of the behavior, in terms of timing, intensity, and shape, can render multiple 'stylistic' versions or vitality affects of the same sign, signal, or action" (Stern, 1985: 159).

The relation to music and the arts is obvious here: "In spontaneous behav-ior, the counterpart to artistic style is the domain of vitality affects" (p. 159). In addition to, or analogously to, this stylistic variation of conventionalized "sign behavior," conventionally expressive phrases of music may also be emotively altered. Phrases that are conventionally judged to be expressive of the "basic" emotions—happiness, anger, fear and sadness (see Kivy, 1990)—may be played in emotively distinct and identifiable ways. It has been shown that, irrespec-tive of training, listeners judge the emotive expressions of musical phrases on the basis of multiple cues with a probabilistic relation to the judgments. This means that "two performers can be equally successful in communicating a particular emotion, despite differences in how they use the expressive cues" (Juslin, 1997). In brief, happiness is associated with fast tempo, high sound level, and staccato articulation; sadness with slow tempo, low sound level, and legato articulation; anger with fast tempo, high sound level, and legato articu-lation; and fear with slow tempo, low sound level, and staccato articulation. Different performers may thus choose different cues when expressing the same emotion, and they may play either "with" or "against" the conventionalized meaning of the melodic contour.

In contrast, consider a whole piece of music, or at least an extensive part of it, experienced as a continuous whole rather than as a number of disconnected phrases placed one after another. We can easily imagine how protonarrative envelopes of various durations underlie melodic lines as well. The "elements of plot" in such cases would be the short melodic phrases and motives of the melody, with their own affective contours, while the protonarrative envelope would be the affective contour of the melody in its entirety, whether this melody be a simple children's song or a complete symphonic movement (or just a brief section thereof). This, I believe, is what Michel Imberty has in mind when speaking about the "macrostructure" of a musical work (Imberty, 1997), and it seems to share affinities with Fred Lerdahl and Ray Jackendoff's (1983) "prolongational reduction," according to which tension and relaxation in a well-formed tonal piece is said to occur as a hierarchy of structural levels, the topmost of which embraces the entire piece (though their theory lacks an account of the affective nature of short phrases).

The protonarrative affective envelope is also what enables us to hear so-called plot archetypes in music. As suggested by Anthony Newcomb (1997), a plot archetype is a more "complex series of actions and agencies" than the expression of conventional emotions. Whereas aestheticians often focus on the "basic" emotions, Newcomb (1992), in a reference to Schiller, speaks of moving toward "renewed harmony to heal the wounds inflicted by mankind's alienation from nature," a progress from "Arcadia forward to Elysium" (p. 131f.), which he regards as pertinent to both Schumann's Second and Mahler's Ninth Symphonies as well as Beethoven's Fifth and Ninth Symphonies. And whereas a plot archetype requires a protonarrative envelope, a basic, "garden-variety" emotion (to use Peter Kivy's phrase) depends on the affect caused by a single melodic contour. (For a discussion of the ethical significance of plot archetypes in terms of "paradigm scenarios," see de Sousa, 1980.) This distinction between basic emotions and plot archetypes also brings to mind Charles Rosen's (1976) observation, when comparing Baroque and classical music, that the former "acts as a dramatic image, not as a scenario" (p. 70). In other words, Baroque music may be expressive of basic emotions, whereas a plot archetype would require the "syntactic art of dramatic movement" (p. 49) that we find only later in music history.

From Affect to Discourse: Music as a Human Cultural Artifact

We can see now that Stern's developmental trajectory has relevance for at least three important aspects of music. First, affect attunement enables the experiencing of musical figures with affective content such as anger, happiness, or sadness. Affective contours have individual characters that enable the infant to recognize its mother's voice, and also the recognition of personal styles of musical performance and emotive alteration of musical phrases with pre-established emotional significance. Second, successions of affective contours that take on thematic consistency may expand into protonarrative envelopes. As such, they provide the underlying affective structure for more extensive musical and narrative unfoldings and lead to expectations of resolution (cf. Rosner and Meyer, 1986).

Nevertheless, we should not assign too much culture-specific content to these kinds of affective experiences. As I have already mentioned, Stern's cautious use of quotation marks when speaking of "forceful" alerts us to the fact that the infant's experience of a gesture as being forceful does not involve any of the conventional associations that such gesturality may invoke through music. I am thinking here of the culture-specific codes of Western classical music as described by Philip Tagg (1979) and Susan McClary (1991), which assign prescribed gender characteristics and ideological content to musical contours and phrases. In Tagg's analysis of the theme music to the TV series *Kojak,* he concludes that the listener (of the 1970s) hears the music as the expression of "a basically monocentric view of the world [in which] the negative experience of a hostile *Umweld* can be overcome by individual action only" (Tagg, 1979: 231). McClary similarly identifies codes that she claims enable listeners to hear the music she analyzes as a hailing of patriarchal principles. These characteristics are quite obviously unavailable to the infant. The same can be said about the plot archetypes mentioned by Newcomb. Any idea of strife toward "renewed harmony to heal the wounds inflicted by mankind's alienation from nature" is over the head of any listener that has not yet advanced developmentally beyond the level of a subjective self.

The explanation of this third aspect of musical experience brings us to the final level of Stern's developmental model, the sense of a verbal self. As we have seen, language is a means of specifying and articulating one's self, history, character, etc. But once again, we are not primarily interested in the various versions of selfhood; we are interested in the development of a "sense of music," and insofar as this sense of music as something *other* develops along a simultaneous route as that taken by our selves, we have here an outline of its trajectory. A *full* sense of music—what we may call music as a human *cultural* artifact—is an analogue to our verbal selves (a sense of self that presupposes and includes the earlier levels of self against and with an other, as well as a subjective self). We may not always have such explicit ideas about the music we hear as we do about ourselves (neither need there be only one full sense of music), but we always have something to say about what we hear that assumes culture-specific knowledge of music. And even if our musical experiences to a large extent parallel those of our non-verbal senses of ourselves—that is, music experienced more or less amodally (or "ineffably"; see Raffman, 1992)—they never do so exclusively. Our musical experiences are always categorized to some extent by the discursive logosphere in which they appear. This holds not only for the individual listener but also for musical cultures at large. To quote Alan Merriam, "it is very doubtful that any people have nothing whatsoever to say about their musical style" (Merriam, 1964: 117).

Mass-Mediated Discursive Content

I have mentioned above that mass mediation blurs the notion of the sender of music insofar as the instance of discourse formulation need not be identical to the one that produced the musical sounds. Hamm's example of the Lionel

Richie hit in South Africa illustrates this point and directs attention to the important question of who gets to formulate the dominating discourses. Who is in charge of discursive power? Whose interests are served by particular discursive contents? To the extent that not only sound recordings but also discursive contents are mass mediated, both musicians *and* listeners tend to become alienated from the ideological processes of discourse formulation. As "brand content providers" (Klein, 2001), the mass media can even be said to exist in a kind of symbiosis with the commercial interests of music production.

This is particularly important as we increasingly use media content to interpret the relationship between the external reality of social structures and our personal experiences in the "life world." In a post-industrial consumer age this leads to a situation where, as Nicholas Garnham (1992) puts it, a social group "largely exists in terms of group identities created via the forms and institutions of mediated communication (magazines, radio stations, record labels) or via consumer-taste publics that themselves use, as their badges of identity, symbols created and circulated in the sphere of advertising."

In spite of counterexamples such as Hamm's, and in line with Tagg's and McClary's findings, the ideological content of music more often functions as a means for maintaining existing social structures than as a means for disruption. In Garnham's (1992) pessimistic formulation, "both the forms and the potential success of resistance can be determined by the system being resisted." Dominated groups may struggle to become the dominating (with the power to manipulate), but the structures of power remain intact as long as public opinions come pre-packaged from a handful of media conglomerates (for a discussion of how intellectual property laws may constrain signifying practices see Volgsten and Åkerberg, this volume; Wallis, this volume).

Whether we paint the picture in all-black colors or not, the importance of music's discursive content is clear. We shall therefore take a brief look at three important agencies of mass-mediated discourse-formulation: academia, popular media (magazines, TV, etc.), and advertising discourse (on the ideological content of orally transmitted music in traditional cultures, see e.g., Feld [1981, 1984, 1986], and Keil [1979]).

Academic Discourse

Considering Western classical music, the ideological task of discourse formulation has to a large extent been taken care of by musicologists (see also Stockfelt, this volume). With scientific intent, they have often claimed that their discourses about music (published in mass-mediated periodicals) are methodologically purged of any external or human interest (as suggested by Meyer's claim that music does not have any external referents). They have elaborated theories and analytical systems that aim to objectively uncover existing principles that presumably underlie musical phenomena. For instance, Meyer locates the affect-causing elements of music, and identifies their syntactical properties.

Other theories are Allen Forte's (1973) pitch set theory, Jean-Jacques Nattiez's (1982) paradigmatic analysis, and Lerdahl and Jackendoff's (1983) analysis of prolongational structure.

Whatever the causal properties of the proposed elements and structures of these theories are (it should be kept in mind that because of their achronic nature, musical structures are not immediately audible, as are their diachronic elements), the resulting analyses suggests a discursive content to the listener, a content that implies ideological assumptions. The implied ideology suggests that the world of music should be viewed as consisting of autonomous, context-free objects that offer themselves to scientific scrutiny. A sociopolitical parallel to this view can be traced in the "social engineering" policies of twentieth-century governments, which tended to ignore contextual factors altogether. The idea of musical *autonomy* is of course of Enlightenment origin, as Dahlhaus (1989) has pointed out. More specifically, Adorno's (1962/1989) analysis of Beethoven shows how the concept of autonomy is articulated musically, revealing the fundamental moral dilemma of the liberal view of the human individual as a free subject (a subject which cannot be thrown under the yoke of a heteronomous or subordinating system without the human rights of free individuals being violated). Although Adorno's is a special case, one need not be an "expert listener" to experience ideological content in music, as analyses of popular music show.

Popular Discourse

A more casual attitude toward music may also involve discursive content. According to Frith, the punk movement relied for much of its intelligibility on verbal discourse: "[I]ts meaning for its subsequent fans was derived not just from the music itself, but also from the various punk images and analyses battling it out in the media" (Frith, 1978: 208). Whether these discourses stem from the listeners themselves, or whether they are a content produced by the mass media, is of utmost concern for the issue of manipulation. As Frith says: "Music papers, indeed, are important even for those people who don't buy them—their readers act as the opinion leaders, the rock interpreters, the ideological gatekeepers for everyone else" (Frith, 1981: 165).

An illustrative case of what is at stake not only in Punk music is given by Sheryl Garratt, commenting on her days as a fan of The Bay City Rollers. As she says: "[M]any became involved not because they particularly liked the music, but because they didn't want to miss out" (Garratt, 1990: 401f.):

> We were a gang of girls having fun together, able to identify each other by tartan scarves and badges. Women are in the minority in demonstrations, in union meetings, or in the crowd at football matches: at the concerts, many were experiencing mass power for the first and last time. Looking back now, I hardly remember the gigs themselves, the songs, or even what the Rollers looked like. What I *do* remember are the bus rides, running home from school together to get to someone's house in time to watch *Shang-a-lang* on

TV, dancing in lines at the school disco, and sitting in each others' bedrooms discussing our fantasies and compiling our scrapbooks. Our real obsession was with ourselves; in the end, the actual men behind the posters had very little to do with it all.

What was talked about among these Rollers fans did not relate to the "music" at all but rather "how to look and what to buy." The world-view held by these girls was largely provided by mass media, which had very little, if anything, to say about such things as musical traditions, performers (Shuker, 1994) or the fact that the Rollers "didn't even play on their early records" (Garratt, 1990). As Garratt puts it, the media "are not interested in music: how or what the artists play—lyrics aside—is usually irrelevant; even the inevitable color posters rarely show the band actually performing. What girls are sold is *a catchy hook,* and an image and lyrics they can identify with. Fantasy fodder" (p. 404, emphasis added).

The musical experience in Garratt's case boils down to not much more—and no less—than a catchy hook (a single particularly attractive, recurring, and attention-invoking affective contour; cf. Burns, 1987), and to sitting in each others' bedrooms discussing fantasies and compiling scrapbooks. The real obsession of these listeners is with themselves, not the persons behind the posters or the details of, or history behind, the musical product. The example may seem puerile, but the ideological function of music does not differ in principle (only in detail) from scholarly discourse, wherein more systematically articulated discourses are likely to be involved. Along with these identificational aspects, we have here (and to some extent this goes for the punk movement too) an ideological imperative prescribing that only the surface appearance of phenomena be valued and attended to, even when the focus of attention is oneself. In other words, the feeling of attained female mass power that Garratt mentions was (and still is) at best a media chimera.

Advertising Discourse

Focusing on a third type of mass-mediated discourse, Claudia Bullerjahn (this volume) describes different ways in which commercial ads parasitize on the positive attitudes and feelings that a particular piece of music, or a piece representative of a particular genre, might generate in the listener. Music, she says, "provides a context that is charged with values," and it is in this context that the consumers' "judgments are made."

Not only do ads feed off of this context; for optimal effect the verbal content associated with the brand name strives to become a part of the musical experience. A good example is Adrian North's reference to Delibes' *Flower Duet.* North says that "to many people in Britain, this music now is British Airways" (North, 2000: 22). For something to "be" British Airways is of course for this something to suggest to people that they spend their money travelling with this company. In other words, Delibes' duet has become an imperative of consumerism. Perhaps one can say the same about the Clash's *Should I Stay or Should I Go*: to many people the music is not only about Levi's jeans; the music *is* Levi's jeans.

These are instances of ideology insofar as the discursive contents sanction certain kinds of action at the expense of others. But the issue of ideology is not restricted to the consumer's choice of a certain brand or company; it is perhaps more importantly about communicating a world-view according to which it is normal and normative to choose between brands and companies. In other words, the moment of choice is the tip of an ideological iceberg whose bottom is the normalizing force of consumerism, copyrighting and branding, and the associated acts of buying brand-name jeans, airplane tickets, and the like.

The Omnipresence of Discursive Content in Music

What we have seen are some brief examples of how music functions ideologically by similar discursive means in different situational uses, whether these are manifested through classical music, watching ads on television, "dancing in the streets" (as in Hamm's case), or attending rock concerts. As both sound *and* discourse become mass-mediated, the possibility of musical manipulation increases.

These discourses need not denote any finer details of the music, as is the case of the categories of musical analysis; general description and mention of the music is enough. But the fact that analytic discourse is absent in a culture or subculture does not mean that the listeners are unable to hear finer details (see Tagg, this volume; DeBellis, 1995). Any or all of a discourse's contents may become part of the musical experience. As Nicholas Cook (1989) says about analytical methods, their role is not so much "to derive strict deductions from undeniable premises, as to persuade the listener to 'hear' or 'see' the music in a certain way" (p. 175).

As an extension of Cook's (1990) thesis—that music analysis *prescribes* ways of hearing music, and that a musical culture is a way, or a set of ways, of doing so—my claim is that *any* discourse related to music may offer a way of hearing this music. Not only strictly analytical discourses but anything from sociological to popular discourses (or what have you) may offer *ways of hearing music*. Although the theoreticians to whom I have referred may disagree, I claim that the mentioned discourses may manipulate the listeners to various extents through the musical experience.

This even goes for the "meta discourses" that I have referred to. For example, irrespective of whether the patriarchal principles unveiled by McClary had any impact on the composers and listeners that she refers to (which I do not doubt), her analyses have the additional function of (re-)actualizing these same discourses. We may or may not subscribe to the values and norm systems of the discourses, but they are nonetheless actualized by her work (something similar can also be said about much ethnomusicological work). But in contrast to analytical discourses, there is a critical edge to these writers' work, since the discursive contents are often problematized and questioned.

Now, an important problem with this claim, that *any* discourse related to music may offer a way of hearing it, becomes apparent in relation to Buller-jahn's discussion (this volume) of recent advertising trends. Bullerjahn says that "advertising devices such as music gain in importance, while the 'content' in the original sense of the word becomes unimportant." Not only do many commercial advertisements increasingly employ minimal verbal messages but our musical experiences appear to be free from discursive content too. We simply do not experience strings of verbal comment when we hear music (at least not usually). So even if there are discourses surrounding our musical experiences, what is to say that there is any verbal content at all in our "real time" musical experiences? Might it after all be that our musical experiences are as "absolute" as Meyer and others have believed?

As is the case in most encounters with music (if we disregard lyrics), the discursive content is to a large extent connoted. Sometimes this content is organized in ways that would not make sense if spelled out verbally (our webs of belief or semantic universes need not be logically consistent, or even verbal, through and through; see Jones, 1984). Tagg (this volume) points to instances where "music arranges our experience into socially constructed categories that hang together musically, not visually or verbally." Again, this does not mean that musical experiences are entirely devoid of discursive content. First of all, music *exemplifies* predicates that denote it (Goodman, 1976). Although music may exemplify sounding categories for which we have no words, there is always some denotative verbal term that the music exemplifies. (A possible instance of Tagg's contention could thus be one where the signified content is differentiated by verbal categories, which in their turn are transferred from their various original semantic domains and reorganized according to a common affective—rather than verbal—denominator, having music as its signifier.) So what does it mean, in this context, that discursive content is to a large extent connoted?

If we look at the cognitive process of music listening, it is important to note that instead of denotation the signifying relation is exemplification; the verbal term that the music signifies is exemplified. Once exemplified, this content may become part of a larger sign, a sign which is simultaneously connoted (on connotation, see Barthes, 1957/1972). Whereas denotation is substituted by exemplification, connotation in music is accounted for by the associative process of metonymy. In this metonymical relation, a part (the exemplified verbal term) comes to stand for a whole. As the examples above show, this metonymically connoted whole may be an entire discourse (in the Foucauldian rather than Habermasian sense), with all the norms and values that constitutes it. Moreover, exemplification and connotation of a discursive content may be either conscious or unconscious. And even if the listener is consciously aware of only the exemplified verbal term, a discourse may simultaneously be connoted through an unconscious process of metonymy.

Cutting across this distinction between exemplification and connotation is the question whether the intended discursive norm system is accepted by the listener. As already said, listeners are capable of critically evaluating discursive content (cf. Eco, 1967/1985; Hall, 1980), and even if a musical sound exemplifies the same verbal term to different listeners, this term may connote discourses that are contradictory on an evaluative level. Hearing Delibes' *Flower Duet* may not persuade the listener to choose British Airways and hearing *The Kojak* theme need not turn the listener into a libertarian.

Activation and "Aesthetic Pleasure"

In support of the claim that discourses are connoted whenever we listen to music, Colin Martindale has formulated a theory according to which related concepts may become activated in our minds without us necessarily being aware of it (though the theory is not formulated explicitly in terms of exemplification and connotation). Simplifying somewhat, one can say that the degree to which a stimulus is categorized by the listener amounts to a corresponding degree of what Martindale calls "aesthetic pleasure": "[T]he more prototypical a stimulus, the greater the preference for it" (Martindale and Moore, 1989: 434). We can specify this by saying that aesthetic pleasure is a function of the activation by this stimulus: "Perception or recognition has to do with exactly which cognitive units are activated, whereas aesthetic pleasure has to do with the net amount of activation of these units" (Martindale and Moore, 1988: 662).

Moreover, associations between objects within the same categorical paradigm are inherently pleasurable (Martindale, 1984). What this means is more easily described if we give names to the different categorical levels that Martindale refers to. Phenomena in a categorical system can be hierarchically sorted into three levels: *superordinate, basic,* and *subordinate.* As an everyday example, beverages belong to the topmost, superordinate level, subsuming for instance white wine at a basic level, the latter of which may subsume Riesling and Chardonnay (or even particular brands) on a subordinate level (cf. Lakoff, 1987).[2] In music, more or less broadly encompassing terms such as "music," "raga," or "blues" stand for superordinate categories, particular songs, phrases and melodic contours are basic level categories, whereas different stylistic renderings of particular songs that require the distinction of fine analytic details such as intonation and rhythmic articulation are categories of the subordinate level. (By "melodic contour" I do not refer to a simple abstract pattern of ups and downs; basic level melodic contours are more or less melodically concrete: each has a particular perceptual quality which does not equal the sum of its parts, and a different arrangement of the same constituent tones will display a different perceptual characteristic, somewhat like a chemical compound; see Warren, 1993.) In the next section we shall see what it is that distinguishes these levels from a cognitive point of view; these distinctions are enough here to clarify Martindale's argument.

Martindale's work shows that *within* the same hierarchical levels, activation (e.g., through exemplification) of the "cognitive units" that demarcate different categorical systems is inhibitory, while activation is strengthened *between* different levels of the same system. This should mean that a certain basic level melodic phrase triggers association with the whole melody and the superordinate style or genre categories to which it belongs, as well as with the subordinate harmonies and genre-specific scales on which it may build. On the other hand, any intervention of closely related phrases from different systems on the (same) basic level will be negatively experienced. Verbal labels should therefore always become activated when they function as superordinate for more basic or subordinate categories, although this activation may of course be unconscious to the listener. By the same token, we can hypothesize that the metonymical relation between the verbal label of the superordinate category and the relevant discourse to which this label belongs should also be marked by a link of aesthetic pleasure.

To show how this network of concept relations may work in a specific case, we can look at a study conducted by North and colleagues (see North and Hargreaves, this volume). North describes how in-store music influences customers' choices. Playing French music in a supermarket that was studied made French wine outsell German wine, whereas playing German music boosted German wine sales. Insofar as the customers were not simply conditioned to drink certain French or German wines when hearing particular French or German pieces of music (in which case no discursive content would be needed, and in which case the consumer need not have any idea at all of national origins), the more or less unconscious association between the music and the wine must somehow have involved the concepts "German" and "French." To be able to categorize music as "German" or "French" one has to have a great deal of cultural knowledge that is language-bound. Although it is impossible to point to any necessary or sufficient information that would grant somebody this knowledge, one must at least have some idea of what a country is, and perhaps of what it means to be a citizen of a country. One has to have some idea that people forming social (and by extension, national) groups develop characteristic similarities that set them apart from other groups. And one also has to have some idea that music originating from a certain nationality or country is likely to exhibit certain characteristic features that set it apart from the music of a different national group. Then one has to have some idea of what music is, what allows it to express those characteristic features, and so forth. The same, of course, goes for the concept of wine that one must have.

Note that the customer need not have any gustatory experience of German wine, or even know that there is such a thing as German wine before he or she sees the bottles in the store. But he or she must understand the word "German," and this is a place where ideological assumptions creep in, since "German" may mean different things to different people. (For instance, I remember being on tour with an amateur Swedish choir in Greece: when we turned from our Swedish and Italian material to Bach, audience members old enough to have experienced World War II left.) In sum, categories such as "German" or "Germanness" are so general and broadly encompassing that they cannot come into existence through simple conditioning or association through mere exposure to "cases."

The hypothesis, then, is that first the music the customers heard in the store exemplified one or more details on the subordinate level which enabled them to recognize the music as being of a certain kind (that is, an intracategorical association between subordinate detail and superordinate kind). The customers need not have been able to name these subordinate details verbally. What they needed was some word for the particular category to which the music belonged. In this case the music presumably exemplified the superordinate category "German," which in turn also subsumed a particular kind of wine (hence the cognitive "fit"). The verbal term (i.e., "German") identifying this superordinate category then connoted a particular discourse (or part thereof) positively value-laden enough to persuade the customer to buy one wine instead of another (it is thus likely that the elderly Greeks at the choral performance would *not* have bought any German wine). Conditioning may of course be the crucial factor in this second step (see Petty and Cacioppo, 1981), but still a discursive content was communicated. Note also that the customers did not need the capacity ("skill" or "knowledge," as Tagg would say) to identify the subordinate gustatory details of German wines; having the superordinate term for the kind was sufficient. Now, is this enough to support the claim that music always exemplifies verbal labels, and that music therefore always connotes some verbal discourse or other?

The Categorization of Sound

The terminology of categorization indicates that it occurs more readily at the basic than at the subordinate or superordinate levels. As Eleanor Rosch and her followers have shown, there are several reasons why the categories of the basic level are the most easily acquired. One reason is that the phenomena categorized have similarly perceived overall shapes. The basic level is also the level at which we use similar motor activity interacting with the categorized phenomena. It is the level at which mental images are most easily evoked and at which we find the highest amount of intracategorical similarity and intercategorical dissimilarity (tellingly, it is at this level that categorization can first be observed in children).

In contrast to the basic level, it is characteristic of the subordinate level that we have to perceive more detailed attributes to distinguish the categories, while at the superordinate level, the categories become increasingly abstract (Rosch and Mervis, 1981; Starkey, 1981; Mervis and Crisafi, 1982).[3] At the superordinate level it is no longer possible to group phenomena on the basis of similarly perceived overall shape, nor is it possible to invoke single mental images that do justice to all instantiations of the category. Action patterns appropriate for some members may be less appropriate for others (a martini may be shaken or stirred; champagne may not). Instead, what enables the acquisition of a superordinate category is language. The reason for this is that the superordinate category and its objects are not clearly distinguished. To illustrate, let me contrast it with an abstract category that does not require language. For instance, an orchestra is a collection of musicians, with the latter being a part of the former. In contrast to the objects of collection categories, which are parts of the collection, the objects when identified by a superordinate category are of that kind. A guitar is an instrument, not a part of an instrument. "We Are the World," "Lush Life," and the *Eroica* are instances, rather than parts of, pop anthems, jazz standards, and symphonies, respectively. While the objects of a collection and the collection itself are clearly distinguished, a superordinate kind and its objects overlap (Markman, 1987). This blurring of perceptual boundaries is the reason why superordinate concepts presuppose language (Horton and Markman, 1980; Benelli, 1988).

My suggestion is that the general term "music" and its counterparts in different human languages, whether they function as nouns or verbs, enable superordinate categorization in that the verbal labels provide the stepping stone for an extension of the musical category. In short, *music* is a superordinate category of the language-dependent kind, and to experience musical phenomena as examples of such general and abstract categories as *ballads*, *ragas*, or *ngoma* requires language. Thus, it is *not* the case that language gives us a term for a perceptual category that we already have (beverage is clearly a limit case). Instead, language is the very capacity that enables us to categorize such different sounding instances as covered by the above terms under single superordinate categories. Together with the assumption, derived from Martindale's work, that the basic and subordinate categories of music always activate their superordinate counterparts, and given the assumption, derived from Merriam, that every music listener has something to say about the music heard, the conclusion is that music always communicates a discursive (verbal) content.

Superordinate Categorization and Musical Pluralism

Music always communicates a discursive content. This discursive content implies an ideology, a norm system. This is so because language is what enables us to distinguish actions from behavior, ascribe intentions to actions, and finally assign values to actions (and types of actions), so that these actions imply moral responsibility on the part of the agent. To be sure, music is not unique in activating a discursive content; it is the way that this content is *affectively articulated* that sets music apart from other arts and expressive behavior. Nor is music the sole source of human morality. Yet, there is a more fundamentally moral aspect of music that I would like to bring to the fore, following from the fact that the connoted discourses involve *superordinate* categories.

This moral aspect of music has to do with the ability to appreciate what I call *musical pluralism*. In short, language provides the listener with general and abstract terms for different genres or styles of musical expression. By doing so, language about music enables the separation of musical sounds and the activities necessary for their production from worldly circumstances such as social function and context. The superordinate categories of language are those that enable the separation of the two parameters (sound and function). On the one hand, they enable the recognition that a totally unfamiliar-sounding foreign music may fulfill the same sociocultural function as does familiar music, and conversely that a foreign music regarded as similar to one's own may nonetheless be understood by the listener as fulfilling a completely different function in its original context. The significance of this is brought to the fore in the explanation of how the newborn comes to recognize its mother's voice.

With reference both to the various attention-evoking qualities of different types of speech contours and to the soothing capacity of lullabies, Sandra Trehub has suggested that these two types of vocalization form prototypical basic level categories (Trehub and Trainor, 1990; Trehub and Unyk, 1991). As we have noted already, basic level categories are easily encoded and remembered; they have similarly perceived overall shapes and show high intracategorical similarity and intercategorical dissimilarity. Trehub suggests that prototypicality of basic level categories is accounted for by gestalt principles such as similarity, proximity, and common direction. In particular, she refers to the law of good continuation. The rising and falling contours, as well as the bell-shaped contour, are said to display *good forms*, which make them particularly easy for the infant to perceive. What is more, the child will also notice deviations from such good patterns more readily than it will notice deviations from less good patterns.

Trehub suggests that this might explain how the mother's voice comes to be recognized. The idiosyncratic deviations from the prototypicality of good patterning that the mother's speech and singing display capture the child's attention and make it possible for the child to categorize, first, the contour properties of the basic level, then subordinate aspects of the mother's voice: "It is possible that infants go beyond a contour processing strategy, encoding the precise extent of the mother's pitch excursions or intervals. This would provide them with a basis for recognizing the mother by her unique yet familiar tunes, which may also be presented in a personalized set of rhythms" (Trehub and Trainor, 1990: 108).

The infant first categorizes the prosodic contours at a basic level and then goes on to categorize individual details at a subordinate level. It is interesting to note that the infant (as well as birds, apes, and whales; see Volgsten, 1999) seems content to categorize socially significant sound at a subordinate level. For the infant, voices other than the mother's seem to be dismissed en masse simply as *other*. A reason for this could be that the infant as yet has no need to categorize any other voices, and that further subordinate categorization would therefore be a waste of cognitive and mnemonic capacity at this early developmental stage. If this is so, and if we may extend the principle to music and culture, it suggests that any musical culture would be capable of developing its own music to a certain extent at the subordinate level, without thereby being able to recognize the fine subordinate distinctions of any different culture.

It is not difficult to imagine cases in which something similar to this occurs. For instance, whereas the uninitiated listener is quite unlikely to distinguish, say, particular instances of hard-core from death metal, classicism from romanticism, Ottoman from Arabic-Andalusian music, the differences are immediately obvious to the accustomed listener. There are probably many of us who have dismissed new or foreign musics as not being music at all, simply for the reason that we cannot categorize what we hear on a subordinate level since the perceptually and aesthetically relevant details differ too much from what we are used to.

What the superordinate verbal category enables—and this is the important point here—is the cultivated listener's ascent from the depths of the identity-marking subordinate categories. It allows the listener to return from the cultural peculiarities of subordinate categorization to the common ground of basic level affective contours, at which music can be said to be a "universal language" for anyone to attune to. The superordinate category functions as a metaphor highlighting the basic level similarities of music that is obscured by dissimilarities at the subordinate level.

This is significant on at least two fronts for the issue of manipulation. On the one hand, it means that we may become receptive to manipulation by music that would otherwise—without language—not even appear to us as music (that is, we would never attune to it). On the other hand, it means that, in addition to familiar music, an abundance of unfamiliar musics become available to us for our own manipulative purposes. The superordinate verbal category allows stylistic pluralism within a culture, where style is understood as referring to functionally similar but perceptually different musics.

This is a human cultural phenomenon. Although non-human animals also engage in subordinate categorization of sound (even the piglet recognizes the sow's voice; see Walser, 1986), they seem incapable of superordinate categorization (Volgsten, 1999). What no animal seems to understand is, first, that the perceptually similar may fulfill different functions: only humans can do this. Humans can conjecture that what sounds similar to their own music may in fact differ in its sociocultural contextual use. Second, by the same token, only humans can come to understand that a culture different from their own (or even another species) can have a different way of performing a social function similar to their own. Without language, one would not be able to understand the significance of a behavior without first internalizing it into one's own repertoire. As Dissanayake (this volume) says: "The peacock is not free to experiment with his display, nor can a robin decide to behave like a peacock. Their partners would not understand such 'creativity.'"

This metaphorical functioning of (in this case musical) terms by way of superordinate categorization is therefore a prerequisite for any kind of cultural pluralism. Not only would it be impossible outside any verbal logosphere for a composer such as Olivier Messiaen or the Kaluli of New Guinea to hear birdsong *as* music—or for the Congo Basongye to say it is not (Merriam, 1964). Verbal language is necessary for acknowledging and understanding other cultures as cultures.

The Ethics of Musical Pluralism

By means of superordinate verbal categories, language enables a decontextualization and recontextualization of the experienced sounds and their requisite activities (Wachsmann, 1961; Nelson, 1988). Listening, one might say, becomes *creative* in that it allows for the imagination of extended functioning (as well as the expansion of existing musical fields—what Blacking [1986] called *radical change*). Thus, in the final instance, it is language that allows the listener both to be manipulated by and to manipulate *foreign* music. It is the superordinate verbal category that makes music a human cultural artifact.

The consequence that follows from this is that listeners, and the musical cultures or subcultures that they belong to, always regard themselves as distinguished from, not just something *other*, but other *listeners* and *cultures*. Regardless of how other listeners and cultures are evaluated by the listening subject, this entailment brings an ethical dimension *into the musical experience*. In contrast to the non-human ritualization that Dissanayake speaks about, the other will be seen as an equivalent by the music listener—recognizing their "common humanity," as Joseph Moreno puts it (this volume)—meaning that the listening subject is turned into a *moral agent*. In non-human ritualization, there may be codes for behavior within the social group, but these are not, indeed cannot be, extended to embrace anyone outside the group. However, as listeners with a full sense of music, we humans have moral responsibility for our actions in the face of others, and the extension of this responsibility to outgroup individuals resides as a potential within the ideological notions of culture and music. It should be noted that to regard some person or group of persons as in some way unworthy of moral respect requires an ideological stance (Gardell, 1996; Lööw, 1999). In other words, without language there would be no xenophobic fanatics in the world (cf. Hare, 1981).

Music as a Human Cultural Artifact

Without superordinate categories we would be condemned to the subordinate exclusiveness of our respective cultures' genre traits. We would never be able to hear anything of significance beyond whatever our own social group had specified at the level of subordinate categorization. With the aid of superordinate categories, we are instead capable of ascending to a level from which we may hear as significant the common, basic level characteristics of *any* music. In addition, we have seen that the superordinate categories are the cognitive units that are always exemplified when we listen to music. By way of connotation, the music ties together with the verbal discourse to which the superordinate category metonymically belongs.

We can also see how this relates to identity formation. Adopting a world-view similar to that of a group of others is a way of identifying with this group and demarcating oneself from those not sharing the same world-view. To the extent that a world-view involves a norm system that differentiates and sanctions certain kinds of actions at the expense of others, i.e., to the extent that it is ideological, it must be more or less discursively articulated. Through the exemplification of superordinate verbal categories, music is a means for the communication and enhancement of such world-views. In contrast to the direct communication of a traditional setting, in a world of mass-mediated discourse music may communicate contents unforeseen by its senders. Still, music enables the listener to *feel* this world-view and norm system, in that the music that we attune to affectively articulates the discursive content that it communicates.

Affect attunement in the early mother-infant dyad is a sort of protomusic. Through the amodal perception of shape and timing, the child experiences the world in a way that is also fundamental to our way of experiencing music. What this means for ideology is that the fundamental basis for our ways of experiencing music is derived from the earliest social interaction encountered by us as human beings. What we trustfully attune to is a *form of life* (Wittgenstein, 1968). Of course, attunement is present in any temporal experience of the outer world (Jones and Boltz, 1989), and at an early age there is no hard-blown distinction between the animate and the inanimate (my oldest daughter used to wave to the tree outside our bedroom window); still, Stern's lesson should be clear: *affect* attunement—which is always present in our musical experiences—is stylistically much more complex and enables significant prediction of action and ascription of motives and intentions to the agent. (A willow might be expressive of sadness, but we will never be able to relate this expressiveness systematically to any reasonable events in the history of the particular tree, and we will never find the willow attuning to us.)

The full sense of self, the sense of a verbal self in Stern's theory, suggests that a full sense of music—music as a human cultural artifact—involves culture-specific verbal discourses about itself. If we adopt this as a premise, and if the above arguments are sound, it follows that language is a necessary (though not sufficient) condition for music. Simultaneously, every musical experience draws on basic human capacities initially developed in mother-infant interaction and in the subsequent development of our selves. Just as "within a particular mother-infant dyad a kind of ritualization of vocalization occurs, such that certain shared meanings can be said to take on a conventional form within a very limited social domain" (Fernald, 1984), so too is sound ritualized in other, more or less limited, musical fields and domains.

Notes

1. In philosophical discourse, an emotion is a mental state with a content toward which the subject has an intentional attitude. In psychology, such states are often called "affect," or "categorical affect," whereas "emotion" denotes states *without* intentional content. In their contributions to this volume, Brown and Dissanayake use "affect" in the latter way, i.e., more or less synonymously with the way "emotion" is used in this essay.
2. Lakoff's examples are furniture at the superordinate level, sofas and chairs at the basic level, and wheelchairs at the superordinate level.
3. What counts as a basic, superordinate, or subordinate level category is not absolute and static, but flexible and modifiable—though within limits and with respect to interest. Hence, it has been observed that basic level categories may differ between adults and their children because of the significance assigned to the various perceived attributes (Mervis, 1984), as well as they may differ between cultures (Dougherty, 1981). As Rosch argues: "Basic objects for an individual, subculture or culture must result from an *interaction* between the potential structure provided by the world and the particular emphases and state of knowledge of the people who are categorizing. However, the environment places constraints on categorizations. Human knowledge cannot provide correlational structure where there is none. Humans can only ignore or exaggerate correlational structures.... Different amounts of knowledge about objects can change the classification scheme. Thus, experts in some domain of knowledge make use of attributes that are ignored by the average person" (Rosch, 1976; for a different example, see Quine, 1992: 6). Similarly, an untrained listener spontaneously taps foot to an intermediate metric level of music (the strong beats), whereas the skilled musician has no problem in attending to and coordinating both higher and lower levels (Drake et al., 1997).

References

Adorno, T. W. (1962/1989). "Mediation." *Introduction to the Sociology of Music*. New York: Continuum.

———— (1970/1984). *Aesthetic Theory*. London: Routledge and Kegan Paul.

Barthes, R. (1957/1972). "Myth today." *Mythologies*. London: Jonathan Cape, Ltd.

Benelli, B. (1988). "On the linguistic origin of superordinate categorization." *Human Development* 31: 20–27.

Berlyne, D. E. (1971). *Aesthetics and Psychobiology*. New York: Appleton-Century-Crofts.

Blacking, J. (1986). "Identifying processes of musical change." *The World of Music* 28: 3–12.

Burns, G. (1987). "A typology of 'hooks' in popular music." *Popular Music* 6: 1–20.

Cook, N. (1989). *Music Analysis and the Listener*. New York: Garland Publishing.

———— (1990). *Music, Imagination, and Culture*. Oxford: Clarendon Press.

Dahlhaus, C. (1989). *The Idea of Absolute Music*. Chicago: University of Chicago Press.

de Sousa, R. (1980). "The rationality of emotions." In A. O. Rorty (ed.) *Explaining the Emotions* (pp. 127–151). Berkeley: University of California Press.

DeBellis, M. (1995). *Music and Conceptualization*. Cambridge: Cambridge University Press.

DeCasper, A. J. and Fifer, W. P. (1980). "Of human bonding: Newborns prefer their mother's voices." *Science* 208: 1174–1176.

Drake, C., Penel, A., Bigand, E., and Stefan, L. (1997). "Tapping in time with musical and mechanical sequences." Proceedings from the Third Triennial ESCOM Conference (pp. 286–291). Uppsala: Department of Psychology.

Eco, U. (1967/1985). "Towards a semiological guerilla warfare." *Travels in Hyperreality.* (pp. 135–144.) San Diego: Harcourt Brace.

Dougherty, J. W. D. (1981). "Salience and relativity in classification." *Language, Culture and Cognition: Anthropological Perspectives.* New York: Macmillan.

Feld, S. (1981). "'Flow like a waterfall': The metaphors of Kaluli musical theory." *Yearbook for Traditional Music* 13: 22–47.

_____ (1984). "Sound structure as social structure." *Ethnomusicology* 28: 383–409.

_____ (1986). "Sound as symbolic system: The Kaluli drum." In C. J. Frisbie (ed.) *Explorations in Ethnomusicology: Essays in Honor of David P. McAllester* (pp. 147–158). Detroit: Information Coordinators.

Fernald, A. (1984). "The perceptual and affective salience of mother's speech to infants." In L. Feagans et al. (ed.) *The Origins and Growth of Communication* (pp. 5–29). Norwood, NJ: Ablex Publishing Corporation.

Fernald, A. and Kuhl, P. (1987). "Acoustic determinants of infants' preference for motherese speech." *Infant Behaviour and Development* 10: 279–293.

Forte, A. (1973). *The Structure of Atonal Music.* New Haven: Yale University Press.

Frith, S. (1996). "Music and identity." In S. Hall and P. du Gay (eds.) *Questions of Cultural Identity* (pp. 108–127). London: Sage Publications.

_____ (1978). *The Sociology of Rock.* London: Constable.

_____ (1981). *Sound Effects: Youth, Leisure, and the Politics of Rock'n'Roll.* New York: Pantheon Books.

Gardell, M. (1996). *In the Name of Elijah Muhammad: Louis Farrakhan and the Nation of Islam.* Durham: Duke University Press.

Garnham, N. (1992). "The media and the Public Sphere." In C. Calhoun (ed.) *Habermas and the Public Sphere.* (pp. 359–376). Cambridge, MA: The MIT Press.

Garratt, S. (1990). "Teenage dreams." In S. Frith and A. Goodwin (eds.) *On Record: Rock, Pop, and the Written Word* (pp. 399–409). London: Routledge.

Giddens, A. (1991). *Modernity and Self-Identity: Self and Society in the Late Modern Age.* Cambridge: Polity Press.

Goodenough, W. H. (1981). *Culture, Language, and Society.* Menlo Park: Benjamin/Cummings Publishing Company.

Goodman, N. (1976). *Languages of Art.* Indianapolis: Hacket.

Hall, S. (1980). "Encoding/decoding." In S. Hall, *et al.* (eds.). *Culture, Media, Language* (pp. 128–138). London: Hutchinson.

Hamm, C. (1992). "Privileging the moment of reception: Music and radio in South Africa." In S. P. Scher (ed.) *Music and Text: Critical Inquiries* (pp. 21–37). Cambridge: Cambridge University Press.

Hare, R. M. (1981). *Moral Thinking.* Oxford: Oxford University Press.

Horton, M. S. and Markman, E. M. (1980). "Developmental differences in the acquisition of basic and superordinate categories." *Child Development* 51: 708–719.

Imberty, M. (1997). "Can one seriously speak about narrativity in music?" Proceedings from the Third Triennial ESCOM Conference (pp. 13–22). Uppsala: Department of Psychology.

Johnson, M. (1987). *The Body in the Mind. The Bodily Basis of Meaning, Imagination and Reason.* Chicago: University of Chicago Press.

Jones, G. V. (1984). "Fragment and schema models for recall." *Memory and Cognition* 12: 250–263.

Jones, M. R. and Boltz, M. (1989). "Dynamic attending and responses to time." *Psychological Review* 96: 459–491.

Juslin, P. N. (1997). "Emotional communication in music performance: A functionalist perspective and some data." *Music Perception* 14: 383–418.

Keil, C. (1979). *Tiv Song.* Chicago: University of Chicago Press.

Kivy, P. (1990). *Music Alone: Philosophical Reflections on the Purely Musical Experience.* Ithaca: Cornell University Press.

Klein, N. (2001). "Interview." *Mediemagasinet, SVT.* 13 March.

Krumhansl, C. K. and Jusczyk, P. W. (1990). "Infants' perception of phrase structure in music." *Psychological Science* 1: 70–73.

Lakoff, G. (1987). *Women, Fire and Dangerous Things: What Categories Reveal about the Mind.* Chicago: University of Chicago Press.

Langer, S. K. (1948). *Philosophy in a New Key.* New York: The New American Library of World Literature.

Lerdahl, F. and Jackendoff, R. (1983). *A Generative Theory of Tonal Music.* Cambridge, MA: MIT Press.

Lewkovicz, D. J. and Turkewitz, G. (1980). "Cross-modal equivalence in early infancy: Audio-visual intensity matching." *Developmental Psychology* 16: 597–607.

Lööw, H. (1999). *Vit maktmusik: En växande industri.* Stockholm: Brottsförebyggande Rådet.

Markman, E. M. (1987). "How children constrain the possible meanings of words." In U. Neisser (ed.) *Concepts and Conceptual Development: Ecological and Intellectual Factors in Categorization* (pp. 255–287). Cambridge: Cambridge University Press.

Martindale, C. (1984). "The pleasures of thought: A theory of cognitive hedonics." *Journal of Mind and Behavior* 5: 49–80.

Martindale, C. and Moore, K. (1988). "Priming, prototypicality, and preference." *Journal of Experimental Psychology: Human Perception and Performance* 14: 661–670.

_____ (1989). "Relationship of musical preference to collative, ecological, and psychophysical variables." *Music Perception* 6: 431–446.

McClary, S. (1991). *Feminine Endings: Music, Gender, and Sexuality.* Minnesota: University of Minnesota Press.

Mehler, J., Bertoncini, J., Barrière, M., and Jassik-Gerschenfeld, D. (1978). "Infant recognition of mother's voice." *Perception* 7: 491–497.

Meltzoff, A. N. (1981). "Imitation, intermodal co-ordination and representation in early infancy." In G. Butterworth (ed.) *Infancy and Epistemology: An Evaluation of Piaget's Theory* (pp. 85–114). Brighton: Harvester Press.

Merriam, A. P. (1964). *The Anthropology of Music.* Evanston, IL: Northwestern University Press.

Mervis, C. (1984). "Early lexical development." In C. Sophian (ed.) *Origins of Cognitive Skills* (pp. 339–370). Hillsdale: Earlbaum.

Mervis, C. B. and Crisafi, M. A. (1982). "Order of acquisition of subordinate-, basic-, and super-ordinate-level categories." *Child Development* 53: 258–266.

Meyer, L. B. (1956). *Emotion and Meaning in Music.* Chicago: University of Chicago Press.

Nattiez, J.-J. (1982). "Varese's 'Density 21.5': A study in semiological analysis." *Music Analysis* 1: 244–340.

Nelson, K. (1988). "Where do taxonomic categories come from?" *Human Development* 31: 3–10.

Newcomb, A. (1992). "Narrative archetypes and Mahler's ninth symphony." In S. P. Scher (ed.) *Music and Text: Critical Inquiries* (pp. 118–136). Cambridge: Cambridge University Press.

_____ (1997). "Action and agency in Mahler's ninth symphony, second movement." In J. Robinson (ed.) *Music and Meaning* (pp. 131–153). Ithaca: Cornell University Press.

North, A. (2000). "The tills are alive" *Music Forum* 6: 22–23.

Papousek, M., Papousek, H. and Symmes, D. (1991). "The meanings of melodies in motherese in tone and stress languages." *Infant Behavior and Development* 14: 415–440.

Petty, R. E. and Cacioppo, J. T. (1981). *Attitudes and Persuasion: Classic and Contemporary approaches.* Dubuque: Brown.

Quine, W.V. (1992). *Pursuit of Truth.* Cambridge, MA: Harvard University Press.

Raffman, D. (1992). *Language, Music, and Mind.* Cambridge, MA: MIT Press.

Rosch, E. (1976). "Basic objects in natural categories." *Cognitive Psychology* 8: 382–439.

Rosch, E. and Mervis, C. B. (1981). "Categorization of natural objects." *Annual Review of Psychology* 32: 89–115.

Rosen, C. (1976). *The Classical Style.* London: Faber and Faber.

Rosner, B. S. and Meyer, L. B. (1986). "The perceptual roles of melodic process, contour and form." *Music Perception* 4: 1–39.

Shuker, R. (1994). *Understanding Popular Music*. London: Routledge.

Spitz, R. (1965). *The First Year of Life*. New York: International Universities Press.

Starkey, D. (1981). "The origins of concept formation: Object sorting and object preference in early infancy." *Child Development* 52: 489–497.

Stern, D. N. (1985). *The Interpersonal World of the Infant: A View From Psychoanalysis and Developmental Psychology*. New York: Basic Books.

_____ (1995). *The Motherhood Constellation: A Unified View of Parent-Infant Psychotherapy*. New York: Basic Books.

Tagg, P. (1979). *Kojak. 50 Seconds of Television Music: Towards the Analysis of Affect in Popular music*. Göteborg: Skrifter från musikvetenskapliga institutionen.

Trehub, S. E. and Trainor, L. J. (1990). "Rules for listening in infancy." In J. T. Enns (ed.) *The Development of Attention: Research and Theory* (pp. 87–119). North Holland: Elsevier Publishers.

Trehub, S. E. and Unyk, A. M. (1991). "Music prototypes in developmental perspective." *Psychomusicology* 10: 73–87.

Volgsten, U. (1999). *Music, Mind and the Serious Zappa: The Passions of a Virtual Listener*. Stockholm: Department of Musicology.

Wachsmann, K. (1961). "Criteria for acculturation." In J. LaRue (ed.) *International Musicological Society. Report of the Eighth Congress, New York 1961* (pp. 197–215). Basel: Bärenreiter.

Walser, E. E. S. (1986). "Recognition of the sow's voice by neonatal piglets." *Behavior* 99: 177–188.

Warren, R. M. (1993). "Perception of acoustic sequences: Global integration versus temporal resolution." In S. McAdams and E. Bigand (eds.) *Thinking in Sound: The Cognitive Psychology of Human Audition* (pp. 37–68). Oxford: Clarendon Press.

Wittgenstein, L. (1968). *Philosophical Investigations*. Oxford: Basil Blackwell.

Manipulation by Music

PART II BACKGROUND MUSIC

Chapter 4

MUSIC IN BUSINESS ENVIRONMENTS

Adrian C. North and David J. Hargreaves

Introduction

This chapter reviews studies of the effects of music in business settings, and argues that the research can be organized according to two basic theoretical processes, namely, psychobiology and knowledge activation. Psychobiological research concerns the effects of music on customer activity, employees in the workplace, and purchasing and affiliation. Knowledge-activation research considers the effects of music on purchasing and affiliation, and also television advertising. Research on music and time perception/waiting time contains elements of both psychobiology and knowledge activation, and is also reviewed. It is concluded that music can be used effectively in business environments, that two basic processes underlie this, and that the effects can be extremely sophisticated. The practical and theoretical implications of the existing research are discussed at length, and the claim is made that the processes of psychobiology and knowledge activation might most usefully be prioritized in future research on the topic.

* * *

While music in commercial environments can be the object of public ridicule, its commercial importance is demonstrated readily by the most recent figures available (National Music Council, 1996), which show that 1995 non-broadcast public performance royalties for music *in the U.K. alone* totalled £53.8 million, with 57.7 percent (£31 million) of this accounted for by music in bars, clubs, restaurants/cafes, and shops. When the cost of installing music reproduction equipment is considered along with the fact that "piped" music can be heard within

---

References for this chapter begin on page 121.

most countries in the Western(ized) world, it quickly becomes surprising that so little independent empirical research was carried out prior to the 1990s (see earlier review by Bruner, 1990). This is particularly so given that the research has direct implications for many disciplines, both within psychology (e.g., consumer/economic psychology, psychology of attitudes and emotions, occupational psychology, psychology of music) and in other domains (e.g., ergonomics, management science, economics, human geography, commercial practice). This dearth of independent studies has led to an extremely disparate literature, a situation the present essay aims to address by providing an overview of the principal theoretical concepts and findings that have driven research to date.

Although university academics have become interested in this field only recently, a large number of studies have been carried out by private sector in-store music providers, most notably the Muzak Corporation. Their publicity literature makes a number of claims that, if valid, suggest that music can have a profound impact on customers and employees alike. For example, it is claimed that music may increase sales, improve productivity, reduce errors and accidents, create a warm and secure environment, make time go faster, reduce absenteeism and lateness, improve vigilance, and aid recruiting. Such claims are extremely provocative, and provide clear hypotheses for independent empirical work.

A number of researchers have responded to this, and it is our contention that the vast majority of studies can be organized into two categories concerning psychobiology and knowledge activation, and that these two processes seem the most promising venues for further research. We begin with a summary of psychobiological- and knowledge-activation-based approaches to explaining the effects of music on people, before then describing research on the former, which has considered the speed of customer activity, the workplace, and purchasing and affiliation. The following section on knowledge-activation-based approaches considers purchasing and affiliation, and television advertising. We then summarize findings on time perception/waiting time, which concern aspects of both psychobiology and knowledge activation, and conclude with the theoretical and practical implications of the existing research.

Theoretical Approaches to Music

Psychobiology

Aristotle wrote in the *Nichomachean Ethics* that "A master of any art avoids excess and deficit but seeks the intermediate and chooses this." This idea perhaps came to maturity in the work of Daniel Berlyne who adopted a psychobiological approach in founding "the new experimental aesthetics" (e.g., Berlyne, 1971, 1972, 1974). He characterized research within this approach as possessing one or more of the following features:

1. It concentrates on collative properties of stimulus patterns. Collative properties (of which more will be said later) are "structural" or "formal" properties, such as variations along familiar-novel, simple-complex, expected-surprising, ambiguous-clear, and stable-variable dimensions.
2. It concentrates on motivational questions (see Berlyne, 1960, 1970, 1971).
3. It studies nonverbal behavior as well as verbally expressed judgments.
4. It strives to establish links between aesthetic phenomena and other psychological phenomena. This means that it aims not only to throw light on aesthetic phenomena but, through the elucidation of aesthetic problems, to throw light on human psychology in general (Berlyne, 1974: 5).

Berlyne (1971) proposed a theory based on this approach that has dominated psychobiological research on responses to music up to the present day. The theory states that responses to artistic stimuli depend upon the extent to which the latter possess "arousal potential," that is, the amount of activity they produce in areas of the brain such as the reticular activating system. Berlyne stated that the stimulus variables that mediate arousal fall into three categories; "psychophysical" variables, which are the intrinsic physical properties of the stimulus such as musical tempo; "ecological" variables, which are the learned associations between the stimulus and other events or activities of biological importance; and "collative" variables which are the informational properties of the stimulus such as its degree of novelty/familiarity or complexity. Berlyne (1971) proposed that the collative variables, are the "most significant of all" (p. 69), and they have dominated research with several studies supporting Berlyne's proposal of an inverted-U relationship between liking and arousal potential, which coincides with Aristotle's and Plato's views described earlier (see reviews by Hargreaves [1986] and Finnäs [1989]).

However, the key point in the context of the present review is that all three classes of variable identified by Berlyne can have a direct influence on activity in the human nervous system. Whenever a piece of music varies in terms of tempo, volume, complexity, or familiarity, for example, it influences the degree of arousal in the listener's autonomic nervous system. A number of the studies reviewed below have related the psychobiological effects of music to various aspects of consumer/employee behavior.

Knowledge Activation

In direct reaction to Berlyne, a number of studies on responses to artistic stimuli conducted since the 1980s have concerned the notion of knowledge activation (e.g., Whitfield and Slatter, 1979; Martindale and Moore, 1988; but see also Boselie, 1991). While much of this research has aimed to explain aesthetic preferences, it is relevant to consumer research because it implicates neural networks in responses to music. The model asserts that the mind is comprised of densely interconnected cognitive units, such that a specific piece of music can activate superordinate knowledge structures. For example, researchers within this approach would argue that people do not respond solely to hearing the "Sgt. Pepper's Lonely Hearts Club Band" album: this album may also be associated with the superordinate category "The Beatles," who may in turn be associated with the superordinate category "1960s pop music," which may in turn be associated with other aspects of the period such as the hippie movement, and so on.

This may explain how music can be effective if it "fits" with a commercial environment. In essence, in-store music should activate related knowledge structures, and this might be expected to prime the selection of products that correspond with that knowledge. More simply, certain types of music might make consumers more aware of certain types of product. Indeed, the intuitive notion that music should activate related knowledge structures has a good pedigree in mainstream research on cognitive psychology. The latter indicates that if information is consistent with someone's existing schema, it elicits faster reaction times and better recall from experimental subjects, and these are both indicative of knowledge activation. Although this research has concentrated on visual rather than auditory stimuli (see, e.g., Macrae and Shepherd, 1991; Nakamura, Kleiber, and Kim, 1992; Nakamura, 1994; Baldwin and Sinclair, 1996; Wansink and Ray, 1996), there are the clear indications that a similar process may operate for music. Indeed, one particularly interesting feature of this research has been the contention that "recall for information within a representation increases as the number of types of interconnections and the strength of the interconnections within a representation increases" (Nakamura, Kleiber, and Kim, 1992: 575). This has direct parallels with the aesthetic research outlined at the beginning of this section.

Preface to the Literature Review

The following three sections review the literature concerning the effects of music in business settings. The first section deals with psychobiological effects of music. Although different studies employ slightly different theoretical frameworks, they all concern the influence of music on human biology and ultimately consumer behavior through properties such as its complexity and tempo. The second literature review section deals with the effects of music on activating product-relevant knowledge. This research has centered around the concept of musical "fit," and the smaller number of studies relative to those concerning psychobiological processes is compensated for by perhaps a greater theoretical coherence. As is clear from this, our basic contention is that most of the literature concerning music in business environments can be seen as concerning psychobiological *or* knowledge activation processes. However, in addition to this, the third literature review section concerns research on music and time perception/waiting time; this research features elements of both psychobiological *and* knowledge activation approaches.

Psychobiological Effects of Music on Consumer Behavior

Customer Activity

Several studies have shown that the tempo of in-store music can mediate the speed of customer activity. In the best known demonstration of this, Milliman (1982) played slow (< 73 beats per minute) and fast (> 93 beats per minute) music in a supermarket, and measured the time it took customers to move between two points in the store. Customers were slower under the slow (127.53 seconds) than the fast (108.93 seconds) tempo conditions, but perhaps because of this they also spent more money at the former pace ($16,740.23 and $12,112.85 respectively). A follow-up study in a restaurant (1986) confirmed these results in that slow music led to longer meal times, and more drinks being bought. These results were supported by Roballey et al. (1985), who found that fast music in a university staff cafeteria led to more bites per minute than slow music (means = 4.40 and 3.83 respectively), and McElrea and Standing (1992), who found that fast music in a bar led to faster drinking than did slow music. In conjunction, these studies indicate that as music becomes faster, consumers act more quickly, but as a consequence of this perhaps spend less money.

How might such apparently consistent effects be explained? One possible answer is provided by a neglected study carried out by Smith and Curnow (1966). They tested their "arousal hypothesis" that a certain noise level will increase activity by playing loud and soft music in a supermarket. Customers shopping to loud music spent less time on average in the supermarket (17.64 minutes) than those shopping to the soft music (18.53 minutes), although there were no differences in sales between the two conditions. This may partly explain the effects of musical tempo indicated by more recent studies. As noted in the previous section, Berlyne and other psychobiological researchers have suggested that various psychophysical properties of music (such as tempo or volume) can influence arousal in the autonomic nervous system. In short, as the tempo or volume of in-store music increases, customers should become more aroused, and in light of this, should indeed act more quickly. Such a conclusion is of course speculative since none of the studies considered here actually measured consumers' arousal. The results are nevertheless clearly consistent with a psychobiological explanation.

The Workplace

Much of the literature on music in business environments focuses on consumers. However, this evidence ignores one other class of people who are exposed to commercial music frequently, namely, staff. Research on the role of music in the workplace is quite disparate, being published in journals of medicine, music therapy, cognitive psychology, and management science. Nevertheless, it is possible to discern two broad themes.

First, there is a growing literature on the effects of music on task performance. Although this research tends to be laboratory-based, it has clear implications regarding the efficiency of, for example, office workers. Although different studies provide slightly different theoretical accounts, almost all may be seen as variants of the psychobiological approach presented by Konecni (1982). He argued that listening to arousing music requires more cognitive processing resources than does listening to relatively pacifying music. Consequently, listening to arousing music reduces the amount of cognitive resource that can be devoted to carrying out some other task. Therefore, the more arousing music is, the worse concurrent task performance should become.

A small number of studies support this view in the context of text comprehension tasks (Kiger, 1989), reading comprehension tasks carried out by introverts and extraverts (Daoussis and McKelvie, 1986), and computer games (North and Hargreaves, 1999a). However, this pattern of results is by no means clear-cut, with some studies reporting that music has *no* effect on task performance (e.g., Wolfe, 1983; Madsen, 1987; Sogin, 1988). Although it is only possible to speculate, it seems that the basic theory of music and task performance as set out by Konecni is likely to be true, but also that several cognitive factors must be incorporated into this, e.g., on-task motivation, attention to the music, etc. Similarly, it seems likely that the difficulty of the task in question will also be important. For example, people doing a simple task may well be so bored that background music will raise their level of arousal and thus improve their performance. This improvement, caused by alleviation of boredom, may more than offset the detriment in performance caused by devoting some attention to the music.

Some evidence concerning this is provided in a field study by Oldham et al. (1995). Their study took place in an office where employees carried out a variety of jobs varying in their difficulty. Over a four-week period, seventy-five employees wore personal stereos as they went about their duties, while the remaining employees did not. The positive effects of stereo use depended on the complexity of employees' jobs. If employees had a simple job, then those with stereos performed at a much higher level than did those without stereos. However, if employees had a complex job, then those with stereos performed at a lower level than those without stereos. Similarly, in the stereo group, employees with a simple job expressed greater job satisfaction than did employees with a complex job. However, this pattern was reversed for those employees who did not have stereos: here, employees with a simple job reported less job satisfaction than did employees with a complex job. As such, this seems to support Konecni's ideas described above. People doing complex jobs can be hampered by music: people doing simple jobs can be helped by music.

It is perhaps also worth noting that several studies were carried out during and after World War II to investigate the effects of music on factory workers' productivity and morale. This work indicated generally that music could decrease boredom, conversation, and absenteeism while improving morale, particularly on repetitive tasks (see, e.g., Kirkpatrick, 1943; Kaplan and Nettel, 1948; McGehee and Gardner, 1949). The effects on productivity were more ambiguous, with some positive and some negative effects. Nevertheless, a few studies found that music could, for example, increase piecework production and decrease scrappage rates (Humes, 1941; Smith, 1947). However, as Soibelman's (1948) review notes, much of the early literature on this topic tends to be characterized by supposition and discussion rather than theoretically driven empirical research. Moreover, it is unclear whether findings from production lines in the 1940s can be generalized to offices many decades later. For these reasons, the results of these 1940s studies are perhaps best viewed with a degree of skepticism, but should nonetheless be the subject of replication studies (see, e.g., North, Hargreaves and McKendrick, submitted).

A second, much smaller group of psychobiological studies suggest that music might influence the immune system through its effects on mood, and particularly anxiety. Although carried out on small samples in laboratory settings, such findings are extremely provocative since they suggest the possibility that workplace music might be used to reduce rates of absenteeism. For example, Rider et al. (1990) either did or did not play subjects 17 minutes of specially composed background music. Compared with the "no music" group, the "music" group showed a significant increase in secretory immunoglobulin A (IgA), which has been used as a general indicator of the strength of the immune system, and protects against upper respiratory infection. The "music" group also had a significantly lower level of symptomatology both three and six weeks later than did the group without music.

A similar study by Charnetski, Brennan, and Harrison (1998) (which was funded by the Muzak Corporation) also found that music could increase IgA. Undergraduates listened to 30 minutes of either Muzak, a radio station playing the same style of music, an alternating tone/click stimulus, or silence. Levels of IgA increased in the "Muzak" and "radio" groups, whereas they decreased in the two remaining groups. Such conclusions must of course be considered carefully; there is a clear need for further research to determine for certain whether music can influence the immune system and how this effect operates, the length of time for which the potential benefits of music last, and whether they operate in a business environment such as an office rather than just the laboratory.

Purchasing and Affiliation

Other psychobiological studies of business music concern customers' purchasing and affiliative behavior, and have drawn on Mehrabian and Russell's (1974) model of environmental psychology. This states that people respond to environments along two principal dimensions, namely, pleasure and arousal. As an environment becomes more pleasurable, people are more likely to demonstrate "approach behaviors" toward it, such as a greater willingness to return, affiliate with others, or, in business environments, make purchases. The arousal-evoking qualities of the environment are claimed to amplify the effects of pleasure. This has obvious relevance to in-store music, which could make the environment more pleasurable and could also influence the extent to which it is arousing.

In applying this model, Dube, Chebat, and Morin (1995) found that customers' desire to interact with employees in a video simulation of a bank was enhanced by high levels of musically evoked pleasure and arousal. Similarly, Baker, Levy, and Grewal (1992) employed a video simulation of a card and gift shop. They found that under certain circumstances, quiet background music and soft lighting led to greater pleasure and willingness to buy from the store than foreground music and brighter lighting. Finally, North and Hargreaves (1996a, 1996b) played several different types of music from a welfare advice stall set up in a student cafeteria. The study showed that disliked music was more noticeable to diners, that no music often had more positive effects than did disliked music but not more than liked music, and that liking for the music was related positively to liking for the cafeteria, willingness to return, the extent to which diners were willing to affiliate with others, and the number of people actually coming to the advice stall. The latter finding suggests that music may be able to attract consumers to a given commercial setting. Also, these effects were predictable partly on the basis of how arousing (and in particular how complex) the music was. Finally, the relative effects of music and no music indicate that retailers must select their music carefully if it is to have commercial benefits. More generally, the results of these three studies seem to support the prediction of the Mehrabian and Russell model that musically induced pleasure leads to affiliation and general approach behaviors toward commercial environments. Evidence concerning the role of arousal in this is less encouraging, although there are some signs that this is also an important factor in determining the probability of customers exhibiting approach behaviors.

Knowledge Activation Effects of Music on Consumer Behavior

Purchasing and Affiliation

Recent research suggests that the effects of music in activating knowledge may also mediate customers' purchasing and affiliative behavior. This research has been dominated by the notion of musical "fit" (see above). First, Areni and Kim (1993) played classical music ("high fit") and Top 40 music ("low fit") in a wine cellar. Although the two types of music did not influence the number of bottles of wine sold, classical music led to customers buying more expensive wine than did Top 40 music, and given the upmarket stereotype of classical music, this finding is consistent with the notion of musical "fit." However, this study does not provide conclusive proof of the effects of "fit." Since only one product was involved, the design does not preclude the possibility that classical music would increase the sales of *any* product, and not just those that it "fits," such as expensive wine. This problem can only be resolved by a study that employs two products and two types of music, with each "fitting" only one product.

This was the basis for a study by North, Hargreaves, and McKendrick (1997, 1999a) in which French and German music were played on alternate days by a supermarket display of French and German wines. The study showed that French and German music activated customers' knowledge regarding these two countries, and that there was a significant tendency to select wine that "fitted" the music. More specifically, when French music was played, French wine outsold German wine by five bottles to one, whereas when German music was played, German wine outsold French wine by two bottles to one. One other interesting finding of this study was that shoppers were apparently unaware (or at least did not want to admit to the researchers) that the music had influenced their product choices, and this issue deserves further investigation.

North and Hargreaves (1998) investigated whether different musical styles could evoke different "images" for the student cafeteria in which they were played, and also influence customer spending. Classical music, pop, easy listening music, and no music were each played over the course of four days. Diners' responses to a questionnaire indicated that classical music led to a sophisticated and up-market image; pop music to a fun and lively image; easy listening music to a rather down-market and "tacky" image; and no music to an image containing elements of all of these. Diners were also asked to state the maximum price that they would be prepared to pay for each of fourteen items on sale in the cafeteria. Pop and classical music led to higher price estimates than did the other two conditions. There was also some indication that this was reflected in diners' actual spending: as compared with the same days during the week before and the week after testing, the pop and classical music conditions led to significantly higher sales, while sales in the other conditions were slightly lower than during the two comparison days.

These results indicate that music can be used to differentiate otherwise similar environments. This should have implications for commercial practice since stores often aim to establish a unique identity even though the goods they sell are very similar to those offered in other stores. The commercial implications of the effect of music on price estimates, and perhaps also actual sales, are obvious. Moreover, they may well correspond with a variation of the notion of "fit" outlined above. While musical "fit" may prime the selection of certain specific products, it may also be possible that the knowledge activated by "fun" and "lively" pop music, or "sophisticated" and "up-market" classical music, can prime more general behaviors such as spending money: spending itself may be a behavior that "fits" with certain musically evoked in-store atmospheres. This would correspond with several non-musical studies demonstrating that affective responses to stores can mediate patronage frequency and money spent (Darden, Erdem, and Darden, 1983; Golden and Zimmer, 1986), store choice (Stanley and Sewall, 1976; Nevin and Houston, 1980; Malhotra, 1983; and Bawa, Landwehr, and Krishna, 1989), and brand loyalty, promotion sensitivity, price sensitivity, and response to new brands (Bawa, Landwehr, and Krishna, 1989). (See also Turley and Milliman (2000) for a review of the effects of store atmosphere on shopping behavior.)

The studies considered in this and the preceding section indicate that music may have immediate effects on in-store purchasing and affiliative behavior. However, one other study by Zullow (1991) deserves mention since it suggests the possibility of longer-term effects. The lyrics of the Top 40 selling songs in the U.S. for each year between 1955 and 1989 were assessed in terms of their depressive content. Variations in this predicted the U.S. government's principal measure of consumer optimism, and this in turn predicted the gross national product with a one- to two-year time lead, such that changes in the song lyrics *preceded* changes in the economy. On the basis of these results, Zullow argued that "[p]essimistic rumination in popular songs ... predict[s] economic recession via decreased consumer optimism and spending" (p. 501). It seems that the prevailing musical environment may be capable of guiding consumers' thoughts in a particular direction on a macro-economic level.

Television Advertisements

Interest in the role of music in advertising increased in parallel with a series of studies in the early 1980s focusing on the concept of "attitude toward the ad" (or *Aad*). This emphasized how consumer behavior could be influenced by the *emotional* consequences of viewing advertising (see review by Brown and Stayman, 1992). In short, the *Aad* approach emphasizes that the likelihood of product purchase is enhanced when advertising leaves the consumer with a positive *feeling* about the product, and advertisement music may serve this purpose by effectively conditioning preferences between products (see Bullerjahn, this volume).

The role of music in classically conditioning product preferences was first illustrated by Gorn (1982) in a study that has since produced considerable comment and controversy. Two hundred and forty-four undergraduates were played music that they either liked (from the movie *Grease*) or disliked (Indian classical music), and were simultaneously shown a slide of either a light blue or beige-colored pen. At the end of the experiment, the viewers were given a choice between either a light blue or a beige pen, supposedly as a reward for having taken part in the study. Seventy-nine percent of the viewers chose the pen associated with liked music, although only five people thought that the music had been an influence on their choice (see also Bierley, McSweeney, and Vannieuwkerk, 1985; Tom, 1995).

There have, however, been several criticisms of this research. First, Pitt and Abratt (1988) suggested that conditioning may not occur when controversial products (in their case, condoms) are involved. Second, demand characteristics may explain conditioning effects, since merely *imagining* liked or disliked music in conjunction with products may elicit conditioning-like effects (Kellaris and

Cox, 1989). Third, conditioning effects may have been exaggerated by the use of still rather than moving pictures in research (Dunbar, 1990).

A second experiment by Gorn (1982) raised another objection to the conditioning approach as a complete explanation. If from the beginning of the experiment subjects were *motivated* to think about which pen they would select, then they tended to choose the one advertised with information about its high quality. This is consistent with the Elaboration Likelihood Model (ELM; see Petty, and Cacioppo, 1981; Petty, Cacioppo, and Schumann, 1983). This states that there are both *central* and *peripheral* routes to persuasion. Attitudes about products are formed via the central route when consumers consider information relevant to the product (e.g., does this pen smudge?). Attitudes about products are formed via the peripheral route when consumers do not actively consider the product. Instead attitudes about the product are formed heuristically when consumers associate it with peripheral cues such as liked or disliked music.

Central route persuasion occurs when the viewer has the motivation, opportunity, *and* ability to think about product information (i.e., "high-involvement" processing). Peripheral route persuasion occurs when the viewer does not have the motivation, opportunity, or ability to think about product information (i.e., "low-involvement" processing). Consequently, playing music that viewers like should be more important when they are unwilling or unable to consider information concerning the product.

Several studies on the ELM have found supporting evidence using nonmusical stimuli such as pictures (e.g., Mitchell, 1986; Stuart, Shimp, and Engle, 1987; Miniard et al., 1991), source expertise (e.g., Yalch and Elmore-Yalch, 1984; Ratneshwar and Chaiken, 1991), and the celebrity status of a product endorser (e.g., Petty, Cacioppo, and Schumann, 1983; Sanbonmatsu and Kardes, 1988). Furthermore, one study by Park and Young (1986) supported the predictions of the ELM in shampoo advertisements employing music. One group was asked to try to learn about the effectiveness of the shampoo (high involvement), whereas subjects in another group were asked to imagine that they had no need to buy shampoo (low involvement). Consistent with the ELM, music had a positive effect for this latter group and a negative effect for people who were thinking about information concerning the shampoo. In short, the ELM seems a promising means of explaining the effects of advertisement music. This is particularly so since it also relates to recent advertising research on the notion of "musical fit."

The ELM states that music could have negative consequences when viewers think about the advertisement because it distracts them from this task. However, MacInnis and Park (1991) argued that music may also have a positive influence when viewers think about the advertisement, providing it "fits" the advertisement (e.g., sophisticated classical music in an advertisement for perfume). MacInnis and Park (1991) provided some initial support for this argument in a study of shampoo commercials: the song "You Make Me Feel Like a Natural Woman" had a positive effect on subjects' purchase intentions.

Moreover, Kellaris, Cox, and Cox (1993) obtained similar results in "radio advertisements" when musical fit was brought about through the instrumental rather than lyrical properties of the music. In short, music may be effective in commercials because it activates knowledge in addition to eliciting emotion. This research is also consistent with that concerning the effect of musical fit on in-store product choices (see above).

This evidence presents a complicated picture for practitioners. However, its business implications might be best summarized as follows. The crucial factor seems to be whether or not viewers consider the advertisement and the product it features. There is some evidence that playing music that viewers like should have a positive influence on their purchase intentions. However, while viewers are thinking about the advertisement, music can have a detrimental effect because it distracts people from the task of processing product relevant information. Yet even if viewers are thinking about information presented by the advertisement, music may have a positive effect if it "fits" the product or the message that advertisers are trying to convey. Under these circumstances, music can activate appropriate knowledge. Two cautionary notes should be added concerning the methodologies employed by existing research. First, these studies tend to use questionnaires to gather data rather than recording participants' actual purchasing subsequent to viewing television advertisements. Second, the viewing circumstances could be more true to real life, given that home-viewing experiments ought to be reasonably easy to set up.

Time Perception and Waiting Time

Research on time perception/waiting time has adopted both psychobiological and knowledge activation approaches, often within single research designs. Businesses often use music in situations where customers are required to wait. The most obvious manifestation of this is on-hold phone music, and several studies have begun to suggest that music may influence actual waiting time and subjective time perception. For example, Ramos (1993) found that the number of people prematurely disconnecting their call to a telephone advisory service was influenced by the style of the on-hold music. North, Hargreaves, and McKendrick (1999b) found that music could lead to significantly longer on-hold waiting times than could a repeated spoken message asking the caller to wait. Palmquist (1990) found that different musical pieces gave rise to significant variations in subjects' estimations of the duration of a 25-second period. Stratton (1992) reported that groups that waited in silence and without music gave higher time duration estimates than other groups. Also, Yalch and Spangenberg (1990) found that background music led under-25-year-old clothes shoppers to report having spent more unplanned time in-store, whereas older subjects showed the same effect when more prominent foreground music was played.

However, many early studies of this phenomenon tended to neglect more theoretical issues. Intuition dictates that "time flies when you're having fun," but in a fascinating series of studies Kellaris demonstrated the opposite, namely, that disliked music seemed to lead to the shortest time estimates. He drew on two cognitive psychological principles in explaining this. First, the "Pollyanna principle" (see, e.g., Matlin, 1989) states that pleasant information is processed and recalled more effectively. Second, time perception is positively related to the number of events that are processed within a given event period (Levin and Zakay, 1989). This means that people hearing music they do not like should encode less information from it, and because of this, subjective time should be shorter than if liked music is heard. So far, this effect has only been demonstrated for females (Kellaris and Altsech, 1992; Kellaris and Mantel, 1994), although other studies (Krishnan and Saxena, 1984; Ramsayer and Lustnauer, 1989) have shown that females are generally less accurate than males when estimating the short durations employed by Kellaris.

However, the commercial applicability of research concerning time perception and musical *preference* is limited: stores and telephone companies usually attract a diverse range of customers, and variations in people's musical tastes mean that preference is an unreliable means by which businesses might influence customers' perceptions of time duration. In light of this, some studies have investigated the effects of structural musical properties on time perception, since the effects of these variables should remain constant between individuals. For example, Kellaris and Kent (1992) applied the notion that "time doesn't fly when you're having fun" to musical mode: affectively positive music in a major key led to longer time estimates than affectively negative atonal music. Similarly, Kellaris and Altsech (1992; see also Kellaris, Mantel, and Altsech, 1996) suggested that loud music caused females to give longer time estimates than did soft music because the former should have required more processing. Structural musical properties such as these can all be characterized in terms of Berlyne's taxonomy and their subsequent psychobiological effects.

In addition to the difficulty of predicting the effects of particular musical pieces because of individual differences in musical taste, research within this approach is also hampered by another problem, namely, that it sometimes fails to produce clearly falsifiable hypotheses. For example, liked music might be expected to lead to longer time duration estimates than does disliked music. However, what if a particular person likes slow, soft music? Music with these structural properties should lead to short rather than long time duration estimates, such that musical preference and the structural properties of the music in question would be expected to pull time duration estimates in opposite directions. Similarly, if a person likes fast, loud music, then is it liking for the music or the structural properties of the music per se that cause elongation of his/her time duration estimates? Indeed, since so many aspects of music can influence its effect on time perception, it is extremely difficult for this theoretical framework to relate any particular effect to one particular property of the music or the listener's response to it. Similarly, any failure to produce effects consistent with the theory can be explained away in terms of some uncontrolled aspect of the music. For example, if liked music fails to produce longer time duration estimates than does disliked music the reason could be that the liked music was also slower or softer than the disliked music.

Indeed, three other studies have produced results that provide much less support for the theoretical approach outlined above. First, Chebat, Gelinas-Chebat, and Filiatrault (1993) found that musical tempo had only an indirect effect on the perceived amount of time spent in a video-simulated bank queue. Second, it is reasonable to assume that actual waiting time will be related to time perception on the assumption that the longer people think they have been kept waiting, so the more likely they are to leave a given place. In an attempt to investigate actual and perceived waiting time within a single research design, North and Hargreaves (1999b) left participants in a laboratory while the experimenter supposedly went to fetch an important piece of equipment required for the "real" experiment. They were told that they were free to leave at any time, and heard either complex music, simple music, or silence while waiting. Subjects waited longest in the silence condition, and this seemed to be because their time duration estimates were the most accurate. Subjects waiting to a musical accompaniment were more likely to overestimate the amount of time they had been kept waiting, and this might be expected to predispose them to leave earlier. However, there were no significant differences between estimates given in the music conditions: this is not what would be expected, since the complex music contained more information than the simple music and should therefore have led to longer time duration estimates and shorter waiting times.

Finally, North, Hargreaves, and Heath (1998) investigated the effects of music on time perception in a more naturalistic situation than the laboratory-based designs employed by other studies. Fast or slow tempo music was played as people worked out in a gymnasium. On leaving the gym, people were told what time they had come in and were asked to estimate the present time. If the perceived duration of a given period is positively related to the amount of information contained in music, then fast music should have led to longer time estimates. The results did not confirm this, although other data collected in the study did show that slow music was perceived as less appropriate for the gym than fast music. Many non-musical studies have shown that contextually inappropriate information is processed less efficiently than contextually appropriate information, and the results of the gym study were consistent with this in that slow, inappropriate music led to time estimates that were less accurate than those made in the fast music condition.

These studies demonstrate three more general points. First, the potential importance of factors such as musical appropriateness indicated that the effects of music on time perception might be related to the *social context* in which that music is experienced. Consumer behavior occurs within particular contexts, and these contexts mediate the effects of music on time estimations. Second, as the above results indicate, while it seems clear that music can mediate time perception and perhaps also actual waiting time, the effects obtained so far by researchers have varied considerably. These diverse outcomes, though not particularly surprising given the likely sophistication of the effect, further emphasize the need for greater theoretical development to account for the interaction between all the factors that have already been shown to be relevant. Finally, these studies also illustrate the point made at the beginning of this section that studies of waiting time/time perception often incorporate psychobiological and knowledge activation approaches within a single research design. For example, North, Hargreaves, and Heath's (1998) gymnasium study considered the effects of musical tempo (i.e., a psychobiological factor) and appropriateness (i.e., a cognitive factor) on time perception. Similarly, the "time doesn't fly when you're having fun" research (described above) suggests that arousal-evoking musical properties (e.g., volume) can activate listeners' heuristics concerning time perception.

Implications

Practical Implications

The review of the literature points to issues that are relevant to practitioners. First, part of the appeal of research on music and consumer behavior is that it often reveals unexpected effects that can be counterintuitive. There are consequently several interesting "trade-offs" that must be considered by businesses when putting findings such as these into commercial practice. For example, retailers could perhaps use liked music to promote liking for a store environment and purchasing, although a further possible consequence of this is that customers may perceive themselves as having spent more time queuing at the checkouts than if disliked music was played. Similarly, retailers may play slow music in an attempt to slow down the speed of in-store traffic flow and increase sales. Meanwhile, this might lead to congestion such that new customers do not enter the premises.

Second, as the previous paragraph demonstrates, businesses may use music to very sophisticated ends. Consequently, it is extremely simplistic to attempt to offer suggestions concerning the "best" music to play in business environments, since this will depend entirely on the marketing strategy of the company in question. To give an obvious example, the type of music played to create an up-market image in-store might be completely different from the type of music played to create a "value for money" image. Furthermore, it is extremely difficult to predict how customers or staff will react to a particular piece of music because any response to music is determined by three interacting factors, namely, the music itself, the listener, and the listening situation.

With regard to the first of these, the field of experimental aesthetics (see Hargreaves, 1986; Hargreaves and North, 1997) has indicated that we need to consider those factors that mediate how arousing the music is, and in particular its complexity and familiarity. With regard to the listener, researchers from many disciplines have been interested in the effects of individual difference variables such as age, sex, and social class on responses to music (see Kemp, 1997; Russell, 1997). In addition to this, it is becoming clear also that the listening situation itself influences responses to music (see North and Hargreaves, 1997): for example, people prefer music that is appropriate for the listening context. This panoply of influences will always render it virtually impossible to predict the "best" music to play in all but the most specific of cases.

Given that the central theme of the present book is manipulation, the research discussed in this chapter raises one final practical issue, namely, ethics. Research on the commercial uses of music might be taken as demonstrating means by which unscrupulous companies can in some way "bend the minds" of unwitting consumers, forcing them into purchasing products and services for which they actually have no real use or desire. Three points should be made in response to such a charge.

First, many stores already employ non-musical environmental variables such as odor or lighting (see Gulas and Bloch, 1995; Kotler, 1973–1974) and other marketer-initiated stimuli such as sales promotions (see Tybout and Artz, 1994) in an attempt to influence consumer spending. Music may or may not ultimately be deemed an unethical marketing tool, but it is even less clear whether this stimulus is any *more* unethical than many others that are in the modern day largely accepted by most consumers. In short, why should music be regarded as a "special case?" Indeed, it may be the case that music functions in fundamentally the same manner as do other forms of marketing. For example, a supermarket playing opera in an attempt to publicize several special offers on Italian foodstuffs may be psychologically equivalent to handing out leaflets at the door that draw people's attention to these goods.

Second, it remains to be determined whether customers are aware of the effects of music on their purchasing. In those few studies that have investigated this issue, the general finding seems to be that customers report being unaware of any effect that music might have had on their behavior. If this is true, then it might suggest that commercial music might indeed be unethical. However, this interpretation of the findings may be rather simplistic, and at least two other interpretations are equally possible and perhaps more appealing in the light of existing findings from experimental psychology. First, perhaps customers do realize that music is used in an attempt to influence their purchasing but do not like to admit to researchers that it has had a direct effect on their own personal behavior. Second, customers may not explain their purchasing in terms of the effects of music simply because this does not seem to them to be a probable cause of their behavior. Instead they may favor other explanations that, although incorrect, seem intuitively more plausible.

Finally, it seems unlikely that in-store music could entirely *determine* shoppers' purchases. Existing research on judgmental biases (see e.g., Bodenhausen, and Wyer, 1985; Krueger and Rothbart, 1988; Macrae and Shepherd, 1989) suggests that the heuristic influence of music would mediate behavior only when there is an element of uncertainty in product choice, or when customers are in a state of low involvement with the decision process (see e.g., Park and Young, 1986; but also MacInnis and Park, 1991). Alternately, when customers have a clear preference for one particular product, or when product selection requires a considerable amount of deliberation, then the effects of music ought to be reduced: a shopper is unlikely to buy a Ferrari rather than a Porsche simply because he/she hears Vivaldi!

That said, it is extremely difficult to create this latter set of circumstances in the laboratory while simultaneously maintaining ecological and face validity. For example, it would be extremely difficult to identify a sample of people who were undecided between actually buying a Ferrari and a Porsche, and even more difficult to persuade their local car dealerships to play experimental music when these potential customers arrived. In short, although more practical from the standpoint of the researcher, the reductionist nature of most experimental research on commercial music can often create precisely those conditions of ambiguity and uncertainty that are most likely to indicate that music can affect consumers. Other circumstances are less likely to indicate that music affects consumers, but these are extremely difficult to create under controlled conditions.

Theoretical Implications

It is also possible to make several theoretical conclusions on the basis of the above literature review. First, there are clear grounds for improving our theoretical understanding of the area. Although the studies reviewed here clearly indicate the potential importance of music in consumer behavior, the many commercial uses to which music is put and the amount of money spent on them far outweigh the extent to which recent empirical research has provided clear theory-based guidance for commercial practitioners. Many of the researchers whose work has been featured here are naturally concerned with the practical utility of their research, and as such there is a strong incentive to carry out field studies or at least investigations with direct practical implications. However, the practical constraints of research in such contexts often prohibits the sophisticated methodologies and controls of the laboratory, and theoretical development has been hampered as a consequence. As such, the field is to an extent torn between its practical applications and its scientific aspirations. We would stress the importance of theoretical development, since this is precisely what allows findings to be generalized into naturalistic business settings.

The reasonably clear-cut division of the literature into approaches concentrating on psychobiology and knowledge activation respectively provides two means by which this increased theoretical understanding might be achieved in a manner that also builds upon existing research. Yet, there are two other obvious approaches to expanding theoretical understanding in the field, although they have scarcely been investigated thus far. First, it is curious that there has been so little overt use of theories of musical behavior. As noted earlier, theorizing on this subject dates back to the Greek philosophers, and so it is likely that modern research on the business uses of music would profit by drawing upon this rich research tradition. Second, there is little evidence of the overt use of mainstream theories of consumer behavior despite their obvious relevance to the role of music in business environments (see reviews by Cohen and Chakravarti, 1990; Tybout and Artz, 1994). Indeed, this neglect of mainstream theories of both musical and consumer behavior seems particularly curious given that both have tended to focus on psychobiological and knowledge activation processes, which are the two approaches adopted by the research reviewed in this chapter.

For the time being, there are also grounds for concern over whether those studies cited here concerning psychobiological and knowledge activation effects do actually demonstrate these influences. Although there are obviously exceptions, the majority of studies fail to collect direct evidence of psychobiological/knowledge activation processes. For example, fast music may increase the speed of customer activity, but this process can only be attributed reliably to specifically *psychobiological* processes through measures of arousal such as pulse rate, etc. Similarly, people may choose products that "fit" with the music played in-store, but a convincing demonstration of knowledge activation also requires specifically *cognitive* evidence, such as a reduction in the time taken to recognize a product in the presence of music that "fits" with it. (It is worth noting that a study we have recently completed has found that *recall* for products is enhanced when ads for them feature music that "fits" the advertiser's message.) Such measures are rarely taken since they are more appropriate to the laboratory than to the field, which reiterates our earlier point concerning the trade-off between theoretically oriented laboratory research and practically oriented field research.

Following from this, research in the field should acknowledge more overtly whether it is based on knowledge-activation, psychobiology, or indeed any other approach. Much of the theorizing presented in the research reviewed here tends to be extremely domain-specific, and fails to draw upon research where the hypothesized processes have been exhibited in other areas of academic inquiry. Drawing on the wider body of available evidence would guide researchers to lines of research that are likely to be (un)successful, and thus allow more sophisticated theorizing. An understanding of the role of music in business settings can be gained by psychologists, management scientists, consumer scientists, economists, human geographers, sociologists, and musicologists. However, few individual studies have employed theories or methodologies from more than one of these disciplines. There is a clear need for interdisciplinary research, and the peer review policies of academic journals should be sensitive to this.

Second, since psychobiological and knowledge activation processes are so pervasive, many aspects of consumer/employee behavior are likely to draw upon them. This means that there is plenty of scope for music to influence a range of hitherto unresearched consumer/employee behaviors. The behaviors reviewed in this chapter may well represent just the tip of the iceberg. Indeed, on the basis of the literature review above, it is not yet possible to make a convincing case for the effectiveness of music in business settings: there are too few studies, and their theoretical bases are frequently underdeveloped. Nevertheless, there are clear positive signs that research on music in business settings may have a range of practical and theoretical benefits that open the way for researcher-practitioner collaboration.

The considerable advances made in this field that have been made over the past five to ten years are largely attributable to two factors. First, there has been an increasing recognition by music researchers that music is a social and cultural artifact that interacts with the listening situation: they are becoming interested in how music can interact with everyday activities. Second, there has been a corresponding recognition by those working in other disciplines that music must be considered in more sophisticated terms than merely its presence or absence, and that responses to music must be treated in much more sophisticated terms than simple measures of, e.g., preference, such that musical knowledge and other cognitive factors are also considered. The effects of music in business settings reflect not just the properties of the music itself but also customers'/employees' processing of the music, the immediate listening situation, customers'/employees' broader cultural understanding of music, prevailing economic conditions, and the financial motives of those companies responsible for playing the music. Such a range of interacting factors and theoretical perspectives is likely to lead to potentially sophisticated business applications of music. The sternest challenge facing researchers over the coming years will be to translate the many influences and approaches to music into commercially useful information while maintaining an emphasis on theoretical development.

References

Areni, C. S. and Kim, D. (1993). "The influence of background music on shopping behavior: Classical versus top-forty music in a wine store." *Advances in Consumer Research* 20: 336–340.

Baker, J., Levy, M., and Grewal, D. (1992). "An experimental approach to making retail store environmental decisions." *Journal of Retailing* 68: 445–460.

Baldwin, M. W. and Sinclair, L. (1996). "Self-esteem and 'if ... then' contingencies of interpersonal acceptance." *Journal of Personality and Social Psychology* 71: 1130–1141.

Bawa, K., Landwehr, J. T., and Krishna, A. (1989). "Consumer response to retailers' marketing environments. an analysis of coffee purchase data." *Journal of Retailing* 65: 471–495.

Berlyne, D. E. (1960). *Conflict, Arousal, and Curiosity*. New York: McGraw-Hill.

_____ (1970). *Motivational Problems*. Prague: Czechoslovak Academy of Sciences.

_____ (1971). *Aesthetics and Psychobiology*. New York: Appleton-Century-Crofts.

_____ (1972). "Experimental aesthetics." In P. C. Dodwell (ed.) *New Horizons in Psychology 2* (pp. 117–135). Hammondsworth: Penguin.

_____ (1974). "The new experimental aesthetics." In D. E. Berlyne (ed.) *Studies in the New Experimental Aesthetics: Steps Toward an Objective Psychology of Aesthetic Appreciation* (pp. 1–26). New York: Halsted Press.

Bierley, C., McSweeney, F. K., and Vannieuwkerk, R. (1985). "Classical conditioning of preferences for stimuli." *Journal of Consumer Research* 12: 316–323.

Bodenhausen, E. V. and Wyer, R.S. (1985). "Effects of stereotypes in decision making and information-processing strategies." *Journal of Personality and Social Psychology* 48: 267–282.

Boselie, F. (1991). "Against prototypicality as a central concept in aesthetics." *Empirical Studies of the Arts* 9: 65–73.

Brown, S. P. and Stayman, D. M. (1992). "Antecedents and consequences of attitude toward the ad: A meta-analysis." *Journal of Consumer Research* 19: 34–51.

Bruner, G. C. (1990). "Music, mood, and marketing." *Journal of Marketing* 54: 94–104.

Charnetski, C. J., Brennan, F. X., and Harrison, J. F. (1998). "Effect of music and auditory stimuli on secretory immunoglobulin A (IgA)." *Perceptual and Motor Skills* 87: 1163–1170.

Chebat, J.-C., Gelinas-Chebat, C., and Filiatrault, P. (1993). "Interactive effects of musical and visual cues on time perception: An application to waiting lines in banks." *Perceptual and Motor Skills* 77: 995–1020.

Cohen, J. B. and Chakravarti, D. (1990). "Consumer psychology." *Annual Review of Psychology* 41: 243–288. Palo Alto: Annual Reviews Inc.

Daoussis, L. and McKelvie, S. J. (1986). "Musical preferences and effects of music on a reading comprehension test for extraverts and introverts." *Perceptual and Motor Skills* 62: 283–289.

Darden, W. R., Erdem, O., and Darden, O. K. (1983). "A comparison and test of three causal models of patronage intentions." In W. R. Darden and R. F. Lusch (eds.) *Patronage Behaviour and Retail Management*. New York: North Holland.

Dube, L., Chebat, J.-C., and Morin, S. (1995). "The effects of background music on consumers' desire to affiliate in buyer-seller interactions." *Psychology and Marketing* 12: 305–319.

Dunbar, D. S. (1990). "Music and advertising." *International Journal of Advertising* 9: 197–203.

Finnäs, L. (1989). "How can musical preferences be modified? A research review." *Bulletin of the Council for Research in Music Education* 102: 1–58.

Golden, L. L. and Zimmer, M. R. (1986). "Relationships between affect, patronage, frequency, and amount of money spent with a comment on affect scaling and measurement." *Advances in Consumer Research* 13: 53–7.

Gorn, G. J. (1982). "The effect of music in advertising on choice behavior: A classical conditioning approach." *Journal of Marketing* 46: 94–101.

Gulas, C. S. and Bloch, P. H. (1995). "Right under our noses: Ambient scent and consumer responses." *Journal of Business and Psychology* 10: 87–98.

Hargreaves, D. J. (1986). *The Developmental Psychology of Music*. Cambridge: Cambridge University Press.

Hargreaves, D. J. and North, A. C. (eds.) (1997). *The Social Psychology of Music*. Oxford: Oxford University Press.

Humes, J. F. (1941). "The effects of occupational music on scrappage in the manufacturing of radio tubes." *Journal of Applied Psychology* 25: 573–587.

Kaplan, L. and Nettel, R. (1948). "Music in industry." *Biology and Human Affairs* 13: 129–135.

Kellaris, J. J. and Altsech, M. B. (1992). "The experience of time as a function of musical loudness and gender of listener." *Advances in Consumer Research* 19: 725–729.

Kellaris, J. J. and Cox, A. D. (1989). "The effects of background music in advertising: A reassessment." *Journal of Consumer Research* 16: 113–118.

Kellaris, J. J. and Kent, R. J. (1992). "The influence of music on consumers' temporal perceptions: Does time fly when you're having fun?" *Journal of Consumer Psychology* 1: 365–376.

Kellaris, J. J. and Mantel, S. P. (1994). "The influence of mood and gender on consumers' time perceptions." *Advances in Consumer Research* 21: 514–518.

Kellaris, J. J., Cox, A. D., and Cox, D. (1993). "The effect of background music on ad processing: A contingency explanation." *Journal of Marketing* 57: 114–125.

Kellaris, J. J., Mantel, S. P., and Altsech, M. B. (1996). "Decibels, disposition, and duration: The impact of musical loudness and internal states on time perceptions." *Advances in Consumer Research* 23: 498–503.

Kemp, A. E. (1997). "Individual differences in musical behaviour." In D. J. Hargreaves and A. C. North (eds.) *The Social Psychology of Music* (pp. 25–45). Oxford: Oxford University Press.

Kiger, D. M. (1989). "Effects of music information load on a reading-comprehension task." *Perceptual and Motor Skills* 69: 531–534.

Kirkpatrick, F. H. (1943). "Music in industry." *Journal of Applied Psychology* 27: 268–274.

Konecni, V. J. (1982). "Social interaction and musical preference." In D. Deutsch (ed.) *The Psychology of Music* (pp. 497–516). New York: Academic Press.

Kotler, P. (1973–74). "Atmospherics as a marketing tool." *Journal of Retailing* 49: 48–64.

Krishnan, L. and Saxena, N. K. (1984). "Perceived time: Its relationship with locus of control, filled versus unfilled time intervals, and perceiver's sex." *The Journal of General Psychology* 110: 275–281.

Krueger, J. and Rothbart, M. (1988). "Use of categorical and individuating information in making inferences about personality." *Journal of Personality and Social Psychology* 55: 187–195.

Levin, I. and Zakay, D. (eds.) (1989). *Time and Human Cognition: A Life-Span Perspective.* Amsterdam: North-Holland.

MacInnis, D. J. and Park, C. W. (1991). "The differential role of characteristics of music on high- and low-involvement consumers' processing of ads." *Journal of Consumer Research* 18: 161–173.

Macrae, C. N. and Shepherd, J. W. (1989). "Stereotypes and social judgements." *British Journal of Social Psychology* 28: 319–325.

_____ (1991). "Categorical effects on attributional inferences: A response-time analysis." *British Journal of Social Psychology* 30: 235–245.

Madsen, C. K. (1987). "Background music: Competition for focus of attention." In C. Madsen and P. Prickett (eds.) *Applications of Research in Music Behavior* (pp. 315–325). Tuscaloosa: University of Alabama Press.

Malhotra, N. K. (1983). "A threshold model of store choice." *Journal of Retailing* 59: 3–21.

Martindale, C. and Moore, K. (1988). "Priming, prototypicality, and preference." *Journal of Experimental Psychology: Human Perception and Performance* 14: 661–670.

Matlin, M. W. (1989). *Cognition.* Chicago: Holt, Rinehart, and Winston.

McElrea, H. and Standing, L. (1992). "Fast music causes fast drinking." *Perceptual and Motor Skills* 75: 362.

McGehee, W. and Gardner, J. E. (1949). "Music in a complex industrial job." *Personnel Psychology* 2: 405–417.

McSweeney, F. K. and Bierley, C. (1984). "Recent developments in classical conditioning." *Journal of Consumer Research* 11: 619–631.

Mehrabian, A. and Russell, J. A. (1974). *An Approach to Environmental Psychology.* Cambridge, MA: MIT Press.

Milliman, R. E. (1982). "Using background music to affect the behavior of supermarket shoppers." *Journal of Marketing* 46: 86–91.

_____ (1986). "The influence of background music on the behavior of restaurant patrons." *Journal of Consumer Research* 13: 286–289.

Miniard, P. W., Bhatla, S., Lord, K. R., Dickson, P. R., and Unnava, H. R. (1991). "Picture-based persuasion processes and the moderating role of involvement." *Journal of Consumer Research* 18: 92–107.

Mitchell, A. A. (1986). "The effect of verbal and visual components of advertisements on brand attitudes and attitude toward the advertisement." *Journal of Consumer Research* 13: 12–24.

Nakamura, G. V. (1994). "Scene schemata in memory for spatial relations." *American Journal of Psychology* 107: 481–497.

Nakamura, G. V., Kleiber, B. A., and Kim, K. (1992). "Categories, propositional representations, and schemas: Test of a structural hypothesis." *American Journal of Psychology* 105: 75–590.

National Music Council. (1996). *The Value of Music*. London: National Music Council.

Nevin, J. R. and Houston, M. (1980). "Images as a component of attractiveness to intra-urban shopping areas." *Journal of Retailing* 56: 77–93.

North, A. C. and Hargreaves, D. J. (1996a). "Responses to music in a dining area." *Journal of Applied Social Psychology* 26: 491–501.

_____ (1996b). "The effects of music on responses to a dining area." *Journal of Environmental Psychology* 16: 55–64.

_____ (1997). "Experimental aesthetics and everyday music listening." In D. J. Hargreaves and A. C. North (eds.) *The Social Psychology of Music* (pp. 84–103). Oxford: Oxford University Press.

_____ (1998). "The effect of music on atmosphere and purchase intentions in a cafeteria." *Journal of Applied Social Psychology* 28: 2254–2273.

_____ (1999a). "Music and driving game performance." *Scandinavian Journal of Psychology* 40: 285–292.

_____ (1999b). "Can music move people? The effects of musical complexity and silence on waiting time." *Environment and Behaviour* 31: 136–149.

North, A. C., Hargreaves, D. J., and Heath, S. (1998). "The effects of music on time perception in a gymnasium." *Psychology of Music* 26: 78–88.

North, A. C., Hargreaves, D. J., and McKendrick, J. (1997). "In-store music affects product choice." *Nature* 390: 132.

_____ (1999a). "The effect of music on in-store wine selections." *Journal of Applied Psychology* 84: 271–276.

_____ (1999b). "Music and on-hold waiting time." *British Journal of Psychology* 90: 161–164.

_____ (Submitted for publication). "The effects of music in the workplace."

Oldham, G. R., Cummings, A., Mischel, L. J., Schmidtke, J. M., and Zhou, J. (1995). "Listen while you work? Quasi experimental relations between personal-stereo headset use and employee work responses." *Journal of Applied Psychology* 80: 547–564.

Palmquist, J. E. (1990). "Apparent time passage and music preference by music and nonmusic majors." *Journal of Research in Music Education* 38: 206–214.

Park, C. W. and Young, S. M. (1986). "Consumer response to television commercials: The impact of involvement and background music on brand attitude formation." *Journal of Marketing Research* 23: 11–24.

Petty, R. E. and Cacioppo, J. T. (1981). *Attitudes and Persuasion: Classic and Contemporary Approaches*. Dubuque, IA: William C. Brown.

Petty, R. E., Cacioppo, J. T., and Schumann, D. T. (1983). "Central and peripheral routes to advertising effectiveness: The moderating effect of involvement." *Journal of Consumer Research* 10: 135–146.

Pitt, L. F. and Abratt, R. (1988). "Music in advertisements for unmentionable products: A classical conditioning experiment." *International Journal of Advertising* 7: 130–137.

Ramos, L. V. (1993). "The effects of on-hold telephone music on the number of premature disconnections to a statewide protective services abuse hot line." *Journal of Music Therapy* 30: 119–129.

Ramsayer, T. and Lustnauer, S. (1989). "Sex differences in time perception." *Perceptual and Motor Skills* 68: 195–198.

Ratneshwar, S. and Chaiken, S. (1991). "Comprehension's role in persuasion: The case of its moderating effect on the persuasive impact of source cues." *Journal of Consumer Research* 18: 52–62.

Rider, M. S., Achterberg, J., Lawlis, G. F., Goven, A., Toledo, R., and Butler, J. R. (1990). "Effect of immune system imagery on secretory IgA." *Biofeedback and Self-Regulation* 15: 317–333.

Roballey, T. C., McGreevy, C., Rongo, R. R., Schwantes, M. L., Steger, P. J., Wininger, M. A., and Gardner, E. B. (1985). "The effect of music on eating behavior." *Bulletin of the Psychonomic Society* 23: 221–222.

Russell, P. A. (1997). "Musical tastes and society." In D. J. Hargreaves and A. C. North (eds.) *The Social Psychology of Music* (pp. 141–158). Oxford: Oxford University Press.

Sanbonmatsu, D. M. and Kardes, F. R. (1988). "The effects of physiological arousal on information processing and persuasion." *Journal of Consumer Research* 15: 379–385.

Smith, H. C. (1947). "Music in relation to employee attitudes, piece-work production, and industrial accidents." *Applied Psychology Monographs* 14. Stanford: Stanford University Press.

Smith, P. C. and Curnow, R. (1966). "'Arousal hypothesis' and the effects of music on purchasing behavior." *Journal of Applied Psychology* 50: 255–256.

Sogin, D. W. (1988). "Effect of three different musical styles of background music on coding by college-age students." *Perceptual and Motor Skills* 67: 275–280.

Soibelman, D. (1948). *Therapeutic and Industrial Uses of Music: A Review of the Literature.* New York: Columbia University Press.

Stanley, R. and Sewall, M. (1976). "Image inputs to a probabilistic model: Predicting retail potential." *Journal of Marketing* 39: 48–53.

Stratton, V. (1992). "Influence of music and socializing on perceived stress while waiting." *Perceptual and Motor Skills* 75: 334.

Stuart, E. W., Shimp, T. A., and Engle, R. W. (1987). "Classical conditioning of consumer attitudes: Four experiments in an advertising context." *Journal of Consumer Research* 14: 334–349.

Tom, G. (1995). "Classical conditioning of unattended stimuli." *Psychology and Marketing* 12: 79–87.

Turley, L. W. and Milliman, R. E. (2000). "Atmospheric effects on shopping behavior: A review of the experimental evidence." *Journal of Business Research* 49: 193–211.

Tybout, A. M. and Artz, N. (1994). "Consumer psychology." *Annual Review of Psychology* 45: 131–169. Palo Alto, CA: Annual Reviews Inc.

Wansink, B. and Ray, M. L. (1996). "Advertising strategies to increase usage frequency." *Journal of Marketing* 60: 31–46.

Whitfield, T. W. A. and Slatter, P. E. (1979). "The effects of categorization and prototypicality on aesthetic choice in a furniture selection task." *British Journal of Psychology* 70: 65–75.

Wolfe, D. E. (1983). "Effects of music loudness on task performance and self-report of college-aged students." *Journal of Research in Music Education* 31: 191–201.

Yalch, R. and Spangenberg, E. (1990). "Effects of store music on shopping behavior." *Journal of Consumer Marketing* 7: 55–63.

Yalch, R. F. and Elmore-Yalch, R. (1984). "The effect of numbers on the route to persuasion." *Journal of Consumer Research* 11: 522–527.

Zullow, H. M. (1991). "Pessimistic rumination in popular songs and newsmagazines predict economic recession via decreased consumer optimism and spending." *Journal of Economic Psychology* 12: 501–526.

Chapter 5

THE SOCIAL USES OF BACKGROUND MUSIC FOR PERSONAL ENHANCEMENT

Steven Brown and Töres Theorell

Introduction

Background music is used in two different kinds of contexts at the social level. First, it is used as a form of "milieu music" in public places to enhance the production and consumption of commercial goods. Second, it is used in a more individualized manner as a form of what we call "personal enhancement background music." The latter includes the uses of background music in clinical and educational settings as well as its ubiquitous use by individuals for the purposes of emotional and motivational control. The current chapter discusses this second set of uses. Four general features of personal enhancement background music are described, including its goals, effects, and mechanisms. Much is shared between the various uses of background music for personal enhancement, not least the hype that accompanies discussions of these uses in the media. Personal enhancement music is based on the notion that "music is good for you," most notably "good" music. We conclude with a discussion of the sociomusicological implications of this notion.

* * *

What do rats and humans have in common? Ten toes. Two eyes. A four-chambered heart. Well, all those things are probably important. But how about the fact that both species show enhanced performance on spatial-reasoning tasks after listening to Mozart's Sonata for Two Pianos in D major, K. 448? *That* is certainly an important point of similarity between the two species—isn't it?

Notes for this chapter are located on page 154.

The current chapter reviews the social uses of background music to improve health and cognition. However, it comes with a warning label attached. Many of the topics discussed herein have been subject to an enormous amount of hype and hysteria in the news media and popular-book literature. Music-listening has been touted as the hottest formula for increasing intelligence and curing all sorts of ailments of the body and soul. There are significant parallels between the approaches of promoters of music for therapeutic purposes ("music cures disease") and those of promoters of music for educational purposes ("music makes people smarter"). Not least among them is their delight in interpreting experiments in which non-human species (including plants) are exposed to classical music. The fact that playing Mozart to rats improves their maze-running performance (Rauscher, Robinson, and Jens, 1998; but see Steele, 2003) is only one of several disturbing trends that have emerged from research into music's cognitive effects. This, in addition to similar work done with monkeys (Carlson et al., 1997; Shaw, 2000) and gorillas (Shaw, 2000), seems to represent a nativist attempt to validate the cross-cultural universality of European classical music without ever bothering to test these effects in a cross-cultural sampling of human beings. There appears to be an unstated dictum that "if it works in rats, it must be a biological effect." Such research raises strong sociocultural concerns that have simply not been addressed by the researchers involved.

In thinking about the social uses of background music generally, we can distinguish two types of uses: (a) those intended to create a certain acoustic environment in public places, something which we will refer to as *milieu music*, and (b) those more individualized uses of music for the purposes of personal improvement, something we will refer here to as *personal enhancement background music* (PEBM). Milieu music includes the background music played in business environments and work settings as well as the "crowd-controlling" music played in elevators, airports, and airplanes. Milieu music operates in public places to create a type of mood or milieu. It is well described as "music that is meant to be heard but not listened to" (Jones and Schumacher, 1992). Milieu music usually has a definite social-control function, often related to economic production and consumption. The chapter by North and Hargreaves in this volume reviews the uses of background music in business settings for economic purposes. In contrast to this, personal enhancement music is the more individualized background music used in both music therapy and educational contexts and for individual listening to music in homes and cars for the purposes of emotional control. It is the kind of background music that is meant to be heard *and* listened to. Personal enhancement music can be used both to restore lost functions (as in music therapy) and to elevate normal functioning beyond some basal level (as in educational settings). It is this area that has generated most of the hype mentioned above about the power of music to do all things useful and good.

We can see a striking contrast between these two forms of background music with regard to their potential for manipulation. Milieu music principally has an economic function, related to the production and consumption of commercial goods. The primary "senders" of this kind of music consist of those people who control the emission (and occasionally live performance) of music in public places. This generally represents a manipulative use of music, a form of mass behavioral control. In contrast, personal enhancement music is used more for personal development or for individual recovery of lost function. It is often self-applied, thereby making the emitter and receiver the same person in many circumstances. This therefore represents a much more altruistic, cooperative, and honest use of music, again suggesting that the uses of music must be analyzed on a case-by-case basis in order to understand how musical communication operates (see the opening chapter by Brown, this volume).

This chapter will be devoted to an analysis of personal enhancement background music and will primarily consider its uses for individualized clinical and cognitive improvement. Far and away the most pervasive use of personal enhancement music occurs in the form of individual listening to music in private settings. Few people need to be convinced of the efficacy of this intervention. Compact disc purchases and digital music downloads give strong indications that individual music listening is on the rise. In addition, people report that music listening is a source of some of their most profound emotional experiences in life (Sloboda, 1991, 1999; Gabrielsson and Lindström, 1993; Panksepp, 1995; Gabrielsson, 2001). Individual listening might be best viewed as the interface between the clinical and cognitive uses of background music discussed in the remainder of this chapter. On the one hand, it serves as a kind of self-medication for emotional catharsis, but on the other, it is often used as mental preparation for other activities.

From the outset it must be stated that this chapter will focus on background music even though most of the uses of music in clinical and educational settings are based on engagement by individuals in active music-making, usually in a long-term program. In both clinical and educational contexts, a distinction can be made between "passive" and "active" formats of use, where the first involves music listening alone—either in a free or guided manner—and the second involves active musical production as well. This categorical distinction is more meaningful in the clinical domain than in the educational domain because passive music listening for educational purposes is not a common activity, except in music courses. The prevalence of active music-making in many clinical and educational programs should not be interpreted as implying that background music is inherently less efficacious at producing effects related to self-improvement but simply that most programs designed to produce these effects involve some level of active musical production. That said, there are certainly conditions where such an activity would be impractical or undesirable and where passive listening is the method of choice. PEBM highlights the ancient idea that music, all on its own, can be wholly efficacious in bringing about effects on people without the necessity of musical production.

Features of Personal Enhancement Background Music

In the remainder of the chapter, we will describe four features of personal enhancement background music in various social contexts. This will serve to highlight the major themes that characterize discussion of this issue in the literature. PEBM (1) has the desired outcome of self-improvement; (2) has both short-term and long-term effects; (3) can have negative effects in addition to positive ones; and (4) may capitalize on common attentional/emotional mechanisms in different contexts. We will conclude with a discussion of the sociological implications of these findings from the persuasion/manipulation perspective presented in this book (see Brown, this volume).

Because of space limitations and in order to give a focus to the discussion, we will take a comparative look at PEBM in two complementary contexts, one clinical and one educational. The clinical one will be the use of background music in the treatment of dementia, and the educational one will be the use of background music to increase cognitive performance in adults. The former examines music's potential to restore normal levels of functioning in light of diminished skills, whereas the latter looks at music's potential to increase cognitive performance above normal levels of functioning. Readers interested in the clinical uses of music outside of dementia treatment should consult standard music therapy textbooks such as Davis, Gfeller, and Thaut's *An Introduction to Music Therapy: Theory and Practice* (1999) or Wigram, Nygaard Pedersen and Bonde's *A Comprehensive Guide to Music Therapy: Theory, Clinical Practice, Research and Training* (2002).

PEBM Has the Desired Outcome of Individual Self-Improvement

Personal enhancement background music is a social use of music designed to produce improvements in functioning and/or quality of life. It is an altruistic and cooperative form of musical communication in which the sender (i.e., emitter) usually has the receiver's best interests in mind. It therefore rarely makes use of manipulation. In the case of recreational music listening, the sender and receiver are generally one and the same person.

PEBM serves as the basis for the popular claim that "music is good for you." Most people describe their personal listening activities as a positive if not essential part of their lives (Panksepp, 1995; Sloboda, 1999; Panksepp and Bernatzky, 2002). PEBM is one of the most socially positive uses of music, especially when viewed alongside forms of milieu music designed to regulate consumer behavior in public places. It is interesting to note that the use of background music in workplaces—which we subsumed under the category of "milieu music"—is often considered to be an altruistic use. It is a means by which employers attempt to humanize the work environment for employees (Jones and Schumacher, 1992), especially those performing repetitive or monotonous tasks. "The point is to make the worker feel better," writes the president of the Muzak Corporation, "because if he feels better, chances are he will work better. It's as simple as that" (quoted in MacLeod, 1979: 23). Whereas increases in productivity may be the ultimate economic driving force for the use of background music in the workplace, an altruistic motive is often expressed by the "senders" of this music, again qualifying it as a situation in which music is thought to be good for people.

Looking to music therapy, the goals typically include "the restoration, maintenance, and improvement of mental and physical health" (National Association for Music Therapy, 1980). Music therapy is done to improve the welfare and functioning of a wide range of patient populations, including autistic children, neurological patients, psychiatric patients, pain sufferers, and mentally retarded people. Music therapy is a twentieth-century discipline, itself derived from diverse forms of "music healing" found in most cultures of the world. There is every reason to believe that healing is a very ancient social use of music (Davis, Gfeller, and Thaut, 1999), and that tribal music healers are the precursors of today's university-trained music therapists. One thing that accompanied the development of music therapy as an academic discipline was the emergence of a branch of research devoted to testing and verifying its effects (see, for example, Wheeler, 1995 or Wigram, Nygaard Pedersen, and Bonde, 2002). Much of what we know about the clinical effects of music comes from this genre of research. However, in the last few decades, a movement of New Age music healing has emerged, making highly exaggerated and unsubstantiated claims about the efficacy of music in curing all sorts of disease conditions. Summer (1996) has provided a critical review of a large number of musical techniques and technologies that claim to cure disease but that come with absolutely no scientific verification of their effects. For example, she exposes hocus-pocus "toning" techniques that claim to cure diabetes, cancer, head injury, and quadriplegia. Moreover, Summer highlights the fact that all techniques that see musical sound as being esoterically and magically efficacious in its effects ignore a critical point about how any therapeutic process works: "What is missing in nearly all of the theories of New Age music healing that I reviewed is personal contact. How can New Age music healers perform their services without personal contact?" (Summer, 1996: 258). One of the earliest written descriptions of the process of music healing is David's regular playing of his harp to help soothe King Saul's melancholia (neurotic depression), as described in the biblical book of Samuel (16:14–23).[1] Suffice it to say that a deep personal relationship—one full of highly ambivalent emotions—existed between these two men (Alvin, 1975).

In contrast to the ancient nature of music's use in healing contexts, the call to use background music for the purposes of increasing cognitive performance and/or general intelligence is a very modern one. Most people who listen to music do so because of an interest in music itself and only rarely use it as a vehicle to make themselves more intelligent. People listen to music for a host of emotional and social reasons (Panksepp, 1995; DeNora, 2001), but few would cite becoming smarter as one of them. The problem with using background music for cognitive enhancement is the age-old realization that learning enhancement is extremely difficult to achieve and verify. In 1993, Rauscher, Shaw, and Ky published a study indicating that 10 minutes of passive listening to Mozart's Sonata for Two Pianos in D Major (K. 448) produced an enhancement in spatial reasoning on a paper-folding-and-cutting task, itself a component of the IQ test. Attempts to replicate this short-term effect led to much controversy among researchers (Rauscher and Shaw, 1998; Chabris, 1999; Steele et al., 1999; Hetland, 2000; Schellenberg, 2003). Unfortunately, this result was immediately interpreted in the press as evidence that listening to classical music makes people smarter, even though this so-called Mozart Effect lasted no longer than fifteen minutes. In a 1995 follow-up study, Rauscher, Shaw, and Ky tested their subjects on five consecutive days but only observed a significant difference between the Mozart condition and the control condition on the first two days of testing. The authors suggested that this may have been due to a ceiling effect, although they did not verify this in later studies.

One popular source that has publicized these findings is Don Campbell's book *The Mozart Effect®: Tapping the Power of Music to Heal the Body, Strengthen the Mind, and Unlock the Creative Spirit* (1997), accompanied by registered trademark as well as a series of Mozart CDs directed at either adults, children, or babies (see www.mozarteffect.com). Campbell's book not only recounts many "miracle stories of treatment and cure" but thoroughly reinforces the mythology of classical music as being all-powerful at improving all aspects of learning, health, and creativity. Given the amount of time that people devote to personal music listening, it might seem odd that they would need a book-length guide to the healing powers of music; by all accounts, people "medicate" themselves musically on a regular basis. However, the nature of the discourse has changed dramatically in recent years. The rhetoric has now become subsumed by brain-talk. Not only is music supposed to produce its well-known effects of relaxation and stimulation, but we are now supposed to believe that it induces long-term changes in the structure and function of the brain, and that only certain musics are effective at doing this. Thus, forget about your favorite pieces of music; listen to Mozart if you want to "heal the body, strengthen the mind, and unlock the creative spirit."

Claims of music-induced learning enhancement attract a lot of attention because they sound so simple. Few people are satisfied with a slow pace of learning in a fast-paced world. If something as effortless as passive listening to background music can really improve learning, then this is something to take notice of. But things are rarely that simple. Most of the brain-claims circulating in the popular press are either false or highly exaggerated. All the published studies with Mozart listening have involved adult subjects and ten-minute listening periods, but this has not held back the flood of recommendations from many spheres of society that children—from fetuses onward—should receive long-term exposure to ambient classical music. Evidence for this is found in the explosion of classical CDs targeted at young listeners, recordings such as *Baby Needs Mozart* (Delos International), *Classical Baby: Mozart* (Wea), *Moving with Mozart* (Kimbo), *The Mozart Effect*—*Music for Babies: From Playtime to Sleepytime* (MMB Music), and *Heigh-Ho! Mozart* (Delos), to name just a few of these recordings (see Habermeyer, 1999).[2]

Personal enhancement music is one of the most socially positive and cooperative uses of music, and yet a new form of social manipulation has taken hold in the form of brain-claims that classical music possesses some unique power to improve intelligence in children and adults. Mozart has been unanimously propped up as the spokesperson for this burgeoning political movement, ostensibly to save music programs in public schools. As we will discuss below with regard to the practice of music therapy, the sad irony about this exclusive promotion of a single style of music for self-improvement is that *personal preferences*—based on individual history, social class, religion, ethnic background, and so on—are an essential consideration in thinking about the enhancing effects of music for any purpose.

PEBM Has Both Short-Term and Long-Term Effects

General Considerations. Personal enhancement background music is a passive counterpart to active forms of musical use, especially in the realm of music therapy. PEBM has both short-term and long-term effects on listeners, where short-term effects generally result from immediate exposure to music, and long-term effects result from chronic exposure. The former include short-term music therapy interventions as well the effects of short-term musical exposure on cognitive-task performance. The latter include longer-term music therapy interventions, the effect of chronic music exposure on learning efficiency, the effect of Muzak on work performance, and the effects of chronic exposure to certain musical styles on behavior and personality.[3] Complementary findings include those discussed by North and Hargreaves (this volume) on the effects of milieu music on behavior in business settings, including purchasing behavior in stores. These will not be discussed in this chapter.

The literature on the short-term effects of music is vast and includes a large amount of research on physiological and psychological effects. *The most prevalent but least studied effects are those that come from daily self-administration of music in order to relieve stress, depression, and boredom.* To the extent that this self-administration occurs on a regular basis, chronic effects can be described, and most people say that music has an important moderating effect on their emotional lives (Gabrielsson and Lindström, 1993; Pansepp, 1995; Sloboda, 1999; DeNora, 2001).

Long-term effects of background music, especially in the educational realm, are poorly studied and much more based on anecdotal reporting than longitudinal scientific studies. Most long-term studies—whether in the clinical or educational domain—involve active music making rather than passive music listening alone. Much of the discussion of the beneficial effects of music making is conceptualized in terms of "transfer effects," or effects in which a skill acquired in one situation carries over to a new learning situation. These claims have been controversial and difficult to reproduce. At one level, the applied uses of music are *only* about transfer effects, about the potential of music to enhance or restore other functions on a lasting basis. It is important to note that many claims of transfer are based on unsubstantiated extrapolations from studies of short-term effects. In examining this literature, one must always keep in mind the distinctions between passive and active formats, short-term and long-term interventions/effects, and intended and unintended outcomes. Too many false claims have circulated due to nonspecialists overinterpreting or misinterpreting the published literature.

Finally, it must be mentioned that music education itself (as opposed to the use of music in schools to improve education in other areas) is based on programs of long-term training involving not just music listening or motor activities but ear training, notation, sight-reading, rhythm studies, memorization, mental rehearsal, and performance, in addition to historical analyses of composers, musicians, performance practices, instruments, musical styles, cultural change, and aesthetics, all this involving close work with a teacher or other role model, countless hours of concentrated practice, and, on many occasions, coordinated performance with a group of peers. While music education is often confounded with music *in* education these days, it is important to maintain this distinction if only because the former places an emphasis on musical aims rather than extra-musical ones.

Clinical Effects. In music therapy research, there is an extensive tradition of comparing short-term and long-term interventions through longitudinal studies and follow-ups. Most of the research literature looks at treatments that last less than three months and at effects that occur within this time frame. Background music has found an increasingly important role in a large number of clinical caregiving situations for numerous purposes, including controlling postoperative pain (Nilsson, Rawal and Unosson, 2003), reducing nausea and vomiting after chemotherapy (Ezzone et al., 1998), handling restrained patients (Janelli and Kanski, 1997), reducing the sensation and distress of labor pain (Phumdoung and Good, 2003), improving postoperative sleep (Zimmerman et al., 1996), reducing stress during immunization of children (Erickson Megel, Wagner Houser and Gleaves, 1998), and decreasing anxiety during ventilatory assistance (Chlan, 1998), to name just a few. Standley (1986) performed a meta-analysis of thirty empirical studies of music therapy, and found that the major use of passive music listening as a form of music therapy is as an *analgesic* and *anxiolytic* device. Background music has been shown to be effective at reducing pain and anxiety in a host of conditions, including cancer, burn, and kidney dialysis. Moreover, music in combination with guided visual imagery (Bonny,

1978) has been shown to be an effective intervention in treating anxiety and depression (Wrangsjo and Korlin, 1995; McKinney et al., 1997). Within nursing, background music has been employed for reducing anxiety and depression, controlling pain, improving motor and cognitive functioning, and reducing aggressive behaviors (reviewed in Snyder and Chlan, 1999).

In the area of dementia in particular, communication by and with patients presents great challenges to clinical staff and family members due to the diminished cognitive skills of the patients. Dementia is a condition in which traditional medical interventions—pharmacological, surgical, physiological, psychotherapeutic—offer little hope for long-term recovery and in which treatment is directed toward maintaining the day-to-day functioning of patients. Music is used extensively to ameliorate communication difficulties with confused, mute, and often aggressive patients. In fact, music is as effective as any intervention for the treatment/care of dementia, and has assumed a major role in helping improve communication between patients and their caregivers, including family members (Clair, 1996). Background music is used extensively with dementia patients in music therapy sessions and caregiving situations, in both individualized and group settings (reviewed in Clair, 1996; Brotons, Koger, and Pickett-Cooper, 1997; Koger, Chapin, and Brotons, 1999; Brown, Götell and Ekman, 2001; Sherratt, Thornton and Hatton, 2004). It has been found to have important effects in decreasing aggressive and agitated behavior (Gerdner and Swanson, 1993; Goddaer and Abraham, 1994; Hoeffer et al., 1997; Ragneskog and Kihlgren, 1997; Clark, Lipe, and Bilbrey, 1998; Gerdner, 2000), increasing food intake during meals (Ragneskog et al., 1996a, 1996b), improving night-time sleep (Lindenmuth, Patel, and Chang, 1992), reducing disruptive vocalizations (Casby and Holm, 1994), increasing bathing cooperation (Thomas, Heitman and Alexander, 1997; Hoeffer et al., 1997; Clark, Lipe and Bilbrey, 1998), and improving mood and social interaction (Lord and Garner, 1993). This general efficacy of background music accords well with studies showing that dementia patients can retain a large degree of musical responsiveness and skill in the face of memory loss, language impairment, and other disabilities (Crystal, Grober, and Masur, 1989; Swartz et al., 1989; Prickett and Moore, 1991; Aldridge, 1996), and that they can be quite responsive to music in caregiving situations (Clair, 1996; Clair and Ebberts, 1997; Matthews, Clair, and Kosloski, 2000; Götell, Brown, and Ekman, 2002, 2003). In addition to this, music in combination with guided visual imagery (Bonny, 1978) has been used with non-demented elderly people to increase emotional control and self-esteem (Summer, 1981).

The contemporary practice of music therapy is based principally on active musical involvement by the patient in conjunction with a music therapist, often making use of guided improvisation (Nordoff and Robbins, 1977; Bruscia, 1987; Aldridge, 1996). Standley's (1986) meta-analysis has shown that many forms of active music therapy incorporate the playing of background music as an important adjunct. For example, preferred music can be combined with various sensory stimulation techniques to increase the responsiveness of patients who are suffering from brain damage or undergoing long-term hospitalization. Music can be used with biofeedback techniques to reinforce or structure physiological responses, such as in the case of epilepsy or coronary heart disease. For dementia treatment as well, active music making is an important component of music therapy, including such activities as singing (Olderog Millard and Smith, 1989; Groene, 1993; Brotons and Pickett-Cooper, 1994; Hanson et al., 1996; Groene et al., 1998), playing instruments (Groene, 1993; Lord and Garner, 1993; Smith-Marchese, 1994; Brotons and Pickett-Cooper, 1994; Brotons and Pickett-Cooper, 1996), and moving to music (Groene, 1993; Brotons and Pickett-Cooper, 1994; Hanson et al., 1996; Brotons and Pickett-Cooper, 1996; Groene et al., 1998). For dementia patients, these are highly effective interventions for increasing awareness, controlling mood, increasing social interactions, eliciting coordinated motor activities, stimulating memory, and bringing out mental coherence, if only on a short-term basis. However, it is important to note that a meta-analysis of research studies of music therapy in dementia by Koger, Chapin, and Brotons (1999) failed to find any advantages of active forms over passive ones, or of long-term interventions over short-term interventions. This accords well with the palliative, here-and-now role of music in dementia care. Music—used either passively or actively—might in fact be as effective as any other treatment to improve the functioning, communicative skills, and quality of life of dementia patients.

Cognitive Effects. Most studies of the effects of background music have dealt with physiological and psychological measurements (reviewed in Barlett, 1996) rather than cognitive performance. They have looked at the effects of music on blood pressure, respiratory rate, heart rate, galvanic skin response, muscle contractility, and the like. The wide diversity of results obtained from such studies has made it clear that music can produce all different types of effects depending on musical style, emotional tone, rhythm, tempo, volume, listening context, duration of exposure, personality variables, cultural background, and so on. All these things are critical considerations in making generalizations about the effects of music on listeners.

In the previous subsection, we discussed studies of the Mozart Effect on performance in a mental paper-folding task. It is important to note that the literature on passive music listening for cognitive enhancement is small and minor. Before Mozart-Effect research appeared on the scene in the 1990s, such questions were given too little consideration, and even then were usually framed in terms of the *distracting* (not facilitative) effects of music. Unlike research on the Mozart Effect—which looks at the effect of *prior* musical exposure on task performance—most other studies have examined the effects of music played *during* a cognitive task. An important naturalistic consideration is whether students typically listen to background music while studying. Daoussis and McKelvie (1986) found that personality type was an important moderating variable:

among those who were classified as extraverts, 50 percent said that they routinely studied to the sounds of background music, whereas among those who were classified as introverts, only 25 percent said they did. Importantly, both groups of students said that while studying to music, they kept the volume either "soft" or "extremely soft," thus minimizing the arousing properties of the music. Daoussis and McKelvie also found that while background music had no particular effect on performance by extroverts on a reading recall test, it significantly disrupted performance among introverts. This important finding suggests that the effects of music on cognitive performance are mediated— perhaps in large part—by individual differences. Crawford and Strapp (1994) extended these findings and showed that vocal music was much more disruptive than instrumental music on cognitive task performance, especially when the demands of the task were high. Looking at an object-number matching task, they found that background music significantly deteriorated performance among introverts but not extraverts, in support of Daoussis and McKelvie's findings on the reading recall task. Crawford and Strapp also found that people who routinely studied to background music performed significantly worse in the *absence* of music than did those who typically studied in silence, again arguing that individual differences are crucial in interpreting studies of the cognitive effects of background music. Other studies have reported that background music can either facilitate, inhibit, or have no effect on various cognitive and motor tasks (e.g., Hallam, Price and Katsarou, 2002; Iwanaga and Ito, 2002). Clearly much work is needed in this area. It is important to reiterate that all studies of the Mozart Effect involve music played *before* the task. It is not at all clear what the practical implications of such an effect are. Should students play music immediately before sitting down to study? Should they bathe themselves in classical music during every free moment away from the books? Again, a reported facilitation *during* music listening would have much greater practical applications if such an effect could be demonstrated.

Such a facilitatory effect has been reported, but this brings us more into the realm of popular science than experimental science. One program that has touted itself as demonstrating that background music can have dramatic effects on building memory is the "Suggestopedia" program developed by the Bulgarian doctor Georgi Lozanov as popularized in the book *Superlearning* (1979) by Ostrander and Schroeder. Not surprisingly for a program of its type, Superlearning comes complete with superclaims: with the incorporation of the appropriate music into the study program, one can learn a foreign language in four weeks, memorize facts and figures ten times faster than normal, perform better in sports, control pain, etc. The music used for this program is quite specific: it is slow, quiet, metric, low-arousal music played in common or triple time, having a tempo of precisely sixty beats per minute. This generally includes instrumental classical pieces of the Baroque period by Bach, Handel, Vivaldi, and others. The use of a regular rhythm is particularly important to the way information is supposed to be presented and memorized. This program is particularly geared toward developing enhanced memory for *lists* of items, such as words in a foreign language. The effects of this commercial study program have not been verified in any scientific publications.

Studies of the effects of *long-term* exposure to music on cognitive function have involved active music making rather than passive listening. In reality there are virtually no analyses of the cognitive effects of chronic exposure to background music (Superlearning aside), and thus little scientific basis for the claim that passive listening to music can increase intelligence. The most celebrated long-term effect reported in the press based on a false extrapolation from a short-term effect was the popular interpretation of the 1993 Mozart Effect study. When publishing their findings, Rauscher, Shaw and Ky presented their results not just as raw test scores but as normalizations in the form of "IQ equivalents," as the paper-folding task was taken from the Stanford-Binet Intelligence Scale. Rauscher, Shaw, and Ky were able to show that the enhancement on task performance amounted to 8 IQ equivalents, representing a statistically significant increase. (Note that the normal IQ score on a standard test is 100, and that the control group in the Mozart study scored 110 IQ equivalents while the Mozart group scored 118 IQ equivalents.) It should come as no surprise that the Zeitgeist in the popular press was that listening to Mozart for 10 minutes could increase IQ score—*and thus general intelligence*—by 8 points. We have no one to blame for this but the Mozart Effect researchers themselves. This transformation of the raw data clearly served as fuel for the media's fire, especially given the fact that the study was published in the world's most prestigious science journal, *Nature*. As mentioned earlier, Rauscher, Shaw, and Ky's 1995 follow-up study showed no improvements after the second of five days of testing, nor did they ever test anything other than 10-minute Mozart exposures or observe anything more than 15-minute enhancements.

Virtually all claims about the long-term effects of music on cognitive function come from classroom studies with *children* in which *active* music programs are instituted on a several-month to several-year basis. In other words, all the evidence for cognitive transfer effects comes from long-term, active studies and nothing else. This leap in reasoning from "passive listening in adults" (e.g., the Mozart Effect) to "active music training in children" is rarely recognized or acknowledged in discussions about the effects of music on learning. Unlike the exclusive emphasis of Mozart-Effect research on spatial reasoning, classroom studies have focused on a host of dependent measurements. Studies to date have provided cautiously encouraging indications that musical training for children can lead to improvements in reading (Barwick et al., 1989; Lamb and Gregory, 1993; Douglas and Willatts, 1994; Gardiner et al., 1996; Standley and Hughes, 1997), verbal memory (Ho, Cheung, and Chan, 2003), spatial-temporal reasoning (Rauscher et al., 1997; Gromko and Poorman, 1998; Costa-Giomi, 1999; Bilhartz, Bruhn, and Olson, 2000; Rauscher and Zupan, 2000), mathematics (Gardiner et, al. 1996; Graziano, Peterson and Shaw, 1999), and social-interaction skills (Weber, Spychiger, and Patry, 1993). However, Schellenberg (2003) provides important caveats in interpreting these classroom studies. Most importantly, he reminds us that it is critical to consider what the no-music, control classroom is doing in place of musical training, because there are numerous potential placebo effects built into musical training that have nothing to do with music per se, factors such as individualized attention, close interaction with an adult role model, higher expectations from parents, the need for increased concentration, increased daily work time, and the like. Controlled classroom studies must be designed so as to distinguish effects that are specific to music from the host of other social and cognitive factors inherent in the music-lesson experience. To date, no consistent trend has emerged from this line of research with regard to protocol or effects. In other words, replicability has been slow, which is not surprising given the laborious and time-consuming nature of classroom studies.

Where musical transfer effects are claimed to occur, it is important to keep in mind that they should exist only when two tasks share a reasonable degree of similarity (Spychiger, 1999; Schellenberg, 2003). Taking a course in jitterbug dancing should provide one with skills that are transferable to a situation in which one learns to dance salsa. But since it is unlikely to be of assistance when studying Indonesian cooking, we should be very skeptical of claims that learning the jitterbug specifically enhances the ability to learn Indonesian cooking. An instructive example in the musical domain comes from Rauscher et al. (1997). In this study, a classroom comparison was done between keyboard training, computer training (an adequate control for instruction, concentration, and adult involvement), group singing, and no extra activity. After six months of these treatments, the keyboard group alone showed significant improvements in spatial-temporal reasoning (but not spatial cognition). No changes were detected in the computer, group-singing, or no-extra-activity groups. It is important to note that this kind of effect reflects a degree of similarity between keyboard training and the spatial skills tested by Rauscher and colleagues: keyboard training (as well as learning staff notation) provides experience with the kind of spatial coordinate systems that may be pertinent to the learning of spatial relations. Group singing, which lacks this spatial component, fails to produce the same type of effect. Such an explanation provides a much more reasonable and convincing model of cognitive transfer than does Shaw's (2000) claim for cortical priming of mental rotation by Mozart listening, in which passive music listening and active mental rotation are thought to share cortical processing mechanisms. Music making is a multimodal and multimedia activity, and so we might expect it to have general effects on cognitive activity. However, the burden of proof will rest on well-designed scientific studies to demonstrate this. It cannot be accepted as an article of faith. Rauscher's study highlights the important need to examine the systematic relationship between the type of music program instituted and the type of cognitive results obtained.

PEBM Can Have Negative Effects in Addition to Positive Ones

General Considerations. Related to the duration of PEBM's effects on people is the *quality* of these effects. Unquestionably the dominant paradigm in discussions of the clinical and educational uses of music is that music is something good for individuals and societies. This is an ancient idea. Since at least the time of Plato, music has been considered an essential part of education, not least of moral education, which has been linked most strongly to the building of a virtuous character. Good music not only comforts the soul but fortifies the moral spirit. And in fact this perspective is alive and well in contemporary clinical and cognitive research, and has received mention throughout this chapter in the credo that "good music is good for you."

However, according to Plato's prescriptions, music is to be rigorously controlled at the social level in order to provide the proper types of scales and rhythms for shaping an individual's character and society as a whole. Bad music is something to be avoided, as it is thought to have all the opposite properties of good music. Bad music leads to moral corruption, posing a threat to society at large (Cole, 1993). It induces immoral thoughts, lascivious behavior, effeminacy in men, social unrest, disruptive actions, and so on. This perspective has served as the basis for musical censorship throughout history (see Korpe, Reitov, and Cloonan, this volume). But to what extent can music be dangerous? What kinds of adverse effects are produced by music?

This book has promoted a "use" perspective as one of its central themes, highlighting the fact that music is very much a mixed bag and music can be used for bad purposes as well as good ones. Sometimes even well-loved music can produce bad effects on people. Consideration must be given to performance style, personal history, performance context, cultural meaning, and the like. What is a good use for one person can simultaneously be a bad use for another. Consider the simple example of a celebration. You throw a party in your apartment to celebrate your birthday and invite all your close friends. For such a celebration to be a success, it is a good idea to play popular music at high volume as this tends to foster a spirit of festivity. However, for the uninvited neighbors on the other side of the apartment wall who are trying to conduct their normal activities, this will be anything but a positive use of music, especially if your party extends into the early hours of morning. In other circumstances, the playing of loud music is not an occasional but unavoidable, celebratory device but rather a socially negative ploy to disturb and annoy. Think of the "boom-boxes" of the 1970s and 1980s. Joseph Martí (1997) has written an interesting account of the "sound[s] and music that people in Barcelona hear but don't want to listen to." Included among the "imposed musical events" that he discusses are the sounds of street musicians, rehearsing music students, music from popular festivals, and music emanating from nearby discos and dance halls. The term "music" cannot be viewed in an abstract sense. Consideration must be given to a host of factors related to its use, meaning, and presentation.

One issue that has entered the political spotlight in recent years is the popular opposition to piped-in music in public places. To many, piped-in music amounts not only to a form of musical pollution that cannot be avoided but to an intolerable bastardization of favorite musical works in the form of Muzak; this "acoustic wallpaper" poisons both music itself and the locales where piped-in music is played. Advocates of a ban on milieu music are quick to point to scientific findings describing just how bad music is for you. According to the British organization Pipedown—bent on banning piped-in music in the United Kingdom—background music "has an adverse effect on human health (it raises the blood pressure and depresses the immune system; it also causes problems for tens of millions of people with tinnitus or other hearing problems)," although absolutely no scientific references are given in support of these claims (see www. pipedown.info). In fact, there is research showing that listening to music can increase levels of the immune molecule IgA, which is associated with *reduced* frequency of illness (McCraty et al. 1996; Charnetski, Brennan, and Harrison, 1998; Hucklebridge et al., 2000). But that will bring little comfort to the 17 percent of the British population who chose piped-in music as "the single thing they most detested about modern life" (cited in www.pipedown.info). For such people, ambient music is unquestionably a situation where "music becomes noise" (Martí, 1997).

Far and away the most controversial claims about the negative effects of music have to do with personal listening and the possible long-term effects that certain musical styles may have on listeners. Like Plato, we cannot judge the moral qualities of music in terms of the sounds alone but must consider the social activities typically associated with a given type of music. There has been concern for the last few decades about the effects of chronic exposure to certain types of music on violent behavior, sexual promiscuity, and suicide. These concerns extend from acoustic considerations (listening to music at high volume can lead to hearing impairment), to content considerations (antisocial messages are promoted in popular songs and their associated videos), to behavioral considerations (hate music is often associated with violent group activities). So the issue is not just the annoying properties of aesthetically displeasing sounds but the association of these sounds with certain messages and behaviors. A well-studied example concerns the effect of musical exposure on the tendency to commit suicide. In 1992, Stack and Gundlach first reported a link between metropolitan suicide rates and airtime devoted to country music, although Maguire and Snipes (1994) and Snipes and Maguire (1995) were not able to replicate these results (but see Stack and Gundlach, 1994, 1995, for replies). A convergence of studies has shown that heavy metal fans are at increased risk for suicide (Stack, Gundlach, and Reeves, 1994; Martin, Clarke, and Pearce, 1994; Lester and Whipple, 1996; Scheel and Westefeld, 1999), while Stack (1998) found that this effect was mediated by the level of religiosity. Looking to yet another musical genre, Stack (2000) found increased suicide acceptability in blues fans. So there is evidence suggesting that long-term exposure to certain genres of music may have adverse consequences on thought and behavior. In contrast to these studies about suicide, very little epidemiological data have been gathered relating musical exposure/preferences to violent behavior, drug use, or sexual promiscuity. Most of the published studies have looked at the effect of watching *music videos* rather than listening to music alone (see Strachan, this volume, for a discussion of music videos).

Clinical Contexts. It is usually assumed that music in clinical contexts has only positive effects on people (sometimes even miraculous ones). However, negative effects are seen as well, although they generally emerge as unintended or unforeseen outcomes of positive uses of music. They are akin to the adverse reactions that people experience in response to medical treatments designed to help them. For example, a lively and happy song used in a music therapy context can elicit bad memories and thus emotional distress in particular patients (Alvin, 1975). For this reason, music therapists make every effort to individualize their selections of music by consulting with patients, family members, and residential care staff. Certain aspects of music may cause discomfort for people. Elderly people in particular have a strong preference for slow and soft music over fast and loud music (Moore, Staum, and Brotons, 1992). Loud music can be especially disturbing for people with hearing problems such as tinnitus. In addition, patients suffering from brain damage can often have a low tolerance for noise, in which case sound levels have to be constantly monitored (Fisher, 1990). One quite adverse and unintentional effect of music is seen in people who experience epileptic seizures in response to music, a condition know as "musical epilepsy" or "musicogenic epilepsy" (Critchley, 1977; Zifkin and Zatorre, 1998; Kaplan, 2003). As Zifkin and Zatorre (1998) describe, "the musical stimulus reported to trigger a musicogenic seizure is often very specific for a given patient, but no common musical characteristics have been isolated for such stimuli as a group" (p. 275). All in all, the adverse effects of music in clinical settings can usually be avoided with suitable individualization of musical selections and presentation practices.

Cognitive Contexts. Background music can be distracting, thereby reducing learning performance. The fact that programs like Superlearning demand such specificity in the choice of music (employing almost exclusively slow and sedate instrumental musical works) suggests that other musics may not only produce no effect on learning but may actually decrease performance, although we have yet to see scientific documentation of any of these effects, positive or negative. Interestingly, music's ability to distract might make it an ideal device to be used *between* study sessions rather than during them. Several study programs suggest using distracters between study bouts, including such activities as juggling. In addition to fostering emotional release, such things may promote the consolidation phase of learning.

One can imagine at least three principal reasons why background music could be distracting and thereby inhibit learning performance. First, the volume of the music might be too high. Volume is a critical concern in all applied uses of music, especially those related to personal improvement. Second, the sound patterns might be too dense or complex for the listener, thus prohibiting the kind of sensory habituation that might foster learning effects. They might be so novel, unusual, or sensitizing as to constantly stimulate attention. Third, the music might be more attractive and rewarding than the lesson to be learned, thus diverting a person's attention from the learning task. Such a fear was expressed by the fathers of the Christian church, who thought that setting prayers to music in the form of songs might be an ideal way to promote the messages of the prayer but, at the same time, realized the tremendous potential of music to take precedence over the verbal messages of the prayer, thereby diminishing their importance. Moderation was thus strongly advised in the use of music in the church (Cole, 1993).

Such moderation has not found its way into animal research. A study by Carlson et al. (1997), describing experiments in which Mozart's music was played either before or during behavioral tests with rhesus monkeys, produced an interesting result. The monkeys not only failed to perform better than controls on a delayed response task but actually performed worse. Whereas the authors of this study argued that "complex music may serve as distraction during tasks requiring attentiveness" (Carlson et al., 1997: 2856), the author of an accompanying commentary suggested that "it is at least conceivable that monkeys have a rudimentary appreciation of some form of music [and therefore that] the monkeys were distracted *because they like Mozart*" (Nordmark, 1997: i, emphasis added). There is little evolutionary plausibility to this. Even Shaw (2000)—the biggest promoter of the use of Mozart for cognitive enhancement—has conceded that langur monkeys and gorillas have little interest in the sounds of Mozart. The important thing to notice, however, is that in a scientific milieu where Mozart is uncritically viewed as having universal effects, a positive Mozart interpretation becomes almost unavoidable. Had the monkeys performed better than controls, this would have been instantly hailed as cross-species evidence for the universality of the Mozart Effect (as the rat studies were; see Rauscher, Robinson, and Jens [1998]). Now that the monkeys were shown to perform worse than controls, the interpretation had to be that the monkeys were so taken by the sounds of Mozart that they were aesthetically distracted from performing the task properly. In either case, Mozart wins, science loses.

A warning to those readers with pet monkeys: don't play Mozart's music in the home. It may make your pet stupid.

PEBM May Capitalize on Common Attentional/Emotional Mechanisms in Different Contexts

This final section looks at the mechanisms by which PEBM brings about its effects, and principally its positive effects. One of the most important questions to address is the specificity of music's effects on clinical condition and learning skill. Does music act by bringing about global changes in cognition, affect, and mood, or does it act in a more specific manner by bringing about changes in particular physiological systems? This question, one of the most important in thinking about the applied uses of music, has scarcely been addressed. As described in the opening chapter of this volume, theories of musical meaning have been traditionally separated into "effect theories" and "semiotic theories," where the former consider music's meaning in terms of the direct emotive effects of musical sound patterns on the listener, and the latter consider it in terms of cultural associations, symbolisms, and interpretations. Suffice it to say that the theories of PEBM discussed in the current chapter fall squarely in the category of effect theories, some of them quite extreme. As such, they place a premium on musical structure over musical symbolism.

If one examines the reasoning behind the Mozart Effect, Superlearning, and the various strands of New Age music healing, one finds many parallel ideas about the mechanisms by which music operates. All see music as a kind of elixir, in a fashion not altogether unlike the mystical theories of thinkers like the sixth-century B.C. Pythagoreans, the sixteenth-century Kabbalists, and the twentieth-century Theosophists. All are rooted in a type of nativist thinking about music based on determinate effects of musical sound on thought, emotion, and behavior, effects that function with almost law-like efficacy. All make reference to rather abstruse ideas about the connection between psychophysics and brain function. All are based on larger-than-life effects of music, whether it be those by which music makes people smarter or those by which music cures terminal illnesses. All ignore social factors such as listening context, personal history, culture, and even species; in other words, all ignore music as a communication system. On the other hand, there is no question that music *can* produce immediate physiological and psychological effects on people, effects that may be both strong and persistent. The question is the extent to which there is a deterministic relationship between a given musical parameter and its effects, independent of cultural mediation and individual experience.

Subjectivity vs. Universality. In reality, issues such as the Mozart Effect or New Age music healing touch upon two different aspects of the psychological experience of music: subjectivity and universality. This distinction is important for any applied use of music, whether it be for learning, therapy, advertising, or dance. A principal tenet of the practice of music therapy is that the music used for a given patient should be tailored to the musical taste and background of that patient. Music therapists spend a great deal of time trying to learn about their patients' personal involvement in music, including their favorite musical works. Thus, individualization is an important concern in the choice of music for therapeutic purposes. It is well known that there are important differences in musical taste and preference that reflect age, gender, social class, ethnicity, religion, and society as a whole (Russell, 1998). Elderly Iranian immigrants living in a nursing home in Stockholm will have different musical preferences and needs than the Swedish teenagers living next door to them. This is not just an acknowledgment of the social construction of musical meaning, but a recognition of the vital role played by familiarity and preference in mediating music's enhancing effects. At some fundamental level, the music used for personal-enhancement purposes must be appealing to the listener. There is no question that at least part of the therapeutic effect of music is to create positive feelings that result from the rewarding properties of listening to appealing music. Music is not supposed to be a bitter pill.

In contrast to this notion of subjectivity is the belief that there are features of musical sound that are universally recognizable and thus universally effective at influencing human behavior. Fast and loud means "excited" (dance a salsa), measured and soft means "calm" or "subdued" (dance a bolero), very slow and very soft means "sad" (don't dance). Despite a great deal of controversy surrounding the topic of musical universals (Nettl, 2000), there do seem to be general cross-cultural trends that characterize the way music is made and used, and there do seem to be features of world musics that have similar interpretive meanings for people of unrelated cultures (Brown, Merker, and Wallin, 2000; Brown, 2000; Brown, in preparation). However, there have been few cross-cultural musicological verifications of these effects. That said, the Mozart Effect is really a brazen statement about the *universality* of Mozart, one that completely ignores interpersonal and cross-cultural variations in the subjective effects of Mozart. Why else would Rauscher, Robinson, and Jens (1998) even bother testing rats?! In reality, the vast majority of human beings have heard little of Mozart's music, and we can assume that a fair proportion of those who have are not particularly fond of it. Personal preferences are important. They highlight not only differences in musical taste among individuals within a given culture but also the gross differences in musical style that occur across cultures. In the end, a balance must be struck between subjectivity and universality in order to provide an adequate explanation of the musical experience.

Even if we accept the plausible idea that there are determinate relationships, at some level, between musical sound patterns and their interpretations/effects (Cooke, 1959; Sloboda, 1991; North and Hargreaves, 1997; Krumhansl, 1997), we have yet to see the kind of analysis of Mozart K. 448 that merits the designation "science." One of the most disturbing aspects of the line research inspired by the Mozart Effect—and the part that makes it most amenable to popular science interpretations—is that Rauscher, Shaw, and others do not seem terribly interested in *dissecting* the Mozart Effect, in determining what feature or features of K. 448 seem to be important for producing the effect. They prefer that K. 448 remain shrouded in the mystery that is Wolfgang Amadeus Mozart: composer, educator, healer, animal tamer.

But dissecting the Mozart Effect would seem to be a more reasonable approach than rushing off to test non-human species. What it is about K. 448 that does the trick? Is it the tempo? The regular rhythm? The timbre of the piano? The D major scale that is used? The harmonic progressions? Some combination thereof? In other words, what is the "active ingredient" in K. 448? Any good educator or researcher would want to know that. But once we knew what the active ingredient in K. 448 was, we would want to know more about how it works. What dose is optimal? How long do you have to receive exposure? Are there side effects? Can it be taken by pregnant women? Are there cross-reactions with other types of music? The problem is if we were to discover what the active ingredient was, the Mozart Effect would cease to have commercial appeal, the kind that sells books and CDs, the kind that makes scientific careers. The handlers of the Mozart Effect have found it necessary to keep K. 448 protected in its pristine, Mozartian state for reasons that have nothing to do with science and everything to do with *marketing* science for popular consumption.

That said, what in fact do we know about the active ingredient in the Mozart Effect? Parsons et al. (in preparation) have made a first attempt at dissecting K. 448, and have discovered that the enhancement seen with Mozart is not produced by music per se but occurs with rhythmic auditory or visual stimuli of diverse kinds, and is primarily localized to operations underlying mental rotation. This provides an important stimulus for further studies whereby pieces of music with rhythmic properties comparable to those of K. 448–most especially those pieces *not* written by Mozart—can be tested for comparison.

The Superlearning program, like the Mozart Effect, is very much based on effect theories of music. For its part, though, Superlearning has been much more open about the parameters of music that supposedly increase memory performance, and they seem to be more or less *opposite* to the fast, regular, rousing sounds thought to enhance spatial-temporal reasoning in the paper-folding-and-cutting task. Superlearning emphasizes slow, quiet, rhythmic pieces, where almost mystical significance is given to a steady tempo of sixty beats per minute. The music used is virtually always instrumental classical music of the Baroque period. Unlike the arousing music used in the Mozart Effect studies, Superlearning takes advantage of low-arousal music, and this difference is probably attributable to the fact that the music in the former studies is played *before* the paper-folding task whereas the music played in the latter memory tests occurs *during* the task. Interestingly, the updated version of Superlearning (Ostrander, Schroeder, and Ostrander, 1994) calls for fast, arousing music to be played *in between* study sessions (but not during them). The common denominator in the musical prescriptions of the Mozart Effect and Superlearning is their use of a regular rhythm (be it fast or slow, arousing or subdued), which is consistent with Parsons et al.'s findings on the paper-folding task. The point of distinction in their musical selections highlights the importance of arousal level in all applied uses of music.

The Importance of Arousal. The moderation of arousal might, in fact, be one of the keys to explaining music's effects. People seem to moderate their arousal level in a negative feedback fashion in accordance with some kind of equilibrium point such that when they are too aroused, they take measures to relax themselves, and when they are too relaxed, they take measures to stimulate themselves. People make frequent use of music in order to do this and select the music in accordance with their needs and social situation. On the other hand, people seem to find moderate increases in arousal as pleasurable and states of either extremely low or extremely high arousal as displeasing. As Anthony Storr (1992: 24) has written in *Music and the Mind*: "Extreme states of arousal are usually felt as painful or unpleasant; but milder degrees of arousal are eagerly sought as life-enhancing." In fact, the relationship between arousal level and reward potential is best described by an inverted-U function, with some level of moderate arousal being optimal, and reward potential falling off as arousal either increases or decreases from that point (Berlyne, 1971). These two classes of observations require reconciliation. On the one hand, people attempt to moderate their arousal about some set point when their arousal level is perturbed from that point, but on the other, they seem to find moderate increases beyond this set point as pleasurable, and seek out *rather than oppose* such increases.

How are we to make sense of this paradox between peoples' tendencies to both moderate arousal and voluntarily perturb it? One way to think about it is in terms of concepts taken from alternative medicine. In that field, a basic distinction is made between *allopathic* and *homeopathic* interventions, where the former refers to treating "like with its contrary," and latter refers to treating "like with like." Allopathic treatment is an attempt to oppose and eliminate a condition by means of interventions that block or reverse the effects. Homeopathic treatment, in contrast, is an attempt to work through a condition by means of direct confrontation or accentuation. Music can be effectively used in both manners (Godwyn, 1987). The properties of the music used will vary in accordance with either allopathic or homeopathic principles depending on the initial condition and desired outcome of the person. In an allopathic intervention, music will be chosen to *oppose* existing arousal levels and restore an equilibrium condition. In a homeopathic intervention, music will be chosen to *match* current arousal levels and accentuate them.

But what determines if an allopathic or homeopathic treatment is most appropriate in a given circumstance? In other words, when do people choose to moderate versus accentuate their arousal levels? Moderation is used in its most straightforward sense as a mood-*controlling* intervention to restore arousal levels to the set point. Accentuation, by contrast, can be used in two very disparate ways: first, it can be used just as in allopathic interventions, as a mood-controlling device to restore baseline arousal levels through a type of "release" mechanism; second, it can be used as a mood-*setting* device to create a socially appropriate environment and emotive state. Let us examine these processes in more detail. Allopathic approaches based on negative feedback regulation probably represent the most common ones during everyday circumstances. Allopathy is an effective guide to the uses of music in most personal listening situations (see Miles, 1997). For example, North and Hargreaves (2000) found that people who had just finished performing vigorous exercise had a significant preference for low-arousal music over high-arousal music, thus suggesting an allopathic or arousal-moderating effect. In general, allopathic interventions are more common when emotional levels are moderate (i.e., modest fluctuations from the equilibrium point).

However, when emotional intensity is very high (i.e., large fluctuations from the equilibrium point), homeopathic interventions are probably the preferred ones. When people feel extreme anger, calming music can be infuriating or at best useless. Likewise, when people experience severe depression, happy and lively music can seem inappropriate and even insulting. To give an example, Summer (1981) suggested that in using music with groups of elderly patients during guided imagery sessions, "the music should match as closely as possible the mood of the group. For example, if the group is generally irritated, a piece such as Mendelssohn's *Agitation, Opus 53, Number 3*, would appropriately echo that feeling in sound" (p. 40). Arousal accentuation can also be a way of creating psychophysiological regulation during particular personal activities. For example, North and Hargreaves (2000) found that people strongly preferred high-arousal to low-arousal music while exercising and the opposite while relaxing.

But in addition to this mood-regulating function, arousal matching in music can be used to create some sense of *fit* to a given social situation. Such a pragmatic goal is seen for all types of social uses of music, be it in ritual, audiovisual or commercial contexts (see Brown, this volume, for a detailed discussion). Situational influences on musical preferences were demonstrated in a study by North and Hargreaves (1996) which showed, for example, that "situations that seem to be arousing in nature (e.g., *jogging with your Walkman on, at an end-of-term party with friends*) seem to be associated with a preference for musical descriptors that should further increase arousal (e.g., *invigorating, exciting/festive, loud*). In contrast, ratings assigned to situations that might be seen as representing a low degree of arousal (e.g., *last thing at night before going to bed*) seem to demonstrate a preference for musical descriptors that would further reduce arousal (e.g., *relaxing/peaceful, lilting, quiet*)" (p. 43, emphases in original). So the homeopathic goal of matching music to arousal level may occur in two very disparate situations: it may occur in a mood-controlling manner when emotional intensity levels are very high, but it may also occur in a mood-setting manner to create a sense of fit to current activities or social situations. This difference can be seen in light of the distinction mentioned earlier between the general desire to moderate arousal levels and the specific desire to produce arousal increases for aesthetic, "life-enhancing" purposes. And in fact, this latter might be one of the principal bases by which aesthetic objects such as music produce their rewarding effects.

Looking further at the aesthetic response to music, we have mentioned Berlyne's inverted-U relationship between arousal and liking, suggesting that there exists an arousal optimum that is maximally rewarding. This would argue that all liked music stimulates arousal, even if it conveys features of peacefulness or relaxation. As Storr (1992) has written: "It is generally agreed that music causes increased *arousal* in those who are interested in it and who therefore listen to it with some degree of concentration.... Lullabies may send children to sleep; but we listen to Chopin's *Berceuse* or the *Wiegenlieder* of Brahms and Schubert with rapt attention" (pp. 24–25, emphasis in original). But more paradoxically, it would suggest that liked music may stimulate arousal even if it produces the psychological *effects* of relaxation. Davis and Thaut (1989) examined the effects of relaxing music on a host of physiological parameters and found that self-reported psychological relaxation was accompanied by physiological arousal responses in autonomic and muscular activity. In other words, relaxing music does not put one into a sleepy state but instead produces a state of "relaxed vigilance" (Alvin, 1975). Brown (1996) has suggested that music's most general response is an "arousing/soothing effect," in other words a coupling between arousing and soothing sensations. This is unquestionably a paradoxical idea. Krumhansl (1997) found that listening to musical excerpts covering a wide range of emotive designations produced a common set of physiological changes—many of which corresponded to the general profile of a state of arousal. Most of the physiological changes were amplified during the course of listening experience. Krumhansl also found that while the musical emotional-states of Sad, Fear, and Happy could be reproducibly differentiated by temporal analysis of dynamic physiological changes, these changes in no way correlated with self-reports of emotions felt by listeners immediately after listening to the musical excerpts, a finding that may mirror the results of Davis and Thaut. So music listening may generally lead to physiological arousal even though the emotions felt and recognized can be variable.

Much more work is needed in this area to disentangle the physiological and psychological effects of music. We suggest that there is a general linkage between arousal level, soothing quality, and rewarding potential that is a feature of the aesthetic response. While the arousing/soothing effect of music can be thought of as a spectrum (with hard-rock music at one end and lullabies at the other), we think it is more appropriate to see it as a simultaneous process occurring during most listening experiences involving liked music.

Are Music's Effects General or Specific? The final question to be addressed is the extent to which music produces effects that are either generalized or specific. In basic terms, we can think about a distinction between a "Music-General" hypothesis and a "Music-Specific" hypothesis. In the first case, music acts by modulating general features such as arousal and attention to enhance a host of psychological processes with little specificity for any one of them, whereas in the second case, music acts by stimulating particular psychological functions and thereby establishing the basis for specific priming and transfer effects. Super-learning is based on a Music-General hypothesis, whereas the Mozart Effect is based on a Music-Specific hypothesis. In reality, most theories of music's mechanisms leave ample room for both kinds of effects, and it would be premature and dogmatic to favor one view over the other. There is emerging evidence (discussed earlier) that musical training in children *can* have carryover effects on non-musical cognitive functions. For example, Rauscher et al.'s (1997) study of schoolchildren found an effect of keyboard training but not group singing on spatial-temporal reasoning, thereby demonstrating the specificity of keyboard playing rather than music *per se* for this reasoning skill. When thinking about transfer effects, we cannot talk about "music" in an abstract sense but must specify the kinds of musical skills and activities involved, as the study by Rauscher et al. demonstrates.

Since this chapter is about *passive* music listening, we would like to skew the discussion in that direction and propose that the Music-General perspective is the most reasonable null hypothesis in explaining music's effects. Unlike music lessons, passive music listening involves no motor activity, no training, and often times little use of language. Instead, it tends to capitalize on attention, emotion, and arousal. As mentioned above, arousal is a key parameter modulated by music listening, and is related to music's rewarding properties in an inverted-U relationship. Given that moderate increases in arousal are perceived as rewarding and that liked music is associated with moderate levels of arousal, then music can be a source of rewarding affective states. What is unclear about this relationship is whether increased arousal is the *source* or *product* of the rewarding emotions associated with music listening. Despite this uncertainty, the final result should be the same: music-induced increases in arousal and positive affect should work cooperatively to bring about improvements in cognitive performance where such improvements are seen.

In order to test some of these ideas, Nantais and Schellenberg (1999) used the typical protocol of the Mozart Effect studies to perform a comparison between listening to Mozart K. 448 and listening to a comparably arousing ten-minute passage from a Stephen King short story. What they found was that both groups of subjects performed comparably on the paper-folding-and-cutting task; that is to say, that both showed an enhancement in performance over subjects who sat in silence for ten minutes. After the experiment, Nantais and Schellenberg asked their subjects which condition they had preferred—the music or the story—and found that subjects who had preferred the Mozart performed significantly better with the Mozart than with the short story, whereas those who preferred the story performed significantly better with the story than with the Mozart. This is evidence that the Mozart Effect is due, at least in large part, to factors related to personal preferences and affinities. It is also important evidence that the Mozart Effect is not dependent on Mozart itself or even music—as Parsons et al. have argued—since comparably arousing conditions, such as listening to a short story, can produce identical effects.

One interpretation of Nantais and Schellenberg's results is that the Mozart Effect can be viewed equally well as a *depression* in performance due to sitting in silence for ten minutes as an enhancement in performance due to listening to arousing music for ten minutes. In order to assess the role of arousal on the paper-folding-and-cutting task, Thompson, Husain, and Schellenberg (2001) performed a comparison between Mozart K. 448 and a piece of music that was expected to reduce psychological (though not necessarily physiological) arousal levels, namely, Albinoni's Adagio for Strings in G minor. The results showed that listening to Albinoni for ten minutes not only failed to produce an enhancement comparable to Mozart listening but actually depressed performance below the baseline level of sitting in silence. After the experiment, subjects were administered two standardized psychological tests—one for mood and one for arousal—and were additionally asked to provide qualitative descriptions of their mood and sense of enjoyment while listening to the two selections of music. What Thompson, Husain, and Schellenberg found was that task performance, arousal, and mood were all strongly correlated: those subjects who listened to the Mozart performed better than controls and showed increases in arousal and positive mood, whereas those subjects who listened to the Albinoni performed worse than controls and showed decreases in arousal and subjective enjoyment. This provides further evidence that the Mozart Effect is largely due to factors related to arousal, preference, and rewarding emotions rather than to a specific effect of music on spatial-temporal reasoning, as Shaw has argued.

There are strong suggestions in the literature that a state of positive affect may have a significant influence on cognitive performance, including creative problem solving, memory recall, and decision making (reviewed in Ashby, Turken, and Isen, 1999). Music might work by creating a rewarding state of relaxed vigilance that favors many types of processes. While music is far from being the only thing that induces such a state, music may take full advantage of creating a state of pleasing arousal. We can imagine a causal chain for the Music-General hypothesis in the following manner:

pleasing music → increased arousal/attention → positive affect → enhancement of cognitive performance

Given that the causal relation between arousal and affect is uncertain, an equally plausible arrangement is:

pleasing music → positive affect → increased arousal/attention → enhancement of cognitive performance

This is in contrast to Shaw's Music-Specific hypothesis, which goes something like:

well-structured music → cortical priming for spatial-temporal reasoning (only) → enhanced spatial-temporal reasoning (only)

With this description in mind, we can summarize much of the research presented in this chapter about personal enhancement background music by stating that whatever learning enhancement, clinical symptom reduction, and individualized recreational listening may entail, they will most likely involve *similar attentional and emotive mechanisms.* Two qualifications must be given to this statement. First, this hypothesis applies only to the passive listening of music. Active musical training unquestionably engages many processes—both general and specific—that might affect non-musical processes as a result of carryover effects due to task similarity. Second, the listening context has a large impact on the effects produced by music. We must not ignore listening context, personality variables, cultural background, and the like in thinking about the mechanisms by which music operates. Individual and cultural variables will have a large influence in moderating both music's positive and negative effects.

Conclusions: Music and Manipulation

This chapter has examined the uses of background music for personal enhancement purposes. Personal enhancement is one of the most positive uses of music at the social level: it is altruistic, cooperative, open, and honest. In addition, much of the music is self-administered (even though the choice of music is strongly influenced by sub-cultural tastes). One theme that has emerged in this chapter is that the universalist claims of, on the one hand, the Mozart Effect and, on the other, New Age music healing, are quite similar. We have devoted much attention to the Mozart Effect in this chapter, and have talked about its unspoken assumptions regarding the universality of the effectiveness of certain types of sound patterns on cognitive function. But the Mozart Effect goes much deeper than a presumed but unverified notion of music's deterministic effects. Elsewhere in this volume, Joseph Moreno recounts a story told by a survivor of the concentration camp Auschwitz: One day a female SS officer requested that a piece by Chopin be played; then, spiritually fortified by the performance, she then went outside and viciously kicked an old woman who had collapsed against the barrack. Certainly Moreno's point was not to characterize the "Chopin Effect" (here, as an inducer of vicious behavior) but to highlight the idea that Western people have a need to believe that the music of the European classical tradition is something noble and good, the kind of thing that works only positively for humankind. In one sense, we are not surprised to learn about the Mozart Effect because we have been brought up with the faith that such a thing must exist. Rauscher and Shaw only scientifically confirm our belief in the power of classical music, our belief that Mozart's music spiritually fortifies us, our belief that great music is a reflection of great societies.

But the "Chopin Effect" and countless other examples like it throughout history are strong evidence that this just can't be so. Music is, at its very root, an emotional manipulator. It can be just as useful for promoting the bad as the good. As the Swedish writer Göran Rosenberg has noted, incidents like the one we are calling the Chopin Effect demonstrate to us "that Bach, Beethoven and Brahms are just as tenuous a link to the nobility of humanity as any three-chord sentimental hit-song" (1995: 124). And in fact the same musical principles that form the foundation of Mozart K. 448 also underlie the construction of propaganda music, battle songs, war songs, hate music, and much more. Music is a moral object, not merely an aesthetic one. We must acknowledge that not only can good music be exploited for bad purposes—such as the charming Strauss waltzes that greeted arriving convoys at Auschwitz—but that much of the music we classify as bad is based on structural-musical principles similar to those of the music we classify as good. Our judgments about the moral value of music must be based as much on the uses to which a given music is put as the sounds that comprise it.

So it is perhaps no surprise that beneath all the hype about the cognitive effects of classical music lurks the Platonic idea that good music is good for people, and that good music (rigorously censored, we should add) makes a society moral. "Good-music-brighter-children" has become the clarion call of those trying to oppose budget cuts for music education in schools. But this laudable goal should not obscure people's judgment of reality. One could easily dismiss the Mozart Effect as a blatant tactic to promote the musical tastes of the dominant class on rationalist grounds. If hard rock music were empirically shown to enhance spatial-temporal reasoning more than does Mozart, would classical-music enthusiasts petition to promote hard-rock music education in schools? The answer seems quite obvious to us.

Herr Mozart is a wonderful salesman for the cause of classical music in both public schools and clinical medicine. But there is something unsettling about this. If the Mozart Effect were simply a code word for the idea that certain types of music can enhance certain types of learning or alleviate certain types of discomfort in certain people under certain conditions, then there would be nothing to worry about. And no reason to buy Mozart CDs! Instead, the Mozart Effect has contributed to the trail of misinformation that accompanied the publication of this finding. "Listening to music for 10 minutes raises your IQ 8 points" is the kind of deceptively inaccurate claim that has routinely made its way into popular books that deal with the topic. What has been systematically ignored is the fact that most claims for cognitive enhancement are based on short-term, passive interventions with adult subjects, having highly short-term effects. The whole notion that music "smartens" or "cures" has little foundation in the scientific literature. In addition, an abundance of historical evidence tells us that the great composers and musicians of the European tradition were among the most sickly, impoverished, and socially unsuccessful people known. Few were towering intellectuals, and few were able to cope with life as social beings. While most were probably as moral as the next person, some, like Wagner, were highly unscrupulous. Gesualdo, the great sixteenth-century innovator in harmony, had his wife and her lover murdered without suffering any legal repercussions.

While the contemporary hysteria over music's supposed cognitive effects has had a tremendous impact on discussions of school curricula, the call for music education in schools is no longer being justified in terms of the cultural importance of music but merely in terms of its efficacy in nurturing non-musical learning skills (e.g., better math scores). But this fails to do justice to theory in the field of music education, and it is perhaps no surprise that a book like Shaw's *Keeping Mozart in Mind* contains not a single reference to the music education literature but instead hundreds to the literatures dealing with theoretical physics and brain physiology. Music education theorists like Zoltan Kodály and Carl Orff clearly saw the promotion of a culture's musical heritage as one of the major goals of music education (Mark, 1996). In fact, Orff—influenced by the theories of his friend Curt Sachs—saw the process of musical development in children as nothing less than the recapitulation of the evolution of music in our species as a whole. Musical education was not seen merely as a means of enhancing nonmusical capacities, nor was it seen purely as a means of training professional musicians. In a basic sense, the programs of Kodály and Orff were designed to develop the musical side of people as an end in and of itself.

Draper and Gayle's (1987) historical analysis of music education textbooks, which analyzes the principal reasons given for teaching music to young children, shows that while certain themes emerged and disappeared as a function of the times, the theme "provides self-expression and creative pleasure" consistently remained the primary justification for teaching music to children over the study period of 1927–1983. The theme "promotes cognitive development and abstract thought" was a minor one up until the late 1970s, but has unquestionably emerged as the dominant theme in our time. However, it is important to keep in mind that this is a thoroughly modern concern, a reflection of a society that is desperately trying to keep pace with ever-accelerating movement along the information superhighway. Shaw (2000) concludes *Keeping Mozart in Mind* in the following utopian fashion: "If I controlled science spending, *I would put 10 billion dollars into a 10-year program to improve our understanding of infant brain development and to learn how to optimize the child's neural hardware for thinking and reasoning*" (p. 319, emphasis in original). Making people smarter seems like a convenient goal for the information age, the kind of popular prescription that characterizes so much public rhetoric in our time. Whether music and music education should be reduced to this level of utility and value is a topic in need of serious discussion. In our opinion, music programs designed to enhance social cooperation skills (Spychiger, 1995, 1999) will turn out to be more valuable to society than those designed to "optimize the child's neural hardware for thinking and reasoning."

The notion that music is some kind of universal elixir that smartens and cures remains one of the most contentious issues in the sociology of music even though it is rarely recognized as such (but see Summer [1996] for a discussion of the ethical aspects of New Age music healing). As the many chapters of this book suggest, the relationship between music and morality is a complex one. Music is a mixed bag. It can be both good and bad for people. We have described in this chapter several types of adverse effects of music on people and society. Some of them, like music's capacity to induce epileptic seizures, are unintentional outcomes of socially positive applications of music. Others, like racist White Power music, are virulent expressions of society's most destructive sentiments. The moral qualities of a work of music are determined not simply by its pitch and rhythmic organization but by its social functions, intended effects, cultural significance, performance context, associated texts, and the like (see also Volgsten, this volume). None of this will ever be conveyed by universalist, cross-species, culture-free theories of musical effects: Rauscher's Mozart-loving rats aren't telling us the whole story. Instead, we have to return to a social view of music that considers how music is used and for what purposes, a theme that dominates much of the present volume. We don't question for one moment the power and glory of music or even the importance of Mozart's own contribution to it, but we do find it very difficult to believe that there is an everyman's (and everyrat's) music, a universal musical elixir. So, yes, we do find much to be alarmed about in this "Mozart Effect." We would feel more comfortable if people like Shaw would simply remind us that every person (and every rat) has his/her Mozart, be that Bob Dylan Mozart, Wolfgang Amadeus Mozart, or Hokwe Zawosa Mozart: something that makes us think more clearly; something that makes us work more effectively; something that eases the pain of living.

Instead, we are bombarded with brain-claims arguing that music is in tune with the inherent dynamics of brain function and therefore that music makes brains into better-tuned thinking machines. Might this become the musical myth of our age? It was once believed that the universe was organized based on musical principles. That idea, long rejected, is now being replaced by the idea that the brain is organized based on musical principles. Whether the music of the *hemi*spheres will turn out to have any more validity than the music of the spheres is yet to be seen. However, we are skeptical.

Notes

1. I Samuel 16:23 reads: "And it happened that whenever the spirit [of melancholy] from God was upon Saul, David would take the harp and play [it] with his hand, and Saul would feel relieved and it would be well with him, and the spirit of melancholy would depart him."
2. MMB Music's catalog description for *The Mozart Effect*—*Music for Children: Tune Your Mind* reads as follows: "Mozart's Violin Concertos may be the most nutritious music ever written for the brain and body. The high frequencies of the violins exercise the ears so that stimulation to the brain is balanced by wonderful harmonies, interesting melodies, and artful rhythms. Listen while doing homework or any time you wish to improve focus and concentration. Use this recording to increase verbal, emotional, and spatial intelligence, improve concentration and memory, and strengthen intuitive thinking skills." All this for under twenty dollars!
3. As these studies tend to focus on the negative effects of music on people, they are discussed in the next section of the chapter.

References

Aldridge, D. (1996). *Music Therapy Research and Practice in Medicine: From Out of the Silence.* London: Jessica Kingsley Publishers.

Alvin, J. (1975). *Music Therapy.* New York: Basic Books.

Ashby, F. G., Turken, A. U., and Isen, A. M. (1999). "A neuropsychological theory of positive affect and its influence on cognition." *Psychological Review* 106: 529–550.

Barlett, D. L. (1996). "Physiological responses to music and sound stimuli." In D. A. Hodges (ed.) *Handbook of Music Psychology.* 2nd ed. (pp. 343–385). San Antonio: IMR Press.

Barwick, J., Valentine, E., West, R., and Wilding, J. (1989). "Relations between reading and musical abilities." *British Journal of Educational Psychology* 59: 253–257.

Berlyne, D. E. (1971). *Aesthetics and Psychobiology.* New York: Appleton-Century-Crofts.

Bilhartz, T. D., Bruhn, R. A., and Olson, J. E. (2000). "The effect of early music training on child cognitive development." *Journal of Applied Developmental Psychology* 20: 615–636.

Bonny, H. L. (1978). *Facilitating Guided Imagery and Music Sessions.* Baltimore: ICM Books.

Brotons, M., Koger, S. M., and Pickett-Cooper, P. (1997). "Music and dementias: A review of literature." *Journal of Music Therapy* 34: 204–245.

Brotons, M. and Pickett-Cooper, P. (1994). "Preferences of Alzheimer's disease patients for music activities: Singing, instruments, dance/movement, games, and composition/improvisation." *Journal of Music Therapy* 31: 220–233.

_____ (1996). "The effect of music therapy intervention on agitation behaviors of Alzheimer disease patients." *Journal of Music Therapy* 33: 2–18.

Brown, S. (1996). "Evolutionary musicology." Working paper of the Institute for Biomusicology.

_____ (2000). "The 'musilanguage' model of music evolution." In N. L. Wallin, B. Merker, and S. Brown (eds.) *The Origins of Music* (pp. 271–300). Cambridge, MA: MIT Press.

_____ (In preparation). "Towards a universal musicology."

Brown, S., Götell, E., and Ekman, S.-L. (2001). "Music-therapeutic caregiving: The necessity of active music-making in clinical care." *The Arts in Psychotherapy* 28: 125–135.

Brown, S., Merker, B., and Wallin, N. (2000). "An introduction to evolutionary musicology." In N. L. Wallin, B. Merker, and S. Brown (eds.) *The Origins of Music* (pp. 3–24). Cambridge, MA: MIT Press.

Bruscia, K. E. (1987). *Improvisational Models of Music Therapy.* Springfield, IL: Charles C. Thomas.

Campbell, D. (1997). *The Mozart Effect*: Tapping the Power of Music to Heal the Body, Strengthen the Mind, and Unlock the Creative Spirit.* New York: Avon Books.

Carlson, S., Rämä, P., Artchakov, D., and Linnankoski, I. (1997). "Effects of music and white noise on working memory performance in monkeys." *NeuroReport* 8: 2853–2856.

Casby, J. A. and Holm, M. B. (1994). "The effect of music on repetitive vocalizations of persons with dementia." *American Journal of Occupational Therapy* 48: 883–889.

Chabris, C. F. (1999). "Prelude or requiem for the 'Mozart effect'?" *Nature* 400: 826–827.

Charnetski, C. J., Brennan, F. X., and Harrison, J. F. (1998). "Effect of music and auditory stimuli on secretory immunoglobulin A (IgA)." *Perceptual and Motor Skills* 87: 1163–1170.

Chlan, L. (1998). "Effectiveness of a music therapy intervention on relaxation and anxiety for patients receiving ventilatory assistance." *Heart and Lung* 27: 169–176.

Clair, A. A. (1996). *Therapeutic Uses of Music with Older Adults.* Baltimore: Health Professions Press.

Clair, A. A. and Ebberts, A. G. (1997). "The effects of music therapy on interactions between family caregivers and their care receivers with late stage dementia." *Journal of Music Therapy* 34: 148–164.

Clark, M. E., Lipe, A. W., and Bilbrey, M. (1998). "Use of music to decrease aggressive behaviors in people with dementia." *Journal of Gerontological Nursing* 24: 10–17.

Cole, B. (1993). *Music and Morals: A Theological Appraisal of the Moral and Psychological Effects of Music.* New York: Alba House.

Cooke, D. (1959). *The Language of Music*. London: Oxford University Press.

Costa-Giomi, E. (1999). "The effects of three years of piano instruction on children's cognitive development." *Journal of Research in Music Education* 47: 198–212.

Crawford, H. J. and Strapp, C. M. (1994). "Effects of vocal and instrumental music on visuospatial and verbal performance as moderated by studying preference and personality." *Personality and Individual Differences* 16: 237–245.

Critchley, M. (1977). "Musical epilepsy: (1) The beginnings." In M. Critchley and R. A. Henson (eds.) *Music and the Brain* (pp. 344–353). London: William Heinemann Medical Books.

Crystal, H. A., Grober, E., and Masur, D. (1989). "Preservation of musical memory in Alzheimer's disease." *Journal of Neurology, Neurosurgery, and Psychiatry* 52: 1415–1416.

Daoussis, L. and McKelvie, S. J. (1986). "Musical preferences and effects of music on a reading comprehension test for extraverts and introverts." *Perceptual and Motor Skills* 62: 283–289.

Davis, W. B., Gfeller, K. E., and Thaut, M. H. (1999). *An Introduction to Music Therapy: Theory and Practice*. 2nd ed. Boston: McGraw-Hill College.

Davis, W. B. and Thaut, M. H. (1989). "The influence of preferred relaxing music on measures of state anxiety, relaxation, and physiological responses." *Journal of Music Therapy* 26: 168–187.

DeNora, T. (2001). "Aesthetic agency and musical practice: New directions in the sociology of music and emotion." In P. N. Juslin and J. A. Sloboda (eds.) *Music and Emotion: Theory and Research* (pp. 161–180). New York: Oxford University Press.

Douglas, S. and Willatts, P. (1994). "The relationship between musical ability and literacy skills." *Journal of Research in Reading* 17: 99–107.

Draper, T. W. and Gayle, C. (1987). "An analysis of historical reasons for teaching music to young children: Is it the same old song?" In J. C. Peery, I. W. Peery, and T. W. Draper (eds.) *Music and Child Development* (pp. 194–205). New York: Springer-Verlag.

Erickson Megel, M., Wagner Houser, C. and Gleaves, L. S. (1998). "Children's responses to immunizations: Lullabies as a distraction." *Issues in Comprehensive Pediatric Nursing* 21: 129–145.

Ezzone, S., Baker, C., Rosselet, R., and Terepka, E. (1998). "Music as an adjunct to antiemetic therapy." *Oncology Nursing Forum* 25: 1551–1556.

Fisher, M. (1990). "Music as therapy." *Nursing Times* 86: 39–41.

Gabrielsson, A. (2001). "Emotions in strong experiences with music." In P. N. Juslin and J. A. Sloboda (eds.) *Music and Emotion: Theory and Research* (pp. 431–449). New York: Oxford University Press.

Gabrielsson, A. and Lindström, S. (1993). "On strong experiences of music." *Jahrbuch der Deutschen Gesellschaft für Musikpsychologie* 10: 118–139.

Gardiner, M. F., Fox, A., Knowles, F., and Jeffrey, D. (1996). "Learning improved by arts training." *Nature* 381: 284.

Gerdner, L. A. (2000). "Effects of individualized versus classical 'relaxation' music on the frequency of agitation in elderly persons with Alzheimer's disease and related disorders." *International Psychogeriatrics* 12: 49–65.

Gerdner, L. A. and Swanson, E. A. (1993). "Effects of individualized music on confused and agitated elderly patients." *Archives of Psychiatric Nursing* 7: 284–291.

Goddaer, J. and Abraham, I. L. (1994). "Effects of relaxing music on agitation during meals among nursing home residents with severe cognitive impairment." *Archives of Psychiatric Nursing* 8: 150–158.

Godwyn, J. (1987). *Harmonies of Heaven and Earth*. Rochester, VT: Inner Traditions International.

Götell, E., Brown, S., and Ekman, S.-L. (2002). "Caregiver singing and background music in dementia care." *Western Journal of Nursing Research* 24: 195–216.

_____ (2003). "The influence of caregiver singing and background music on posture, movement and sensory awareness in dementia care." *International Psychogeriatrics* 15: 411–430.

Graziano, A. B., Peterson, M., and Shaw, G. L. (1999). "Enhanced learning of proportional math through music training and spatial-temporal training." *Neurological Research* 21: 139–152.

Groene II, R. W. (1993). "Effectiveness of music therapy: 1:1 intervention with individuals having senile dementia of the Alzheimer type." *Journal of Music Therapy* 30: 138–157.

Groene II, R., Zapchenk, S., Marble, G. and Kantar, S. (1998). "The effect of therapist and activity characteristics on the purposeful responses of probable Alzheimer's disease participants." *Journal of Music Therapy* 35: 119–136.

Gromko, J. E. and Poorman, A. S. (1998). "The effect of music training on preschoolers' spatial-temporal task performance." *Journal of Research in Music Education* 46: 173–181.

Habermeyer, S. (1999). *Good Music, Brighter Children: Simple and Practical Ideas to Help Transform Your Child's Life Through the Power of Music.* Rocklin, CA: Prima Publishing.

Hallam, S., Price, J., and Katsarou, G. (2002). "The effects of background music on primary school pupils' task performance." *Education Studies* 28: 111–122.

Hanson, N., Gfeller, K., Woodworth, G., Swanson, E. A., and Garand, L. (1996). "A comparison of the effectiveness of differing types and difficulty of music activities in programming for older adults with Alzheimer's disease and related disorders." *Journal of Music Therapy* 33: 93–123.

Hetland, J. (2000). "Listen to Mozart enhances spatial-temporal reasoning: Evidence for the 'Mozart Effect.'" *Journal of Aesthetic Education* 34: 105–148.

Ho, Y. C., Cheung, M. C., and Chan, A. S. (2003). "Music training improves verbal but not visual memory: Cross-sectional and longitudinal explorations in children." *Neuropsychology* 17: 439–450.

Hoeffer, B., Rader, J., McKenzie, D., Lavelle, M., and Stewart, B. (1997). "Reducing aggressive behavior during bathing cognitively impaired nursing home residents." *Journal of Gerontological Nursing* 23: 16–23.

Hucklebridge, F., Lambert, S., Clow, A., Warburton, D. M., Evans, P. D., and Sherwood, N. (2000). "Modulation of secretory immunoglobulin A in saliva: Response to manipulation of mood." *Biological Psychology* 53: 25–35.

Iwanaga, M. and Ito, T. (2002). Disturbance effect of music on processing verbal and spatial memories. *Perceptual and Motor Skills* 94: 1251–1258.

Janelli, L. M. and Kanski, G. W. (1997). "Music intervention with physically restrained patients." *Rehabilitation Nursing* 22: 14–19.

Jones, S. C. and Schumacher, T. G. (1992). "Muzak: On functional music and power." *Critical Studies in Mass Communication* 9: 156–169.

Kaplan, P. W. (2003). "Musicogenic epilepsy and epileptic music: A seizure's song." *Epilepsy and Behavior* 4: 464–473.

Koger, S. M., Chapin, K., and Brotons, M. (1999). "Is music therapy an effective intervention for dementia? A meta-analytic review of literature." *Journal of Music Therapy* 36: 2–15.

Krumhansl, C. L. (1997). "An exploratory study of musical emotions and psychophysiology." *Canadian Journal of Experimental Psychology* 51: 336–352.

Lamb, S. J. and Gregory, A. H. (1993). "The relationship between music and reading in beginning readers." *Educational Psychology* 13: 19–27.

Lester, D. and Whipple, M. (1996). "Music preference, depression, suicidal preoccupation, and personality: Comment on Stack and Gundlach's papers." *Suicide and Life-Threatening Behavior* 26: 68–70.

Lindenmuth, G. F., Patel, M., and Chang, P. K. (1992). "Effects of music on sleep in healthy elderly and subjects with senile dementia of the Alzheimer type." *American Journal of Alzheimer's Care and Related Disorders Research* 2: 13–20.

Lord, T. R. and Garner, J. E. (1993). "Effects of music on Alzheimer's patients." *Perceptual and Motor Skills* 76: 451–455.

MacLeod, B. (1979). "Facing the Muzak." *Popular Music and Society* 7: 18–31.

Maguire, E. R. and Snipes, J. B. (1994). "Reassessing the link between country music and suicide." *Social Forces* 72: 1239–1243.

Mark, M. L. (1996). *Contemporary Music Education.* 3rd ed. New York: Schirmer Books.

Martí, J. (1997). "When music becomes noise: Sound and music that people in Barcelona hear but don't want to listen to." *The World of Music* 39: 9–17.

Martin, G., Clarke, M., and Pearce, C. (1993). "Adolescent suicide: Music preference as an indicator of vulnerability." *Journal of the American Academy of Child and Adolescent Psychiatry* 32: 530–535.

Matthews, R. M., Clair, A. A., and Kosloski, K. (2000). "Brief in-service training in music therapy for activity aides: Increasing engagement of persons with dementia in rhythm activities." *Activities, Adaptation and Aging* 24: 41–49.

McCraty, R., Atkinson, M., Rein, G., and Watkins, A. D. (1996). "Music enhances the effect of positive emotional states on salivary IgA." *Stress Medicine* 12: 167–175.

McKinney, C. H., Antoni, M. H., Kumar, M., Tims, F. C., and McCabe, P. M. (1997). "Effects of guided imagery and music (GIM) therapy on mood and cortisol in healthy adults." *Health Psychology* 16: 390–400.

Miles, E. (1997). *Tune Your Brain: Using Music to Manage Your Mind, Body, and Mood.* New York: Berkley Books.

Moore, R. S., Staum, M. J., and Brotons, M. (1992). "Music preferences of the elderly: Repertoire, vocal ranges, tempos, and accompaniments for singing." *Journal of Music Therapy* 29: 236–252.

Nantais, K. M. and Schellenberg, E. G. (1999). "The Mozart Effect: An artifact of preference." *Psychological Science* 10: 370–373.

National Association for Music Therapy (1980). *A Career in Music Therapy* (brochure). Washington, DC: National Association for Music Therapy.

Nettl, B. (2000). "An ethnomusicologist contemplates universals in musical sound and musical culture." In N. L. Wallin, B. Merker, and S. Brown (eds.) *The Origins of Music* (pp. 463–472). Cambridge, MA: MIT Press.

Nilsson, U., Rawal, N., and Unosson, M. (2003). "A comparison of intra-operative or postoperative exposure to music: A controlled trail of the effects on postoperative pain." *Anaesthesia* 58: 699–703.

Nordmark, J. (1997). "A hairy thumbs up for Mozart." *NeuroReport* 8: i.

Nordoff, P. and Robbins, C. (1977). *Creative Music Therapy.* New York: John Day.

North, A. C. and Hargreaves, D. J. (1996). "Situational influences on reported musical preference." *Psychomusicology* 15: 30–45.

_____ (1997). "Liking, arousal potential, and the emotions expressed by music." *Scandinavian Journal of Psychology* 38: 45–53.

_____ (2000). "Musical preferences during and after relaxation and exercise." *American Journal of Psychology* 113: 43–67.

Olderog Millard, K. A. and Smith, J. M. (1989). "The influence of group singing therapy on the behavior of Alzheimer disease patients." *Journal of Music Therapy* 26: 58–70.

Ostrander, S. and Schroeder, L. (1979). *Superlearning.* London: Sphere Books.

Ostrander, S., Schroeder, L., and Ostrander, N. (1994). *Superlearning 2000.* New York: Delacorte.

Panksepp, J. (1995). "The emotional source of 'chills' induced by music." *Music Perception* 13: 171–207.

Panksepp, J. and Bernatzky, G. (2002). "Emotional sounds and the brain: The neuro-affective foundations of musical appreciation." *Behavioural Processes* 60: 133–155.

Phumdoung, S. and Good, M. (2003). "Music reduces sensation and distress of labor pain." *Pain Management Nursing* 4: 54–61.

Prickett, C. A. and Moore, R. S. (1991). "The use of music to aid memory of Alzheimer's patients." *Journal of Music Therapy* 28: 101–110.

Ragneskog, H. and Kihlgren, M. (1997). "Music and other strategies to improve the care of agitated patients with dementia: Interviews with experienced staff." *Scandinavian Journal of Caring Sciences* 11: 176–182.

Ragneskog, H., Kihlgren, M., Karlsson, I., and Norberg, A. (1996a). "Dinner music for demented patients: Analysis of video-recorded observations." *Clinical Nursing Research* 5: 262–277.

Ragneskog, H., Bråne, G., Karlsson, M., and Kihlgren, M. (1996b). "Influence of dinner music on food intake and symptoms common in dementia." *Scandinavian Journal of Caring Sciences* 10: 11–17.

Rauscher, F. H., Robinson, K. D., and Jens, J. J. (1998). "Improved maze learning through early music exposure in rats." *Neurological Research* 20: 427–432.

Rauscher, F. H. and Shaw, G. L. (1998). "Key components of the Mozart Effect." *Perceptual and Motor Skills* 86: 835–841.

Rauscher, F. H., Shaw, G. L., and Ky, K. N. (1993). "Music and spatial task performance." *Nature* 365: 611.

_____ (1995). "Listening to Mozart enhances spatial-temporal reasoning: Towards a neurophysiological basis." *Neuroscience Letters* 185: 44–47.

Rauscher, F. H., Shaw, G. L., Levine, L. J., Wright, E. L., Dennis, W. R., and Newcomb, R. L. (1997). "Music training causes long-term enhancement of preschool children's spatial-temporal reasoning." *Neurological Research* 19: 2–8.

Rauscher, F. H. and Zupan, M. A. (2000). "Classroom keyboard instruction improves kindergarten children's spatial-temporal performance: A field experiment." *Early Childhood Research Quarterly* 15: 215–228.

Rosenberg, G. (1995). "Theresienstadt: Culture and barbarism." In L. Makarova (ed.) *Theresienstadt: Culture and Barbarism* (pp. 122–124). Stockholm: Carlsson Bokförlag.

Russell, P. A. (1998). "Musical tastes and society." In D. J. Hargreaves and A. C. North (eds.) *The Social Psychology of Music* (pp. 141–158). Oxford: Oxford University Press.

Scheel, K. R. and Westefeld, J. S. (1999). "Heavy metal music and adolescent suicidability: An empirical investigation." *Adolescence* 34: 253–273.

Schellenberg, E. G. (2003). "Does exposure to music have beneficial side effects?" In I. Peretz and R. J. Zatorre (eds.) *The Cognitive Neuroscience of Music* (pp. 430–448). Oxford: Oxford University Press.

Shaw, G. L. (2000). *Keeping Mozart in Mind.* San Diego: Academic Press.

Sherratt, K., Thornton, A., and Hatton, C. (2004). "Music interventions for people with dementia: A review of the literature." *Aging and Mental Health* 8: 3–12.

Sloboda, J. A. (1991). "Music structure and emotional response: Some empirical findings." *Psychology of Music* 19: 110–120.

_____ (1999). "Music: Where cognition and emotion meet." *The Psychologist* 12: 450–455.

Smith-Marchese, K. (1994). "The effects of participatory music on the reality orientation and sociability of Alzheimer's residents in a long-term care setting." *Activities, Adaptation and Aging* 18: 41–55.

Snipes, J. B. and Maguire, E. R. (1995). "Country music, suicide, and spuriousness." *Social Forces* 74: 327–329.

Snyder, M. and Chlan, L. (1999). "Music therapy." *Annual Review of Nursing Research* 17: 3–25.

Spychiger, M. B. (1995). "Rationales for music education: A view from the psychology of emotion." *Journal of Aesthetic Education* 29: 53–63.

_____ (1999). "Can music in school give stimulus to other school subjects?" *MCA Music Forum* August/September: 19–22.

Stack, S. (1998). "Heavy metal, religiosity, and suicide acceptability." *Suicide and Life-Threatening Behavior* 28: 388–394.

_____ (2000). "Blues fans and suicide acceptability." *Death Studies* 24: 223–231.

Stack, S. and Gundlach, J. (1992). "The effect of country music on suicide." *Social Forces* 71: 211–218.

_____ (1994). "Country music and suicide: A reply to Maguire and Snipes." *Social Forces* 72: 1245–1248.

Stack, S. and Gundlach, J. (1995). "Country music and suicide: Individual, indirect, and interaction effects: A reply to Snipes and Maguire." *Social Forces* 74: 331–335.

Stack, S., Gundlach, J., and Reeves, J. L. (1994). "The heavy metal subculture and suicide." *Suicide and Life-Threatening Behavior* 24: 15–23.

Standley, J. M. (1986). "Music research in medical/dental treatment: Meta-analysis and clinical applications." *Journal of Music Therapy* 23: 56–122.

Standley, J. M. and Hughes, J. E. (1997). "Evaluation of an early intervention music curriculum for enhancing prereading/writing skills." *Music Therapy Perspectives* 15: 79–85.

Steele, K. M. (2003). "Do rats show a Mozart effect?" *Music Perception* 21: 251–265.

Steele, K. M., Dalla Bella, S., Peretz, I., Dunlop, T., Dawe, L. A., Humphrey, G. K., Shannon, R. A., Kirby, J. L. Jr., and Olmstead, C. G. (1999). "Prelude or requiem for the 'Mozart effect'?" *Nature* 400: 827.

Storr, A. (1992) *Music and the Mind*. London: HarperCollins.

Summer, L. (1981). "Guided imagery and music with the elderly." *Music Therapy* 1: 39–42.

_____ (1996). *Music: The New Age Elixir*. Amherst, NY: Prometheus Books.

Swartz, K. P., Hantz, E. C., Crummer, G. C., Walton, J. P., and Frisina, R. D. (1989). "Does the melody linger on? Music cognition in Alzheimer's disease." *Seminars in Neurology* 9: 152–158.

Thomas, D. W., Heitman, R. J., and Alexander, T. (1997). "The effects of music on bathing cooperation for residents with dementia." *Journal of Music Therapy* 34: 246–259.

Thompson, W. F., Schellenberg, E. G., and Husain, G. (2001). "Arousal, mood, and the Mozart effect." *Psychological Science* 12: 248–251.

Weber, E. W., Spychiger, M., and Patry, J.-L. (1993). *Musik macht Schule*. Published in abridged English translation as "Music Makes the School." Essen: Die Blaue Eule.

Wigram, T., Nygaard Pedersen, I., and Bonde, L. O. (2002). *A Comprehensive Guide to Music Therapy: Theory, Clinical Practice, Research and Training*. London: Jessica Kingsly Publishers.

Wheeler, B. L. (ed.) (1995). *Music Therapy Research: Quantitative and Qualitative Perspectives*. Phoenixville, PA: Barcelona Publishers.

Wrangsjo, B. and Korlin, D. (1995). "Guided imagery and music as a psychotherapeutic method in psychiatry." *Journal of the Association for Music and Imagery* 4: 79–92.

Zifkin, B. G. and Zatorre, R. J. (1998). "Musicogenic epilepsy." *Advances in Neurology* 75: 273–281.

Zimmerman, L., Nieveen, J., Barnason, S., and Schmaderer, M. (1996). "The effects of music interventions on postoperative pain and sleep in coronary artery bypass graft (CABG) patients." *Scholarly Inquiry in Nursing Practice* 10: 153–170.

PART III AUDIOVISUAL MEDIA

Chapter 6

Music, Moving Images, Semiotics, and the Democratic Right to Know

Philip Tagg

Introduction

Although about a third of all music heard by the average Westerner comes through television, TV music has been virtually neglected as an area of serious inquiry. Since the logistics of TV production tend to demand that music for the medium be (1) cheap and quick to produce or acquire, and (2) efficient and unequivocal in communicating the intended mood and connotations, television constitutes a highly suitable area for the study of musical "meaning" in everyday life. TV music affects its listeners in several ways, one being the nonverbal, nonvisual formation of attitudes, emotional and ideological, toward particular types of people, environments, and actions. Although such communication does not in itself constitute manipulation, its involuntary and unquestioned influences do. Such manipulation can be partially but effectively counteracted by research and by simple improvements in general education.

* * *

Over the last ten years, the first lesson in my course on "Music and the Moving Image" has begun with a well-tried commutation trick. I have attempted to focus attention, as tangibly as possible, on music's ability to bring about radical changes in our interpretation of the images it accompanies. This old trick consists of playing the same thirty-second sequence three times in succession, first with no music, to establish the visual sequence of events, then with the music written expressly for the sequence, and finally with music of contrasting character. It is worth describing this procedure in more detail in order to concretize

---

Notes for this chapter begin on page 183.

music's power in influencing our interpretation of concurrent events. That power is both manifest and elusive, and it is necessary to identify this contradiction if we wish to address the question of manipulation in relation to music and the moving image.

The musical commutation trick I play uses the title sequences from the original series of the British TV soap *Emmerdale Farm* (Hatch, 1972). This footage consists almost entirely of one single, slow, smooth helicopter pan, shot from a few hundred feet in the air looking right and diagonally downwards. This visually legato pan takes the viewer from right to left over rolling green hills, over irregularly and "organically" shaped fields bordered with stone walls (Yorkshire Dales in northern England); it continues, all in the same take, over a small village nestling in the valley, its houses built in gray stone, its churchyard flanked by large, round leafy trees (not winter). In the mid distance of the same helicopter sweep, a small car moves slowly, also left to right, past the village green. A final soft fade, the only edit in the thirty-second sequence, points the viewer towards a gray-stone farmhouse and farmyard set against a green hillside.

The original music for these sequences, Tony Hatch's *Emmerdale Farm* theme (1972), belongs unquestionably to the same basic European tradition of pastoral music as do *Dawn* from Grieg's *Peer Gynt*, or the idyllic herding section in Rossini's *William Tell* overture, or the pastoral symphony in Händel's *Messiah*. Like those pieces, the *Emmerdale Farm* signature is in 6/8 time and performed at a leisurely pace (dotted quarter note = 72 beats per minute). The title music's *legato e cantabile* oboe tune, which moves mainly in quavers, and whose individual phrases span an octave, is, with the exception of short suspensions that are immediately resolved, accompanied by piano arpeggios reminiscent of Beethoven's *Moonlight Sonata*. The circle-of-fifths progressions heard in the piano part are padded out by a full string orchestra playing held chords (Tagg and Clarida, 2003). The pastoral sphere of connotation was recognized from the music on other occasions, when it was played without visual accompaniment to respondents unable to identify the piece. Asked to write down the most likely scenario for this music, almost all of them provided one of the following associations: country(side), British, romantic, melancholy, nostalgia (see chapter 6 of Tagg and Clarida [2003] for more details).

The music of contrasting character that replaces the pastoral music in the third viewing of the same visual sequence is a ten-second phrase, repeated three times and consisting of a quiet, high, held dissonance played by violins, and punctuated by low brass stabs playing a chromatic line with irregular note values in no discernible meter. Such high, held dissonances have been used countless times for effects of extreme mental tension, as in extracts from music for *In Cold Blood* (Jones, 1968), *Eyes Cold from Fear* (Morricone, 1971), *Love is the Devil* (Sakomoto, 1998); similarly articulated chromatic bass lines are used to create a mood of (usually male) physical violence, be it consistent and unstoppable, as with Darth Vader in *Star Wars* (Williams, 1977), or erratic and unpredictable as in the underscore from *The Assassination* (Morricone, 1972), or a combination of both as in the title theme for *The Untouchables* (Morricone, 1987). In fact, the track we used as contrasting underscore was Trevor Duncan's "Transcenics 2," a library music piece described by its producers as "ominous, agitated" and included on a tension and horror music album containing such other titles as "Knife Chase," "Blood Run," "Urge To Kill," "The Hate Drug," "Two Neuroses," "Two Psychoses" and "Psychotic Transients."

Students subjected to this commutation trick for the first time generally exhibit a combination of instant recognition and bemused embarrassment. Indeed, instantly recognizable to anyone belonging to our culture is the fact that the two different music scores create two completely different narratives from the same visual sequence. Narrative One is that of a pastoral idyll. It draws our visual and affective attention to smooth movement over rolling hills past a pretty stone village in the valley. Nature tamed by humans comes across as a source of relaxation, and most viewers/listeners seem to interpret the lack of people on screen as a positive sign of rest and recreation—"far from the madding crowd." Even the car being driven at a leisurely pace past the village green to the idyllic farmhouse cross-faded into the hill at the end of the footage comes across as a pleasant and relaxed activity.

Narrative Two is that of a horror story. This time the slow pace of the helicopter sweep and the absence of movement from people, animals, or other foreground figures all come across as threatening, not as signs of pleasant rural relaxation. Typical comments from seminar discussion about this emptiness in the second narrative are "perhaps a plague has struck or maybe there's been radioactive fallout or an invasion by aliens." The only sign of human life is the slowly moving car whose driver we do not see and whose pace now seems more funereal than leisurely. One student thought that it would most likely be Jack Nicholson, a diabolical grin on his face, driving that old car with unnerving sang-froid toward the farmhouse whose cellar another student assumed to be concealing "a stack of dismembered bodies." "The farmhouse looked nice before," said someone else; "now it looks really grim." "All the colors seem darker," remarked yet another seminar participant.

Most people in our culture are as competent as the students just mentioned at decoding the sounds of the music they hear accompanying moving images: they clearly recognize difference of narrative in the same visual sequences on the sole basis of musical difference. Now, finding out that you share values and interpretations of cultural phenomena in common with others is usually a process that brings a sense of relief, reinforces a sense of community, and provides a sense of sociocultural security. Indeed, belonging to any definable population—a fan club, a trade union, a political party, a nation—relies on such realization of shared values and meanings in comparison to others who share other sets of values, interests, and experiences. However, as recurrently observed in the seminars at which I have presented the *Emmerdale Farm* commutation trick, recognizing that you share the same musical ability as your peers to react in a culturally competent fashion seems to cause embarrassment as well as relief. Why should this type of realization differ from other situations in which individuals belonging to the same basic culture discover shared values and meanings?

One plausible reason for this embarrassment is that the type of cultural ability exhibited in interpreting the two music tracks to the same visuals is something we share with practically anyone living in a world whose cultural fare is largely provided by moving images with their concomitant sound and music. The point is that while extreme metal fans or political party members, for example, may be acutely aware of their shared values because they are constantly reminded of their difference to those of other known groups of people, it is almost impossible to imagine that other members of contemporary Western mass culture would not interpret the two music tracks for *Emmerdale Farm* in more or less the same way as ourselves (see Tagg and Clarida [2003] for a more detailed discussion). As one postgraduate put it: "[T]he differences are so obvious, so you never think about them." In short, first-time recognition of this particular type of cultural competence begs previously unasked questions of cultural specificity and relativity, for example: Which cultures do *not* pattern musical notions of rurality, leisure, fear, and horror as we do? What values are mediated musically in relation to which phenomena in our own Western, globalized mass-media culture? *How* are they mediated? Do we really agree with those values? If unasked, let alone unanswered, these questions are bound to provoke unease and embarrassment rather than a sense of security and familiarity. Put tersely, it is patently obvious that identifying and questioning the apparently obvious can be quite unsettling.

Another plausible reason for the embarrassment usually emerges in discussion following the commutation trick. It relates to the fact that, in our culture at least, most people's everyday expertise in understanding different messages from different sorts of music, as with the *Emmerdale Farm* example, is not matched by commensurate competence in terms of understanding how and why such musical communication actually works. This incongruence between high ability in musical response and low ability in understanding the mechanisms underpinning such response is particularly embarrassing when highlighted in the context of education or research. The problem here is that our tradition of knowledge tends to differentiate so radically between "understanding mechanisms" and "responding emotionally" as distinct modes of experience that they are shunted into separate institutions of learning. This notional and institutional division of musical competences lies at the heart of problems relating to musical manipulation.

As shown in figure 6.1, by *music as knowledge* is meant knowledge *in* rather than *about* music, i.e., knowledge that relates directly to musical discourse and that is both intrinsically musical and culturally specific. This type of musical knowledge can be divided into two sub-types: (1a) "music-making competence," i.e., the various abilities involved in creating, producing, composing,

Figure 6.1 Music as Knowledge, Knowledge about Music, and Musical Manipulation

Name	Explanation	Seats of learning
1. Music *as* knowledge (knowledge *in* music)		
1a. Music-making competence	creating, originating, producing, composing, arranging, performing, etc.	conservatories, colleges of music
1b. Musical interpretative competence	recalling, recognising, distinguishing between musical sounds, as well as between their culturally specific connotations and social functions	-
2. Metamusical knowledge (knowledge *about* music)		
2a. Metamusical discourse	'music theory', identification and naming elements and patterns of musical structure	departments of music(ology), academies of music
2b. Interpretative metamusical discourse	explaining how musical practices relate to culture and society, including approaches from semiotics, acoustics, business studies, psychology, sociology, anthropology, cultural studies.	social science departments, literature and media studies, 'popular music studies'

arranging or performing music; and (1b) "interpretative competence," i.e., the ability to recall, recognize and distinguish between musical sounds, as well as between their culturally specific connotations and social functions. Neither type of musical knowledge just mentioned relies on any explicit verbal denotation and they are both more usually referred to as skills or competences rather than as "knowledge." Knowledge type 1a depends, of course, on competence in knowledge type 1b—but not vice versa. The fact that our culture refers to these immanently musical types of knowledge in terms of "skill" or "competence" further underlines the same sort of epistemological split that makes the statement "carnal knowledge" (as in "Adam knew Eve") seem rather archaic.

Knowledge about music, on the other hand, is by definition metamusical and always entails explicit verbal denotation. However, like "music as knowledge" (type 1), "knowledge about music" (type 2) is culturally specific and can also be divided into two categories. Knowledge type 2a, "musical metadiscourse," is often referred to as "music theory" and entails the ability to identify and name elements and patterns of musical structure, while type 2b, "interpretative metadiscourse," involves explaining how musical practices relate to the culture and society that produce them and which they affect. This fourth aspect of musical knowledge (type 2b or "interpretative metadiscourse") covers everything from music semiotics to acoustics, from business studies to psychology, sociology, anthropology, cultural studies, and so on, and has until now been predominant in popular music studies.[1]

The institutional underpinning of division between these four types of musical knowledge is strong. For example, in tertiary education, the first ([1a], "music-making knowledge") is generally taught in special colleges (i.e., pop and jazz conservatories, performing art schools, and the like), the third ([2a], "music theory") in departments of music or musicology and, to some extent, in pop and jazz conservatories, and the fourth [2b] in practically any humanities or social science department, but less so in conventional musicology and even less in performing arts colleges.

Observant readers will notice that knowledge type 1b is missing from the list just presented. The omission is intentional because the ability to distinguish, without recourse to words, between musical sounds, as well as between their culturally specific connotations and social functions, i.e., the widespread and popular form of musical competence so clearly evidenced in the *Emmerdale Farm* example, is generally absent from institutions of learning.

Of course, assuming everyone to be an expert in area 1b, it is neither surprising nor injurious that there are specialists in areas 1a, 2a, and 2b. The only problem is that while music today is received, heard, and used by most people as one integral unit—often in the same experiential package as words, images, patterns of social behavior and other human phenomena—its teaching is subject to the institutional divisions just mentioned. Such parceling of music studies may once have had a valid purpose, but today it obstructs us from understanding, for example, how we react to the music in an advertisement or a film, or to a pop song, to a classical concert, to background music in pubs, shops or restaurants, or to the underscore in a party political broadcast, or a chat show signature, or quiz show music and so on. There is in other words a clear sense in which our society's conceptual and institutional division of musical competences deprives its citizens of access to aspects of knowledge that could allow them to understand and, by extension, control how and to what extent music communicates values and attitudes that they are expected to assume in relation to the people, actions, locations, cultures, and other phenomena that the music accompanies. Such knowledge is in other words a matter of power.

The popular meaning of "manipulation" also implies a relation of power: "manipulate: to manage (a person, situation, etc.) to one's own advantage, esp. unfairly or unscrupulously" (*Concise Oxford Dictionary*, 1995). There is an obvious ethical aspect to this sense of the word: *manipulation* involves undue and unjust coercion, a power relation in which the stronger party manipulates the weaker. Of course, this does not mean that when composers or musicians try, consciously or unconsciously, to influence our state of mind that they exert undue or unjust coercion on us. On the contrary, music is *supposed* to influence our feelings, our state of mind, our actions, without our having to think about or analyze what is happening to us. No, the type of manipulation we are dealing with is embedded in the power relations of the culture to which we belong: the weight and inertia of hegemonic convention and belief systems represent the stronger party, while those of us who need to discover and formulate alternative values more appropriate to the changing nature of the society we live in can be seen as representing the weaker party in the power relation. In other words, the manipulation under discussion cannot be personalized: it is endemic in the system, and the fact that individual manipulators can rarely be held to account for intentionally undue and unjust coercion makes the power relation all the more insidious and manipulative.[2]

Now, since ignorance constitutes a particular form of human weakness, it could be argued that the *unwanted and unnoticed* modification of our behavior as listeners (our *manipulation*) is more likely to occur if we remain *unaware*, not just of the mere fact that we respond competently to music on an everyday basis but also of how that competence is used to influence our evaluation of phenomena associated with the music, as in the *Emmerdale Farm* example. In other words, the embarrassment caused by conflict between familiarity of musical response and unfamiliarity of reflecting on that response raises the question of manipulation. It is as if the students exposed to the commutation trick feel cheated, as if caught with their epistemological pants down. At the same time we know that music by its very nature affects listeners at non-verbal, non-analytical levels of cognition in terms of gesture, movement, emotion, mood, attitude, etc. It would therefore be absurd to think of musical communication as intrinsically manipulative in the sense of managing listener behavior unfairly or unscrupulously. It is only the *potential* for unfair influence through music that increases if listeners are unaware of music's semiotic mechanisms.

It is, for example, worth remembering that Hollywood Westerns, both films and TV series, used a lot of crude "savage Injun music" stereotypes to underscore the appearance of Native Americans on screen, at least until the release of *A Man Called Horse* in 1970. It is also worth noting that music for male crime-busting heroes changes radically, from the anguished minor-key jazz themes for the equally anguished 1940s *film noir* detective via James Bond, to the brash pop figures of 1970s police dramas. This musical change relates just as closely to change in mainstream notions of the white male in American society as the change from "savage Injun music" to the music of Native Americans themselves marks a change in white mainstream American ideology vis-à-vis other peoples and cultures.[3] In other words, music may be just as important as words or pictures in communicating how we should value, despise, admire, fear, love or hate other people or ourselves, other cultures or our own. The only difference is that while education may help us, if we are lucky, to reflect upon and criticize messages that come to us through visual and verbal media, we are not trained to reflect upon or criticize musically mediated ideology. We are in this sense more open to manipulation through music than through most other channels of mediating meaning.

However, the risk of manipulation can, as we shall see, be reduced through educational reform, particularly in the areas of music and of media studies. One goal would be to incorporate musical knowledge type 1b, i.e., the sort of knowledge evidenced in the *Emmerdale Farm* commutation trick, into our education system; another would be to integrate that type of competence with the other three aspects of musical knowledge mentioned earlier. However, these educational goals will not be attainable without the establishment of viable teaching methods for this new area. Such methods can in their turn only be developed if they are based on the kind of wide-ranging information and well-founded argumentation that comes from serious research. In what follows next it is argued that music for film and TV represents a useful and important field of study for such research.

Researching Film and TV Music

There are three main reasons for advocating the serious study of film and TV music. The first is democratic or demographic; the second and third are both methodological. The first and most obvious reason for advocating the serious study of television music is that a lot of people hear a lot of it. In fact, as recent work has shown, music is present during over one third of all standard terrestrial TV programming between six o'clock and midnight on an average evening in the UK. Bearing in mind (1) that programming for the particular evening chosen for the study included two complete football matches; (2) that satellite TV, not included in the study, features both movie and music video channels; and (3) that the average UK household leaves the television on for two hours every day, then we are liable to hear around one hour of music every day from that source alone.

The second reason for choosing music and the moving image as a serious object of study is methodological. It relates to, and can help overcome, conventional European musicology's problems with the notion of music as more than just *tönend bewegte Formen*.[4]

I have previously argued that European musicology evolved in the nineteenth century as an intellectual strategy to propagate a basically anti-intellectual view of music. One of its main aesthetic spin-offs was the establishment of a sliding scale of excellence ranging from the musically "trivial" and socially utilitarian (low) to the musically "great" and (allegedly) socially transcendent (high) (see chapter 1 of Tagg and Clarida, 2003).

One problem with music studies in Europe for many years was that only the latter (the highbrow) was generally considered worthy of inclusion in higher education, while most of the music heard most of the time by most of the people in most of the world was excluded. Another problem with the notion of "absolute" music was of course, as several scholars of the European classical tradition have noted (e.g., Rosen, 1976; Ford, 1991), that instrumental music in the European classical tradition was clearly rooted in a sense of affect that had taken hundreds of years to evolve in conjunction with, not in spite of, dramatic or verbal narrative.

Film and TV have continued a long-standing tradition of what Austrian film composer Hans Jelinek (1968) termed "invisible music," i.e., multimodal or multimedia situations where the non-verbal sound does not necessarily constitute the primary focus of the presentation and where musical performance is rarely a visual issue. In the historical context of institutionalized music education and research it is unfortunately often still necessary to emphasize that "invisible" music has always been much more common than its "visible" counterpart, to explain that over 99 percent of music heard comes out of loud-speakers or headphones and most of that music is not primarily envisaged as performed on stage.[5]

In the early twentieth century, feature film music developed largely from European classical music's vocabulary of cultural connotations and sense of dramatic narrative. Silent film music collections in the US and elsewhere were produced by conservatory-trained musicians with an intimate knowledge of the European classical repertoire (Rapée, 1924/1974; Becce and Erdmann, 1927)—an overwhelmingly "classical"-"romantic" repertoire, of course (Berg, 1976; Pauli, 1981; Thiel, 1981; Miceli, 1982; Schmidt, 1982; Anderson, 1988). Many prewar sound film scores by such figures as Erich von Korngold and Max Steiner made extensive use of the expressive vocabulary of nineteenth-century opera, ballet and tone poems, and when music was required almost instantly to provide the appropriate mood for newsreels and animated film, library music collections could rely on an existing set of codes that had already been used for several generations in various audiovisual contexts (film, opera, ballet, etc.). Library music, along with most music for American/British film and TV, was of course subsequently influenced by other styles (jazz, rock, avant-garde, folk and "world" music, etc.), which were gradually grafted onto a basically European classical core style. By "library music" or "mood music" is meant those produc-tions, consisting of several hundred phonograms and an extensive catalogue, in which recorded music is classified under headings for use in such audiovisual situations as advertising and low-budget film, TV or video.

Library music's main customers today are in advertising, broadcasting and low-budget program production, not least for TV. The logistics of audiovisual production in capitalism (particularly true if low-budget) tend to demand that appropriate music be easily accessible as well as efficient in communicating the intended mood and connotations. Such considerations favor the tendency to use well-established musical "signifiers" so that the mainstream audience's rec-ognition will be instantaneous and homogeneous when it comes to the musical representation of, for example, male, female, love, threat, urgency, crime and mystery, fin-de-siècle Paris, imperial Japan, warp speed travel, Celtic mists, eighteenth-century high society in Europe, opening, rising, closing, ending, bridging, and so on. Although neither such categories nor the vast majority of musical traits assumed to act as operative "signifiers" for those categories remain constant from one cultural context to another, there is nevertheless sufficient practical coherence within one general cultural context to study the mechanisms of signification in film and TV music in some detail (Tagg, 1982, 1989a, 1993). In short, since film and TV music by definition accompanies images, actions and words, it is impossible to dissociate from whichever par-ticular dramatic purpose it is supposed to serve. This means that musical struc-ture cannot be explained without reference to communicative function. Such symbiosis between musical structure and communication is a prerequisite for any discussion of musical manipulation. It could be argued that this tenet might be salutarily applied to any music either canonized or parading as "absolute."

The third methodological reason for studying the everyday use of music for the moving image relates to the demographic considerations mentioned earlier, for not only is film and TV music heard a lot by a lot of people, not only is it exceedingly difficult to dissociate from the general type of visual and verbal narrative it accompanies: in its popular, everyday areas of use it also represents a well-established set of semiotic functions. Now, if we accept that it makes more sense to base general observations about the mediation of meaning on what appears to be common practice, i.e., on the "rule" within one culture rather than on its exceptions, then music for film and, in particular, TV can be regarded as constituting an important part of that rule. (No one in their right mind would suggest basing a general semiotics of modern colloquial English on Shakespeare sonnets, or on the works of T. S. Eliot. However, several early music semiotics came up with the equivalent, basing quite broad theories of musical signification on works from the European art music classical canon or avant-garde [e.g., Ruwet, 1972; Nattiez, 1976].)

Researching the Everyday Semiotics of Music for Film and TV

In earlier publications (Tagg, 1982, 2000a, 2000b) I have demonstrated various models intended to facilitate the semiotic analysis of music in the modern media. However, despite copious amounts of musical and paramusical evidence, neither the title theme to the 1970s TV series *Kojak* (Goldenberg, 1973, Tagg, 2000b) nor the Abba song *Fernando* (Abba, 1975; Tagg, 2000a) were ever subjected to any analysis of listener responses: interpretations of musical "meaning" were based solely on hermeneutic-semiotic method. In order to confront this method problem head-on I conducted a series of listening tests during the early 1980s.

Ten title themes for film or television, each lasting between thirty and sixty seconds, were selected as test pieces and played to persons attending a lesson or lecture for which I was responsible (for full details of this study, see Tagg and Clarida, 2003). Respondents were told they would hear some pieces of music that had been used in film or on television; they were asked to write down what they thought might be happening on the screen along with each tune. The results were collected and reduced to single concepts. Each concept from each respondent for each tune was interpreted as a "visual-verbal association" (VVA). Thus, for the person who saw the first tune in connection with a girl in a white dress running in slow motion through a meadow in nice summer weather as part of a shampoo advertisement, the separate VVAs were "girl," "white," "dress," "run," "slow motion," "through," "meadow," "summer," "nice weather," "shampoo" and "advert."

It should be noted that this test procedure is one of free induction, meaning that respondents had to actively imagine pictures which they then had to put into words. There is consequently a far greater spread of response for each piece than would have been the case if multiple-choice method had been used. It also means that each answer has greater cultural and symbolic significance, since each response was actively created with the music as sole stimulus and not with the aid of ready made alternatives. Despite the use of free induction, Poisson analysis of the results showed extensive clustering of responses, this suggesting that there was significant consistency of response and a very low degree of random spread over the various tunes. To this extent the results can be considered as reliable indicators of differences in mood and scenario between the ten pieces, as expressed by the respondents in the form of VVAs to solely musical stimuli in the test situation. Since the results and statistics of these reception tests are voluminous, I shall concentrate here on a few general aspects of the material and on certain musical and visual-verbal stereotypes of particular anthropological interest.

Classification of Visual-Verbal Associations (VVAs)

Now, free induction produces a wide spread of individual responses which impedes the use of directly quantitative statistical methods. Therefore, if the results of the reception test are to be presented in a meaningful way, they must be grouped together in semantic fields larger than those represented by each VVA. Thus, even some of the most common VVAs, such as *love* and *romantic* (each of which accounted for only 4 percent each of the total sum of responses given to all ten tunes), are bracketed together into the same general category of Love/Kindness. However, since *love* is a broader concept than *romantic love* and therefore warrants a wider range of different musics than the latter, *love* and *romantic love* falls into two separate subcategories, both contained under the more general Love/Kindness section (Tagg and Clarida, 2003). There is no room here to present the extensive listing of VVA categories, let alone the taxonomic rationale behind its construction. However, three aspects of response classification criteria are relevant to the question of musical meaning and, by extension, to that of musical manipulation.

The first of these criteria consists of widely accepted systematizations of the functions of film music, more specifically those codified by Lissa (1965: 115–256). (For discussion of other film music function classifications, see, for example, Julien [1987: 28–41]; Gorbman [1987]; and Karlin and Wright [1990].) Particularly important symbolic categories influencing our VVA classification are, freely translated, what Lissa calls Emphasizing movement, Stylizing real sounds, Representing location, Representing time (of day, in history), Expressing psychological experiences (of actors), and Providing empathy (for the audience). The second major influence on our system of response categories comes from classifications of musical moods made by compilers of library music (see above) or of anthologies of music for the silent film (Rapée, 1924/1974). We are referring here in particular to such synoptic classifications as Animals,

Bright, Bucolic, Children, Comedy, Danger, Disaster, Eerie, Exotic, Fashion, Foreign, Futuristic, Grandiose, Happy, Heavy Industry, Humor, Impressive, Light Action, Melancholy, Mysterious, National, Nature, Open Air, Panoramic, Pastoral, Period, Prestigious, Religious, Romance, Sad, Scenic, Sea, Serious, Solitude, Space (cosmos), Sport, Suspense, Tenderness, Tension, Tragic, Travel, Water, and Western, rather than to episodic functions like Openings and Closes or to generic classifications like Classical, Rock or Jazz.

The third response classification procedure relies on musical common sense acquired as members of this culture and on some skill in hermeneutics. We had to ask ourselves whether a particular VVA would, according to our experience as musicians, musicologists, composers and listeners, warrant different music to that corresponding to any of the categories we had listed up to that point. For example, we had to split up cities and towns, putting "big city" and "small town" into separate categories because they are different in terms of musical symbolization, although both verbally categorizable as "urban" (see Tagg, 1989b). Particularly striking was, however, the clear musical and para-musical profiles cut by the cultural categories Male and Female.

Male and Female

During the process of category classification sketched above, it became clear that our respondents had seen/heard more male and less female figures in connection with four tunes, more female and less male in connection with four others. For purposes of brevity I will refer to the four title tunes in response to which people associated to far more male than female figures as "the male tunes," and to the four others as "the female tunes." The first two columns in figure 6.2 show, as percentages, occurrences of words or phrases denoting male and female humans in relation to all responses for each of the eight tunes. The third column sums columns one and two to show the percentage of all

Figure 6.2 "Male" and "Female" Responses

Tune	male	female	total	male%	female%
'Male' tunes					
The Virginian	36.9	0.7	38.0	98.2	1.8
Sportsnight	16.3	1.6	18.0	90.9	9.1
Owed to 'g'	22.1	1.4	23.0	94.1	5.9
Miami Vice	11.4	1.0	12.0	70.0	30.0
'Female' tunes					
Dream of Olwen	0.5	12.7	13.0	3.7	96.3
Romeo & Juliet	4.8	17.2	22.0	21.9	78.1
Emmerdale Farm	—	4.1	4.1	—	100
Sayonara	4.1	13.1	17.0	23.8	76.2

responses to each tune were categorizable as either male or female. The last two columns show, as percentages of the sum in column three, the proportion of male to female associations provided by respondents for each tune. Some of the basic musical differences between the male and female tunes are then summarized in figure 6.3.

The basic structural differences between recordings of the eight pieces listed are striking and suggest that men and women, as represented by the music in question, can be interpreted according to the characteristics enumerated in figure 6.4. In order to see whether the music really presented such a stereotypical view of gender, it seemed wise to check what other associations our respondents had made to the eight tunes and to see whether those other responses created any patterns refuting or confirming the somewhat sexist hypotheses of figure 6.3. Figure 6.5 summarizes some of those other responses. In fact, our respondents provided us with some rather drastic statistics:

Figure 6.3 Some Musical Characteristics of "Male" and "Female" Tunes in the Test

musical characteristic	male tunes	female tunes
average tempo	109 bpm	83 bpm
surface rate	c. 400	c. 180
phrase length	short	long
phrasing	staccato	legato
repeated notes	common	none
volume change	none	some
bass line	active and angular	quite static
offbeats and syncopation	common	rare
melodic instrumentation	electric guitar, guitar synth, trumpet, xylophone	strings, flute, mandolin, oboe, piano
accompanimental instrumentation	guitar riffs + strum, brass stabs, sequenced synth, percussion	strings, piano, woodwind, no brass, no percussion
tonal idiom	rock, (diluted) jazz common	classical, romantic common

Note: By "surface rate" is meant the general speed of the quickest notes, i.e., the "diddly-diddly" factor rather than the "boom-thwack" rate of tone beats (= pulse or tempo). Some of *The Virginian's* Fender guitar tune is doubled by oboe, and the major key section is led by lively unison strings.

Figure 6.4 Polarities of Gender Hypothesized from Characteristics Listed in Figure 6.2

male	female	male	female	male	female
fast	slow	sudden	gradual	active	passive
dynamic	static	upwards	downwards	outwards	inwards
hard	soft	jagged	smooth	sharp	rounded
urban	rural	modern	old times	strong	weak

Figure 6.5 Visual-Verbal Associations to "Male" and "Female" Tunes in Order of Responses Frequency

male tunes (1)	male tunes (2)	female tunes (1)	female tunes (2)
cars	bustling†	love*	19th century
chase	crowds	sad*	ending
city	rebellious†	couple	destiny*
young people	threat†	countryside	coast*
action	video†	grass	evening
Western†	sports†	parting*	neutral
fast†	smoke	melancholy*	flowers*
detective†	slums	loneliness	against will... *
riding	about to...	summer	Russian*
USA†	motorways	syrupy	dark*
horses	thriller†	scene	fog
cowboys	comedy†	calm	remembering
excitement	business†	pastoral	small town
tough†	performance†	tragic*	kissing*
modern	disturbing†	sea	always has been*
rock music†	shooting†	sunrise*	two people
stress	disaster†	walking	sitting*
traffic†	robbery†	British	sailing
cruel	space†	beautiful	white*
cigarettes	the future†	emotion	rivers*
social rejects†	living it up†	family	springtime*
driving	war	crying*	gliding
hard†	planning†	old times	lakes
spies	alcohol	after something*	ecstatic
introduction	ladies	sun	secluded* spot*
concrete†	'hot stuff'	meeting	park*
desert	bad	nostalgia	France*
streets	machines	sentimental*	waves*
aeroplanes	chromium	green*	wind
villains	pulse	boats	harmonious*
night	skyscraper	death*	upper class*
heroes	to and fro	caressing*	outdoors

† VVA exclusive to "male tunes"
* VVA exclusive to "female tunes"

- women are twice as likely as men to be associated with the outdoors;
- women are 7 times more likely than men to be related to seasons or the weather;
- women are 12 times more rural than men;
- women are 13 times more likely than men to be associated with quiet and calm;
- women are 25 percent more likely than men to be associated with love;

- women are never asocial and never carry weapons;
- women may often be sad, melancholic or nostalgic;
- men are 8 times more urban than women;
- men are 9 times more likely to be indoors than women;
- men are 20 times more likely than women to be associated with cars;
- men are 35 times more likely to be in clubs and bars than women;
- men are 33 percent more likely than women to be in meetings, parades, etc.;
- men are 50 percent stronger than women;
- men are never seen or heard in isolated or secluded spots;
- men can be asocial and carry weapons: women do not;
- men are never sad.

It should be noted that these figures result from what a few hundred respondents imagined seeing when listening to eight short pieces of title music (for a detailed description of respondent populations and test situations, see Tagg and Clarida, 2003). Of course, the stereotypical character of the tunes is bound to tie in with the respondents' previous experience of equally stereotypical visual narrative accompanying such music. However, it should also be remembered that any such narrative and its archetypal personalities, props, scenarios and patterns of action were elicited by *instrumental music alone* and that it would be highly unlikely for a similar test based on a comparable series of, say, photographs, paintings or short poems to produce the same results.[6] Why? Because tall grass, rolling hills, shampoo, a light breeze, sea swell in the sunshine, long hair, Austria, flowing dresses, slow-motion takes, cornfields, couples caressing, billowing sails (all recurrent associations to *The Dream of Olwen*) are *verbally and visually incongruent* entities: hills just do not resemble hair, nor shampoo a cornfield, nor Austria the sea. However, all those verbally and visually incongruent associations are highly congruent in terms of emotion, touch, gesture, etc., and music is famed for its ability to arrange such aspects of our experience. Thus, *The Dream of Olwen* elicited a set of associations that the respondents heard, either directly or indirectly, as representing emotional, tactile and corporeal qualities of slow, smooth and pleasantly wavy motion in culturally specific sonic terms. Indeed, the results from the whole experiment suggest that music arranges our experience into socially constructed categories that hang together musically, not visually or verbally, even though there may be the occasional synaesthetic overlap.

If these short observations on the specificity of music as a symbolic system are of any use, and if the thin slice of research dealing with musically mediated notions of male and female are not worth less than the paper they are written on, then it might be wise to accord the analysis of musical "texts" a little more space in general education. For, even though there has been no room here to provide more than a small taster of the empirical materials and theoretical issues involved, it should be clear that music—even without words or accompanying visuals—is capable of creating and communicating semantic fields of considerable ideological potential.[7] If this is true, and if, as suggested earlier, we are as listeners unable to understand the basic mechanisms by which music manages to influence our attitudes towards such phenomena as male, female, nature, Native Americans, etc., then we can also be manipulated by music in connection with moving images. The question is how to combat manipulation in this field without depriving music of its intrinsic ability to influence our thoughts, feelings, attitudes and behavior in its intrinsically direct, non-analytical manner.

Combating Manipulation through Education

It is possible to identify four main interrelated areas of education and research that can help combat media manipulation through music: the epistemology of music, semiotic music analysis, musical creativity and ideological critique.

Epistemology of Music

The *Emmerdale Farm* example gave proof of a clear epistemological gap: listeners understood the music by responding in a culturally competent fashion to the different music tracks set to the same visual sequences while exhibiting embarrassment at their inability to grasp the mechanisms underpinning that competence. A similar kind of epistemological contradiction emanates from the reception test results discussed above: while respondents formed clear ideas about the difference between the cultural spheres of male and female merely by listening to particular pieces of instrumental music, the ideology of gender is rarely discussed in its musically mediated guise (but see work by McClary [1991] and Ford [1991] for notable exceptions to this tendency). The capacity to understand music as a cultural influence on our feelings, attitudes and behavior obviously demands that music be studied as such, i.e., that it be reintegrated into our understanding of culture as a whole.

This volume has provided ample evidence that our understanding of music as a means of influencing (and manipulating) our fellow humans can be radically improved when existing disciplinary boundaries are radically transgressed. At the same time the necessity of this volume provides an eloquent indictment of the institutional "normality" in which most of us must work, a normality in which there is little or no dialogue between natural and social scientists, where there are often endemic misunderstandings between social scientists interested in music and musicians or musicologists interested in society, not to mention the mistrust with which musicians often view musicologists or the mutual disdain that seems to exist between the music industry and higher education in music. In this epistemological context of combating manipulation I can do no more than highlight two interrelated questions calling for particularly urgent attention: the defalsification of our own music history and the anthropological relativization of our own music culture(s).

By the defalsification of European music I mean combating such phenomena as its misrepresentation as an ethereal and suprasocial phenomenon. In one of the most rigorous musicological studies of recent years, Martinez (1997), drawing on Blacking (1976), Merriam (1964), Seeger (1977) and others, proposes a holistic approach that, while allowing discussion of intramusical structure and signification, refutes the "autonomous" music aesthetic that still holds sway in many conservatories and departments of musicology. Such musical "absolutism" can still sometimes be found in the company of a kind of cultural reductionism according to which other music cultures are regarded as essentially more rhythmical, more corporeal and more tightly linked to ritual and social functions than our own. Of course, such reductionism is historically false and can easily degenerate into various types of racism.[8] By the relativization of our own music culture I mean therefore the ability to see ourselves, as well as others, anthropologically, and to lay bare the underlying social and ritual functions of our music beneath the veneer of illusions like "autonomous music" or "pure entertainment" (see Tagg, 1989a).

The Semiotic Analysis of Music

Studies of film and TV music's relative coherence of signification within Western culture have been a useful starting point in the development of a widely applicable semiotics of music (Tagg, 1987, 2000a; Tagg and Clarida, 2003). Indeed, over the past ten years, I have found two methodological procedures, developed from earlier research, to be of particular use in classes explicitly aimed at creating awareness, among students of both music and other subjects, of music's specificity as a means of communication.[9] One such trick is called *interobjective comparison*, a procedure involving the use of other music and of musical commutation, not of words or images, as the primary step in relating the music under analysis to anything outside itself (see Tagg, 2000a, 2000b). The other trick employs a simple *sign typology* of music developed not from linguistic or from general cultural theory but from consistent relationships, observed in extensive empirical research, between musical structure and paramusical phenomena (Tagg, 1992).

Depending on the grain of analysis, these simple and well-tried analytical procedures allow for varying degrees of awareness into the mechanisms underpinning musical communication in the modern mass media. Such insight can in its turn make all the difference for listeners between manipulation and affect, for example between, on the one hand, just feeling, thanks to some discordant music, that the Native Americans shown on screen are savage villains and, on the other, knowing that what the music has told you to feel about them may not be what you really feel or think. Such insights allow you to reject other musically mediated ideological stereotypes, for example those described in the reception test summary; they allow you to object when heroic music tells you to side up with a macho slob, or when those romantic strings ask you to get involved in a claustrophobic on-screen relationship. This kind of insight can also be useful when *making* music: it makes it much easier to identify whether you want to go with the standard use of musical structures or to opt for something different, either in terms of musical structure or with regard to how music relates to the images, words or actions it accompanies.

Music Making

The third area of activity in which we can combat musical manipulation is that identified by Swedish poet Göran Sonnevi:

> Musiken
> kan inte bortförklaras.
> Det går inte ens att säga emot,
> annat än
> med helt ny musik.
>
> Music
> cannot be explained away.
> It cannot even be contradicted
> except by
> totally new music.

One way of interpreting this aphorism is to say that the risk of musical manipulation will be least when everyone has equal power over the means of musical statement and production, the same potential to exert musical influence, the same right to "talk back" at music by making music yourself, so to speak. Now, it would be unrealistic to envisage an imminent return to live communal music making, and inadvisable to advocate the introduction of compulsory violin or classical singing lessons. It is, however, hardly unreasonable to consider recent developments in media technology and in some popular music cultures as indicative of a democratic potential in music making. Indeed, sampling, digital sound formats such as MP3, "composer jukebox" sites on the Internet, Web distribution, and so forth, all seem to bode well for the spread rather than demise of musical activity in industrialized society (see also the chapters by Wallis and by Volgsten and Åkerberg, this volume).[10] The ability to make music need no longer be the sole preserve of traditionally trained musicians: it could now in effect be open to all. And yet educational provision of music-making skills has been slow to realize this potential, being still largely restricted to those considered musically talented in conventional terms, with far fewer institutions using the new technologies to provide music-making education for all.[11]

Although some traditionally schooled musicians may regard sampling and prerecorded archetypal soundbytes as a disingenuous means of making music, such phenomena are no more than modern technology's variants of the compositional building block. Just as Mozart or Beethoven relied on existing musical idioms and forms to create their own music, just as Charlie Parker relied on established harmonic formulae to construct his improvisations, just as Frank Zappa relied on pop stereotypes to create his innovative musical and social critiques, and just as Morricone is often able to juxtapose everyday sounds against orchestral texture and both of these against moving images in a highly original fashion, there is similarly no need to believe that anyone using samples or other prerecorded soundbytes as compositional building blocks is automatically innovative or derivative. After all, it is not the novelty of building materials that constitutes innovation but how the building blocks are organized into patterns of simultaneity, sequence, repetition and, variation, i.e., what is constructed or *composed.*

As audiovisual digital technology becomes increasingly affordable, and as the music business (in its traditional sense) becomes an increasingly peripheral part of the global entertainment industry, music will become increasingly treated as just one of several ingredients in film, TV, games, and so on. (For example, by the mid 1990s turnover in the games industry had far outstripped that of the international music business.) It is therefore important that particular educational attention be devoted to both the production and analysis of music for moving images.

Ideological Critique

This essay has attempted to illustrate ways in which manipulation may occur when music accompanies moving images. In so doing, it has been necessary to question the self-evident: "How come our interpretative skills are so obvious but the mechanisms behind those skills so elusive? Or why are those skills not institutionalized as knowledge in the same way as familiarity with verbal forms of statement?" Questioning the apparently obvious entails by definition some ideological critique, since asking "Why are things this way?" implies that a different state of affairs may be preferable. Proposing changes in music research and education constitutes a more obvious form of ideological critique: if nothing was wrong, no change would be necessary. Indeed, the whole concept of manipulation and the formulation of means to avert its risks involves, as stated earlier, an ethical dimension that includes the notion of unjust coercion and the abuse of power.

The most obvious sources of manipulation in today's industrialized world are corporate sectors such as advertising, branding, marketing. (Klein, 2000), but manipulation through advertisements, including their music, is just the tip of the iceberg. Beneath the surface lies a culture of fear in which the mysteries of "free" competition, "free" enterprise, the something-for-nothing syndrome,[12] and the American Dream all serve to maneuver many of us into the belief that it is our own fault that there is something wrong with us as individuals if we do not amass wealth at the expense of others. Now that capitalism has ruled the world unchallenged by any other geopolitical system for over a decade, it has become more difficult to visualize alternatives to this seemingly monolithic culture of greed and fear. Some conservative politicians even claim that society and social classes no longer exist, despite the fact that the gap between rich and poor in the industrialized world, not to mention the great divide separating us from the majority of the world's population in the developing countries, has widened alarmingly over the same decade.

Under such circumstances it is all the more essential to actively seek out alternatives with which to challenge the clearly unjust world system in which we live. More than ever before, critical thinking needs to play a central role in education, and it is in this context that the kind of music-teaching reforms sketched above can play a small but important part. Indeed, twenty years of teaching "Music and the Moving Image" as well as the semiotic analysis of music have amply demonstrated to me that there is broad interest among young people (not just among music students) in understanding how they are affected by music, both duly and unduly (the latter constituting manipulation). This interest, combined with considerable everyday experience of music and moving image acquired ever since TV and the video player were first used to babysit them, has produced a remarkable competence in distinguishing nuances of connotation brought about by nuances of structural difference in the music they hear and of the context in which that music is heard.

In my day-to-day work I try to provide these young people with some sort of anti-manipulative first-aid kit that will, I hope, at least allow them to understand the basic mechanisms of communicating moods and connotations through music. Together with greater knowledge of musical manipulation from the business side, with the democratic potential of new technologies, with a truly anthropological approach to our own culture (not just to other cultures), with a reevaluation and defalsification of our own continent's music history, with new insights into matters audioneurological and bioacoustic, I would hold that the aims and methods mentioned in this chapter can be useful in attempts to diminish the risks of musical manipulation. I also hope that they can empower young people to make their own choices about which emotional messages, musical or not, they want to create, accept or reject. Like it or not, it is they, not we, who will be bombarded by media messages in the unjust and manipulative future that we seem to have prepared for them.

Notes

1. As IASPM founder member Franco Fabbri put it in 1995: "[M]usic and musicians seem to have become some kind of troublesome appendage to popular music studies. Where is music and where are the musicians?" For further details, see Tagg (1998a).

2. These observations apply not least to the realm of music, as will be seen in subsequent sections about music for Native Americans in Hollywood productions, and about "male" and "female" music for the moving image.

3. See Tagg (1998b), which traces a line from the minor-key jazz of Ellington (1940) and Gershwin (1935) via *Harlem Nocturne* (Hagen, 1940), via *A Streetcar Named Desire* (North, 1951) and *The Man with the Golden Arm* (Bernstein, 1955), through the "James Bond Theme" (Norman, 1962) to the demise of bebop cool in *The Pink Panther* (Mancini, 1964) and a Philadelphia Cream Cheese advertisement (Horowitz, 1989). Its replacement by brasher, more rock/pop-oriented detective music is the subject of a vast research project that would need to cover TV work from the early 1970s until the present day.

4. Literally: "sounding forms in motion." In *Vom musalisch-schönen* Hanslick states that "tönend bewegte Formen sind einzig und allein Inhalt und Gegenstand der Musik." See also Schönberg ("the work of Art has its own existence" from *Style and Idea* [1950/1975]) and Stravinsky's objection to the idea of music expressing anything at all. Here we are referring also to the type of "normative" structural analysis criticized by Bengtsson (1973: 226–228) and as exemplified by Schenker and Reti (1961: 31–55).

5. House and early techno music's tendency to draw attention away from musicians and vocalists as foreground figures represents a particularly interesting example of music's "invisibility" in that the pop music industry, previously used to thinking of marketing "acts," was slow to find new ways of gaining control of mass-market mediation for those types of music (see Tagg, 1994).

6. The construction of such association tests, based on a verbal or visual starting point, ought indeed to be a task for future research. The unlikelihood of such tests producing the same results can be attributed to certain axioms about the specificity of musical communication, for example the indexical quality of most musical signs (Karbušicky, 1986) and to the relative rarity of sonic anaphones in most musical discourse (Tagg, 1992).

7. For instance, instead of accounting for "male" and "female" in title music, we could have discussed musical categorization of other broadly connotative concepts, some of which—like "Hero," "Nature," "Time," or "Death" (Tagg, 2000b: 185–200, 1982, 1984, 1989b)—might even be anthropologically basic enough to qualify as archetypes, in the Jungian sense of the word (Jung, 1964; Henderson, 1964).

8. For a critique of the mechanistic inversion of this aesthetic, see Tagg, 1989a.

9. For more information about these courses, visit www.tagg.org/courses.html

10. This democratic potential may be quite restricted from a global viewpoint: not only, in 1999, did less than 10 percent of UK households currently own a computer hooked up to the Internet, the vast majority of people in the developing world were also, at that time, unable to use a computer at all. Moreover, the Internet's democratic potential cannot be assured unless the actual hardware (telecommunications, satellites, etc.) is under popular control.

11. Traditional rock band musicianship also requires specific motor skills for performance on specific instruments. Even singing with a rock or pop ensemble demands specific skills of projection and of microphone technique. Although the roles of composer and performer are less distinct here than in classical music making, there is nevertheless a sense in which performance, with all its concomitant motor skills, is at the forefront of the music-making process. But with skills in MIDI, sampling, synthesizer use, and multitrack home recording, the role of performer is virtually nonexistent, and that of the composer paramount. However, the public "face" of the music as performance, the "act" (to use the music business term) of much current popular music produced in this way (e.g., techno) is *not* the

composer; instead it is the DJ who intervenes as a sort of performer, presenting the music to its fans in its social context.

12. The something-for-nothing syndrome can be illustrated by the omnipresence in advertising of words or exhortations like "win," "save," "n +1 for the price of n," "free with every x you buy," "y percent off," "free z percent extra," "reduced," "sale," "everything must go," "bargain." These consumerist illusions are founded on fallacies of shareholding and finance capitalism, namely, that money, the abstraction of human labour, can increase in value without any investment of anyone's labor or without causing harm to anyone.

References

Abba. (1975). *Fernando*. Epic EPC 4036. Also on *Abba's Greatest Hits* (Epic 69218, 1976), and on *The Hits*. Vol. 2 (Hit Box Vol. 2; Pickwick PWKS 500, 1988).

Anderson, G. B. (1988). *Music for Silent Films 1894–1929*. Washington, DC: Library of Congress.

Becce, G. and Erdmann, H. (eds.) (1927). *Allgemeines Handbuch der Film-Musik (Band I)* unter Mitarbeit von Ludwig Brav. Berlin-Lichterfelde and Leipzig: Schlesingersche Buch- und Musikhandlung Robert Lienau.

Bengtsson, I. (1973). *Musikvetenskap*. Stockholm: Esselte.

Berg, C. M. (1976). *An Investigation of the Motives for and Realization of Music Accompanying the American Silent Film 1896–1927*. Chicago: Arno Press.

Bernstein, E. (1955). "Clark Street: The Top." *The Man with the Golden Arm*. MCA Coral ORL 8280 (1959). Also on *Filmmusik* (1982).

Blacking, J. (1976). *How Musical Is Man?* London: Faber.

Concise Oxford Dictionary (1995). 9th ed. Oxford: Clarendon Press.

Duncan, T. (n.d.) "Knife Chase," "Blood Run," "Urge To Kill," "The Hate Drug," "Two Neuroses," "Two Psychoses," "Transcenics" (1–8), "Psychotic Transients" (1–17), "Hallucinations" (1–5). On *Recorded Music for Film, Radio & TV*. Boosey & Hawkes SBH 2986.

Ellington, D. (1940). "Koko." On *Take the 'A' Train*. Success 2140CD-AAD (1988).

Filmmusik. (1982). Edited by H.-C. Schmidt. Bärenreiter Musicaphon BM 30 SL 5104/05.

Ford, C. (1991). *Così? Sexual Politics in Mozart's Operas*. Manchester: Manchester University Press.

Gershwin, G. (1935). *Porgy and Bess*. New York: Chappell.

Goldenberg, W. (1973). *Kojak* (Main Theme), orchestral arrangement no. 2. Universal City Production No. 40400 (as used in episode "Dark Sunday" rerun by Swedish TV1, 1983).

Gorbman, C. (1987). *Unheard Melodies: Narrative Film Music*. Bloomington, IN: Indiana University Press.

Hagen, E. (1940). *Harlem Nocturne*. New York: Shapiro Bernstein & Co.

Hatch, T. (1972). "Emmerdale Farm" (Yorkshire TV). On Hatch, 1974.

———— (1974). *Tony Hatch and his Orchestra: Hit the Road to Themeland*. Pye NSPL 41029.

Henderson, J. L. (1964). "Ancient myths and modern man." In C. Jung and M.-L. von Franz (eds.) *Man and His Symbols* (pp. 95–156). New York: Dell.

Horowitz, D. (1989). "Petty Larceny" (Philadelphia Cream Cheese Advertisement). Chicago: J. Walter Thompson Agency.

Jelinek, H. (1968). "Musik in film und fernsehen." *Österreichisches Musikzeitschrift* 23: 122–135.

Jones, Q. (1968). "In Cold Blood" (extract). On *Filmmusik* (1982).

Julien J.-R. (1987). "Défense et illustration des fonctions de la musique de film." *Vibrations* 4: 28–41.

Jung, C. G. (1964). "Approaching the unconscious." In C. Jung and M.-L. von Franz (eds.) *Man and His Symbols* (pp. 1–94). New York: Dell.

Karbušicky, V. (1986). *Grundriß der Musikalischen Semantik.* Darmstadt: Wissenschaftliche Buchgesellschaft.

Karlin, F. and Wright, R. (1990). *On the Track: A Guide to Contemporary Film Scoring.* New York: Schirmer.

Klein, N. (2000). *No Logo.* London: HarperCollins.

Lissa, Z. (1965). *Ästhetik der Filmmusik.* Berlin: Henschelverlag.

Mancini, H. (1964). *The Pink Panther.* United Artists UA 3376/6736 (1964).

Martinez, J. L. (1997). *Semiosis in Hindustani Music.* Imatra: Acta Semiotica Fennica V.

McClary, S. (1991). *Feminine Endings: Music, Gender and Sexuality.* Minneapolis: University of Minnesota Press.

Merriam, A. P. (1964). *The Anthropology of Music.* Evanston, IL: Northwestern University Press.

Miceli, S. (1982). *La Musica nel Film: Arte e Artigianato.* Florence: Discanto Edizioni.

Morricone, E. (n.d.). *Time for Suspense.* Vivi Musica Soundtracks.

_____ (1971). "Gli occhi freddi della paura: Titoli." Morricone (n.d.).

_____ (1972). "L'Attentato: Tradimento pubblico." Morricone (n.d.).

_____ (1987). *The Untouchables* (Paramount). CIC Video VHR 2288 (n.d.).

Nattiez, J.-J. (1976). *Fondements d'une Sémiologie de la Musique.* Paris: Ugé.

Norman, M. (1962). "The James Bond Theme." On *Il terzo uomo e altri celebri film* (n.d.). RCA Cinematre NL 43890.

North, A. (1951). "A Streetcar Named Desire (extracts)." *Fifty Years of Film Music.* Warner 3XX 2737 (1973).

Pauli, H. (1981). *Filmmusik: Stummfilm.* Stuttgart: Klett-Cotta.

Post, M. (1974). "The Rockford Files." On *Television's Greatest Hits 70s & 80s* (1990).

_____ (1980a). "Magnum, P.I." On *Television's Greatest Hits 70s & 80s* (1990).

_____ (1980b). "Hill Street Blues." On *Television's Greatest Hits 70s & 80s* (1990).

_____ (1993/1998). "Theme from NYPD Blue." Steve Bochco Productions; recorded off air 1995. Also available on *Les meilleures séries TV du cable et du satellite.* TV Toons TVT Reecords PL 980442-3036492 (1998).

Rapée, E. (1924/1974). *Motion Picture Moods for Pianists and Organists.* New York: Arno Press.

Reti, R. (1961). *The Thematic Process in Music.* London: Faber.

Rosen, C. (1976). *The Classical Style.* London: Faber.

Ruwet, N. (1972). *Langue, Musique, Poésie.* Paris: Editions du Seuil.

Sakomoto, R. (1998). "Fall." On *Love is the Devil.* Asphodel Asph 0987 BBC/BFI.

Schmidt, H.-C. (1982). *Filmmusik für die Sekundar und Studienstufe.* Kassel: Bärenreiter.

Schönberg, A. (1950/1975). *Style and Idea: Selected Writings of Arnold Schoenberg.* Leonard Stein (ed.). London: Faber and Faber.

Scott, T. (1975). "Starsky & Hutch ('Gotcha')." On *Television's Greatest Hits 70s & 80s* (1990).

Seeger, C. (1977). *Studies in Musicology.* Berkeley: University of California Press.

Snow, M. (1993/1996). "Theme from *The X Files.*" Fox TV; recorded off air 1996. Also available on *The Truth and the Light: Music from the X Files.* Warner Brothers 9362-46448-2.

Tagg, P. (1982). *Nature as a Musical Mood Category.* Göteborg: IASPM. Online as www.tagg. org/articles/nature.pdf

_____ (1984). "Understanding 'time sense'." *Skrifter från Musikvetenskapliga Institutionen* (Göteborg) 9: 21–43. (Revised and expanded version online at www.tagg.org/articles/timesens.pdf

_____ (1987). "Musicology and the semiotics of popular music." *Semiotica* 66: 279–298.

_____ (1989a). "Open letter: Black music, Afro-American and European music." *Popular Music* 8: 285–298.

_____ (1989b). "An anthropology of television music?" *Svensk Tidskrift för Musikforskning* 71: 19–42.

_____ (1992). "Towards a sign typology of music." In R. Dalmonte and M. Baroni (eds.) *Secondo convegno europeo di analisi musicale* (pp. 369–378). Trento: Università degli studi di Trento.

_____ (1993). "'Universal' music and the case of death." *Critical Quarterly* 35: 54–85.

_____ (1994). "From refrain to rave: The decline of figure and the rise of ground" *Popular Music* 13: 209–222.

_____ (1998a). "Analysing music in the media: An epistemological mess." In T. Hautamäki and H. Järviluoma (eds.) *Music on Show: Issues of Performance* (pp. 319–329). Tampere: Department of Folk Tradition.

_____ (1998b). "Tritonal crime and music as 'music'." In S. Miceli and L Kokkaliari (eds.) *Norme con ironie: Scritti per i settant' anni di Ennio Morricone* (pp. 273–312). Milano: Suvini Zerboni.

_____ (2000a). *Fernando the Flute* 2nd ed. New York: Mass Media Music Scholars' Press.

_____ (2000b). *Kojak: 50 Seconds of Television Music.* 2nd ed. New York: Mass Media Music Scholars' Press.

Tagg, P. and Clarida, B. (2003). *Ten Little Title Tunes.* New York: Mass Media Music Scholars' Press.

Television's Greatest Hits 70s & 80s. (1990). TeeVee Toons TVT 1300.

Thiel, W. (1981). *Filmmusik in Geschichte und Gegenwart.* Berlin: Henschelverlag.

Williams, J. (1977). *Star Wars.* Twentieth Century 6641679.

Chapter 7

Music Video and Genre
Structure, Context, and Commerce

Rob Strachan

Introduction

Music video has become a central component of the promotional strategies of the global entertainment industries, and the body of writing on the subject has addressed its visual and structural conventions. However, there has been little academic work that addresses how the structural elements of music video are inextricably linked to the ideological constructions and marketing processes of popular music. The multinational music industry's need for genre classification demands that the successful video must be adept at tapping into well-established visual and cultural associations. There is thus a need to locate the musical text within certain contextual parameters in order for the viewer to "place" it within the relevant frame of reference. At the same time, the visual elements must work effectively with the music to produce a synchronous audiovisual text that can be understood (relatively) autonomously. This chapter discusses how the characteristics of music video are related to the structures of musical signification but are also grounded in the visual tropes and social conventions of individual genres. It centers around two video extracts from differing genres: "indie rock" and contemporary dance music. These examples serve to open a discussion on how far these conventions can be viewed as a manipulation that strives to further the ideological and commercial aims of the entertainment industry.

* * *

Music video has become such a crucial component of the promotional strategies of the global entertainment industries that it is impossible for a popular

---

Notes for this chapter are located on page 204.

music act to achieve major commercial success without an accompanying video clip. Correspondingly, the number of videos made and the budgets accorded to them have risen dramatically since the widespread development of music video as a key marketing tool. Although the first promotional videos appeared intermittently as early as the mid 1960s, from the late 1970s onward investment in this media form by record companies rose steadily. Banks (1998) estimated that from the early 1980s to the early 1990s, the average budget for videos rose from around US $15,000 to $80,000. Banks pointed out that by the late 1980s, 97 percent of songs on the Billboard music chart had accompanying videos, and that the US record industry alone was spending upwards of $150 million per year on their production. The late 1990s saw a further increase in video budgets to the point where it became not uncommon for individual videos in genres such as contemporary R&B and Hip-Hop to command production budgets of $1 million (Zimmerman, 1999). Video has also been central to the creation of an increasingly globalized market for popular music. Specialist music-television broadcasters have become powerful players in the global media market, and the proliferation of specialist cable, digital, and satellite channels has vastly widened the platform on which music video is shown. The major music television broadcaster MTV (Music Television), for instance, transmits to 83 countries and territories and reaches nearly 300 million households worldwide (Klein, 2000), while Rupert Murdoch's pan-Asian company Channel V claims to reach around 70 million households in China and India alone.

This promotional importance of video in the context of the recording industry is central to the way music video differs from many of the topics relating to combinations of sound and vision under discussion in this volume. Music video is unlike, for instance, underscore in film or advertising music in television, which are used to stimulate the viewer's attention, reinforce an intended message, or evoke emotion within a visual text. The primary focus of music video (at least on a surface level) is on the musical product itself rather than on the promotion of an unrelated commercial product or the evocation of a particular emotion in the context of a visually led narrative. Videos are essentially a means of selling an act, creating an image, and framing a sound. Mundy (1999) pointed out that "as a cultural form they remain essentially authorless texts. What matters is the presence and the persona of the musical performer" (p. 243). This chapter proposes that the music video is also concerned with placing the musical text within popular cultural reference points that imbue the text with a sense of credibility, and that even if the performers do not actually appear in their promotional video, an "image" is still evoked by the manipulation of very specific signs and sign systems in order to increase the salability of the musical product.

The Study of Music Video

Music videos have been studied using a variety of methodological and disciplinary approaches. Within sociology, cultural studies, psychology, and musicology, the body of academic work on music video has addressed, respectively, video's history, cultural significance, effects on attitudes and behavior, and visual and structural conventions. From the inception of MTV in 1981, work within cultural studies was quick to evaluate the rise of music video and television in the light of critical paradigms of the day. Music television and video were read as symptomatic of postmodern culture through its supposed abandonment of grand narrative structures, its use of intertextuality and pastiche, and its blurring of chronological and historical distinctions (Wolfe, 1983; Lynch, 1984; Kaplan, 1987). From the mid 1980s onward, a dominant argument in this scholarship was that the rise of music video made the "image" more important than the music and hence detracted from the experience of music by tying down the meaning to the visual representation of the video (see Straw, 1993). Subsequent scholars have argued that these assessments of music video did not make full account of how music works within the audiovisual text of the video, and that there has been an over-readiness to see MTV and music videos as indicative of an all-pervading rise of postmodernism in popular culture. Methodologically, these assessments have been criticized for applying constructs borrowed from disciplines such as film theory to what is essentially a music-driven text (Goodwin, 1993; Straw, 1993). As Björnberg (1994) points out, the tropes and techniques common in the music video format are better understood in relation to the syntactical characteristics of popular music. That is, they are traits and editing techniques that attempt to visually echo and reflect the rhythmic, structural, and melodic properties of a given musical text.

A common methodological approach to the study of music video is "content analysis," which attempts to chart the ways in which gender, sexuality, religion and violence are commonly represented in music video. Pardun and McKee (1995) analyzed thirty hours of music television programming, and found that a significant portion of the sample combined sexual and religious imagery within the same video, and that religious images were more likely to occur alongside sexual imagery than without it. Likewise, studies of themes such as the portrayal of women across a number of clips (Vincent, 1989; Seidman, 1992) have demonstrated the recurrent representation of females as either sex objects or passive characters. Conversely, Lewis (1990) outlined preferred (and specifically gendered) modes of address common to music video in the 1980s. He argued that audiences are interpretative and reflexive, and that music video provided a cultural space in which differing gendered identities could be explored, discussed, and played out.

There have also been a number of audience studies that have analyzed viewers' reactions to and understanding of particular music videos. Studies in experimental psychology have attempted to measure the effects of music video on viewers' attitudes and behavior in areas such as sexual permissiveness (Strouse, Buerkel-Rothfuss, and Long, 1995), violence (DuRant et al., 1997), race (Rich et al., 1998), and gender roles (Kalof, 1993, 1999; Sommers-Flanagan, Sommers-Flanagan, and Davis, 1993; Toney and Weaver, 1994). Hansen and Krygowski (1994), for instance, attempted to measure physiological arousal and the priming effects of sexually themed music video in an "ambiguous" television commercial. They found that participants' perceptions were modified after viewing rock videos in that they were more likely to identify sexual connotations in the test commercial. Similarly, Kalof (1999) found that exposure to the depiction of traditional gender roles in popular music videos could affect acceptance of stereotypical and reactionary sexual attitudes. These psychological accounts are interesting in terms of reception, as behavioral and survey research in this field appears to show a stronger connection between "various attitudinal and behavioral indices than any other media genre" (Strouse, Buerkel-Rothfuss, and Long, 1995: 508). Such studies also provide some evidence of the suggestive powers of music video, albeit in very specific research contexts.

Although this type of research is useful in attempting to measure the physiological and behavioral effects of music video, it fails to take into account the nuances of the symbolic fields of reference that make up an audience's understanding of a popular cultural text. Interestingly, the issues of context and familiarity may be linked to what have been traditionally seen as the "problems" of empirical studies of audience reception of media texts, namely, that there are numerous variables that may affect their results: for example, whether the respondents in a study view music videos regularly in their day-to-day lives, whether the artist in the chosen video is popular at the time of the study, or whether there are fans of the artist in the viewing group. Empirical studies of audiences, such as that of Brown and Schulze (1990), have suggested that factors such as race, class, gender, and fandom have a major bearing on an audience's interpretation of music video. In other words, the reading of a media text should always be understood as an active social process affected by a number of variables. Andrew Goodwin (1993) took this reasoning one stage further by arguing that these "variables" are precisely the factors that *should* be taken into consideration, as they constitute an important part of the "content" of a given text. Meaning here is contingent on areas of expertise beyond the traditional limits of the "text," such as familiarity, fandom, and fashion.

Despite the range of scholarly analysis of music video, there has been little academic work demonstrating how the structural and symbolic makeup of music video is inextricably linked to the ideological constructions and marketing processes of popular music. As Leonard (2000: 159) pointed out, "editorial decisions on music videos are geared toward meeting the demands of the marketplace. The fast cutting between scenes is not only an aesthetic choice, but also a financial imperative ensuring that the videos are suitable for television broadcast." While the approaches outlined above are undoubtedly valuable, and while the musicality of individual texts, audience reception, and psychological effects are all aspects of the music video that should always be taken into account, additional questions must be asked: How do the structural elements of music video (and the structural relationship between sound and vision) relate to the context in which popular music is produced and consumed? How do they reflect, uphold, and construct the discourses of popular music? Such questions confront music video's status as a promotional tool for the sale of a commercial product and how this relates to its content. The specific project of this chapter, then, is to examine how the semiotic and structural elements in music videos attempt to reach a particular target market and, importantly, how these elements differ according to *who* is being targeted.

The Generic Visual Tropes of Popular Music Genres

In order to contextualize the music video within its generic and commercial parameters, we need to appreciate that popular music has always been closely linked with images and the visual, and that all contemporary popular music genres have visual histories and well-established visual conventions. Music has undergone mass dissemination through television and film since the beginnings of these forms. For instance, films shown at the 1900 Paris World Fair featured theater actors performing sketches with synchronized gramophone accompaniment (Wallis and Malm, 1988). A number of performance films using this method appeared in the first two decades of the twentieth century, such as those made and shown in Sweden between 1905 and 1914. Technological advancements in sound-on-film in the 1920s, such as Movietone and Vitaphone, were perceived by major American film studios as a way of tapping into popular music markets. Albert Warner of Warner Brothers envisaged that "radio music programs" on film would be a principal use of these new technologies (Chanan, 1995: 72). Indeed, *The Jazz Singer* (1927), the film generally accepted as being the first full-length sound film, acted as a star vehicle for Al Jolson. These early examples are indicative of the way in which the symbiotic relationship between the audio and visual media-industries has been and continues to be crucially important to the marketing and dissemination of popular music and to the construction and maintenance of its discourses. While film and television have capitalized on the popularity of musicians and have traded in (and reinforced) the mythologies surrounding popular music, these depictions have also enhanced the popularity of performers and affected musical and subcultural practice. Rather than being a revolutionary moment that transformed the relationship between sound and vision, the widespread production of the music video and the rise of music television in the 1970s and 1980s should be seen as a natural progression of an existing relationship.

These developments suggest that throughout the history of the mass dissemination of popular music, the visual and the aural have been entwined in popular cultural memory, and that throughout the twentieth century the musical and the visual combined to make an impact on the "meanings" of popular musical texts. To take an obvious example, it is impossible for us to imagine the figure of Elvis Presley without evoking various visual connotations. It is significant that he is as often referred to in a visual sense (as "iconic") as he is in a musical one. While I am not arguing for an overriding primacy of the visual in popular music culture, I am suggesting that many artists and, indeed, musical genres are so bound up by their dissemination through visual media that the visual has become an integral part of the way in which they are marketed and understood. This is not to suggest any great level of homology but, instead, to posit that there are certain socially constructed conventions of dress, performance style, and associated imagery that have evolved over the history of popular music. Capitalizing on this, the project of music video is to tap into these existing connotations and conventions while at the same time maintaining a strong relationship to the structural elements of the musical text it is made to accompany. Any understanding of music's relationship to the visual, moreover, must consider the specifics of generic parameters. Generic conventions do not rely solely on formal elements of particular musical texts but are made up of constructed discourses that have "material consequences for how [the] music is produced, the forms it takes, how it is experienced, and its meanings" (Horner, 1999: 18). Within this conceptualization, the "meaning" of music depends not just on stylistic or structural elements but also on the way that music is represented, discussed, and understood. The visual here is vitally important, as the ideologies of genres are codified not only through musical style and discursive practice but also through visual performance.

Simon Frith (1988) has pointed out that record companies usually use three categories of music video: performance, narrative, and conceptual videos. *Performance videos* are those that show a live performance of an act and attempt to evoke the excitement of attending a live event. *Narrative videos* show a particular sequence of events that is usually resolved at the end of the clip. Cathy Switchenberg (1992: 124) defines *conceptual videos* as those that "underscore and reinforce the primacy of popular music through the rapid movement of visuals." However, one could argue that, in effect, all music videos utilize this technique and that the term refers to any clip that does not fit in the previous two categories; that is, it does not attempt to replicate performance or present a clear narrative. The specificities of differing musical genres are borne out by the fact that certain types of videos are used more commonly to promote artists working in particular musical genres. For instance, country music videos rely heavily on performance or narrative modes whereas dance music videos are generally conceptual.

Videos are also generically distinct in terms of the type of imagery used, the narrative, and the situation. As Leonard (2000) pointed out, the distinctiveness of imagery within particular genres is so encoded, and those conventions so established, that "when one is shown a reel of videos with the sound turned town, one is easily able to identify the musical style and genre from the mode of presentation" (p. 160). Furthermore, these visual elements usually reinforce the ideological constructions and discourses of particular genres. For instance, in the 1980s the format of performance video dominated the promotion of heavy metal music relying on a limited scope of visual imagery. Robert Walser (1993) argued that this prevalence was intended to evoke a sense of collectivity and community among the viewing audience, and that the visual was highly signifi-cant in upholding certain images of dominant masculinity that were central in the genre's discourse. Likewise, Fenster (1993) described how country music vid-eos differentiated themselves through set design, costumes, and the singer's style or performance, and how the narrative conventions tended to echo ideological dimensions of the genre, such as integrity, authenticity, and family values.

These generic parameters, in turn, must be placed in the context of the mar-ketplace. The promotional nature of the music video means that its form and content are inherently linked to the commercial concerns of the international recording industry. This is reflected in the way that videos are produced and in the balance of power of their conception and production. Negus (1992) pointed to the meticulous process that occurs even before a video has been shot. He argued that owing to decisions made by record companies, artists, and marketing staff, and to the employment of professional stylists, this is the point of the most "critical assessment" of an artist's image to date in the music industry process. Banks (1998) pointed out that the balance of power in the production of music videos almost always lies with the record compa-nies, and that directors and producers have limited "bargaining leverage … during contract negotiations, compelling the video clip makers to consent to contracts weighted in favor of the record companies" (p. 295). Furthermore, Banks argued that this situation encourages imitation in visual style and edit-ing techniques because record companies are keen to echo previously "success-ful" combinations of sound and image. Video is therefore by its very nature involved with manipulation, in that its codes and conventions are constructed and indeed necessitated by the need to successfully frame and present a musi-cal product for commercial ends. The questions are: How does this attempted manipulation take place in textual terms? And how successful is it?

The generic elements outlined above are necessary to the process of successful marketing. In order to "place" a musical text correctly, the video has to fit within certain generic parameters. Visual representations generally relate to particular ideologies intrinsic to various musical genres. What I am suggesting is that one of video's primary purposes is the reinforcement of a musical act as authentic within a particular genre or subculture. I should make it clear that I am using "authentic" as a relative term. The discourses of particular genres are grounded in "authenticity paradigms" that tend to be in keeping with widely disseminated and idealized notions of "sincerity," "cultural autonomy," "street cred," or "cool." The record industry is concerned with the manipulation of already-existing and socially constructed signifying systems that connote particular values and therefore have specific appeal in particular markets. The central problem is how we make sense of the process through which this manipulation is attempted. It would be impossible in the limited scope of this chapter to propose a comprehensive theoretical model to explain every aspect of this problem. However, I would suggest that semiotic analysis is useful in any attempt to understand the constituent parts of a text, in order to trace how particular symbolic systems are utilized in the economic process. By way of illustration, I will devote the remainder of this chapter to two video examples that are anchored in very specific cultural reference points. While I am not suggesting that my conclusions apply to all rock and pop videos, I believe that the illustrative nature of these examples highlights the crucial importance of very specific contexts.

"Indie Rock" and the Visual Encoding of Ideology

The first illustration is a video produced for the American "indie rock" group Built to Spill to promote their 1994 release "In the Morning." Formed in Boise, Idaho, Built to Spill recorded material for a variety of independent labels before signing with the major label Warner Brothers Records in the mid 1990s. Because it falls within the generic category of "indie rock,"[1] the group provides a particularly pertinent example of the structural relationship between the aesthetics/discourses of a genre and the industrial processes of popular music.

The term "indie" began to be used in the 1980s to denote music (rather than its previous reference to recording companies) released on post-punk independent labels. This grouping constituted a loose definition bounded by the methods of production and distribution of its record labels, encompassing a wide range of genres, including artists influenced by such diverse source musics as punk, psychedelia, rock, and country. Indeed, Hesmondhalgh (1996) remarked that the generic term "indie" was significant because "no music genre had ever before taken its name for the mode of production of its recordings" (p. 111). Hence, implicit in the very term "indie rock" is a critique of the way in which the music industry operates. The genre has thus been popularly perceived as possessing ethical and ideological dimensions that mark artists and labels as different from the products of major record labels. This polarization implies that these ethical and musical agendas are discrete and (to a certain extent) mutually incompatible. "Indie" here connotes a primacy of artistic expression over profit, immediacy over expensive production, and a democratization of business practice in which artist and consumer are treated fairly and respectfully. While such conceptions can be viewed as ideological constructions in keeping with well-worn discourses occurring throughout the history of rock music,[2] they should be understood as having an important bearing on the way in which musical (and audiovisual) texts in this genre are understood.

Shot on 16 mm film, the video has a low-budget feel and shows members of the band and choreographed dancers in a rural outdoor location intercut with an often bizarre set of images, such as a toy rubber pig, chickens in a barn, and cut-outs of a body builder and a brain floating in a stream. It uses a combination of well-worn directorial and editing techniques common to many pop and rock videos to echo structural elements in the musical text. Images frequently echo lyrical components or the general mood of the song, fast cutting echoes its rhythmic elements, and changes in images are synchronous with the overall structure. In a useful attempt to produce a critical taxonomy of music video techniques for use in semiotic analysis of such texts, Goodwin pointed to the common devices of "illustration," "amplification," and "disjuncture" (1993: 85–97). *Illustration* refers to the basic technique of matching a song lyric with a particular image, be it the video narrative replicating the story of the lyrical narrative or a particular lyric being literally represented. Illustration can also refer to a literal representation of a song lyric that exhorts the listener to feel in a particular way: "sexy," "dancing," and so on. According to Goodwin's model, *amplification* is used to add visual aspects that are not apparent in the lyrics but may add to the narrative of the song. Finally, Goodwin proposes the term *disjuncture* to describe instances where there is no apparent relationship, or where a conscious jarring occurs, between the mood or lyrics of a song and the visual images.

The *In the Morning* video makes clear use of the techniques that Goodwin proposes. For instance, there is extended use of illustration throughout the clip with individual lyrics such as "mind," "body," "ocean," and "eyes" all being represented literally as the lyric is being sung. Goodwin also uses the term "illustration" to refer to editing techniques that may be used to replicate structural elements of the song. A clear example of this in the Built to Spill video is the way in which the instrumental break after the second chorus is strongly singled out through use of slow motion and a concentration on one image (chickens, in this instance). I would like to suggest that in the Built to Spill video, the techniques that Goodwin describes are used not only to echo elements of the musical text but also specifically to reflect and reinforce its particular generic discourse. For instance, the use of disjuncture is generically placed, working to manipulate existing, culturally encoded signs. The clip features a high degree of ironic play, such as the use of wholesome American images, wherein cheerleader-style dancers are dressed in stereotypical "slacker" clothing, and tropes reminiscent of advertising (see the following chapter by Bullerjahn), such as the lead singer and a young woman licking their lips in the style of a Wrigley's chewing gum ad. These elements are disjunctive in that they seem apparently at odds with the lyrical theme and the sonic texture of the musical text. The lyrical theme, concerned with alienation and depression ("Today is flat beneath the weight of the next day in the morning feeling half-right … appearing normal ignoring my condition"), is delivered by a smiling singer and a toy pig puppet accompanied by choreographed dancers. This disjuncture indicates an ironic distance and suggests to the viewers that the video should be understood as tongue-in-cheek. However, the disjuncture also has to be viewed in the light of certain cultural constructs, mainly, that the text falls within the American indie rock genre and that irony is one of the principal characteristics in the wider so-called alternative American culture to which the genre is central. Stephen Duncombe (1997) argued that "[f]or those in the cultural underground, using irony is a pragmatic response to commercial culture that eats up any positive statement, strips it of its original meaning and context, and reproduces and disseminates it as an affirmation of its own message of consumption" (p. 146).

A successful decoding of the text, however, requires a highly developed level of media literacy, and with it, an implied critique of the means and strategies of the media industries. It requires a "codal competence"[3] by which the viewer is familiar not only with the particular musical style of the genre but also with its ideological dimensions. I am proposing that there is at the same time a dominant *and* oppositional understanding of the visual signs at work here. Signified meanings can be split into two distinct sets, related to different generic codes in the text. First are the "normal" signified meanings of the images, that is, their dominant "meanings" in mainstream American culture. Second are the signified meanings that rely on their new setting within an indie rock video. The latter depend on the receivers' ability to decode the first "message" in a successful way and then understand or decode the second, "ironic" meaning. The second set of signified meanings is thus formed through an appraisal and value judgment of the first set. It relies on the understanding of the fact that the text is part of an alternative or underground culture whose texts often imply a critique of mainstream culture. These visual representations are grounded in notions of subcultural identity with its classic ideas of identity formation through opposition to a mainstream, polarizations of "hip" and "square," etc. (Becker, 1963; Thornton, 1995).

Built to Spill can be located within a particular subgenre of indie rock that in the late 1980s came to be referred to as "Lo-Fi" through critical appraisal and marketing. This term is an abbreviation for "low fidelity," alluding to the fact that many recordings in the subgenre use cheap technology and home recording to produce a sound understood as "immediate," "direct," and "homespun." As Daly and Wice (1995) pointed out, the stylistic characteristics and production values of Lo-Fi emerged because many indie rock bands could not afford to use industry-standard instrumentation and recording techniques. However, as the sub-genre gained critical and popular acclaim, "a significant number of bands [began] adhering to its strictures out of choice" (p. 134). Lo-Fi as a subgenre thus inverts the professional industry aesthetic in that it constitutes a purposeful rejection of major label standards, which in turn construct the particularities of its authenticity paradigm. It is a consciously ideological as well as purely musical rejection. The politicized rejection of the independent *bêtes noirs* of "corporatism" and "selling out" is embodied in how the music sounds in terms of vocal characteristics, instrumentation, performance style, and recording techniques. Because they do not adhere to "industry" aesthetics, the sonic attributes of indie rock texts provide a built-in critique of the musical means of production. It is, in a sense, a subculture of negation; it is defined by what it is *not*. These are traits that can also be directly related back to the visual representations in the *In the Morning* video: its irony, its sense of opposition and underground identity, its critique of mainstream values, and its low-budget feel all serve to generically place the text and to construct and reinforce its ideologies.

The music and the visuals are presented in such a way as to appeal to "alternative" sensibilities and hence tap into certain (albeit very specific) markets. The production values of both the music and video set the text up as independent and oppositional even though the group's music was released via the multinational recording company Warner Brothers. What is important here is the *appearance* of independence, cultural autonomy, and authenticity. Indeed, if the *In the Morning* video were a product of what Duncome (1997) calls the "cultural underground"—i.e., if it were a video promoting an independently produced and distributed record—it is extremely unlikely that it would be shown in the programming of mainstream broadcast media. Banks (1998) pointed out that it is highly unusual for a video released by an independently distributed label to be given any level of exposure on music television channels such as MTV. Thus, the *In the Morning* video benefits from the distribution and promotional channels opened up to it by its status as a product of the multinational recording industry while at the same time maintaining its *appearance* as an independent production.

This is not to suggest that the use of certain traits that signify "independence" or alternative sensibilities is merely a reflection or even commodification of a "pure" youth subculture, but rather that there is a multidirectional flow of symbolic information between the mass media, music, and youth cultures. This concurs with Thornton's (1995) argument that there are no authentic, unmediated layers of subcultures that are subsequently exploited by the mass media. On the contrary, media coverage (both positive and negative) is vital to the life of youth subcultures and participates in their "assembly, demarcation and development" (p. 32). Hence, media coverage may be seen to "legitimise and authenticate youth cultures" (p. 32). *In the Morning* was released at a time when there was widespread media coverage of the so-called Generation X and Slacker phenomena, of which alternative and indie rock was seen as a central component.[4] In addition, the video was predated by the international mainstream success of the "alternative rock" or "grunge" group Nirvana, which was consistently marketed and represented with reference to the politics of independent and alternative culture. The widespread media dissemination of the ideologies of "alternative" culture meant that the ideas invoked in the video had wide-ranging currency among media-literate viewers. The idea of the anti-establishment, anti-work, twenty-something youth was already in the public consciousness.

Furthermore, at the time of the record's release, these subcultural sensibilities and attitudes had already been incorporated into the promotional logic of mainstream corporations, and the symbolic attributes of Generation X culture had been used to sell everything from soft drinks to automobiles. Music and its attendant discourses were used to target a particular age group or to fit advertisements into particularly inclusive or exclusive frames of reference. Frank (1995) described an early 1990s advertisement that appeared in American business papers promoting the advertising potential of MTV. The advertisement, which depicted a youth dressed in "grunge" clothes (associated with American alternative rock culture), read: "Buy this 24 year old and get all his friends absolutely free.... He knows a lot. More than just what CDs to buy.... He knows what car to drive and what credit cards to use. And he's no loner. What he eats, his friends eat. What he wears, they wear. What he likes, they like" (p. 112). The *In the Morning* video, then, must be understood within very specific cultural and temporal contexts in that it constitutes a package that trades off the semiotic mediations of contemporaneous trends in fashion, lifestyle, and consumption. It must be recognized not only as an illustrative audiovisual text but as a constituent of wider patterns in youth consumption.

"Leaky Boundaries" and Contemporary Dance Music

To illustrate this point further, I will present a second example, this time from contemporary dance music. Such a comparison is useful as this genre is bounded by a differing set of generic parameters than the first one: hence the visual representations used to promote dance-music acts utilize a different set of symbolic reference points. Much contemporary dance music is purely instrumental (i.e., it contains no lyrics) or uses disembodied snatches of lyrical phrases. Added to this, many dance acts do not primarily use images of themselves to promote particular releases; indeed, they are often referred to in media criticism as "faceless." The dance video, then, is generally more concerned with structural elements and representations of musical components in the musical text than with a depiction of a particular act.

Video within this genre is thus necessarily more tied to conceptual video making than are other musical genres. Many dance videos use purely abstract images cut in time with the music. For instance, from the emergence of dance culture in the late 1980s, there was widespread use in dance-music videos of fractal imagery generated from chaos-theory computer programs or computer animation. During the early 1990s, hundreds of fractal videos were marketed for home video viewing rather than rotation on MTV. Indeed, these domestic video cassettes became so popular that MTV Europe began to produce its own fractal shows during this period. However, these were not arbitrarily selected images, and their often psychedelic nature can be linked to the drug culture that surrounds dance music. In so far as the use of such images can be related to the widespread use of ecstasy in dance clubs, it may be thus seen as an attempt to replicate the drug experience in a domestic setting. In effect, it constitutes a codified imagery that connotes an understanding of the wider culture of dance music. References to drugs or drug-induced imagery serve to contextualize the videos within "underground" scenes or to denote a certain amount of insider knowledge of those cultures.

The discourses of contemporary dance culture, however, are not solely grounded in drug culture. They can also be related to wider trends in popular culture related to lifestyle and consumption, such as fashion, the visual arts, television, and technology. For instance, in a manner similar to the way Generation X became a targeted demographic for marketing, the importance of trends in dance music audiences has been widely utilized in the strategies of large companies. Since the 18–30 age group is regarded by the advertising industry as a taste leader in the general market, trends in consumption not immediately associated with music or youth can often be branded as having a relevance to youth lifestyles. The marketing manager of the Ericsson mobile phone company, for instance, justified an ad campaign for the company that used dance music and culture by explaining that "young people, especially clubbers, dictate trends [which are] followed by the rest of the population" (quoted in Doward, 1999: 6).

In order to illustrate both the conceptual nature of dance videos and the manipulation of symbolic capital associated with contemporary fads and fashions, I will discuss the video used to promote a 1997 release by the French "house music" group Daft Punk entitled *Around the World*, which was directed by Michel Gondry. *Around the World* presents us with a good demonstration of Frith's (1988) argument that the structural elements of video—that is, the movement and editing—act as a "metaphor for sound."

The musical track consists of a constant 4/4 drumbeat at the standard house-music tempo of 120 beats per minute, a sampled funk style bass line, keyboard figures played on an analogue synthesizer, and a sampled disco guitar riff overlaid with a synthesized vocal using a vocoder repeating the song's title. In the video, there are no images of the group members themselves, and the visual element primarily attempts to echo the linear nature of the track and the evolution of its melodic and harmonic structures. The video is a closely choreographed whole in which four groups of four dancers dressed in differing costumes move around a single circular set made up of steps and a dance floor. Each set of dancers is choreographed to "represent" individual musical parts, so the video works as a direct illustration of the structural and musical components of the sound recording. The percussion in the track is represented by dancers dressed as Egyptian mummies, the bass by African-American Hip-Hop dancers, the electronic vocal by dancers dressed as robots, the keyboard line by young women in swimsuits, and the guitars by dancers in skeleton suits. Changes in the musical phrases are, in turn, illustrated by the choreographed movements of individual figures, and rhythmic variations are mirrored by particular dance moves. It is a choreographed visual map of the elements in the recording. Tagg (1997) uses the word "museme" to mean a "minimal unit of musical discourse that is recurrent and meaningful in itself within the framework of any one musical genre" (p. 22). In the Daft Punk video, each museme is choreographed to a particular group of dancers and dance moves in the video in a kinetic representation of musical structure, melody, and harmony. For instance, ascending and descending bass and keyboard patterns are choreographed to their respective dancers moving up and down stairs on the soundstage set.

The Daft Punk video is not solely concerned with echoing the structural and melodic components of the musical text. Indeed, it is significant that this semiotic "cashing in" is done in a very particular way. The visual signifiers used are specifically grounded in popular cultural discourse and amount to more than just a representation that is synchronic with the musical elements. Despite the fact that the band members do not actually appear in the clip, the visual representations in the video are essential in building an image for the artists. They are successful in tapping into cultural references, current trends in music and fashion that frame the musicians within those reference points. The video appropriates kitsch cultural signifiers such as 1950s science fiction and horror, 1970s discotheques, Busby Berkeley musicals, and the then-current vogue for 1980s American Hip-Hop culture. (There is specific intertextuality[5] in that the dance moves and the mode of dress of the Hip-Hop dancers are lifted directly from videos of the 1980s American act Run-DMC.)

These visual elements act to place the record generically and imbue it with a sense of popular cultural currency. The overall look of the video could be described as "future retro," a media term used to describe the appropriation of representations of the future from the popular past, to ironic effect. When the video was made in 1997, the concept of "future retro" had received much media coverage on youth television programming and in style and music magazines. The term was a buzzword used to denote particular trends in fashion, music, and media, such as the appropriation of "futuristic" designs of the 1950s in fashion and design, early synthesizer music of the 1970s in contemporary music genres, and images of 1950s science fiction movies in advertising, music video, and film.

These visual and musical signs can be seen in light of what John Fiske (1989) calls "leaky boundaries": through their intertextuality, popular texts flow into each other and everyday life, and thus can only be understood within this context. Thus, while the action in the Daft Punk video can be admired in terms of its choreography, the visual signifiers that are employed also act as references to other contemporary trends and discourses. The video can be understood as pure spectacle *and* as a link to fads and fashions relating to contemporary uses of past popular culture. Moreover, the specific images used in the *Around the World* clip are intertextual in two ways: first in the sense that they are appropriated from other, *past* sources of popular culture; and second (and crucially) by the reuse of those images in other forms of *current* popular culture. This reuse means that these are already decodable signifiers imbued with fashionable credibility. Successful decoding of these elements implies a very distinct (although limited and relative) form of what Bourdieu (1986) calls "cultural capital" to describe lifestyle choices and cultural hierarchies articulated through the consumption of cultural forms.

This is not, however, merely a mapping of currently fashionable signifiers onto an inappropriate musical text in order to imbue it with popular cultural capital. The visual signs could not operate successfully without a close relationship to the music. Many of the dance moves echo a gesturality that has become culturally encoded in elements of the music. The elements of break-dancing, for example, are synchronic with the bass line, which is reminiscent of the 1970s American disco/funk group Chic, one of the most sampled groups in Hip-Hop music. The visuals thus present a musical "fit" in the sense that the visual appropriation of selected elements of popular culture echo the sonic texture of the record and the group's image. The intertextual nature of the musical text, through its use of antiquated analogue synthesizers and samples from previous musical movements, is echoed in the visual representation of the video. Hence, the text as a whole fits in with generic parameters and taps into subscribed constructions of "hip" in that genre, even as it relates to wider, mediated trends in fashion and popular culture. This analysis moves away from a model of one-way flow of meaning from video producer to viewer. The viewer cannot be considered purely in terms of a manipulated consumer. Instead the visual codes illustrate that the aesthetic choices made by the video director anticipate the successful decoding by a media-literate audience. The video ultimately participates in a visual language that is specifically related to popular music practice and consumption.

Conclusions

While this chapter has concentrated on discrete and culturally specific examples, it has gone some way toward illustrating how generic conventions in popular music video constitute a component part of the discourses of particular genres. Music video's structural and visual conventions uphold and reflect the socially constructed discourses that affect the meaning of a musical text. Furthermore, both the music video's production and reception should be understood in light of the manipulation of these discourses in the context of the commercial nexus where the production and consumption of popular music take place.

Just as the musical text is polysemic (i.e., its "meaning" is not fixed, it can have several signifieds, and its understanding may relate to the listener's a priori knowledge, age, race, gender, etc.), so the video can be seen to work in the same way. The meanings are not fixed but are refracted through the inner speech of the viewer (see Volgsten, this volume, for a possible explanation of how ideological discourses tie on to music). A duality can be highlighted here. On one level, videos such as *Around the World* or *In the Morning* work on a general level; they can be understood simply as audiovisual texts in which the visual images complement the music and the visual editing follows rhythmic and structural elements of the song. On another, they utilize a complex layered set of visual signifiers that serve to contextualize and reflect the music in very specific ways. These reference points can be decoded if one is *au fait* with certain aspects of dance culture or indie rock culture, if one is involved in certain subcultural practices, or even if one subscribes to certain magazines or watches certain television programs. In other words, they are dependent on signification systems based in culturally specific spheres of Anglo-American culture.

These connotations are important in that the music industry is essentially concerned with the trade of symbolic goods and capital. Furthermore, it strives to produce a rapid turnover of its product mitigated through fads and fashions. However, the visual must at the same time retain its relationship to the music in a music video. Indeed, music and image cannot be separated, for if the images from either of the two examples were used in the promotion of, say, a country music recording, something would jar. They would not fit with the extra-musical field of reference that is constantly connoted and evoked in audiovisual representations of that genre. The two examples illustrate the cultural relativity of any understanding of the audiovisual text. Moreover, such an understanding is dependent on socially constructed variables based on the viewer's codal competence and grounding in specific socially constructed sign systems. These examples constitute a manipulation in that they illustrate that through music video the music industry attempts to play on these variables.

These texts ultimately rely on a manipulation of "cool" as a salable commodity, a commodity that is a premium asset in the advertising, music, and media industries. They are an appeal to what Thornton (1995) (following Bourdieu) calls "subcultural capital" to describe the way in which identity and social distinction are formed within group cultures through the assessment of social interactions and symbolic goods against a set of group-specific values. Forms of behavior, style, and consumption are markers of inclusion within taste cultures and are expressive of internalized identities. Subcultural capital, then, "confers status on its owner in the eyes of the relevant beholder" (p. 11). The relationship between producer and consumer in this context belies a variable economy of cultural signs in which subcultural capital is not only a powerful component in the construction of identities but also a highly valuable commodity in the marketplace. More specifically, it is valuable within the youth market that the music industry encourages to part with its money. Furthermore, the music video taps into youth cultures and authenticity paradigms that are global in reach. As Savan (1994: 89) pointed out: "Marketers believe that modern communications have spawned a 'global teen,' kids who have more in common with kids halfway across the earth than they do with other generations in the next room." In this context, music is used to associate products with cosmopolitan attributes and non-localized values (although it may be argued that these are often Western values). This idea is borne out in Gillespie's (1995) ethnographic study of young London Punjabis, in which she formulated a hierarchy of desirable values from her respondents' reactions to certain advertisements. At the top of this hierarchy lie conceptions of "coolness." Likewise, Cannon (1994) used focus groups in North America and Europe to examine common attitudes among geographically dispersed young people. He concluded that "they are joined together not by a common ideology but rather a sophisticated knowledge of consumer products" (p. 2) and that "specialist knowledges are constantly traded among young people and represent a kind of status symbol to those who possess them" (p. 7).

Ultimately, music is a central way in which these conceptions are constructed and disseminated on a global scale. Its nonlinguistic nature has combined with the global predominance of a limited number of multinational record and entertainment conglomerates to render music an unparalleled vehicle for transmitting and denoting these values and associations. Klein (2000) noted that a marketing survey of 27,600 teenagers in forty countries found that the "most significant factor in contributing to the shared tastes of the middle class teenagers it surveyed was TV—in particular MTV, which 85 percent of them watched every day" (p. 120). Ultimately these videos are designed by the entertainment industry to appeal to certain notions of cultural exclusivity in their target audience. To decode particular elements in the text, viewers require a certain degree of codal competence in their respective subsystems of signification; the act of understanding is an act of re-affirmation of one's own subcultural capital.

While this chapter has demonstrated that aesthetic decisions of music video should be seen in the light of economic considerations and that they are informed by a notion of who their audience is, it must be remembered that viewers too are also active in the production of meanings, and indeed that their interpretations cannot always be anticipated by video makers. Hence, the question of manipulation is a difficult one. For a manipulation to take place, the audience must buy into these constructions of authenticity and credibility in order to be "good consumers." Yet, the relationship between consumption and identity is complex and cannot merely be conceptualized as a one-way flow in which audiences passively consume the symbolic reference points and goods they are offered. Indeed, many critics (Frith, 1981; Lewis, 1990) have pointed out that audiences are critical, creative, and reflexive with mass-disseminated cultural goods. At the same time, the fact that the media industries spend billions of dollars every year on marketing and promotion makes it clear that trading in symbolic capital works in an economic sense *and* has an impact on the subjectivity and identity of the individual. Further understanding of the intricacies of this relationship will require much wider empirical research and analysis—analysis which simultaneously takes into account audience reception, semiotics, and the political economy of the media industries.

Notes

1. As Leonard (2000: 289) points out, the generic categories of "indie rock" and "alternative rock" are often used interchangeably. For the purposes of clarity, I will refer to the genre as indie rock throughout this chapter.
2. Critics such as Frith (1981), Laing (1985), and Harron (1988) have pointed out that the art-versus-commerce debate was central to the formation in the late 1960s of a new dominant "folk art" aesthetic of rock in which rock music was understood as possessing a direct emotional capacity that transcended its dissemination through the "commercial" structures of the culture industries. Within these ideological constructions, to be seen as pandering to capitalism or "the market" was to be seen as "selling out."
3. Tagg (1997: 9) proposes the term "codal competence" to describe the interaction between socially constructed symbols, sociocultural norms, and musical texts in a process of semiosis. In order to decode a particular text "successfully," the receiver of that text must be grounded in a particular culture and be familiar with a store of symbols common to that culture. While Tagg's primary use of the term is concerned with the differing musical conventions of certain ethnic, national, and local cultures, the term is also useful in understanding semiosis with regard to group cultures, taste cultures, and subcultures. Furthermore, the term may also be used to denote levels of media literacy and familiarity with particular generic conventions.
4. In the wake of Douglas Coupland's book *Generation X* and Richard Linklater's film *Slacker* in 1991, both terms became widely mediated categories to describe attitudes, taste cultures, and demographic movements within the 18–30 age group in the US. It should be noted that both "Generation X" and "Slacker" became contested and oft-ridiculed terms as they became appropriated by the advertising industry.
5. Intertextuality has been used extensively in post structuralist analysis to refer to the way in which the meanings of particular texts are negotiated with reference to other artistic works. In the context of this chapter, the term is used to describe the way in which texts allude directly to and explicitly reference each other.

References

Banks, J. (1998). "Video in the machine: The incorporation of music video into the recording industry." *Popular Music* 16: 293–309.

Becker, H. (1963). *Outsiders: Studies in the Sociology of Deviance.* New York: Free Press.

Björnberg, A. (1994). "Structural relationships of music and images in music video." *Popular Music* 13: 51–74.

Bourdieu, P. (1986). *Distinction: A Social Critique of the Judgment of Taste.* London: Routledge.

Brown, J. D. and Schulze, L. (1990). "The effects of race, gender and fandom on audience interpretations of Madonna's music videos." *Journal of Communication* 40: 88–101.

Cannon, D. (1994). *Generation X and the New Work Ethic.* London: Demos.

Chanan, M. (1995). *Repeated Takes: A Short History of Recording and its Effects on Music.* London: Verso.

Coupland, D. (1992). *Generation X: Tales for an Accelerated Culture.* New York: St. Martin's Press.

Daly, S. and Wice N. (1995). *Alt.culture: An A—Z Guide to the 90s Underground, On-line and Over the Counter.* New York: Harper Perennial.

Doward, J. (1999). "Music to the ears in the quest for cred." *The Observer* 2 May: 6.

Duncombe, S. (1997). *Notes from Underground: Zines and the Politics of Alternative Culture*. London: Verso.

DuRant, R. H., Rich, M., Emans, S. J., Rome, E. S., Allred, E., and Woods, E. R. (1997). "Violence and weapon carrying in music videos: A content analysis." *Archives of Pediatric and Adolescent Medicine* 151: 443–448.

Fenster, M. (1993). "Genre and form: The development of country music video." In S. Frith, A. Goodwin, and L. Grossberg (eds.) *Sound and Vision: The Music Video Reader* (pp. 109–128). New York: Routledge.

Fiske, J. (1989). *Reading Popular Culture*. Boston: Unwin Hyman.

Frank, T. (1995). "Alternative to what?" In R. Sakolsky and F. W.-H. Ho (eds.) *Sounding Off: Music as Subversion/Resistance/Revolution* (pp. 103–120). New York: Autonomedia.

Frith, S. (1981). *Sound Effects: Youth, Leisure, and the Politics of Rock 'n' Roll*. London: Constable.

_____ (1988). "Video pop: Picking up the pieces." In S. Frith (ed.) *Facing The Music* (pp. 88–130). London: Pantheon.

Gillespie, M. (1995). *Television, Ethnicity and Cultural Change*. London: Routledge.

Goodwin, A. (1993). *Dancing In The Distraction Factory: Music Television and Popular Culture*. London: Routledge.

Hansen, C. H. and Krygowski, W. (1994). "Arousal-augmented priming effects: Rock-music videos and sex object schemas." *Communication Research* 21: 24–27.

Harron, M. (1988). McRock: Pop as commodity. In S. Frith (ed.) *Facing the Music: Essays on Pop, Rock and Culture* (pp. 173–220). London: Mandarin.

Hesmondhalgh, D. (1996). *Independent Record Companies and Democratization in the Popular Music Industry*. Unpublished doctoral dissertation. Goldsmiths College.

Horner, B. (1999). "Discourse." In B. Horner and T. Swiss (eds.) *Key Terms in Popular Music and Culture* (pp. 18–34). Oxford: Blackwell.

Kalof, L. (1993). "Dilemmas of femininity: Gender and the social construction of sexual imagery." *Sociological Quarterly* 34: 639–651.

_____ (1999). "The effects of gender and music video imagery on sexual attitudes." *Journal of Social Psychology* 139: 378–385.

Kaplan, E. A. (1987). *Rocking Around the Clock: The Televisual Apparatus, Advertising and Schizophrenia in Music Television*. London: Methuen.

Klein, N. (2000). *No Logo*. London: Flamingo.

Laing, D. (1985). *One Chord Wonders: Power and Meaning in Punk Rock*. Milton Keynes: Open University Press.

Leonard, M. (2000). *Gender and the Music Industry: An Analysis of the Production and Mediation of Indie Rock*. Unpublished doctoral dissertation. University of Liverpool.

Lewis, L. (1990). *Gender Politics and MTV*. Philadelphia: Temple University Press.

Lynch, J. (1984). "Music videos: From performance to Dada-surrealism." *Journal of Popular Culture* 18: 53–57.

Mundy, J. (1999). *Popular Music on Screen*. Manchester: Manchester University Press.

Negus, K. (1992). *Producing Pop: Culture and Conflict in the Popular Music Industry*. London: Edward Arnold.

Pardun, C. J. and McKee, K. B. (1995). "Strange bedfellows: Symbols of religion and sexuality on MTV." *Youth and Society* 6: 438–449.

Rich, M., Woods, E. R., Goodman, E., Emans, E., and DuRant, R. H. (1998). "Aggressors or victims: Gender and race in music video violence." *Pediatrics* 101: 669–674.

Savan, L. (1994). *The Sponsored Life: Ads, TV and American Culture*. Philadelphia: Temple University Press.

Seidman, S A. (1992). "An investigation of sex-role stereotyping in music videos." *Journal of Broadcasting and Electronic Media* 36: 209–216

Sommers-Flanagan, R., Sommers-Flanagan, J., and Davis, B. (1993). "What's happening on music television: A gender-role content-analysis." *Sex Roles* 28: 745–753.

Straw, W. (1993). "Popular music and postmodernism in the 1980s." In S. Frith, A. Goodwin, and L. Grossberg (eds.) *Sound and Vision: The Music Video Reader* (pp. 3–21). New York: Routledge.

Strouse, J. S., Buerkel-Rothfuss, H., and Long, E. C. J. (1995). "Gender and family as moderators of the relationship between music video exposure and adolescent sexual permissiveness." *Adolescence* 30: 505–521.

Switchenberg, C. (1992). "Music video: The popular pleasures of visual music." In J. Lull (ed.) *Popular Music and Communication* (pp. 116–133). London: Sage.

Tagg, P. (1997). *Introductory Notes to the Semiotics of Music.* Version 2. Course materials used at Griffith University, Brisbane.

Thornton, S. (1995). *Club Cultures: Music Media and Subcultural Capital.* London: Polity.

Toney, G. T. and Weaver, J. B. (1994). "Effects of gender and gender-role self-perceptions on affective reactions to rock-music videos." *Sex Roles* 30: 567–583

Vincent, R. C. (1989). "Clio's consciousness raised? Portrayal of women in rock videos, re-examined." *Journalism Quarterly* 64: 750–762.

Wallis, R. and Malm, K. (1988). "Push pull for the video clip: A systems approach to the relationship between the phonogram/videogram industry and music television." *Popular Music* 7: 267–84.

Walser, R. (1993). "Forging masculinity: Heavy metal sounds and images of gender." In S. Frith, A. Goodwin, and L. Grossberg (eds.) *Sound and Vision: The Music Video Reader* (pp. 153–184). New York: Routledge.

Wolfe, A. (1983). "Rock on cable: On MTV, music television the first music video channel." *Popular Music and Society* 9: 41–50.

Zimmerman, K. (1999). "Rising marketing cost cause a rethink on the number of releases." *MBI Special Report 1999: The US Report* (p. xi). London: Music Business International.

Chapter 8

THE EFFECTIVENESS OF MUSIC IN TELEVISION COMMERCIALS
A Comparison of Theoretical Approaches

Claudia Bullerjahn

Introduction

Advertising devices such as music are used in a systematic fashion to influence a target group's purchasing behavior. Various models have been proposed to explain the effect of advertising on behavior and to clarify the relationship among the different components of the influencing process. Older "step models" presume a hierarchical sequencing of the components of the influencing processes. Such processes are assumed to occur automatically and unavoidably. The newer "involvement models," on the other hand, require neither obligatory sequences nor hierarchical structuring. In addition, they do not require directed attention to commercials, which is more in line with today's television-viewing behavior. The "elaboration likelihood model" of persuasion provides a link between these two approaches. By considering the recipient's level and type of involvement, this model posits that information can be processed either consciously or casually. In the latter case, nonverbal advertising cues such as music increase in salience, whereas the ad's "contents"—in the crude sense of the term—diminish in importance. The effectiveness of music in television commercials is generally studied using memory measurements, determinations of attitudes and tastes, and questionnaires about product preferences and purchasing intentions. Experimental studies predominate, whereas behavioral observations in naturalistic contexts are rare. The present chapter provides an overview of studies dealing with the effectiveness of music in relation to general advertising mechanisms, discussing their practical utility, and pinpointing important gaps to be filled in future research.

Notes for this chapter are located on page 233.

* * *

[M]usic in advertising is a commonplace. Jingles, rock-star endorsements, and "needledrop" music [prefabricated, multipurpose, and highly conventional stock music] are a trivial easily understood part of the daily cultural discourse. Children sing "Keep on, keep on, keep on moving with Twix" in the school yard. Parents smile, shaking their heads. A moon-headed piano player flies across television skies crooning "Mack the Knife," and the audience laughs, recognizing Ray Charles. Pepsi yanks Madonna's commercial to avoid offending the Catholic church. The next morning, columnists raise their eyebrows knowingly. Advertising music is a shared experience we can parrot and parody together. (Scott, 1990: 223)

The commercial use of music in television advertising constitutes one of the principal sources of our everyday exposure to music in the Western world. The advertising industry and its corporate clients spend billions of dollars annually on royalty payments for the use of music in television advertisements. The importance of music to the effectiveness of television commercials seems to be obvious. It is reported that music is present in at least 42 percent of representatively large samples of television advertisements (North and Hargreaves, 1997). When considering advertisements screened internationally, music is in fact typically the predominant element in about 90 percent of them. It is therefore astonishing to consider that so little research has been devoted to the study of music's effectiveness as a marketing tool in television. As a consequence, the practical use of advertising music has often occurred in a very "haphazard and unplanned way" (Dunbar, 1990: 201; see also Vinh, 1994).

Current Trends in Television Commercials

No matter what people think of the omnipresent fact "advertising," advertising has long since become a permanent component of our everyday culture. With its fast modifications in the 1980s, it set about becoming a cultural factor that requires more than the arrogant curiosity of intellectuals. Science and society will have to deal more intensely with advertising in the near future if this socio-economic sector of growth with cultural time fuse is not to be left to itself in a more or less natural way. It is true that serious questions about advertising requiring our undivided attention have been asked in many places: will advertising develop into an alternative to art and culture in capitalist society? Will the TV commercial develop into an independent art genre? Is 1980s advertising a secular translation of the post-modern period? Does life imitate the TV commercial? Does advertising need products anymore?[1] (Schmidt, Sinofzik, and Spieß, 1991: 142f.)

Product-oriented advertising, and especially television commercials, underwent fast development in the 1980s and 1990s in terms of both quality and quantity. This boom was the product of two major factors: first, the development of private television stations (especially in Europe) financed exclusively by advertising, and second, the explosive growth of new stations in both Europe and the US in the form of cable and satellite networks (Kloepfer and Landbeck, 1991). The niche in which commercials could be employed was greatly expanded, and advertisers sought to place as many commercials as possible in these new and open spaces. They generally employed two strategies in doing so. On the one hand, they tried to embed lucrative commercials in attractive program slots; on the other, they have moved increasingly in the direction of entertaining and aesthetic commercials in order to blur the lines of demarcation between program and advertisement.

The latter strategy derives from the fact that several studies in the 1980s demonstrated that a person's attitude toward the *ad* is generally a more important determinant of purchasing intentions than their attitude toward the *product*. In other words, people purchase products not necessarily because they are favorably disposed to the product itself but because they are favorably disposed to the ad (see Brown and Stayman [1992] for a meta-analysis). Furthermore, consumer behavior appears to be enhanced by message-appropriate moods (Alpert and Alpert, 1989, 1990). Therefore, one approach to television advertising is to create ads that leave the consumer with a favorable though not necessarily conscious feeling about the product, something that can be accomplished with the use of appealingly fitting music, humorous devices, and attractive people, among many other things.

The most striking feature of the new kind of television commercial is its resemblance to the music video, i.e., the advertising medium of the popular music industry. This is partly due to the increasing orientation of television advertisements to adolescent and young-adult target groups. The result has been that informative (i.e., linguistically argumentative) commercials have increasingly given way to less informative but emotionally charged commercials. While conventional commercials employ musical devices such as jingles or product-specific songs to create mnemonic links with the advertised product or to enhance the more or less convincing argumentation of the ad message, the new commercials rely solely on the mood-modulating power of music. For simplicity's sake, we will employ a distinction between the conventional kind of "product-oriented" commercial and the newer kind of "entertainment-oriented" commercial. The latter was pioneered in 1986 by Levi Strauss's *Laundrette* commercial for 501 jeans, with other commercials following this lead (Bullerjahn, Bode, and Mennecke, 1994).

Another important trend to highlight is the ever-vanishing distinction between advertisements and artworks. On the one hand, graphic artworks assume the form of advertisements (e.g., Andy Warhol's soup can) and motion pictures borrow their aesthetic from commercials (e.g., *9 1/2 Weeks*) or consist of series of product placements (e.g., *Fire, Ice and Dynamite*). On the other hand, commercials themselves are often produced like artworks, quoting known artworks' details—making them look unusual—or using stylistic devices that were developed in artistic domains (Schmidt, 1990). French advertising directors in particular have been outstanding in their resource-fulness, a prime example being Jean-Claude Goude's celebrated *Égoïste* commercial (Bullerjahn, 1993). The artistic importance of commercials is reflected in the fact that a large audience pays to see the annual *Cannes Role*, with the award-winning commercials appearing at the acclaimed *International Advertising Festival*. Allusions to art and cinema are also typical of many music videos, a good example being *Express Yourself* by Madonna (Bullerjahn, 2000). The close relationship between advertisement and music video is also evident in Madonna's video *Like a Prayer*, where the song was simultaneously used in a television commercial by Pepsi Cola. A more recent example of the hybridization of form and content that has blurred the boundaries between video and commercial is Sting's *Brand New Day*, which ironically plays with advertising elements (e.g., the product placement of a detergent).

Models of Advertising Effect

> *Entertainment* is not the product, but simply a tool of the trade. The true product of broadcast media is the audience; and the true consumers are the advertisers. (Huron, 1989: 559, emphasis in original)

Advertising devices such as music are used in a systematic and strategic fashion to influence a target group's purchasing behavior, as measured by several criteria (Brosius and Fahr, 1996). Changes in purchasing behavior are believed to be mediated by a host of mechanisms, including stimulation of attention or interest, grouping of the ad message into information chunks, evocation of emotions, improvement in memory performance, presentation of cognitive schemes, and manipulation of opinions and attitudes. Various models have been proposed to explain the impact of advertising on behavior and to clarify the relationship among the different components of the influencing process. The two basic types of models are referred to as step models and involvement models (see Brosius and Fahr, 1996).

Step models, established in the tradition of the stimulus-response paradigm, presume a hierarchical sequencing of the components of the influencing processes. Such processes are assumed to occur automatically and unavoidably, having the same impact on all viewers. A well-known example is the so-called AIDA model (Tauchnitz, 1990; Brosius and Fahr, 1996). According to this scheme, a commercial should (in sequence) excite Attention, arouse Interest, generate a Desire, and thereby lead to a (purchasing) Action. It is assumed that consumer behavior is predictable according to rational-choice considerations, where all relevant information is contained within the commercial itself. Music plays but a secondary role in such a scheme, where its principal task is to arouse and remind but not to accompany the linguistic argumentation of the ad. In this respect, music that is signal-like (i.e., concise and intense) and that starts and ends abruptly is the kind that is most efficacious in increasing vigilance and in triggering an "orienting reflex" in the viewer. Musical forms typically associated with such a role are the "advertising fanfare" and the jingle.

In contrast to this, the more recent *involvement models* require neither obligatory sequences nor hierarchies of components and instead focus on the viewer's involvement level as a critical variable. As such, they do not require directed attention to the commercial, which is more in line with today's television-viewing behavior. Indeed, television commercials are perceived quite casually and are frequently avoided in an active manner by being zapped with remote controllers. This behavior is probably attributable to the ever-increasing number of television commercials in Europe and America. But in addition to this, consumers generally have only minimal need for product information and, especially in the case of routine purchasing, are usually uninterested in such information given the minor material differences among low-priced products of everyday use. Hence, the consumer is "weakly involved" in the commercial and will tend to ignore the arguments of the commercial's message. Even the production quality of the commercial may only merit slight attention from the viewer. For this reason, music—as a powerful emotion-triggering and attachment-promoting medium—plays an important role in commercials that people might otherwise avoid altogether. It also helps establish a product's image and create points of apparent distinction even where no objective differences between brands exist. This way of functioning is indicated by the fact that music and other non-verbal aspects of an ad are more easily and quickly processed than the verbal elements (Alpert and Alpert, 1990).

The "elaboration likelihood model" of persuasion by Petty and Cacioppo (1983) provides a link between these two approaches (schematically presented in figure 8.1). Depending on the recipient's level of *involvement* (i.e., his/her motivation, desire, and/or readiness to process the brand information in an ad), the product information is processed either in a conscious and elaborated manner (referred to as the "central route" of information processing) or in a casual and affective manner (referred to as the "peripheral route" of information processing). Especially in the case of the peripheral route to persuasion, nonverbal advertising cues such as music increase in salience, whereas the ad's "contents" diminish in importance.

In an important theoretical paper about general advertising effects, MacInnis, Moorman, and Jaworski (1991) described the significance of three key consumer variables—namely, motivation, opportunity, and ability—for the processing of brand information in ads. These three variables mediate the relationship between the ad's executional cues (i.e., all manipulable aspects of the ad, such as the visuals, hedonic symbolisms, celebrity endorsers, humor, music) and viewer/listener processing of the ad (i.e., the extent to which the viewer/listener allocates attention and processing resources to comprehend and elaborate on information in the ad). Music as an executional cue can easily influence these three consumer variables in ad processing:

Figure 8.1 The Elaboration Likelihood Model of Persuasion

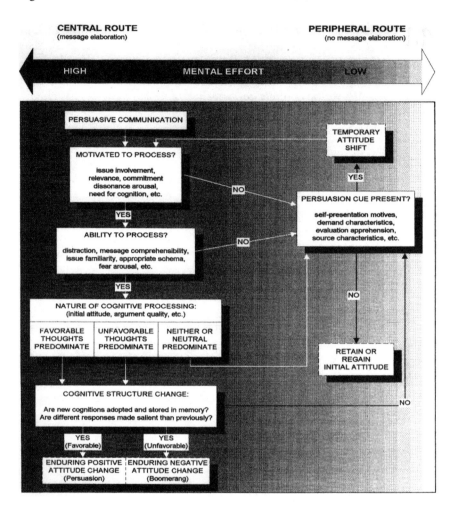

This figure is a schematic summary of the dominant paradigm in experimental research on attitudes and persuasion. As shown in the figure, either persuasive messages can be processed in an attentive way through the central route, leading to message elaboration, or they can be processed in an inattentive way through the peripheral route, leading to little direct elaboration of the verbal message. Most central processing involves linguistic arguments. Music, in contrast, is considered a *peripheral persuasion cue* (see the right side of the figure) that is processed by the peripheral route. One consequence of music being a peripheral cue—at least according to the elaboration likelihood model—is that it should be capable of producing only weak attitude change, which probably makes it an ideal persuasion device for contexts such as television commercials. Adapted from Petty and Cacioppo (1983), with permission.

1. Music can enhance the *motivation* to process the ad through increases in attentional levels, e.g., when loud, arousing, novel and/or pleasing music is played or when a sudden silence is introduced.
2. Music can increase the *opportunity* to process the information when the advertisement's cognitive load is reduced (e.g., by playing slow or familiar music) and when the redundancy of the brand information in the ad is increased. For example, a jingle or product-specific song can repeat and thus reinforce information already present in the ad, thereby increasing processing opportunity.
3. Music can increase the *ability* to process the ad by enhancing cues that access relevant knowledge structures about the product, e.g., when music that "fits" the product and that serves as a context for interpreting the brand information is played.

MacInnis, Moorman, and Jaworski (1991) draw attention to potential trade-offs between motivation, opportunity, and ability in ad processing: "[C]ues designed to enhance motivation to process the *ad* may reduce opportunity to process the *brand*" (p. 46, emphases in original). For example, sexual images that enhance motivation to process the ad can simultaneously reduce recall for the brand. Furthermore, "[T]he same cue that enhances processing opportunity or ability may reduce subsequent processing motivation" (p. 47). For example, frequent repetition of commercials with a simple or familiar advertising song may guarantee the opportunity to process the ad but may also result in a "wear-out" effect, thereby diminishing motivation to process the ad. In reality, it is impossible to find a musical piece that optimizes motivation, opportunity, and ability in equal measure.

Several researchers have attempted to build a framework that integrates all the key moderators of musical influence in advertising (see, for example, Alpert and Alpert, 1991). In my book on the principles of the effects of film music (Bullerjahn, 2001), I introduced an interdisciplinary model (modified for the present chapter) to explain the effects of advertising music in television commercials. The model is based on the analysis of around 70 research reports about musical effects in the audiovisual media, including television commercials. As shown in figure 8.2, the model involves three interacting levels, which include not only musical and effect variables but characteristics of the consumers as well, such as their personality, prejudices, and demographics. Total manipulation of a group of people through music alone is certainly impossible. Individual differences always moderate the effects of music on people. For example, Vinh (1994) pointed out the significance of the variable "age": it appears that the verbal/cognitive content of an ad is much more important for older people than for younger ones. Vinh also examined the significance of the collative variable "surprise": unusual combinations of product and music were better remembered than more commonplace ones (see below).

Figure 8.2 A Model of the Effects of Advertising Music

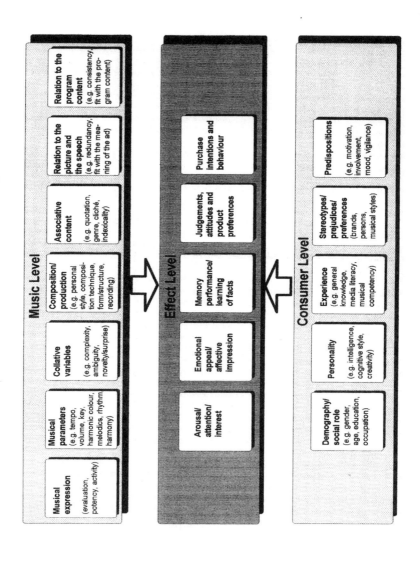

Note for Figure 8.2: A Model of the Effects of Advertising Music. The figure shows how the effect of music on advertising is moderated not only by the properties of the music (and its connection with the image and verbal content) but also by those of the consumer. These two levels, then, converge on a series of mechanisms discussed in this chapter, such as attention, emotion, memory, attitude formation, and purchasing intentions. Adapted from my book, *Grundlagen der Wirkung von Filmmusik* (Fundamental Principles of the Effects of Film Music, 2001).

Comparing advertising music with film music, we see further effect-variables of importance, such as the frequency of contact with a commercial, the viewing context, and the placement of a commercial within an ad block. For example, the employment of an identical or similar song in commercials for two different products will unquestionably lead to consumer confusion (Vinh, 1994). Englis (1991: 112) suggested that music-television as a viewing context for commercials may create unanticipated effects on consumer attitudes because of the strong emotions evoked by the music videos themselves. This is especially true in the case for "low-involvement" cognitive processing of ads.

Advertising music works not only by influencing affect but also by conveying and highlighting relevant *information* in the ad. This idea implies that music is not only about conveying emotional connotations, and second, music's ability to connote emotion must be seen within the context of the listener's capacities for interpretation, mediation, and judgment. Music, as an advertising device, plays on a whole slew of cultural associations with musical styles and musical works. In more abstract terms, a link exists between persuasion and "the extent to which messages resonate … with the schemas assigned by recipients to attitude objects" (Brannon and Brock, 1994: 169). Scott (1990) provided one of the very few cultural analyses to date of music in television commercials. She persuasively argued that empirical research on television commercials overlooks "the communicative meaning that a musical piece may have" and thereby "negate[s] the complex functionality of music" (p. 225). Furthermore, researchers' underlying faith in the universality of the interpretive effects of musical structural-devices "precludes consumers' ability to judge and understand various styles and melodies as appropriate and communicative in particular message contexts, exclusive of personal taste" (p. 226). David Dunbar (1990), for instance, highlighted the fact that music seems to communicate on three principal levels: the sensual, the emotional, and the intellectual. The results of his small pilot study show that music does change the way that ordinary people see the products, persons, etc. presented in ads. Like Scott (1990), Blair and Hatala (1992) emphasized that music cannot be separated from its social context or from meanings that are culturally shared. They proposed examining advertising music from an "anthropological/sociological perspective." Following Gottdiener's model of mass culture, they attempted to explain how rap music as "a social statement about life of oppressed youth in the ghettos becomes so acceptable to the mass culture that it is used by many white advertisers to sell products" (Blair and Hatala, 1992: 720).

Such cultural analyses are especially applicable in cases where well-known musics—classical or popular, in original form or rearranged form—are used in commercials. In these situations music is reused in manners it was not originally intended for. This is perhaps the most extreme instance of music being exploited for its previously established connotations and cultural meanings (see chapters by Stockfelt and Volgsten and Åkerberg).

Empirical Studies of the Effectiveness of Music in Television Commercials

Because it is not possible to directly measure the impact of television commercials on the financial success of an advertised product, indirect means must be employed to examine the effectiveness of advertising elements like music. A variety of effect-variables assumed to have a positive influence on advertising success are used as indicators. The typical variables that are measured include: attention to the ad message; recognition of the product; retention of the information conveyed in the commercial; affective impressions of the commercial and the advertised product; attitude toward the commercial and product; product preferences; and purchasing intentions. Although the majority of television commercials use music—indicating that the advertising industry has extraordinarily high expectations with regard to music's effectiveness—scientific research has only just begun to analyze its effects. Experimental studies predominate in this area, whereas behavioral observations in naturalistic contexts are rare. The current section of the chapter analyzes empirical studies in this area. Its five subsections are organized in parallel to the five stages of the "effect level" presented in figure 8.2.

Arousal, Attention, and Interest

There can be no response to advertising if an individual's attention is not stimulated at some level. Attention is selective, and this selectivity is guided by the degree of personal relevance. Individuals are highly selective in concentrating on particular elements of their surrounding environment, and this applies to their attentiveness to television commercials. Pre-attentional processes filter irrelevant information and help individuals determine which environmental elements merit further information processing. Music in particular can serve as an attention-catching device. Although low-involvement consumers generally pay little attention to an ad, music with striking characteristics may nonetheless affect their attentional resources.

MacInnis and Park (1991) examined the extent to which musical characteristics had an impact on attracting attention in relation to levels of consumer involvement. A previous study by Park and Young (1986) had shown that under conditions of high cognitive involvement—in which subjects were required to focus on attributes of the product described in the ad—music served as a *distracter*, thereby diminishing attention to the product information. In contrast, under conditions of low cognitive involvement—in which subjects were required to focus on personal thoughts quite removed from the advertised product—the same music served as an *enhancer*, improving attention to product information. MacInnis and Park (1991) wanted to find out if there were conditions under which music could enhance rather than distract attention during high-involvement processing. In order to do so, they manipulated two important variables of the music: fit (i.e., the extent to which the music was felt to be congruent with the advertised product) and "indexicality" (i.e., the extent to which music aroused emotion-laden memories based on past experience with the music). What they found was that high fit had a positive effect on attitude toward the brand for *both* low-involvement and high-involvement viewers, most likely through an effect on attention toward the message. If music fits the message, it facilitates a consumer's focus on the message, which in turn enhances message-encoding and memory. It allows all the elements of the ad to work cooperatively rather than competitively so as to create a coherent whole. In addition, the message was perceived as more credible by high-involvement subjects.

The situation with indexicality was different because in general indexicality directs the attention toward the music. High indexicality enhanced attitude toward the brand during conditions of low-involvement processing but not during high-involvement processing. By stimulating previously held emotions about the piece of music, indexicality served as a weak distracter during high-involvement processing. On the one hand, the strong emotions associated with high-indexicality music must have enhanced low-involvement consumers' interest in the ad message. On the other hand, the high-indexicality music used by MacInnis and Park was unrelated to the advertised message, and therefore the retrieval of past emotions might have interfered with high-involvement consumers' message processing.

While musical fit may be an important factor in enhancing attention to the ad, Olsen (1994) proposed that silence—the absence of music and other audio effects, aside from an announcer's voice—could separate an advertisement from the "noise" generated by television programs and other advertisements, thereby producing greater attention to the ad's content and in turn enhancing the listener's retention of the message. Furthermore, Olsen suggested that a piece of information could stand out more effectively if it first appeared in a noisy context after which a cut to silence would suddenly occur. Rehearsals of information might be encouraged in such a context of silence. A survey of creative directors on the use of silence in advertising revealed that most of them were convinced of its effectiveness in generating attention. However, these subjective beliefs should not be seen as a substitute for systematic research.

Emotional Appeal and Affective Impression

Television commercials often provide little objective product information but instead evoke feelings and/or images to be associated with the product. As a result of what Tauchnitz (1990: 68) called the "affective turn" in consumer research, music has achieved a new significance in advertising practice. It is overwhelmingly used to create feeling states, influence consumer moods, and generate an affective impression of the product. Bruner (1990) performed a meta-analysis of studies on musical expression and concluded that the emotional impressions associated with particular musical parameters could be determined in a predictable manner. For example, sadness is associated with slow tempos, soft volume, minor keys, dissonant harmonies, etc. The caveat to this principle is that familiarity with a piece of music may have a constraining effect on its interpretation in a commercial setting, as the listener may have already acquired particular affective impressions of the music in connection with earlier life experiences.

In measuring affective impressions, researchers generally rely on verbal indicators of emotion, such as adjective checklists and semantic differentials (i.e., pairs of adjectives having contrasting meanings with degrees in between). Evaluations are usually made for the musical and visual levels as well as for the brand and commercial. The fact that music can have an emotional influence on people's visual impressions of television commercials is highlighted in several studies. Wintle (1978) used semantic differentials to measure three dimensions (evaluation, potency, and activity) of people's audiovisual impressions of an ad and found that music could have either an enhancing or inhibiting effect on each of the three dimensions studied. Tauchnitz (1990) too used semantic differentials to measure audiovisual impressions of an ad but inquired into brand impression in addition. Like Wintle, Tauchnitz showed that music could have an enhancing or inhibiting effect on audiovisual impressions of the ad but found that this had only a minor correlation with subjects' brand impression, which did not appreciably change. Music's effects were apparently covered by the advertising medium's visual impressions.

Morris and Boone (1998) pointed out interpretive problems that may arise when adjective checklists or semantic differential scales are used to access emotional responses, such as in the studies of Wintle (1978) and Tauchnitz (1990). The precise meaning of the emotional words in these lists varies from person to person. Using open-ended questions—such as "Please describe your feelings about the product"—as an alternative to checklists requires that respondents access a metacognitive level at which they may lack the appropriate vocabulary to express their feelings precisely. In response to this, Morris and Boone (1998) created a visual "Self-Assessment Manikin" (SAM) as a nonverbal means of describing feeling states (see figure 8.3), which is based on the three-dimensional PAD approach (Pleasure, Arousal, Dominance). Subjects were asked to signify their emotional assessments by *marking the picture*

Figure 8.3 The "Self-Assessment Manikin" of Morris and Boone

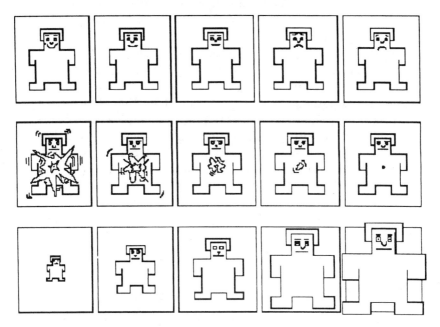

The manikin presents a cartoon character in fifteen different emotive states, and provides subjects a means of expressing emotional evaluations without using words. This therefore circumvents problems associated with the use of verbal descriptions of emotion. Reprinted from Morris and Boone (1998), with permission.

that came closest to their feelings. This was done for the three dimensions of pleasure, arousal and dominance. In the experiment, subjects were asked to view transparencies of twelve print advertisements for thirty seconds, where half the subjects also heard music that was congruent with the content of the ad. The results showed that music had no effect on subjects' attitude toward the brand or their purchasing intentions. However, for half of the ads, subjects showed significant differences in their emotional responses as a function of the presence of music. Interestingly, music was especially efficient at bringing out negative feeling states, although it could also enhance positive feelings when contemporary pop songs were used.

Memory Performance and Learning of Facts

Advertising experts generally assume that music has a positive influence on the memorability of a brand name. The results of existing research on the use of music as an audiovisual mnemonic device, however, do not lend unqualified support to this assumption. While several studies have found an improvement in memory performance using music, most have found either no effect or a negative one (Tauchnitz, 1990: 16ff.; Vinh, 1994: 59ff.). It is important to point out that different studies have used different means for assessing memory performance, and that their outcomes may vary in significant ways as a function of this. The three major methods that are employed are called free recall, aided recall, and recognition. In *free recall*, subjects are asked to recall the content of a previously seen commercial without any type of memory aid to assist them. In *aided recall*, subjects are provided with reference cues (such as the product slogan or the background music) to help them recall the commercial's contents. In the case of *recognition*, the subjects are presented with a multiple-choice list that includes the correct response as one of the possible choices. Different kinds of scientific results can be obtained as a function of the memory method used.

The general influence of music on memory performance can be viewed from various perspectives:

1. Music in commercials can direct attention to the relevant details in the ad, organize the material in the ad, and label this material emotionally as context information, thereby stimulating elaboration. Acting as an emotional reference, a mnemonic cue, or a recall stimulus, music can improve access to stored product information. Furthermore, it may provide an important means for rehearsal: "As the listener hums a tune or sings a jingle, he or she engages in a rehearsal strategy that results in a better memory" (Macklin, 1988: 225).
2. When conveying a message via the visual and auditory channels, music can lead to improved information processing because of an increase in overall "channel capacity" (la Motte-Haber and Emons, 1980: 204). The redundancy that results from simultaneously using two sensory modalities can have a positive effect on verbal storage of factual knowledge. Gestalt-psychological considerations predict that the multimodal coupling of music and image should have a stronger mnemonic impact than either modality alone.
3. In thinking about all these considerations, it is important to keep in mind that music also has the capacity to serve as a distracter and to interfere with a limited capacity for processing. This is especially true for the combination of music with speech, both of which share the acoustic modality of information processing. Such a caveat applies especially to children and the elderly. In addition, music can impair visual memory.

Academic and advertising professionals frequently claim that a sung slogan, a so-called jingle, enhances the memorability of the product information. However, one complicating consideration is the fact that verbal material presented in a jingle is more likely to be processed *phonetically* than semantically, which might impair comprehension of the ideas expressed in its lyrics. Research on mnemonic aids reveals that jingles are most useful in situations where there are few cues for retrieving verbal information. Where other cues are available (such as in a recognition test), jingles are of little benefit. In a study on the efficacy of jingles, Yalch (1991) provided empirical support for these caveats. With a single exposure to a given ad, the addition of a jingle led to a significant improvement in aided recall of the product name compared to when no jingle was used (see figure 8.4, One Exposure). However, when *recognition* tests were used, in which several cues were simultaneously present, there was no significant difference between the jingle and no-jingle conditions. In addition, Yalch found that the relative benefits of a jingle as a mnemonic device decreased with increasing exposure to the ad (figure 8.4, Two Exposures).

A different approach to studying the effect of music on product recall was taken by Stewart, Farmer, and Stannard (1990) in an "advertising tracking" study, a protocol that is much closer to a naturalistic study than to an experimental one. In this tracking study, 2,956 people were contacted by telephone through a "random digit dialing procedure" over a nine-month period. Two weeks after the interviews started, a new advertising campaign for a well-known

Figure 8.4 The Effect of Jingles on Brand Recall

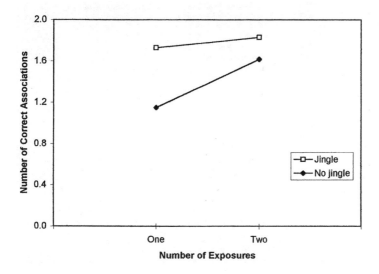

This figure shows the number of correct associations of brand names and advertising slogans by the use of a jingle as a function of the number of exposures in an aided recall procedure. Note that during a single exposure, the use of a jingle improves memory over no jingle but that after a second exposure, the jingle condition shows no relative advantage. From Yalch (1991). Copyright © 1991 by the American Psychological Association. Adapted with permission.

car began, and its commercials were continually shown during the course of the study. Each telephone interview began with general questions about the product category (i.e., cars). This was then followed by specific questions about the campaign's actual commercials using an aided recall approach in which the product's name was mentioned (the verbal cue). Finally, the respondents were asked to listen to a ten-second tape of the music used in the commercial in question (the musical cue); this was a hard-rock song that had been composed for the campaign. The results showed that while only 62 percent of the people sampled could remember the commercial after the verbal cue, 83 percent of them recognized the music. "More interesting, however is the finding that only 12 percent of respondents who stated they had seen advertising for the product in response to the verbal product-cue stated that they were unfamiliar with the music. In contrast, 29 percent of the respondents who indicated that they had not seen the advertising in response to the verbal product-cue indicated that they recognized the music" (Stewart, Farmer, and Stannard, 1990: 43). If only the last three months of the study are taken in consideration, nearly all respondents recognized the musical cue (Stewart and Punj, 1998: 45). Figure 8.5 shows the development of recognition for the verbal and musical cues over the course of the nine-month study. While the number of people remembering the commercial after the verbal reference-cue changed only slightly during the campaign (from 56 to 68 percent; note that the product had been advertised regularly before the study began and was thus known to people), the number of people recognizing the musical cue (used for the first time during this campaign) rose from 0 to 90 percent. "Music cues appear to be more sensitive than verbal cues both as absolute measures of memory and as a means for detecting changes in awareness over time" (Stewart, Farmer, and Stannard, 1990: 47).

Stewart, Farmer and Stannard (1990) also asked their respondents to describe what they could remember seeing or hearing in the ad. The degree of elaboration of the respondents' descriptions increased over time, but more importantly, there was a significant difference in the types of features they described depending on the type of cue that was used. "Respondents were two to three times more likely to use words referring to people, setting, or actions in response to the musical cue" than to verbal ones (Stewart, Farmer, and Stannard, 1990: 46). Amazingly, "references to imagery in response to the product name cue appear to be independent of references to imagery in response to the musical cue. There appears to be a 'verbal imagery' factor and a 'nonverbal imagery' factor that are unrelated to one another" (Stewart and Punj, 1998: 46). These results offer empirical support for a "dual coding" hypothesis, which argues that verbal and nonverbal information are processed by separate routes, and that the information coded along these two routes is complementary and nonredundant.

Hahn and Hwang (1999) looked at another factor involved in message processing, namely, cognitive load. They examined the effects of tempo and familiarity of background music on verbal message recall for a television advertisement. They provided evidence that the relationship between the tempo of

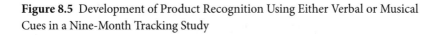

Figure 8.5 Development of Product Recognition Using Either Verbal or Musical Cues in a Nine-Month Tracking Study

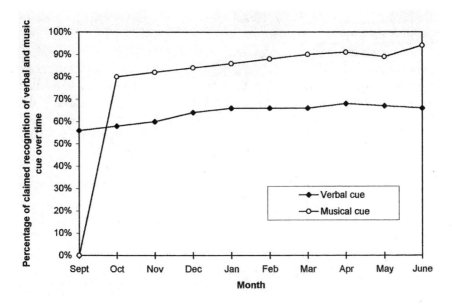

The figure shows the results of an advertising tracking study in which people were interviewed by telephone and asked if they recognized an advertised car after being given a verbal cue (the brand name) or a musical cue (the music used in the television commercial). While the number of people remembering the commercial after the verbal cue changed only slightly during the campaign (from 56 percent to 68 percent), the number recognizing the musical cue rose from 0 percent to 90 percent. Note that the starting point for the verbal cue was 56 percent as the product was already known at the outset of the study. By contrast, the original song played in the commercial was used for the first time in this particular ad campaign. Reprinted from *Journal of Advertising* © Copyright 1990, by the Advertising Research Foundation.

the background music and message recall is an inverted-U shape: there is an optimal recall response at some intermediate tempo value, while both faster and lower tempos lead to fall-offs in response. While no interaction between tempo and familiarity was observed in the recall test, such an interaction was recorded in a recognition test. Only in the case of high-familiarity music was there an optimal tempo level that maximized message processing. Hahn and Hwang (1999) interpreted their results for the high-familiarity music in terms of a "resource-matching" hypothesis that states that message processing is optimal when the resources demanded by the processing task match what people are able to make available. "If the information load of advertising messages is light, faster-tempo music may be preferred for better message recall. If it is heavy, slower-tempo music may be adequate" (Hahn and Hwang, 1999: 672). In contrast to these results showing an efficacy of well-known, high-familiarity music for message recall, Tom (1990) did a direct comparison of original musics composed for a commercial, parodies of popular songs, and actual popular songs and found that original musics were most effective at aiding subjects' recall of the brand name (77.6 percent recall score), whereas popular songs in their original form were the *least* effective (only 23.6 percent).

An important factor to consider in all memory tests is the age of the subject. Young adults and elderly people differ significantly in their ability to process information. Research focusing on the growing elderly population shows that the elderly exhibit a strong preference for informational television programs and advertisements, although they experience difficulty with selective attention and information processing, especially when the information is presented in fast-paced manner. Any type of distraction, such as music, can make it especially hard for them to pay attention to and process relevant information in the ad. By presenting television commercials to a sample of elderly people, Gorn et al. (1991) demonstrated that music interfered with the acquisition of explicit verbal product information while at the same time improving recall of visual details.

Vinh (1994) showed television commercials of different types to members of either youth groups or senior citizens' organizations, where the commercials were embedded in a program-context that was appropriate to the age of the subjects. Using a free recall method, he examined the extent to which the respondents remembered the contents of the program, the advertised product, and the brand name. Contrary to his hypotheses, he found with entertainment-oriented commercials that neither the popularity of the advertisement music nor that of its performer had any impact on memory performance in either group. However, with product-oriented commercials, the unusual combination of a product with a music style *not* matching the stereotype (e.g., sneakers with baroque music) led to better recall performance than did a typical combination of product and music (e.g., sneakers with techno music). This finding seems to contradict the above-mentioned finding of MacInnis and Park (1991) that increased musical fit leads to improvements in the processing of brand information.

Judgments, Attitudes, and Product Preferences

Purchasing decisions are almost always made at a point in time that is quite removed from the viewing of an advertisement. Therefore, some latent construct is required to maintain the effect of the advertisement over time in a relatively enduring fashion: the *attitude*. The impact of commercial music on attitude formation is usually explained by the fact that music provides a context that is charged with values. It is in this context that attitudes are formed. The additional information provided by music influences the strength of an opinion, and shows the advertised product (or the commercial itself) in a better light. For this reason, commercials often use musical styles or works that advertisers hope will correctly match the musical preferences of the target group.

One must, however, avoid committing the error of thinking that listeners/viewers are helpless, impressionable, emotionally vulnerable beings without fixed convictions or desires, who exist precariously at the whim and mercy of omnipotent advertisers. It is often forgotten that commercials only rarely convey completely unknown contents. As a rule, every viewer has certain attitudes or, at the very least, stereotyped ideas about the products shown in commercials. Persuasion research has shown that if a viewer has a stable attitude about something, no music, be it popular or "emotionalizing," can change it. Music and other peripheral cues are much more effective at bringing about attitude change when attitudes are lightly held and labile. Under conditions where people have a negative bias toward the brand but happen to like the music in the ad, a form of "cognitive dissonance" develops between these two conflicting attitudes. Such a conflict can be resolved by changing one's attitude toward the brand, changing one's attitude toward the music, or both. When people have no particular bias toward or against the brand, aesthetically pleasing commercials (including appealing music) have the potential to increase a viewer's predisposition to purchase the advertised product. In addition, in situations where ad music is based on familiar "oldies," such songs can re-emerge on the pop charts. This can have an "agenda-setting" effect: the use of classical music in commercials apparently has the effect of advancing sales of the music, as a glance at the classical music charts confirms. The most effective commercials for music pretend to advertise other products.

While some researchers only used a scale of "pleasantness" to register attitudes (e.g., Tauchnitz, 1990), others use semantic differentials in the form of multidimensional measurements. Tauchnitz (1990) was unable to show an effect of music on attitude to the advertised product or the ad by using musics differing in affective quality. In contrast, Vinh (1994) showed that the use of popular music in an entertainment-oriented commercial led to a more positive attitude toward the ad and product provided that the product was known and that no explicit disinterest in it existed.

Blair and Shimp (1992) pointed out the risks of using well-known music in commercials. While it is true that well-known music represents the best means for accessing attention and capitalizing on positive carryover effects, it is also true that the probability of negative associations rises with increasing popularity: "[T]he commercial use of a golden-oldie tune may stir pleasant nostalgic memories in many audience members who were teenagers when the music was popular, but for others the same music may be associated with an unpleasant time of confusion, low self-esteem, and perhaps unrequited love" (Blair and Shimp, 1992: 41). Blair and Shimp used second-order classical conditioning procedures to test this idea. Some of the subjects in their study were pre-exposed to a "new age" instrumental composition (*Thanksgiving* by George Winston), that was rated by people as neutral with regard to interest. During five time-consuming and bothersome sessions, subjects had to evaluate business programs on cassette tape, all of which began and concluded with the musical stimulus as theme music. Obviously, subjects who had endured this unpleasant experience developed a distaste for the music. The results indicated that the pre-exposed subjects held less favorable attitudes about a proposed brand name for a fictitious line of sportswear than did subjects who only heard the music in the context of conditioning trials, which also included the same music.

A study by Tom (1995) showed that a change of attitude about an object through music did not even require attention to the object: music could condition preferences even when subjects were unaware of the stimuli. Tom used "liked" music as an unconditioned stimulus, and found that it could significantly establish the formation of preferences for both attended stimuli (two pens of different color presented on slides) and unattended conditioned stimuli (Chinese ideograms presented using a tachistoscope for 0.02 seconds). As figure 8.6 shows, liked music led to a preference for the presented item, whether attended to or not, while disliked music led to a rejection of the presented item, whether attended to or not. In other words, classical conditioning was demonstrated only when the unconditioned stimulus was "liked." An explanation may be that the disliked music employed in this study was also perceived as inappropriate for the advertisement; in other words, it did not have a good *fit* for the ad.

Purchasing Intentions and Behavior

The influence of music on decision-making and behavior can be explained by many types of mechanisms depending on the use and the context. One

Figure 8.6 Classical Conditioning of Product Preferences Using Music

	Music condition	
	"Liked" music: Kenny G, *Song Bird*	"Disliked" music: John Lennon, *Number 9 Dream*
Attended stimuli: **Pen preference**		
Advertised pen	60.36%	46.36%
Unadvertised pen	39.64%	53.64%
Unattended stimuli: **Ideogram preference**		
Advertised ideogram	58.56%	44.55%
Unadvertised ideogram	41.44%	55.45%

The numbers in the figure refer to the percentage of subjects in each condition who preferred the item listed (either a pen or an ideogram). Notice the reversal in the preference trends for liked versus disliked music: when liked music is used, people show a preference for the advertised item, but when disliked music is used, they show a preference for the other item. This occurs whether the stimulus in question is attended to (the pens) or not (the ideograms). This table is a modification of data tables from Tom (1995). Adapted with permission.

important mechanism for advertisers is a form of associative learning referred to as classical conditioning. As shown schematically in figure 8.7, classical conditioning involves the pairing of two types of stimuli: an "unconditioned stimulus" (US), something that is intrinsically rewarding (for example, food), while a "conditioned stimulus" (CS) is hedonically neutral. An unconditioned stimulus leads to an "unconditioned response" (UR), which is a response that occurs naturally and automatically without learning: salivation in response to the presence of food is a type of unconditioned response. The goal of classical conditioning is to create a conditioned response (CR), in other words to make the CS—something that initially produces no response because it is perceived as being completely neutral—produce the same response as the US. In advertising studies, the CS is the advertised product, for which people initially have no particular feelings. The US can include a large number of rewarding stimuli such as beautiful people, attractive scenery, and not least, pleasurable music. Through classical conditioning, the appropriate pairing of the CS and US in a relation of contiguity changes the response to the CS from nothing to something that is essentially identical to the UR. In other words, what used to be a neutral commercial product now is now a product of great interest and intention as a result of being coupled with a rewarding stimulus in the ad. The

Figure 8.7 Classical Conditioning with Advertising Music

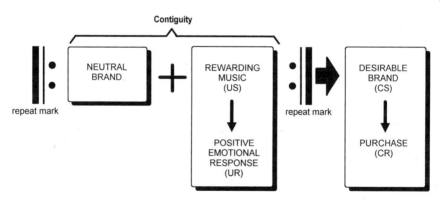

The figure presents a model of how music can condition preferences for commercial products in advertisements. Music is considered here to be an "unconditioned stimulus" (US), even though it certainly acquired its intrinsic rewarding properties in a learning process as part of musical socialization. An unconditioned stimulus generally leads to an unconditioned response (UR), such as stimulation of attention in this case. The commercial product is the conditioned stimulus (CS), as it is something that has to be learned to be liked; it is not intrinsically rewarding the way an unconditioned stimulus is. The repeated contiguous pairing together of an unconditioned stimulus like music with a conditioned stimulus like a product can lead to a conditioned response (CR): a preference for the now positively associated product (CS). Thereafter, presentation of the CS (the product) should lead to a desire for the product, which may result in a purchase (CR).

product has acquired an additional benefit: an emotional value. This can have an impact on purchasing behavior.

Because unconditioned stimuli are often unrelated to the behavior at hand, people do not often realize or accept the impact of classical conditioning when it comes to purchasing behavior. People even frequently think that they are strictly rational. In a pioneering study, Gorn (1982) tried to uncover possible classical-conditioning effects that might have been "underestimated and under-reported in self-reports" (p. 95) of advertising effects. Slides of pens were shown to subjects as music played in the background. The color of the pen was varied (light blue or beige), as was the music (excerpts from either the then-popular and well-liked film musical *Grease* or Indian classical music that pre-tests had predicted would be disliked). Subjects were then asked to choose one of the two pens as a gift for participating in the study. The results showed a significant preference for the pen color that had been associated with the "liked" music, that is, the popular music (79 percent). Only 30 percent of the test subjects chose the pen connected to the "disliked" music. Another experiment by Gorn (1982) showed that in situations where subjects were forced to make a product choice, information provided by the commercial was given more weight than peripheral cues such as music, the latter holding greater influence in situations that did not call for decisions: "[M]usical conditioning seemed to operate when subjects had no reason to evaluate the advertised brand, whereas product information seemed to be more important when they were motivated to process brand-relevant information" (North and Hargreaves, 1997: 271).

Several groups tried to replicate Gorn's findings, either using the identical protocol or employing methodological modifications (Bierley, McSweeney, and Vannieuwkerk, 1985; Pitt and Abratt, 1988; Tom, 1995). Gorn's results could not always be replicated, which led Kellaris and Cox (1989) to search for "demand artifacts" inherent in Gorn's study. Their research confirmed that in a study designed the same way as Gorn's, subjects could have effectively intuited the experimenter's hypothesis and thus given the response that they thought was being sought. In other words, subjects could have been reacting more to the experimenter's *instructions* than to the experimental *stimuli*.

Over the past years, there has been growing criticism of Gorn's methods and theoretical interpretation (Tauchnitz, 1990; Vinh, 1994). First, Gorn's protocol of using a slide format does not correspond to the usual conditions of viewing advertisements, especially in that the subjects directed their attention to the simulated ad. Second, a set of confounding factors cannot be excluded since they were not controlled in the experiments. This holds especially true for the question of whether the music variants were felt to be appropriate or inappropriate, which might have influenced behavior beyond the context of music preferences. Third, proper control groups were not included in the experiment. Fourth, more fundamental concerns have been raised about the possibility of true classical conditioning occurring in Gorn's study. Classical conditioning is impossible when the stimulus that is to be conditioned (the pen) is combined only once with an unconditioned stimulus that is, biologically speaking, not terribly relevant (the musical pieces chosen for the experiment)! Furthermore, Gorn presented the pens and music at the *same* time, a procedure that does not usually produce strong classical conditioning; it is best to present the pen (CS) before the music (US). For these reasons, Tauchnitz (1990) suggested that the effects discerned by Gorn were more likely explained by associative-learning mechanisms other than classical conditioning, or even by instrumental conditioning. The fact that Gorn's experimental findings may not be explainable in terms of classical conditioning does not rule out the possibility that classical conditioning may be an important force when using music in commercials. It only means that further research with stronger experimental designs is needed.

In a later study, Gorn et al. (1991) dissociated themselves from the paradigm of conditioning and sought to orient their work in the context of the "elaboration likelihood model" of persuasion, such as the above-mentioned work of Park and Young (1986). The focus was on the distinction between an information-oriented presentation (emphasizing the product's advantages) and a music-oriented presentation (focusing more on musical emotionality and less on the product's advantages). Senior citizens aged 60 to 84 were asked to assess a 20-minute extract of a program for the elderly. In the experimental condition, the program included a 30-second commercial for apple juice that was repeated one time. Subjects saw either an information-oriented commercial without music, the same commercial with music, or a musical-entertainment-oriented commercial without much substantive information. Following the program, the subjects were given a choice of beverage coupons. The perception of information-oriented commercials had a significant impact on the choice of coupons for apple juice. It even seemed that the combination of information and music produced a better result than information on its own (48.7 compared to 41.7 percent) although explicit memories were found to be disturbed by music. On the other hand, both the absence of product information and advertising media-contact led to poorer results (26.8 percent compared to 12.16 percent). It can be concluded that the preferences of senior citizens are significantly influenced by information content.

Alpert and Alpert (1989, 1990) examined the influence of background music on purchasing intentions and found that it could be best explained as an effect on consumer mood. Experimental subjects were exposed to slides of three different friendship greeting-cards (pre-tested and rated as happy, sad, or neutral), accompanied by two Preludes from Book I of J. S. Bach's *Well-Tempered Clavier* (pretested and rated as happy or sad). Although the music did not produce significant variations in the perception of card moods or overall card impressions, cards appearing with sad music were significantly more likely to be selected than those with happy music (figure 8.8). Sad music, possibly by evoking feelings of melancholy, seemed better suited for sending greeting cards to distant

Figure 8.8 The Effect of Music on Purchasing Intentions

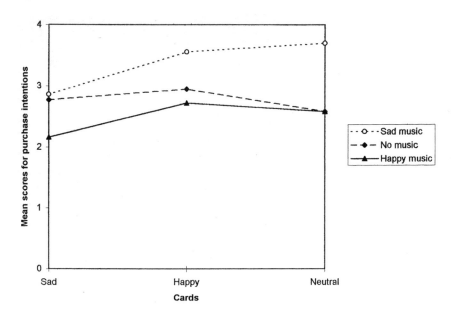

In this study, three different music conditions (sad music, happy music, or no music) were paired with the appearance of three different types of greeting cards (sad, happy, or neutral). Sad music appeared to have a stronger influence on purchase intentions for all three types of cards than happy music or no music. Note that the purchase intentions were evaluated in a 5-step semantic differential. The subjects had to answer the question "If you are going to send a card to a friend, how likely is it that you would buy this card?" (5 = would buy it, 1 = would not buy it). Redrawn from Alpert and Alpert (1990) with permission.

friends than did happy music. Presumably, the affective link between music and the ad message was decisive for the subjects' purchasing intentions.

In contrast to this, Middlestadt, Fishbein, and Chan (1994) questioned the primacy of affect in influencing purchase intentions. Students were exposed to one of two versions of a television commercial for a brand of apple juice. The versions differed only in the presence or absence of instrumental background music. All in all, addition of music led to a significantly more positive affective and evaluative reaction toward the ad, and students viewing the ad with music were significantly more positive about the notion of drinking the advertised brand than those who viewed the video-only version. Further analysis found that those in the video-plus-music condition had more numerous positive arguments for (but not more negative arguments against) drinking the apple juice than did those exposed to video only; the presence of music resulted in the juice being perceived as significantly better tasting and more natural. In other words, music influenced *beliefs* as well as affect. The authors thus concluded that changes in purchasing intentions occur by way of altering underlying beliefs rather than by way of affective change alone.

Outlook

It is mistaken to assume that consumers passively receive advertising messages. Over periods of time, consumers become sensitive to the means by which advertisers establish authority. As viewers become more cognizant of the means of appeal, advertisers are forced to seek new techniques to overcome viewer scepticism. The meanings of advertisements are necessarily linked *dynamically* to particular times and the past experience of viewers. There results a kind of escalation or inflation—what might be called an "authority spiral." (Huron, 1989: 569; emphasis in original)

I have described how new trends in the production of television commercials go hand in hand with new theoretical and advertising approaches. We can see how the role of music in commercials has changed: from its humble beginnings as the ephemeral jingle, music has now become a total acoustic backdrop for many if not most commercials. A four-minute commercial break can be filled almost completely with the sound of music. I have already discussed the synergy between commercial and music video. The nearly nonstop presence of music in commercials nowadays permits advertising at two levels: advertisement for the product but also advertisement for the music itself. To the best of my knowledge, the influence of commercials on the marketing success of music (phonograms) has not been researched systematically.

Advertisers often choose popular music that they think their target audience will find appealing. However, contrary to advertising practice, several research findings remind us that "popular music is not necessarily a panacea and may even be a liability under certain conditions" (Blair and Shimp, 1992: 42; see also Tom, 1990). This suggests the need for more vigilant (and less haphazard) selection of music in commercials and more concerted study of the effectiveness of popular music in television commercials. Television viewers from all age groups and all walks of life amass important experiences of musical styles, including classical music, through the medium of commercials. This can be an opportunity for cultivating musical literacy (Czypionka, 1999), but on the other hand, it may contribute to a disturbing form of musical stereotyping, as many music educators fear. However, this idea has yet to be researched.

An important problem in studying the effects of music in advertising involves the choice of indicators (e.g., attention, recall, preference) used to measure these effects. Not only has the independence of these indicators not been established, but it is unclear to what extent they have a direct impact on the actual economic success of the advertised product. There are lingering doubts, especially in the measurement of memory, as to whether the most salient aspects of the advertising process are even registered: "[A]dvertising research … formulates an audience searching for product information, compliantly forming positive brand attitudes, and resolving intentions to purchase. A more accurate formulation might be television viewers who roll their eyes, sigh, and go for a snack when the commercials come on" (Scott, 1990: 227). Overall, it has to be stressed that music has the capacity to increase advertising impact, yet music alone cannot guarantee marketing success. Music is but one of a wide range of advertising elements that work in concert to produce effects (see North and Hargreaves, this volume).

There are other factors that should be considered in future research. One is a consideration of large-scale musical schematas. Until now, research has focused on the effects of individual musical parameters (volume, tonality, rhythm) but not on more meaningful semiotic features, like the kinds of schematas discussed in Philip Tagg's chapter in this volume. Studies with new methodologies and the careful handling of the experimental music must be done in order to investigate these factors. The combination of qualitative and quantitative approaches (triangulation) is particularly recommended.[2] In addition, studies of advertising music must be broadened to include a larger subject population. Commercials are usually aimed at a large audience with average processing capacities and media literacy. Most studies use college students as subjects, thereby limiting themselves to a very narrow demographic group. To date, little attention has been accorded to individual differences in responsiveness to advertising music (Haase, 1989). This should definitely be a priority of future research. An interesting factor to consider for the digital age is the ability to customize advertising music. In the same way that commercial web sites come complete with visual advertisements popping up all over the place, these ads will probably be accompanied by music in the not-too-distant future. And just as visual ads are customized to the viewers of such sites, it is to be expected that the music for these advertisements will be individualized to the user.

Finally, what of the question of "music and manipulation," the subject matter of this volume? It seems obvious that advertisers *are* attempting to effect some form of mass manipulation via their production of commercials and in their widespread use of music in them. As mentioned in the opening of this chapter, advertisers are among the largest *users* of music in Western society. It seems equally clear, though, that music's effectiveness in television commercials is hard to measure and hard to verify. The results to date have provided a very mixed message. The art of music in commercials is anything but a science. What does seem clear is that music's role in commercials has definitively shifted from the level of the two-second jingle to that of the thirty-second background score. Music is increasingly becoming the central focus of commercials, and we should expect this trend to continue in the coming years. In addition, television commercials are increasingly developing the form and feel of music videos, the small difference being that they are advertising some product other than the music itself. The synergy between television commercial and music video has already developed a complex history. There seems to be no question that television commercials, like music videos, have changed and will continue to change the way we perceive music. When a contemporary band covers another group's hit song from the 1980s, people welcome it as an entertaining bit of nostalgia. However, when a television commercial for ketchup employs a classical symphony as its background music, lovers of the symphony call it an abomination. The reuse of well-known music in commercials confronts deep-seated feelings about moral rights and cultural protection. All of this suggests that the use of music in television commercials will be a topic of great interest and importance in the years ahead.

Notes

1. All German quotations translated by the author.
2. Research by Hung (2000, 2001), who uses a mixed design integrating features of qualitative and quantitative methods, suggests that music comprises a sign system that adds meanings to advertising. The viewer's knowledge of cultural texts forms a reference point for reading a commercial: depending on the cultural context cued by music, some meanings embedded in visual ad elements can be acquired by the viewer while other meanings can become less apparent. Music in particular, which is congruent with visual ad components, reinforces the connecting cultural context to communicate meanings by supporting a relevant schema. Furthermore, some meanings embedded in visual ad components may be changed, as when the viewer experiences the commercial in an alternative cultural context cued by incongruent music. The findings suggest that music can help viewers organize complex visual materials into meaningfully cross-modal gestalts.

References

Alpert, J. I., and Alpert, M. I. (1989). "Background music as an influence in consumer mood and advertising responses." *Advances in Consumer Research* 16: 485–491.

_____ (1990). "Music influences on mood and purchase intentions." *Psychology and Marketing* 7: 109–133.

_____ (1991). "Contributions from a musical perspective on advertising and consumer behavior." *Advances in Consumer Research* 18: 232–238.

Bierley, C., McSweeney, F. K., and Vannieuwkerk, R. (1985). "Classical conditioning of preferences for stimuli." *Journal of Consumer Research* 12: 316–323.

Blair, M. E. and Hatala, M. N. (1992). "The use of rap music in children's advertising." *Advances in Consumer Research* 19: 719–724.

Blair, M. E. and Shimp, T. A. (1992). "Consequences of an unpleasant experience with music: A second-order negative conditioning perspective." *Journal of Advertising* 21: 35–43.

Brannon, L. A. and Brock, T. C. (1994). "Test of schema correspondence theory of persuasion: Effects of matching an appeal to actual, ideal, and product 'selves.'" In E. M. Clark, T. C. Brock, and D. W. Stewart (eds.) *Attention, Attitude, and Affect in Responses to Advertising* (pp. 169–188). Hillsdale, NJ: Lawrence Erlbaum Associates.

Brosius, H.-B. and Fahr, A. (1996). *Werbewirkung im Fernsehen: Aktuelle Befunde der Medienforschung*. Munich: Verlag Reinhard Fischer.

Brown, S. P. and Stayman, D. M. (1992). "Antecedents and consequences of attitude toward the ad: A meta-analysis." *Journal of Consumer Research* 19: 34–51.

Bruner II, G. C. (1990). "Music, mood, and marketing." *Journal of Marketing* 54: 94–104.

Bullerjahn, C. (1993). "Kulturelle Duftmarken eines Egoisten." In K.-E. Behne, H. de la Motte-Haber, and G. Kleinen (eds.) *Musikpsychologie: Empirische Forschungen—Ästhetische Experimente. Jahrbuch der Deutschen Gesellschaft für Musikpsychologie* (pp. 137–141). Wilhelmshaven: Florian Noetzel Verlag.

_____ (2000). "Do music videos stir up sex and violence in our teenagers?" *Music Forum* (Australia) 6: 26–29.

_____ (2001). *Grundlagen der Wirkung von Filmmusik* [Fundamental Principles of the Effects of Film Music]. Augsburg: Wißner-Verlag.

Bullerjahn, C., Bode, A., and Mennecke, M. (1994). "The Sound of Fashion: Rockmusik, Zeitgeist und Jugendlichkeit in Fernsehwerbeclips." In J. Frieß, S. Lowry, and H. J. Wulff (eds.) *6. Film- und Fernsehwissenschaftliches Kolloquium/Berlin '93* (pp. 81–88). Berlin: Gesellschaft für Theorie und Geschichte audiovisueller Kommunikation e. V.

Czypionka, A. (1999). "Musikalische Repertoirebildung durch Werbung." In M. L. Schulten (ed.) *Medien und Musik. Musikalische Sozialisationen 5–15 jähriger* (pp. 198–238). Münster: LIT Verlag.

Dunbar, D. S. (1990). "Music, and advertising." *International Journal of Advertising* 9: 197–203.

Englis, B. G. (1991). "Music television and its influence on consumers, consumer culture, and the transmission of consumption messages." *Advances in Consumer Research* 18: 111–114.

Gorn, G. J. (1982). "The effects of music in advertising on choice behavior: A classical conditioning approach." *Journal of Marketing* 46: 94–101.

Gorn, G. J., Goldberg, M. E., Chattopadhyay, A., and Litvack, D. (1991). "Music and information in commercials: Their effects with an elderly sample." *Journal of Advertising Research* 5: 23–32.

Haase, H. (1989). "Werbewirkungsforschung." In J. Groebel and P. Winterhoff-Spurk (eds.) *Empirische Medienpsychologie* (pp. 215–246). Munich: Psychologie-Verlags-Union.

Hahn, M. and Hwang, I. (1999). "Effects of tempo and familiarity of background music on message processing in TV advertising: A resource-matching perspective." *Psychology and Marketing* 16: 659–675.

Helms, S. (1981). *Musik in der Werbung*. Wiesbaden: Breitkopf und Härtel.

Hung, K. (2000). "Narrative music in congruent and incongruent TV advertising." *Journal of Advertising* 29: 25–34.

_____ (2001). "Framing meaning perception with music: the case of teaser ads." *Journal of Advertising* 30: 39–49.

Huron, D. (1989). "Music in advertising: An analytic paradigm." *The Musical Quarterly* 73: 557–574.

Kellaris, J. J. and Cox, A. D. (1989). "The effects of background music in advertising: A reassessment." *Journal of Consumer Research* 16: 113–118.

Kloepfer, R. and Landbeck, H. (1991). *Ästhetik der Werbung. Der Fernsehspot in Europa als Symptom neuer Macht*. Frankfurt am Main: Fischer Taschenbuch Verlag.

la Motte-Haber, H. de and Emons, H. (1980). *Filmmusik: Eine systematische Beschreibung*. Munich: Carl Hanser Verlag.

MacInnis, D. J., Moorman, C., and Jaworski, B. J. (1991). "Enhancing and measuring consumer's motivation, opportunity, and ability to process brand information from ads." *Journal of Marketing* 55: 32–53.

MacInnis, D. J. and Park, C. W. (1991). "The differential role of characteristics of music on high- and low-involvement consumers' processing of ads." *Journal of Consumer Research* 18: 161–173.

Macklin, M. C. (1988). "The relationship between music in advertising and children's responses: An experimental investigation." In S. Hecker and D. W. Stewart (eds.) *Nonverbal Communication in Advertising* (pp. 225–243). Lexington, MA: D. C. Heath.

Middlestadt, S. E., Fishbein, M., and Chan, D. K.-S. (1994). "The effect of music on brand attitudes: Affect- or belief-based change?" In E. M. Clark, T. C. Brock, and D. W. Stewart (eds.) *Attention, Attitude, and Affect in Responses to Advertising* (pp. 149–167). Hillsdale, NJ: Lawrence Erlbaum Associates.

Morris, J. D. and Boone, M. A. (1998). "The effects of music on emotional response, brand attitude, and purchase intent in an emotional advertising condition." *Advances in Consumer Research* 25: 518–526.

North, A. C. and Hargreaves, D. J. (1997). "Music and consumer behavior." In D. J. Hargreaves and A. C. North (eds.) *The Social Psychology of Music* (pp. 268–289). Oxford: Oxford University Press.

Olsen, G. D. (1994). "The sounds of silence: Functions and use of silence in television advertising." *Journal of Advertising Research* 34: 89–95.

Park, C. W. and Young, S. M. (1986). "Consumer response to television commercials: The impact of involvement and background music on brand attitude formation." *Journal of Marketing Research* 23: 11–24.

Petty, R. E. and Cacioppo, J. T. (1983). "Central and peripheral routes to persuasion: Application to advertising." In L. Percy and A. G. Woodside (eds.) *Advertising and Consumer Psychology* (pp. 3–24). Lexington, MA: D. C. Heath.

Pitt, L. F. and Abratt, R. (1988). "Music in advertisements for unmentionable products: A classical conditioning experiment." *International Journal of Advertising* 7: 130–137.

Schmidt, S. J. (1990). "'All images will soon be interchangeable' (J. Gerz) or What advertising can tell scholars of empirical aesthetics." Keynote address to the XIth International Conference of Empirical Aesthetics. Budapest, August 22–25.

Schmidt, S. J., Sinofzik, D., and Spieß, B. (1991). "Kulturfaktor Werbung: Entwicklungen und Trends der 80er Jahre." In C. W. Thomsen (ed.) *Aufbruch in die Neunziger: Ideen, Entwicklungen, Perspektiven der achtziger Jahre* (pp. 142–170). Cologne: DuMont Buchverlag.

Scott, L. M. (1990). "Understanding jingles and needledrop: A rhetorical approach to music in advertising." *Journal of Consumer Research* 17: 223–236.

Stewart, D. W., Farmer, K. M., and Stannard, C. I. (1990). "Music as a recognition cue in advertising-tracking studies." *Journal of Advertising Research* 30: 39–48.

Stewart, D. W. and Punj, G. N. (1998). "Effects of using a nonverbal (musical) cue on recall and playback of television advertising: Implications for advertising tracking." *Journal of Business Research* 42: 39–51.

Tauchnitz, J. (1990). *Werbung mit Musik. Theoretische Grundlagen und experimentelle Studien zur Wirkung von Hintergrundmusik in der Rundfunk- und Fernsehwerbung.* Heidelberg: Physica-Verlag.

Tom, G. (1990). "Marketing with music." *The Journal of Consumer Marketing* 7: 49–53.

———— (1995). "Classical conditioning of unattended stimuli." *Psychology and Marketing* 12: 79–87.

Vinh, A.-L. (1994). *Die Wirkungen von Musik in der Fernsehwerbung.* Ph.D. diss. St. Gallen, Hochschule für Wirtschafts-, Rechts- und Sozialwissenschaften. Rosch-Buch. Hallstadt.

Wintle, R. R. (1978). *Emotional Impact of Music on Television Commercials.* Ph.D. diss. University of Nebraska UMI 79-01, 953.

Yalch, R. F. (1991). "Memory in a jingle jungle: Music as a mnemonic device in communicating advertising slogans." *Journal of Applied Psychology* 76: 268–275.

PART IV GOVERNMENTAL/ INDUSTRIAL CONTROL

Chapter 9

MUSIC CENSORSHIP FROM PLATO
TO THE PRESENT

Marie Korpe, Ole Reitov, and Martin Cloonan

Introduction

The current chapter describes the motivations and mechanisms of music censorship from both a historical and cross-cultural perspective. It focuses especially on religion and government as the two principal censorial agents, where
censorship is generally driven by a desire to control mass behavior. While censorship has been applied to everything from musical intervals to musical genres
to performance contexts, the most clear-cut examples are those in which musicians themselves are restricted, persecuted, imprisoned, expelled, or killed as a
result of their musical activities. Along these lines, we examine a series of case
studies of musicians who have been under fire in such diverse locales as Algeria,
Afghanistan, South Africa, Nazi Germany, the former Soviet bloc, and modern-
day America. While music censorship is generally viewed as a straightforward
manipulation of music, it ultimately turns out to be a mixed bag, especially in
cases where the expression of hateful and violent sentiments represents a direct
threat to the livelihood and security of minority groups within a society. The
topic of music censorship, therefore, touches on a wide range of moral issues.

* * *

Censorship and propaganda represent two of the major means by which music
undergoes manipulation at the social level (Korpe, 2003; Vidal-Hall, 2003).
While these two processes are highly intertwined, the current chapter focuses
on censorship, which is often rooted in political and religious ideologies
underlying such divergent practices as nationalism, racism, traditionalism, and

Notes for this chapter begin on page 260.

sexism. Censorship is a form of cultural protection and intended mass behavioral control. It can be implemented by a wide range of institutions, including governments, mass media, religious authorities, industries, business firms, school systems, retailers, musical groups, parents, and even individual musicians (Cloonan, 1996; Martin and Segrave, 1988; Owen, Korpe, and Reitov, 1998; Korpe, 2001; Cloonan and Garofalo, 2003). The targets of music censorship are equally diverse, and include musical systems (e.g., musical intervals, rhythms), associated texts (i.e., song lyrics), musical instruments, musicians, performances, performance contexts, individual musical works, and musical genres (see Bremberger [1990] and Cloonan [2003] for an extensive discussion of music censorship and its terminology).

Although the effects of censorship can be easily identified in cases where composers and performers are imprisoned or killed, the social and economic repercussions of censorship are more difficult to measure. A culture deprived of its artistic creations and musical heritage clearly loses an important link to its history and identity. However, no study has been conducted thus far on the social or economic consequences of music censorship. We will concentrate here on investigating why, where, and how music—either on its own or in combination with words—is condemned, banned and persecuted. In particular, we will focus on the two principal agents of music censorship—religion and state—both of which are strongly concerned with regulating mass behavior. They often do so through control of the symbolic elements of a culture. Cultural artifacts carry with them the power to influence the minds and motivations of the masses, and with it, the power to divert people from an awareness of and compliance with the normative behaviors of a society, as dictated by religious and political ideologies. The control of culture is thus a major concern for both clerics and politicians.

The first significant written account of a proposal to censor music is found in Plato's *Republic*, written in roughly 375 B.C. In one of the most famous passages of ancient literature to deal with music, we find Socrates, Plato's mentor and mouthpiece, engaged in a dialogue with Adeimantus (an elder brother of Plato), describing which of the eight musical modes he would eliminate from the training regime of the rulers ("guardians") of his ideal state. Socrates speaks first:

> "But we agreed as far as the words are concerned to dispense with dirges and laments did we not?"
> "We did."
> "Tell me then—you are a musician—which are the modes suitable for dirges?"
> "The Mixed Lydian and the Extreme Lydian and similar modes."
> "Then we can reject them," I said: "even women, if they are respectable, have no use for them, let alone men."
> "Quite right."
> "But drunkenness, softness, or idleness are also qualities most unsuitable in a Guardian."

"Of course."

"What, then, are the relaxing modes and the ones we use for drinking songs?"

"The Ionian and certain Lydian modes, commonly described as 'languid.'"

"Will they then," I asked, "be of any use for training soldiers?"

"None at all," he replied. "You seem to be left with the Dorian and Phrygian."

(*The Republic* 398d–399a; Plato, 1987: 99–100)

Socrates then goes on describe the musical instruments and rhythms he would include and exclude from this ideal city.

Why all this fuss about modes? It seems clear that it wasn't the modes themselves but instead the *activities* associated with musics using these modes that were the objects of Plato's condemnation. The modes themselves were only symptomatic of a larger social problem associated with reckless uses of music. As ancient Greece and later the Roman empire saw the emergence of many religious cults that combined music, alcohol, and sex, Plato had a particular interest in banning the Bacchic cults of his day. In his good society, citizens required the guidance of a specially trained and morally superior class of "guardians" who could judge the good from the bad in music (and all other domains, for that matter). As Curt Sachs (1943) pointed out, Plato almost certainly depended on even older authorities for his arguments: "In the fifth century B.C., Herodotos had related that Egyptian youths were not allowed to learn music at random, only good music was conceded, and it was the priests who decided what good music was. In the same order of thought ... melodies of bad tonality were avoided, while those particularly appropriate to steering the character took precedence" (p. 243).

Lippman (1964: 81) noted that Plato decried musical excess "as the ruin(ation) of the state; musical degeneracy leads to degeneracy in morals. The effect of bad music, he holds, is like the effect of bad company. Confusion, or lack of definition, in the meaning of music is only a step removed from clearly vicious content." He continues that, in an important passage from *The Laws*, Plato discusses the difference between the nature of law and freedom: "[T]he discussion turns at once to music, for in music, it is maintained, lies the origin and foundation of both good order and lawlessness" (p. 83). Plato was referring to the laws of music and the process whereby order is gradually succeeded by a situation in which performers start mixing styles, leading to bad music. Plato had a severe distrust of poets and believed that they composed licentious works that inspired the masses to lawlessness and disrespect for their rulers: "The gravest charge against poetry still remains. It has a terrible power to corrupt even the best characters" (*The Republic* 605c; Plato, 1987: 374). Plato was highly concerned about this, and sought to control the bad in music, thus becoming the first major scholar to step down the long historical road to the "music police."[1]

Reese (1940), in his research on ancient and medieval music, suggested that the ideas of Plato and his followers were the precursors of Christian (and later Muslim and Communist)[2] hard-line attitudes toward music. He pointed out that "Porphyry [a neo-Platonist], though a defender of paganism and violent opponent of Christianity, came to exercise a definite influence upon the Church Fathers. An ardent advocate of asceticism, he disapproved of the sensuous pleasure afforded by music and placed dramatic spectacles and dances, with their music, in the same class as horse-races" (p. 59). As we shall see, ideas that highlight the potential of music to cause social upheaval recur throughout the various justifications to censor music. As modern nation-states emerged from the beginning of the seventeenth century, so too did the sophistication of music censorship (and, conversely, of the means of avoiding it). Prior to this, the main censorial agent was organized religion, to which we now turn.

Implementing God's Will? Religion and the Censorship of Music

In thinking about the religious censorship of music, it is important to keep in mind that religion is actually one of the great propagandizing forces that exists, designed to create homogeneity of belief, attitude, and behavior. It is to be expected, then, that religious authorities should want not only to take advantage of the power of music to bring about obedience and conformity but also to regulate its ability to divert people away from the straight path outlined for them by religious doctrine. The story of religious censorship, therefore, is really the dual tale of imposing one type of music while simultaneously blocking all others. Censorship ranges from urging the faithful not to partake of various forms of music through to outright bans on music at times when clerics have themselves been in power or had strong influence with ruling regimes. In particular, societies in which Christianity and Islam have been the dominant religions have seen the articulation of doctrines identifying music as a central cause of undesirable (e.g., sexual) behavior and a detraction from religious practice and a virtuous lifestyle (see Godwin 1985, 1988 for just one modern example of such arguments).

The Work of the Devil?

A common idea that pervades Jewish, Christian, and Muslim writings on the topic is that music causes sensual feelings of pleasure and that such feelings lead unerringly to debauchery and thoughtlessness (Shiloah, 1992). Yet music is not to be prohibited altogether, for it clearly has a great capacity to enhance worship; it is a source of joy that can fortify faith in God. This dichotomy often takes form in such a way that the positive uses of music are seen as the grace of God, whereas those that lead to debauchery are seen as the work of the Devil. Music must therefore be rigorously controlled so as to enhance its positive effects while at the same time preventing its sensual effects. This line of thought has generally taken the form of a code whereby devotional music that is explicitly tied to worship—and especially music associated with religious texts of some kind—is accepted, whereas music that occurs outside the context of worship—and especially instrumental music associated with dance—is generally forbidden because of its sensual qualities.

The great Jewish scholar Maimonides (1135–1204) provided a systematic summary of prohibitions against music, listed here in increasing order of severity: listening to a song with a secular text; listening to a song that is accompanied by an instrument; listening to a song whose content includes obscene language; listening to a string instrument; listening to passages played on such instruments while drinking wine; and, finally, listening to the singing and playing of a woman (Shiloah, 1992). The only musical instrument that is currently allowed to be played as part of Jewish worship is the *shofar* (a ram's horn), which is only played during the High Holiday prayers. While instruments were unquestionably a part of Jewish worship in the days of the temple in Jerusalem, rabbinical scholars called for a ban on instrumental music in the synagogue, ostensibly as a gesture of mourning for the destruction of the second temple in 70 A.D. But can we perhaps imagine that this prohibition was simply a convenient means of eliminating what may have been the sensual consequences of instrument playing in the temple?

A similar situation was found during the formation of the Christian church. Music was thought of as a source of sin, vice, paganism, obscenity, lasciviousness, and all things secular. Therefore, every attempt was made to keep music outside the church. But as mentioned, music was also recognized as something having an unprecedented power to unify people and create a special link with God. Music that was used in the appropriate manner could be a transcendental source of beauty. What was important was that the music be subordinate to the words, as was true for Judaism and even in Plato's own thinking. Basil the Great, the influential fourth-century Greek Christian scholar, wrote: "What did the Holy Spirit do when he saw that the human race was not led easily to virtue and that, due to our penchant for pleasure, we gave little heed to an upright life? He mixed the sweetness of melody with doctrine so that inadvertently we would absorb the benefit of the words through gentleness and ease of hearing, just as clever physicians frequently smear the cup with honey when giving the fastidious some rather bitter medicine to drink" (quoted in Cole, 1993: 54). So music did end up having a place in the Christian worship, though as with the Jews and later the Muslims, only in association with liturgical texts.

The end result was a distinction not only between religious and secular music but between acceptable music and dangerous music. Many forms of non-devotional music, especially those associated with sensual behavior, were attributed to the workings of Devil. In cultures dominated by the Judeo-Christian-Islamic religions, pagan rituals were often said to the be the product of the Devil, and this was sufficient basis to officially censor music in a given society. Every student of classical music knows that the interval of the tritone (i.e., the augmented fourth or diminished fifth) was called "diabolus in musica"—the Devil in music—and was officially prohibited from Church music. As Godwin (1987: 51) pointed out, "the Devil's musical skill serves one purpose only: the seduction of souls." Myths about the Devil's relationship to both music and musical instruments can be found in ancient cultures throughout the Mediterranean:

> The God Pan, whose original representation was in the invisible world of sound of the forest and who was subsequently represented in animal form with horns, was called *Faunus* by the Latins and *Cernunnos* by the Celts. These characters perpetuated once again the horned Paleolithic shaman, guide and protector of the wild animals and the forest and inventor of the flute, who became confused with the Devil by the medieval Christians. Bacchus, Dionysius—bestower of knowledge of fertility, sex and the plant world—for the Greeks, raised by Pan's nymphs in a cave similar to Shiva in India, is the mythical cultural hero, bestower of knowledge of the plant world, particularly wine and psychoactive substances which lead to ecstasy, as well as the dancers and the music of Bacchanalia. In the course of the Roman cults of Pan, Bacchus, Cybele, Jupiter and Venus, very ancient instruments were used … buzzers, horns, sounding stones and the flute. (Maioli, 1996: 5–6)

Thus, Pan as proto-Devil served as a source of many notions that music was dangerous and in need of the strictest control.

There are many recorded incidents of songs being banned by religious authorities because they were thought to foster superstition or undermine public order. One such song was the "Media Vita," which ran afoul of the French authorities in the thirteenth and fourteenth centuries. "The melody achieved the rank of an ecclesiastical folk-song. Miraculous powers were ascribed to it. When in the year 1263 the Archbishop of Treves appointed a certain William to be Abbot of the Monastery of St. Matthias against the will of the monks, they prostrated themselves on the ground and said the Media Vita and other prayers, and thus hoped to get protection from the Abbot who was being forced upon them.… The Council of Cologne in 1316 forbade the Media Vita to be sung against anyone without the archbishop's permission" (Reese, 1940: 129).

Censorship of music extends well beyond the borders of individual societies to all those places where these societies exert a cultural influence. While it is safe to assume that the conquerors in all conflicts in human history have tried to impose their culture on the conquered, the period of European colonialism that began in the fifteenth century offered unprecedented opportunities for cultural imposition. With that, music censorship moved from being an internal matter of individual nations to being the mission of the new colonial powers bent on extending their reaches to all parts of the world. Royalty, religion, and trade joined hands in bringing "civilization" to previously unconquered continents, and with the spread of colonialism came many new forms of cultural and religious imperialism, as those who sought to control cultural life at home now sought to do so in distant lands. Wherever Christian missionaries moved, an intense war was declared on all forms of traditional, pagan culture, including (and especially) the music and dance rituals.[3] From Greenland to

Latin America, drums and other traditional instruments were burned and the performance of traditional music and dance forbidden. In Western Greenland, for example, a whole culture of drum dancing was completely destroyed by Danish missionaries, whereas in remote Eastern Greenland, the traditions survived despite many attempts at eradication. Several missionaries in Greenland simultaneously performed the roles of police, judge, and executioner, and conducted public lashings when they observed the use of ritual frame drums.

Such practices also contributed to the bringing of Christianity and civilization to the native Eskimo/Inuit population in the 1720s. In 1728, a Norwegian-born priest, Hans Egede, set out on behalf of the Royal Kingdom of Denmark to christianize the Eskimo population. He was well known for punishing and beating performers of shamanistic rituals and for destroying or burning their traditional frame drums. The missionaries reported back to the Missionary College in Copenhagen during their stay. In one report, Niels Egede (Hans's son, who was equally active in missionary work) wrote of an incident that took place on 9 March 1740 when, during a visit to a small Eskimo community with a certain Mr. Drachardt, an Eskimo provoked Drachardt by beating a frame drum. Egede reported: "So I took the drum away and beat them [the Eskimos] hard. I myself got a share of the beating, but when they realized my superiority, they became very humble and I could get them to do whatever I wanted" (Missionary Report, 1744: 136). In the book *On the Greenlanders*, written in 1769, Egede reported that certain Eskimo/Inuit songs and festivities were strongly forbidden by the clergy (cited in Hauser, 1992).

The impact of colonialism on traditional music is part of a broader story in which Christian authorities were implicated in attempts to censor culture via eradication. Another aspect of this story concerns internal missionaries. As late as the end of the nineteenth century, internal missionaries in Sweden recommended that traditional fiddlers burn their instruments as these were considered "the tools of the Devil." This recommendation was followed by several musicians (Malm, 1985: 160). Another good example involves the form of Christianity practiced by the Society of Friends, or Quakers, who are revered today for their altruistic ethos and pacifist principles. In the early days of their movement in the seventeenth century, the Quakers "were strongly opposed to music, as to all the arts. George Fox, founder of the movement, denounced all such amusement and regularly attended fairs 'to preach against all sorts of music'... although he also sanctioned the (unaccompanied) singing of psalms. The Quaker's Yearly Meeting and Epistle of 1846 speaks of the practice and acquisition of music as 'unfavorable to the health of the soul' and as leading to unprofitable and even pernicious associations, and, in some instances, to a general indulgence in the vain amusement of the world" (Baily, 2001: 41). In more contemporary times, as the roles of missionaries have gradually changed in the postcolonial era, various Christian organizations have continued in their attempt to suppress different types of music. In part, the history of popular music in the twentieth century is also that of attacks on jazz, rock 'n' roll, pop, and rap music by a variety of clerics and religious organizations. Sometimes such attacks formed part of overtly racist ideologies, and more often than not they occurred in combination with explicit political agendas.

The Land of the Free?

Some of the most vociferous attacks on music have occurred in the United States, where religious groups and family associations, inspired by seventeenth-century Puritan attitudes, have had a long history of lobbying for censorship. To cite just one example from the 1920s: "Anne Shaw Faulkner of the General Federation of Women's Club—a bulwark of American Protestantism—published the article 'Does Jazz put the Sin in Syncopation?'" in the *Ladies Home Journal* in August of 1921 (D'Entremont, 1998: 34). Shaw characterized jazz as "the accompaniment of the voodoo dancer, stimulating the half-crazed barbarian to the vilest deeds" (p. 34). Christian organizations have often been at the forefront of the public debate about music and the attempt to "cleanse" American culture, to the point that it is now difficult to disentangle political censorship from overtly Christian censorship. In some instances, right-wing Christian groups have attacked rock music for being "communist and hypnotic."[4] In others, as examined by Godwin (1985, 1988), Jones (1988), Pyle (1985), and MacKenzie (1987), the beat of rock has been identified as the direct work of Satan.

In the mid 1980s, Ronald Reagan's America witnessed what was arguably the most successful censorial campaign yet attempted by religiously inspired groups. This was an anti-obscenity campaign that centered on the work of the Parents Music Resource Center (PMRC), a pressure group formed in 1985 by the wives of a number of leading politicians (Chastanger, 1999; Nuzum, 2001). The most prominent of these was Tipper Gore, wife of later Vice President and presidential candidate Al Gore. She was moved to action after finding her eight-year-old daughter listening to the song "Darling Nikki" from Prince's *Purple Rain* album, which tells of a young woman masturbating with a magazine in a hotel lobby. Another prominent founder was Susan Baker, the wife of then Secretary of the Treasury James Baker. While not directly affiliated with religion, the PMRC had a number of direct contacts with religious groups and drew upon their literatures in their own campaigns (Sullivan, 1987). The organization sought to get the music industry to adopt a more responsible attitude toward the contents of its output. It organized what became known as the "porn rock" Senate hearings in September of 1985 (Chastanger, 1999: 184), during which record industry figures were called on to defend their industry's product. In November of 1985, the Recording Industry Association of America (RIAA) signed an agreement with the PMRC to place warning labels on albums containing "explicit" lyrics. As a result of this, warning stickers saying "Parental Advisory: Explicit Lyrics" started to appear on albums, as they do to this day in the US and its sites of exportation.[5, 6]

This had an important impact. America's largest retail chain, Wal-Mart, soon responded to lobbying groups by deciding not to sell CDs with warning labels in its 2,300 outlets. Because of its financial clout in America, Wal-Mart was able to demand special censored versions of CDs for its stores, a demand that most of the major companies complied with. In recent years, religious groups have systematized their attacks on controversial musical groups—usually rap and heavy-metal artists—as well as influenced school authorities to deny performance possibilities to certain bands. The introduction of warning labels has also led to several cases of self-censorship by the record industry, as some record companies have refused to sign on acts that they believed might require warning labels on their recordings (Cloonan, 1996: 59). The financial effects of American censorship, however, are difficult to analyze. Many banned groups seem to find their own distribution channels and may even benefit from the media coverage associated with bans. As Jones (1991) has argued, politicization of music through bans or warning labels often stimulates people's curiosity about the banned music and thereby increases sales of the album. Nonetheless, it seems clear that religiously motivated censors from the Christian right will continue in their attempt to shape the content of music within the US and beyond.

Music and Islam

Christianity is not the only world religion whose censorial agenda has had a strong political impact. Recent concern in the West about freedom of expression in Islamic countries can be traced back to 1989 and the vociferous attacks that were waged against the book *The Satanic Verses* and its author Salman Rushdie. In examining the place of music in Islam, we confront two apparently contradictory pictures. One is of absolute dedication to music: millions of people in the Arab-speaking world tuning in to Radio Cairo on the first Thursday night of every month, year after year during the 1930s to 1950s, to revel in the magical voice of Egyptian singer Oom Kalthoum (Umm Kulthum). The other is a picture of absolute condemnation of music: Islamic scholars rejecting music as the work of Satan (see Malm, 1985: 160) and the public beating of musicians and the banning of musical performances in 1980s Iran under Ayatolah Khomeini and 1990s Afghanistan under the Taliban. In Afghanistan, Taliban officials maintained a ban on music by arguing that "music has a corrupting influence on the sexes, distracting them from their real duties: to pray to and praise Allah" (Baily, 2001: 39), and many incidents were reported of musicians being beaten, instruments officially burned, and music lovers jailed for possession of audio cassettes.[7] There were also cases where musicians have had to pay with their own lives.

In November 1994, a religious primary school teacher went into the Musicians' and Singers' Club in Omdurman, Sudan, and stabbed to death Khogali Osman, a popular singer. This incident was the culmination of an anti-music campaign launched by the governing National Islamic Front (NIF), as publicized on national radio. "The NIF both fears and seeks to manipulate music and musicians. As a result, periods of repression alternate with periods of coercion, both of them designed to gain control of one of the most potent popular forces in the country" (Verney, 1998: 77). Two months before Osman's killing, seventy-five wedding guests were arrested in northern Sudan for protesting against a ruling dictating that wedding parties (and their accompanying music) end before the sunset prayers. In a society where music, dance, and weddings had been cultural cornerstones for centuries, the introduction of "Islamic law" and the attacks on music that followed created a great deal of tension (Verney, 1998). The campaign for the "Islamization of art" included other violent attacks on musicians, not to mention the demolition of retail cassette shops, the downgrading of the Sudan Institute of Music and Drama, and the erasing of valuable recordings from the radio archives.[8]

However, it is important to keep in mind that music censorship in the Muslim world is not always driven by religious motivations, as there are several well-documented cases of prohibitions inspired by political and ethnic factors. Prominent examples include the bans on Kurdish music in Turkey and Berber music in Algeria, which can be seen as having predominantly political and nationalistic overtones.

The Quran, Music, and a Musical Hierarchy

A number of Muslim scholars—like their counterparts in other religions—have claimed that religion cannot be separated from politics and that religious texts, in this case the Quran, must guide and regulate all aspects of life, including musical practice. In order to understand the relationship between music and Islam, therefore, we must examine Islam's scriptures and their interpretations in order to see what they reveal about the religion's attitude toward music. The Holy Quran does not, in fact, say anything at all about music or music making. The contemporary abstract concept of music did not exist during the times of Mohammed (570–632). For that reason, religious scholars typically make reference to the "Hadith," which contains the sayings and actions attributed to Mohammed during his lifetime. A millennium-long debate continues over how certain incidents and quotations of the Prophet, as described in the Hadith, come to bear on the practice of music in society, and therefore how music should be controlled.

Writing in 1910, Mustafa Sabri, a prominent Ottoman scholar, expressed his own attitude toward music this way: "Music is a useless activity which, in fact, is a state of passiveness.... The benefit and pleasure taken from music involves a meaning of deep slavery in passion.... If the effect of music on feelings must indeed be an important need for the soul, the recitation of the Quran serves that need in a much more dignified way."[9] Variants of this viewpoint have been expressed by Islamic thinkers since the ninth century. Amnon Shiloah, perhaps the most renowned scholar of music in the world of Islam, summarized the general ambivalence of Islam toward music thus:

> [W]hen music is considered a spell inspired by the devil, it calls into question the basic concept of a transcendental divinity with absolute rule over the world and the deeds of men. Acting as an irresistible force, music can be identified with magical powers that oppose religious elements which presumably have an independent capacity to guide man's destiny. These arguments would imply rejection of all music. In fact, the total prohibition involves only art music, which displays man's vanity and primarily furthers interest in mundane, worldly concerns. It does not apply to folk tunes or, by extension, to certain forms used in religious music which are not regarded as music *per se* and are not even called music. This is due to the predominance of the text in religious or folk music, wherein the combination of sounds is relegated to a secondary role, or is a device mainly designed to support the words and enhance their meaning. (Shiloah, 1995: 37)

There has thus been a theological debate within Islam concerning how music should be defined and which categories of music should be deemed acceptable. If music is used in the service of religious devotion, it is permissible. However, as soon as it becomes part of entertainment or an art form in of itself, controversy reigns. In particular, so-called sensuous music is condemned by traditionalists in a manner reminiscent of many Jewish and Christian traditionalists. In essence, two and only two forms of chant constitute the religiously sanctioned forms of musical expression in Islam, yet they are not considered to be music at all by Muslim definitions. Music—in the Western sense of the word—refers instead to the realm of the profane, such as popular music, dance music, and all wordless instrumental music. As with Judaism (and probably because of Judaism), Islam gives an overwhelming priority to "the word" and only sanctions those uses of music that enhance and glorify the word; all other uses are highly suspect. The two forms of chant that are officially sanctioned are referred to as *adhan* and *tadjwid*. *Adhan* is what is conventionally known as the "call to prayer," which is sung by a *muezzin* five times a day from the minaret of a mosque. The *adhan* is essentially a signaling device that beckons worshipers to the mosque at the time of prayer. *Tadjwid* refers to the chanting of the Quran, and is itself predated by a conceptually similar system employed by Jews for chanting the Torah (Shiloah, 1992) using ascending or descending musical lines and melismatic embellishment. The *adhan* and *tadjwid* constitute the only compulsory music of the mosque and thus the only officially acceptable expressions of what Westerners refer to as music. Again, Quranic recitation is considered to be neither singing nor music by Muslims.

This presents a categorical distinction between religious chant and all the rest that Westerners think of as music, which is often given the catch-all designation *musiqa*. While this term usually refers to purely instrumental music—and to certain secular musical genres in particular—the mass media and modern technology have influenced people living in Muslim countries today so that they understand the term "music" in much the same way as Westerners do. There is thus an understanding of the typology of musical categories found in the West, such as religious music, classical music, popular music, and dance music. In the mid 1980s, at a peak of the controversy about music in Muslim countries, researcher Lois Lamya' al-Faruqi (1989) developed a hierarchical scheme charting the status of music in the Islamic world (see also Stokes, 1992: 208). She differentiated between "legitimate" music (or *halal musiqa*) and controversial or prohibited music (*haram musiqa*). While much of the latter consists of instrumental music, a notable exception consists of the musical practices of the Sufi Muslims, who, like their Hasidic counterparts in Judaism, find instrumental and wordless music to be an essential channel for communicating with God. One form of Sufi music that has attracted international attention is "Qawwali" music, which is a type of mystical and devotional music performed by Sufis in Pakistan. It is not uncommon to find performances of Qawwali music in Europe's concert halls and music clubs nowadays despite its overriding religious import. The relationship between music and Islam remains a complex one, and we now examine some case studies of the control of music and musicians in Muslim countries.

Algerian Rai

Censorial practices in Muslim countries have the potential to confuse many Western observers. For example, "Rai" music has for many years been the favorite of the youth of Algeria as well as a central feature of the "world music" explosion. The music has often been described as rebellious or even revolutionary in Western media, as the term "rai" literally means "opinion." However, many Rai artists distance themselves from politics, at least in the formal sense. The most renowned international Rai artist, Khaled, living in exile in Paris, said: "I don't sing about politics. I sing about love, alcohol, sex and the liberation of women. It is the *integristes* [i.e., those who want to integrate religion into every aspect of life] that mix religion and politics.... I respect religion but I don't want an Imam as Prime Minister" (Reitov, 1992). The fact that Rai artists have been banned from public appearance and the media at various times has been seen by many Westerners as a political ban, whereas in the Muslim context it is seen as a case of *haram musiqa* (see above), music that is sensuous and on a par with prostitution and decadent lifestyles. It is thus condemnable in the religious manner of distinguishing good from bad taste rather than from a purely political perspective (see Schade-Poulsen, 1999).

Finally, the ideological and physical attack on musicians in Muslim countries is only the tip of the iceberg. As in the West, musical censorship in most Muslim countries is also carried out by record companies and radio stations. While modern technology provides global access to all kinds of information via cables, satellites, and the Internet, most people outside of the industrialized world are still at the mercy of regulated national media, which are often times nothing more than mouthpieces for the ruling regime. Where the media are under autocratic political control, strong forms of musical censorship can be effected. In the following section, we turn our focus to state control of music.

Rocking the State

The power of religion to shape the beliefs and values of a society has been superseded in recent years by the power of nation-states to do so. Censorial prerogative has thus shifted from the domain of clerics to that of politicians. Control of popular culture and, in particular, of the airwaves has become a preoccupation of those in power. Most nation-states have sought to exert some level of control over the airwaves by means of state-run broadcast media, which provide not only entertainment but official versions of news events for the masses. Even countries such as the United States, which have never opted for the use of state-run broadcasting services, have passed legislation controlling the activities of the mass media, including regulations that broadcasters remain compliant during times of national emergency. Censorship by nation-states, moreover, has taken the form of anti-obscenity laws, such as the UK's Obscene Publications Act (1959), which has been used to censor music (Cloonan 1996: 75–95). Several forms of popular culture have been at continual loggerheads with these laws (de Grazia, 1992; Matthew, 1994). Thus, while it is usually assumed that the totalitarian regimes of the twentieth century—with their desire to control *all* media—provide the starkest examples of censorship, it is also the case that censorship battles have taken place in the liberal democracies of the West, such as the United States (Martin and Segrave 1988; Winfield and Davidson, 1999) and the UK (Cloonan, 1995, 1996).

The story of state and quasi-state censorship of popular music is a long and complicated one (Ramet, 1994; Cloonan and Garofalo, 2003). As far back as the early fifteenth century, England was home to music censorship when King Henry V issued an edict dictating that "No ditties shall be made or sung by minstrels or others" (cited in Hillman, 1968: 15). This edict was canceled in 1422, but in 1553, at the time of the upheavals that accompanied the Reformation, a royal proclamation called for the suppression of "ballads and rimes and other lewd treatises in the English tongue." A 1543 edict banned all printed ballads for worry that they might "subtly and craftily instruct the king's people and especially the youth of the realm," a ban that was lifted by Edward VI, reinstituted by Mary, and lifted again by Elizabeth I (Hillman, 1968). But by the end of the sixteenth century, ballads were again censored for being overly lewd.

Such prohibitions against songs with lewd lyrics can be seen as the precursors of today's anti-obscenity laws. However, these benign edicts of the sixteenth century were to be strongly overshadowed by the extreme ideological censorship that emerged in the twentieth century with the rise of two major political ideologies, namely, Nazism and Communism. In the case of Nazi Germany, various forms of musical expression, especially those by Jewish, black, and modernist composers and performers, were labeled "degenerate" and completely prohibited. In the Soviet Union, similar attacks on "formalist" music led to harsh bans against modernist composers and their works. We consider these two cases in greater detail below. We also examine a more poorly documented case, that of apartheid South Africa, where censorial policies were upheld under a regime that was highly authoritarian though not fully totalitarian.

Nazi Germany

Music censorship under the Third Reich is well documented (Kater, 1992; Levi, 1994; Dümling, 1995). The authorities in Nazi Germany set their sights on a number of musical enemies—Jews, modernists, the Romani—and made it their mission to quash their musical activities through a variety of means. Censorship in Nazi Germany is instructive not only because of the extensive institutional infrastructure that drove it but because of the intimate link that was established between censorship and propaganda. With the formation of the Reich Music Chamber (Reichsmusikkammer or RMK) as part of the Reich Chamber of Culture (Reichskulturkammer or RKK), its president Joseph Goebbels took commanding control over the cultural policy of Nazi Germany. The RKK encompassed all members of the creative professions, and composers were forced to become members of the RMK if they wished to work. Membership was refused to "undesirables" such as all Jews. For propaganda purposes, Richard Strauss was made president of the RMK in 1934; he was forced out of this position in 1935 for having collaborated with a Jewish librettist, Stefan Zweig, on his opera Die schweigsame Frau. This opera was banned after only a few performances (Levi, 1994). As a result of the work of Goebbels and other ideologues like Alfred Rosenberg, strict anti-Semitic laws were set in motion that prevented Jewish composers and musicians from having any role at all in the musical life of Germany and the occupied territories.

An essential part of the National Socialist agenda was the construction of a racially pure Aryan identity. This was effected in the cultural realm through a joint propaganda/censorship program designed, respectively, to promote German culture and to eradicate all art that was viewed as being incompatible with German ideals. A radical musical manifestation of this agenda was the war against modernism, a program known as "Entartete Musik" or degenerate music. In 1938, an exhibition of Entartete Musik took place as part of the Parade of German Musical Life (Reichmusiktage) in Düsseldorf. This was no doubt inspired by the spectacular success of an exhibition of degenerate art that had been held the year before in Munich. The Düsseldorf exhibition presented portraits and musical works (on gramophone) of modernist and non-Aryan composers such as Schoenberg, Weil, Stravinsky, Hindemith, and many others. The exhibition's organizer, Hans Severus Ziegler, wrote in the program book that "[t]he Entartete Musik exhibition presents a picture of a veritable witch's sabbath portraying the most frivolous intellectual and artistic aspects of Cultural Bolshevism ... and the triumph of arrogant Jewish impudence.... Degenerate music is thus basically de-Germanised music" (quoted in Levi, 1994: 96). At the Parade of German Musical Life, Goebbels laid out ten rules for German musical creativity and stated that "the battle against Jewishness in German music [is] our primary duty at present, never to be abandoned" (quoted in Dümling, 1995: 10). As Ludwig (1998: 158) pointed out, "[T]he *Entartete* Programme became a policy of censorship that supported the ethnic and political cleansing of German society." Some composers, like Schoenberg, were able to flee into exile. Hanns Eisler, an active Marxist, found temporary asylum in the US, only to fall victim to cold-war McCarthyism. Driven from the US, he eventually became the leading composer of East Germany—ironically enough a state that had instituted its own harsh system of ideological music censorship (Wicke and Shepherd, 1993). But other composers were not as lucky as Schoenberg and Eisler. Among them were several renowned Jewish composers who were prisoners in the concentration camp Theresienstadt (Terezín), located 30 kilometers outside of Prague. In fact, the Nazi's most insidious form of music censorship was genocide.

Theresienstadt was unique among the concentration camps in that it served as a propaganda showpiece for the Nazis. Its most notorious achievement was to manipulate a visiting delegation from the International Red Cross into believing that rumors about extermination camps being "the final solution" for the Jews were completely unfounded, and that the worst fate facing the Jews was life in wholesome-looking work camps like the one Theresienstadt was made out to be (Karas, 1985). The Red Cross visit was filmed, and these images were incorporated into a propaganda film entitled "The Fuhrer Gives the Jews a City" (1944). But the reality was quite different. Theresienstadt was actually a transfer camp for people en route to the extermination camps in Poland. The prisoners lived in deplorable conditions. Fully 95 percent of its 140,000 prisoners, including all the children, either were killed in the death camps or died in Theresienstadt itself. Because of Theresienstadt's function as a propaganda set, the Nazis freely encouraged the prisoners of the camp to develop an active and rich cultural life, something that would be exploited in the presence of international inspectors. This included an incredible program of concerts, theater performances, painting classes, lectures, and much more (Makarova, 1995). Among the musicians imprisoned in the camp were Viktor Ullmann (a former student of Schoenberg), Hans Krása (a former student of Zemlinsky), Pavel Haas (a former student of Janacek), and the pianist/composer Gideon Klein. The musical works that these and other composers created in Theresienstadt are virtually the only notated musical remains of the concentration camps. This music, including Ullmann's bold opera *The Kaiser from Atlantis* and Krása's moving children's opera *Brundibar*, served as a source of hope and fortitude for the doomed inmates of Theresienstadt. However, outside of this camp, music was used in the other concentration camps as an insidious tool for humiliation, deception, and torture, as described in detail by Moreno (1999; see also Moreno's chapter in this volume).

The Soviet Union

Music censorship in Soviet Russia, while not oriented toward the genocidal practices of the Nazis, still involved severe restrictions on the activities of composers and musicians. The major targets of these activities, as with Nazi Germany's *Entartete Musik* program, were modernist composers and, in later decades, rock 'n' roll musicians. Stalin came to power in the late 1920s. Soon after that, in 1932, the Union of Soviet Composers was created to shape the content and form of music in the Soviet Union. What is often cited as the turning point for Soviet music was an unsigned 1936 article in the newspaper *Pravda* entitled "Chaos Instead of Music," which provided a damning condemnation of Dmitri Shostakovich's 1934 opera *Lady Macbeth of the Mtsensk District*. The case against *Lady Macbeth* was a strong personal attack against Shostakovich, one that he accepted with resignation. By the time the *Pravda* article come out, the opera had already received nearly 200 performances. However, the article appeared just days after a Moscow performance of the opera that Stalin had attended and walked out of. The opera was immediately withdrawn, as was Shostakovich's ballet *The Limpid Stream*. According to the new Stalinist ideology of "social realism," the "social and moral aspects of music were eventually given precedence over purely aesthetic considerations, so that, for the first time in any society, music was drawn into the direct service of government policy.… [M]usical works should have a socialist content and should be expressed in a readily understood language addressed to the people at large. The Party promoted national feelings and the use of folk materials" (McAllister, 1980: 384–385). In this new milieu, the chief enemy of wholesome music was "formalism" (as modernism was usually called). The modernist works of Schoenberg, Hindemith, and others were banned from performance, and those of Russian composers such as Stravinsky and Prokofiev were disowned by the authorities.

If the 1936 censure of Shostakovich represented a personal attack against a single renegade composer, the next censure was to have a much more collective and devastating impact. The end of World War II was accompanied by ideological purges of music even greater than had occurred during the 1930s. In one of the worst excesses of that period, Andrei Zhdanov, Stalin's personal emissary, in his capacity as chair of the First Congress of Soviet Composers, equated "formalism" with "decadent Western influences." A decree passed in February of 1948 by the Communist Party's Central Committee accused Shostakovich, Prokofiev, Khachaturian, Myaskovsky, Shebalin, and others of formalism in their music. Their compositions represented "formalistic perversions and anti-democratic tendencies in music," namely, the "cults of atonality, dissonance and discord … [and] infatuation with confused, neurotic combinations which transform music into cacophony" (quoted in Schwarz, 1986: 179–180). Their music was considered to be "alien to the Soviet people." This decree had devastating consequences for all the named composers. For example, many of Prokofiev's early works were banned from performance. His newer works did not find favor with the Union of Soviet Composers, and this unquestionably contributed to his failing health (McAllister, 1986). He died in 1951, only three years after the Zhdanov decree.

A post-Stalin easing of restrictions on classical composers in later decades was accompanied by strong censorial practices in the realm of rock and jazz music (Starr, 1983; Bright, 1985; Ryback, 1990). Such practices were seen not only in Russia but in all the countries of the Soviet bloc, including Poland, Czechoslovakia, East Germany, Hungary, the Baltic Republics, Yugoslavia, Romania, and Bulgaria, all of which experienced severe restrictions on performances and recordings of popular music. This manifested itself in the form of state control over the activities of local musicians—through licensing systems for live performance and control over access to recording studios—as well as bans on foreign recordings. For example, in 1984 the Russian Ministry of Culture banned the recordings of a number of local and international artists, including the Ramones, Elvis Costello, the Who, the Sex Pistols, and 10cc. Rock music was simply considered to be a danger to society, in large part because of its symbolic representation of democracy and free expression in the West.

Wicke (1992) provided a telling example of how state-run music censorship actually backfired and led to the downfall of a highly repressive regime. Not long after rock music appeared on the scene in East Germany, it came under the control of a state-sponsored dependency system designed to depoliticize what appeared to be the subversive nature of the music and its song texts. In September of 1989, some 100 musicians signed a manifesto rallying the public against the "inflexible political line" of the social system and calling for "an immediate dialogue with all relevant parties" on the hostilities and contradictions of the current social situation. The regime viewed the statement as a crime against the state and canceled all important public performances in order to prevent the reading of this manifesto. But the ploy backfired. "On October 7, 1989, the 40th anniversary of the founding of the GDR [German Democratic Republic], during performances by rock musicians, singer-songwriters, and other artists throughout the whole country, the statement was read publicly. It precipitated an unprecedented degree of solidarity between performers and audiences.... [A] course of action had been set in motion which could not be stopped" (Wicke, 1992: 90). Not long after this, the Communist government in East Germany tumbled.

Apartheid South Africa

While sharing many similarities with the cases of Nazi Germany and Soviet Union, music censorship in apartheid South Africa (1948–1994) sprang up from a mixture of racism and Calvinistic ideology. Although it did not make use of such terms as "degenerate music" and "formalism," the main idea behind apartheid music policy under the ruling National Party was that certain types of music—especially racial and stylistic hybrids—should be prohibited, leaving the racially divided sectors of society to listen to and develop only their own types of music. In practice this involved the development of forms of censorship targeting performances, recordings, and airplay. The net result was a plethora of bizarre events. As mixed audiences and black performances for white audiences were banned in the early years of the apartheid regime, several musicians were caught in a paradoxical situation. A growing young white audience took an interest in black popular music, but as (white) music clubs were not allowed to have black musicians perform, bars developed a system of "shadow players." Black musicians would dress up as waiters and play music behind a screen, while in front of the screen, white performers mimed the music for the white audience. If the police ever appeared, the "shadow" musicians would immediately pick up a tray and walk around as if they were waiters. Black musicians working as such shadow players faced heavy risks within their own communities if it was ever found out that they had been working for "the white enemy" (Reitov, 1998b).

Although the ban on mixed performances was eventually lifted in the mid 1980s, musicians continued to be harassed by the police and military forces. The paranoia of the South African secret police led it to plant musician-spies in the band of Anton Goosen, a white singer-songwriter whose socially critical songs were considered a danger to the apartheid system.[10] In an interview with one of this chapter's authors (O.R.), he said: "At Houtstock, [we] had a bomb at a big concert. And me, personally, in '89–'90, the security police followed us. They knew what we were doing. They were listening to conversations with me and my girlfriend on the phone, sometimes interrupting, making their own little remarks. Yeah, we were watched … we were watched very carefully.... There was a spy in my band, not only one, there were two of them. The drummer was ex-security police, and his big mission was to try to get information from the Conservative Party's diaries. And the other one's girlfriend, the guitarist's girlfriend, was working for national intelligence" (Reitov, 1998a). Ray Phiri, best known as a guitarist on Paul Simon's *Graceland* album, also found out that one of his former managers was a spy (Korpe, 2001). Under the apartheid system, several black musicians were forced to leave the country. Some of them, such as Miriam Makeba, Hugh Masekela, and Abdullah Ibrahim (Dollar Brand), went on to gain worldwide recognition, while those who stayed behind and spoke up against the policies of apartheid, like Ray Phiri, did so at great personal risk.

So did some white musicians. A key example of this was Johnny Clegg, a white social anthropologist and musician who was imprisoned several times as a teenager when he started mixing with Zulu musicians. He was threatened by the police and military, and took great risks by performing with a racially and culturally mixed group, Juluka, which he formed with his Zulu musician-friend Sipho Mchunu in 1976. While some musicians gave in to these forms of censorship, which were based on a combination of state oppression and market forces, others tried to subvert or bypass the system by using metaphors in their lyrics. This allowed them to make political points while avoiding state censorship, something Clegg approved of and practiced. Clegg and his band had several concerts banned, and the state-owned South Africa Broadcasting Corporation (SABC) censored several of his songs. In this case, the censorship related not so much to the cultural mixing in Clegg's music (which clearly violated the apartheid idea of racial purity) but to the lyrics.

Apartheid Media

Censorship of the radio in South Africa involved control over what type of music could be aired to certain groups of listeners residing in racially demarcated areas. As part of the apartheid government's goal of dividing the masses, a plan for "Bantu Radio" was developed in 1962. It constituted "a cynical exercise in apartheid wish-fulfillment: broadcasting was to be harnessed as a propaganda tool to foster 'separate development.' In the cities, monolingual programming would encourage ethnic identity while in the rural 'bantustans,' radio would provide the voice of incipient nationhood. It was intended that the rural stations would feature exclusively the traditional music of their regions in order to encourage ethnic separatism" (Allingham, 1994: 377). However, the apartheid regime did not succeed in its mission, for rural stations found that they had to include (officially unacceptable) forms of popular music in order to attract listeners.

At the same time, harsh censorship of lyrics was introduced, and the SABC gradually developed a very efficient control system, beginning with its record libraries. Under this system, record companies had to submit lyrics for all the records that were to be delivered for airplay. A group of program directors would meet once a week and decide which records would be banned and which would be allowed. The SABC record librarians would then mark or destroy records that contained banned lyrics. The SABC developed a set of thirteen guidelines to direct the censors in their decisions,[11] including the banning of all "lyrics that may inflame public opinion" and "lyrics [that] propagate the usage of drugs." Although the SABC was a highly politicized body, to which intelligence officers often paid visits, the former censor Cecile Pracher reported that the record library was so efficient in performing its duty that intelligence never bothered to pay the censor board a visit (Korpe, 2001: 21–44). One well-known example of a banned song was Pink Floyd's "Another Brick In The Wall," which was banned by the SABC in 1980 after it became a great favorite among student demonstrators in Soweto. The song's lyric "we don't need no education" became "we don't want your education" in demonstrations against the so-called Bantu education program, whose aim was to give black students a practical non-university education. Pink Floyd's album *The Wall* was banned after having sold thousands of copies. According to several informants, it was initially a surprise to the regime that black students would even listen to the music of a white British rock band.

When thinking about the censorship of music, it is perhaps simplest to focus on the short-term effects brought about by governments and media organizations. However, it is also important to take a broader, longer-term approach to the problem in order to ascertain the full impact of censorship. Internal censorship in South Africa unquestionably crippled creativity and thus the development of the music industry there, especially as the new genre of "world music" made its dramatic appearance on the world stage in the 1980s, becoming an influential and financially profitable force in the global music market. Unable to participate fully in this development, South African musicians lost many years of financial and creative access to the world market for several reasons: the censorship within the country, the cultural boycott imposed by the United Nations and most Western countries, and also the comparative underdevelopment of its own industry. Democratic South Africa has thus had to cope with the cultural as well as the financial legacy of apartheid.

Conclusion

This chapter has focused on the religious and political manipulation of music, and examined a number of relatively straightforward cases of censorship. We wish to end by stressing that there is a flip side to our discussion of censorship as a purely repressive and manipulative force. An ongoing debate over music censorship is taking place in democratic countries in response to the explosive rise of hate music, including so-called white noise music (Lööw, 1998a; Barber-Kersovan, 2003). The rise of neo-Nazis and other white supremacist groups in Europe and America has created problems for states that seek to defend free speech while simultaneously aiming to defend the rights and security of minority groups. To what extent should a democratic government tolerate the intolerant? When does censorship shift from being a form of mass manipulation to being a form of humanitarian protection?

International and national legislative codes are in certain ways both internally contradictory and incompatible with one another on this point. Article 19 of the International Covenant on Civil and Political Rights states that "everyone shall have the right to freedom of expression." But Article 20 of the same document states that "any advocacy of national, racial or religious hatred that constitutes incitement to discrimination, hostility or violence must be prohibited."[12] These sentiments are difficult to reconcile. In Sweden, for example, the authorities have stopped several concerts organized by neo-Nazi groups, citing the music as part of an expression of Nazi views that is not permitted under the Swedish Criminal Code (Lööw, 1998b). This latter code outlaws the expression of views or the dissemination of information that acts to threaten or express disrespect for any particular race, ethnic group, or other grouping of people. In a 1996 trial, the Swedish High Court ruled that it was unlawful to wear Nazi symbols because their association with the Nazi persecution of Jews gave them the capacity to incite hatred against certain groups. However, such protective legislation has not been easy to put into action in Sweden. It is not until some direct threat against individuals or groups has been established that these laws become effective. In fact, Sweden has traditionally been one of the countries with the strongest laws guaranteeing freedom of expression, which explains why it is currently one of the major producers and exporters of Nazi music recordings and print-propaganda, not to mention home to many Nazi web sites. So there is an important sense in which Swedish law is internally contradictory. This example merely shows that governments in liberal democracies are grappling with the problem of, on the one hand, providing freedom of (cultural) expression for its citizens and, on the other, providing protection for minority groups that are the objects of blatant expressions of hate and violence.

Meanwhile, the power of lobbying organizations to control censorship has been amply illustrated in the United States. Although the First Amendment to the US Constitution guarantees freedom of expression, local authorities and lobbying groups have long been able to influence social policy regarding music. The many cases of music censorship in American schools and the American recording industry are testament to the power of religious and political lobbying groups, whose influence has spread well beyond the US and into Europe. Countries subject to religiously dominated regimes, such as many Arab and Asian countries, apply censorship to music; the net effect, though, is always undercut by economic differences across the society, since the richer residents can generally acquire access to world media-products by means of satellite dishes and the Internet while poorer people from these same countries are solely dependent on national media that are strongly controlled by the government and under constant pressure from religious groups.

Another factor that complicates the face of music censorship is self-censorship, an interesting example being the voluntary ban on the public performance of Richard Wagner's works in Israel, which lasted nearly 60 years. Wagner was a highly vocal and unapologetic anti-Semite. His music, though composed many decades before there was ever such a thing as National Socialism, became an emotional symbol of Hitler's crusade to destroy Jewish culture through ethnic cleansing. Wagner, both because of his personal views about Jews and because of his connections to the Nazi regime decades after his death, became in the eyes of Israelis the ultimate anti-Jewish composer, one whose music was seen as unfit for performance in a Jewish state. In October of 2000, the Rishon Leztion Symphony Orchestra, under the direction of Mendi Rodan—himself a Holocaust survivor—performed Wagner's *Siegfried Idyll* in a regularly scheduled concert near Tel Aviv. Well before the concert took place, strong protest was voiced by many Israelis, most especially Holocaust survivors. One 83-year-old survivor even went to the courts to appeal for a restraining order to stop the concert. In the end, the Israeli Supreme Court refused to stop the concert, and the performance went ahead as scheduled.

These examples demonstrate the inherently contradictory nature of censorship. Democratic governments are supposed to guarantee freedom of cultural expression but are also supposed to set limits on these expressions when they infringe on the rights of others. Censorial practices can be bypassed by members of certain strata of society, making their effects unequal. Self-censorship can be effected for purely emotional (and perhaps even irrational) reasons. In many ways, the power of nation-states to carry out censorship is being undermined as global communication networks expand and international trade barriers crumble. This means that it is becoming more difficult for governments to control what their citizens have access to; however, history suggests that nation-states will be reluctant to relinquish control. Likewise, adherents of timeless religious beliefs are unlikely to give up their efforts to regulate spiritual purity. But as church and state decline in importance in the control of music, another censor appears quite ready to step in to fill the censorial void—namely, the market. And there is no guarantee that it will prove to be any less censorious than its religious and political predecessors.

Notes

1. The term "music police" has been used in various contexts as a metaphor for scholars or reviewers who claim to know the rights from the wrongs in musical expression. The term was often used in the fevered debate about traditional music during the 1960s and 1970s.
2. Perris (1985: 99) suggested that Mao Zedong's early readings included Plato's *Republic*, and therefore that Mao was aware of the potential harm that music could cause.
3. Similarly, attempts were made to prevent contamination of domestic culture from "alien" sources. Thus, many attacks on early rock 'n' roll music in the United States concentrated on its alleged alien origins. For example, in his anti-rock tract, Pyle (1985) wrote of being told by missionaries in Haiti and Africa that "the beat and the movements of their pagan and sensual dances in these so-called heathen lands are exactly the same as the beat and movements of the rock 'n' roll dances over here in so-called civilized America" (p. 10).
4. In 1965, the Reverend David A. Noebel published a pamphlet called "Communism, Hypnotism and the Beatles" for the right-wing John Birch Society. In it, Noebel outlined his fear that rock music would make "a generation of American youth useless through nerve-jamming, mental deterioration and retardation." For more on this, see Sullivan (1987).
5. Several web sites have published Senate hearings and included details on parental advisory campaigns. The most consistent documentation of music censorship in the US is done by Mass MIC at www.massmic.com. A parental advisory program jointly introduced by the Recording Industry Association of America and the National Association of Recording Merchandisers has aimed at avoiding local state legislation by employing education campaigns. See Fischer (2003) and www.ericnuzum.com/banned for more about attempts to legislate musical content in the US.

6. Editors' note: one of the artists called to defend their art was Frank Zappa, who later used sampled portions of the hearings on his album *Frank Zappa Meets the Mothers of Prevention* (see Volgsten, 1999).
7. These dark images contrast with the picture in another Muslim country, namely, music-loving Mali, where people have the highest regard for female griot singers and where some of the major figures on the world music scene, such as Salif Keita and Ali Farka Touré, had their start. Combining these latter musicians with Senegal's Youssou N'Dour, Algeria's Khaled, and Pakistan's Nusrat Fateh Ali Khan, we see that the Muslim world contains a rich musical diversity that ranges from classical music to ecstatic religious music to folk music to global pop.
8. See www.dr.dk/p1/censorship/listen.htm for a discussion of music censorship in Sudan.
9. The text is available at www.wakeup.org/anadolu/05/4/mustafa_sabri_en.html.
10. See www.freemuse.org/04artist.html.
11. The SABC guidelines can be found at www.freemuse.org/03libra/subjects/aparth02.html.
12. See www.hrweb.org/legal/cpr.html.

References

al-Faruqi, L. L. (1989). "The Shari' ah on music and musicians." *al-ʿilm* 9: 33–53.
Allingham, R. (1994). "Township jive." In S. Broughton, M. Ellingham, D. Muddyman, and R. Trillo (eds.) *World Music: The Rough Guide* (pp. 373–390). London: Penguin.
Baily, J. (2001). *Censorship of Music in Afghanistan*. Copenhagen: Freemuse.
Barber-Kersovan, A. (2003). "German Nazi bands, censorship and (state) repression." In M. Cloonan and R. Garofalo (eds.) *Policing Pop* (pp. 188–206). Philadelphia: Temple University Press.
Bremberger, B. (1990). *Musikzensur: Eine annäherung an die Grenzen des Erlaubten in der Musik*. Berlin: Verlag Schmengler.
Bright, T. (1985). "Soviet crusade against pop." *Popular Music* 5: 123–148.
Chastanger, C. (1999). "The Parents' Music Resource Center: From information to censorship." *Popular Music* 18: 179–192.
Cloonan, M. (1995). "Popular music and censorship in Britain: An overview." *Popular Music and Society* 19: 75–104.
_____ (1996). *Banned! Censorship of Popular Music in Britain, 1967–1992*. Aldershot: Arena.
_____ (2003). "What is the censorship of popular music?" In M. Cloonan and R. Garofalo (eds.) *Policing Pop*. (pp. 13–29). Philadelphia: Temple University Press.
Cloonan, M. and Garofalo, R. (eds.) (2003). *Policing Pop*. Philadelphia: Temple University Press.
Cole, B. (1993). *Music and Morals*. New York: Alba House.
de Grazia, E. (1992). *Girls Lean Back Everywhere*. New York: Random House.
D'Entremont, J. (1998). "The Devil's disciples." *Index on Censorship* 27 (6): 32–39.
Dümling, A. (ed.) (1995). *Entartete Musik*. Berlin: City of Berlin Department for Cultural Affairs.
Fischer, P. (2003). "Rock, rap, and Rehnquist: American challenges to popular music as expression." In M. Cloonan and R. Garofalo (eds.) *Policing Pop* (pp. 223–239). Philadelphia: Temple University Press.
Godwin, J. (1985). *The Devil's Disciples*. Chicago: Chick.
_____ (1987). *Harmonies of Heaven and Earth*. London: Thames and Hudson.
_____ (1988). *Dancing With Demons*. Chicago: Chick.
Hauser, M. (1992). *Traditional Greenlandic Music*. Copenhagen: Kragen/Ulo.
Hillman, B. C. (1968). "When the king banned pop songs." *The Times,* 3 August, p. 15.
Jones, R. (1988). *Stairway to Hell*. Chicago: Chick.

Jones, S. (1991). "Ban(ned) in the USA: Popular music and censorship." *Journal of Communication Inquiry* 15 (1): 73–87.

Karas, J. (1985). *Music in Terezín.* Stuyvesant, NY: Pendragon Press.

Kater, M. (1992). *Different Drum: Jazz in the Culture of Nazi Germany.* New York: Oxford University Press.

Korpe, M. (ed.) (2001). *1st World Conference on Music and Censorship.* Copenhagen: Freemuse.

_____ (ed.) (2003). *Shoot the Singer! Music Censorship Today* London: Zed Books.

Levi, E. (1994). *Music in the Third Reich.* New York: St. Martin's Press.

Lippman, E. A. (1964). *Musical Thought in Ancient Greece.* New York: Columbia University Press.

Lööw, H. (1998a). "White-power rock 'n' roll: A growing industry." In J. Kaplan and T. Bjørgo (eds.). *Nation and Race: The Developing Euro-American Racist Subculture* (pp. 126–147). Boston: Northeastern University Press.

_____ (1998b). "White noise." *Index on Censorship* 27 (6): 153–155.

Ludwig, M. (1998). "Tales of Terezín." *Index on Censorship* 27 (6): 156–165.

MacKenzie, R. (1987). *Bands, Boppers and Believers.* Harare: Campaign for Cleaner Rock.

Maioli, M. (1996). "The music of ancient Rome." Notes to the CD *Music from Ancient Rome,* vol. 1. Amitata Records ARNR 1396.

Makarova, E. (1995). "Introduction." In E. Makarova (ed.) *Theresienstadt: Culture and Barbarism* (pp. 112–124). Stockholm: Carlsson Bokförlag.

Malm, K. (1985). *Islam: Religion-Kultur-Samhälle.* Stockholm: Statens Historiska Museum.

Martin, L. and Segrave, K. (1988). *Anti-Rock: The Opposition to Rock and Roll.* Hampden, CT: Archon Books.

Matthew, T. D. (1994). *Censored!* London: Chatto and Windus.

McAllister, R. (1980). "Russian art music." In S. Sadie (ed.) *The New Grove Dictionary of Music and Musicians* (pp. 384–387). London: Macmillan.

_____ (1986). "Sergey Prokofiev." In G. Abraham, H. Macdonald, G. Norris, R. McAllister, and B. Schwarz, *The New Grove Russian Masters 2* (pp. 109–171). New York: Norton.

McDonald, J. (1989). "Censoring rock lyrics: A historical analysis of the debate." *Youth and Society* 19 (3): 294–313.

Missionary Report (1744). *Continuation af relationerne betræffende den Grønlandske Missions tilstand og beskaffenhed.* Copenhagen: Missionskollegiet.

Moreno, J. (1999). "Orpheus in hell: Music and therapy in the Holocaust." *The Arts in Psychotherapy* 26: 3–14.

Nuzum, E. D. (2001). *Parental Advisory: Music Censorship in America.* New York: Harper Perennial.

Owen, U., Korpe, M., and Reitov, O. (eds.) (1998). "Smashed hits: The book of banned music." *Index on Censorship* 27 (6).

Perris, A. (1985). *Music As Propaganda: Art to Persuade, Art to Control.* London: Greenwood Press.

Plato (1987). *The Republic.* Translated by Desmond Lee. London: Penguin.

Pyle, H. (1985). *The Truth About Rock Music.* Murfreesboro, TN: Sword of the Lord.

Ramet, S. (ed.) (1994). *Rockin' the State.* Boulder, CO: Westview Press.

Reese, G. (1940). *Music in the Middle Ages.* New York: Norton.

Reitov, O. (1992). Interview with Khaled. Stockholm.

_____ (1998a). Interview with Anton Goosen. Johannesburg.

_____ (1998b). Interview with Pops Mohamed. Copenhagen.

Ryback, T. (1990). *Rock Around the Block.* Oxford: Oxford University Press.

Sabri, M. (1910) "A topic of dispute in Islam: Music." *Beyan-ul-Haq* 63 (3): www.wakeup.org/anadolu/05/4/mustafa_sabri_en.html.

Sachs, C. (1943). *The Rise of Music in the Ancient World East and West.* New York: Norton.

Schade-Poulsen, M. (1999). *Men and Popular Music in Algeria: The Social Significance of Raï.* Austin: University of Texas Press.

Schwarz, B. (1986). "Dmitry Shostakovich." In G. Abraham, H. Macdonald, G. Norris, R. McAllister, and B. Schwarz, *The New Grove Russian Masters 2* (pp. 175–231). New York: Norton.

Shiloah, A. (1992). *Jewish Musical Traditions*. Detroit: Wayne State University Press.

_____ (1995). *Music in the World of Islam: A Socio-Cultural Study*. Aldershot: Scholar Press.

Starr, S. (1983). *Red and Hot*. Oxford: Oxford University Press.

Stokes, M. (1992). *The Arabesk Debate: Music and Musicians in Modern Turkey*. Oxford: Clarendon Press.

Sullivan, M. (1987). "More popular than Jesus: The Beatles and the religious far right." *Popular Music* 6: 313–326.

Verney, P. (1998). "Does Allah like music?" *Index on Censorship* 27 (6): 75–78.

Vidal-Hall, J. (ed.) (2003). *The A-Z of Free Expression*. London: Index on Censorship.

Volgsten, U. (1999). *Music, Mind and the Serious Zappa: The Passions of a Virtual Listener*. Stockholm: Department of Musicology.

Wicke, P. (1992). "'The times they are a-changin': Rock music and political change in East Germany." In R. Garofalo (ed.) *Rockin' the Boat: Mass Music and Mass Movements* (pp. 81–92). Boston: South End Press.

Wicke, P. and Shepherd, J. (1993). "The cabaret is dead: Rock culture as state enterprise—The political organization of rock in East Germany." In T. Bennet, S. Frith, L. Grossberg, J. Shepherd, and G. Turner (eds.) *Rock and Popular Music: Politics, Policies, Institutions* (pp. 25–36). London: Routledge.

Winfield, B. H. and Davidson, S. (eds.) (1999). *Bleep! Censoring Rock and Rap Music*. London: Greenwood Press.

Chapter 10

ORPHEUS IN HELL

Music in the Holocaust

Joseph J. Moreno

Introduction

The contradictory role of music in the Holocaust is demonstrated in the ways music was used by the Nazis and for the intentional abuse of concentration camp prisoners for such purposes as deception, humiliation, and control. At the same time, the presence of music sometimes had clear therapeutic value for both the prisoners and their captors. Prisoner orchestras were organized in the camps primarily to perform military marches to accompany the long processions of prisoners departing for and returning from their daily work details, but they were also utilized to play regular concerts for the SS and their families. For these officers, the incongruous use of music in these places of killing seemed to improve their quality of life in the remote camps that were otherwise devoid of such entertainments. By contrast, for prisoner musicians in these ensembles, music making became a path to survival. For ordinary prisoners the music often had mixed meanings. For some, its associations with the positive aspects of a normal life irretrievably lost added to their suffering, while for others it symbolized something to hold onto, a hope for a better future. The emotional compartmentalization that enabled the Nazis to genuinely respond to sentimental music, while involved daily in the murder of thousands of innocent prisoners, remains a paradox that is difficult to comprehend.

* * *

It is now more than sixty years since the end of World War II and that period between 1933 and 1945 that is now referred to as the Holocaust. The Holocaust

Notes and references for this chapter begin on page 285.

saw the purposeful and systematic murder of six million Jews and other minorities as part of Hitler's infamous "final solution," and still stands as one of the most horrifying events in human history.

In considering the endless atrocities of the Holocaust, one might well imagine that it would be an unlikely place to find anything that would hint at a therapeutic role for music. And yet, music often played a significant and even therapeutic role, not only for the victims of the Holocaust but for the perpetrators as well. Indeed, music was used by the perpetrators in ways so incongruous and bizarre that they raise fundamental questions about the deepest meanings of music and its relation to human emotions.

For the victims of the Holocaust, the role and meaning of music is clearer and more in line with what one would expect. At best music provided a degree of support, something positive to hold on to in the worst possible circumstances and, for some, even a means of survival. However, these people were also subjected to musical torments and manipulations, and in those perverted circumstances, their musical experiences were anything but positive.

By contrast, if we look at the meaning of music for the perpetrators of the Holocaust and the extreme ways in which it was used to deceive, humiliate, and manipulate the victims, questions arise that are far more difficult to understand. How could genuine musical sentiment and mass murder comfortably coexist? How could the citizens of the country that gave us Bach, Beethoven, and Brahms not only have been Hitler's willing executioners, but even used that very same music to aid in the extermination process of millions of Jews and many other victims?

It requires a total reversal of medical ethics to comprehend the fact that the mass murders in the death camps were directly supervised by fully qualified German physicians (Lifton, 1988). In one characteristic example of the association between music and murder carried out by a physician, an SS doctor in the Buchenwald camp in Germany "finished off a whole row of prisoners with injections of sodium evipan and then strolled from the operating room, a cigarette in hand, merrily whistling 'The End of a Perfect Day'" (Kogan, 1980: 149).

The best-known of the Nazi German physicians involved in the Holocaust was Dr. Josef Mengele, who carried out selections of the arriving transports at Auschwitz, the most infamous of the Nazi death camps. In a typical selection of about 1,500 people, as many as 1,200–1,300 would go directly to the gas chambers. During this process, Mengele would often sit whistling his favorite music. His preferences included Mozart, Wagner, Verdi, Puccini, and Johann Strauss (Lengyel, 1947). A "long-time lover of opera and classical music," the "music-mad" Mengele was in many ways a cultured man whose passion for music well preceded his involvement in the death camps (Lengyel, 1947: 144). This contradictory behavior of making music while selecting victims for the gas chambers exemplifies the Holocaust's evocation of many disturbing questions about the meaning of music and its relationship to human feelings. Mengele's whistling during the selections was probably not done in a taunting manner; more likely he just sought the simple pleasure that any person might get from whistling a familiar melody as he works.

Mengele was obsessed with carrying out pseudo-scientific medical experiments on sets of twins that he was able to retrieve from the arriving transports. He was whistling when he first met one particular set of twins. Since both boys had studied classical music in Hungary, they recognized the music as Mozart's and told this to Mengele. He was very pleased and continued to enjoy discussing music with them, even as he went on to use them as subjects for his brutal medical experiments (Lagnado and Dekel, 1992).

Perhaps the most incongruous role of music in the concentration camps was that of the prisoner orchestras. When the SS commanders of a camp decided to form an orchestra, it was easy to recruit musicians from the thousands of transports that arrived daily. Those who were recruited upon arrival were often surprised to imagine that they could be utilized for playing music, as opposed to what they may have initially perceived as laboring in a work camp. Those who had been in the camps for any length of time well knew that their inevitable fate would soon be death by exhaustion, starvation, and gassing; for them the opportunity to be involved in a camp orchestra was a path to survival. Once accepted into a performing group, camp musicians were generally exempt from normal work details and had opportunities to have more and better food than the other prisoners. So long as they played satisfactorily for the SS, they had a chance to stay alive, literally "playing for time," as expressed in the title of the autobiographical book by Fania Fenelon (1977) describing her experiences in the women's orchestra in Birkenau, a part of the Auschwitz camp complex.

Music in the Transports

Even in the cattle cars transporting the prisoners to their final destinations, spontaneous music making often arose as a way of trying to sustain morale. A typical example of music as group support is the story of Alfred Werner, who was thrown into a train boxcar for transport to Dachau. The men were packed so tightly together they could not move and there were no toilets. Werner noticed the despair around him and started singing Yiddish songs. The others joined in and the songs helped them to cope, at least for the moment (Mizrachi, 1994). A similar experience is described by Roman Mirga, a Romani survivor of a group that was sent to Auschwitz in the cattle cars (Ramati, 1985). Suffering from thirst during the long trip, the Romani prisoners tried to persuade the train guard to bring them water, but he completely ignored them. In their despair, one woman began a Gypsy song, "From village to village Gypsy girls are strolling." Other women picked up the tune and, noting his attention, began to direct their singing to the guard. He enjoyed their singing, applauded, and asked for more. They then asked him again for water, and this time he obliged. The women's music served a useful purpose in a kind of exchange of music for water. As for the guard, his behavior seemed to be motivated by the musical reward rather than any basic humanitarian concern for the prisoners who were suffering from extreme dehydration. In one transport of all women, one woman was singing to her five-year-old daughter who was traveling with her. All were suffering, and this woman was singing so beautifully she comforted the others. She sang, in German, a song with words that translate as "I'll buy you a pink crinoline, my child, when you and I go to your first ball together." Full of emotion all the women in the car joined in the song. In the end, the mother, her daughter, and nearly all the rest were gassed on arrival in Auschwitz.

Music as Humiliation and Torment

The prisoner musical ensembles served different functions at different times, pointing to the many paradoxical roles that music played in the death camps. For example, in the Belzec camp in Poland, a six-member musical group was used both for entertainment of the SS men and during the extermination of the transports. The musicians were set up in the area between the gas chambers and the burial pits and were compelled to play during the transfer of the corpses from the gas chambers to their graves (Arad, 1987). For arriving transports from the Polish city of Zamosc, the orchestra was forced to play such popular German songs as "Everything Passes, Everything Goes By" (Reder, 1946: 42–44). This music, which most people associated with life and happiness, was here used to torment and further humiliate the prisoners, underscoring the horror of their situation. In a similar manner, before getting their food in the afternoon, prisoners from Belzec were forced to sing while the orchestra played and other prisoners were being herded into the gas chambers (Arad, 1987).

In the Sobibor camp, another Polish death camp that was part of the Aktion Reinhard camps alongside Belzec and Treblinka, the commandant would force the prisoners to sing a song that described how happy they were, how wonderful the food was, and so on. Prisoners who dared to sing with insufficient "enthusiasm" were whipped for this infraction (Arad, 1987: 200). A famous German-Jewish star of the musical stage, Kurt Gerron, was forced to sing the song that had made him famous, the "Canon Song" from the *Threepenny Opera*, while being marched to the gas chamber (Kater, 1992). In another example, prisoner workers in the Sonderkommando in Auschwitz, assigned to pulverize with wooden mallets the burned bones just removed from the crematoria, were forced by the SS to sing throughout the process (Nahon, 1989). A group of Jewish prisoners, naked in the middle of the winter, was forced to enter a deep canal that ran through the camp. Trembling with fear and cold, they were compelled, for the amusement of the SS guards, to dance and sing a specially composed song with the words "We are the damned Jews who are destroying the world" (Whissen, 1996). This torment was continued for more than two hours, and those that survived were sent straight to their deaths. However repugnant, these examples demonstrate that the perpetrators intuitively recognized that music was something that the victims cherished and with which they had positive associations, which enhanced its potential for torment when forced upon them in these terrible circumstances.

This perverted use of music to humiliate is not confined to the Nazi Holocaust. In the more recent war of genocide in the Balkans there have been instances of Serbian soldiers forcing Muslim prisoners to sing Serbian songs simply as a form of torment before killing them. For example, in the words of one survivor of a Serbian massacre: "I remember one man on crutches who was ordered to sing Serbian songs. If any soldier didn't like the way the guy was singing, he would beat him with his own crutches." This man was then beaten to death (Stover, 1997).

Musical Censorship

Tacitly recognizing the positive powers of music, the Nazis banned the performance of music by any and all Jewish composers in Germany as well as the occupied territories. If German audiences had been left to enjoy the music of composers such as Mendelssohn, Mahler, or Schoenberg, or even Offenbach, whose popular melodies were actually removed from the hurdy-gurdies on the street, then they might have been forced to begin to accept the Jews as people and recognize their common humanity. Performing or even listening to jazz music associated with Afro-American and Jewish performers and composers was similarly forbidden.

In the same manner, Jewish musical performers and conductors who had formerly held high musical posts in Germany were all banned from public performance and teaching posts long before "the final solution" was implemented. The recent film, *The Pianist,* based on the memoirs of Polish concert pianist Wladyslaw Szypilman (2003), shows how a previously successful artist had to remain in hiding in Warsaw throughout the war in order to survive. Similarly, another Warsaw pianist, Marion Filar, barely survived incarceration in Mazdenek, Buchenwald, and other camps. As described in his memoir (2002), Filar, like Szypilman, went on to have a notable postwar career as a performer and teacher.

When violinist Szymon Laks auditioned for the men's orchestra in Auschwitz, he played some passages from the Mendelssohn violin concerto. His auditioner was not musically educated enough to recognize the piece. Had he done so, Laks might have been rejected and immediately sent to his death for presuming to play the music of a Jewish composer (Laks, 1948).

Music as Deception

Toward the end of the war, the Nazis decided that all the prisoners in one group of camps would shortly be killed. To distract these prisoners from thinking about their end or contemplating the possibilities of resistance, the SS then strongly encouraged the orchestra to entertain the prisoners. This demonstrates that the music was, in a sense, intended to be "therapeutic," distracting and providing temporary comfort for the prisoners. But it was, of course, a deceptive and malevolent "therapy" meant only to lull the prisoners into a false sense of complacency. As described by one survivor of Sobibor: "[T]he SS men were interested in keeping up our spirits so that we should not be depressed and we would work better. They organized concerts for us, music was played and we were entertained. The purpose was that we should not feel that we were doomed for extermination and think about an uprising" (Arad, 1987: 230f.). In the end, almost all of these prisoners were killed.

In Sobibor the orchestra was intended to create an illusion about the place, presumably to deceive and calm the arriving transports; moreover, music accompanied the entire extermination process. The sounds of Sobibor combined the "cries of the women and children, shouts and wild laughter of the SS men, the noise of the working engines, and music played by an orchestra" (Arad, 1987: 228). The prisoners were forced to sing as they marched to work, singing as they would directly pass by their family, friends, and others being led to the gas.

Another well-known deceptive use of music by the Nazis was the playing of very loud music from loudspeakers. In the death camps, this was done to drown out the sound of gunfire as Jews were shot en masse so as not to arouse other prisoners' suspicions, which might lead to panic or rebellion. One description reads: "As the Jews passed between the chain of reserve policemen into the camp, music blared from two loudspeaker trucks. Despite the attempt to drown out the other noise, the sound of steady gun fire could be heard from the camp" (Browning, 1992: 138). As a climax to the Nazi occupation of Kiev, then capital of the Soviet republic of Ukraine, and on the pretense of a resettlement action, the Jews of the city were ordered to report to a certain train station; as they arrived by the thousands they were herded to the nearby ravine of Babi Yar for the purposes of mass execution. In the massacre at Babi Yar, 34,000 Jews were killed in two days in September 1941. The victims were pushed along a road leading to the edge of a deep ravine, where "loud speakers bellowed dance melodies which drowned out the screams of the victims" (Berenbaum, 1997: 145).

Depicting yet another case of deception through music, the French woman Claude Vaillant Courturier recalled how deportees were greeted upon their arrival in Birkenau prior to being sent directly to the gas. "To render their welcome more pleasant at this time—June, July, 1944—an orchestra composed of internees, all young and pretty girls dressed in white blouses and navy blue skirts, played during the selection on the arrival of the trains gay tunes such as *The Merry Widow*, the Barcarolle from *The Tales of Hoffmann*, etc. They were then informed that this was a labor camp and, since they were not brought into the camp, they only saw the small platform surrounded by flowering plants. Naturally, they could not realize what was in store for them" (Gilbert, 1985: 686).

As Lengyel (1995: 84) described it: "While the deportees were being disembarked, the camp orchestra, inmates in striped pajamas, played swing tunes to welcome the new arrivals. The gas chambers waited, but the victims must be soothed first. Indeed, the selections at the station were usually made to the tune of languorous tangos, jazz numbers, and popular ballads." One writer-musician recalled that at the time of his arrival, "we were greeted in Auschwitz by a full, first-class symphony orchestra playing Richard Wagner's Lohengrin" (Kater, 1992: 180).

Music as Distraction and Masking

Music was also used as a form of distraction and masking for the SS themselves. For example, in the Treblinka camp, the SS men organized an instrumental trio of prisoners who would perform for them during meals, in the evenings, at their parties and for special guests. They also were required to play to help drown out the unpleasant screams of those who were being whipped and prodded in their final run to the gas chambers (Arad, 1987). In Buchenwald, on occasions of public punishments by whipping, the prisoners would often scream and moan in pain. When this noise sufficiently annoyed the SS officers, they would order the band to play a march, and in one instance an officer even placed an opera singer by the whipping rack to sing operatic arias that would cover up the sounds of people being tortured (Kogan, 1980).

The Prisoner Orchestras

A well-known Jewish conductor of cafe orchestras in Warsaw, Arthur Gold, was pulled at the last moment from the line to the gas chambers, naked and freezing, and recruited to organize a full-scale prisoner orchestra in Treblinka. There was no shortage of musical instruments in the camps as they often were taken from those who arrived in the transports. Gold also put together a jazz ensemble and a mixed choir of men and women. The orchestra, complete with specially created band uniforms, was expected to present elaborate music revues with prisoner singers and other performers. It was also involved as part of the daily prisoner roll calls, when punishments and selections were all accompanied by music. At the end of the roll call, the prisoners were forced to sing the *Treblinka Anthem* that Gold had been forced to compose before being dismissed (Kogan, 1980).

What of the mentality of the SS, those whose daily work revolved around the direct oversight of the killing of thousands of people a day for years on end but who at the same time were able to genuinely enjoy the music that they heard? This was not only martial music aggressively supporting a militaristic and sadistic mentality, which would perhaps have been more understandable. Rather, the SS often chose to hear sentimental music that could move them to tears. For example, one SS officer in the Birkenau camp always requested orchestral performances of Schumann's *Reverie*, a beautiful and sentimental piece that he enjoyed particularly after a hard day of selections and gassing (Fenelon and Routier, 1977). There is no reason to suppose that the musical enjoyment of SS men such as this individual was superficial or less than that of any other music lover. One might say of the SS that this music was their therapy. The orchestras often played music they had specifically asked for, the music they loved. The music relaxed them; the camp officers even took a certain pride in the quality of "their" prisoner orchestras. And yet, the music apparently did not move them in any significant way to feel a humanizing compassion toward those whom they murdered on a daily basis. The music may have somehow supported their denial, distracting them from their own behavior and the reality of what was before them. Music seemed to sedate rather than stimulate their misgivings, as one might expect in more normal circumstances. Henry Rosner, a violinist, was compelled to play for the Commandant Amon Goeth at parties and other social occasions at the Plaszow camp in Poland. Often he would play for Goeth after one of his frequent killing sprees of prisoner victims. At his bedside, he played the German songs Goeth preferred, perhaps, as Rosner stated, "to ease his conscience" (Brecher, 1994).

The SS did sometimes interact with musicians in a less brutal way than they did with the ordinary prisoners. They occasionally accorded them a limited level of civility and human regard even as they killed their fellow Jews daily, and saw no problem in this bizarre distinction. However, in the end, they had no reservations about the eventual extermination of these same musicians when they were no longer needed (van Weren 1995).

Gaston, in his 1968 book *Music in Therapy* (in the chapter "Man and Music"), states that "Music is one of those areas of organization that stands at or very near the apex of man's humanness" (Gaston, 1968: 12). Gaston seems to suggest that music could have a humanizing effect but obviously the opposite was true in the Holocaust experience. Music may have the potential to reach and sensitize human feelings, but only in a context in which it is specifically directed in that way, as in some music therapy practice, and with receptive listeners. In the Holocaust, the positive potentials of this aspect of music were so abused that all such norms became irrelevant. Further, the Holocaust amply demonstrated that musically induced humane feelings could be neatly compartmentalized with sentiment and nostalgia apparently comfortably coexisting with denial and indifference to the suffering of others.

The best-known book describing the experience of the prisoner orchestras is Fania Fenelon's *Playing for Time* (1977), about her experiences performing in the women's prisoner orchestra at the Birkenau extermination camp. Fenelon describes how she received word that they were seeking musicians to be part of a newly formed prisoner orchestra, for which she volunteered. It is difficult even to try to imagine the level of intimidation one would feel during such a musical audition, so typical of the Holocaust musical context. If you are successful, you live; if not, you die. Having been a pianist and cabaret singer in France before her imprisonment, Fenelon mastered what was needed to successfully sing and accompany herself in an aria from Puccini's *Madama Butterfly* that was requested and therefore managed to save her life.

The primary role of the prisoner orchestras in Auschwitz was to play German military marches outdoors. These were performed for the prisoner work details as they were marched to work in the morning and then returned again at the end of the day (Laks, 1948). This martial music helped to create a sense of order and discipline within the camp for the SS commanders. Again, the incongruity is horrifying: the contrast between the agony of the slave laborers who were starving, suffering, barely managing to stay alive; and the benign character of the lively marches that were the musical accompaniment to the prisoners' parades to and from work details. The prisoners were often forced to march in rhythmic cadence, even when many of them could barely walk.

Most could survive the camps only a few months at best, until they too were gassed and replaced by other, able-bodied prisoners from the next arriving transport. The music, selected by the SS, probably meant little or nothing to the prisoners under those conditions. It has even been suggested that the music, with its cheerful demeanor, may have further demoralized the prisoners, making their lot that much more difficult (Laks, 1948). As one survivor put it: "[L]istening to them play was heartbreaking. It reminded us so much of normal life ... the life that other people still led" (Lagnado and Dekel, 1992: 62). In fact, some prisoners cursed and swore at the orchestra members for having privileged positions and not sharing the fate of the others.

Writer and survivor Primo Levi wrote that years later, the blood would freeze in his veins when he heard or remembered some of those marching tunes and became aware once more of how lucky he was to have escaped death in Auschwitz. Levi also described the ceremonial hanging of a prisoner who had been part of an attempted sabotage in Birkenau: in the center of the camp, hundreds of prisoners were forced to witness the event which was accompanied by a band performance (Levi, 1960).

Survivors of the women's orchestra talk about the horrors of having to perform marches for the emaciated prisoners on their way to work, of playing against the background of the smoke and smell of the crematoria, and in sight of the arriving transports. However, during the hours that the orchestra members spent rehearsing in the barracks, the music did have some genuine therapeutic value for them (Tichauer, 1995).

The women's orchestra at Birkenau, a group of forty-five to fifty players and the only female ensemble ever organized in any of the concentration camps, was principally conducted by a famous European violinist, Alma Rosé, a niece of the composer Gustav Mahler. On arrival at Auschwitz, before being recognized as a well-known artist, she was first placed in Block 10 in Birkenau, a part of the Experimental Block with a horrific reputation for using women as subjects in medical experiments that usually proved fatal. "Believing that she was going to her death, Rosé asked one of the overseers of Block 10 to grant her the condemned person's customary final request. She asked to play the violin for a last time" (Newman, 2000: 222). It was easy enough to find a violin for Rosé from among the camp's stolen properties. Her playing in Block 10 "transported the prisoners to the world outside of Auschwitz far from hate and inhumanity" (Newman, 2000: 223). The series of nightly cabarets she organized in Block 10 also served to bring her presence and talents to the attention of important persons at Birkenau, notably Maria Mandel, the most senior woman SS officer in the women's camp. Mandel, a passionate music lover, was committed to developing the fledgling women's orchestra and transferred Rosé from Block 10 to the Music Block to become its new conductor.

Rosé conducted the orchestra with dedication and discipline, typically rehearsing at least ten hours a day in addition to the twice-daily performances for the slave laborers and the Sunday concerts, and effectively kept herself and the other orchestra members alive for several years. As she repeatedly warned her "orchestra girls" (as they were known): "[I]f we don't play well, we'll go to the gas" (Newman, 2000: 5). On some occasions the orchestra played for the sick in the infirmary to distract them. However, the patients for whom they played in the morning would inevitably be gassed in the afternoon. Those patients, although sometimes moved by the music, would typically find it too difficult to bear and would scream at the musicians and plead with them to leave and let them die in peace. Yet, some prisoners did glean positive feelings from the orchestra concerts, "citing the music as one of the only elements of beauty in their circus of death ... a reminder that there still was something such as family, home and artistry outside Auschwitz" (Newman, 1995). The bizarrely contradictory ethos of one of these orchestral performances was poignantly described by Szmaglewska (1947: 287): "Another transport has arrived. It is night. A messenger is sent to bid the orchestra, come to the gate and play. The music stands are set up in the darkness and leaping flames light the notes and the concert begins. Shouts of the SS men, moans of the beaten, crying children coming from railroad cars mix with the melodies of Spanish dances, serenades, and sentimental songs." This after-hours performance, specifically organized for the occasion of a newly arrived transport, lends credence to the still disputed idea that the orchestra was being purposely utilized to deceive and provide a false sense of security for the prisoners.

In New York I interviewed Mrs. Yvette Lennon (1993), a Greek-Jewish woman who had played in Rosé's orchestra. Lennon initially played accordion, but later her place in the orchestra became threatened because a second, better accordionist had arrived. She was then encouraged by her sister and by Rosé to play the string bass, a needed instrument in the orchestra. Since she didn't know how to play the bass, it was actually arranged for a bass player from the men's orchestra to go to the women's camp to give her a series of bass lessons—a strange example of music education in Auschwitz.

Szymon Laks, a violinist and conductor of the Auschwitz men's orchestra, survived to publish his memoirs (Laks, 1948). Laks addressed the contradictions inherent in the role of music in the camps when he asked how "music, that most sublime expression of the human spirit—also became entangled in the hellish enterprise of the extermination of millions of people and even took an active part in this extermination" (Laks, 1948: 5). In general, Laks thought that the music, if it helped anyone, helped the musicians who did not have to endure hard labor and ate a little better than the others. For the rest, he believed the music had little value. For the ordinary prisoners, music was a luxury that, for the most part, they could not begin to appreciate in that context.

Shoshona Kalisch (1995), a Hungarian Jew who spent years at Auschwitz, talked about the informal singing that sometimes broke out in the barracks, where the prisoners would sing their national songs to each other, happy as well as sad, which she and others said served as a kind of therapy and sustenance for them. Alec Ward was a teenage prisoner in the Flossenburg camp in eastern Germany. Enduring physical brutality and starvation, he remembered his friend, Artek, "who helped me enormously to keep up my morale there. My friend had a most wonderful voice and very often we would sing together to while away our painfully hungry time" (Gilbert, 1996). In another example, when asked why she was constantly singing in the barracks, one prisoner replied: "Manci, I am so hungry: when I sing I don't feel it so much" (Brecher, 1994).

Lex Van Weren was a Dutch trumpet player and violinist who played in the Auschwitz orchestra. He described how the orchestra often played while the prisoners were being led into the gas chambers (Van Weren, 1995). Since none of those prisoners survived, there is no way to know if the music provided them with some level of momentary security. The waiting prisoners may have sensed their fate: they were not sure if they were being led into a shower and delousing room, as they were told, or if something more ominous lay in store. They were anxious and did not understand what was happening to them. Van Weren felt that it was certainly possible that the music did provide them with a false sense of momentary security, again on the level of a brutally deceptive kind of "therapy."

He recalled the commandant of Auschwitz/Birkenau, Franz Hossler, a music lover for whom Van Weren played his favorite numbers, such as "Bei Mir Bist du Schön" (To Me You Are Beautiful), "Alexander's Ragtime Band," and other popular music selections. Van Weren describes how, at such times, Hossler would speak to him about some of the normal things in life, of his wife and children and other ordinary subjects. In a very limited way, for brief periods of time, the music would humanize him in his relation to the performers. But this certainly did not extend to the view of his role in the daily mass murders.

Louis Bannet was another Dutch trumpet player, a jazz musician who survived by performing in the Auschwitz prisoner orchestra (Axelrod, 1989). Having played in an ensemble for two years, he eventually found himself in the terrible position of having to see his own mother arrive in a transport as he performed. Bannet describes some of the usual scenes of musical humiliation, such as when a prisoner who had escaped was later caught and killed. The killers put the dead body in a chair and forced the musicians to look at it as they played, to serve as a kind of deterrent.

Perhaps one of the most horrific musical auditions from the Holocaust was that experienced by Shony Alex Braun (1985). After initially spending some time in Auschwitz, he was later transferred to Dachau. Braun had been a violin prodigy in Romania before the war, and was only thirteen at the time of his imprisonment. He had spent his first year in the camps as an ordinary prisoner-worker and had had no occasion to play his instrument. After several days in Dachau, he had reached his limits; his life hung by a thread. At that point, an SS officer entered his barrack with a violin in hand and offered food to any prisoner who could play to his satisfaction. Braun volunteered, along with two others. As Braun describes it, the violin was first handed to the oldest prisoner, Feher, a man in his forties who had been a famous violin virtuoso. He began by playing Bach and, according to Braun, played superbly, but apparently not to the SS officer's taste. He signaled the capos, and "[o]ne took the violin out of Feher's hands, while another picked up a thick iron pipe and smashed his head with such tremendous force that his skull cracked open. Blood and brains splattered the room. He died instantly" (Braun, 1985). The violin was than handed to the next prisoner, a man of about twenty-five, who was understandably so shocked that he couldn't play, and he too was beaten to death.

Without any opportunity to defer, Braun was obliged to play next. He had planned to play some work by Kreisler or Dvořák, but in that bloodied room, and in terror, his mind went blank. He stood frozen for several seconds. He saw the capo again reaching for the pipe to crush his skull and knew that he was about to be killed. Braun had never before played a full-sized violin and hadn't played for a year, and his fingers felt too weak to depress the strings. And yet, perhaps inspired by a lucky intuition about the kind of music the officer was likely to relate to, he began to play Strauss's *Blue Danube Waltz*. To this music the officer responded positively and gestured to the capo to pick up his guitar to accompany him. The encounter gave Braun a new role in which he was eventually able to entertain the SS in exchange for food, providing the margin of strength that enabled him to survive until his liberation.

The mentality of the officer, capable of such extreme brutality and yet fully able to take pleasure in a Strauss waltz at the same time, is another paradoxical example of the distorted values and emotional compartmentalization that prevailed in the Holocaust. One can refer to psychological concepts such as splitting, dissociation, denial, reaction-formation, and so on, in attempting to understand these behaviors. However, the extreme nature of such actions exceeds the boundaries of our usual understanding.

There are endless similar examples. As described by one of Rosé's players: "[T]he Music Block became a special refuge for the SS officers, a place to relax and be entertained. Suddenly an SS woman would ask for Chopin, hear it, and upon leaving, kick an old grandmother. Commandant Hess would ask for an aria from Butterfly, then go off on a selection" (Newman, 2000: 266).

German Musicians and the Holocaust

What about German musicians who had the opportunity to play in and around the death camps? Did their prior musical experiences somehow make them more sensitive to the suffering of the prisoners than the ordinary SS men? Apparently not.

On the night before a planned mass murder of thousands of Jews in Poland by German Police Battalion 101, one officer remembered: "On this evening an entertainment unit of the Berlin police—so called 'welfare for the front'—was our guest." ("Welfare" here apparently meant a kind of sedative music therapy to help suppress whatever misgivings the officers might have had in relation to their daily killing.) He continued: "[T]his entertainment unit consisted of musicians and performers. The members of this unit had likewise heard of the pending shooting of the Jews. They asked, indeed even emphatically begged, to be allowed to participate in the execution of the Jews. This request was granted by the battalion" (Browning, 1992: 112). Equipped with guns provided by the battalion, the musicians formed their own firing squads: even their prior lifetime experiences with music did not sensitize them to this horror and brutality.

A Dr. Schönfelder, a German physician who specifically instructed the men of Police Battalion 101 in the techniques of killing Jews, was remembered by one member of the unit, a violinist, as someone who "played the accordion marvelously and did so with us frequently." The men of the battalion enjoyed musical afternoons in the city of Meidzyrzec (Poland), a "site of their most frequent and largest killing operations" (Goldhagen, 1996).

Music in Theresienstadt

Among the concentration camps, one camp was different from all the rest, and that was the Theresienstadt camp in Czechoslovakia, about 30 kilometers from Prague (Berenbaum, 1993). Aside from its role as a transfer camp for transports to the east, it was the one concentration camp that was used by the Nazis as a model camp for propaganda purposes. In response to pressures from the International Red Cross and other organizations investigating rumors and allegations that prisoners in the concentration camps were being abused, Theresienstadt was eventually developed as a kind of showcase intended to deceive outside observers about the real fate of concentration camp prisoners. In Theresienstadt, the prisoners were encouraged to develop an active community and cultural life. Since many talented musicians and composers were imprisoned in Theresienstadt, a vital musical culture thrived there. Meanwhile, all the performers knew well enough that they lived under the shadow of death and that whatever was allowed them could be destroyed at any moment. They knew that they could and probably would ultimately be transported to their deaths in Auschwitz. In fact, almost all the prisoners of Theresienstadt met this tragic end.

There were many notable and highly accomplished Czech-Jewish musicians in Theresienstadt. These included the talented pianist-composer Gideon Klein, the conductor Rafael Schacter, and the composers Viktor Ullmann, Pavel Haas, and Hans Krása. The scope of the musical life in Theresienstadt was extraordinary under the circumstances. Theresienstadt supported four concert orchestras, and several small ensembles for popular music as well as chamber music ensembles, solo recitals, choral music performances, and even an active jazz ensemble (Karas, 1985).

Hans Krása wrote a wonderful children's opera, *Brundibar*, which premiered in a boys' orphanage in Prague in 1941 and was revived in Thereisenstadt in 1943. This happy and buoyant piece, melodic and charming, served as the perfect performance vehicle to deceive the observers from the International Red Cross Committee and was also highly popular with the Theresienstadt prisoners. Tickets were extremely hard to come by in the prison community and *Brundibar* had a run of fifty-five performances. The opera also had a great deal of symbolic meaning. For the prisoners, children seemed to represent hope for the future, and the story line symbolized the ultimate triumph of good over evil. The sad reality is that the children who performed in the opera and the orchestra players, the composer, and most of those prisoners who heard and enjoyed these performances, perished in the death camp at Auschwitz.

Although the music of the best Czech composers from Theresienstadt is now of special historical interest because of the circumstances of its creation, it is also recognized as a repertoire of genuine musical value regardless of its source. However, in listening to this music today, it is difficult to disassociate it from the poignancy of the time and place in which it was conceived.

Even Adolph Eichmann enjoyed attending musical events in Theresienstadt when he had business there. These included performances of Verdi's *Requiem* presented by the prisoners as a requiem for themselves as well as, ironically, a Christian requiem for Jews to convey the full awareness of their circumstances to their captors. Predictably, these performances had no effect whatsoever on Eichmann's continuing policies of deportation and extermination (Karas, 1985).

Music in the Ghettos

One cannot consider the role of music in the concentration camps without also giving consideration to the role of music in sustaining hope, culture, and group solidarity for those Jews imprisoned in the urban ghettos of Warsaw, Lodz, and other occupied cities. In a sense, life in the ghettos was similar to life in Theresienstadt, although the conditions were generally far worse from a strictly physical point of view. The common element of stress for those living in the ghettos was the constant quota of forced daily deportations to the death camps. Yet, as in Theresienstadt, musical life flourished in the ghettos. As one survivor put it: "[T]he song was the only truth. The Nazis could take everything away from us, but they could not take singing from us. This remained our only human expression" (Flam, 1992: 1). Whereas performing in the prisoner orchestras of camps like Auschwitz was a way of playing for physical survival, singing songs in the ghettos became a kind of singing for spiritual survival, a form of music therapy.

The rich cultural activity within the Lodz ghetto included a variety of entertainments that had their origins in prewar Jewish cultural life, such as symphonic concerts, street music, and other less formal music making (Flam, 1992). Many ghetto survivors recalled singing at home as a kind of domestic music therapy activity. As one survivor described it: "[W]e did not give up singing; it was singing for its own sake. We sang all kinds of songs. Actually, we did not have any good news to talk about. We tried to forget the bad times, so we sang. It worked wonderfully! I think that was one of the things which helped us to survive" (Flam, 1992: 156).

Music and Memory

Among the innumerable music-related Holocaust memories detailed in survivor accounts, the following are particularly poignant.

Violetta was an Italian Jew in Birkenau. During their first days there, the prisoners had no idea what had happened to people they no longer saw. One day while they were working, the SS women guards ordered them: "Italian women, sing." The women started to sing the popular sentimental Italian song "Mama" (Bixio, 1943) in the hopes that their parents might hear them and know they were alive. Then the Polish girls laughed and asked them if they wanted their mamas to come out of the chimneys that were always smoking. That was when Violetta realized what was happening to the people whom they no longer saw (Robbins, 1994).

Miriam describes this memory: "When we went out of the camp, we were always told to sing so that if there were trains arriving on the tracks, the people would hear singing (no doubt to provide them with a false sense of security, again a deceptive use of music). One day we were asked to sing and we saw cattle wagons lined up on the tracks. We saw little faces peeping through the barred windows of the cattle wagons. We knew that they were our Jewish children. We felt utter helplessness and despair. We could do nothing; we could only murmur to ourselves and hang our heads in shame that there was a world outside this camp that knew about this and allowed it to happen and that there was no help coming from anywhere. I shall never forget this sight" (Robbins, 1994).

Roman Mirga, an Auschwitz survivor, was the son of the Romani violinist, Dmitri Mirga. He remembered listening to his father play daily in a Gypsy string orchestra, accompanying the endless lines of prisoners on their last walks to the gas chambers (Ramati, 1985). For a period, the Gypsy camp was spared, but in the end it too was set for extermination. Mirga remembered the night the Gypsy children were sent to the gas chambers, hearing their own Gypsy music in their last moments. They were later followed by the rest of the camp, including Mirga's own family. He especially remembered the time when the music that he had heard every day for a year—indeed, for his whole life— suddenly stopped forever as all the orchestra members, including his own father, were sent to their death in the gas chambers.

Shortly after arriving at Birkenau in 1943, Jacques Stroumsa, a Greek-Jewish violinist, responded to a call in his barracks for accomplished musical instrumentalists. Having been handed a violin, he asked the block chief what he wanted to hear: Mozart, Haydn, or Beethoven? Told to play whatever he wanted, he tuned the violin, began to play, and continued for 20 minutes without pause. In the context of Birkenau, surrounded by his newly arrived prisoner friends from Thessaloniki, Greece, the music had a dramatic impact. All were filled with painful emotions, the music being so very much associated with their former life as free men and its stark contrast with their present circumstances. Stroumsa was then escorted to the "conservatory" barracks, where he was appointed first violinist of the Birkenau orchestra (Stroumsa, 1993). He later became known as "The Fiddler of Auschwitz," and fifty years after his liberation, in 1995, he returned to Auschwitz to play his violin there once again, this time as part of a Holocaust memorial ceremony.

Stroumsa also recalled a day in Auschwitz on which, between the morning departure of the prisoners to their forced labor and their evening return to the camp, he had had several hours free from his responsibilities of playing with the orchestra. On this occasion, he had the impulse to go to the infirmary and play some solo violin selections of Mozart and Schubert for those essentially condemned prisoners, in the hope of giving them a moment of comfort and respite. The music seemed to have been well received, but the story does not end there. Some forty years after his liberation, Stroumsa had settled in Jerusalem. He was sitting in a café enjoying coffee with friends when a man suddenly ran up to him and embraced him, in tears. This man had been one of the prisoners in the Auschwitz infirmary on the day Stroumsa played there. He had never forgotten that music, and felt that it had somehow provided him with the moral strength that enabled him to survive.

Musical Transcendence: Present and Past

Transcending the Present

An incident of music that briefly helped to mitigate terrible circumstances was related by Olga Lengyel. Laboring in Auschwitz, she was assigned to sort the luggage that had been taken from a group of Americans that had just been killed. In one suitcase, she and her fellow prisoners found some phonograph records. Hungry for music, they began to play one on a portable phonograph that was also in the luggage. The recording was of "Silent Night" sung by Bing Crosby, and the prisoners were transfixed. A German guard heard the music, rushed into the room, and destroyed the record. Lengyel (1995: 102) recalled: "For a few moments the American crooner had helped us to forget our predicament."

The cellist Anita Lasker-Wolfisch recalled that "Alma Rosé, through her compulsive drive to create a professional-sounding ensemble from a group of primarily amateur players, helped herself and her musicians to symbolically escape through the pursuit of musical excellence. What she did achieve, with the discipline she imposed on us, was that our attention was focused away from what was happening outside the block—away from the smoking chimney and smell of burning flesh—to an F which should have been an F sharp" (Newman, 2000: 270).

Transcending the Past

Zvi Klein, an Auschwitz survivor, was one from the hundreds of sets of young twins who endured the sadistic medical experiments carried out by Joseph Mengele (Lagnado and Dekel, 1992). After his liberation, Klein grew up to become a man tortured by recurring, terrifying memories of Mengele and the traumas to which he had been subjected. He traveled the world as a sailor, in a driven way, but remained unable to escape his obsessive dreams of the death camp. He movingly describes how, during a stop in New York, he wandered into a bar that had a band featuring Louis Armstrong. He was there for only an hour before he had to leave but became fully engaged in the music. He never forgot that hour and remembered it in a way that reflects the most positive power of music to assist us in transcending painful experiences: "Yes, I was happy then! In fact, never in my life have I been as happy as during the hour I spent inside that dive on the West Side. Because for one whole hour, I actually managed to forget Auschwitz and Dr. Joseph Mengele" (p. 27).

Music as Self-Affirmation

Music also provided death camp prisoners with a symbolic way of maintaining their sense of personal identity, a kind of affirmation of their essential humanity and the existence of a better world outside the confines of the camp. As

Geve, a youthful prisoner in Auschwitz, explained (1958: 90): "[A] prisoner's best friends are melodies. To us youngsters the best way to dream ourselves away was to sing. We sang when penned up in our block during the many curfews, whilst having our weekly shower baths or out of loneliness. Our songs were many and varied: Gypsy melodies, ditties about love, folk songs from all over Europe and partisan marches. Those who had picked themselves a favorite would hum it as a kind of signature tune, something they would be known by" (Geve, 1958: 121). Geve picked a sentimental French song as his own, and later he wrote, movingly: "[E]very time I hummed this, my own private melody, I was overcome with the feeling that, despite all, I was still alive. After a whole year of concentration camp, I had remained my own self. Even though I could not see my face, for mirrors were denied to us, I could still hear my signature tune. It was the proof of my existence" (Geve, 1958: 122).

Conclusions

What does all of this teach us? What is the relevance to us today of these contradictory roles of music in the Holocaust? For one, they demonstrate how deeply important music is to people in general and, particularly, to those in crisis. Camp prisoners who had even a modicum of quality of life beyond total starvation and suffering from disease sought out music for comfort. Songs sung in the ghetto provided hope and comfort as well as the courage to resist. Music in the ghettos was also a way of sustaining a rich culture and sense of community and, perhaps, a fleeting sense of well-being. Those marching into the gas chambers singing songs such as "Hatikva" in their last moments of life affirmed their shared identity and faith through group solidarity, a spontaneous moment of the kind of supportive group music therapy embraced by prisoners who sang together in the barracks for mutual comfort. In these examples, we see how people sought out music in what were, literally, some of the most extreme situations possible. When it is not provided, people will often create their own music therapy, a human need that is basic and essential.

In a more organized form, Herbert Zipper, a Viennese-Jewish musician imprisoned in Dachau in 1938, managed on his own to create a secret volunteer string ensemble of fourteen players. He composed original music for this group, and they gave a series of clandestine concerts in an unused latrine. For the players, as well as for the audience of twenty to thirty prisoners, these concerts revived a sense of "reaffirming something worthwhile" and "exerting some freedom of the will," in otherwise totally dehumanizing circumstances (Cummins, 1992: 86).

Judith Isaacson (1991), a Hungarian Jew in Auschwitz, fell asleep in the mud after an interminable pre-dawn roll call in cold and rainy weather. She was later awakened by a warm rain and the spontaneous singing of several thousand women prisoners, all joining in an anonymously created song: "Above me weeps the sky Darkly, I wing, I fly My loved ones are waiting at home" (p. 76). She joined in this singing, both desperate and hopeful at the same time, and later said that no music had ever moved her more.

In the end, then, how can we begin to understand the men and women of the SS, murderers who could still be touched by music and saw no contradictions in this? Perhaps some insight is provided by the following case, a strange and haunting story that can be interpreted in different ways. A group of Hungarian Jewish women were packed into a cattle car for two weeks on their way to Auschwitz. At one point, a woman in the train (who had been a well-known opera singer in Budapest) began to sing. All the women became still in the train car, as she helped to temporarily distract and comfort them in their terrible immediate circumstances.

The story of this singer continued in Auschwitz where, for a time, she survived as a prison worker. She sometimes sang in the barracks at night, again comforting those around her, the same women with whom she had traveled to Auschwitz in the train transport.

The SS woman supervisor for this barrack had apparently heard her singing to the other prisoners at night. One day, at a lunch break, she abruptly approached the opera singer and said, "Sing for me!" Then, she directed her to sit on a box in the middle of the floor. The singer sat down and began to very softly sing a popular German song, "Du, du, du Bist Mein Herr" (You, You, You, Are My Man). The song was a romantic one, in waltz time, and as her voice grew stronger the whole group of prisoners was entranced. At the end of the song, she stopped. And then, for no apparent reason, the SS woman, in tears, began to beat her, hitting her on the head, arms, and back with a metal soup ladle she had grabbed from the pot. When the beating stopped, the singer managed to pull herself up and return to work. A few days later the incident was repeated, and the pattern continued on a regular basis, several times a week: the other prisoners sat down to eat, the woman was ordered to sing, the SS woman's face became covered in tears, and the singer was beaten.

How can we interpret this behavior? What was it about this woman's singing, or the words of the song and its associations, that so enraged the SS supervisor? Was it because the song celebrates "having a man," which perhaps she did not? Did it evoke painful memories of a man from her past? What was it about this music that brought her to tears? What led her to hate the person who aroused those emotions? Was it like hating a therapist, in this case a symbolic music therapist, who forces you to confront some painful truths? Was she angry at some inner vulnerability of her own that was somehow unacceptable to her? There are no clear answers to these questions. However, it is axiomatic that when one person has total control over another and there are no ethical or behavioral boundaries, instinctive actions that would ordinarily be repressed are carried out.

One day the SS woman beat the singer particularly brutally over the head with a heavy club. This time, the singer couldn't get up. The SS woman was furious, kicking and cursing the woman until she saw that she was finally dead. She then left, with a final insult: "That damn bitch!" (Bernstein, 1997: 224ff.).

It may be that any human being, however evil or corrupt, still has the capacity to feel music. Many ordinary people can be cruel in small ways and enjoy music. Even in the Holocaust, where we find the ultimate expressions of human cruelty, the worst perpetrators retained their feeling for music. Perhaps this is only a question of degree.

For people who have reached that level of criminality, abandoning one's defenses is an overwhelmingly self-destructive proposition. Were they to do so, they would be obliged to move from a position of self-esteem—believing in the rightness of their actions—to a totally reversed position, in which individuals realized that they had in fact been monsters of evil. One can readily understand that many would avoid taking such a threatening psychic leap. As with any other people, music for the SS could stir sentimental feelings for love of home, family, country, and so on. Still, it did not break down the power of their internal defense systems.

Music and the Holocaust Today

One implication of the current discussion relates to music as therapy and the potential of utilizing music from the Holocaust period as part of music therapy interventions in work with Holocaust survivors. For those who survived but have repressed many feelings that still remain too painful to acknowledge, music and imagery therapy, with music of the Holocaust period as a background stimulus, could facilitate the process of associative recall on a deep emotional level. This experience could help such survivors to directly confront and work through such feelings as fear, grief over the loss of loved ones, anger, guilt at having survived when so many others perished, loss of confidence in one's personal autonomy, loss of trust in others, and so on. This same principle would also apply to other, more recent victims of torture and related traumatic abuses in which music associated with their experiences could assist the victims to fully come to terms with their feelings and begin a process of personal reintegration.

Even today, there are Holocaust survivors who have been unable to accept the music of the anti-Semitic composer Richard Wagner. Many European Jews were led to an association between Wagner's music and the Nazi movement through exposure to his music in Nazi parades, rallies, and newscasts. As a result, they were negatively conditioned to connect his music with their Holocaust-period experiences. This demonstrates just how powerful and enduring such musical associations can be, a principle long recognized by music therapists. In the autumn of 2000, the Rishon Letzion Symphony Orchestra conducted by Mendl Rotan, a Holocaust survivor, performed Wagner's "Siegfried Idyll" in a chamber music series. Still highly controversial in Israel, this event was based on the premise that "we can despise Wagner as a man, but appreciate him as a musician" (Sontag, 2000). But can we really separate a person from the music he or she creates, especially the music they compose? And if we do so, are we not again creating another kind of musical-emotional compartmentalization? As this concert was about to begin, a noisy rattle was swung in protest by a man in the audience, an 80-year-old Polish Jew whose family had died in the Holocaust. He was quieted by the audience and the performance took place.

It would be heartening to conclude, with the Holocaust now more than sixty years behind us, that the world has learned from the experience and is now a more peaceful and better place. Unfortunately, we need look no further than the more recent wars in Rwanda and the Balkans to see that genocide, violence, and ethnic hatreds are still very much with us. In their own music, a kind of rock-hate genre, neo-Nazi groups still persist in penning lyrics that support their ideas. Bound for Glory, an anti-Semitic white power rap group in the United States, recorded the song "A Call to Arms," with the following lyrics:

> Zionist illusions, state of confusions
> Are decaying away my mind
> Feelings of hate, can't get it straight
> Am I the only one of my kind?
> Massive inflation by the radical infestation
> Has turned our streets to decay.
> Racial domination, swift termination
> Has become the only way.
> Close the border, start the New Order.
> Gather your guns, it is time to fight, a call to arms!
> (Suall, I., 1994: A16)

Even when music is misused to support negative ideologies, its power to unite and inspire remains undiminished.

If there is a positive message to be learned from all this, it may be that the power and significance of music in human culture has essential meaning within the human psyche. We cannot blame music for the hatred that has its origins in the most formative social, familial, and cultural experiences. Music does not create hatred; it can only support a hatred that is already there. Although the elimination of racism and other bigotry is beyond our capacity as music therapists, we are privileged to work with a medium so basic, pervasive, and universal that when guided by the highest ethical standards, it has the potential to help people be the best that they can be.

Notes

This chapter is a modified version of a 1999 article by the same author previously published in *The Arts in Psychotherapy* 26: 3–14, with permission.

References

Arad, Y. (1987). *Belzec, Sobibor, Treblinka: The Operation Reinhard Death Camps.* Bloomington: Indiana University Press.

Axelrod, T. (1989). "A musician's best friend: sounds of life and death." *The Jewish Week, Inc.*

Berenbaum, M. (1993). *The World Must Know.* New York: Little Brown.

_____ (1997). *Witness to the Holocaust.* New York: HarperCollins.

Bernstein, S. T. (1997). *The Seamstress.* New York: G. P. Putnam's Sons.

Bixio, C. A. (1943). *"Mama."* Milan: SAM.

Braun, S. B. (1985). *From Concentration Camp to Concert Hall.* Los Angeles: Shony Alex Braun.

Brecher, E. J. (1994). *Schindler's Legacy.* London: Hodder and Stoughton.

Browning, C. R. (1992). *Ordinary Men.* New York: HarperCollins.

Cummins, P. (1992). *Dachau Song.* New York: Peter Lang.

Fenelon, F. and Routier, M. (1977). *Playing for Time.* New York: Atheneum.

Filar, M. and Patterson, C. (2002). *From Buchenwald to Carnegie Hall.* Jackson: University Press of Mississippi.

Flam, F. (1992). *Singing for Survival: Songs of the Lodz Ghetto.* Chicago: University of Illinois-Urbana Press.

Garcia, M. (1994). Personal communication.

Gaston, T. E. (1968). *Music in Therapy.* New York: The MacMillan Company.

Geve, T. (1958). *Youth in Chains.* Jerusalem: Rubin Mass.

Gilbert, M. (1985). *The Holocaust.* New York: Henry Holt.

_____ (1996). *The Boys: The Untold Story of 732 Young Concentration Camp Survivors.* New York: Henry Holt.

Goldhagen, D. J. (1996). *Hitler's Willing Executioners.* New York: Alfred A. Knopf.

Isaacson, J. M. (1991). *Seed of Sarah: Memoirs of a Survivor.* 2nd ed. Chicago: University of Illinois Press.

Kalisch, S. (1995). Personal communication.

Karas, J. (1985). *Music in Terezín.* New York: Beaufort Books.

Kater, M. (1992). *Different Drummers: Jazz in the Culture of Nazi Germany.* New York: Oxford University Press.

Kogan, E. (1980). *The Theory and Practice of Hell.* New York: Berkeley Books.

Lagnado, L. M. and Dekel, S. C. (1992). *Children of the Flames: Dr. Joseph Mengele and the Untold Story of the Twins of Auschwitz.* New York: Penguin Books.

Laks, S. (1948). *Music of Another World.* Evanston, Ill.: Northwestern University Press.

Lengyel, O. (1947/1995). *Five Chimneys: The Story of Auschwitz.* Chicago: Academy Chicago Publishers.

Lennon, Y. (1993). Personal communication.

Levi, P. (1960). *Survival in Auschwitz.* New York: Summit Books.

Lifton, R. J. (1988). *The Nazi Doctors.* New York: HarperCollins.

Mizrachi, N. (1994). Personal communication.

Nahon, M. (1989). *Birkenau: The Camp of Death.* Tuscaloosa: The University of Alabama Press.

Newman, R. (1995). Personal communication.

_____ (2000). *Alma Rosé: Vienna to Auschwitz*. Portland, OR: Amadeus.

Ramati, A. (1985). *And the Violins Stopped Playing: A Story of the Gypsy Holocaust*. London: Hodder and Stoughton.

Reder, R. (1946). *Belzec Centralna Zydowski*. Krakow: Komisja Historycyzna.

Robbins, G. (1994). Personal communication.

Sontag, S. (2000). "Israel plans a test for Wagner." *New York Times*, 8 April.

Stover, E. (1997). "The grave at Vukovar." *Smithsonian* 27: 41–51.

Stroumsa, J. (1993). *Geiger in Auschwitz*. Constanz, Germany: Hartung-Garre Verlag.

Suall, I. (1994). "Letter to the editor." *New York Times,* 22 February.

Szmaglewska, S. (1947). *Smoke over Birkenau*. New York: Henry Holt.

Szypilman, W. (2003). *The Pianist: The Extraordinary True Story of One Man's Survival in Warsaw, 1939–1945*. New York: Picador.

Tichauer, H. (1995). Personal communication.

Van Weren, L. (1995). Personal communication.

Whissen, T. (1996). *Inside the Concentration Camps: Eyewitness Accounts of Life in Hitler's Death Camps*. Westport, CT: Praeger Publishers.

Chapter 11

THE CHANGING STRUCTURE OF THE MUSIC INDUSTRY

Threats to and Opportunities for Creativity

e⁓

Roger Wallis

Introduction

Digital production and distribution technology, in theory, provide powerful opportunities for creators and performers of musical works to reach a potential global audience without dependence on the series of intermediaries that is so typical of the established music industry. However, this does not appear to have occurred in practice via players in the traditional industry. This chapter looks at the resilient nature of the established music industry value chain and describes some of the forces that tend to support elements of the status quo. Many early assumptions concerning electronic commerce suggested that digital networks would guarantee a greater range of choice for consumers and higher financial returns for suppliers/producers. A further assumption was that products that can easily be transferred from the physical form to the virtual via the process of digitalization would be at the forefront of e-commerce.

The experience of the music industry shows that such claims were oversimplifications. On the contrary, current data suggest that the power structure in the music industry serves to maintain a status quo under which different players in the value chain can retain their power and revenue structure, even when their contribution in terms of value added has changed beyond recognition. Such developments suggest that the age old tensions between concentration and diversification have not been markedly altered by the introduction of digital networks and production technology. The jury is still out. Maybe the Internet will prove to be ideal for niche expressions of culture seeking a small but globally diversified audience, while the mainstream products of the global commercial music industry will seek other routes to an audience that is willing to invest in products that are currently in favor with global media distribution companies.

* * *

Current Trends in the Global Music Industry Arena

Current changes in the music industry—as in all media industries—result from a mix of technological, economic, and cultural factors, with the latter including both social and legal aspects. The music industry is of particular interest as we focus on the world of information delivery through digital networks. Music is the glue that holds many complex media-products together. In the face of uncertainty about the future, music is often the sector chosen by the media industries for experimentation, following the principle that it might be better to learn from mistakes with media products that include only sound, rather than those that require multibillion dollar investments, such as feature films. On the other hand, even the music industry has gone through a period of concentration of ownership among international corporations, with resources being focused on a smaller number of global superstars. The stakes in the music industry, in other words, have grown even higher as up-front investments in talent have increased. A number of authors have described these developments in the academic literature (Wallis, 1990; Malm and Wallis, 1992; Hirsch, 1992; Frith, 1992; Choi and Hilton, 1995; Burnett, 1996).

In addition, we can observe an increased degree of both formal and informal integration within and between different sectors of the media industries. This includes, significantly, the amalgamation of organizations that produce recorded music (record or "phonogram" companies) and organizations that own the copyrights to the music that is recorded (music publishers) (Wallis and Malm, 1984; Wallis, 1994). These trends have shaped an increasingly consolidated industrial landscape. As a result of a wave of mergers and takeovers during the 1980s and early 1990s, a few multinational media corporations "own" most of the superstars as well as a very large repertoire of music copyrights. In 2003, these were Sony (Japan), Universal-Vivendi (France), AOL Time Warner (US), EMI (UK), and BMG (Germany), five "majors" who consistently account for 70 to 80 percent of global music sales. In 2004, AOL-Time Warner sold its music recording and publishing interests to a group of investors headed by Edgar Bronfman (of the Canadian Seagram dynasty), including the brand name Warner Music. BMG and Sony also received regulatory approval for the merger of their recording businesses to produce BMG-Sony. Recent developments under the General Agreement on Tariffs and Trade (GATT), and the North American Free Trade Agreement (NAFTA), and in the

European Union (EU), such as extension of the term of copyright protection to a minimum of 70 years after an author's death in both the EU and the US, have made such rights even more attractive as long-term investments. EMI's music publishing in the year 2000, for instance, accounted for only 14.6 percent of its turnover, but 32 percent of its operating profit, according to the well-informed trade newsletter *Music and Copyright* (Anonymous, 2001).

This was certainly a major factor in the attempt to merge the music businesses of Time Warner and EMI at the start of the present decade. The merger failed to clear the regulatory hurdles in the EU mainly because of concerns about what the regulators term "collective dominance," i.e., the implications for both vertical integration and overall market dominance in certain music business areas. EMI and Time Warner withdrew their application to merge in late 2000. Had they joined, their publishing businesses would have had a market share of around 50 percent in Sweden and nearer 70 percent in Finland. Globally, EMI and Time Warner enjoy average market share of around 13 percent each, with large variations between geographical regions. EMI has traditionally been strong in Europe, and Time Warner has held a similar strong position in the US. Despite initial concerns about the possible negative effects of collective dominance, regulators in Europe and the US approved the merger of Sony and BMG's record companies as long as their respective publishing divisions remained separate entities in the two parent corporations.

In parallel to these trends of concentration and integration, a dramatic change has transformed channels that convey music. During the 1980s, many Western governments sought to deregulate the media, resulting in a proliferation of new local radio channels and television channels, including cable and satellite broadcasting. More recently, the Internet has exploded as a communication medium. The Internet by its very nature is largely unregulated: there is no "The Internet Company" to turn to when seeking redress. This raises a number of largely unresolved issues regarding responsibilities in "cyberspace," including privacy, security, and copyright (Hugenholtz, 1996; Hulsink and Tang, 1997). Ready access to sites where music is stored and made available in an established and convenient data format (e.g., as MP3 files) has caused major problems for those controlling large up-front investments in artists. File-sharing applications such as Napster and Kazaa were eagerly embraced by consumers but fought in the courtrooms by the major players in the music industry. Many of these legal tussles have already been resolved, either out of court (e.g., the agreement between some major record companies and MP3.com) or via collaborative deals seeking to make the new applications "legal" (e.g., between Bertelsmann [parent company of BMG Records] and Napster prior to Napster's bankruptcy). Moral panic has chosen a route, via the courts, to a state of pragmatic solutions, as highlighted in a typical trade paper leader entitled "Napster Shows the Way Forward" (Anonymous, 2000a). By late 2003, the owners of Kazaa, Sharman networks, reported that over 240 million copies of their "Fast Track" software had been downloaded, an all-time world record.

Deregulation, which has fostered and been fostered by changes in technology, has had a heavy impact on the media industries. At one time, television and radio transmission required large up-front investments in capital equipment. Now, a local radio station can be set up for as little as $50,000, a cable television station need not cost much more if the delivery infrastructure is available, and distribution on the Internet is virtually free. Similarly, new technology has emerged to make it easy to produce CDs and cassette tapes, affecting both legitimate and illegitimate users. Unlike analog recordings, material in digital form can be copied time and time again without any loss of quality. This raises an interesting legal question as to whether such processes result in "copies" (which allows the person involved some freedom as regards personal use) or whether they result in "clones" and should be treated as new reproductions (Kretschmer and Wallis, 2000).

These developments are significant in the context of the changing ways in which music and culture are distributed. One of the most important trends concerns the structure of intellectual property right (IPR) revenues. IPRs in this context refer to the rights of creators or their representatives to control and demand remuneration for the use of their creations. When works of music are publicly performed or exploited by record companies on CDs, then the owners of these IPRs have a right to demand compensation.[1] Not only has there been a general growth in the IPR revenue stream, but the revenue base has shifted from profits earned in the physical distribution of tangible carriers, such as the sale of CDs and tapes, to income from licensing fees for the use of music in media channels. The factors of the growth of music television, the proliferation of private radio stations, and the use of music in advertising and game products have made actors in the global media arena increasingly dependent on *immaterial rights* as sources of revenue (Qualen, 1985; Roe and Wallis, 1989; Rutten, 1991). Transactions via the expanding electronic media are more difficult to monitor than sales of tangible items, which means that the establishment and coherence of intellectual property rights has become a more pressing issue than ever before (for further discussion of copyright, see Volgsten and Åkerberg, this volume).

Let us sum up the main current trends in the music industry:

- New digital technologies for recording and distribution, providing wider access to technology with satisfactory quality at an affordable price.
- The deregulation of existing analog channels and the growth of the Internet and new digital channels for conveying music to consumers.
- The irrelevance of national boundaries in distribution (through satellite and Internet distribution), leading to globalization of media products.
- Increased revenue flows from intangible as opposed to tangible sources, with many people predicting the demise of physical carriers such as the CD but little evidence so far to show this actually happening.

These trends became apparent in the latter half of the 1990s, in an environment characterized by a high level of faith in the inevitability of digital network technology to facilitate a major shift to electronic forms of commerce. Such rhetoric was strongly supported by a range of interest groups: politicians, business prophets, and of course, the information technology (IT) industry. The traditional recording industry, on the other hand, was and still is very dependent on a well-established value chain that in some aspects bears little relation to reality or to the opportunities offered by the digital environment (Wallis, 2001; Wallis and Wikström, 2002)

The Music Industry Value Chain: Myths, Facts, and Lost Opportunities

At the height of the IT/dot.com boom, e-commerce (i.e., electronic commerce over digital networks) developed its own form of conventional wisdom, much of which has been shown to suffer from severe flaws in practice. A few of the beliefs underpinning faith in some form of "frictionless capitalism" (as Microsoft founder Bill Gates put it) are:

1. Each seller can find an attractive buyer/price and vice versa.
2. Technology encourages rational behavior.
3. Intermediaries are made redundant (i.e., "disintermediation").
4. Content can only become cheaper or free.
5. Everything will become global.
6. Technology can solve all issues of trust and security.

By about 1990, some American academics had put forward the argument that information technology would change many traditional rules of the economic marketplace: market*space* theories would replace market*place* theories. Such theories were strongly supported by leading consultants and high-profile academics such as Professor Negroponti of the MIT Media Lab. Many positive predictions emerged from academia during the first half of the 1990s (Cohen and Levinthal, 1990; Parsons, Zeisser, and Waitman, 1996; Peterson, Balasubramanian, and Bronnenberg, 1997). Conventional wisdom at the time was that network computer technology would create a new, transparent market space in which buyers and sellers could be matched speedily, at minimum cost (Malone, Yates, and Benjamin, 1989). This view led to widespread belief that traditional intermediaries would be made redundant and that price competition would be radically stimulated, leading to lower prices for the consumer. Acceptance of these tenets often combined with an almost blind faith in the ability of new technology to encourage rational behavior among consumers as well as to solve softer issues of commerce, such as trust and security. This euphoria received generous support by the media and the IT industry, which saw huge opportunities for new business. However, the fact that basic aspects of the human nature of commerce and other human systems change only very slowly seems to have been ignored (Wallis et al., 1998). Venture capital flowed in spate into e-commerce start-ups, but by 2000 many had lost their luster or had even gone bankrupt.

Even a very modest interpretation of the opportunities provided by digital networks would have predicted an inevitable shake-up in the traditional music industry value chain. But as we shall note later, this does not appear to have transpired. The opportunities for e-commerce produced two very different reactions in the music industry. First, the major record companies and publishers, not surprisingly, reacted to the e-commerce prophecies by strongly countering moves to make recorded music available over digital networks. They saw a clear risk of losing control over their copyrighted products, as well as of being bypassed in their role as intermediaries between creator and consumer. Anyone sharing music over the Internet was a pirate, essentially in the same class as an owner of an illegal CD factory, an argument the general public found hard to accept.

The second reaction came from independent recording companies that were keen to test the new technology. They saw the Internet as an amazing opportunity for music creators to discover the shortest distance to a potential audience anywhere in the world. Often working with lesser known artists or less popular musical genres, these companies naturally saw such opportunities to bypass the mainstream industry as particularly attractive. Even here, though, success was limited. Consumers showed little willingness to pay for digital downloads of recorded music. Their propensity to pay was decreased even further by the emergence of companies such as MP3.com and file-sharing applications such as Napster, which made recorded music available "for free." That said, there is evidence that the increased availability of music in virtual form as MP3 files leads to an increased consumption of physical products such as CDs. For example, in an address to the annual PopCom music trade fair in Germany, the forecasting company Jupiter presented findings suggesting that 26 percent of those who used Napster while searching for music online actually increased their purchases of CDs, whereas the corresponding figure for non–Napster users was only 16 percent (Ahlgren, 2000). More recently, there has been a marked increase in live revenues from concerts and music festivals, suggesting that consumer spending is shifting from physical products such as CDs to "physical" experiences, and that the Internet plays an important marketing role in this process. That the major record companies have violently opposed file-sharing over the Internet becomes more understandable in the light of this development—few record company contracts with artists have traditionally included a share of concert revenues.

It is important to consider the current "value chain" in the mainstream music business (see figure 11.1). Music is created by a composer and finds its

Figure 11.1 The Music Industry Value Chain: From Composer to Consumer

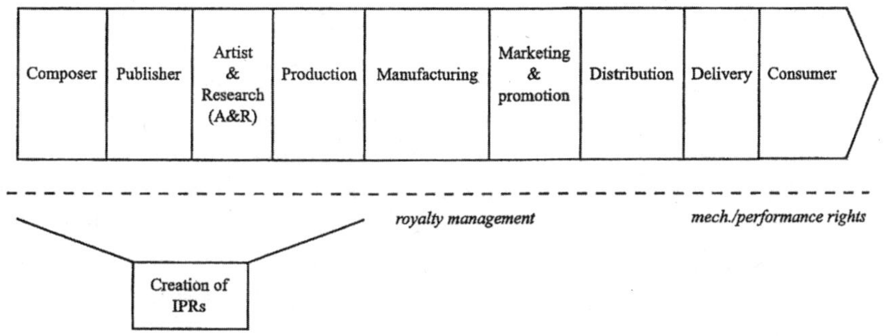

Composer	Publisher	Artist & Research (A&R)	Production	Manufacturing	Marketing & promotion	Distribution	Delivery	Consumer

royalty management   *mech./performance rights*

Creation of IPRs

Intellectual property rights are established when composers create and performers record. These generate revenue flows when recordings are sold or performed in public (e.g., when broadcast).

way into the bottom end of the industry "food chain." Together with a lyricist and the occasional music arranger, it is the composer who provides the essential input to start the process moving through the chain. The chain has hardly changed since the 1930s, when publishers established themselves as intermediaries between composers and performers/record companies. The publisher would print sheet music, search out new artists, and push songs to would-be record companies. A 50/50 share of the royalties was not unusual. There are many anecdotes of composers receiving a small down payment and nothing more, particularly in the heyday of the New York "publishing street" known as Tin Pan Alley.

As the business matured, publishers, either directly or via collecting societies, collected (and still collect) so-called mechanical rights revenues from record companies for the use of the songs. These revenues are based on the actual sales of records, and are shared between the publisher and the composer(s). Other rights that generate revenue for publishers and composers include "performance rights" (e.g., fees from radio stations for broadcasting music) and "synchronization rights" (e.g., fees paid for the use of music in films, television programs, and commercials). These rights are discussed in further detail below. Record companies' expertise in the value chain has traditionally been in the area of "artists and repertoire" or A&R—the process of selecting the right combination of artists and works to be recorded. Record companies record, manufacture, market, and distribute the resulting products, which are then delivered to music stores or other retail channels such as record clubs for sale to consumers. They also perform many promotional activities, including "plugging" recordings to broadcasters.

Over the years, a number of developments have occurred that make the existing value chain appear somewhat archaic even though it still reflects business relationships:

- Numerous artists record their own songs (in the singer-songwriter tradition).
- Through horizontal integration in the industry (i.e., buying up firms with similar activities, for example, Polygram Records buying Decca Records back in the 1970s), publishers and recording companies have become larger in size while medium-sized to large companies have become fewer in number.
- Through vertical integration (i.e., firms buying other players in the value chain, for example, a record company buying a publishing company), different parts of the value chain have ended up having the same owners. The Big 4 record companies (Universal, Sony-BMG, Warner and EMI) are divisions of the same five corporations that own the five major music publishers. These same corporations have also increased their control over broadcasting via ownership of radio and television networks, satellite and cable networks, and so on. For example, the AOL Time Warner amalgamation in 2000 resulted in an integration of physical and non-physical distribution channels. The European Union's competition regulators have recently begun to use the term "collective dominance" when referring to possible negative effects of vertical integration on competition resulting from such combined dominance over various parts of the value chain in the same industrial sector.
- Vertical integration has allowed record companies and publishers to "bundle" contracts: a singer-songwriter has to sign away publishing rights to a publisher in the same corporation in order to get a recording contract with them.
- The division of work between different entities in the chain, and indeed between different specialists within it, has changed. Only a minimal number of publishers rely on sales of sheet music for their income. Many have moved into the A&R arena, contracting singer-songwriters, establishing their own recording studios, and discovering "talent" according to the traditional record company role. The gap has narrowed between recording artists and recording engineers, with artists (and sometimes composers) recording their own works, and recording engineers playing an increasingly creative role in the production process.
- Many publishers function as investment houses, where rights are purchased with the knowledge that they can, in many cases, generate income for decades to come since they are valid up to seventy years after a composer's death.

It is surprising that such changes have not markedly altered the structure of the music industry value chain. If one considers the theoretical opportunities digital technology provides for shortening the value chain between creator and consumer, this sluggishness becomes even more remarkable. On the other hand, the very nature of existing contracts (which are essentially unaffected by many changes in the music industry environment) is probably one of the factors hindering speedy change. Publishing contracts, for instance, are particularly vague as regards any obligations of the publisher to demonstrate more than their best efforts to achieve success in the marketplace; it is hard for composers to extract themselves from such contracts. Many recording contracts with major companies include terms restricting the artist's use of his or her own home pages on the Internet.

Control Over the Use of Copyrighted Musical Works

Vertical integration, producing larger and larger music and media corporations, has meant that the traditional, "personal" nature of the relationships between creator and exploiter has inevitably changed. The traditional publisher-composer relationship (and indeed many contracts regulating such relationships) assumes close ties between the creator and publisher, with the publisher being entirely independent of, say, the recording industry. At the same time, the example of EMI quoted earlier shows that copyright revenues are an increasingly important contribution to the revenues generated in the music industry value chain. When publishing musical works, composers transfer rights to exploitation (i.e., use) to publishers, who then represent them. As publishers have grown in size, the relationship between creator and publisher has typically shifted from personal to impersonal. For example, the largest publisher in Sweden controls almost 600,000 works. Clearly, such an organization can inject personal effort into promoting only a small percentage of these works. This situation can result in three different types of control:

1. *active promotion* of particular works;
2. *neutral participation:* little activity, but retention of a share of copyright incomes when such works happen to be exploited, for example, broadcast on the radio; and
3. *negative control:* de facto blocking access of a large number of copyrighted works to the market so as to establish higher rates for exploitation. In their objection to the EMI–Time Warner amalgamation, the Disney Corporation complained to the European Commission (EC) that the combined publishing outfit would have a major dominance over the sale of music for use in films and commercials, and could thus manipulate market prices by withholding materials and not accepting current prices.

In the Internet world, control over a work's use becomes far more difficult once a recording has found its way onto digital networks. Conditions are also complicated by tensions between different rights holders, with publishers controlling music copyrights and record companies controlling the rights to specific recordings. Vertical integration is characterized by the integration of the ownership and the exploitation of rights. In the distribution of IPR revenues, a cost for one division of a global media company (the record company, for example) is a source of revenue for another division (the publishing division, for example). Synergy values, in other words, can only be achieved by decreasing payments to actors outside this synergy relationship, which in essence forces consumers to pay more or creators to receive less.

Pressures on the Music Collection/Protection Societies

The question of necessary intermediaries between creators and consumers is of particular interest. Is there a need for both record companies and publishers? Do they add the value that is reflected in their share of revenues? Above all, what should be the role of the so-called collecting societies (also known as performing rights societies or rights societies) created by authors, publishers, and in some cases performers to collect and distribute revenue from users of music? Are they essential intermediaries? Could other entities—e.g., telecom operators, financial services companies, or even IT companies—replace existing actors? Most music authors, including lyricists and arrangers, rely on the efficient functioning of music collecting societies to regulate the flow of IPR revenues between themselves and music exploiters. Historically, such societies were founded by authors. Publishers can be members of their boards but their influence varies from society to society, depending on the influence of composers and their organizations. In the Nordic area, for instance, composers' associations are part owners of their national collecting societies, a situation not found in any other music territory.

Copyright organizations need to be capable of handling four categories of data: a register of members whose rights they represent, details of registered works (titles, authors, publishers), details of users with whom agreements are signed, and details of music use by such users. Such demands involve huge amounts of data. The Swedish collecting society STIM, for instance, has no fewer than 47,000 registered associate members in Sweden and a register of over 5 million works (2004). Radio alone in a small country like Sweden can account for several million performances of musical works per year. All this has to be analyzed as efficiently and cheaply as possible, with the moneys being distributed to rights holders in a manner that is deemed as correct as possible by rights holders, users, and other observers. Collecting societies, as intermediaries, have to satisfy a number of demands from three major sources (see figure 11.2): from copyright owners (who want efficiency and success in hunting down music users), from music users (who do not, as a rule, enjoy paying copyright dues), and from various official watchdogs monitoring their behavior as de facto monopolies. The EU competition authorities have been particularly critical of some aspects of collecting society operations (Temple Lang, 1997).

Figure 11.2 Demands on Collecting Societies

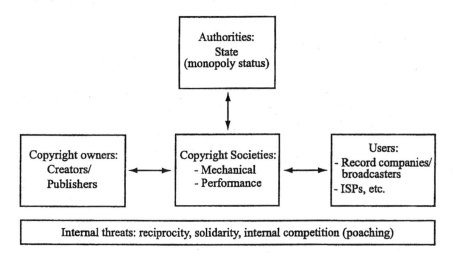

Internal threats: reciprocity, solidarity, internal competition (poaching)

Collecting societies are experiencing a number of pressures: from competition authorities (national and international), from powerful users, and from influential copyright owners. Users can be traditional players such as radio and TV broadcasters or newer actors such as Internet service providers (ISPs).

Most collecting societies in Europe are de facto monopolies. This is generally accepted by exploiters of music as a practical advantage since it allows them to sign "blanket licenses" giving them access to virtually "all repertoire." A system with competing collecting societies, such as that in the US, can cause problems for users who do not know which agreements relate to which repertoire. A bar pianist playing requests, for instance, can hardly be expected to check in advance whether the song a customer wants to hear is represented by one or another collecting society.

Collecting societies control a number of different types of rights. Figure 11.3 shows the remuneration flow connected with performance rights and synchronization rights. These are economic rights that entitle a rights owner to authorize and prohibit the use of the copyrighted music. Remuneration generally occurs in the form of licensing fees paid by users and consumers. There are also *moral rights*, which allow a rights owner to refuse certain forms of use that conflict with his or her integrity (see Volgsten and Åkerberg, this volume). Such rights are usually featured in contexts involving religion, politics, or pornography. Moral rights can also function as economic rights if they are used as an argument for raising the price of acceptance when, say, an advertiser wishes to use a piece of music in a particular commercial context.

The international collecting society system is held together by the principles of *reciprocity* and *solidarity*. Composers in country A can be certain that

Figure 11.3 The Origins and Flows of Different Types of IPR Revenues

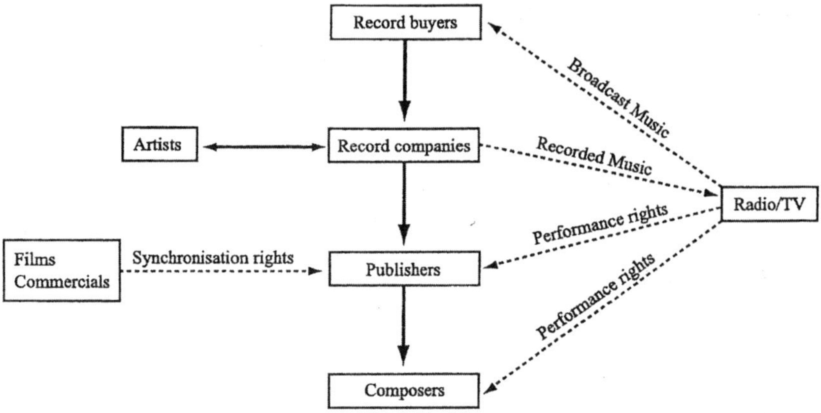

The recording industry provides broadcasters with recorded music. Broadcasters pay for the right to broadcast music (a performance right). Record companies pay mechanical rights dues for the right to reproduce musical works. Synchronization rights are valid in cases where music is synchronized with images (e.g., in films or TV commercials).

their rights are looked after by the local collecting society in country B, and vice versa; administrative costs are more or less shared by all rights owners. Reciprocity is similar to the workings of the VISA credit card: if composer X from country A has music performed in country B, then country B's collecting society will pay money to X via country B's society, and vice versa. Solidarity implies that administrative charges are spread evenly over all composers and rights holders, where foreign composers are treated in exactly the same manner as domestic composers. This is analogous to the operations of the Postal Service and its principle of universal service based on communication being an "essential right." As monopolies, collecting societies have traditionally seen themselves as intellectual and cultural guardians of the system, in other words as essential facilitators or intermediaries. Since monopolies are open to abuse of power, various safeguards have been introduced to prevent abuse. In Sweden, for example, the state appointed the chairman of the board of STIM and two of its governors from the early 1940s through to 2003. From 2003, these government appointees were replaced by two independent, externally recruited board members. This move was a reflection of the shift in official focus from the justice department overseeing a national legal institution to the working of an independent organization in a market subject to the scrutiny of the national competition authorities. In some countries (Denmark, for example), tariffs have to be cleared with a government ministry. Otherwise the boards generally consist of composers and publishers.

The principles of solidarity and reciprocity have eroded in recent years as a result of a number of moves by larger players (i.e., the major record companies and publishers) demanding increased efficiency from the societies and, in some circumstances, preferential treatment (see Wallis et al., 1998, for a more detailed discussion). Three of the most important of these moves are Central European Licensing, cultural deductions, and the Casino or Cannes Agreement.

Central European Licensing

CEL, introduced in the late 1980s and later renamed Central Licensing Agreements or CLA, began when one large record company offered to pay in all its mechanical rights dues to one collecting society only, irrespective of where the recordings were manufactured. The deal involved a discount on the agreed percentage of the retail price of the recording, in other words, an apparent decrease in the cost of copyright. The Dutch mechanical collecting society accepted the deal, thus undermining the reciprocity principle (Montgomery, 1994). With moneys being redistributed via other societies to locally resident composers/publishers, collecting societies were forced to accept a lower commission rate, essentially increasing the costs of distribution for those outside the CEL area.

A similar type of move was then tried by EMI Publishing, which attempted to set up an independent "society" to handle all the incomes from mechanical rights for several songs published by the group Simply Red. This was discontinued but nevertheless succeeded in rocking the boat. The power of EMI Publishing is illustrated by the fact that the costs of discontinuing EMI's pending new organization were partly covered by the established collecting society in the same territory. The group U2 also requested a shift from the rigid principle of solidarity by demanding better deals for returns on income from its own live concerts. They argued that since they were playing their own works, the costs of handling the distribution process were minimal and therefore societies should charge them a lower rate than for concerts by other groups whose repertoire would require more effort to identify the works performed. At least one society has agreed to this demand.

Cultural Deductions

International agreements between collecting societies allow them to deduct up to 10 percent of their national income and use it for "cultural purposes." Such deductions have been heavily opposed by some British and American composers and publishers, who claim they are a way of "stealing" their money. Continental European societies would argue that the deductions are used in a way that strengthens respect for copyright and thus benefits everyone, irrespective of nationality.

Casino

Casino, or the Cannes Agreement of 1995, stemmed from the major publishers' demands for a general decrease over time of the commission rates charged by the mechanical collection organizations for handling revenues from Central Licensing Agreements. The alternative would have been a move by at least one major publisher (Polygram Publishing) to bypass parts of the international system, using the British mechanical rights organization MCPS to move moneys, where relevant, from Polygram Records to Polygram Music (i.e., in cases where songs published by the publishing arm were released on discs by the Polygram recording arm). To be able to fulfill the terms of the Cannes Agreement, some smaller societies were forced to charge higher commission rates for the distribution of payments from copyrighted materials on smaller record labels (outside the CEL system). In the case of the Nordic Copyright Bureau or NCB (which collects royalties for Sweden, Finland, Denmark, Norway, Iceland, and recently also the Baltic states Estonia, Latvia and Lithuania), the society deemed it necessary to charge 12.5 percent—as opposed to 3.9 percent, falling to 2.4 percent, on revenues due to rights holders from CEL records—in order to balance the books. The major publishers, in essence, demanded lower commission rates for the distribution of their revenues from mechanical rights arising from CEL records, in other words from records released by recording divisions of their own corporations. This would apply, of course, to all composers and publishers released on smaller labels, even the major publishers, weakening the principle of solidarity.

The Cannes Agreement ran out in July 2001. The major publishers wished to renegotiate the terms so as to gain greater representation on the boards of the mechanical collecting societies. This rather complicated relationship between the distribution institutions (the collecting societies), the recording divisions of the major global music corporations, and their sister publishing divisions illustrates how vertical integration supports the power of the major players while putting smaller, independent players at a financial disadvantage.

Vertical Integration Leading to Instability

From the outside of the music industry, it would appear that collecting societies play a pivotal role in the operations of the industry (figure 11.4), controlling tariffs and regulating the flows of money between exploiters (record companies, broadcasters, etc.) and rights owners (authors, publishers). But as is shown in the above discussion about pressures on collecting societies, this is a gross simplification of the actual working of the industry. The actual entanglements are rooted in the move toward vertical integration, when the same corporation aims to control both publishing and recording activities and,

Figure 11.4 A Traditional View of the Role of Collecting Societies as Intermediaries

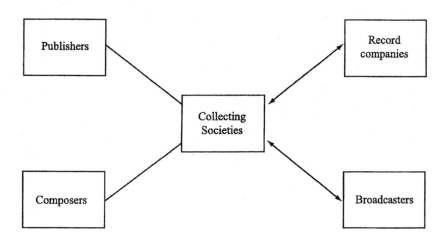

The collecting societies represent rights owners when negotiating with exploiters of music (record companies, broadcasters). This model assumes that collecting societies enjoy a large degree of independence and power (and that users are independent from rights owners).

in some cases, even broadcasting. For example, the amalgamation of AOL and Time Warner in 2000 added considerable Internet and cable access to the areas under AOL Time Warner control.

Figure 11.5 illustrates how the role of the collecting society has been diminished (compare figures 11.4 and 11.5). Major publishers who are members of these societies inevitably have dual loyalties, to the collecting society and to their corporate bosses. Such publishers, via their ownership links to major record companies and broadcasters, enjoy preferential information not available to individual creators or smaller independent companies. More recently, broadcasters and even some advertising agencies have started their own "publishing houses," which often demand that composers who are offered commissions to write music for television programs or commercials have to give away their publishing rights to the broadcasters' or the agencies' "publishers." In effect, this cuts the remuneration to the composer by up to 50 percent. As a rule, these "pretend" publishers are generally administered by one of the major multinational publishers, which probably explains why the collecting society regime has not been able to question their validity. The BBC publishing arm, for instance, is administered by BMG Publishing, itself owned by BMG Music. Sweden's national commercial television network TV4 has a publishing arm administered by Sony Publishing. British media composers have heatedly opposed this development but have enjoyed little success in their efforts to reverse it. In a speech to the 1999 congress of

Figure 11.5 Vertical Integration Involving the Dominance of Large Media Corporations

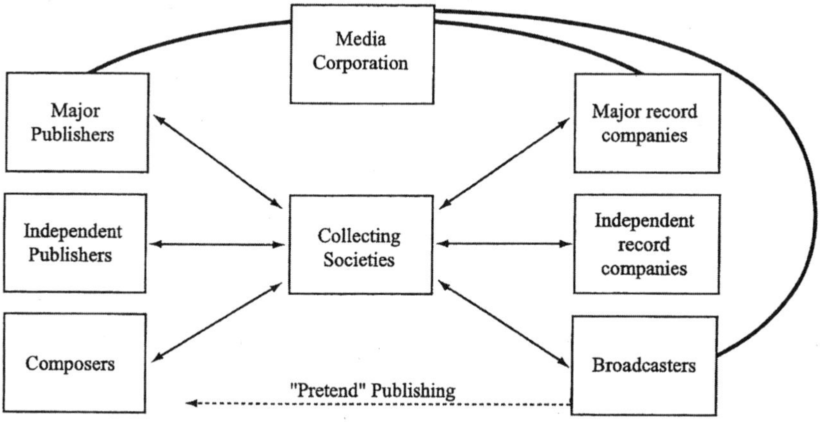

With record companies, publishers, and even broadcasters being controlled by large media corporations, the power and independence of collecting societies becomes heavily curtailed. Broadcasters can even create "pretend" publishers, the sole purpose of which is to recoup copyright dues via publishing works composed specifically for radio or television.

the International Confederation of Musical Authors, Mark Fishlock of the British Academy of Composers and Songwriters maintained: "We've made virtually no progress on this issue over the last 20 years: what began as a shady practice is fast becoming the industry norm. One of the main reasons is the problem of getting beyond contractual considerations. The argument composers are forever hearing is: 'if you don't like it, don't sign the contract.' This is all very well, but the composer's bargaining position has never been weaker. So the reality is, if you don't accept their [the music industry's] terms, you don't get the job" (Fishlock, 1999). In late 2004, after a period of collecting and analyzing evidence, composers' organizations in both the UK and Sweden filed complaints about these business practices with their respective competition authorities. These documents asked for an investigation of the effects of "pretend publishing" on competition in the music publishing market.

Another problem affecting the system is internal rivalry among collecting societies, particularly as the larger societies strive to become even larger. Smaller societies, however, have a number of advantages: they have local expertise, they can be nimble, and traditionally they have been able to collect more IPR revenues per capita than societies with larger territories (Wallis, 2000).

The Music Industry in the Brave New World of e-Commerce

As this book goes to press, e-commerce is still a dominant, if not somewhat tarnished, buzz phrase. A number of academic theorists predicted in the late 1980s and early 1990s that the introduction of digital networks coupled with Internet/Web technology would inevitably revolutionize the way people engage in commerce. This would apply both to commerce between companies (business-to-business, or B2B) and to dealings between commercial enterprises and individuals (business-to-customer, or B2C, also known as e-commerce). Traditional physical sales entities would be bypassed ("disintermediated") as suppliers made direct contact with individual consumers via the Internet. Where physical products or services could be transformed into digital ones, the new virtual forms would take over. The change would be linear and irreversible (Wallis and Holtham, 2000). These theories were heavily backed up by IT companies keen to sell solutions, consultants eager to present themselves as experts on the "new economy," and, not least, the media. No self-respecting journal could fail to provide a special section on e-business. This in turn led to a spate of venture capital funds and a myriad of so-called dot-com companies.

The music industry was a key area of focus in this development. It seemed to present an opportunity to offer a greater range of products at a cheaper price (the driving force behind companies such as Amazon.com). Moreover, music could be easily transformed from a material form to an immaterial form via compression standards such as those used in MP3 files. This naturally opened a Pandora's box in the Internet, since music lovers could exchange files individually or gain access to files via companies such as MP3.com and file-sharing applications such as Napster and Kazaa. The major players in the industry saw an obvious threat. They might lose control over their copyrighted materials and run the risk of getting lower returns on their heavy, up-front investments in international superstars.

The overall result was a mixture of commercial ventures—many of which appeared unable to make a profit—coupled with legal and technological moves by the major players to control the digital distribution of music. Third-quarter 2000 results for a number of companies in the Internet music business were published in the October and November 2000 issues of the trade publication *Billboard*. Many showed significant losses:

MP3.com	Loss 48.7 million dollars (19.9 same period 1999)
Blockbuster	Loss 19.3 million dollars (19.1)
Emusic	Loss 17.3 million dollars (14.2)
Loudeye technologies	Loss 9.5 million dollars
Preview Systems	Loss 5.4 million dollars (4.1)
Amazon.com	Loss 240.5 million dollars (197.1)

The Internet book- and music-seller Amazon claimed that their book- and CD-sales division was at last returning an operating profit. This profit, however, did not include technology and some financial costs.

An in-depth study of four Swedish-based e-music companies with strategies ranging from sales of physical products to sales of digital downloads (work-by-work) came to the following conclusions (Ahlgren, 2000):

- The Internet does provide an opportunity for suppliers of niche music genres to reach an international audience. The main challenge concerns choice of marketing strategy in a noisy information environment.
- There is no evidence of high consumer demand for mainstream music (work-by-work) purchased via digital downloads. Whether this is the result of plentiful access to "free" music files via the Internet or a gap between supply and perceived consumer needs/convenience is unclear.
- There is considerable evidence that the availability of multiple free copies of songs via the Internet encourages consumers to purchase physical products (although it does not encourage them to purchase digital downloads of the same recordings).
- In all the case studies examined, technical problems have been underestimated, particularly those that involve integration of different systems and applications.
- Development (and analyses) has been complicated by the fact that major players in the music industry have relied on both legal and technological means to control their copyrighted materials in the Internet environment. At the same time, however, these players have become involved, via settlements or share purchases, in companies and applications that make music available over the Net, in other words in the very companies they are seeking to oppose.
- Many e-retailers grounded their models in the belief that bypassing a traditional bricks-and-mortar outlet (i.e., a standard music store) could free up resources sufficient to offer both a wider range of choice as well as lower prices for physical products such as CDs. They ignored the significance of other necessary physical expertise (logistics and warehousing). They also underestimated the problems of growth pains and cultural difficulties that can arise from speedy international expansion.
- Sudden changes in the availability of venture capital funds can have a critical effect on e-commerce initiatives that rely on such capital for speedy expansion.
- There is no evidence so far that musical creators (i.e., composers and artists) have enjoyed any financial benefits at all from the shorter value chain made possible via disintermediation. Some may, however, have been able to reap publicity benefits from an Internet presence.

An interesting example of a major player's strategy to control use of music on the Internet is the case of the file-sharing application company Scour.com. Like Napster, it offered a "file swapping" application that allowed users to share music (and even video) titles stored on their computer's hard disk. The music and film industries claimed that this was the same as stealing, since it would seem to discourage users from buying physical products or even paying for digital variants. File swapping adherents claimed that it was merely a digital equivalent of lending a personal CD to a friend. Scour was sued by both the Recording Industry Association of America (RIAA) and the film industry in July of 2000. To alleviate its problems, Scour filed for bankruptcy and offered to sell its assets to another e-commerce firm, listen.com. All five major record companies have a financial interest in listen.com. A spokesperson for the RIAA said that cancelation of the suit against Scour would depend on its new owner, listen.com, shutting down its "file exchange service and search engine" (Anonymous, 2000b). BMG, via its parent company Bertelsmann, applied an even more direct strategy to come to terms with file swapping companies. In 2000, Bertelsmann did a deal directly with Napster while a legal case for damages driven by the RIAA was still in progress. Shortly afterwards, Napster was allowed to go bankrupt. The brand name was sold later to Roxio, a firm specializing in producing software for so-called CD-burners. Napster was then relaunched by Roxio in 2003 as a subscription-based legal downloading site for digital music files. About the same time, Apple computers launched its iTunes site. The prime driving force was not the sale of digital music per se, but to encourage the sale of Apple's iPod digital storage device.

Legal suits and buy-ups have been one part of the majors' strategy. Another has involved encryption and watermarking technologies that block file copying and follow files as they move around networks. An industrial consortium was formed to agree on standards for these technologies. It was hoped the new standards would be introduced into music players (e.g., MP3 players) by the consumer electronics industry. The so-called Secure Digital Music Initiative (SDMI) attracted almost one hundred different collaborators, many with very divergent agendas. To prove its invincibility, in 2000 the consortium challenged hackers and computer scientists to crack the codes. Within a week, brains at Princeton University had done so, picking up a $10,000 reward. As predicted by a number of observers, SDMI folded in late 2000 (Prast, 1999). Legal sales initiatives offering music over the Internet were introduced by the major record companies in 2001 (PressPlay and Musicnet). Both of these failed. PressPlay was later sold to Roxio, a US company that develops, amongst other things, software for CD burners. Roxio also bought the Napster brand name from BMG in 2003. The first reasonably successful "legal" (i.e., satisfying the demands of related copyright owners) digital delivery system for music files was provided by a computer manufacturer, Apple, in 2003, probably with the intention of using it to market a piece of consumer electronics hardware, the iPod storage device.

Superstar Composers, New Entrants, Niche Experimenters, and the Future

Business schools often claim that an 80/20 rule applies to a majority of industrial activities, with 80 percent of the revenue being accounted for by 20 percent of the products. In the copyright world, distributions from collecting societies suggest that a relatively small number of authors, perhaps 15 percent, account for around 85 to 90 percent of IPR revenues distributed to individuals. This does not necessarily reflect the actual use of music, as was observed by Britain's Monopolies and Mergers Commission (1996) in studying the British collecting society PRS. Results can become skewed because heavily performed works are easier to identify when analyzing music use. Works performed less often require a greater degree of manual analysis, thus increasing the administrative costs for the society.

A comparison of "cumulative income" to "percentages of composers" is illustrated with a Laurentz curve in figure 11.6. Such a graph indicates the cumulative payments over the spectrum of recipients. If all recipients got the same remuneration, then the curve would be a straight line at an angle of 45 degrees. The figure illustrates that a small percentage of members receive the largest spoils. In the middle are all the composers who enjoy "average" use of their music (as identified by the collection societies' administrative processes). Here we also find new entrants and the "stars of the future." Finally, on the right side, we find special cases, such as those working with experimental music, whose usage is both scarce and hard/expensive to identify. The Monopolies and Mergers Commission study of the PRS questioned whether the steep slope of the curve reflected the reality of music use.

In an e-commerce business environment, one can consider three different business models for music, pertaining essentially to the three different segments of the Laurentz curve. The first category consists of superstars. If mainstream products are to generate revenue in the anarchic Internet environment, then the major music industry players will have to exert far more control over activities such as file swapping. They will also have to link the use of virtual forms of distribution to the sale of physical products or experiences. A problem here is that many traditional record company contracts do not include control over "merchandising" (e.g., the sale of T-shirts). The move by some record companies, notably Sony Music, to stipulate control over artists' Internet home pages (bitterly opposed by many artists' managers) can be interpreted as an attempt to move in this direction. The large category of middle-rank players, new entrants, and future stars probably needs a far less rigid approach to the Internet. Attracting publicity and building communities of interest are far more important initial priorities than protecting revenues from file swapping. A model that migrates from publicity to revenue generation is still more attractive. Finally, there are the special cases, the experimenters, who clearly require some

Figure 11.6 A Fair Distribution of IPR Incomes?

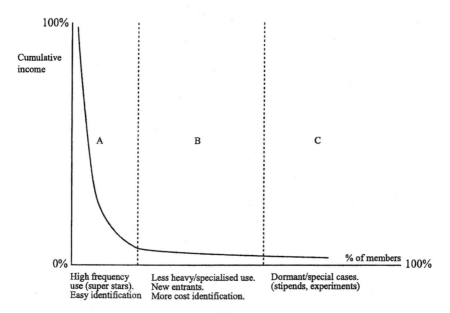

As much as 85 percent of a typical collecting society's revenue can be distributed to less than 10 percent of members (A). This is partly the result of the easy identification of heavily used works. In the middle segment (B) we find less frequently performed works, music by new entrants, etc. The third segment (C) reflects works that are dormant or performed in contexts that are hard to identify. Any move to cut administration costs is likely to enhance the dominance of highly popular works/composers (A).

form of cross subsidization. After all, they are the research and development (R&D) workers of the music industry. Collecting societies have traditionally funded this activity via cultural deductions, described earlier. The British and American societies actively lobbied against such activities for about a decade, but as of the early 2000s, this view seemed to have mellowed. The British collecting society PRS now takes a cultural deduction of 10 percent of the money it returns to Sweden for the performance of Swedish works in the UK.

Final Thought: Will Anything Change?

At the turn of the millennium, the "new economy" was all the rage among academics, journalists, consultants, and IT suppliers. With many dot-com companies having collapsed, sales of physical products holding up reasonably well, and file-sharing activities either being subject to head-on attacks or being amalgamated into the world of the major players, can one expect any change in the music industry value chain? Will the same major players still rule the playing field in the near future?

Many of the questions posed in this chapter still have relevance. A 2004 study by Jupiter Communications (Anonymous, 2004a) found that CD sales will not be replaced by digital downloads in the immediate future, predicting digital sales of no more than 12 percent of consumer music spending by 2009. About half of a sample of adults interviewed by Jupiter claimed that music recorded on a physical disc was more valuable than the digital downloaded equivalent.

The strategies of the major record companies to file-sharing activities on the Internet are ambivalent. Record companies have enlisted the help of anti-piracy experts to flood the file-sharing network Kazaa with millions of so-called spoof files (false files) to disrupt would-be downloaders. At the same time, the same major companies are buying intelligence information from "P2P sniffers," companies that track Internet requests for downloads, not only for identifying individuals who share copyrighted materials, but also to plan their own marketing of physical products (Anonymous, 2004b). More evidence suggests that the initial rapid growth of legal downloads noted in 2003 could be slowing down. *Music and Copyright* noted that "one of the striking features of the emerging online music market is that, despite the widespread excitement it generates, it is the technology, and in particular the iPod, rather than the content, i.e., the music, that has been celebrated. With the launch of iTunes, Apple was widely heralded in the media as the saviour of the music industry by singularly creating a legitimate online music market. It now seems more accurate to note that iTunes and iPod have become the saviors of Apple Computer Inc." (Anonymous, 2004c).

As regards the fortunes of different actors in the music industry, much will depend on the activities of the collecting agencies that collect and distribute "intangible" revenues to artists, publishers, composers, and producers. They have extensive databases of artists, composers, and works. They can, in theory, offer new platforms through which creators can find shortcuts to users, both business users and individual consumers. The Spanish collecting society has invested heavily in an Internet site known as Portalatino, offering composers the ability to create their own home pages and make recordings available to consumers who visit the site, without the involvement of intermediaries such as record companies and publishers. The society was taken to court by the major publishers, who claimed that this was a misuse of members' funds, since they too are members of collecting societies such as SGAE. Another interesting initiative is the Phonofile digital base in Norway, which allows commercial users to browse among and purchase over 25,000 digitized recordings, mainly from independent Norwegian record companies. Such initiatives, though not much appreciated by sectors of the existing music industry value chain, would seem to be the only way to date to shorten the route between creators and listeners in the digital environment.

Such hopeful propositions assume an inherent driving force behind human beings that seeks a constant widening of horizons, with new experiences being the object of an active in-built search function. In 1984, this author (together with colleague Krister Malm) considered a very similar set of alternatives. Would the growth of the global music industry, coupled with the emergence of new technologies such as the music cassette, provide us with a greater or a more limited range of available music experiences? In Wallis and Malm (1984), we concluded with the following questions, which were probably just as provocative then as any positive analysis of Napster might still be to the established music industry now. We asked whether the interaction of cultures and technology would result in "a to and fro movement where more and more musical features will become more and more common to more and more music cultures [with] a little satisfaction to a lot of people and a lot of satisfaction to very, very few" (p. 323). An alternative outcome, we suggested, might be "the emergence of a multitude of types of music arising out of new living conditions and new music technologies" (p. 324).

The degree of the concentration of power effected in the music and entertainment industry via vertical and horizontal integration in the latter half of the 1990s is extraordinary compared to the situation we were describing back in 1984. In curbing those who wish to assume global control, ownership of rights and means of production and distribution, the role of regulators will be critical, as will be the interaction between people and new technology. Fortunately, the interaction of people and technology in the media field always seems to result in applications that were never foreseen by either the inventors or the financial forces that seek to exploit the same technologies.

Notes

1. The business term "exploitation" refers to the *regular* use of recorded music in such media as radio and television. When a recorded song is broadcast on the radio, it is being "exploited" (according to business jargon). This should not be confused with exploitation as *abusive* use.

References

Ahlgren, B. (2000). *Electronic Trade in Music: The Shift from Physical to Non-Physical Products.* Masters thesis, Department of Media Technology and Graphic Arts, Royal Institute of Technology (KTH), Stockholm, Sweden.

Anonymous. (2000a). "Napster shows the way forward." *Music Business International* 10: 9.

Anonymous. (2000b). "Scour forced to close search engine." *Billboard* 111: 10.

Anonymous. (2001). "EMI sees 12% increase in revenues." *Music and Copyright* 206: 4.

Anonymous. (2004a). "Subscription-based music will drive sales." *Cnet News.com* 12. http://news.com.com/Study+Subscription+services+ to+drive+digital+music/2100-1027_3-5473153.html.

Anonymous. (2004b). "Digital music market comes of age but will it bring significant profits to the record industry?" *Music and Copyright* 287: 2.

Anonymous. (2004c). "Labels peer at pirates for insights." *Billboard*, April 24, p. 73.

Burnett, R. (1996). *The Global Jukebox: The International Music Industry*. London: Routledge.

Choi, C. J. and Hilton, B. (1995). "Globalization, originality, and convergence in the entertainment industry." In L. Foster (ed.) *Advances in Applied Business Strategy* (pp. 76–89). Greenwich, CT: JAI Press.

Cohen, W. M. and Levinthal, D. A. (1990). "Absorptive capacity: A new perspective on learning and innovation." *Administrative Science Quarterly* 35: 128–152.

Fishlock, M. (1999). "The relationships between authors and publishers." Speech presented at the *1999 congress of the International Confederation of Authors of Musical Works (CIAM), Helsinki, Finland.*

Frith, S. (1992). "The industrialisation of popular music." In J. Lull (ed.) *Popular Music and Communication* (pp. 53–77). Beverly Hills: Sage.

Hirsch, P. M. (1992). "Globalization of mass-media ownership: Implications and effects." *Communication Research* 19: 677–681.

Hugenholtz, P. B. (ed.) (1996). *The Future of Copyright in a Digital Environment*. The Hague: Kluwer.

Hulsink, W. and Tang, P. (1997). *The Winds of Change: Digital Technologies, Trading Information and Managing Intellectual Property Rights*. Management Report No. 44. Rotterdam: Rotterdam School of Management.

Kretschmer, M. and Wallis, R. (2000). "Business models and regulation in the electronic distribution of music." In B. Stanford-Smith (ed.) *E-Business: Key Issues, Applications and Technologies* (pp. 197–204). Amsterdam: IOS Press.

Malm, K. and Wallis, R. (1992). *Media Policy and Music Activity*. London: Routledge.

Malone, T., Yates, J., and Benjamin, R. (1989). "The logic of electronic markets." *Harvard Business Review,* May–June, pp. 166–170.

Monopolies and Mergers Commission (1996). *Performing Rights*. London: HMSO Cm 3147.

Montgomery, R. (1994). "Central licensing of mechanical rights in Europe: The journey towards a single copyright." *European Intellectual Property Review,* pp. 45–65.

Parsons, A., Zeisser, M., and Waitman, R. (1996). "Organizing for digital marketing." *McKinsey Quarterly* 4: 1.

Peterson, R., Balasubramanian A., and Bronnenberg, B. J. (1997). "Exploring the implications of the Internet for consumer marketing." *Journal of the Academy of Marketing Science* 25: 329–346.

Prast, J. (1999). "Rights of passage: Digital music strategies." MBA thesis, Department of Information Management, City University Business School, London, UK.

Qualen, J. (1985). *The Music Industry: The End of Vinyl*. London: Comedia.

Roe, K. and Wallis, R. (1989). "One planet, one music: The development of music television in Europe." *Nordicom Review* 1: 35–41.

Rutten, P. (1991). "Local popular music on the national and international markets." *Cultural Studies* 5: 294–305.

Temple Lang, J. (1997). *Media, Multimedia and European Community Antitrust Law*. Working paper of the European Commission Competition Directorate (DGIV).

Wallis, R. (1990). *Internationalisation, Localisation and Integration: The Changing Structure of the Music Industry*. Working paper of the Department of Mass Communication, Gothenburg University.

_____ (1994). "The future of radio as seen from the outside." *Nordicom Review* 2: 43–47.

_____ (2000). "The music industry and the digital environment seen through the eyes of a smaller collecting society." In J. Turton and E. Lauvaux (eds.) *Legal and Commercial Effects of Digitisation on the Music Industry* (pp. 221–232). Apeldoorn, Netherlands: Maklu Publishers.

_____ (2001). "Business as usual or a real paradigm shift in the value chain? The example of the music industry's response to e-commerce technology and ideology," In B. Stanford-Smith and E. Chuizza (eds.). *E-Work and E-Commerce: Novel Solutions and Practices for a Global Networked Society.* Amsterdam: IOS Press.

Wallis, R. and Holtham, C. W. (2000). "From the physical to the virtual and back again: Relationships between tangible and intangible products, devices and experiences and their relevance in the digital environment." Proceedings of the Third International Conference on Telecommunications and Electronic Commerce (ICTEC) (pp. 147–159). Dallas: South Methodist University.

Wallis, R., Kretschmer, M., Holtham, C., and Skinner, C. (1998). "Credibility capital: The new logic of electronic markets." Proceedings of the First International Conference on Telecommunications and Electronic Commerce (ICTEC). Nashville: Vanderbilt University.

Wallis, R. and Malm, K. (1984). *Big Sounds from Small Peoples: The Music Industry in Small Countries.* London: Constable.

Wallis, R. and Wikström, O. (2002). "Re-visiting the Dot.com fallout in search of lessons learned and values created." In B. Standford-Smith, E. Chiozza, and M. Edin (eds.). *Challenges and Achievements in E-business and E-work* (pp. 1447–1454). Amsterdam: IOS Press.

PART V CONTROL BY REUSE

Chapter 12

Music and Reuse

Theoretical and Historical Considerations

Ola Stockfelt

Introduction

"Classical music" is often used in commercial advertisements, as background music in public places, and in various audiovisual contexts—computer games, TV shows, cartoons, various genres of "popular music," and so on. The music that is used often consists of extracts, rearranged and remixed to fit these situations. This reuse of well-known music is subject to criticism from not only a copyright perspective but also various moral positions. I suggest that this criticism is worthy of serious discussion and that its claims highlight some crucial aspects of contemporary musical life, not least the functions and utility of traditional musicology. The dominant, commonsense view of music history over the last couple of centuries—reified not only in popular textbooks but also in phonogram editions and legal texts—is not only historically false but also increasingly inadequate and impractical for dealing with pressing problems related to copyright in a digital society. Alternative criteria must be established to specify what elements constitute a piece of music and who could and should be regarded as its composer. Such an approach, however, will clash with several well-established myths in our society as well as with fundamental economic and professional interests.

* * *

Classical music is used in television commercials. The fact that this was obviously not the intention of the composers has often been presented both as an example of manipulation of music and of manipulation by music. So what?

Notes for this chapter begin on page 334.

What do we expect? *Everything* is used in television commercials to sell products, from the most banal to the most unthinkable things: violence, sex, bliss and misery, art and trash, high and low standards, high and low quality presentations, tragedy, classical dramas, guilt, loneliness, sociability, and on and on. Sometimes even solid arguments. And of course all kinds of music. Well, almost. So why not classical music?

Within the sphere of musicology, I do not think that anybody is too upset today by hearing the continuo from a duet of a Bach cantata underscoring a verbal presentation telling you how to show the love, affection, and responsibility your cat deserves by providing it with a specific brand of ground canned meat as picturesque kittens happily prance about on the TV screen in the soft colors of a cozy home, shot with point-of-view close-ups from mostly low angles. Musicologists today usually excel in reflexive relativism rather than in the defense of any specific brand of expert listening or autonomous aesthetics. Nothing is really allowed to shock us anymore—least of all J. S. Bach, no matter what the context.

But the fact of the matter is that while, in all probability, neither the average attentive viewer of a cat food commercial nor the average up-to-date musicologist will be at all bothered by the use of excerpts or arranged fragments of "classical" music in such a context, significant (or at least audible) groups of people actually *do* give expression to a deep and honest moral indignation that they claim to experience in such situations. These attitudes are not only held by the small stratum of elderly people who grew up in a social context wherein the famous Adornian expert listeners' standards were supposedly unquestioned. In such a context, classical music was not to be tainted; considerable cultural capital as well as certain fundamental views of the world were often dependent on the eternal values of "classical" music being kept pure and unquestioned. In fact, many young students, and not only those studying music or musicology, frequently hold similar attitudes. So might highly competent colleagues working in other academic disciplines.

Each year I get telephone calls from journalists asking for statements or information that they can use to write articles or produce radio programs about the manipulation of (and by) music as "Muzak" or in commercials. Their interest and what it represents are seen from a new angle in the context of the following questions:

- What is the nature of the repulsion that some people feel about the use of "classical" music in undesirable contexts? Whose intentions are being disregarded?
- Which uses of music are considered to be negative manipulation of music and which are not?

Let us confront the queries of these questioning and questing journalists. I have never really taken their questions and prejudices so seriously before, which, matters of etiquette aside, might have been a mistake. On the one hand, the questions they ask and the views they express are probably not significantly representative of the general population's view on the subject. Journalists have angles, interests, and problems connected with their special need for quick production of easily digestible information and infotainment. Nevertheless, I think that they can provide a starting point for a more general discussion. Besides, the views they express have a good chance of entering into the sphere of mass-media-based common knowledge—"what everybody knows"—and of perpetuating existing views.

These journalists obviously expect me to be willing and able to confirm a set of basic opinions that would help them construct good headlines and nicely rounded articles. They are just as obviously disappointed when I fail to conform to their needs.

- They want me to say that background music is bad.[1]
- They want me to say that it is a way of manipulating people to act against their own interests.
- They want me to tell them that using adapted, "manipulated" classical music as background music in commercial environments is a way of depriving music of intrinsic value, a value that will make you into a better person if you could just learn to appreciate music in the right way, as performed in the "originally intended" fashion.
- They want me to say that it is a means of disregarding the composer's intentions and of falsifying what the composer/author wanted to "say" with his (or, on rare occasions, her) music, a sort of lie, and therefore something detestable on indisputable moral grounds. The truly old "classics" like Bach and Mozart seem most prone to elicit this kind of concern.
- They might even hope that I will say that this is a sure sign that Western civilization is going swiftly down the drain.

I do know that they want me to say these things as several of them have actually tried to put the very words in my mouth. Each of them seems to have read some report, or some article about some report, that provides scientific proof that listening to Mozart turns us into civilized and intelligent people (at least for a while), whereas listening to death metal turns us into destructive, suicidal brutes. They want me to comment on this, and preferably to confirm it beyond any reasonable doubt. Sometimes they apparently want my confirmation in order to expose conservative academia, against which they could contrast streetwise, commonsense attitudes. Journalists love simple, straightforward conflicts between two opposing camps, no matter what the subject. But just as often, they obviously want me to say these things because they themselves honestly believe them to be truths to live by and seek affirmation from a reliable authority. In either case, I let them down. Sometimes they write an article or make a radio program anyhow, but they do not come back. Other journalists, perhaps inspired by the first journalists' articles, take their place in the never-ending trickle of such callers.[2]

Let us confront the issue. I will start by discussing the manipulation of music and mentioning the composition of new music for different contexts. I will then make a short detour into the areas of music and moving images and music and narration, and touch very briefly on the problem of musical historiography. I will conclude with a short discussion of what really might be bothering this new generation of journalists, students, and others. This will be accomplished mainly by pointing (not pounding) at a number of already open doors. Please bear with me if I take some time to state what might be fairly obvious to most of you. I think my point lies in the combination of these obvious facts and in what ought to be done about it.

Manipulation of Music

Manipulation of music can be given a wide range of definitions. Its defining characteristics here is that it either changes the musical material in some more or less fundamental manner, or places the musical material in a context that makes it appear to be more or less fundamentally changed. Both cases involve the musical material's retention of some sort of basic identity or identifiability. Thus, the idea of manipulation presupposes some sort of "original" form and context that somebody other than the "original composer" might appropriate and alter. How, when, and where does the form and context of "classical" music appear? When is the music actually created? What constitutes the identity of a piece of music and why? Since these questions are obviously too large, too fundamental, and possibly too naive to tackle directly, this chapter will go at them from one angle and basically limit itself to one question: How is our conception of the existence of a musical work established?

In the late 1980s, I completed a rather large study on how Mozart's 40th symphony had been performed, disseminated, and received during the span of its (then) exactly 200 years of existence (Stockfelt, 1988). Some of that study's conclusions are relevant to the current discussion; others were not drawn in the context at the time but now appear significant in hindsight. One discussion that really ought to have been developed involves the problem of the actual identity of the work. There is no question of whether Mozart actually did write the symphony. He did, beyond any reasonable doubt. Twice, in fact, or at least in two different versions. During the two centuries that have passed since then, the symphony has appeared (in print, in performance, in recording) in an immense number of different versions and contexts. Easily demonstrated and quite obvious is the fact that, throughout its life span, the piece has never actually been performed for or been received by an audience in a way corresponding to the intentions and expectations Mozart could have had when he thought it out and wrote it down. The only possible exceptions were these: (1) the legendary concert of April 1791 in Vienna, when at least parts of the clarinet version may have been performed; and (2) one or two other performances that may or may not have taken place in the very last years of the eighteenth century. The music had to be radically changed, both in content and context, before it could become part of the "standard repertoire" of concert halls and be recognized as a piece of "classical music." In short, it had to be manipulated.

The size and composition of the orchestra were changed. The timbre and intonation of various instruments were changed. Tempi and dynamics were changed. Instrumental and orchestral articulation, i.e., the actual tones played by the musicians and the ways they were expected to execute those tones, changed radically. And the music's setting—the cultural context, the setting of performances, the listeners' interests, expectations and perspectives—was changed beyond reasonable comparison by, for example, the construction of a "standard repertoire" of "classical works" and of "box office" concert halls as we now know them. Once it landed on the list of canonized music works, the symphony continued to undergo further changes in order to stay there, clinging to its nominal position as the context underwent further radical changes. Such changes have, since then, been a constant feature of all performance and reception of "classical music," as the music has had to conform to: (1) the tendency toward standardization of formats, (2) the establishment of new formats, and (3) social and technical changes in society.

A few of these many changes might actually have been in harmony with Mozart's intentions and ideals. There are some aspects of how the symphony is written that perhaps indicate that he would in fact have preferred a more "modern" practice of, for example, intonation and orchestral coordination than could reasonably have been expected at the time and place of inception. Thus, in some cases and in some ways, later performances might have been *more* in accordance with the composer's intentions than Mozart could have expected from any ensemble or orchestra of his day. But these aspects are the interesting exceptions. For the most part, the changes over time dictated by different orchestral standards, performance practices, performance contexts, expectations of performers and audiences, and other transitory factors transformed the composition into something Mozart had no reasonable possibility of envisioning, much less intending. Possibly even more important is the fact that what was originally intended, performed, and received as a rather revolutionary, dramatic, inordinately big and complicated piece of avant-garde culture, directed toward a specific and small cultural elite, was transformed into a generally well-known and recognizable, classical, small, rather simple piece of stock repertoire for mass consumption. In sum, the work was transformed by historical context into a very different kind of commodity.

During the time it took to establish this music as a piece of the classical standard repertoire and make it fit into that (then) newly constructed slot, consideration of the actual composer's views and intentions was rare or nonexistent. He wasn't there; he was dead. The first recorded public suggestion of consideration for Mozart's possible intentions did not appear until June 1830, when the symphony was forty-two years old. The critic who first invoked Mozart's possible intentions, and even suggested that they might be considered, wrote:

> Wir leben freylich im Posaunenzeitalter. Aber, fragen muss man doch: kann denn gar kein Tonwerk mehr ohne Posaunen Wirkung machen?... Die G moll-Symphonie scheint mir ein solches Werk.

> We are after all living in the age of trombones. But you still have to ask: can't a work of music produce effects without trombones?... The G minor Symphony seems to me to be such a work. (Unsigned review in *Allgemeine Musikalische Zeitung* 22, Halle, June 1830)

The critic had never heard the piece without a prominent trombone ensemble, and he was curious to know how Mozart himself might have intended it to sound. This question remained open, but the subsequent decades witnessed the development of yet another kind of modern ideal performance practice, declared by academia to be the way the "classic composers" actually wanted their works to be performed. This new practice was possibly even further removed from any intentions Mozart himself might have harbored.[3] It also differed considerably from any of today's practices, although we might prefer to downplay the differences. So, in view of the music's constant, more or less radical changes from time to time and context to context, how do we know we are still talking about the same composition? Mozart wrote the score, but to what extent did he also construct the Symphony No. 40, K. 550 as we know it?

Identifying the Work of Music

One small but significant detail involves the way the identity of the work is manifested in its appearance *as* a work, illustrated by the very name of the piece of music: No. 40, K. 550. We all know that Mozart wrote forty-one symphonies, and that this is the next-to-last one, the big G minor, the centerpiece of the threefold fulfillment of his symphonic legacy. But Mozart didn't know that (and neither did the critic quoted above). Not only was it not Mozart who numbered the symphony in that fashion, but the very label "symphony" did not have the same meaning during his lifetime as it would acquire during the century following his death. The very process of numbering music meant something quite different as well. The present way of identifying this music is a rather recent invention that took an impressive amount of time and work to establish.

During most of the nineteenth century, this particular piece of music was mainly known as symphony No. 2. That is the number you find—when you find any number at all—on most of the arrangements, of varying complexity and content, that appeared in large numbers from 1810 onwards, for piano (for two, four or even eight hands) and for different ensembles (including some very surprising combinations). It also has a number of other designations and numbers. In Luigi Della Croce's study of Mozart's symphonies, it is given the number 64 (Della Croce, 1977). According to this study, only one of the eleven pieces of symphonic music written by Mozart after the "No. 40" (or "64") was to get into the history books and stock repertoire as a symphony (namely, No. 41, the *Jupiter*, K. 551), with all the word's present-day connotations, cultural prestige, and market value. Thus, No. 40 is the "next-to-last" symphony. The handle "No. 40" has become well-established, and we all seem to know which music we are talking about when we name it. You just have to look at any history book or record catalog to find out that Mozart wrote forty-one symphonies. Questioning such a basic fact would only elicit laughter or contempt. The fact that Mozart himself might have had a different opinion on the matter does not bear any weight at all. Thus, of the thirty-four Mozart symphonies that Della Croce analyzed in his study, only those that have already appeared as symphonies on the CD shelves in the shops will ever have a chance of being seen as such. The first Haffner serenade from 1776 never did make it as an officially numbered symphony, although it sometimes was presented and performed as such during the nineteenth century. It was probably considered too unruly, with its seven or eight different movements, of which the trios and the Adagio (I suspect) did not fit the cataloguers' conception of how a symphony should be constructed. The second Haffner serenade from 1782 did fit the format, however (not quite, but well enough), and got symphony status as "No. 35."

The academic and commercial canons are far too well established to allow any significant changes, such as renumbering of the records on the shelves or radical rewriting of the dictionary entries. Some pieces of music are supposed to be regarded, used, and listened to as symphonies while others are not. These criteria have little to do with the intentions of the composers of these works, who could not possibly have suspected or predicted future developments. But they have much to do with the principles used when the works of the masters were repackaged, catalogued, and sold during the following century.

Creating Works of Music

The rather recent needs for works of music to be catalogued and packaged in an unambiguous manner presupposes a need to keep music in stock and under control, for one purpose or another, over an extended period of time. Of the many demand-oriented perspectives from which the concept of music has had to be reconsidered, I want to focus on three that were firmly established during the course of the nineteenth century. Although one can find earlier examples of each of them, they could not really be combined to constitute an unquestionable normative force until that time.

Creation by the Market

The first reconceptualization of music involves the demands of the market. When pieces of music became salable commodities, distributors needed to be able to identify, brand, catalog, and control their goods, as well as to defend their sole rights to possession. This, of course, limited the acceptability of uncontrolled reuse by others. The mass production of printed scores—especially those of piano arrangements for different social settings—made the copyright problem obvious. The mass production of physical recordings a century later made it crucial (as does mass accessibility of music in virtual formats today). In any case, the market had a perfectly legitimate need to create commodities out of music, and thus to create and stabilize the forms of the music's public appearance as singular, identifiable, and controllable entities. This constituted one form of interest to which the concept of the musical work had to be adapted.

Creation by Listeners

The second conceptual evolution involved the needs of musicologists and of bourgeois public discourse on art. For convenience, the two are united in the current context although they might elsewhere be dealt with separately. The different discourses existing and being developed during the nineteenth century for the production and narration of the history, analysis, and value judgments of music demanded, among other things, definitions of creators and creations, doers and deeds, composers and works. One can follow the development of this discourse by reading through, for example, the fifty years of *Allgemeine Musikalische Zeitung* (1798–1848), or the works of Fetis, A. B. Marx, Hanslick, Wagner, or Riemann. Such studies reveal how a new and very different category of composer was being established (and given retroactive validity), with a few undisputed geniuses serving as exemplars and an ever larger number of masterpieces being recognized, catalogued, and "exegeted" by the knowledgeable. Disputes over how a piece of music was to be understood, as well as instructions for the right way to understand music in order to behave as a cultured member of society, created normative criteria for the production and consumption of music. This led to the fixation of "correct" editions of masterpieces and ideal ways of performing and appreciating them. In this way, new music, both in performance and perception, was in fact created in the guise of old works, using the scores as a kind of blueprint—a form of "inverted plagiarism"—which definitely complicates any discussion of moral and economic rights.

In the nineteenth-century atmosphere of rapidly developing information technology, cultured citizen-consumers developed legitimate claims within both the commercial and academic spheres of music cataloguing and reification in order to protect the value of their cultural investments. The masterpiece one bought as a concert-goer, piano player, record owner or certified knowledge possessor should retain the lasting value it was given by the authorized "dealer." Truths and eternal values should not be temporary, nor should the benefits garnered by possessing them. When music became something to be not only enjoyed but studied, recognized, and talked about in order to enhance and manifest one's cultural capital, an unambiguous tag was needed to connect the knowledge gained from this new genre of expert writing on music with the actual music one listened to and was expected to express opinions about. And when music could become a collector's item, gaps had to be discussed and filled in order to make a collection complete. These different interests constituted a new, perfectly legitimate set of needs for music's public appearance as singular, identifiable, and collectable entities, as a different type of commodity requiring new perspectives on the concept of the work of music.

Creation by Composers

The third perspective under discussion here involves the needs of the actual composers. When music was conceived of as a salable commodity, it could, as a consequence, be stolen. Pragmatically speaking, a creation must be protected from thieves, and, if subjected to theft, must be identifiable and recoverable. Preferring not to starve (at least not to death), composers had an urgent need to support the new definition of their compositions as fixed works, and of themselves as free-market composers. To defend their property and livelihood, to strengthen their positions in negotiations, and to influence legislation, they had to unionize. This did not encourage a humble attitude toward the collective creation of recognized and valuable pieces of music. Rather, it demanded a view of the work of music as the original and singular brain-child of a sole individual.

The scope of this chapter does not permit further exploration of composers' initiatives, although several more categories could be added. It is, on the other hand, necessary to address the question of the distinction between economic rights and moral rights.

Economic Rights and Moral Rights

Music could of course be "stolen" long before the emergence of a free market for music as a commodity. A musical invention such as a theme or a tune could be used in various situations by somebody pretending to have invented it. For this reason, moral rights are distinct from economic rights. The introduction of the market economy and the artists' needs for daily sustenance led directly to the whole process of unionization and the creation of legislation for the defense of composers' economic rights. However, these economic rights also were (and are) often motivated by an unquestionable moral imperative. Moral rights fit in neatly with the modern idealized view of the artistic creator, which focuses on the artist as a person of original and enlightened thought, rather than as a person working hard and needing to eat. Thus, confusion over the boundary between these two fundamentally different types of rights is based on a historical need (on the role of discourse for any music, see Volgsten, this volume; on moral versus economical rights and the issue of theft, see Volgsten and Åkerberg, this volume).

Creating Consensus

The point is that, for a variety of reasons, a variety of needs seemed to converge in what appeared to be the same direction: a new definition of the identity of a work of music as a singular, unambiguous piece of original production by a composer. Music, furthermore, was to be viewed as an autonomous art created by a number of single individuals and consisting of reified works of lasting identity and value, dependent on the existence of masters and masterpieces. Each discrete concept in this network of concepts had to be redefined and accommodated to changing market conditions. Since the very concept of eternal, unchanging values was central to the network as a whole, the changes themselves became, almost by definition, impossible to fully acknowledge (see Stockfelt and van der Lee, 1998).

Perhaps the music business was helping the field of musicology by distributing the results of musicological research and increasing the general accessibility of music. Perhaps musicologists and music historians were providing salable legitimization for the music business and increasing the exchange value of its products by creating a noncommercial discourse, cataloguing the goods and digging out new salable jewels from the historic archives they created and explored. On the other hand, the academic and commercial segments of musical life were perhaps engaged in a head-on struggle between "real" cultural music appreciation and commercial, manipulative "debasement." This marriage versus confrontation of interests has since been a matter of much discussion. It is obvious that genuine and assumed conflicts were abundant; indeed, they remain so. Academic musicologists have often denounced commercial musical life and denied playing any part in it. Composers and the representatives of the commercial market traditionally differ over such issues as reasonable prices for music products and methods of product control.

It is also obvious that parallel activity took place on both sides in defining the very field of conflict, the categories involved. In the process of reifying the work of music, both as a piece in the historically canonized repertoire and as a basic unit in contemporary musical life, these two camps contributed to the same general discourse. Their conflicts helped to reify the battleground's characteristics as perceived by the combatants. And together they helped create the conception of these new categories as precisely "eternal," not new—and as adequate for all real music. Music that did not conform to these ideals was not seen as threatening to the relevance of these ideals but as somewhat less "music" than the music that did conform. The conception became a qualitative, not a chronological or sociological, category.

Thus, much of the traditional praxis of music making—rearranging, piecing together different parts of music for the conditions of a specific setting or context, using the most appropriate music available and remaking it to fit, composing new parts where necessary—was reduced under these conditions of discourse, not only to a qualitatively lower form of music making than "true" composing, but to a parasitic form of music life, stealing the brain-children of great men and manipulating them to fit profane purposes. The competence to perform within the traditional praxis described above came to be seen as less valuable, and sometimes even suspect, compared to the competence to live up to the new expectations of individual composition. This became the case not only in theory and in the consensus of explicit discourse but also within musicology, as well as those segments of the music market that thrived off sales of "original" music commodities.

Mixing and Remixing

The practice of mixing criteria from different and partly conflicting interests that appear to move in tandem must not be taken to mean that these criteria are identical or even mutually supportive under all conditions. In fact, it appears that any conditions of mutual support are long gone today. The many questions we face concerning the identity of a work and the moral and economic rights to a work (including the demands of the questing journalists I mentioned earlier) cannot hope to be resolved if we do not review and recognize these conflicts and "unholy" alliances so as to analyze them from the perspectives of differing interests and criteria.

It is an interesting complexity and an illustration of the multidimensionality of cultural life that the very idea of eternal artistic value in music commodities itself quickly became not only a social and commercial tool but also a tool of artistic expression, and as such a form of commodity in its own right. What might have started out as a myth, serving a multitude of converging and diverging purposes, became a very tangible, verifiable fact as it was worked into the fabric of social discourse and institutionalization. Thus, the task is not just to expose the myth as a myth but also to deal with it as a concrete historical and social fact. Caryl Flinn's excellent study on the way that music's "utopian" character was used as a means of expression in the formation of the Hollywood film-music format is a very useful illustration (Flinn, 1992).[4]

Music in film can never really be autonomous, except when, in the film narrative, it is nonautonomously representing autonomous values. But to say that music is nonautonomous does not necessarily mean that it is subordinate to any other form of expression. Music in film is subordinate to the purpose of the film, usually the narrative. (Films usually have multiple purposes. The rather common purpose of selling well and creating a handy profit might require a hit song or a tune, which allows the use of the name of an already famous and successful artist rather than music instrumental in the straight intrinsic narrative. But that is perhaps a different discussion.) When that narrative is mainly carried by visuals and/or dialogue, music becomes supportive of them. Sometimes music is the main carrier of the narrative, or even the only carrier, for a shorter or longer period of time (see Stockfelt, 1998). Sometimes it is obvious when music should be seen as "just supportive," whereas at other times it is entirely up to the viewer/listener to decide.

But when subordinating music to the purpose of a film that is meant to be seen and heard by a wide audience, it is often practical to do what composers and musicians have done in similar circumstances since time immemorial: use music with a reasonable chance of contributing in a predictable manner to the experiences of the audience. This involves using the available music that best fits the purpose by adapting it to the situation, or creating what is not available or cannot be found in order to fulfill the music's intended functions in that context. This is rational, professional behavior if your main interest is to deliver the intended results, especially if you are pressed for time.

> Mountain peaks invariably invoke string tremolos punctuated by signal-like horn motifs. The ranch to which the virile hero has eloped with the sophisticated heroine is accompanied by forest murmurs and a flute melody. A slow waltz goes along with a moonlit scene in which a boat drifts down a river lined with weeping willows. (Adorno and Eisler, 1947/1994: 13)

> We murdered the works of Beethoven, Mozart, Grieg, J. S. Bach, Verdi, Bizet, Tchaikovsky and Wagner—everything that wasn't protected by copyright from our pilfering. (Winkler, 1951)

The "autonomy" of art music, and the utopias it paradoxically refers to, provide just one of several means of music-cinematic expression. This of course makes film music doubly damnable—not only do its composers refuse to live up to the rules of "autonomous" music, but they sometimes publicly flout the rules in several ways simultaneously for their own purposes.

This behavior of film music composers (and theater music composers, and composers of different kinds of "popular" music—and if you want to point out that any number of baroque, classical, and romantic composers actually did the very same thing, you do it at your own risk) clashed rather violently with the process of reification of autonomous music. Thus, music for films, not surprisingly, was seen as a qualitatively less valuable kind of music than music for the concert hall (and the phonogram). When this music was on occasion manipulated to fit the autonomous concert format—by being rearranged as orchestral pieces—it was judged as being more valuable. Conversely, when music with reified autonomous value within the refuge of the concert scene was manipulated in order to fit the film format, it was seen as less valuable, and was often judged as debasement, manipulation, and theft.

Using and Hiding Blueprints

This difference between lowly esteemed film music and highly regarded concert music has nothing whatsoever to do with the actual original creative deeds of composers within these different "genres." It is perfectly possible to argue that, during the twentieth century and beyond, film music has been far more influential in the artistic development of autonomous music formats than vice versa. The various attitudes toward adaptations in the two directions have little or no foundation in differences in the actual processes of composition. Rather, they are closely related to the reification of value-norms discussed above. And like the utopian immortality of music, this myth in praxis has become a concrete and verifiable fact.

In the present context, then, when film music is sold in huge quantities on CD, composers who wish to wind up on top rather than in court face an expanded list of problems to be solved during the process of composition. They must now consider how to live up to the idea—held by the market, by legislation, critics, colleagues and by themselves—of what aspects of a work, in which contexts, make it constitute a piece of original composition. Furthermore, they must avoid "simple plagiarism"—manipulation and theft—while still managing to address the problems the music is intended to resolve in the construction of the film. This is often no simple deed. Interviews with prominent film composers show how close to the edge they have to, or choose to, walk; reviews (and lawsuits) show how far they might fall. In an interview about composing music for the film *The Beast* (see Carlsson, 1999), the film composer Don Davies said:

> There are techniques that are effective when illustrating drama which involves brutal, unrelenting action.... Those techniques include pounding rhythmic figures in the percussion and low brass, lots of forceful French horn lines, and high ostinato figures in the violins and trumpets—in other words, featuring each instrument in its most advantageous region—all the while outlining a tonality based on a symmetrical scale of alternating half-steps and whole-steps. The blueprint for this kind of writing is Stravinsky's "Rite of Spring." ... The JAWS approach was discussed a great deal during the production, but the obvious connection to the JAWS story (both films were adaptations from novels by Peter Benchley, and involved similar plot lines and scenarios) was cause for concern. The actual shark motif from JAWS is so simple (it's essentially two alternating notes a half-step apart) that any musical reference to it amounts to plagiarism. So I came up with a squid motif that was an upward-moving French horn figure, which is actually more along the lines of a Jerry Goldsmith approach (via the "Rite of Spring" blueprint), so the score evolved in that manner.

The *Rite of Spring* is "the blueprint," and is frequently used as such by Goldsmith, Davies, and many others. The Williams *Shark* motif is so simple that virtually any use of it renders a composer a plagiarist. (Even if "plagiarism" were allowed culturally and legally, the reuse of the simple *Shark* motif would be impractical except as irony or comedy, in that it would require heavy disguising in order to be effective as a dramatic component, except possibly in cartoons for small children.) Using such "blueprints" and "manuals"[5] to create music is considered cheating, unless you do it with great and explicit reflection.

A Case of Creation and Reuse

When Waldo de los Rios arranged a sort of *Readers' Digest* version of some "classical masterpieces" for modern entertainment orchestra and in 1971 recorded it as *Symphonies for the Seventies* (looking forward), he actually did something rather new that inspired a large number of followers. Of course, the project was deemed a severe debasement of the music and of the original composers' intentions, with the *Readers' Digest* aspect of it regarded as an especially demeaning manipulation (by myself at the time as well as by the majority of other self-appointed defenders of traditional values).

The same year, Louis Andriessen made a tape composition by cutting the beginning of the first part of Mozart's big G minor symphony to pieces and patching it together again with spots of silence that gave the resulting composite the same rhythmic structure as Stravinsky's *Rite of Spring*. He published the recording as *Im memoriam* (looking backwards), thus celebrating the memories of Mozart and the recently deceased Stravinsky. Andriessen's piece was deemed an original composition of high standing (I felt that way at the time and still do), in spite of the fact that it was actually de los Rios's version that had been cut to pieces and patched together according to the *Rite of Spring* blueprint. Perhaps the acceptance of the piece was due to Andriessen's success in bringing the symphony back to the virtual concert situation of a serious recording.

What Andriessen could do in 1971, working in an exclusive studio, copying music and rhythmical parameters from two different works of music in order to combine them into a third, which was then hailed as an original composition, anybody can do today owing to the development of technology and the resultant general accessibility of musical material for use in such processes. Such a process thus is no longer deemed an art but a lowly form of manipulation. Anybody can do it. It does not require a certified artist. All it takes is a versatile computer program and a download or two of music, the will to do it, and an appropriate channel to disseminate the result. This illustrates some fundamental changes in how music has been created since the advent of the phonogram, when recordings became music's prime form of identity fixation and distribution.

Another Case of Creation and Reuse

In my hometown of Gothenburg (Sweden), there is a depressed, angry, and rather poor composer of rock songs who claims to have written one of the 1990s' major Swedish international hits. I present this case as a concrete example of a situation that is far from unique. In short, he recorded some songs he had written on a cassette and sent it off to a major record company. The tape remained there, apparently unused, for a rather long period of time. It took repeated contacts with the company to finally get the tape back, whereupon they informed him that they were not at all interested in recording his songs. A short time after that, a famous Swedish artist connected to that record company had a huge hit with a song that was in some ways quite similar to one of the songs on the composer's tape.

Everyone has heard this story before, or at least one very much like it. Somebody has a hit; somebody else claims that the tune was stolen from him or her and that he or she should have a due share of the credit and the money. Whether this particular song was actually stolen is moot. I couldn't say. The two songs are in some ways very similar, but so are lots of songs. The tape was available at the record company, but there is no proof that the recording artist in question ever heard it, although he might have, since he did spend quite a lot of time listening to music in the place where the tape was stored. If he did happen to hear it, we do not know if he was inspired or influenced by it when he made his hit. If he was in fact influenced by it, we do not know if it was a case of intentional plagiarism or one of unavoidable subconscious inspiration. There is no way of determining whether or not this was a case of theft—unless, of course, the recording artist admitted to it. The interesting point has to do with the criteria used for establishing the identity of a piece of music in such a situation. What was the basis for our poor composer's claim that his song was stolen, and what was the basis for the rejection of his claim by the composers' union, the legislative system, and other bodies who heard him (he did try to take the case all the way to the top)?

Some differences between the songs in question are obvious. The text differs. Every aspect of the verbal content, including the names of the songs, is different, except for a certain similarity in the way the lyrics change back and forth between different voices in the refrain. The melodies differ as well, not in their general outlines but in actual notes. Yet, the number of phrases is virtually identical, as are the relationships between the phrases and the contours of the individual phrases. While many of the actual notes unequivocally differ, if you play them together (which I have done), it almost appears as if the hit song more often than not is a second singer on top of the non-hit song, mostly a interval of a third apart. Or the other way around, if you prefer. The harmonies are almost identical, though not quite. The key differs, of course, unless you pitch it, but that is easy to do and of lesser importance.

The two songs have all these similarities in common with a lot of other songs. Both rely heavily on the reuse of traditional turns and phrases. All these phrases, including most of the verbal phrases, can be easily found in earlier instances of popular music. Each of the two songs is thus a collection of earlier, functional material, combined to make a new whole. The two new entities are done in quite similar fashion, with almost identical results. There is basically only one thing that makes these two songs stand out from earlier mainstream songs—one rather original turn in the combination of chord-shifting and phrasing in the refrain, linking a couple of easily recognized clichés together in a new and quite original fashion. It sounds natural and not particularly remarkable when you hear it, but it stays in the mind. No matter how I have tried to find an earlier song with the same turn, I have not been able to come up with a single example. This was the very heart of the composition. The poor composer had worked quite a bit at figuring out this thing through a long process of trial and error. When he finally found it, he was extremely pleased with the result and with himself, sensing that this, at last, had the makings of a real hit. He was right. A hit it was, but not his. That is why he is so angry and depressed today, and why he will not renounce his claim.

Musicological expertise was called for, and the musicologists involved gave their judgments. The clichés in both songs were so very obvious that it was deemed impossible to say that the one was a copy of the other. This conclusion was both reasonable and completely unreasonable. The significant work of the composer consisted not in the reuse but in the original use of clichés, the invention being the way they were combinated and linked. As in Andriessen's work, a new composition had been created by cutting and joining of old ones in an unforeseeably novel manner.

An added complication is that the second version became a hit (and got recorded in the first place) only partly because of the actual invention within the song. Probably at least as important were the name and reputation of the (alleged?) composer, his channels for marketing, and the identity of the singer. These are elements that, especially since phonograms became an important channel for music about a century ago, have long been self-evident parts of the music; yet they still are seldom if ever counted as integral parts of the actual composition. In all probability the song would never have become a hit if it had not appeared in the second version, by the established artist. Still, it is easy to see why the composer in Gothenburg got depressed, hearing his own hard-won musical solution being played on the radio and MTV and knowing that an already rich and famous artist got all the credit and all the money for it.

Musicologists still lack the basic, relevant tools for extracting and describing the actual content of original creative compositional work in such a situation—although we are working on it. Our traditional tools are perfectly suited for describing and analyzing music and significant aspects of the process of composition of music that conform, in form and use, with the traditional myths of the individual composer creating autonomous pieces of original works of music with unambiguous identities. They are, however, less than adequate to describe and appreciate the original qualities manifested in the reuse of old music in new contexts or in the creation of new connections and meanings between and in already well-known phrases and turns. Our tools are inadequate for isolating the small, possibly unnoticed but significant details that make old music function anew in a different situation—such as its adaptation to specific popular artists and marketing situations. Still, the belief in the possibility to establish the unique identity any work of music lives on, while the creative activities of resetting, rearranging, and reuse are downplayed.

In the end, musicological expertise was unable to produce an effective "ruling" on the similarities between the two pieces of music; thus, the matter of possible theft was dropped. The task was rendered too complex by at least two obstacles, both of which were inordinately challenging. It would have required a public invalidation of the relevance of available tools and parameters (including a loss of prestige for the discipline of musicology) and an ad hoc development of new, relevant tools and parameters. In addition, such a ruling probably would have led to strife within the discipline over the adequacy of these new tools and parameters. In any case, the process of establishing what was what, and what made the hit version a hit, fell mainly outside the reaches of traditional musicology.

The Role of Musicology

We musicologists all acknowledge our limitations with a reasonably reflective perspective on the current capacities of our discipline. We know that the changes in musical life have dramatically outpaced the development of theoretical understanding. And we know that many of the elements that determine the experienced qualities of a piece of music—any piece of music—lie in the interrelation with contexts that do not quite fall within the traditional reaches of our field. Awareness of these limits tends to be tacitly guarded as expert knowledge within the academic sphere. Or rather, the propagators of the "traditional" view are louder and manage to get more air time.

Certainly, the questing journalists seem not to know it. They want to have traditional values confirmed, perhaps slightly adapted to fit new genres, and are disappointed with us when we do not conform to their expectations. The "musicological" tradition—fostered not by musicologists but by the commercial market—exercises a tremendous pedagogical force in conserving the aspects of musicological discourse that function as legitimization of past and present profitable myths. This, I think, is a real case of unambiguous manipulation of music, and thus by music. It needs to be addressed forcefully, not just by musicologists who work with popular music, youth culture, music sociology, or any other "niche" branches, but also by musicology experts firmly and manifestly embedded in the "traditional tradition" of musicology.

We can be quite certain that Bach never intended his music to sell cat food (although some of his music quite possibly did sell some coffee in his day). But he did not intend it to sell records either. What is the straight answer: Why is one market considered a worse commercial debasement and manipulation than the other? In neither case is the music performed in a manner conforming to what the composer might possibly have envisioned in either content or context. What is happening when we hear pieces of highlights from the first part of Mozart's 40th symphony, in an arrangement for circus orchestra accompanying and encouraging the performance of a group of trampoline artists, quickly flashing by in a trailer for a French television program to be shown a week later as a part of public service television's Christmas programming in Sweden? Is this better or worse than hearing the symphony's main theme in a tram or as a ringer on a cellular telephone? Or looped as part of the background track of a rap artist? Some sorts of rights are obviously being violated. But whose rights? And what rights? Whose intentions are being disregarded? How can we define those intentions? And should we care? In what ways do performances of those kinds differ, as violations of the composer's intentions, from the selling of a recording of the same symphony played in a concert hall by a modern, large, standardized symphony orchestra, an interpreting conductor, and a silent or nonexistent audience?

In what respects are economic and moral rights involved? When it comes to protecting present-day composers' moral rights, or even some late nineteenth-century composers' intentions, there might be an obvious point in the type of reactions elicited by the cat food commercials. However, the same negative, strident judgment is made indiscriminately of all uses of "classical music," as defined not by musicological criteria but by the commercial market for non-experts. This includes, more or less, all music that is not seen as "popular," "folk," or "world" music, from Vivaldi through Beethoven and Brahms up to a number of present-day prestigious composers and hailed soloists.

What's Bothering Those Journalists?

It is definitely not the disregard for the actual composers' intentions that bothers the questing journalists, although the problem is likely to be presented as such. Rather, it is the rupture between their own unquestioned, idealized view of the composers' intentions and their own attitudes toward commercials. Basically, they do not enjoy having their clean utopia sullied by mashed meat for cats. This attitude does not actually mirror concern for any ideal property rights that composers might choose to exercise. In fact, it is the opposite, namely, a demand that composers form their public images in accordance with the dictates of the market. Thus, composers are expected to create music with intentions that can be used to uphold the idealized views held of them, as well as the commodifiable nature of their pieces of work. This attitude does not reflect a genuine concern for the composers' economic rights, since the "right" to exercise such rights presupposes conformity to an idealized mode of production. The commodified "utopianism" Caryl Flinn analyzes in Hollywood film music is just as present on the record shelves of music shops. And in the same doubly concealed manner, it succeeds in preventing constructive discussion about the manipulation of music.

Of course, the composer (and the artist, author, etc.) should earn a fair return on his or her labor. Legislation of some kind is needed to ensure that this occurs, especially with regard to the rights of the less established composers and artists who are most easily exploited by strong commercial actors. But *whose* rights are we ready to respect if we continue to disregard the actual composer? How do we determine the actual composer? Is the category of moral right even theoretically possible, and important, to uphold? The mythscape (Stockfelt and Björnberg, 1996) within which the different kinds of property rights can be seen as fully coinciding has disappeared, except possibly in the myth of utopian discourse.

Classical music is used in television commercials. Whereas this was obviously not the intention of the composers of the music, it is completely in accordance with the tradition that made the music "classical" in the modern sense of the word. If we want to prohibit the illicit or morally offensive use of music, the "composers' intentions" argument will not suffice. If we want to defend the composers' rights to credit and having some measure of control over the music, then we must fundamentally question the system that primarily makes music into a fixed commodity among other commodities. *This can hardly be accomplished by defending the legal and intellectual system that provides the very categories that uphold music's status as such a commodity.* Musicology helps provide and spread the criteria essential to keep alive the myth of music as commodity. The field has not helped to form necessary criteria for creating adequate legislation. The present legislative structure claims to protect something that no longer exists—if it ever did—while in fact it upholds the very forces it should protect against. The expanding possibilities of computer technology foretoken the imminent breakdown of the present system. This need not be a problem for the creative artists themselves: however, it is a problem of great magnitude for the record companies and the owners of commercial rights (see the chapters by Wallis and by Volgsten and Åkerberg, this volume). The situation may even lead to some sort of a constructive breakthrough.

The current general opinion about how and where a piece of "classical" music, such as a symphony by Mozart, could and should be played is the result of a multifaceted struggle two centuries long. Among the factors in play are: orchestras' needs to present themselves and to acquire music to play, the fact that musical scores allow and disallow different treatment in different contexts, the huge body of writings on what constitutes good music and how it should be appreciated, and the commercial needs of printers, arrangers, producers, distributors, and others, as well as radio and TV companies' attempts to entertain and educate. We seem to perceive it as offensive when the music:

1. is used as a commercial means for something that does not, within this complex tradition, appear to have anything to do with the music as such (e.g., not being publicity for Mozart, an orchestra, a conductor, an edition, the cities of Salzburg and Vienna, etc., but rather for things like cat food, ice hockey, James Bond, or circus acrobats, just to name a few current examples);

2. is presented in a format where it is cut and/or rearranged to fulfill this purpose, in a way that is radically different from the practice of performance that has been established in concert halls and "classical" recordings; and

3. appears in contexts that are radically different from those that function as manifestations of the spheres of society that claim prime possession of the music (such as when it appears in circuses, sports arenas, action movies, or food stores).

But otherwise, we seem to believe it is quite all right.

Thus, the question "Is it morally right to allow artistically intended music to become a symbol for commercial products?" itself conceals a moral question. Only rarely does its asking have anything at all to do with fidelity to the actual composer; instead, it concerns the manifestation and defense of social norms and myths. It is a question of whose social rules should be allowed to dominate, whose myths should be taken as reality. The questing journalists want to keep their own mythscape of utopian views of the accessibility of inherent qualities of great art untainted. They really do fear that civilization as they know it is going down the drain. They might even be right, although in a rather roundabout way. They definitely should be taken seriously—and addressed.

Notes

1. I will not comment further on the uses of background music in this context. See Stockfelt, 1985, 1986, 1987, 1988, 1994, 1997.

2. Please note that this is intended *neither* as an attack on journalism (which I might provide in another context) *nor* one on journalists, who are usually very *decent* people. And some journalists do have more reasonable quests, and often actually do come back for more.

3. While this new "academic" tradition of redefining the piece took place, the actual music continued to provide material for a variety of musical and social settings.

4. My own rather extensive writing as a symphonic music critic might be viewed as another example of the same type of myth becoming and being presented as real and tangible experience.

5. See also Lord Rock and Time Boy (1988). Although it would lead too far astray, it might be very interesting to discuss the KLF manual in this context. In "the manual," the authors promise that if you just follow their Golden Rules—reusing slightly older music in line with their explicit matrix, and relying heavily on the creative competence of studio personnel and their handling of marketing forces—you will have one huge hit. Being part of the larger KLF project, this manual functions as a sort of reflective artistic legitimization of their own

hits (in line with, for example, their infamous public burning of money). Several of the artists who have claimed to follow the manual have actually gotten hits and have thus gained some fame and money—although very little "cultural capital"—in the process. The activity KLF promotes in this manual is in many ways more similar to the activity of the parties that defined ideal performance practices of the classical canon than to the actual or idealized activities of the "actual" composers of the works of this canon.

References

Adorno, T. W. and Eisler, H. (1947/1994). *Composing for the Films*. London: Athlone Press.

Carlsson, M. (1999). "Anything is possible. Don Davis talks to Mikael Carlsson." *Music from the Movies* Web site. http://www.musicfromthemovies.com/pages/davis_don_interview.html.

Della Croce, L. (1977). *Le 75 Sinfonie di Mozart: Guida e analisi critica*. Torino: Edizioni Eda.

Flinn, C. (1992). *Strains of Utopia: Gender, Nostalgia, and Hollywood Film Music*. Princeton: Princeton University Press.

Lord Rock and Time Boy (1988). *The Manual (How to Have a Number One the Easy Way)*. KLF Publications. http://klf.life.eu.org/Misc/the-manual.txt.

Stockfelt, O. (1985). "The listener's 'view' on background music in a Swedish factory." Paper presented at the conference of the International Association for the Study of Popular Music, Montreal, Canada.

_____ (1986). "Samtal med mannen bakom bakgrundsmusiken; Arbetsmaterial [Talks with the man behind the background music]." Working paper of the Department of Musicology, Gothenburg University.

_____ (1987). "Varför finns det bakgrundsmusik i varuhus? [Why is there background music in department stores?]." Working paper of the Department of Musicology, Gothenburg University.

_____ (1988). *Musik som lyssnandets konst. En analys av W. A. Mozarts symfoni No. 40, g moll K. 550*. [Music as the Art of Listening: An Analysis of Mozart's Symphony No. 40, g minor K. 550]. Ph.D. diss., Department of Musicology, Gothenburg University.

_____ (1994). "Cars, buildings, soundscapes." In H. Järviluoma (ed.) *Soundscapes: Essays on Vroom and Moo* (pp. 19–38). Tampere, Finland: Tampere University Printing Service.

_____ (1997). "Adequate modes of listening." In D. Schwartz, A. Kassabian, and L. Siegler (eds.) *Keeping Score: Music, Disciplinarity, Culture* (pp. 129–136). Charlottesville: University Press of Virginia.

_____ (1998). "Intermezzo: ett musikaliskt narrativ i svensk 30-talsfilm. [Intermezzo: A musical narrative in Swedish film of the 30s]." In E. Hedling (ed.) *Blågult Flimmer: Svenska Filmanalyser* (pp. 69–92). Lund: Utbildningshuset Studentlitteratur.

Stockfelt, O. and Björnberg, A. (1996). "Kristen Klatvask fra Vejle: On Danish dance and 'local camp.'" *Popular Music* 15: 131–147.

Stockfelt, O. and van der Lee, P. (1998). "The beginning and the end of the eternal values of music." *Svensk Tidskrift för Musikforskning* [Swedish Journal of Musicology] 80: 53–83.

Winkler, M. (1951). *A Penny from Heaven*. New York: Appelton-Century-Crofts.

Chapter 13

Copyright, Music, and Morals

Artistic Expression and the Public Sphere

Ulrik Volgsten and Yngve Åkerberg

The rights to you are sold.

Frank Zappa, "I'm the Slime from Your Video" (1973)

Introduction

We begin this chapter with a few examples highlighting how moral intuitions are frequently violated in the production and consumption of music. To prevent such infringements, laws exist that specify the rights and obligations of musical senders and receivers. These include intellectual property rights, which consist of economic rights (or copyrights) and moral rights. The basic question we ask is: What can these rights do to prevent the violation of moral intuitions? We then briefly trace the notion of intellectual property throughout history, discuss its relations to other kinds of rights, and then analyze arguments for and against musical copyright, including arguments for the revision of today's copyright laws. Rather than moral intuitions, it turns out that the strongest incitement for copyright legislation has been the commercial potential of mass mediation. Finally, we discuss whether the notion of rights is a fruitful one and the only possible point of departure for coming to terms with the ethical problems faced by musicians, listeners, and producers of music in a twenty-first-century public sphere. Put differently, are rights right?

* * *

When the management of CNN Partner Hotels commissioned background music for one of its international TV commercials, its choice of a melody

---

Notes for this chapter are located on page 361.

and sonority similar to that of Mascagni's *Cavalleria Rusticana* was hardly a coincidence. The producer of the music knew quite well that such a melody would convey an impression of high culture and a romantic ambience. With a decisive melodic line and similar harmonies, the effect sought was one of culture and class.

But Mascagni certainly never expected his music to be used for marketing commercial hotels, neither in its original form nor in a modified version. One effect of the ad that the CNN Partner Hotels probably did not foresee—however marginal it may have been from an economic standpoint—was the negative response the many opera lovers of the world might experience on hearing a familiar work of music used in such a way. Or perhaps they did consider such a negative effect but simply judged it to be of little serious economic consequence (for similar examples, see Edström, 1998).

In contrast to this distressing situation, and to the delight of countless fans of classical music, the end of the millennium witnessed the completion and world première performance of Edward Elgar's Third Symphony as well as the rediscovery and performance of Grieg's C minor symphony of 1863. Although both of these works received critical and popular acclaim, the performance of the music in both instances went against the expressed wishes of their composers. With regard to the Third Symphony, Elgar requested, in a well-known letter to a friend, not to "let anyone tinker with it" (quoted in Kent, 1982). Likewise, Grieg wrote on the title page of his score that the symphony must never be performed ("må aldrig opføres"). However, these clearly expressed wishes do not seem to have bothered the musicologists responsible for the completion of the two works.

A musical scholar of a different genre, Alan Lomax, was responsible for a somewhat different treatment of his sources. Lomax edited and added new material to traditional folk songs, as performed by the famous musician Leadbelly, for the sake of compiling a song book. By adding a few words here and a chord there, Lomax was able to copyright Leadbelly's entire repertoire. Leadbelly received ten dollars for a contract that gave him "the right to 'sing any of the songs,'" while at the same time depriving him of "any self-respect as well as any rights to possible future Royalties" (Young, 1997; see Feld [1994] on Paul Simon's copyrighting of traditional musicians' performances).

What we see from the above examples is, first, how an important artistic symbol of one culture can be exploited without any respect for the possible meanings and values assigned to the musical symbol in question—in this case Mascagni's opera—and the potential offense it might cause to the members of that culture. This is a major moral issue since musical reuse exists on a rampant scale and since well-known music occupies an important place in any society's cultural heritage. As noted by the editors of this volume, "In the same way that people don't want their Bibles used as paperweights they don't want their most beloved pieces of music used as associative symbols for commodities to which they assign no positive value, or performed in a manner that betrays the original feel of the music" (Brown and Volgsten, 2000; for a critical view, see Stockfelt, this volume). In other words, the first example seems to be a case of what could perhaps be described as a collective offense against an entire culture or listening public.

With the second pair of examples, we have cases of music users ignoring the clearly expressed wishes of composers. The issue here is the extent to which composers should in fact have the last word regarding the treatment of their products. Bruckner, Mahler, Schubert, and Beethoven are yet other composers whose sketches were completed by enthusiastic scholars. While the artistic results may vary in quality, a question, which many might regard as purely rhetorical, still remains: Irrespective of whether they are dead or alive, should composers' opinions count for anything at all?

Perhaps the most common issue involving rights is the one exemplified by the third example. Should composers and musicians have rights to any profits that result from their musical work(s)? To the Leadbelly example we could add a huge list of jazz and blues artists who never earned anything from the sale of their music. The biggest offender here is not the academic scholar but the music industry. From the 1940s to the 1960s, major labels such as Capitol and Mercury and independents such as Atlantic and Imperial offered contracts with royalty rates as low as 1 percent of actual retail price. And many artists "who recorded for independent labels such as Savoy agreed to receive no royalties whatsoever, in return for lump-sum buyouts of $200 or less" (Begle, 1994: 9). As the editor of the leading music-industry magazine in the US ashamedly admitted:

> One of the music industry's best-kept secrets for decades centered on an ugly period of economic injustice often perpetrated by owners of masters and song copyrights against artists and songwriters who mainly made their way (if not much of a living) in the R&B and blues fields. Among them were acknowledged influences on today's pop music, which generates a major portion of a multi-billion-dollar music industry in the U.S. and further billions in other markets. Yes, many acquiesced to legal, though morally questionable, contractual obligations. Others, through their own ignorance, ineptitude, or corrupt representation, accepted paltry fees in signing away the product of their creativity, with little knowledge that they could have retained a measure of ownership in their works. Denied proper financial recognition in the prime of their careers, they were also denied future economic protection for themselves and their families. (Anonymous, 1995: 79)

One might wonder why the industry acknowledged this mistreatment so late—in the mid-1990s—a time when most of the artists in question were already dead and the sales had already passed their peaks; and why there is no mention of the fact that similar kinds of questionable contracts are still being offered by today's leading companies (see Wallis, this volume).

The Digital Revolution: Sampling, Digital Audio, and MP3

Since the early days of sound recording, much has happened with regard to the technology of music. New inventions and new technologies, such as digital technology, have gradually though strikingly increased the possibilities for using and reusing fixed works and performances. The original version of a fixed performance cannot only be copied, distributed, and transmitted all around the world but it can also be reused in whole or in part, far beyond what was initially expected or intended by the original composer or performer. It can be incorporated into many different media, from CDs and videos to MP3 files on the Internet, and can also be adapted and modified to fit new musical contexts. Even a single tone of an instrument, a short vocal phrase, or a high C by a famous singer can be sampled and reused, and can thus possess commercial value as a building block for a new piece of music. Since digital sampling has become a tool in almost everyone's hands, album producers do not even need to deal directly with the musicians whose music ends up in record stores and on radio stations. Therefore, digital technology has given rise to new moral dilemmas.

Let us begin with digital sampling. Digital sampling is the exact duplication of a portion of a musical work that can be reused in any number of new musical contexts. The duration of the sampled fragment may vary considerably, ranging from the sound of a single tone to an extensive segment of a composition. For the former, the common procedure is to "get a recording of your favorite player, find a good isolated sound, and record it carefully into your digital sampler" (Alvaro, 1986: 10). The sampled sound may then be played by anyone via, for instance, a synthesizer keyboard. Whereas sampling was once an activity reserved for an exclusive group of sound engineers and mostly used by rap musicians, the uses have now broadened: "The use of digital music sampling, once the province of a limited segment of the music business, such as rap artists with 'gangster' images, has expanded considerably. It is now being used by mainstream pop music artists like Janet Jackson, whose single *Got Till It's Gone* incorporates part of Joni Mitchell's song *Big Yellow Taxi* in the chorus" (Upton Douglass and Mende, 1998: 23).

A striking instance of the sampling of larger musical segments and the moral problems associated with it comes from the album *Deep Forest*. On this recording, traditional music of Ghana, the Solomon Islands, and Central African Pygmy tribes was fused with techno-house dance rhythms of the mid-1990s. This raised a special problem regarding the distribution of royalties. Although the album cover warned that all rights were reserved and that "duplication is a violation of applicable laws," no credit was given to the musicians of the Solomon Islands. And although some portion of the profit from the album (which sold more than two million copies) was reportedly routed to a particular "Pygmy fund," this fund was devoted to the preservation of a Pygmy tribe that was not represented on the album. In other words, the royalties of this album went to the wrong people (Mills, 1996).

A similar case concerns the Ami tribe of Taiwan (Taylor, 1999). A ritual weeding song by the Ami was sampled from a copyrighted ethnomusicology CD and incorporated into a song by the pop group Enigma. Although a licensing fee was paid to the record company that issued the CD, the Ami musicians were never asked permission. In addition, the Ami musicians claimed that they had made their recording exclusively for the purposes of cultural preservation and not for pop-music commercialism. In essence, they claimed that their moral rights had been violated. So whereas the Pygmies of the *Deep Forest* example did not receive their due royalties, the Ami musicians presumably did but felt their moral rights were violated by the change in the context of their music.

Digital technology, then, is both an asset and a liability in that "it makes 'cloning'—not mere copying—possible, because it preserves the quality of the original recording instead of delivering a second-hand copy" (Gramatke, 1996: 4). From the vantage point of copyright, a particularly problematic case is the dissemination of CD-quality music through digital audio broadcasting. Japan's digital radio station Star Digio 100 provides more than 100 channels of music of various genres to over 76,000 subscribers for a price of approximately nine dollars per month. Star Digio operates by playing music from CDs "without disc jockeys or other interruptions, repeating programmes up to six times a day" (Lawson and Steed, 1999: 16): "Subscribers to the service were sent facsimile schedules, detailing the play list of songs on the service, down to the second. This made it easy for subscribers with digital equipment, such as MiniDisc systems, to create unlicensed, near CD quality recordings of entire albums at minimal inconvenience and cost" (p. 16). Several record companies, including Sony and Toshiba-EMI, initiated legal proceedings against Star Digio, "claiming that the Star Digio service is not a broadcasting service but an unlicensed record distribution which infringes the reproduction right of the record companies" (Lawson and Steed, 1999: 16). In May 1999, this led to a suspension by Star Digio of their facsimile service; however, their output continued unabated.

Digital technology is also a precondition for the distribution and exchange of music via the Internet. In the case of the Internet, the increasing popularity of MP3 technology and file exchange programs like the pioneering Napster and Gnutella (and later Kazaa) brought the issue of intellectual property rights to its logical and technological extremes. MP3 can be described briefly as "a non-patented freely available technology which is able to compress audio by removing inaudible information without perceivable loss in sound quality" (Lawson and Steed, 1999: 17). This means that minimal memory storage is required for the downloading of sound files.

Along with MP3, there are the so-called P2P (peer to peer) programs. Both Napster and Gnutella allowed their users to share files without the files having to go through a central server. Napster required the user to log on to its server, and then it searched its database for other users who were online. If Napster found a match for a sought song, it connected the user who wanted a certain file with a user who had it, and the file was downloaded directly from one to the other. Gnutella did not require the user to log on to a central server. Once the software was downloaded, it enabled the user to search the Internet for other users with the same software, who were in turn programmed to extend the search to further users with the same software, and so on. Once a temporary network of users was located and identified, the request for a certain file was delivered across the network, enabling anyone who had this file to transmit it directly.

The increasing availability on the market of cheap portable devices for storing MP3 files, together with the relative ease with which anyone can distribute files over the Internet, enables consumers to download extensive portions of recorded music without any royalties being paid to the copyright owners. In short, anybody can produce their own favorite music compilations without paying anything. Attempts have been made in the US to impose a royalty fee of 2 percent on the distribution of MP3 recording devices, but overall it has proven difficult to prohibit such products so long as they can be used for purposes other than making serial copies. As long as the technology can be used for private purposes, copyright law is not enough for prohibition.

That the free distribution of music via the Internet upsets copyright owners around the world should come as no surprise now that anyone with a PC can become a virtual "music pirate." Neither should it have come as a surprise that Napster was shut down after having lost a lawsuit filed against it. Indeed, the issue is all but trivial. As Atlantic Records co-chairman Val Azzoli said, "I don't know how to stop it. It's not just music I'm worried about. It's all intellectual properties. If you can take music, you can take everything else too" (quoted in Greenfeld, 2000: 67). But as the case of MP3 recording devices indicates, it is the mass-mediating potential of the technology that is the crux of the matter.

From Moral Intuitions to Statutory Rights

We have seen in the examples above how the moral intuitions of people can be violated by various reuses and manipulations of music. We have the cases of the Mascagni opera, the completion of composers' unfinished scores, and the ritual songs of the Ami tribe, all examples of people who feel their moral rights have been violated in some way. In the cases of Leadbelly and the Pygmies from *Deep Forest*, as well as the general distribution of music on the Internet, we have examples of music makers not receiving anything close to the fair share of the profits that their musical activities generate. The moral intuition here is that the performers and composers should receive royalties whenever their music is played in public. Then there are the copyright owners, who need not be directly involved in the production of the music. Shouldn't the owner of the right, whoever it may be, be safeguarded against piracy and illegitimate use?

As will be shown, the law makes a distinction between economic rights and moral rights. In the case of economic rights, this distinction leads to some rather counterintuitive outcomes regarding rights. Let us therefore take a look at the various rights that sit under the wide heading of intellectual property. Beginning with moral rights, a moral right is the right to be credited for one's work and the right to preserve the integrity of one's work. The Bern Convention (Article 6) puts it thus: "Independently of the author's economic rights, and even after the transfer of the said rights, the author shall have the right to claim authorship of the work and to object to any distortion, mutilation, or other modification of, or other derogatory action in relation to, the said work, which would be prejudicial to his honour and reputation" (quoted in Karlen, 1993: 38).

Regarding economic rights, at least five types of rights are distinguished: performers, mechanical, distribution, communication, and synchronization rights (Garofalo, 1999; Stannow, Åkerberg, and Hillerström, 1999; Wallis et al., 1999; Wallis, this volume).

1. Performers rights ensure the right to authorize and prohibit *the public performance of a work* (live or recorded; sometimes the terms "performing rights" and "performance rights" are used to distinguish between the rights to the work and those to the recording).
2. Mechanical rights (fixation and reproduction rights) entitle the copyright owner the right to authorize and prohibit *the fixation of a work or live performance,* such as recording it, and the reproduction (i.e., the making of copies) thereof.
3. and 4. Distribution and communication rights provide the right to authorize and prohibit *the making available of ("fixed") works and performances* to the public by either physical copies (such as CDs) or by other means (such as broadcasting).
5. Synchronization rights apply when music is combined with other art forms such as videos or movies.

It should be noted that these rights concern the right to *authorize* and *prohibit* the uses of music in various forms. These rights are only subsequently granted to users by contracts and against payment. For instance, the rights of communication and public performance of a fixed performance of a work are, within the field of so-called neighboring rights, mostly replaced by a right to a single equitable remuneration, which then entitles the performers and phonogram producers to a royalty when their recordings are played publicly.

Lastly, we can also distinguish between "natural" and "non-natural" (or conventional) rights. A natural right is a principle grounded on the order of nature and cannot, due to its divine or natural origin, be disputed. In the words of William of Occam (following Aristotle), a natural right is "a power of conform to right reason without an agreement or pact" (quoted in Melden, 1988). Human rights are generally regarded as natural rights. In contrast, conventional rights are regulated by convention and may therefore be changed as legislative authorities deem necessary.

Whereas the various versions of copyright are of primary interest in most discussions about the workings of the music industry, the distinction between natural and conventional rights will prove to be of importance when we discuss the ethical issues of the manipulation of music. What can be immediately observed is a possible clash between moral rights and economic rights. This is illustrated by the aforementioned case: the pop group Enigma obtained a license from the copyright owners to use a traditional Ami song; however, the copyright and the moral right belonged to different people. The problem here is the prioritization of these rights: should moral rights be the ultimate source for permission for reuse, or should it be the entitlement that comes with the copyright? Perhaps the time has come for a case that judges whether such a use is an infringement on the musicians,' or even the entire culture's, moral rights.

The Historical Background of Intellectual Property Rights

Whether the moral issues of the type we have identified can be solved by any of the principles of rights mentioned above is a key question that should be addressed by anyone who takes recourse to the notion of rights in situations of social controversy, be the issues musical or otherwise. In an attempt to address this question, we will find it instructive to look at the historical background of the notion of intellectual property rights. What we shall see is that copyright is strongly tied to the commercial potential of mass mediation.

Rights to music are a fairly recent phenomenon, whereas rights to literary manuscripts are a more established practice historically. Benedictine monasteries were already charging payment for the right to copy their manuscripts in the Middle Ages. Nevertheless, medieval Europe was primarily an oral culture. As Ronald Bettig has pointed out, because medieval musicians and listeners were more respectful to the form of information than to its source of authorship, "it was difficult for the *troubadours* and *jongleurs* to protect their work from copiers and imitators" (Bettig, 1992: 135):

> The real historical events upon which the poems and songs of the Middle Ages were based belonged to a literary commons from which anyone could draw. Nor could the oral performance itself be kept or owned in any way. For an oral poet, the moment of composition takes place at the time of performance, and each actualization of the songs and stories is different. Thus, there is no "original," only a combination of formula, spontaneity, and forgetfulness, a "creative artist making the tradition." (p. 135; Bettig quotes Lord, 1960)

Bettig also points out that the "corporate structure of medieval society meant that people saw themselves primarily as members of a group rather than as individuals" (p. 136). Economic interests were therefore primarily protected by guilds, which preserved the art of a profession of a limited group rather than the rights to individual works. Not until the dawn of the European Renaissance did the individual achieve the attention necessary for the concept of authorship to emerge. A crucial step toward assigning priority to the individual as a moral agent, separate from the collective of family and village, occurred as late as the fourteenth century, when an increased awareness and importance of the Day of Judgment and a corresponding weighing of good deeds against bad forced people to acknowledge their individual biographies and personal narratives (Ariès, 1981). That a concern about the individual in no way suffices for the concept of authorship to be established is shown by the fact that it never arose in Ancient Greece, although the individual acquired increased focus from the sixth century B.C. onwards (see Bettig, 1992: 132f.). When considering music, Martin Scherzinger dates the idea of an autonomous composer of an original work "to nineteenth-century romantic assumptions about imagination, genius and inspiration" (Scherzinger, 1999: 106). Scherzinger refers to the still widespread myth of the divinely inspired genius creating an original musical work in a process that is devoid of heteronomous, mundane influence (see also Stockfelt, this volume).

As many authors have pointed out (e.g., Bettig, 1992; Garofalo, 1999; Stannow, Åkerberg and Hillerström, 1999), it was the advent of the book printing technique in Europe and its improvement by Johann Gutenberg around the middle of the fifteenth century that ignited the concept of copyright. By enabling duplication—and thus mass mediation—of an increasing number of titles, Gutenberg's printing press immediately gained economic interest (see Mumford, 1999). One reason for this was that Gutenberg's press opened the door for piracy. Because no copyright protection existed at the time, a book printer next door could easily make parallel editions of the most economically attractive works. Although the first book printer regarded it as theft, there was nothing he could do about it. The need for some kind of legal protection for his investment became increasingly pressing.

This is how the concept of copyright originated: with printers and publishers rather than authors and artists. An early attempt to regulate the copying of literary works occurred in 1557 when a printers guild was created in England. Nevertheless, Gutenberg's invention was 250 years old when authorship was acknowledged and copyright legislation was finally passed. Thus, in the Statute of Queen Anne of 1709, "[a] literary work was considered the author's personal property for the first time" (Mills, 1996: 57). In France, following the French revolution, a first exclusive right of authors (*droit d'auteur*) was passed in 1791–1793. But these agreements concentrated mainly on literary works. Although Johann Christian Bach (the youngest son of J. S. Bach), working in London, was able to defend the right to one of his published pieces as early as 1777 (Wallis et al., 1999), the first legal protection of musical rights was enacted with a supplement to the British Copyright Act of 1842 (Laing, 1993). At first, music was classed under the extended category of "books," and it was not until 1882 that the law came to regard music as an independent art form (Mills, 1996).

The Bern Convention of 1886 marked the first multinational agreement on the intellectual property rights of music (to which some 130 nations have now adhered). Interestingly enough, the United States had a less than idealistic attitude toward the reciprocal principles of international copyright legislation. As Laing points out, "United States publishing interests were antagonistic to attempts to enforce payment to foreign authors when the US itself had little copyright material for export. It was not until the 1890s, when the songs of Stephen Foster and others had gained substantial popularity and sheet music sales in Britain, that the US government agreed to protect the rights of foreign composers and publishers. Prior to this, the prevailing view in the US was that such royalty payments would be a 'tax on knowledge' and would cause a balance of payments deficit in the cultural field" (Laing, 1993: 23).

The British Copyright Act of 1842 and the earliest version of the Bern Convention dealt only with published musical works. Before the start of broadcasting and the inventions of recording technology, there was no need for any kind of protection for performers. Much as in medieval times, the performance continued to exist only during the moment it was made and in which the audience was in direct contact with the performer. This was still the situation at the beginning of the twentieth century. Along with radio broadcasting, the replacement of the phonograph by the gramophone and soundtracked film opened the way for the live performance to be recorded, repeated, duplicated, and transmitted to audiences and listeners far beyond the confines of concert halls and theaters. Even more so than with printed scores, broadcasting and recording enabled mass mediation of music. Although performers had already started to claim their rights to protection before 1930, an international instrument for neighboring rights was not created until the ratification of the Rome Convention in 1961.

Considering the performance rights inherent in musical recordings, the US Copyright Act of 1906 excluded music rolls and gramophone records from copyright legislation. And whereas the US would wait until 1995 to sign a law regarding performance rights (Pollack, 2000), France and Canada still have not done so, which means that playing a CD in public or on the radio in these countries does not yield any royalties whatsoever to the copyright owner (Frith, 1987).

Finally, collecting societies warrant a mention. Copyright owners noticed early on that the protection of their rights was a cumbersome affair. Thus, the mid-nineteenth century saw the birth of the first societies devoted to the collection of royalties for their members. During the twentieth century, national nonprofit collecting societies were the principal instrument by which copyright owners received their royalty incomes. In addition to the collection and distribution of royalties to its members, these societies also administer the licensing of rights for various uses and users. In Sweden, for instance, different collecting societies represent different groups of copyright owners, such as composers, arrangers, and publishers (STIM); phonogram and video producers (IFPI); and musicians and performers (SAMI) (see Edström, 1998, Wallis et al., 1999; Lundberg, Malm, and Ronström, 2000; Wallis, this volume).

Moral Issues versus Economical Interests

Bettig (1992) mentions that both authors and publishers often referred to popular notions of every man's natural right to the product of his labor as they sought to define the concept and practice of intellectual property rights. In other words, there was a tendency to refer to moral intuition when deciding about the economic benefits of copyright. In spite of its relative importance for the continental *droit d'auteur*, Bettig concludes that the idea of natural rights was of secondary importance for the Anglo-Saxon development. What counted above all was economic interest. In particular, it is the commercial potential of mass mediation that urged on and continues to urge on copyright: "This history of the origins and development of the concept of literary property demonstrates the essential function of copyright as an economic right of capital. The incorporation of elements of an author's moral or natural right into copyright principles has since obscured the separate interests of authors and publishers" (p. 149).

Although there were legal cases in Britain in which the courts "recognized the author's natural copyright as common law" (p. 145), the British saw no need to supplant the Statute of Queen Anne, which assigned copyright to publishers. In the US, some states, such as Massachusetts, passed acts that based copyright on the author's natural rights, whereas others, such as Pennsylvania, saw copyright as a property that could be freely exchanged between author and publisher.

The consequence of this development, Bettig argues, is a situation wherein media corporations increasingly pressure present-day artists to sell the rights to their work (see also Wallis, this volume). Bettig writes about authors who must "give up claim to copyright ownership in the work they do.... Even best-selling novelists must sell the rights to their stories" (p. 150). In the music business, the situation is similar. Martin Kretschmer (2000) mentions how copyright, although it is "initially vested in the individual creator ... rarely remains there for long": "In the process of bringing music to the market, the creator trades exclusive rights against resources s/he does not have: a specific promotional muscle, global distribution, access to risk finance" (Kretschmer, 2000). This development should be seen in light of Roger Wallis's observation (this volume) that copyright has become an increasing source of income for the major music corporations, as "a few multinational media corporations now 'own' most of the superstars as well as a very large repertoire of music copyrights," and that for a company such as EMI, the music publishing part accounts for about 15 percent of its turnover but almost 32 percent of its revenues. Likewise, Simon Frith describes how these corporations regard each piece of music as a "basket of rights," and that they see it as their task "to exploit as many of these rights as possible" (Frith, 1987: 57).

Not only is this—the power of capital to force musicians to give up their rights—a moral problem in itself; the practice also discloses an important inconsistency in the notion of intellectual property rights, at least as this notion has developed in relation to music. This inconsistency resides in the relations between the different notions of rights and the notion of music. We have already seen how moral rights and copyrights may conflict when they are assigned to different parties. However, we should first question on what grounds a right—in this case a copyright—can be sold at all. That goods and services can be sold usually comes as no surprise, but *can one really sell a right?*

The source of the issue seems to be the notion of natural rights as it was developed by John Locke in the seventeenth century. Locke elaborated the idea of a "state of nature," in which individuals are claimed to be in "a state of perfect freedom to order their actions and dispose their possessions as they think fit, within the bounds of the law of nature, without asking leave or dependency upon the will of any other man" (quoted in Nozick, 1974: 10). Because every individual owns himself, this state of "perfect freedom" (which differs radically from the state of nature envisioned by his predecessor Hobbes) entails a natural right of an individual to the product of his labor: "[T]he labour of his body and the work of his hands, we may say, are properly his. Whatsoever then he removes out of the state that nature hath provided and left it in, he hath mixed his labour with, and joined to it something that is his own, and thereby makes it his property" (quoted in Bettig, 1992: 141).

The popular notion of a natural right, referred to by authors and publishers alike when fighting for intellectual property rights, was largely influenced by Lockean ideas. The problem seems to be Locke's notion of property. We cannot enter into an exegesis on this point, but it seems as if Locke, on the one hand, spoke about the products of a man's labor and the rights to the products of this labor in the same terms, that is, as an instance of property. Man has the natural moral right to decide about his property-as-commodity. Should he decide to sell his property-as-commodity, the property-as-right will be transferred too. On the other hand, Locke argues forcefully against the disposal of human rights: "For a man, not having the Power of his own life, *cannot*, by Compact, or his own consent, *enslave himself* to any one, nor put himself under the Absolute, Arbitrary Power of another, to take away his Life, when he pleases. No Body can give more Power than he has himself; and he that cannot take away his own Life, cannot give another power over it" (quoted in Nergelius and Zetterquist, 2001: 35).

One's life is not property, and so cannot be sold, although one has a natural right to it. In grounding both his ideas of property rights and human rights (as it were) on the same notion of a state of nature, Locke provides what might be the source of confusion between a right and a commodity as both being properties of a person. Although Jürgen Habermas (1989) notes that "Locke's basic formula of 'the preservation of property' quite naturally and in the same breath subsumed life, liberty and estate under the title of 'possessions'" (p. 56), natural rights seem to be transferable only through the exchange of the goods to which one has these rights. Insofar as we remain with Locke, we cannot maintain that copyright is a natural right and at the same time accept that this right is being transferred, lest we let it go together with the musical commodity. Let us assume for the moment that the same holds true if copyright is seen as a conventional right; in such a case we still have to sell the musical commodity if we want to transfer the right to it. The question we must then ask is this: What is a musical commodity?

The Reification of the Musical Work

In the words of Bettig: "[T]here is an essential connection between the rise of capitalism [and] the extension of commodity relations into literary and artistic domains, and the emergence of the printing press" (Bettig, 1992: 131). We have seen that the development of the notion of copyright is the result of economic interests rather than of moral or ethical concerns. Copyright was developed along with the commercial potential of mass mediation. Moreover, copyrights seem to be governed by conventional statutes rather than by principles of natural rights, as the Bern Convention indicates in its very name. The Bern Convention even treats moral rights as optional (Laing, 1993), and moral rights are not recognized at all in US law (Mills, 1996: 84). But what does Bettig mean by saying that commodity relations are extended into the domains of the literary and artistic?

Simon Frith brings us one step toward an answer in his reference to the British Copyright Act of 1956, according to which "a musical work (and any associated lyrics) acquires copyright protection immediately when it is committed to paper or fixed in some other material form, such as a recording" (quoted in Frith, 1987: 63). "What then," Frith asks

> is a "musical work?" This is not defined in the 1956 Act, though the 1902 Act referred to "any combination of melody and harmony or either of them." ... There can be copyright in the arrangement of a piece of music (if it involves sufficient "skill and labour") but not in particular instrumental sounds or rhythmic combinations. Bo Diddley, for example, could not copyright the familiar Bo Diddley Beat and, to cite a recently controversial case, Paul Simon could use US law to acknowledge and reward his South African collaborators' melodic contributions to *Graceland* but not their musically more significant instrumental sounds. As these examples make clear, copyright law defines music in terms of nineteenth-century Western conventions and is not well suited to the protection of Afro-American musician's improvisational art or rhythmic skills. (p. 63)[1]

Carl Dahlhaus traced the idea of music as an "*opus absolutum,* a work in itself, freed from its sounding realization in any present moment," to Listenius in 1537 (Dahlhaus, 1982: 11). Still, as Frith rightly points out, it was not until the nineteenth century that this idea gained widespread currency in the West. More precisely, it was in the change from the general conception of the classical music of the Enlightenment to the organic works of romanticism that the idea became fully developed. This change involved a successive transition from the notion of music as a type of activity to that of music as a type of object.

As pointed out by Dahlhaus (1989), Mark Evan Bonds (1991), and others, during the eighteenth century, composers established unity and order among musical sounds mainly by molding musical material according to the rules of rhetoric. Music was seen, at this time, as a wordless oration (albeit in the service of the sung word), and the task of the composer was to persuade the listener. Through a rhetorically ordered presentation of various passions, the successful composition enabled the expression of a certain sentimental character that was to be accepted by, or to affect, the audience. Music was a means to an end, and the form of the composition had to be graspable by the listener, since it was the listener's positive verdict that was the outcome sought.

During the following century, this view of music changed dramatically, allowing ultimately for a conception of music as an organism that exists in its own right. From being rejected as more or less nonsensical or superficial (unless serving such ends as exhibiting the virtuosity of the musician or accompanying dance), instrumental compositions now were elevated to "absolute music" (Dahlhaus, 1989). Whereas in the eighteenth century composers were regarded more or less as craftsmen and the outcome of their toil a crafting of preexisting material, the nineteenth-century composer was hailed by the romantics as a divinely inspired genius, whose organic offspring aspired to a higher status than the transience of their mortal forerunners. And while the form of a pre-romantic composition was largely determined by genre—the harmonic plan being a way of ordering a preconceived thought—in the music of the nineteenth century, this underlying thought came to be equated with the formal outline of the work itself. Whereas content had earlier been determined mainly by a text (and the thoughts or passions it conveyed), content subsequently found itself incarnated in the individual form of the composition. The general thereby became particular. The event was turned into an object—in a movement that curiously replaced the expression of individual passions with that of an ineffable feeling—and the identity of the work was to be found in the achronic harmonic structure of a score rather than, as before, in the temporal unfolding and exposition of an "extramusical" idea (which ultimately enabled the jettisoning of emotional content in music altogether, see Hanslick, 1955).

We can hereby see that when Bettig talks about the medieval focus on form rather than sources of authorship, form (as Bettig uses the term) should be understood as genre rather than as structure. Transposed to music history, we can say that since the nineteenth century an instance of Western music has come to exemplify a particular work, before that time it exemplified a particular genre (Dahlhaus, 1982: 15). In particular, this change in conception involves a reification of the musical work as a commodity, which is a prerequisite for copyright law to apply. Without this historical shift, copyright law would hardly apply to musical phenomena the way it does today.

Solving Moral Problems with Recourse to Intellectual Property Rights

Copyright law defines musical works in terms of nineteenth-century Western standards. It requires the reification[2] of musical objects that are identified primarily by their mass-media potential: either the printed score, or, since 1956, the fixation of sound in a recorded medium. In addition to this process of reification, we have observed copyright law's reliance upon notions of authority that likewise stem from culture-specific European thought. This compels us to rethink the ontological status of music and question the very foundations of musical copyright. If the notion of a musical commodity is a cultural construct (with a fairly brief history at that)—if the notion of a musical "work" is of a nominal rather than a natural kind—what reason is there, if any, to let this culturally and historically contingent notion serve as the foundation for any concept of musical right? Perhaps more to our point: Are existing intellectual property right laws capable of solving the moral issues that we have examined, and if so, can this serve as an argument in favor of the former? Or should present copyright laws be revised? Or should they be done away with altogether?

With these queries in mind, it is interesting to note that a steadily growing number of voices have, in some way or another, been raised against copyright. There was recently some excitement in the Swedish business community when the minister of free trade encouraged youths and other economically non-dominant groups to download music from the Internet so as to circumvent the record companies' copyrighted sources of profit. The argument for the invitation to such obviously illegal action was that when only a few companies control the output, the result is inevitably conformity in price setting and cartel-like development of the market.

Other critics, such as Rosemary Coombe (1998) and Naomi Klein (2000), claim that copyright is an infringement on the democratic right to use one's symbolic environment in free expression. They focus on the saturation of today's societies by copyrighted trademarks and logotypes, from Disney's Donald Duck[3] to the case of Bette Midler, who successfully sued against the imitation of her vocal style in a commercial advertisement for cars (see also Gaines, 1993; on the relation of this issue to sampling, see Schumacher, 1995; Porcello [1991] refers to several studio technicians who believe that the sound of a voice, such as Ella Fitzgerald's, can be owned by the artist, whereas a particular drum sound, such as that of Phil Collins, cannot be). Coombe and Klein both show that copyright is used to prohibit musical reuse on economic, rather than moral, grounds. Klein (2000) describes a case in point:

When Beck, a major-label artist, makes an album packed with hundreds of samples, Warner Music clears the rights to each and every piece of the audio collage and the work is lauded for capturing the media-saturated, multi-referenced sounds of our age. But when independent artists do the same thing, trying to cut and paste together art from their branded lives and make good on some of the info-age hype about DIY culture, it's criminalized—defined as theft, not art. This was the point made by musicians on the 1998 *Deconstructing Beck* CD, produced entirely by electronically recontextualizing Beck's already recontextualized sounds. Their point was simple: if Beck could do it, why shouldn't they? Right on cue, Beck's label sent out threatening lawyers' letters that quieted down abruptly when the musicians made it clear that they were gunning for a media fight. Their point, however, had been made: the prevailing formula for copyright and trademark enforcement is a turf war over who is going to get to make art with the new technologies. And it seems that if you're not on the team of a company large enough to control a significant part of the playing field, and can't afford your very own team of lawyers, you don't get to play. (p. 179f.)

To add to these issues, Frith has described copyright law as "a key plank in Western cultural and commercial imperialism," a plank which can "increasingly [be] seen as a weapon used by the multinationals against small countries" (Frith, 1993). We have already referred to Frith saying that Western copyright law defines music in terms not well suited to the protection of music based on improvisation, rhythm, or musicians' individual sounds. And as a comment to the *Deep Forest* sampling case mentioned above, Sherylle Mills adds: "Through the simple process of recording and transcribing, a recorder exerts enough intellectual effort to secure a copyright over field recordings. The traditional community, however, is denied ownership rights over their music if they cannot produce the requisite 'writing' or 'author.' ... [Since it is] extremely difficult for the [traditional] community to actively monitor the music's use ... a recorder gains almost exclusive *de facto* control over the dissemination of recorded [traditional] music" (Mills, 1996: 67).

This argues for the extensive revision of copyright laws. Since different countries have different laws and regulations, and laws are constantly being revised, it is impossible to give a comprehensive overview here, but some suggestions can be mentioned. Regarding sampling, it has been suggested that specific licenses with uniform rates be introduced for brief samples (up to five seconds), which would simplify licensing and thus reduce illegitimate use (Brown, 1992). In order that members' access to their culture not be constrained, a "threshold requirement" has been suggested that would demand compelling reasons from copyright owners who wish to withhold the licensing of their music (Falstrom, 1994: 376). For similar reasons, it has been suggested that the range of copyright be reduced to a maximum of fifteen years, and only "where it can be shown that it is essential to enable investments in products which otherwise would be immediately copied at marginal costs" (Kretschmer, 2000).

Considering cases such as *Deep Forest* and the Ami, Mills suggests that copyright be ascribable to entire communities, since individual composers are seldom identifiable. For instance, the Suya of South America regard plants and animals as the original sources of their music, which is traditionally handed down through the generations by "keepers" rather than by interpreters, composers, or authors. To control the use of field recordings, Mills suggests that ethnomusicologists copyright their recorded material. Instead of division of the access to the music into mechanical and performing rights, she suggests that ethnomusicologists have a "secondary" right that entitles them to the full protection of copyright law and the right to license and instigate infringement suits. The community should have the "primary" right to the music (as long as the community has members who inherit the right), which would mean that the "secondary" rights owner would need the approval of the first party to exercise its right (Mills, 1996; see also Malm, 1998; for a criticism of Mills, see Scherzinger, 1999).

Arguments for Copyright

We have examined suggestions made for the revision of existing copyright laws. Let us now examine some of the pro's and con's regarding musical copyright. Since copyright law has been a subject of concern for several centuries, it would perhaps be naive to try to single out a core justification for it. Nevertheless, at the base of the claims for copyright there seem to be at least two lines of argument (the six motives for copyright mentioned in Stannow, Åkerberg, and Hillerström [1999] can be subsumed under these two lines of argument). The first is that, without copyright, people would cease to be musically creative. (A weaker version of this claim states that, without copyright, the opportunities for creativity would decrease.) The second claim is that copyright infringement is theft. Let us begin with the claim that without copyright people would cease to be musically creative.

According to the US Constitution, copyright is intended "[t]o promote the Progress of Science and Useful Arts, by securing for limited Times to Authors and inventors the exclusive Rights to their respective Writings and discoveries" (quoted in Mills, 1996: 61). This statement is rather weak since it assumes no more than that copyright may promote the progress of "useful arts." A stronger claim is the argument that the European Commission should "improve intellectual property rights" in the European Community (Shackleton, 1998: 16). Reference to the Maastricht Treaty's aim of "creating an ever closer union among the peoples of Europe" (quoted in Shackleton, 1998: 16) implies that copyright is a condition for music's capacity to unite people. It is also claimed that copyright protection "makes it possible to guarantee maintenance and development of creativity in the authors, the cultural industries, consumers and the community as a whole" (Shackleton, 1998: 18). Accordingly copyright guarantees the maintenance and development of creativity as a matter of fact. Stronger still, and more specifically related to music and its copyright protection on the Internet, is the British Music Rights Manifesto,[4] which claims that "[u]nauthorized use and cloning of music on-line will, if unchecked, destabilise the commercial basis of the music business. Without strong enforceable copyright legislation the continuing ability of British music publishers to invest in new British talent will be undermined. Without strong copyright, music cannot operate as a profession.... Without adequate protection, creating music in Britain, as elsewhere, will revert to being a pastime for enthusiastic amateurs rather than serious and respected business" (Rigg, 1998: 41).

Although the British Music Rights Manifesto speaks about music's ability "to promote personal values, interpersonal sensitivity, imagination and analytical and critical thinking, teamworking, coordination and self-discipline" (Rigg, 1998: 42), it does not say much about the promotion of art or the development of creativity but rather implies a "commercial basis" and "respected business" as the source of musical creativity. Thus, the claim that "British Music Rights was established to ensure that British music and British music creators and publishers are able to flourish through electronic trade in music" (Rigg, 1998) may be understood as a claim about economic rather than artistic flourishing. But if we don't read any assumptions about artistic merit into the notion of "creativity," we can treat it as synonymous with "productivity." According to such a reading, copyright is a precondition for musical productivity.

The second line of argument equates copyright infringement with theft and is logically supportive of the first: if what is justifiably the musical property of a musician or composer is stolen from him or her, this will diminish his or her motivation and/or inspiration to produce. Opinions on this matter are often more explicit, perhaps because infringements are experienced as instances of moral offense. For example, in one of the first court decisions on unlicensed sampling ("Alone Again" by rapper Biz Markie, built on a sampled section of Gilbert O'Sullivan's "Alone Again (Naturally)," the judge opened his final statement with the Bible quotation "Thou shalt not steal," after which the defendant was proclaimed guilty of stealing copyrighted musical property (see Upton Douglass and Mende, 1998; Falstrom, 1994). This was entirely in line with the case made by the plaintiff's lawyer, who claimed that "[the issue] is dirt simple.... You can't use somebody else's property without their consent.... [Unlicensed sampling] is a euphemism ... for what anybody else would call pickpocketing" (quoted in Falstrom, 1994: 364).

The same opinion has been expressed almost verbatim by Bryan Bell, a technician who worked with artists such as Carlos Santana and Herbie Hancock: "Copying without paying is a pretty simple issue. Theft is theft. I don't know how any musician whose livelihood depends on royalty income can feel good about taking something from a fellow artist without permission" (quoted in Alvaro, 1986: 10). But what exactly is being stolen? Irrespective of whether we are speaking about a sampled sound, a sample (or a copy, or a pastiche) of a more extensive portion of music, or a downloaded song from the Internet, we can think of various entities being stolen. When, for instance, it is said that "[s]amplers somehow deprive the creators of the sampled sounds of the fruits of their labors"

(Falstrom, 1994: 373), the fruits in question may be either the musical object, the right to use the music, or the economic benefits of the music.

If any of these are stolen, we are dealing with an instance of theft. This is analytically true. But are musical objects ever stolen? Are rights ever stolen? Are economic benefits (other than hard cash or hardware) ever stolen? In the next section we will examine some answers to these questions.

Arguments against Copyright

We have already traced the history of musical reification. This is the history of how the general becomes particular, how the event is turned into an object, and how the identity of the musical work (the musical commodity) is to be found in the achronic formal structure of a score, rather than as before, in the temporal unfolding of sound. This is essentially the history of Western art music. According to Charles Keil, the extent to which many indigenous cultures have nouns at all in their musical terminologies (the grammatical category for denoting commodities such as reified musical objects and formal structures) is largely due to the influence of Christian missionaries (Keil, 1998, personal communication; on the role of discourse in music, see Volgsten, this volume). So the answer to the question of whether musical objects are ever stolen depends on whether musical objects can be stolen at all, a question whose answer depends on whether we can consistently speak of musical objects.

A strong argument against copyright has been presented by the Dutch composer Godfried-Willem Raes (1988). Echoing the American nineteenth-century view that royalty payment is a tax on knowledge, Raes claims that music is not an object; it is information (or what others would call a "meme"; see Dennett, 1990). Information is defined by Raes as "a set of perceivable forms of matter or energy." "As such," Raes continues, "any form is transferable to any material or energetic substratum or carrier. This is a logical consequence of the notion of information itself. [This becomes] evident when we apply it to such things as knowledge: It simply means that I can tell you something I know, that I can also write it down or store it as a sequence of bytes in a computer. The basic property of information seems to be that its transfer and multiplication is possible without taking away anything from the source. When I tell you something, I don't lose anything from what I'm telling you" (Raes, 1988: 146). From this it follows that information cannot be produced. Its material substrate can of course be produced, but the information itself cannot. As Raes says: "[T]hinking is not producing.... An idea is not a product." And even if it is impossible to communicate information and ideas "without producing shaped substrata ... the distinction remains fully correct." Thus, "[a] score is the result of real production, just as making (and I mean, playing) music is" (p. 146).

This means at least two things for the issue of musical theft. First, if music is information and not an object, music cannot be stolen. Of course, physical scores can be stolen, as can physical recordings of musicians playing music, but the music itself cannot be. Second, if music is not an object and is not produced, and thus cannot be lost or stolen, it cannot be considered property: "If you can't lose something, you can't consider it to be your property either. Property, after all, is something you can lose" (p. 146). What Raes brings to the fore is not exactly disputed by the industry. As Gerald Levin, president of Time Warner, put it: "The material actually becomes more valuable over time. It can be sold and resold, over and over again. There are very few businesses I know that have those characteristics" (quoted in Sadler, 1997: 1930). Note that Levin does not talk about "letting out" the music, since music need not be taken back in order to be sold again. Still, he quite understandably would not laud Raes's conclusion that "any legal limitation on the reproducibility of information is an infringement on the proper character of information" (Raes, 1988: 147).

To further show "[t]he absurdity of copyright" (p. 145) when applied to instances of information, Raes makes a comparison between the composing and playing of music and the formulation and use of physical laws: "Who would say that Einstein owned the general relativity theory? Or stronger, who would find it logical to pay a fee to Einstein (or his heritors) every time 'his' knowledge would be used for something" (p. 147). Underlying this difference in attitudes toward musical works and physical laws is of course the romantic myth of the musical genius who creates a work of his own, whereas physical laws are popularly considered to have been discovered. In this view, the laws of nature are objectively "there" as truths for the scientist to find, whereas music has to be created (the classical refutation of this naturalized view of scientific truths is Kuhn, 1962). The absurdity lingers if we change the example from physical laws to an everyday commodity such as cars. Who would accept paying a fee to Volvo or General Motors every time they drove their car to work? And with regard to economic benefits, should car producers have a right to benefit from the profit of, say, a taxi driver?

Raes's answer to such questions is an emphatic "no." Music cannot be stolen. But what about rights or economic benefits: Can they be stolen? It can be seen in our earlier discussion of Locke that rights are not objects either but instances of information (memes). If anyone is to be accused of theft in this context, it would rather be the agents of the corporate music industry who construct and push its compulsory deals forcing musicians to sign away their rights and economic benefits. As Kretschmer has pointed out: "[R]ights accounting for 70 to 80 percent of global revenues end up in the hands of only five companies: EMI (UK), Bertelsmann (Germany), Warner (US), Sony (Japan) and Universal (France)" (Kretschmer, 2000). The common argument within the industry is that without copyright revenues "there will be no money for reinvestment." The words are those of Rupert Perry, CEO of EMI Europe (quoted in Kretschmer, 2000), and Gerald Levin readily admits as well that "copyright is the underlying principle that safeguards the value of Time Warner's products" (quoted in Sadler, 1997: 1930).

Taking into account Kretschmer's observation that in the UK "80 percent of composers earn less than £1000 per year from copyright royalties" (Kretschmer, 2000; on similar conditions in Sweden, see Wallis and Malm, 1984), it becomes increasingly clear that copyright is an instrument that primarily serves the industry itself (as Bettig indicated) and a modest number of "stars." This is also the conclusion drawn by Keil, who says that "[t]he only people who profit from copyright are the huge, ever-growing companies and an ever-smaller cluster of superstars" (Keil and Feld, 1994: 314). So when the industry raises concerns about the free distribution of music via the Internet, its concern is not so much to safeguard the creative and economic basis for musicians and composers, as the official line goes, as it is to safeguard its own oligopolistic grip on the market. By preventing the free exchange of MP3 files on the Internet, copyright is a way of securing the industry's power over the distribution channels. With the extension of the application of copyright from fifty to seventy years, which has already been enacted, the ability to "sell and re-sell music, over and over again" is significantly extended. Copyright thus "constitutes a money making machine far beyond the amortisation of initial investments" (Kretschmer, 2000).

Nevertheless, copyright is not a money-making machine for the majority of the world's musicians and composers, and it is doubtful if it ever will be. Will copyright ever be a precondition for musical creativity and productivity? In this case, the issue over copyright on the Internet can be compared with the anti-tape-recording campaign of the 1970s. The industry's slogan then was that "home taping is killing music." In retrospect, we know that home taping did not kill musical creativity; nor did it have any negative effects on record sales. It is therefore unlikely that the digital revolution, with its sampling devices and MP3s, will have any negative effects on creativity.

In addition to copyright's inadequacy as a source of income for the majority of musicians and composers, Keil points to the negative effects of marketing on artistic creativity. In their hunt for potential super-sellers, corporations tend to promote only a small number of stars and styles: "Currently, the control justifies the hype. If you have the copyright and think it can be defended legally in court, then you can put hundreds of thousands of dollars behind saying that this punk rock excrescence is the one to promote this spring. You can risk all kinds of money trying to shape people's consciousness to like a particular music" (Keil and Feld, 1994: 318). Moreover, as Kretschmer (2000) points out: "The creative base of the music industry is financed by other means [than copyright]: session payments, concerts, teaching, grants." And as Raes adds: "[I]n everyday practice, the vast majority of new [i.e., "art-"] music composers generally compose within the time they are already paid for by our social institutions: radio-stations, music schools, universities, etc." (Raes, 1988). If this were not enough, "we see that throughout most of human history there existed no concept of intellectual property rights, yet technological and cultural artefacts were still produced" (Bettig, 1992: 146).

What would happen without musical copyright, Raes predicts, is rather that small-scale regional music would experience a recovery. Because there would be less financial gain in the playing of old hits, new music would become much more attractive and the small-scale, regional music industry would increase at the expense of the big multinationals. In other words, musical creativity would be significantly promoted (cf. Peterson and Berger, 1975). As Raes puts it:

> [V]ery probably the whole industry would collapse pretty fast.... Small-scale music production everywhere would flourish.... So many more musicians would get chances to play more musics. Nobody would make music only for the royalties anymore—no more top hits. Reproduction of music would no longer be in the financial interest of the record-producer, so he would to a much lesser extent put media under pressure to program it. Also radio and TV would become substantially cheaper, which would render regional TV and radio a lot more interesting. (Raes, 1988: 148f.)

Raes's prospect may seem utopian, perhaps even naive. Nevertheless, what the issue of copyright boils down to is very much the questioning of the status of the music industry. The British Music Rights Manifesto makes no secret of this in its constant reference to music as "a serious and respected business" (Rigg, 1998: 41). However, Klein and Coombe both demonstrate how the industry constrains the availability of expressive means through its appropriation of copyright. The outcome is a diminished public sphere (cf. Habermas, 1989). As Thomas Schumacher (1995) says: "Copyright is enabling of certain forms of discourse while prohibiting others in the ideological balance of 'free expression' and profitability.... In other words, [through its appropriation of copyright] capital is able to control the patterns of signification that are most suited to its needs" (p. 267). In the end, it is a question of democracy: Who is allowed to say what, where, and when?

All this, Raes would say, shows that copyright should be abolished. As is true of all information, music cannot be owned. On the contrary, like information, music requires the exchange of ideas. Any knowledge that can be transmitted via (in)formed matter is "a capacity of a system, and its transferability is even a criterion for its being knowledge" (p. 146). Without communication, ideas such as music would simply die out. To paraphrase Wallis (this volume), inhibiting the free circulation of music represents not an opportunity for but a *threat* to musical creativity. Raes's conclusion, that copyright is an infringement on music's status as information, "an epistemological lie [that] is purely immoral towards society" (p. 147), is echoed by Gilberto Gil, musician, minister of culture in Brazil, and winner of the 2005 Polar Music Prize: "A world opened up by communications cannot remain closed up in a feudal vision of property. No country, not the US, not Europe, can stand in the way of it. It's a global trend. It's part of the very process of civilization. It's the semantic abundance of the modern world, of the postmodern world—and there's no use resisting it" (quoted in Dibbell, 2004).

What does this mean for the claim of the European Commission lobbyists that improvement and harmonization of copyright is a condition for music's capacity to unite people?

The Metaphorical Basis of Morals: Are Rights Right?

In the shift from the Enlightenment conception of music as a rhetorical oration to the romantic view of music as an organic structure, we witnessed a shift from the view of music as being chiefly a temporal event, or activity, to an objective view: music is a thing rather than an activity. To say that music is either an oration or an organic structure is to speak metaphorically, since in a sense, music is neither. By applying either the term "rhetoric" or "organic structure" to a sound event, one transposes a whole domain of relationships onto it. And insofar as the metaphor proves successful, a sound event is regarded as an acceptable instance of music only if it complies with the metaphor. In the first case, the relationships transposed are those of rhetoric; accordingly, an acceptable piece of music has to display a correct rhetorical plan. Thus, the exposition, development, and recapitulation of a pre-romantic sonata correspond to the exordium, narratio, and confirmatio of rhetoric (though Mattheson required six parts in a "well developed composition," see Bent and Drabkin, 1987: 8). In the second case, the organic work of romanticism, the dispositional parts of a sonata, are seen as the surface of an organism whose elements are all structurally related to a tonic center (Solie, 1980).[5]

As Mark Johnson has shown, metaphors are also responsible for our conceptualization of morality. According to Johnson: "We understand morally problematic situations via conventional metaphorical mappings," and "Our most important moral concepts (e.g., will, action, purpose, rights, duties, laws) are defined by systems of metaphors" (Johnson, 1993: 33). It is not our purpose here to go into the metaphorical bases of the concept of rights, as they are analyzed by Johnson. Suffice it to say that Locke's "confusion," mentioned earlier, can be seen as a case of a metaphorical mapping of objects onto rights; that is, Locke's notion of rights requires reification by an ontological metaphor. What we want to emphasize, rather, is the relativistic and culture-specific foundations of both music and morals. True, music or morals of different cultures would not be radically incommensurable, but the point is that both music and morals rest on human basic levels of categorization (see Volgsten, this volume), which nevertheless are conceptualized in culture-specific ways.

What Johnson questions is any ethic whose purpose is "the figuring out [of] the relevant moral laws" that would determine "how we ought to treat ourselves and others" in particular situations (p. 21). Morality is not governed by absolute laws that hold universally for all humans. Instead, Johnson's analysis of the metaphorical bases of moral thinking focuses on "the imaginative activity that is crucial to human moral deliberation" (p. 31). This imaginative aspect of moral deliberation allows the coexistence of different systems of moral logic. "The crucial point is that many, if not most, people will have ... competing sets of values and their corresponding notions of reasoning that they will bring into play in a given situation" (p. 116). We all know this from our own experiences and perhaps even condemn it as a weakness of the will. Johnson wants us to see this pluralism of values and norms as an indication of our capacity as creative imaginative beings.

Without metaphorical moral thinking, Johnson says, "we would be doomed to habitual acts" (p. 33). As an existing alternative to "[a] morality of rights, rules, and justice-as-fairness [that] requires a procedure for calculating what is due to each individual in a situation and thus determin[es] the right rule to follow," Johnson draws our attention to a different moral logic. This alternative is a "morality of care, relationships, and cooperation [that] seeks a way to preserve and enhance relationships and community in the face of conflict and competing interests" (p. 114).

> There is a different locus of moral reasoning here. Unlike the previous example, it is not a calculation of rights, duties, and obligations according to universal rules. Instead, it is a logic of cooperation, of figuring out how to work together—to be responsible to and for others—in the presence of conflict. The best course of action is determined by what is required to preserve certain relationships and to promote the growth of harmony and community.... With the maintenance of relationships as primary, it might actually be necessary to forgo something to which, from the perspective of a morality of rights and justice, one has a right or entitlement. (p. 116)

Again, it is not a question of determining which of these systems of moral logic conform to a universal law. Johnson's point—which we want to bring to the fore—is rather that "[m]ost of us do not live exclusively by one such set of values or the other. We have both of them, as well as others, woven together in our complex moral understanding" (p. 116). Having established that we have both of them, Johnson also recommends that we become aware of both of them. Focusing exclusively on the logic of rights results in "an extremely narrow definition of what counts as morality" (p. 246). According to the rights version of morality, "[m]orality is a set of restrictive rules that are supposed to tell you which acts you may and may not perform, which you have an obligation to perform, and when you can be blamed for what you have done. It is not fundamentally about how to live a good life, or how to live well. Instead, it is only a matter of "doing the right thing—*the* one right thing required of you in a given situation" (p. 246; emphasis in original).

Questioning the existence of "*the* right thing to do" is not, however, a call for moral nihilism. Neither is it an argument in favor of a radical relativism according to which anything goes. As Richard Rorty (1983) says: "The view that every tradition is as rational or as moral as every other could be held only by a god, someone who had no need to use (but only to mention) the terms 'rational' or 'moral,' because she had no need to inquire or deliberate." Since we fully acknowledge the epistemological limits of any "point of view," as well as the human need to inquire and deliberate, we would, rather, argue for a free circulation of information and ideas, built on the idea of communication and dialogue as a human precondition.

From Economic Rights to Moral Rights

In the context of intellectual property rights, Johnson's view of morality has interesting consequences. It suggests a strengthening of moral issues vis-à-vis economic rights, insofar as the latter impel the players in the arena of musical production to calculate what is due to them and to determine which rule others should follow when using their music. In contrast, an increased focus on the logic of care would situate music at the center of a good life—a good life which we do not owe to others, but wish on them all the same. It would emphasize respect for others not as a duty or imperative that a moral law confers on us but as an ideal: "[R]espect for ourselves and others becomes an ideal for treating people (and perhaps animals and the environment?) in a way that makes it possible for us to live together with some measure of harmony" (Johnson, 1993: 256).

An increased focus on a logic of care would not require the abolition of copyright law altogether (the two authors of this chapter have differing views on the advisability of such a move), but it would put new emphasis on moral rights. It would expose the notion of rights as dependent on convention and on the cultivation of one particular moral logic at the expense of others. Considering the Ami case, for instance (given that copyright is maintained in some form or another), a possible compromise would be to say that once a moral-rights holder decides to release a piece of music to a commercial market, or in any other way make it public, he or she must accept the rules of the game, including the transfiguration of the music into a common good for mass mediation. Since they were never so released, the manuscripts of Elgar and Grieg would therefore be left alone, or at least be held outside the access of the general commercial sphere (one may indeed wonder whether mass mediation is not implicitly taken for granted in the moral intuitions mentioned at the outset). However, the right to release music on the market should never be transferable from the participants of the relevant culture, meaning that rights could never be signed away. Copyright transfer is a convention that should be rejected on both epistemological and moral grounds.

But don't moral rights, as Stockfelt (this volume) claims, also rest on the idea of a reified musical work? What we have just said should not be interpreted as an attempt to ground moral rights on any kind of universal law by sneaking it in through the back door. We rather subscribe to some version of "deliberative democracy" in a world of free access to information. Rather than stressing consensus or majority decisions based on preestablished values and attitudes, it stresses our attention to different points of view. As Bernard Manin puts it: "[A] legitimate decision does not represent the *will* of all, but is one that results from the *deliberation of all*. It is the process by which everyone's will is formed that confers its legitimacy on the outcome, rather than the sum of already formed wills" (quoted in Thompson, 1995: 296). But whatever the outcomes of such deliberation in issues of copyright, we still emphasize that great music is never exclusively the result of an inspired genius or a possessed soul—and this brings us back to the issue of the unification of peoples (of Europe or anywhere else); it is the result of the world's listeners investing both emotional and monetary value, without which there would be no great composers, musicians, and singers. As Keil says: "[Y]ou can't put a monetary value on being the voice of your people. It doesn't commodify or compute.... [T]he gift must always circulate. Musicians have to keep moving the money around that comes out of people's emotions and their best instincts, their love vibe, their spiritual aspirations, their thirst for justice, their thirst to hear certain words expressed in a certain way.... [E]verybody's music belongs to everybody else" (Keil and Feld 1994: 321f.).[6]

Notes

1. On the priority accorded to melody at the expense of rhythm and harmony in copyright infringement suits, see Croonin (1997).
2. The term "reification" is used here primarily to indicate the process by which an abstract entity is conceived as a concrete object (objectification). A different use of the term is to refer to the process whereby a cultural phenomenon is conceived as natural (naturalization). To conceive of rights (or truths) as natural may be seen as an instance of the second use.
3. A significant case is that of Charlie Christensen, "author" of the Swedish character Arne Anka (Arne Duck, a Donald Duck™ look-alike), whom the Disney Company threatened to sue for exploiting their copyrighted character. Arne Anka is a rambling, sexually frustrated scoundrel who passes his nights in the bars of Stockholm. When Disney threatened legal action, Christensen simply turned his duck into a goose, who in one strip enters a well known toy store in Stockholm to buy himself a Donald Duck™ false beak. Dressed up like Donald Duck™, Arne lives on and has long since become a cult personality in the Swedish world of comics.
4. The British Music Rights Manifesto was formed by the British Academy of Composers and Songwriters, the Music Publishers Association, the Mechanical-Copyright Protection Society, and the Performing Right Society.
5. Of course, the discourses implicit in these metaphors may vary depending on the beholder of the music and the discourses the music exemplifies by way of these metaphors. For instance, when they first occurred, the two structural metaphors mentioned did not appear in such an explicit form as they do here; rather they were intertwined, with the one successively replacing the other. In addition, there were other parallel, partly related views according to which "music is a narrative," as well as formalistic descriptions of music in terms of organisms growing out of a single thematic kernel.
6. "The members [of a society] do not own this knowledge, but they share it, change it, contribute to it, recombine it, transform it and ... can only give it back (i.e., let it know) to society" (Raes, 1988).

References

Alvaro, S. (1986). "What is musical property? The ethics of sampling." *Keyboard* 10: 157.

Anonymous. (1995). "All must address past moral failures." *Billboard* 107: 79.

Ariès, P. (1981). *The Hour of Death*. London: Allen Lane.

Begle, H. (1994). "Pioneer R&B artists deserve back royalties." *Billboard* 106: 9.

Bent, I. and Drabkin, W. (1987). *Analysis*. London: Macmillan.

Bettig, R. V. (1992). "Critical perspectives on the history and philosophy of copyright." *Critical Studies in Mass Communication* 9: 131–155.

Bonds, M. E. (1991). *Wordless Rhetoric: Musical Form and the Metaphor of Oration*. Cambridge, MA: Harvard University Press.

Brown, J. H. (1992). "'They don't make music the way they used to': The legal implications of 'sampling' in contemporary music." *Wisconsin Law Review* 6: 1941–1991.

Brown, S. and Volgsten, U. (2000). "Controlling the music; controlling the listener." *Music Forum* 6: 23–25.

Coombe, R. J. (1998). *The Cultural Life of Intellectual Property: Authorship, Appropriation, and the Law*. Durham: Duke University Press.

Croonin, C. (1997). "Concepts of melodic similarity in music-copyright infringement suits." *Computing in Musicology* 11: 187–209.

Dahlhaus. C. (1982). *Esthetics of Music*. Translated by W. Austin. Cambridge: Cambridge University Press.

_____ (1989). *The Idea of Absolute Music*. Translated by R. Lustig. Chicago: University of Chicago Press.

Dennett, D. C. (1990). "Memes and the exploitation of imagination." *Journal of Aesthetics and Art Criticism* 48: 127–135.

Dibbell, J. (2004). "We pledge allegiance to the penguin." *Wired* 12. http://www.wired.com/wired/archive/12.11/linux.html

Edström, O. (1998). *Harmoniskt samspel. Sjuttiofem år med STIM*. Stockholm: STIM.

Falstrom, C. A. (1994). "Thou shalt not steal: Grand Upright Music Ltd. v. Warner Bros. Records Inc. and the future of digital sound sampling in popular music." *Hastings Law Journal* 45: 359–381.

Feld, S. (1994). "Notes on 'world beat.'" In C. Keil and S. Feld. *Music Grooves* (pp. 238–246). Chicago: University of Chicago Press.

Frith, S. (1987). "Copyright and the music business." *Popular Music* 7: 57–75.

_____ (1993). "Introduction." In S. Frith (ed.) *Music and Copyright* (pp. ix–xiv). Edinburgh: Edinburgh University Press.

Gaines, J. M. (1993). "Bette Midler and the piracy of identity." In S. Frith (ed.) *Music and Copyright* (pp. 86–98). Edinburgh: Edinburgh University Press.

Garofalo, R. (1999). "From music publishing to MP3: Music and industry in the twentieth century." *American Music* 17: 318–353.

Gramatke, W. D. (1996). "Digital future needs safeguards." *Billboard* 108: 4.

Greenfeld, K. T. (2000). "Meet Shawn Fanning." *Time,* 2 October: 65–70.

Habermas, J. (1989). *The Structural Transformation of the Public Sphere: An Inquiry into a Category of Bourgeois Society*. Cambridge, MA: MIT Press.

Hanslick, E. (1955). *Om det Sköna i Musiken*. Translated by B. Collinder. Uppsala: Almqvist och Wiksell.

Johnson, M. (1993). *Moral Imagination: Implications of Cognitive Science for Ethics*. Chicago: University of Chicago Press.

Karlen, P. H. (1993). "Co-ownership of moral rights." *Copyright World* 36: 38–41.

Keil, C. (1979). *Tiv Song*. Chicago: University of Chicago Press.

Keil, C. and Feld. S. (1994). "Commodified grooves." In C. Keil and S. Feld. *Music Grooves* (pp. 313–324). Chicago: University of Chicago Press.

Kent, C. (1982). "Elgar's third symphony: The sketches reconsidered." *Musical Times* 123: 532–537.

Klein, N. (2000). *No Logo*. London: HarperCollins.

Kretschmer, M. (2000). "In defence of piracy: Music copyright and creativity in the digital environment." *MICAZINE* 11: 1–10.

Kuhn, T. S. (1962). *The Structure of Scientific Revolutions*. Chicago: University of Chicago Press.

Laing, D. (1993). "Copyright and the international music industry." In S. Frith (ed.) *Music and Copyright* (pp. 22–39). Edinburgh: Edinburgh University Press.

Lawson, E. and Steed, A. (1999). "Sounds unlimited 2: Music and copyright in cyberspace: An update." *Copyright World* 5: 16–20.

Lord, A. (1960). *The Singer of Tales*. Cambridge, MA: Harvard University Press.

Lundberg, D., Malm, K., and Ronström, O. (2000). *Musik, Medier, Mångkultur: Förändringar i Svenska Musiklandskap*. Hedemora: Gidlunds.

Malm, K. (1998). "Copyright and the protection of intellectual property in traditional music: A summary of international efforts." *Music, Media, Multiculture: Today and Tomorrow* (pp. 110–132). Stockholm: Musikaliska Akademien.

Melden, A. I. (1988). *Rights in Moral Lives*. Berkeley: University of California Press.

Mills, S. (1996). "Indigenous music and the law: An analysis of national and international legislation." *Yearbook for Traditional Music* 28: 57–86.

Mumford, L. (1999). "The invention of printing." In D. Crowley and P. Heyer (eds.) *Communication in History: Technology, Culture, Society* (pp. 85–88). New York: Addison Wesley Longman.

Nergelius, J. and Zetterquist, O. (2001). "Kontraktsteorier." In J. Nergelius (ed.) *Rättsfilosofi: Samhälle och Moral Genom Tiderna* (pp. 21–58). Lund: Studentlitteratur.

Nozick, R. (1974). *Anarchy, State, and Utopia*. Oxford: Blackwell.

Peterson, R. A. and Berger, D. G. (1975). "Cycles in symbolic production: The case of popular music." *American Sociological Review* 40: 158–173.

Porcello, T. (1991). "The ethics of digital audio sampling." *Popular Music* 10: 69–84.

Pollack, W. M. (2000). "Tuning in: The future of copyright protection for online music in the digital millennium." *Fordham Law Review* 68: 2445–2488.

Raes, G.-W. (1988). "The absurdity of copyright." *Interface* 17: 145–150.

Rigg, N. (1998). "British Music Rights Manifesto." *Copyright World* 9: 40–42.

Rorty, R. (1983). "Postmodernist bourgeois liberalism." *The Journal of Philosophy* 80: 583–589.

Sadler, D. (1997). "The global music business as an information industry: Reinterpreting economies of culture." *Environment and Planning* 29: 1919–1936.

Scherzinger, M. (1999). "Music, spirit possession and the copyright law: Cross-cultural comparisons and strategic speculations." *Yearbook for Traditional Music* 31: 102–125.

Schumacher, T. G. (1995). "'This is a sampling sport': Digital sampling, rap music and the law in cultural production." *Media, Culture and Society* 17: 253–273.

Shackleton, E. (1998). "Culture and the music business within the European Union." *Copyright World* 4: 16–19.

Solie, R. A. (1980). "The living work: Organicism and musical analysis." *19th-Century Music* 4: 147–156.

Stannow, H., Åkerberg, Y., and Hillerström, H. (1999). *Musikjuridik: Rättigheter och Avtal på Musikområdet*. Stockholm: CKM.

Taylor, T. (1999). "Credit where credit's due." *Songlines*, Summer/Autumn, pp. 26–27.

Thompson, J. B. (1995). *The Media and Modernity: A Social Theory of the Media*. Stanford: Stanford University Press.

Upton Douglass, S. and Mende, C. S. (1998). "Music sampling: More than digital theft?" *Copyright World* 82: 23–28.

Wallis, R., Baden-Fuller, C., Kretschmer, M., and Klimis, G. M. (1999). "Contested collective administration of intellectual property rights in music." *European Journal of Communication* 14: 5–35.

Wallis, R. and Malm, K. (1984). *Big Sounds from Small People: The Music Industry in Small Countries*. London: Constable.

Young, I. G. (1997). Untitled and unpublished paper.

AESTH/ETHIC EPILOGUE
Is Mozart's Music *Good*?

Steven Brown and Ulrik Volgsten

The title of this epilogue refers to the relationship between aesthetics and ethics: Is something that is aesthetically pleasing necessarily morally proper as well? What is the general relationship between aesthetics and ethics?

As pointed out by aestheticians and art historians, aesthetics as a discipline was not originally intended as a theory of art. Founded in 1750 by Andreas Baumgarten, it was meant as a logic of the senses (see Gross, 2002). Nor did a unified concept of *fine art* emerge until the eighteenth century (Kristeller, 1980). Moreover, what became central concepts of aesthetics as it turned into a theory of art—beauty and disinterestedness—were derived from the ethics and metaphysics of previous ages (Stolnitz, 1961a, 1961b; Tatarkiewicz, 1972). From antiquity came the idea that beauty is the harmonious ordering of diverse parts into a unified whole. The principles for such ordering were first codified as laws of society; then as natural laws, by the Pythagoreans; and only thereafter, at the time of Plato and Aristotle, as principles for music, dance, poetry, etc. (von Wright, 1994).

The cosmic foundation of beauty became subject to theological revision by the Christian Church during the Middle Ages. Along with geometry, arithmetic, and astronomy, music theory was defined as a liberal art. Hence, medieval thinkers attributed true beauty to the music of the spheres rather than to any *musica instrumentalis*. With the Renaissance, attention was drawn from the divine toward human activities. Whereas beauty was initially discussed only in relation to the visual arts (Tatarkiewicz, 1972; Kristeller, 1980; Dahlhaus, 1982), it soon found its way to music in compositional treatises specifying the rules of musical genres (Dahlhaus, 1982; Lippman, 1986).

The end of the eighteenth century brought with it a questioning of this primacy of genre, praising instead the *autonomous* work (on this transition, see Volgsten and Åkerberg, this volume). As result of the Enlightenment's "inward turn" and its focus on disinterested contemplation, aesthetic imagination was already struck by both the sublime and the ugly (unrelated, Burke claimed, to either proportion, harmony, or unity), which for beauty meant that it was successively seen as only one aspect of "taste" among others. With Kant's critiques, aesthetics and ethics were firmly separated (while norms were turned into categorical imperatives), and the two would not be rejoined until postmodern thinkers paid them due attention (e.g., Shusterman, 1992; Muelder Eaton, 1997; Welsch, 1997; Huijer, 1999). Nevertheless, music was the member of the fine arts that—in its Austro-German and subsequently American formalist versions—most persistently cultivated classical beauty (in contrast to the postmodern focus on the sublime) in its focus on *organic unity*.

What this shows is that the similarity between aesthetics and ethics runs deep. Both systems seem to be underlain by a common psychological process that can be referred to (with a provisional neologism) as an *aesth/ethic* perception mechanism. The classical operation of this perception mechanism can be phrased as a simple equivalence rule: What is beautiful is good, and what is good is beautiful. (Likewise for the ugly and the bad.) This process can be thought of as a "gut-level" system that mediates various affective, perceptual, and cognitive evaluations that occur in forming both moral and aesthetic judgments. These evaluations are the responses we experience when we perceive something that strikes us as good or bad, such as when we view a scene of war or hear a beautiful piece of music. Seeing a bloody corpse at the site of a massacre may convince us of the evil of war simply by being so aesthetically repulsive. In like form, listening to a sheeringly beautiful piece of music may convince us of the moral goodness of the work and its composer. So it would seem that both moral and aesthetic perceptions, as emotional responses, arise from a common psychological core devoted to aesth/ethic perceptions, a level at which what is morally proper and what is beautiful are strongly intertwined. This would imply that moral responses have a definite aesthetic character to them and that aesthetic responses have a definite moral character to them.

It is important to point out that such a mechanism is subject to strong degrees of cognitive dissonance. This occurs, for example, when we learn that the massacre in question was part of a battle to liberate innocent hostages, or that the beautiful piece of music was written by a malevolent person. Clashes between moral and aesthetic responses create strong feelings of cognitive dissonance because they violate the state in which the right and the beautiful are consonant and parallel. What is bad or unfair should be ugly to behold; what is right or just should be beautiful to experience. We often have great difficulty believing that a beautiful piece of music could be the product of an evil soul, or that a repulsive work could be the output of a wholesome society. The point to underline is that the relationship between aesthetics and morality is frequently violated in everyday life, and that the psychological repercussions are generally severe.

The aesth/ethic core of this perception mechanism can be thought of as involving an evolutionarily ancestral affective system that mediates evaluative responses of an moral-aesthetic kind. We can posit that from the starting point of this common core, both moral and aesthetic systems—as higher-level conceptual systems of codes and norms—emerged through a type of branching process, one dealing with normative codes of behavior (guided by aesthetic considerations) and the other dealing with evaluative codes of object-attractiveness (guided by moral considerations). How could this emergence of moral and aesthetic systems have come about during human evolutionary history? One clue lies in the fact that aesthetic systems and moral systems are united by their involvement in collective belief systems (codifying affiliations and alliances) tied to ritual and religion (cf. Nietzsche, 1969; Deleuze and Guattari, 1983). The appearance of art is intimately related to the emergence of ceremonial rituals in human societies, an important function being to establish and reinforce the moral codes and practices of a society (Dissanayake, 2000). At this level, the moral and the aesthetic are inseparable, and countless premodern societies whose aesthetic systems have been described by ethnographers attest to this fact.

From this perspective, the moral and the aesthetic are true collaborators. And what they collaborate in achieving (we propose) is a sense of *social harmony*. This concept of social harmony suggests that a well-functioning society must be beautiful as well as just. However, a society's beauty is not found in the buildings and monuments that fill its public spaces but in something that, for lack of a better term, could be called a sense of "flow" characterizing its way of life, that is, the manner in which the members of the society engage in their world and with one another when they are at their best. Social harmony does not preclude power relations (in Foucault's sense), although it should always admit of their rearrangement. As Brown points out in his contribution to this volume, consensus and conflict are the "flip sides" of the same social coin (no cosmic order without a Pythagorean comma, as it were).

What we want to highlight is music's contribution to this harmony. Music primarily contributes not by revealing noumenal purposefulness nor by serving as a means to educational ends or as a standard for aesthetic self-production, but rather as a form/content transgressing medium for social relations at both the group and individual levels (Frith, 1996). "The relevance of the beautiful" in music (to use Gadamer's [1986] phrase) is its invitation to *attune* to it. Not only do we affectively attune to music, but our communication with other persons builds on proto-musical attunement (see Volgsten, this volume). And to the extent that our psychological selves are composed of a polyphony of different voices (Emerson, 1983; Bakhtin, 1994; Shotter and Billig, 1998), this pre-linguistic dialogue is their primary condition and orchestrator.

The current volume has examined relationships between music and morality. As has been argued in many of the contributions, an important aspect of music (perhaps the most important) is its capacity to create bonds within social groups, whether it be for inclusive expressions of universal love or exclusionist outbursts of ethnocentric resentment. While many people believe that music is something that is good for individuals and societies, the use of music in the world today is characterized by cognitive dissonance. Mozart's music may be an elixir for the soul, but it may also be an effective commercial device for selling upscale cars. A particular formulaic pop song may be the zillionth love song to hit the charts, or it may be a profound expression of protest coming from the most oppressed corner of the world. All we can say about this is that, at the psychological level, there does seem to be a natural tendency to equate the beautiful with the proper and the ugly with the wrong, and that the social uses of music both strongly reinforce and strongly challenge our deepest aesth/ethic intuitions. We go through life constantly trying to weed out the good from the bad. When we are lucky, the moral and aesthetic walk hand in hand, but in too many circumstances they simply do not.

And so, at the end of this journey, we are left with no choice but to ask ourselves the following question: Is Mozart's music good … or is it perhaps evil?

References

Bakhtin, M. (1994). "Discourse in the novel." In S. D. Ross (ed.) *Art and Its Significance: An Anthology of Aesthetic Theory* (pp. 484–497). Albany: State University of New York Press.

Dahlhaus, C. (1982). *Esthetics of Music*. Translated by W. Austin. Cambridge: Cambridge University Press.

Deleuze, G. and Guattari, F. (1983). *Anti-Oedipus: Capitalism and Schizophrenia*. Minneapolis: University of Minnesota Press.

Dissanayake, E. (2000). *Art and Intimacy: How the Arts Began*. Seattle: University of Washington Press.

Emerson, C. (1983). "The outer word and inner speech: Bakhtin, Vygotsky, and the internalization of language." *Critical Inquiry* 10: 245–264.

Frith, S. (1996). "Music and identity." In S. Hall and P. du Gay (eds.) *Questions of Cultural Identity* (pp. 108–127). London: Sage Publications.

Gadamer, H. G. (1986). *The Relevance of the Beautiful*. Translated by N. Walker. Cambridge: Cambridge University Press.

Gross, S. W. (2002). "The neglected programme of aesthetics." *British Journal of Aesthetics* 42: 403–413.

Huijer, M. (1999). "The aesthetics of existence in the work of Michel Foucault." *Philosophy and Social Criticism* 25: 61–85.

Kristeller, P. O. (1980). "The modern system of the arts." In *Renaissance Thought and the Arts* (pp. 163–227). Princeton, NJ: Princeton University Press.

Lippman, E. A. (1986). *Musical Aesthetics: A Historical Reader*. Vol. 1. New York: Pendragon Press.

Muelder Eaton, M. (1997). "Aesthetics: The mother of ethics?" *The Journal of Aesthetics and Art Criticism* 55: 355–364.

Nietzsche, F. (1969). *On the Genealogy of Morals*. Translated by W. Kaufmann and R. J. Hollingdale. New York: Vintage Books.

Shotter, J. and Billig, M. (1998). "A Bakhtinian psychology: From out of the heads of individuals and into the dialogues between them." In M. M. Bell and M. Gardiner (eds.) *Bakhtin and the Human Sciences* (pp. 13–39). London: Sage Publications.

Shusterman, R. (1992). "Postmodern ethics and the art of living." In *Pragmatist Aesthetics: Living Beauty, Rethinking Art* (pp. 236–261). Oxford: Blackwell.

Stolnitz, J. (1961a). "'Beauty': Some stages in the history of an idea." *Journal of the History of Ideas* 22: 185–204.

———— (1961b). "On the origins of 'aesthetic disinterestedness.'" *Journal of Aesthetics and Art Criticism* 20: 131–143.

Tatarkiewicz, W. (1972). "The great theory of beauty and its decline." *Journal of Aesthetics and Art Criticism* 31: 165–180.

von Wright, G. H. (1994). "Paideia." In *Att förstå sin samtid* (pp. 39–82). Stockholm: Albert Bonniers Förlag.

Welsch, W. (1997). *Undoing Aesthetics*. Translated by A. Inkpin. London: Sage Publications.

INDEX